Shanghai

ALSO BY DAVID ROTENBERG

Shanghai

DAVID ROTENBERG

The Ivory Compact

VIKING
CANADA

VIKING CANADA

Published by the Penguin Group

Penguin Group (Canada), 90 Eglinton Avenue East, Suite 700,
Toronto, Ontario, Canada M4P 2Y3 (a division of Pearson Canada Inc.)

Penguin Group (USA) Inc., 375 Hudson Street, New York, New York 10014, U.S.A.
Penguin Books Ltd, 80 Strand, London WC2R 0RL, England
Penguin Ireland, 25 St Stephen's Green, Dublin 2, Ireland
(a division of Penguin Books Ltd)
Penguin Group (Australia), 250 Camberwell Road, Camberwell, Victoria 3124,
Australia (a division of Pearson Australia Group Pty Ltd)
Penguin Books India Pvt Ltd, 11 Community Centre,
Panchsheel Park, New Delhi – 110 017, India
Penguin Group (NZ), 67 Apollo Drive, Rosedale, North Shore 0745, Auckland,
New Zealand (a division of Pearson New Zealand Ltd)
Penguin Books (South Africa) (Pty) Ltd, 24 Sturdee Avenue,
Rosebank, Johannesburg 2196, South Africa

Penguin Books Ltd, Registered Offices:
80 Strand, London WC2R 0RL, England

First published 2008

1 2 3 4 5 6 7 8 9 10 (RRD)

Manufactured in the U.S.A.

Library and Archives Canada Cataloguing in Publication data available upon
request to the publisher.

Visit the Penguin Group (Canada) website at www.penguin.ca

Special and corporate bulk purchase rates available;
please see www.penguin.ca/corporatesales or call 1-800-810-3104, ext. 477 or 474

We have just enough religion to make us hate,
but not enough to make us love, one another.

—Jonathan Swift, 1667–1745

Contents

Book One—From the Holy Mountain

Part One

Part Two

CONTENTS

* * *

Book Two—A Man with a Book

* * *

Book Three—The End of the Garden

book one ∗ part one

From the Holy Mountain

Wherein two prophecies are put forward;
one proceeds, the other is fulfilled,
and a city at the Bend in the River grows.

chapter one

The Ivory Compact

January 207 BC

As the late-afternoon winter sun slid behind the towering dark clouds, a shadow swelled across the beautiful but usually desolate foothills of the Green Mountain, the Hua Shan. In the murky light, thousands upon thousands of rebel troops readied themselves to spring a trap that would end the life of the most powerful man the world had ever known, or very possibly would ever know—Q'in She Huang, China's First Emperor.

A village fisherman raced to the far side of a partially frozen upland lake where his prized eels were supposed to be hibernating in their underwater pen. As he approached, the water was roiling and rich with blood. Females had slithered up onto an ice floe and were giving birth while the thicker, more powerful males thrashed the open water as they gorged themselves on their young. The fisherman watched in shocked silence, then turned his eyes upward, toward the darkening sky. Just down the winding mountain path a hunchbacked farmwife smacked the ice from a blanket she had hung to dry on the bamboo stand the night before and was amazed to find that the coverlet, although frozen stiff, was hot to the touch. Farther back in the foothills, a toothless peasant pinched the night-soil collector's product between his thumb and forefinger and brought it to his nose. To his amazement, the product was as fresh as the man had claimed it to be. He dropped the human fecal matter to the ground and stared at the night-soil collector. Then he looked to the black clouds, sniffed the air, turned, and ran.

Peasants always recognize the distinctive ozone reek that precedes change.

But as they retreated to their huts and drew their children close to them, none knew the nature of the change that was beginning, not in the foothills with the rebel troops but on the upper plateau of the Hua Shan, the Holy Mountain. Change conceived and brought into being by the renowned Q'in She Huang himself.

* * *

"YOU THINK ME MAD," China's First Emperor said in a hoarse whisper. "You—all three of you—think I am beyond my wits. That I was tempted here in the depths of winter to this lonely mountaintop to ..." His voice trailed off. For a moment, Q'in She Huang allowed himself to look toward the vine-covered mouth of the cave behind him. He took a deep breath and let it out slowly in a fine line of white mist.

His breath dusted the faces of the three people he trusted most on this earth, his Chosen: his personal Body Guard; his head Confucian; and Jiang, his favourite concubine. *What are you thinking now, in your secret hearts?* he wondered, then put the thought aside. He knew there was no way to know another's hidden self. There was no way to find the mind's construction in a person's face.

He raised his arms, setting the abalone shells sewn into his silk coverlet tinkling. Then he spoke loudly. "Do you believe that I, who had the Great Wall built, I, who receive personal tribute from the barbarian lands far to the west, from the cruel kingdoms of the south and the arrogant men of the island called Nippon, that I, who united the Middle Kingdom for the first time, am now beyond my wits?"

The Confucian noted the subtle shift in the First Emperor's language. No longer was he using the immoderate style of the ancient writers. Now his words were succinct and to the point. More importantly, his thoughts weren't the erratic, unpredictable rantings of a man insanely searching for the secret to eternal life. These were the lucid, considered thoughts of the man who had designed the longest man-made waterway in the world, joining the Yangtze River with Beijing, who had standardized the character writing distinctive to the Black-Haired people and created the Mandarin system of examinations that had led to the world's first organized civil service. This was the First Emperor he had known as a young man, not the one who had burned Confucians along with their books—a madness that he had witnessed and written about in his private journal.

"Do you believe that I am now infirm of mind—mad? That I brought you here to this barren place in search of some mountebank's charade, some alchemist's folly—a stone that would grant me eternal life? Do you believe that is why we now stand here and shiver in the cold while below the rebel troops surround this mountain? Do you believe that of me?"

Yes, thought the Body Guard, *that is precisely what I believe. It all began with your madness—your madness within madness. Then its seductive strands slithered beneath the latched door of your chamber and out into the world.*

For in Q'in She Huang's madness, his imperial madness, he had somehow eternally bound them all to him. But none of them then understood that. All they knew was his lunacy, his screams for light in the darkness, for them to "Find it. Find it for me now!" And now these new orders. Two porters to be hobbled and then their flesh slashed so that "their blood will bring to light that which will be."

The sun, almost at the western horizon, broke through the dense cloud cover and instantly banished the gloom. Suddenly the massive clouds were in furious motion, racing away to the north.

Q'in She Huang looked up and marvelled at their speed. Shortly, the sky was perfectly clear—and still, so still. *As if some deity had swept it clean with one great breath,* he thought. Then a cold wind, all the way from the Gobi Desert, swept up the mountainside and blew the long plaits of his lacquered hair against his cheek, creasing the wind's sudden howl with a sharp *thwap, thwap, thwap.*

Jiang, the concubine, wrapped her woven shawl tightly around her, but still the cold entered her, hurt her, like an angry lover. She looked to her last angry lover, Q'in She Huang, and remembered his exacting instructions about the way to reveal a sacred relic. She shivered involuntarily at the memory. More madness!

The First Emperor turned to face the coming cold. "Even nature is in harmony with my intent," he said softly, and was tempted to smile—but didn't.

———

At the western base of the mountain, the rebel general's Mongolian pony stirred beneath him as the desert wind engulfed them. From the desert. Madness wind, he thought.

A tear formed, then fell from his left eye. The malformation of the socket, like that of his father and his father before him, prevented the eyelid from fully covering the pupil. The gusting wind found the point of access to his eye and the irritation always brought tears. It infuriated him.

He turned to his adjutant. "Are our men in place?"

"Yes, General."

"Their orders?"

"As you commanded, to kill on sight anyone who comes down from the Holy Mountain."

The rebel general was about to retort that there were no holy mountains but was distracted by the commotion of the horses behind him. The unfamiliar desert wind was frightening the animals. "Hold your ranks," he ordered. "Every man is to control his horse on pain of death!" Then he bellowed, "Q'in She Huang either freezes to death on the mountain or is slain as he comes down. His infamy dies with him and his followers this night."

A cheer rose from his men.

As it did, the sibilant voice of the court's Head Eunuch, Chesu Hoi, whispered in his ear, "There are caves, great General." Even with the swirling desert wind, the general smelled the jasmine-scented breath of the half-man. He didn't like the Eunuch to be so close to him, but he managed a smile. The First Emperor's Head Eunuch had powerful allies at court.

"Your meaning?"

"The mountain's white stone is porous."

"What?"

"The Hua Shan is riven with caves and tunnels, General. If Q'in She Huang has a proper guide, he could perhaps escape through ..."

"You knew of this before but "

"I was not asked, Great General. I am, as you have said so often, merely a court creature," Chesu Hoi said with a barely concealed smile.

The rebel general looked toward the mountain. The sun was setting. The cold seemed to be rising from the ground itself.

He turned in his saddle. His army was spread across the foothills, one great, living thing. With them behind him he was strength itself. China's new emperor. Then why was he filled with such misgiving? Suddenly he was off his horse and shouting orders and running—running toward the Holy Mountain.

* * *

THE SHARP REPORT of snapping branches came from the thick vines that obscured the cave's mouth behind Q'in She Huang. An elderly man hacked through the vines with a short scythe. Behind him, two barefoot porters carried a large, silk-covered object on their shoulders.

The Emperor caught his Body Guard's eye and nodded slightly. *So these are the two,* the Body Guard thought as he stepped back and to the side.

Q'in She Huang barked at the porters, "Come forward and put down your burden." The men emerged from the darkness of the cave and then carefully leaned forward from the waist and placed the long, heavy object on the frozen ground.

The Body Guard leapt forward and in one motion slit the porters' hamstrings. They crumpled to the ground beside their load. The desert wind plucked their cries of pain and flung them eastward, off the mountain, toward the sea.

"Make known the relic," Q'in She Huang said.

Jiang, the concubine, stepped between the two hobbled men and knelt as the First Emperor had instructed her. For a moment she allowed her fingers to luxuriate on the surface of the black silk that covered the long, curved, tubular object on the ground. She took a deep breath, then reached for a far corner with her right hand and pulled it between the second and third fingers of her left. It whispered her name as it moved— *Jiang, Jiang, Jiang*—as Q'in She Huang had so often whispered in her ear as he reached for the clouds and rain.

She pulled at the sheer blackness again and the wind snatched the silk from her hands and lifted it high in the air. And there the silk hung for a moment, like a canopy over all of this.

The First Emperor looked up. Through the black silk he saw the last rays of the weak winter sun—the last sun rays he would ever see. His role was almost completed, destiny's portal within sight.

"When you leave here, a black trail will appear in the sky. Look for it. Follow it. It will point the way." The Chosen Three stared at their Emperor, but before any of them could speak, he continued, "Now, cast your eyes down."

At their feet lay a five-foot length of ivory tusk clamped at each end to a square jade stand. At its thickest it was as big around as a young man's thigh, at its point, the size of an infant's clenched fist.

"Narwhal?" asked the Confucian. Astonishment arched his voice.

"Tribute from the far north. It dwarfs the ivories we have from the beasts of Annam. This may well be the largest intact piece of ivory under the heavens. It is beyond doubt the single most powerful object in the world of men and gods." He nodded to the Body Guard. The man shoved one of the porters to his knees, then slid his swalto blade across the man's throat—the man's cry was nothing more than a liquid burble. Then the Body Guard grabbed a handful of the dying man's hair and pulled hard. The neck wound gaped open, and blood, like the falling water upriver from the great gorge, sprayed over the whiteness of the Narwhal Tusk. Quickly the Body Guard repeated the process with the second porter.

Thousands of slender lines of filigree etched on the Tusk's surface guided the blood toward an oblong pool at the thicker end of the ivory. Every eye followed its progress. The pool bulged slightly above its lip, then overflowed its lower rim in a thin, even, crimson curtain.

Beneath the blood, the surface of the narwhal ivory began to change, from something solid and opaque to something delicate and translucent. Shadows of hundreds of tiny carved figures lurked in the Tusk's interior, as if ready to be born.

Then beneath the blood a crack appeared in the ivory. And another. Then the entire surface beneath the blood curtain fell away, revealing an intricately carved world within.

"Strike a taper."

The flickering light brought to vibrant life what appeared to be hundreds of drunken Han Chinese men with unusually long pigtails and bizarrely shaven foreheads and lengthy reeds coming from their mouths. Some stood, many were lying on pallets. Servants carrying trays and small braziers dotted the tableau. But it was the drunken, pigtailed Han Chinese men that dominated the montage.

The Three gasped as one. "This is the future," the First Emperor said. "This is what I have seen and why we are here. Now, listen to me carefully. For many years to come, the Middle Kingdom will rule supreme. The kingdom will divide, then divide again. Invasions will follow, and at times barbarians will sit on my throne, but we will control them—never them us. The great Sea of China will salt every river." He pointed to the scene carved within the Tusk. "Until this." He paused to allow his listeners a moment to take in his words. Then, he repeated himself. "Until this." He glanced at the dancing figures. "This is the Age of White Birds on Water. It will be the beginning of the darkness. The onset of China's decline into chaos. With the arrival of the White Birds on Water your challenge begins—your families' challenge begins."

He scraped the long, yellowed nail of his baby finger along the Tusk's length, from the blood-filled pool, past the unmarked middle pool, to the far end. He rubbed the surface there. "The Age of White Birds on Water begins the darkness." Then he tapped the ivory sharply and two large panels slid to the frozen ground. Behind the panels was a vista of great structures on the far side of a bend in a river. Structures in shape and design the likes of which had never been seen. Some shot straight up and then curved, others were wide at the base and then rose in two towers, while others seemed to balance magically on almost invisible pedestals. "This is the Age of the Seventy Pagodas. It signifies the end of the darkness, the rebirth." He looked at his Chosen Three. They did not meet his eye.

Q'in She Huang continued, "It is your families' responsibility, when the Age of White Birds on Water begins, to make the darkness come. There will be great resistance. There will be efforts all around you to prevent the darkness, but you must complete your task. The darkness must come or there will be no light. You must force the darkness to come or a more sub-tle, much more dangerous darkness—a contagion—will creep upon our land, and if it does, it will never end. We will be enslaved to others, for-ever, and the Age of the Seventy Pagodas will never arrive."

The First Emperor stood and looked down at his Chosen Three. "Each of you must pass down to your succeeding generations the secret of the Ivory Tusk—of the compact you will enter into on this day on this Holy Mountain. Each family is to give the responsibility of carrying on the com-mitment to one family member only. That family member is to pass it on to another as age takes him—and so on through time. If any of them fail, then we, the Black-Haired people, will be swept away. China will be no more.

"The period of darkness will be long, but we will find our way through the darkness to the light. To a rebirth the likes of which the world has never seen. One that will dwarf even my achievements—the Age of the Seventy Pagodas."

All three of the Chosen noted that Q'in She Huang had passed by the centre of the Tusk.

The First Emperor looked at them and said, "There is a middle window, but it can be opened only when the Age of White Birds on Water is upon the land. Those who experience the darkness will know how to open that portal." He shifted to watch the final rays of the final sun that he would ever see. When the last of the last rays were no more, he said, "Keep the Tusk a secret from all others. It is sacred. These are either the words of a madman or a seer—that is up to you." Q'in She Huang looked back the way they had come up the mountain. "Remember that guile is your great-est weapon. People want to believe in whimsy—and madness. I let it be known that I sought the stone of eternal life. I screamed for it night after night from my bedchamber. I sent messengers to the far reaches of our kingdom to find it. I executed hundreds when they failed to bring me the stone of eternal life. I allowed the people to believe me mad to give the Carver time to complete my visions in the Tusk—which I now commit to you. You are here to lead, not follow. Use your insight, endurance, and will." He took a deep, wheezing breath, then said, "Now put your hands on the Narwhal Tusk."

Each of the Three did. The blood on the Tusk was still thick and warm.

"And bind you one to the other—and the leaders of your families one to the other—until the Age of the Seventy Pagodas arrives, when the rebirth will be complete."

Murmurs of assent rose in the throats of all three.

"Now take the Tusk and go. The Carver will lead you down through the caves. Once you are across the river, look for the black trail in the sky to lead you."

"But Emperor ..."

"My voyage is finished. I bound this country together. I united it with canals and laws and language. Now it is yours to see that China enters the darkness so that it will one day see the light. I have been granted a glimpse of the future—it is in the Tusk. Make this happen and China will be great. Fail and we will be picked apart by carrion birds, never to taste greatness again." He let out a long, heavy sigh, then said, "Now go."

With that the most powerful man the world had ever known, or very possibly would ever know, turned from his Chosen Three, removed his clothing, knelt in the cold, and awaited his death—like a great slab of rock ready to accept the first snows of winter.

And that is how the rebel general and his troops found Q'in She Huang. A naked, kneeling, frozen figure alone on the high plateau of the Holy Mountain.

—

Shortly, exhausted runners from the east side of the mountain reported to the General that no one had been seen coming down the mountain. Everyone on that desolate mountaintop understood that the First Emperor's Chosen Three had managed to escape. The night quickly took on a tension that loosed icy tendrils of chaos into the air. A leaderless Middle Kingdom was the worst of all possible outcomes.

The rebel general ordered a huge bonfire built. When the fire had pushed back the darkness, he ordered the First Emperor's body thrown on the blaze. The smell of sizzling flesh entered every nostril. It calmed the mountaintop—the First Emperor was truly gone, the new emperor in control.

The rebel general, for the first time that day, allowed himself a moment of calm. Then his teary left eye widened in horror as the First Emperor's head turned on the embers and faced him. Q'in She Huang's dead eyes held the rebel general's until flames engulfed the head in an intense blaze, seemingly of its own making.

A chill ran through the rebel general. "Cut down every tree, burn everything. Build a fire to drive away the night and obliterate for all time what happened here." His voice was thin, girlish. It infuriated him.

* * *

THE CHOSEN THREE and the Carver sat on the far bank of the river and looked east. The first rays of the cold sun announced a new day—a new, dangerous world. The Narwhal Tusk lay at their feet.

"What should we do now?" asked the Body Guard.

"Q'in She Huang is no more, hence ..." began the Confucian, but he stopped when he saw Jiang stand and move up the bank, away from the river's edge.

For a long moment she stood completely immobile. Then she pointed west, over their heads, toward the Holy Mountain. They turned to see what had drawn her attention. And there, coming from the Hua Shan, was a dense cloud of dark smoke. As Q'in She Huang had promised, there was a black trail in the sky. It was showing the way, eastward, toward the sea and the bend in the river—to a place that would eventually be called Shanghai.

chapter two

Approaching the Yangtye

The opium addict does not make masterpieces, he becomes one, or rather he becomes the canvas upon which the masterpiece takes place.

—FROM RICHARD HORDOON'S LETTER OF AUGUST 6, 1837, TO THOMAS DE QUINCY

North China Sea
October 1841

Richard Hordoon holds the pipe in both hands. Its polished cane stem, a dense black from years of use, is silken to his touch; its turned water buffalo horn mouthpiece a pleasure on his tongue; the six inches of silver inlaid with copper at the far end a magical thing in the flickering brazier light. Just past the midway point of the foot-and-a-half-long tube, in a three-inch-wide cavity, sits a turnip-shaped porcelain bowl. The bottom of the bowl is intricately patterned with a series of tiny holes, perfectly placed to convey the smoke to the smoker.

A long needle pierces, then plucks a sticky ball of opium from the bronze tray and holds it over the spirit lamp. The black resin pales, softens, then sputters. The needle deposits the bubbling ball in the bowl of the pipe.

A puff, a second, a third, then the process is repeated with the next molten orb from the bronze tray, and the next— until time shimmers, then slips. Rancour crystallizes, then opens and blooms roses and hydrangeas. Richard's neck elongates and his head swivels. His mouth opens and he catches a fine tendril of the far-off scent of desert air. It swirls round and round his teeth, then plunges down his throat.

And his being turns and spirals after it, down and down as a soft wind whispers up into his face and he floats on the gentle draught from the bottom of nowhere.

11

And the pipe is in his hands again, a cool, sensual smoothness, a swan's neck.

"*Zhangzui,*" the voice says in Mandarin. It is the wrong word. The speaker means "*Xiqi,*" breathe, not "*zhangzui,*" which means open your mouth. But Richard knows what is meant. He opens the two large holes in the bottom of his back and draws the serpent smoke down deeper.

Wings sprout from his sides and, filling with air, the skin that joins his ribs and his arms rounds and pulls taut. And he rises.

He is gliding up a river delta with the majesty of a four-master in full sail, riding with God's breath at his back. He recognizes the waterway. It's the Bogue, the access channel to Canton. The familiar cliffs of Linten Island approach fast. He speeds past the British bark, the *Red Rover,* and the American clipper, the *Water Witch,* at anchor, their sides teeming with pyjama-bottomed Chinamen carrying mango-wood caskets from the English ships to their native bumboats, since no *Fan Kuei* is allowed to set foot on the sacred soil of the Celestial Kingdom.

He holds up a hand—or at least in his mind he holds up a hand—and stares at his palm. For a moment he is lost in the lines of his life.

"Turn your foolish mitt, damn you," he snarls, surprised how quickly his English has taken on a cockney twist. His hand slowly turns to face the other way—and so does he. Now the *Water Witch* and the *Red Rover* are behind him, the deep, navigable passage to Canton straight ahead.

"Up!" he commands, and his palm turns skyward—and so does he.

And the smoke purrs and seeks and finds the hidden entrance within him. His death and the haunting cry of a young girl beckon him to go deeper and deeper into the opium tunnel.

"*Zhangzui!*" The wrong word again.

The smoke turns. It is suddenly angry, liquid fury. Thick leather straps slap across his chest and thighs as iron buckles cinch tight.

"Breathe!" A voice. A different voice. Not in Mandarin. Farsi this time. "Breathe!"

This time insistent. Calling him back, back from the tunnel. From the cool depths of himself and his search.

"Breathe! Richard, we've turned north toward the bloody Yangtze, brother mine. No more time for dreaming."

And he was there. Maxi. And it was fading—the secret access to the tunnel lost until the next time the pipe is in his hands … and he is brave enough to search again.

* * *

THE SOUTHERN CROSS was just visible on the western horizon as Richard carefully stepped up onto the midship deck of the flagship of Queen Victoria's Expeditionary Force, HMS *Cornwallis*. His red-haired, white-skinned brother disappeared down a grapple line and boarded the two-man Chinese junk that awaited him there. He tied a red kerchief around his neck, waved goodbye to Richard, then loosed the junk's moorings and headed toward the British steamer HMS *Nemesis*, a mile or so off the port side.

Richard took a deep breath, allowing the salt air to expand his lungs. *Fifteen years in China,* he thought, *and finally it is all about to really begin.* He watched Maxi's junk catch the wind and bolt shoreward and he laughed aloud. Who would have thought it possible? Richard and Maxi Hordoon in the employ of the British Expeditionary Force, heading toward the mouth of the mighty Yangtze River! Who would believe such a story? Who would dare dream the dream that he and his brother were now living?

On board, mariners scrambled up the rigging to secure the single top-gallants, the royals, and even the skysails on the three towering mainmasts. The anchor was secured to the forecastle cleats, the gantry cranes pulled on deck and tied down. As Admiral Gough emerged from the coach house and mounted the steps to the raised quarterdeck, the jib, outer jib, and flying jib were hoisted in the bow and the boat completed its turn into the wind. The men all around Richard worked with a vigour he had not seen before. They all knew that if they could make it to, then up, the Yangtze River to Nanking, there would be riches for one and all. The seamen and soldiers aboard the ships of the armada had already spent more than a year with little to show for their labours. They had seen comrades die in hideous, shrieking agony, poisoned by Chinese cooks; watched helplessly as kidnapped shipmates were executed in public squares as the Manchus led the throngs in cheers and song; stood by while hundreds died from suppurating wounds that would not heal in the tropical heat; and could do nothing as many more shat themselves to death with the dysentery or burned up with the malaria, or both. These seven hundred soldiers and mariners in the Expeditionary Force were battle tested and disease hardened. And despite the Queen's personally appointed diminutive idiot politician, Governor General Robert Pottinger, who had nominal command of the entire enterprise, they still believed in their military commander, Admiral Hugh Gough.

The mariners looked up as the sails momentarily luffed while the ship headed into the wind. Then they passed by the headwind and the sails bloated, the mighty man-o'-war heeled to starboard, and the ship headed due north toward the Yangtze. The men smiled. They were ready for a reward.

chapter three
The Vrassoons

London
November 1841

More than two thousand miles to the west, the patriarch of the powerful Vrassoon family, the Duke of Warwickshire—Eliazar Vrassoon by name—sat in his London study overlooking the Mall. He, too, was thinking about rewards. "Just rewards for very hard work" is the way he would have put it, had he been inclined to speak his mind aloud—but he wasn't so inclined, and had never been.

Runners were constantly in and out of the enormous outer office carrying messages from the far-flung ends of his vast mercantile empire. But it was one specific message that he awaited.

The eldest of his four sons, Ari, an elegant, perfumed man in his late twenties, entered and assumed his position over his father's left shoulder, his embossed notepad in his immaculately manicured hand. He hoped that this business could be completed quickly, as his man had informed him that a certain young—very young—beauty awaited his pleasure in the room above the Southwark Inn. Just another kind of reward for a hard day's labour. Ari wanted to smile, but wisely chose to keep his lightly powdered face neutral.

Two older workers, the firm's most trusted China hands, slid into the office soundlessly and closed the door behind them. One took his place at a writing desk, pen and ink at the ready, while the other stood silently beside him.

No one spoke. The silence stretched out, broken only by the *clop-clop* of horses' hooves and the hawking of fishmongers from the cobblestone streets below. A train whistle sounded sharply, and for just a moment Vrassoon's eldest son felt inexplicably weak in the knees.

The Vrassoon Patriarch sat with his fingers steepled in front of his face. They all waited. They had all waited many times before for Eliazar Vrassoon to speak. Finally he unsteepled his fingers and scraped the long fingernails of his right hand across his freckled scalp beneath his thinning grey hair. He remembered the glory days in Baghdad, riding with his father to one side of the Grand Vizier—the power around, behind, and through the throne. Then had come the expulsion. Of course they had known it was going to happen and had already transferred their assets to London and Paris and, most importantly, to Calcutta. *To Calcutta,* he thought wistfully. "Calcutta before …" he said aloud. He said the word *before* a second time—as if it were a time very, very long ago. Then he cast aside the thought, because now China loomed on the horizon. *The mother of all jewels,* he thought, lapsing into the purple prose of his native Farsi.

It was getting late, and Eliazar needed to see the mad girl shortly, as he did at this hour every Thursday since he had taken the baby from her. He owed her at least that—although the meeting always distressed him, and Bedlam was so far away.

He turned to Ari and signalled him to approach. The younger man did and leaned down to his father.

"How long after the treaty is signed will the land auction take place?" Eliazar asked.

"There is the hope that it will happen shortly after the conflict ends, whenever that may be. In the early spring, perhaps, but it is hard to know how much resistance the Manchu Emperor will mount. The details of several prospective dates are being finalized by the Foreign Office."

"By *our* people in the Foreign Office?"

"Naturally, Father."

"And how long after that to extraterritoriality?"

The younger Vrassoon hesitated.

The Vrassoon Patriarch shook his head. Not for the first time, he wondered whether his first-born was strong enough to hold together all that he had wrought. He doubted it. Fortunately, his youngest seemed to be made of sterner stuff. The Patriarch looked to the elder of the two China hands. "Cyril, your thoughts."

"At first it all seemed so simple, sir. The Chinese took to opium ships in their harbours the way the Scots would take to a freighter loaded down with Glenlivet sailing up the Firth of Forth."

If this was intended as a joke, no one laughed. Finally the Vrassoon Patriarch said, "And now?"

"Now, not so simple, sir."

"Why should it be simple, Cyril? You have been in my employ for almost twenty years. When did we last make an important decision that was not complicated?"

"Granted, sir. But the Chinese are different from the Mesopotamians or the Hindus. They are arrogant. They actually believe that they are winning the war."

The Vrassoon Patriarch thought about that for a moment. He glanced at his watch fob. The mad girl would be waiting for him. "Nothing stops demand, Cyril. If a product is wanted—desired, yearned for—there is no force on earth able to stem the tide." He thought, *The sale of dreams is unstoppable,* and nodded. Then he said, "If governments would only learn that lesson, the world would be an easier place—and more peaceful. Legalize it and tax it and we all win."

"Agreed, sir. But the Chinese do not accept that their populace both does and will always demand vast quantities of our opium."

"Fools! Do they believe they can change human nature? That they are gods on earth?"

"Perhaps, sir, perhaps they believe that. More likely they are just practical. They are willing to engage in lengthy wars and to lose in the present in order to win in the future. Their entire history supports that kind of thinking, sir. They have, in fact, been ruled by Manchus, who are not Chinese at all, for over two hundred years. But the Chinese culture long ago seduced the Manchus, who are now more Chinese in many respects than the Han Chinese."

"Then surely these foreign authorities can be undermined."

"Absolutely. For a decade, over a decade, we have all but openly traded our opium at Canton. More recently we have managed to move past the silliness of anchoring off Linten Island and having the Chinese skiffs come out and off-load our product—but, despite all our years of trading and our contacts, we have not moved very far past that. With the exception of the three hundred acres the Manchu authorities assigned to foreigners in the marshes south of the city upon which we have warehouse space—as do the Americans, Scottish, British, and even those damnable Hordoons—it remains an offence punishable by death for any non-Chinese to set foot on Chinese soil. The Mandarins, although they take our bribes, have always resisted our request for real land in the Celestial Kingdom."

"I've warned you not to use that phrase!" The Patriarch's voice was hard. "There is only one Celestial Kingdom, and it is not on this earth."

Silence again seeped into the room. The stern religious views of Eliazar Vrassoon were well known and forced upon everyone who worked for the massive, octopus-like company, even to the farthest reaches of the Vrassoon empire.

"Sorry, sir."

"This company has fed you and yours and made you wealthy. It can just as easily impoverish you and yours. Is that clear?"

There was a moment of real shock in the room. The Patriarch did not issue idle threats.

"I want to know when extraterritoriality will be realized."

"Father," his son began, "we haven't even forced a treaty from the Manchu Emperor yet."

"A foregone conclusion," his father snapped. "If Britain can rule the hordes of India, it can force land concessions from these Buddhist heathens."

The son heard the edge of panic in his father's voice. How much of the company's fortune had his father committed to the British expedition that was heading toward Nanking? Even he didn't know the details of that. He had, in the past, watched in horror as his father endangered the entire wealth of the company, first by a dangerous stock offering and then by vast expenditures in Calcutta. But both had proved, in the long run, to be brilliant business decisions. *Why then am I so concerned about this Chinese venture?* the young man asked himself. And the answer flooded into his mind: because of the Chinese—because of their arrogance, because of their vast numbers, and because there was something else at play here that neither he nor any other person here understood.

A furious knocking at the door sounded loudly in the room.

"In!" the Vrassoon Patriarch shouted.

A dust-covered man, still stinking of horses, held out a fingerprint-stained envelope, then left the room. The Patriarch grabbed it and turned toward the window. The London haze was lifting; for the first time in weeks there was an inkling that the sun might pierce through the fetid air. Eliazar Vrassoon flicked open the seal, read the progress report quickly, and turned to the others.

"Assuming they've kept the same pace reported in this document, our boats should be approaching the Yangtze River even as we speak."

"Our boats, Father?" Ari asked.

"The British Expeditionary Force—*our* boats."

chapter four
Maxi

North China Sea
Mid-November 1841

The grease-covered man swore viciously as blood shot from the gash on his hand and splatted against the exposed pistons of the steam engine. His cussing startled the English mariners in charge of the boiler room and engine, not because they were unused to foul language, but because the angry expletives were in a polyglot of Farsi, Hindi, cockney English, and a language none could identify—Yiddish.

The man's extraordinary linguistic tirade finally ended with a triple denunciation of the female genitalia, all in Farsi, preceded by a very common English verb used in its all too common gerundial form. Then the man took the red kerchief from his neck, swiped the blood from his hand across his filthy shirt, and said, "Start her up, gents. See if my blood larded her enough."

Moments later the damnable engine turned over and HMS *Nemesis,* for the first time in a day and a half, began to move. The men gave a cheer for the odd, red-haired Baghdadi Jew whom they knew only by his Christian name, Maxi.

Maxi Hordoon smiled, his large white teeth seeming even whiter in his grease-smeared face. He gave the engine a little kick with his boot and headed for the deck. Under his breath he said, "Fuckin' steamboats almost did us in, they did."

And they had. Years earlier, in a desperate move to increase their opium sales to northern China, Richard, over Maxi's objections, had leased two sidewheeler steamers.

"They're garbage, brother mine," Maxi had said.

"But they can make three round trips from Canton to northern China before the weather sets in," Richard had claimed, "as opposed to the two that's the maximum for even the fastest clipper. Come on, Maxi, think what we could do with fifty percent more profit each year. Fifty percent more, Maxi!"

Despite his reservations and his well-earned fear of monsoon season at sea, Maxi said, "Let me at least take a look at these new mechanical marvels before you throw our money away."

Maxi examined the two sidewheelers, and although they were better than the ones constructed by Miller and Symington, they weren't as secure as Henry Bell's version, called the Comet. Maxi spent almost a week with the boiler men, concerned about the transfer of steam to the pistons. Then he questioned the use of sea water in the boilers but was assured that as long as the boilers were cleaned after each trip, the salt residue wouldn't hurt the mechanism. He nodded but wasn't thrilled.

In the end, Richard leased two of the steamships from their agent in Hong Kong, Barclays Bank of London.

Things went well at first, but the turnaround time after each leg of the trip was just barely enough to give the boilers a cursory cleaning, so that the last leg of the third trip took longer—a lot longer than expected. Less than a day's steaming from the Bogue entrance to Canton, the monsoon caught up with them.

Maxi did his best to get more speed from the engine, but the salt residue buildup in the boiler proved too much. They just couldn't outrun the storm. It fell on them with a fury that felt personal. The tilt of the boat in the mountainous waves pulled the paddlewheel out of the water over and over again. Then the sea snapped open the hatches and quickly swamped them. Maxi could still feel the swirling water rising around him as he tried to restart the engine of the lead ship. But the water had gotten into the piston shafts, and the boiler fires had been snuffed out by the cold sea water.

Maxi was the last to leave the ship. He had actually considered going down with it, then thought better of it. "God'd laugh if I died in this piece of crap," he said as he dove off the stern of the sinking vessel.

He and Richard lost not only the two steamships, but also all the silk, silver, and tea they'd accepted as payment for their opium. It almost ended them. The other trading houses circled round them like vultures waiting for a gutted soldier to finally die. But Richard held out, dodging one creditor after another, begging space on one ship and securing it with supposed goods from another. Richard kept them alive. He was smart and shrewd, and the Hordoon brothers made it to the next trading season, although they still owed Barclays Bank for both of the steamships.

Maxi would never forget when Vrassoon's man approached them and, with a smile, offered them work at a shilling on the pound. Richard had to hold Maxi back. Maxi wanted to pull the man's head off and cut him into little pieces.

"Liver of blaspheming Jew," Richard said.

"Wha'?"

"Just a quote, Maxi."

Maxi thought about asking where the quote came from, but decided instead to say, "You read too much, brother mine. You ought to take care about that. Too much of that reading and yer dick'll fall off, and imagine what our local chefs would make outta that."

Richard laughed. Maxi smiled.

He smiled again now as he watched the Chinese coastline slip past, and wondered at his life. Who would ever have believed that he, Maxi Hordoon, would be standing, legs apart, hands on hips, on the foredeck of the steamer HMS *Nemesis* of the British Expeditionary Force—as it made its way to the mouth of the mighty Yangtze River?

chapter five
The Master Carver

At the Bend in the River
Late November 1841

The village of Shanghai's noonday sun streamed through the slatted shutters of his workshop as the Master Carver limped in. Three journeymen carvers were working on different large chunks of third-quality jade, held in place by wooden vises. The sounds of their cutting and smoothing tools produced a gentle whistle in the air. Since he was a boy, the Master Carver had always loved that sound.

Near the south-facing, open window, his older son was completing a large, complex piece carved from the interior of a bull elephant tusk. It had taken him almost two years, and now it was nearing completion. The Master Carver put both of his aged hands on the sculpted ivory top of his cane and leaned forward to view the work, and encourage his son. Although it was clear to him that this son did not really have the true carver's gift, fortunately his younger boy did.

The Master Carver hobbled to the very back of the shop to watch his gifted son learning the art of painting intricate country scenes on the interior of small, narrow-necked glass bottles. Not only did he have to manipulate the extremely slender paintbrushes with great care, he also had to paint upside down. The Master Carver remembered his own struggles with this art. The young man looked up from his labours and grinned at his father. The boy was alive with delight. It lit up every angle of his sharply defined facial features. The Master Carver put a hand gently on his son's

21

forehead and smiled. He would tell this one of the Narwhal Tusk soon. But not now.

The Master Carver left the workshop. From the other side of the high wall he heard the chatter from the open-air hot-water shop and the distant song of the dumpling hawkers. For a moment he thought of leaving the family compound and calling over one of the street vendors, who would cook up a dumpling-and-soup meal right there for him. But he decided against it and made his way past the storage shed toward the compound's bamboo stand. Pushing his way through the dense front row of canes, he stepped into an open, grassy glade. To one side was a sheer wall of rock covered with vines. He pulled back the dense vegetation and descended the steep concealed stairway there.

At the bottom of the stairway he used his hands to guide him along a long corridor that was cut from the rock itself. Twice he hit his head on outcroppings from above, but he did not dare light a taper. Finally the passage took a sharp turn to the right, and then a long gentle curve to the left, and opened to a wide, tall space.

He pressed down on his cane, stood up to his full height, and lit the torch affixed to the wall. The large, beautifully crafted mahogany box, sitting on its stone stand in the centre of the chamber, seemed to draw the light.

The Master Carver took a deep breath of the mineral-rich air and thought, *First the* Fan Kuei *ships sail up our coast, then they dare enter the great river. Maybe now is the time.*

When the Round-Eyed barbarians had begun to arrive in the south down by Canton, almost four generations ago, some of the Chosen's descendants had believed it was the time of White Birds on Water. But the Master Carver of that time had rejected this conclusion. Although the arrival of the British and their ludicrous desire to trade trinkets was a new reality in the Manchu-ruled Middle Kingdom, it was not the appointed time.

The Long Noses had tried to trade with the Middle Kingdom for many years thereafter but had always been rebuffed. What did these intensely ugly men have to offer China? Their goods were inferior to those readily available throughout the Middle Kingdom. Their manners were appalling, few spoke even the rudiments of the Common Speech, and none could read.

The Carver flipped open the latches of the mahogany box on the stone pedestal. They made reports like a firecracker in the underground space. He paused and then opened the case. The Narwhal Tusk, now deeply yellowed with age, nestled on its plush purple silk pad. Perhaps his talented son would be the one who would have to make a replica of the Tusk. Hopefully he would be up to the task.

The Carver leaned down and looked in the first of the three windows in the Tusk: hundreds of Han Chinese men with shaved foreheads and pig-tails seemingly dancing with long reeds in their mouths. "What must have seemed fanciful back then is common now," he said aloud to the empty space.

The arrival of the pale foreigners' opium did not begin the Age of White Birds on Water, although it was surely the precursor of change. The Master Carver of that time had indeed readied himself. But although there was noted change in some of the Middle Kingdom, there was no real change here. Not at the Bend in the River, where the black cloud in the sky had led the first Carver. There had even been sightings of a very young, violent, teary-eyed general from Beijing. But not here—not in the agricul-tural backwater where they had been told—no, *promised*—that the rebirth would happen.

Everyone in the Middle Kingdom felt the creep of the darkness that had begun some three or four generations before.

But Q'in She Huang's order was to allow the darkness in. To foster it. Just as only the brutality of winter cleanses the earth for the spring's planting, so the darkness would have to deepen to permit the arrival of the light.

And the darkness was surely intensifying. The Confucian, who was the nominal proconsul for the district, had lost one of his sons to the drug, and his overly proper wife was so addicted that she once sold herself to a cotton merchant to get the money she needed for her daily pipes. The Confucian, no doubt, thought that the predicted darkness had already arrived.

But it was not the Age of White Birds on Water. Not yet. *There is no darkness here,* the Master Carver thought, *but the time approaches.*

The Master Carver allowed his fingers to trace the supple firmness of the ivory, lingering on the centre section for just a moment. Only in ivory could such carving exist. Only its malleable density, its exquisite solidity could permit such work. And narwhal was the purest form of ivory in the world—and so very hard to find. Almost thirty years ago he had secured a tusk and stored it away carefully should it ever be needed to produce a replica. Now he wondered if it would.

Q'in She Huang's vision in the Tusk had last been seen by the Chosen Three over seventy years ago, when the first Round Eye had ventured into the hamlet. His black robe and raving made him a source of laughter for most of the village's residents, but not for the descendants of those who were bound by the Ivory Compact.

Even as this Jesuit was making a grotesque mockery of the Common Tongue, to the delight of the hamlet's children, the Chosen Three sought out the Carver and viewed again the "life within"—the vibrant tableau of figures beneath the filigree inscription: The Age of White Birds on Water.

But that was so long ago that once again—as the Carver had hoped—the very existence of the Tusk had fallen first into dispute, then into open ridicule. Secrets were best thought to be nothing but whimsy.

I feel it is near, the Carver thought, *and will shortly be upon us. The darkness and pain will begin. We must endure this. The three descendants of the Chosen must force this darkness on the people if the rebirth is ever to come to pass.*

The Carver took a deep breath, then closed the box and snapped the latches shut. He was tempted to take the Tusk out of its box a second time and stare at the future, but he resisted temptation and walked back into the corridor. There, deep in a crack in the rock, was a large statue. The Carver put the torch in front of it and knelt in prayer—prayer to the man who had first enlisted his ancestor to carve Q'in She Huang's vision in the Tusk and then had protected his ancestors from the wrath of the teary eyed rebel general—Q'in She Huang's Head Eunuch, Chesu Hoi.

Shanghai was little more than a large trading village at the Bend in the River in 1841. It would soon change—for the worse.

chapter six

Near the Bend in the River

The Yangtze River
December 1841

The great swaths of white sails draped on the sides of the British man-o'-war, HMS *Cornwallis*, rippled in the breeze with the dawning light. With the rising sun at its back, the expanse of white canvas provided a degree of camouflage for the great fighting vessel—and those that followed. After narrowly avoiding a confrontation near Woosung at the mouth of the Yangtze, the British had taken precautions. They had finally realized the significance of entering a main artery that could lead directly to the heart of China.

The wind picked up and the halyards snapped to. Overhead the mizzen-mast's sails caught the wind first and swelled. They were quickly followed by the fore-course, topsail, and topgallant, and the great ship heeled hard to port, its miles of hemp rope drawn taut, its block-and-tackle systems straining to keep control as its starboard canvas and flying jibs flapped wildly.

All eyes on the ship were trained on the water ahead. All but those belonging to Richard Hordoon, the Expeditionary Force's translator. His eyes were locked on the text of a letter from the famous English opium eater Thomas De Quincy. He read the great man's beautifully penned words several times, folded the letter, and placed it carefully in his personal journal. Then he strode to the port rail on the quarterdeck, stared ahead at the approaching bend in the river, and smiled. The wide arc of the mighty

25

Yangtze, as it swung past the mouth of the Huangpo River, was the best natural harbour Richard had ever seen.

A two-man Chinese junk came about and nestled into the side of the ship. Maxi, his face and bare arms covered in engine room grease, pulled himself up, hand over hand, on the rope hung from the quarterdeck, spotted his brother Richard, flung his arms open, and called out, "Mission accomplished! Another damned engine works as well as a Baghdadi farts."

Richard shook his head and signalled his brother to follow him astern.

Maxi's antics drew sidelong looks from several mariners and a few of the officers. Two of the senior midshipmen stepped forward, but Maxi turned to them and challenged them in Yiddish. "Something to say to me, gentlemen?"

The midshipmen muttered something about decorum, but the red-haired Jew ignored them. Although the British didn't like Maxi, they needed him. Not just because he was a genius in a boiler room—and the new steamships were proving temperamental in China's tropical heat—but also because he led the expedition's irregulars—a fighting unit that in a hundred years would be called guerilla fighters. The British army had learned much since its disgraceful defeat by the Americans in 1776 and the ensuing stalemate in 1812. Its leaders understood that fighting in formation was still a powerful battlefield tactic, but the regimental stand, shoot, kneel, and reload approach to warfare needed to be supported by advance attack teams that had to be local. Since the British didn't trust the Chinese, let alone the Manchus, the next best thing was this noisome Mesopotamian Jew and his band of opium traders—the irregulars.

Maxi's men always preceded the Expeditionary Force on the battlefield. Sometimes they scouted; more often they tested enemy defences and emplacements and reported back to Admiral Gough. Sometimes they didn't bother reporting back. They took some casualties, but not many. Maxi knew his men. He even knew some of their children. They all worked for the Hordoon trading company out of Canton. These men were the "unwanted," not good enough for the classier opium traders, like the Dents, the Jardine Mathesons, the Oliphants, and the damnable Vrassoons. These men owed their very existence to the ingenuity of the Hordoon brothers, and they knew it. They understood Maxi and thought of him as one of them—an outcast. He never recklessly endangered their lives, and yet he never shied away from a legitimate fight. He knew how to lead, and they followed.

Maxi caught up to his older brother near the stern of the quarterdeck just past the gig, the Captain's personal boat, which sat on iron deck crutches, its suspension launch wires looped like coiled snakes on a pair of side bollards. Over Richard's shoulder he saw Admiral Gough on the command deck, a full seven storeys above the orlop deck where Maxi and his men were billeted.

Richard was leaning against a deck winch, with one foot on a brass capstan. He stared at the shoreline.

"What do you see, brother mine?"

"Eyes, Maxi. Eyes watching."

"The Chinamen always watch, Richard, so what's so different now?"

These eyes are expecting us, Richard wanted to say, but he stepped away from his brother. Some thoughts were too dangerous, even for family. Family. He allowed himself the luxury of thinking about his twin boys in Malaya, already so strong and wiry at three. They were evidently a handful for their *amah.* Them so strong, and at the end their mother so weak. An image of his wife's final gasps for life in the birthing room came to him, as it did so often.

"Boys, Sarah, two boys," he'd said. But her eyes were wild with fear and pain. She'd grabbed him by the hand and yanked him down to her, then spat out, "Why? What have you done, Richard? What have you done?" He'd pulled his arm free and her fingernails had left four crimson lines on his forearm. He tried to calm her, "Sarah, please ..." but she'd shrieked back at him, "Tell me, what have you done?" She'd died in the bed, but her pain-contorted face and her terrified question—"What have you done?" lived on in Richard's head.

Like so many other questions, he thought.

"Do you think they'll fight, or will it be more of that marching up and down *mishagas?*"

"What ...?"

"Will the Chinese fight this time or just do that parading nonsense?" Maxi repeated.

The extraordinary pre-battle theatrics of the enemy had taken them all by surprise. The Chinese appeared that first morning on the battlefield wearing elaborate Chinkiang silks and then proceeded to parade up and down and slap each other on the back as a few of the soldiers pantomimed acts of supposed ferocity. It seemed that the Chinese believed that all they had to do to win a battle was to behave as if they were already victorious. Evidently they felt that the actual details of the fighting were beneath their concern, so they left them to the imagination of their enemy. Why bother with the fine points if you have already won the engagement? Their display lasted for almost ninety minutes.

When, apparently much to the surprise of the Chinese, the British didn't turn tail and run, the Celestials began the second act of their little war drama. Soldiers wielding ancient swords and shouting strange cries and various terms of opprobrium moved forward and performed somersaults and other acrobatic feats—all from a distance, but well within firing range of the fully arrayed forces of the British Expeditionary Force.

Maxi, as the leader of the irregulars, was closer to the show than the army itself and was shocked when he heard shots—two of them—whistle over his head. Instantly the closest acrobat-warrior paused in the air, mid-somersault, and, as if someone had cut his strings, crashed to the ground, his ancient sword beneath his body. And lay very, very still. Maxi sprang to his feet to see which of his men had fired, disobeying his orders, and was astounded to see the Queen's man, the diminutive Pottinger, jumping up and down in celebration thirty yards behind him.

"Bagged him. Bagged him like a partridge, I did." The man's upper-class lisp seemed to saw through the heavy air.

Then everything moved quickly. The Manchus' bannered troops raced forward and the battle was joined. But the Chinese weaponry was not up to the task. Many men carried only rattan shields with painted heads of devils or wild animals on them for protection. Some wore tiger-head caps. Neither was any match for a bullet manufactured in Manchester or Leeds. The Chinese had no artillery worthy of the name. Their muskets were of the antique matchlock design and were as likely to send the small-calibre shot backward as forward. Cromwell had used better weapons when he'd forced the King from his throne two hundred years earlier. And although it was the Chinese who had invented gunpowder, they hadn't perfected it. Twice Maxi had set full kegs of Chinese gunpowder alight only to find the damage done was less than what two of his rifle men could have inflicted in five minutes.

After an initial successful foray, Maxi had moved his irregulars to one side. He had real appetite for a fight but none for a slaughter.

"They will fight the way they fight, Maxi. Nothing more," Richard said at last.

"Won't they fight to protect their homes?"

"Why should they? Invaders have come before—shite, Tartars rule them now—but China remains as Chinese as ever, and I think it always will. Eventually the Middle Kingdom opens its legs and simply takes us in."

Maxi wanted to pursue this, but Richard turned away, thinking, *Fifteen years, fifteen years to get here*. During that time he had had more direct dealings with common Chinamen than any other foreigner. He spoke their languages better than any non-Chinese except the accursed Jesuits, who were now *persona non grata* in the Middle Kingdom, and he and Maxi had ventured up the coast well before the others. A fact that made them no friends in the world of the English, Scottish, and American opium traders in Canton.

The first time he'd set foot in Shanghai, Richard had known it was the key to everything for which he had worked. He had performed a full kowtow before the purple-robed chief government official, the Mandarin—the *Ch'in-ch'ai*—and then invited him onboard his ship. The man had declined his offer but was clearly interested in the Foreign Devil who spoke the Common Tongue. Through the Mandarin, Richard met Chen, and things had begun—things, plans. For the next two years he'd devoted himself to learning their complex dialect. Even with his tremendous facility for languages, he had found it hard going—but rewarding. And he had kept the glorious harbour at the Bend in the River at the centre of his plans. And now they were here.

"Say that thing about spreading the legs again, brother mine. It's a nice change to hear you talk of such things," Maxi said, showing off his large white teeth.

"They'll put up a show. But they don't think they need to defend themselves against barbarians like us. We'll win the battle and get what we think we want. But ultimately we'll do their bidding. It has always been thus here."

"You're a God-eating philosopher, brother."

And you're enjoying all this too much, Richard wanted to say, but he held his tongue. He would need his brother's fury if he were to break free of the detestable House of Vrassoon and trade in the China smoke on his own terms up here in Shanghai. For he had no doubt that once the port was open, once the fighting was done, the mongrel Vrassoons would be there with their self-serving rules and their political friends in London, their damnable monopoly on direct trade from England to China, and their base of power in India. Their cohorts in crime, the Kadooris, might even follow them, using their monopoly on rubber in Siam to wedge their way into the new market—and no doubt this *was* the new market. Not the old Canton routes that were littered with outstretched palms at every turn demanding squeeze. No. Now that the British navy had been lured into war there would be new treaty ports. And these new treaty ports, especially Shanghai, would offer real access to the interior—and the north of China, the heart of the Celestial Kingdom.

He sighed. *Patience,* he thought. *Patience.* It had taken him a decade and a half to get here; a few more years meant nothing. Soon he'd have a foothold, and his twin boys would join him, just up ahead, at the Bend in the River.

chapter seven
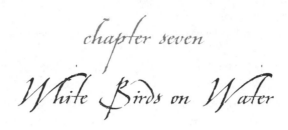
White Birds on Water

The Village of Shanghai
December 1841

THE BODY GUARD

"It hurts, Papa."

"Don't touch it, and it will heal more quickly."

"But it hurts."

Despite himself, the Body Guard said softly, "Yes, it does." He smiled at his ungainly son. The boy, if left alone, would spend all his time with their baby cormorants. He refused to hunt, reluctantly fished, and only went through the motions of his fighting lessons so he could return to the birds. Often the Body Guard found the boy in the bird coop singing to the young chicks. He would have slept with the birds if his father had permitted it. The boy's gentleness won the birds' hearts—and grudgingly his father's as well.

"Ouch!" the boy said as he picked at the scab.

"Leave it alone and allow it to heal."

"But it hurts."

"And it will for the rest of your life."

"For the rest of my life?"

The boy's shocked expression made the Body Guard laugh out loud. "Come," he said. He held out his left hand. The tattooed cobra on the back of his hand stood out even more starkly than usual in the rising sun.

The Body Guard's son made his way carefully to the stern of the rocking boat where his father sat, the handle of the wedge-shaped piece of carved wood that acted as both paddle and rudder held securely in his other hand. The boy knew better than to ask his father to leave his position of control of the boat while their birds were still underwater fishing.

"Why do I have to have this?" the boy said, pointing at the tattoo.

"Because you are the eldest."

"But what if I don't want it?"

The Body Guard remembered a similar conversation he had had with his own father almost twenty-five years before. At the time, he had taken some solace when his father said, "It may mean nothing. It hasn't meant anything for more years than anyone can count. It will have meaning only when the White Birds on Water approach."

He reached over and patted his son's cheek, feeling the velvet softness of his skin.

The boy, for a moment, enjoyed his father's touch, then moved his head away from the callused, rough palm. "It's not funny, Papa, it hurts."

"I know it does, son. Once we call back our cormorants, put your hand in the water. It's cold enough to help."

"Is mine going to be a cobra like yours?"

"Yes, once the scab comes off."

"What does it mean, Papa?"

He was about to repeat what his father had said to him, then stopped himself. The signs were everywhere. The first of the White traders had arrived at the Bend in the River on the very day of his grandfather's birth. Since then there had been English and Portuguese traders who had anchored offshore from time to time, but none brave enough to break the Manchu law against setting foot on the sacred soil of the Celestial Kingdom. Thanks to the traders, there was now opium to be had in the village. Not much, but some. Through darkened windows, pigtailed Chinese men with shaven foreheads could be seen sucking on long bamboo reeds. The arrival of the raving Black Robe with his stupid book fifteen years ago had raised more alarms—perhaps a further sign. Now there were two of them in the village—but they were not White Birds on Water. Three years ago Commissioner Lin's men had actually boarded an English trading ship in Canton Harbour and thrown twenty thousand opium caskets into the sea. Afterwards, Commissioner Lin had organized formal prayers begging the water's forgiveness for polluting it. The tale was told as a show of Chinese power, but the Body Guard thought of it as just another sign of the approaching darkness.

The eldest cormorant broke the water's surface not four feet from the boat. The Body Guard slapped the gunwales twice and the bird approached. Reaching over the side, he carefully plucked his old friend from the cold waters of the Yangtze.

As he put the bird on the plank in front of him, he noticed the lack of new moult and the frayed tail feathers. He reached out and touched the metal ring around the base of the bird's neck that stopped the cormorant from swallowing his catch. Then he smoothed down the bird's neck feathers and applied a gentle pressure just above the neck ring. Two wriggling, plump fish burped up the bird's neck, out of its mouth, and onto the bottom of the wooden boat.

The boy quickly picked up the fish and packed them into the reed basket at his side.

The Body Guard looked from the old bird to his young son—one ending, another just beginning.

He had sculled his slender carrack out farther than usual, past where the Huangpo River emptied into the mighty Yangtze. The current here was strong and the water cold. Good for fishing at this time of year, but treacherous. The light was growing all around them. He had no desire to be caught in the open water when the sun was fully awakened.

He reached into the water and slapped the side of the boat three times, hard. Quickly his four remaining birds made their way to the boat. He pulled on the rudder and turned the boat so that the side with the birds was away from the Yangtze and toward the much calmer Huangpo. "Come, help me," he told his son. "It's time to bring breakfast home for your mother and brother." He reached into the water and plucked out one young cormorant, then a second. "Pinch out the fish and put them in the basket." He didn't at first notice that his son hadn't responded. He quickly lifted the last two birds from the cold Yangtze water, then turned to the boy, who was standing on the boat's single plank seat with his hand over his eyes, looking toward the rising sun.

"Help me, boy."

"Papa, what are those?"

His eyes followed his son's outstretched hand and there, coming out of the rising sun, just taking the large bend of the mighty Yangtze, were four massive ships in full sail—their decks and sides draped with white canvas.

These were not the trading ships he had seen before. These were warships heading upriver toward Nanking. But it wasn't even that which so concerned the Body Guard. He drew his son close to him and held him tight as their boat rocked in the wash from the four great fighting ships.

"What is it, Papa? Why are you afraid?"

"I'm not afraid, son," he said, although he felt the blood rush into the cobra tattooed on his hand and the one he had never shown his son, which was etched in scar tissue on his back. *So it has begun,* he thought. *All the stories from my father and grandfather of the Narwhal Tusk and a task for our family. Finally the day has come.* He instinctively rubbed the tattooed cobra and stretched his fingers. Then he thought of his younger brother's son and made a tight fist. The cobra's hood opened as the blood gushed into the veins on the back of his hand—and made the scar tissue on his back turn a flaming red. The cobras were gorged and ready to strike, to choose which of the boys was strong enough to carry the family's responsibility, carved into the surface of the Narwhal Tusk.

"Sit by me, son. Your test is approaching. It is time for me to explain the tattoo on the back of your hand."

THE CONFUCIAN

He saw them first reflected in his great-grandfather's ebony writing stone, which he had mounted on the wall of his study. The white image glided across the darkness of the stone.

He carefully allowed the ink from his brush to return to the well on his desk, then powdered the document he had just finished. He waited for the ink to set, then shook off the powder. It sifted to the polished hardwood floor. He rolled the rice paper and sealed it with a wax imprimatur from his ring—the etching of a scholar sitting beneath a tree in a concubine's garden—then placed it atop a small pile of other scrolls. *Few of the candidates would be admitted to the civil service from this lot,* he thought. Over the years he had noticed a marked decline in qualified candidates. It had worried him, but looking up at the white reflections moving stately across the darkness of the ebony writing stone, it occurred to him that his worry was severely misplaced.

He took a deep breath and turned away from the reflections and walked out onto the balcony that overlooked the north reach of the Yangtze.

The glistening of a crane's expansive wings in the first rays of the rising sun drew his eye. He watched as it gracefully descended to the point where the great river made its final turn toward the sea. Shortly the bird melted into a tiny black dot on the horizon. He leaned against the hardwood railing and smelled the incoming ocean—and waited.

Something came around the bend in the river. Everything shifted. And there they were, four great men-o'-war, four masts apiece, in full sail. Four white birds on water—and he knew they would not be the last. Without thinking, he fell back into the patterns that his grandfather had written of in the ancient journal. *Do not be fooled by the exterior of a thing but do not ignore it either. See the thing—breathe in the thing—then sense its vital essence. Speak that essence aloud to understand what you have seen. Then write in the book what you have spoken.*

He spoke. His voice was strong and carried on the morning wind. "Ships, within whose cannons is the explosive stuff of change.

"So it has begun at last—the prophecy, the Ivory Compact, is finally in motion. The Age of White Birds on Water is upon us." He took his brush and made an entry in the secret journal that had been passed down to him by the previous Confucians of the Ivory Compact.

The cries of birds drew his eyes from his writing.

Below him, in the hundreds of flooded rice paddies that separated him from the river, peasants were attaching long reeds to the feet of hundreds of tiny starlings. The birds screamed in protest. On a signal the starlings would all be released to fly skyward with their reeds clattering beneath them, in order to frighten away devils that could hurt the tender newly planted rice plants.

The Confucian wanted to laugh. *There are more serious devils approaching than those that would destroy your rice,* he thought. "And these devils will not be frightened away by the silly clatter of reeds beneath tiny birds." This last he said aloud.

In response, an ancient voice sang in his head, and he knew that his ancestors were calling in a debt made all those years ago on a far-off holy mountain. And the paying of that debt would change everything.

JIANG, THE CONCUBINE

Jiang carefully disentangled herself from the fat salt merchant and slipped on a silken robe. The scent of opium lingered in the hot air of the stuffy bedchamber. She flung open the wooden shutters of the third-storey room and for a moment thought the opium was still alive in her blood, causing her to hallucinate. But that moment quickly passed. She had seen what she had seen. A great warship, draped all in white, entering the Huangpo River.

She picked up her leather pouch of silk ropes and her two-stringed arhu from the table, then quickly made her way down the stairs.

Outside, the morning streets were already alive. The men from the night-soil wagons were quickly collecting the round, red honeypots from each house, then emptying the contents into the wagons. A second set of men gave the night-soil pots a quick rinse and returned them to the appropriate homes. Jiang knew that although night-soil collection was the lowliest of professions, it also paid the highest financial rewards. Because of that, Jiang's family always married their first daughter into the Zhong clan that controlled this lucrative business. In the meantime, she was happy that she was upwind of the night-soil cart.

She turned a sharp corner and a five-spice egg seller fish-eyed her, then put one nasty finger to a nostril and blew hard. Green snot splatted to the ground inches from the pot. "Missed," the egg seller chortled. "Was his spear big?" she asked Jiang with feigned innocence.

"He would have split you in half, old lady," Jiang quipped.

"Only if he entered the dark passage. In the sacred lotus I can take a stallion." She laughed at her own joke and again blew her nose. This time some of the green mass went in the pot.

"Ah!" Jiang shouted.

"Special ingredient," the five-spice egg seller chimed back.

All around Jiang the morning smell of porridge escaped from coal-fired braziers. She usually didn't care to eat at this hour, but the subtle smell of a steamed pork bun drew her down an alley on her way toward the water. The gentle woman selling the buns allowed her hand to linger just a moment too long on Jiang's smooth skin before she took Jiang's half-*tael* piece.

The first bite of the bun filled Jiang with an old joy. *When I get old I can have as many of these as I want. Fat. Fat. Ah, to be free enough and old enough to be fat,* she thought.

She avoided the accusatory looks of the women in the streets as she ran out of the alley, past the fish sellers and the wooden tables thick with wriggling eels ready to be sliced. For a moment she paused in front of the snake seller. Did she need more man in her now? she wondered.

"Cobra?" she asked.

"Man's food," the toothless vendor replied.

"Most days I agree," Jiang said, "but not today."

"Expensive," he prompted.

"How much?"

He quoted an astronomical figure—the laughing price—and she promptly laughed in his face and turned to go. He chased after her and said, "So tell me, how much are you willing to pay?"

She quoted an outrageously low price—the crying price—and he made appropriate protestations.

Five minutes, two threats to leave, and one threat to kill her later and they had settled on a price.

The snake man reached into his burlap bag and withdrew a king cobra as fat around as a man's arm. He adjusted his hand to secure his grip on the back of the reptile's head.

She nodded.

The snake lashed out with the full strength of its six-foot body, but the snake seller was expert at his craft. He knelt in front of a thick log sticking out of the ground. With one quick motion he forced open the cobra's jaws and the fangs scissored out of its mouth. Just as the poison tipped the end of the fangs, the man slammed the cobra's head down onto the cut end of the log. The fangs dug deep into the soft wood. The body of the snake thrashed viciously at the air, but it was firmly secured to the log by its fangs. The snake seller looked up and smiled a toothless grin, then withdrew a slender blade and made his first cut.

Jiang enjoyed the skinning of the snake. She had seen it done many times before, but it never failed to surprise her when the snake seller threw the skin high into the air. It landed on the ground and thrashed—thrashed as if it were still somehow alive. *Very male,* Jiang thought. *With the arrival of the ships I'll need all the masculine blood in me that I can manage.*

She gave the tail third of the flesh to the beggars standing to one side, who ate it raw. The rest she tucked into a package, and then she raced toward the river.

She got there just as the second ship rounded the west bend.

She watched the great ships—and she knew that nothing would be the same, ever again.

A clatter of birds above her made her look up. The starlings from the rice paddies were falling in ever-narrowing spirals, the weight of the reeds dragging them earthward. A tiny bird crashed to the ground on the path ahead of her. She ran to retrieve it, only to be caught in a hail of hundreds of falling, screaming starlings.

She put up her lovely hands to protect her face, and as she did she looked to the high ridge.

There she saw the Body Guard and the Confucian, both staring at the ships.

Then she heard the sound of the Chinese artillery—all three did. And all three of the Chosen knew that their job was to usher in the darkness, not defeat it with cannons.

chapter eight
Shanghai

At the Bend in the River
December 1841

As Richard contemplated his future at the Bend in the River, the mizzen-mast let out a shriek and the single topgallant sail ripped into shreds like so much tissue. The long canvas strands were quickly picked up by the strong wind and snapped angrily.

A second gingall blast from the shore battery slammed into the bowsprit.

"Cannon on the south shore!" screamed two seamen in unison from their respective crow's nest perches.

Orders were shouted. A sailor's torn body was quickly covered with sheeting, as all hands ran to battle stations and the great ship came about, its massive expanse of canvas luffing in the momentary calm.

The hills on the south side of the river just past the widest part of the arc were lined with long-barrelled, small-calibre cannons: gingalls. But there were enough of them to do some damage. Once the ship was broadside to the land, the mariners dropped anchor both fore and aft—then the port side gun ports slammed open.

The grind and screech of iron wheels against oaken floorboards filled the air as the ship's cannons moved forward and stuck their snouts out of their respective gun ports. Then all noise ceased. The wind seemed to pick up, but the anchors held the great ship still in the water.

Admiral Gough stared at the shore and, as far as Richard could tell, said a prayer. Then he straightened his waistcoat and gave an order to his adjutant, who promptly called out: "Fire!"

The heavens opened as the thunder of the ship's twenty-six wide-bore port side cannons transformed the Chinese gun emplacements into the muddy, blooded places where men's lives come to an abrupt end. Richard watched, and the horror of lives lost entered his head. For an instant he thought of his last moments with his mother in the hovel in Calcutta—her life slowly flowing from her emaciated White Russian body, her red hair so thin that he saw more scalp than hair. Then his wife's dying cry of "Why? What have you done!" echoed through his head. He turned—and he was with her again.

———

"What have you done, Richard?" Sarah asked as she turned slowly in the morning light of their Malay bedroom, showing off her large, pregnant belly to her handsome husband.

Richard sat up in their bed and put on a face of mock horror. "My goodness," he said, pointing at her belly, "could I have had something to do with that?"

"Only a very little something—a very, very little something," she said as a lascivious grin creased her full lips. Then she posed demurely, although completely naked, against a foot post of their four-poster bed.

Richard laughed, then said, "It's a work day, Sarah" and got to his feet.

"Really?" she asked, pointing at his tented pyjama bottoms. "That kind of work I could, perhaps, help you with."

"Really?"

"Really, my darling!"

Richard held out his hand, and she took it. He guided her onto the bed, then stood back. Another aghast look crossed his face. "I do believe that the dirty deed was done on these very premises."

But Sarah knew differently. It had been the day on the south island when she had insisted on a picnic. There on the beach, as the sun set, they had made slow, easy love. And she had connected to the ground and the sound of the waves rolling in and a new life within her. That night they'd slept beneath the stars and she had felt it—the earth spin. And she had spun with it.

Richard positioned the pillows to support her back, and she mounted the high bed, then held her arms out to her fine husband, the father of that which grew within her.

"Promise me something, Richard?"

"Anything."

"That you'll write something for me. Just for me."

"I've already—"

"Something new. After I give birth. Something to celebrate me becoming a mother. And be sure to give it to our child."

"As you wish, Sarah." He breathed the words into her mouth. "As you wish."

Then, as their energies came together and they brought what Asians call the clouds and rain, she whispered in his ear, "What have you done, Richard, what have you done?" But Richard heard more than just a coy come-on in the words. He heard the beginnings of an accusation.

———

The cannonade lasted for hours, despite the fact that it had been some time since the shore batteries had returned fire.

Before the landing party had fully disembarked, Richard took Maxi aside. Jollyboats, cutters, bumboats, and colourful skiffs were in constant motion between the large troop transports and the landing site. As usual, the Chinese hadn't deigned to defend against the foreigners' landing.

"They may fight as you get closer to the centre of the city," Richard said. "The walls you should be able to scale with no problem. In the first skirmish, head toward the south gate."

"You've told me three times, brother mine."

"Fine, Maxi, but I need you to listen carefully. I don't think the armada is going to stop here. To them, Shanghai is insignificant. It's the mouth of the Grand Canal and Nanking that they want. And they'll need me to translate when the Emperor has finally had enough and decides he wants a treaty. So I won't be with you in the city."

"On my own am I, then?" said Maxi with a grin.

"Not really. Chen will meet you there and lead you to the Warrens. There he'll introduce you to the other Chinese power-brokers. You'll recognize some of them from our earlier trips, but there are bound to be those you don't know. Let Chen do the talking—even your pidgin is godawful, and they'll take it as an insult. Which, by the by, it is. When will you finally—?"

"Never, brother. It was hard enough for me to learn passable English. This Mandarin is well beyond me. You have the gift to pick up these odd tongues, not me."

"Just keep your mouth shut, but listen carefully, and get Chen to translate everything. Everything. Don't push for anything. Just remind Chen that I am on my way and that we have been good as our word for better than five years with him. We've made him a wealthy man, Maxi, and now it's time for him to return the favour. We want access to any survey plans of the city. We won't be allowed to live within their walls, but then again we don't really want to. We need to know who owns the land next to the river and exactly who has access to the wharves. Get Chen to begin negotiations with whoever that is. He won't sell anything yet, but we'll have our foot in the door."

"Do you want me to stay in Shanghai?"

"Not unless you have to."

"That'd technically make me break my contract with the British Expeditionary Force, brother mine."

"Would it?"

"You know it would."

"Does that bother you, Maxi?"

"Not much," he said as a darkness crossed his face "You'll be with the real action, though, won't you, brother mine?"

"Bureaucrats will decide the important things in the Celestial Kingdom. Battles are just for show, I'm afraid."

"Men die for show?"

"Yes, Maxi, and it won't be the last time for that." Maxi scowled and Richard readied himself for a fight. But none came. "I'll be at the treaty table, since none of our ninnies speak a word of the Common Tongue." He paused, then added, "I'll be there to make the sacrifices of those lives mean something."

Maxi nodded but didn't speak. Orders were being shouted all around them.

"After we take Chinkiang, I think it's just a matter of endless negotiations until Shanghai is opened up—and I want us ready to move as soon as it is."

Maxi nodded again.

"One more thing?"

"What, brother mine?"

"Control yourself."

Maxi gave the smile that had for years terrified his enemies and made ladies swoon. "Knife in its sheath, dick in me pants. Right?"

"Right, Maxi, right."

* * *

AFTER THE TROOPS were put ashore, steamers pulled two warships up the Huangpo River and the siege of Shanghai began. The mariners and infantrymen, Maxi at the head of his irregulars, made their way overland on an all-night march that swung them all the way around the city, ending at a ridge north of the city gates.

The morning came up fast and caught the British advance contingent unawares. The long march had exhausted the troops, and many had curled up on the ground and slept without taking off their boots.

Maxi never slept the night before battle. He climbed to the far side of the ridge and watched the sun rise. Then he saw them, small, crouched silhouettes coming from the east, not from the city at all. He watched as they skirted the British encampment and flanked out in small groups. He was too far away to give a warning cry and a gunshot would have been lost at that distance, so he began to run.

* * *

THE EAST PERIMETER SENTRY SIGHED. His watch was almost over. He thought of good British ale and his young wife. Then he lit a cardboard-wrapped Turkish cigarette and breathed in deeply—and felt the smoke somehow come out his neck! He turned, and a wiry Chinaman, clad all in white, smiled at him. In his long fingers a slender, blood-slick knife twirled round and round. *How does he do that?* the sentry thought, then watched helplessly as the knife sank deeper into his throat then tore sideways.

"Wake up, you slackers!" Maxi screamed as he crested the nearest hill. Quickly, two Chinese assassins were on him, then on the ground writhing in pain. Maxi's second shot awoke the camp, and screams quickly followed.

Maxi saw the Manchu banner and raced toward the man carrying it. The man saw Maxi and ran at full speed toward him. Three yards from Maxi he lowered the banner and, to Maxi's surprise, planted it in the ground and pulled himself up and over it as his feet thrashed at Maxi's head. One of the blows landed squarely, flattening Maxi's nose and sending him smashing to the ground.

Maxi hit, then immediately rolled. Only the friction of the banner whistling through the air saved him from the downward thrust of the lance at its end. It stuck several inches deep in the soft ground. Maxi rolled again and came up with a pistol cocked and aimed at the banner-man's head.

The man took his hands from the banner and stood very still. He said something—calmly, totally without fear. Maxi wished Richard were at his side to tell him what the brave man had said, but he wasn't. The man repeated himself. Not arrogant, clearly accepting what was going to happen to him. *The way the opium farmers accepted their lives in India,* he thought.

Maxi reached down and pulled the banner from the ground and handed it to the man. The man canted his head, Maxi matched the head bob precisely, then each turned and left—the bannerman to his army, Maxi to the south gate of the city.

Chen met Maxi just outside the south gate and signalled the *Fan Kuei* to follow him.

Maxi did, through the rickety streets of the Old City, then down a particularly long alley and through a hovel, then down a wooden ladder into a web of tunnels that Maxi knew were called the Warrens. The massive web of underground passages ran beneath the west section of the walled city, all the way to the river.

Maxi knew that above him was the old walled town, with the Huangpo River on the east and the Suzu Creek to the north. To the west were lakes and canals that led back into the southern reaches of the country. Cotton grew down by the delta, and rice paddies came right up to the southern walls.

Even beneath the ground Maxi could sense the energy of this place. After the first hundred yards or so, he saw lit torches in carved niches in the walls. Chen picked up his speed and Maxi matched him stride for stride. The walls were wet to the touch, but the tunnels had been well tended, and many places were worn smooth from the endless years of running feet.

After many turns and cut stone stairs both up and down, Chen held up his hand and Maxi stopped close behind him. Chen whistled a single, shrill, high-pitched note. Moments later, after the echo had ceased, a low-pitched whistle responded and a rope ladder was lowered from directly overhead. Chen and Maxi climbed it. At the top, strong hands grasped their wrists and hauled them up to a mahogany-floored chamber.

It took a moment for Maxi's eyes to adjust. The room was large and quite cold. A formal lacquered table stood to one side. Behind it stood a High Mandarin and three lesser authorities, all wearing the flowing silk robes and conical hats that were their badges of office. One of the officials, dressed in the purple robe of a scholar, was a certain Confucian.

All eyes were on Maxi.

He bowed low, then got down on one knee and performed the formal kowtow that Richard had taught him. When his forehead touched the wooden floor, his broken nose sent shards of pain through his entire body, but he didn't wince. Finally finished with the elaborate prostrations, he stood.

The Mandarin crossed to the table, reached into his long sleeve, and extracted a map.

As he did, the Confucian thought, *Here is my first deed in fulfilling my family's commitment to the Ivory Compact and returning Confucians to their rightful place in China.*

Maxi accepted tea from Chen—and the planning began.

* * *

LATER THAT AFTERNOON, the British, following Maxi's instructions, entered the city by climbing over the roof of a hut built illegally close to the outer wall—and owned by a certain courtesan named Jiang. Resistance in the city melted away as the man with the cobra tattooed on his hand advised against "overt action." The dawn sally of assassins from the walls proved the total extent of the defence mounted by the Shanghainese to protect their city.

By noon a delegation of the wealthiest merchants had come from the city walls and set up a large silk tent. Inside, on shiny black lacquered tables inlaid with designs made from mother-of-pearl, they served tea and fine sweetmeats to the British—then agreed to pay three million silver dollars in return for the safety of their city of two hundred and fifty thousand souls.

Maxi stood in the back of the tent, a cloth to his broken nose. He saw their man, Chen, at the conference table and wondered if he'd had something to do with the ease of the city's capitulation. The entire city had cost the British three dead and sixteen wounded.

The city's Jesuit translator made some final amendments to the document of Shanghai's surrender as the head merchant chattered on, seemingly no more concerned than if he had been bargaining for a slightly better price for the summer's second rice crop.

The money was put on the treaty table. Pottinger's representative, a chubby man named McCullough, didn't deign to touch it, acting as if such trifles were beneath a man of his station in life.

McCullough waited for the head merchant to sign the last of the documents, then stepped up to the table and took up the quill pen. He dunked it in the ink and poised it over the parchment. Then he turned to his lieutenant, who fired a shot through the silk roof of the tent. Before anyone in the tent could respond, a loud explosion caused them all to turn to the city.

The south gate of the city flew into bits, killing several Chinese bird and fish merchants whose stalls were adjacent to the gate.

"Just to show these Celestials who runs this town now," he announced, then turned to the Jesuit and ordered, "Translate that for your friends." Before the Jesuit could comply McCullough placed his pen on the signature line of the peace agreement and dashed off his name with some considerable flourish. When he'd finished, he turned to the interpreter again and said, "Three of my men were murdered this morning before dawn by your heathens. I will expect ten times that number handed over to me for execution by sundown—or the rest of your city will be put to the torch." Then he inexplicably switched to pidgin, despite the fact that the Jesuit's English was missionary-school perfect. "Understandee, boy? Quickee, go go, chop chop."

When the Shanghai delegation left, the tent flap was momentarily held open by the wind—and there in the bright sunlight stood the bannerman Maxi had encountered that morning. He glared at Maxi—and Maxi believed he had never seen so much hate in the eyes of any individual in his life.

Later, as Maxi lay on the surgeon's table in the belly of HMS *Cornwallis*, he thought that the hate in the bannerman's eyes was totally justified. Then the surgeon yanked the cartilage of his broken nose back into place and the pain that rocketed through his body removed any sentimental feeling Maxi had for the bannerman, the man's children, if he had any, or the lowliest beast of burden in the Middle Kingdom.

* * *

FOUR FULL DECKS ABOVE Maxi, in the Captain's well-appointed quarters, Gough reported on the securing of Shanghai to Governor General Pottinger, who was perched like an old owl over a table covered with river charts.

"We'll leave a battle frigate in this harbour and send another back to here," Pottinger stated, pointing to the mouth of the Yangtze by the village of Woosung.

That made sense to Gough, and he nodded.

"Glad you agree, Admiral," Pottinger said, then added, "I want the commander of the frigates to be instructed to intercept and sink any and all Chinese vessels heading up or down the river." He lifted his head from the charts.

"A blockade, sir?" Gough asked incredulously.

"Yes. That's the word I've been searching for. A blockade." Pottinger seemed to be tasting the word. He smiled, an ugly thing to witness as it exposed the diminutive creature's rotted front teeth. Then Queen Victoria's appointed man in China mumbled something unintelligible and abruptly left the cabin.

For a moment Gough didn't know what to do, then he raced after Pottinger and managed to corner the Governor General on the forecastle deck. "I have misgivings about a full blockade, sir."

Pottinger turned to Gough and a quizzical look crossed his surprisingly large facial features. "Are you questioning my command, Admiral?"

"No, sir. But why can we not allow trade in common goods to continue?"

Her Majesty's representative in China drew himself up to his full five-foot, four-inch height and said, in his fulsome Oxford lisp, "We will take no half measures, my good sir. We have come to this God-forsaken place to accomplish a task, and nothing, nothing, will stand in the way of our endeavour. Our period of operations is limited. The government and people of England look to me for decisive results. We will let the monkey emperor see that we have the means, and are prepared to exert them, of increasing pressure on his damnable country to an unbearable degree." A small smile creased his glistening lips. "Once the armada is fully on the river we will stop and loot every Chinese vessel we come across. Is that clear?"

Gough understood the advantage of raiding Chinese coal vessels to take the coal for their own steamers, but why all the vessels? And had the Queen's representative in China really legitimized looting? Finally he said, "We want to trade with the Chinese, not starve them to death." He added the word *sir* just in time to avoid a formal reprimand.

Pottinger thought about that for a moment, then replied, "A few starving Chinamen might prove advantageous—very advantageous."

chapter nine
A Vrassoon at Bedlam

London
December 1841

The Vrassoon Patriarch signalled for the matron to take the beautiful mad-woman from his arms. "Gently, gently now," he cooed after her as the matron took her and marched her back across the room.

The beautiful madwoman broke free and ran back to Eliazar, clutching at his arm. "Will you dance with me?"

"Surely. Surely I will dance with you," he said, removing her nailless fingers from his coat and turning her to face the matron once again. "Be gentle with her. She's not dangerous."

The matron ignored him and yanked the bedraggled creature by the fleshy part of her upper arm. Two stalwart guards stepped forward and reaffixed the buckles and belts of her outer restraining garment.

Vrassoon looked away. He wanted to wash his hands, but not while she could see him. He owed her that, at least.

"Why bother seeing her at all?" It was his elegant eldest son, Ari, who thought of the woman as his mad older cousin.

Because she's my heart, Eliazar wanted to say but didn't dare. Then he turned on his son. "How dare you interfere with my privacy?"

"I had no choice, Father."

"And why exactly is that? Why are you here?"

"There's news. News that couldn't wait for your return to the office."

Vrassoon raised a single bushy eyebrow. His son signalled him to follow.

Ten minutes later they were in the family's luxurious carriage. The company's two China hands sat across from the Vrassoons. The Patriarch demanded, "They've been authorized by the government to do what?"

"To blockade the Yangtze if they see fit, sir," said the elder China hand, then added, "so that not a single ship can get into the river. And on the river itself they've been given permission to stop every boat—to take the goods and burn the vessels."

"They're fools, Father," said Ari.

Eliazar Vrassoon looked out the carriage window and thought about that. The men on the British Expeditionary Force were men in search of riches, not so different from himself. He reached out and flipped the latch. The window folded outward. The stink of London entered the carriage. Finally he asked, "Will there be hunger?"

"Surely," the younger China hand replied.

"Starvation?" Vrassoon asked.

"Probably."

The Patriarch tapped his fingers against the leather-upholstered side of the carriage. The rain was coming down in sheets. *So there would be hunger. Much hunger.* He thought about that, then about prayer and faith and the willingness to believe. He thought about the mad girl who had shared his bed, whose daughter was now in her fifth year with the farm family in Hereford. The wind shifted and the rain came at the carriage on a slant. He reached out and pulled the window back into place. The wind shifted again and the rain suddenly beat on the roof of the carriage so loudly that it was hard to hear anyone speak. Eliazar Vrassoon nodded. *There will be hunger and starvation—and the world will change,* he thought. *So be it.* Then he turned to the others in the carriage and said loudly, "Do you think it will ever stop raining?"

The men were actually stunned by the question. Was the Patriarch of the Vrassoon family chatting about the weather? Did he expect them to respond?

Before any of them could speak, Eliazar Vrassoon answered his own question. "Everything stops eventually, gentlemen, and something new arises. It has been and will be forever thus."

There was a palpable sense of relief in the carriage as it raced past the rain-soaked beggars and drunkards of East London on its way to the centre of the Vrassoon company's seat of power, its offices on the Mall.

chapter ten

Hunger

On the Yangtze River
December 1841

Richard moved silently away from Gough and Pottinger. He knew a great deal more about hunger than they did. He passed by the deck watch unchallenged. As the expedition's translator, he had a temporary commission as a sub-lieutenant and pretty much free rein of the ship, so long as he stayed away from the crew quarters.

Richard stood at the port rail mid-deck and watched the fires on the shore as the great ship headed upriver. He turned his face to the wind and breathed deeply. Then he thought of the people on either side of the great river who might well soon be hungry. Some of whom might, in fact, shortly begin the lengthy process of starving to death.

"Starving's nothing special, boychick. It's just not eating."

Richard wasn't surprised to hear his dead father's voice. Lately, as he neared the completion of his plan, his deceased father's words, spoken in his unique mix of old-fashioned formal Farsi and Yiddish, often popped into his head. Although he had not seen his father for almost twenty years, he remembered exactly when his father had said those words to him.

"They're trying to starve us into leaving, Papa."

"That they are."

"Why?"

"Because they don't want us here, *boychick.*"

"You mean the dung-eating new caliph doesn't want us in Baghdad any more? Because he claims some stupid book said we are monkeys?"

"Dogs and monkeys, actually, Richard. Important to remember that. Not just monkeys, but dogs and monkeys. In fact, the progeny of dogs and monkeys," his father said. The deep cut on his forehead opened slightly when he laughed. The man could find humour in anything.

"We should just rip off the old idiot's beard and shove it down his stupid throat."

"This from a fourteen-year-old? A fourteen-year-old wants violence? Violence! It is my decision to leave Baghdad. Mine. It's a good time."

"A good time? A good time to leave our home?"

"Richard!"

Richard stared for a moment at the fool of a man in front of him, but he chose not to speak. His father might be willing to leave their ancestral home like a beaten mule, but Richard and Maxi were not so inclined. Even as children they had been unafraid. The Baghdadi boys' stones and taunts had never frightened him, and for Maxi they were just an excuse to attack.

There had been fires in the Jewish quarter two Friday nights before—naturally, on a Friday night. The Hordoons had escaped harm because they didn't live in ostentation like the Vrassoons and the Kadooris. The rich had been the first to feel the new caliph's wrath—or rather the rage of the countless Baghdadi poor, ignorant, and gullible. But last Monday while Richard was at school, his father's small leather tanning stall in the bazaar had been set afire—with the old man in it. Luckily Maxi had been nearby. He'd dragged their father to safety and then stood his ground as three grown men tried to loot the stall. Maxi was small in stature, but he was a giant in a brawl. Every ounce of him was muscle and sinew, and he loved a fight. When he balled his surprisingly small fists his eyes would go glassy hard, and the smile that the Moslem boys had learned to fear curled his lips. He could take more punishment than any man Richard had ever met, and he was only twelve years old—and extremely pale white, white skinned and red-haired like their Russian mother. When Richard finally found them, his father had the large gash across his forehead and Maxi was covered in blood—other men's blood. Maxi smiled, his large white teeth showing through his parted, swollen lips. He pointed to the ground, to the three grown men moaning in the dirt—one with an arm bone showing sickly white through his swarthy skin, another with an eye missing, and the third with a reddened crotch that did not bode well for his contribution to future generations.

Remembering, Richard smiled and nodded.

"Why are you nodding? What are you agreeing with, *boychick?*"

"Nothing—everything."

"Good. Agreeing is good," his father said, and grinned.

Richard took a deep breath, then asked, "So when have you decided that we leave Baghdad?"

"Tonight—late—after moonset."

So they were going on foot. No trains ran that late. "Where?"

"Where what, *boychick?*"

"Where are we going, Papa?"

"South."

South! Not west to Europe but south! He felt his muscles cramp with anger. Then he thought of Maxi—the wild one—and he knew how they'd spend their last night in old Baghdad.

* * *

THE TWO-STOREY COURTYARD was centred on an ancient well. The gate in front was made of sturdy metal bars with sharpened tips, but they posed no problem for the Hordoon boys.

Once over the gate they pressed their backs against the wall, in the deep shadow cast by the full moon. Richard sensed rather than saw Maxi at his side, then sensed him gone. Richard reached into the darkness for his brother, but he wasn't there. Minutes passed. Sounds of family life from the rooms across the way and the scent of highly spiced chickpeas found their way to his hiding place. Then Maxi was back, as silently as he had left.

"Teacher's home, brother mine."

"You know …?"

"Where he sleeps with his new boy." Maxi pointed toward an ancient stone arch.

"How do—?"

"Are we here to ask questions or say goodbye to this Jew-hating sodomite?"

"Let's go."

They crept along the compound wall. A dog barked, then fell silent. A few women came to the well carrying stoneware and a large clay pot. The boys went through the arch, turned a corner, and ran down a corridor into another interior courtyard. Across the way was a set of time-worn stone stairs. The boys took a step forward and froze. Something had moved in the courtyard. They both stood completely still. Then a peacock darted out from the shadows.

It took Richard a moment to identify the danger, but Maxi pounced on the animal and grabbed it by its neck. A breathy burp came from the bird rather than the usual piercing cries that would have alerted the whole compound. For a moment Maxi stood in the very centre of the courtyard, in full moonlight, holding the large, squirming creature by the neck. Then he flashed his smile and whipped the bird around his head twice. The bird's neck made a slight popping sound, then its body went limp. Maxi plucked two large tail feathers and threw the limp carcass high over the wall.

Then, he headed toward the stairs.

At the top of the steps a narrow hallway faced the boys. Down the hall they saw a heavy door barring their way into what Richard assumed was a bedroom. This was obviously a private part of the compound, and it was ghostly quiet. No cooking here, no cleaning—just a man's place—and a boy's.

Maxi kicked open the heavy door.

The boy was face down, spread-eagled on the bed, his arms and legs tethered by leather thongs to the bed's four posts. Teacher, who always referred to Maxi as the "retarded pig" whenever he called upon him in class, squatted over the terrified boy, whose pants were down around his ankles.

Teacher spun round and squinted toward the door. His thick glasses were on the night table. Maxi jumped forward and, grabbing the man by the hair, threw him to the ground while Richard stuffed yards of the bed sheets into the man's mouth to ensure his silence. Maxi sauntered over to the night table while Richard tied Teacher's hands behind his back. He took the thick glasses and returned to Teacher. Leaning down, he put the glasses on the man's face, "Want you to see us, Teacher. See what the Hordoon brothers are doing to you."

Richard cut the boy loose. "Leave without a sound," he whispered. The boy nodded, grabbed his clothes, and ran from the room.

Once the boy was gone Richard and Maxi lifted Teacher to his feet and frogmarched him to the squatter in the water closet.

The hole in the ground between the porcelain footholds was just large enough, after a bit of tile lifting and prying, to fit a grown man's head— Teacher's head. The boys hoisted squirming Teacher in the air and held him over the reeking hole. Maxi shoved the peacock's tail feathers between Teacher's toes. "Hold these," he ordered.

Richard looked at Maxi. "How did you know where his room …?" But he didn't need an answer, he understood.

Maxi shrugged his shoulders and said, "He would have had either you or me. I let it be me."

Richard nodded, then the Hordoon brothers turned Teacher upside down and shoved him head first into the hole—and left. Perhaps his God would save him. Perhaps He wouldn't.

A few hours later the Hordoon family snuck out of the city that eight generations of their forefathers had called home. All they took with them was what they could carry on their backs.

Seventeen weeks of hard travelling later, they staggered into the squalor of Calcutta.

The day they arrived, Richard wrote the first entry in the journal that he would keep for the rest of his life. It read: *How do I explain Calcutta— a dream within a nightmare; a song without end; the glory of darkness and shade while the sun roasts the earth. Then the rain comes. And everywhere palaces—ancient dilapidated palaces slowly but inevitably falling into the river.*

Richard thought about that first journal entry he had penned, when he was barely fifteen years old, as he crossed the foredeck of the *Cornwallis* and the White Birds on Water made their way up the mighty Yangtze River—and changed the course of Chinese history.

chapter eleven

At the Grand Canal

The Yangtze at the Grand Canal and Farther West

No nation had ever dared to enter the mighty Yangtze in such force as the British did in the last month of 1841. But although the British were virtually unopposed, the Yangtze itself proved a formidable enemy. The British had seventy-five vessels in their armada. Eleven were men-o'-war under sail, ranging in size from the enormous flagship *Cornwallis* to a small ten-gun brig. There were also four troopships, ten steamers, two survey schooners, and forty-eight transports.

The great river, although ten miles across at places, seldom had a navigable channel of any significant width, and Nanking was two hundred miles upriver. Shallow draft steamers went ahead and attempted to buoy the channel, but it proved trickier than anyone had anticipated. Several ships ran aground and needed to wait for high tide to dislodge themselves. Quickly the armada broke into its component parts. Some of the bigger ships needed to be pulled by steamers. Eventually the armada found itself spread over a thirty-mile area, as much as six days of sailing apart from each other. The biggest problems were the flagship, the *Cornwallis,* and a disgusting old tub called the *Belleisle.*

And, of course, Governor General Pottinger insisted that the flagship lead the way.

After the first sixty or seventy miles the banks of the Yangtze suddenly narrowed, sharp bends became common, and the current quickened. The ships found it hard going, and this far upriver the tide was negligible, so any ship that erred in its charting and went aground needed to offload its entire cargo—cannon included—before it could hope to refloat itself.

Not a single ship managed the voyage without grounding at least once; with some it was almost a daily occurrence.

Despite this, the British met little military resistance. The odd shore battery attack was feeble even for the Chinese. However, if mariners ventured ashore—especially if they were ill—they were immediately attacked by brigands or the locals, and these attacks often ended with British heads on the ends of sharpened pikes. So, although the British controlled the water, they were prisoners on their own ships.

Richard stared at the murky water of the great river. They were approaching Chinkiang, at the southern entrance to the First Emperor's Grand Canal, which connected Beijing with the Yangtze. *Surely the Chinese will defend the waterway to the heart of their nation,* Richard thought.

As the walls of Chinkiang came into view, Richard stood back from the railing and tried to stretch the tension from his muscles. As he did, the railing upon which he had been leaning only a moment before splintered and the wall behind him flew into a thousand bits. The morning air filled with the high, whistling shriek of flying chain and scrap metal as ranks of gingalls fired from their shore batteries. Richard stood staring at the splintered railing until an officer screamed "Battle stations!" and the decks and rigging, as if by magic, filled with mariners.

The *Cornwallis* turned into the wind and dropped anchor. Five other ships followed suit. Gough shouted "Port side gun ports!" and "Siege flags!"

The ports slammed open and battle flags raced up the bowsprit. All around him Richard watched the men of the Royal Navy preparing their positions for battle. He felt his heart race. For a brief moment he wondered where Maxi was, but then he cast aside his concern. If there was anyone who could look after himself in a fight it was his brother. No doubt he was readying his irregulars to lead Her Majesty's troops into battle.

Richard flinched when the first cannon roared beneath his feet. Then over a hundred cannon from five different ships brought the wrath of the British navy to bear on the gingall emplacements that were intended to guard the mouth of Q'in She Huang's Grand Canal. For three hours, without cease, the British shelled the Manchu batteries, and when they fell silent the gunners raised the angle on their weapons and bombarded the walled city itself.

Then, without warning, the guns fell silent. At first Richard couldn't tell, since his hearing had left him hours earlier. A sharp slap across his back caused him to spin around. "You're to prepare yourself for a landing in General Gough's party," mouthed the adjutant. Richard looked down. Below him the water was quickly filling with shuttle boats heading toward the shore. Richard thought he could make out the red kerchief that Maxi always wore around his neck on days of battle. Naturally he was in the lead boat, almost at the rocky beach. Maxi was always first to a fight.

A half hour later, seven hundred mariners and armed seamen formed ranks on the shoreline just east of Chinkiang. For some of them it was the first time their feet had touched the sacred soil of the Celestial Kingdom. Shortly afterwards, the horses were brought to join the infantry, and a man from Maxi's irregulars came running up to General Gough.

"It's clear, General, from here to the city. Not a single battery is left, sir."

The man's English was so highly accented that Gough turned to Richard. "What language is he speaking?"

"Farsi-accented English."

"English?"

Richard repeated the irregular's message in his impeccable English, then asked the man in Farsi, "And the city?"

"The gates are closed and barred. No sign of them coming out to meet us in the field."

Richard translated, and Gough asked, "Anything else?"

The irregular looked to Richard and said in Farsi, "Your brother suggests that you tell your British friends to take a close look at the Chinese weapons. There are some surprises."

Richard passed this on to Gough, who turned to a lieutenant and issued an order.

An hour later they were on a battery emplacement hill examining two pieces of Chinese artillery.

"Sir?" Richard asked.

"They're clever. Look at the pivot on that gingall. The weapon itself is poorly constructed and only a little more effective than their shields with the savage pictures and the character writing painted on them."

Richard's ability to read Chinese characters was limited, but he knew the characters on the Chinese shields had epithets like "Thief's Judgment," "Red Hair Tamer," and "Subduer of Foreign Devils." He didn't think it was worth telling Gough.

Gough knelt and looked at the iron apparatus on the back of the narrow-barrelled gingall. Two corners of a metal triangle were bolted to the back of the weapon while the third was welded to a large metal ring.

"It's a pivot apparatus," Gough said as he circled the thing. "Take a large spike and hammer it through the ring into the ground, then the gun can be moved on an arc by as few as two gunners. Look at the wheels. They can be set forward and back or in a curve left to right. We need five men to change the basic positioning of our cannon. This is a legitimate advance. Lucky they don't use them strategically or we'd have lost a ship, maybe two."

A lieutenant ran up and saluted. "Sir, the monkeys' handboats are in the western cove."

Richard bridled at hearing the Chinese referred to that way, but he let it pass.

In the western cove Richard watched Gough once again admire the ingenuity of the enemy. In the water, close to the shore, were seven sleek boats with side wheels. "They're hand-powered," the lieutenant said as he showed Gough how a single man could move the boat with a simple arm motion.

Again Gough quickly realized how fortunate they had been. "If they'd filled these with pitch and then set them ablaze ..." He didn't need to say the rest. Fire on a wooden sailing ship was a frightful thing, and clearly these small boats would have been hard to stop. "If they'd known where our magazines ... well, they didn't," he said, but Richard noted a strong hint of both fear and respect in the man's words.

When Gough turned from the cove he was surprised to see Maxi standing on the rise beyond the beach, clearly waiting for him, his kerchief just slightly redder than his hair.

Gough accepted the man's worth, but he was a gentleman, and this Persian was ... was a Persian. "Report," he ordered.

Maxi smiled. "The city's silent, but I'd watch your flanks as you approach the walls."

"Sir!"

"Sir," Maxi added grudgingly. Richard noted the pulsing vein in his brother's forehead, like a thick worm caught beneath the flawless pale skin.

"No resistance?"

"No resistance yet ... sir."

Gough dismissed the Persian.

Maxi turned and headed back the way he had come.

* * *

THE NEXT DAY, on the morning of July 21, 1842, General Gough led two full brigades of his men confidently toward the walls of Chinkiang.

As they got within sight of the walls his adjutant said, "There seems to be no defensive positioning at all, General."

Gough didn't like it, but he didn't know what else to do. He needed to secure the mouth of the Grand Canal if he had any chance of forcing the Emperor to the treaty table. Still, the silence was disconcerting, and his own private alarms were ringing like the church bells of his home parish on Easter morn.

He turned back toward his ships and bit his lip, drawing a thin line of blood. Then he reminded himself that he couldn't afford to return to England empty-handed, since he had invested what was left of his family's dwindling fortune in the possibility of plunder from this expedition.

"Should we move the brigade forward, sir?"

The land in front of them was hard-packed clay, with grass growing to the height of a man's waist in the distance; to the left were flooded rice paddies. On the right was a grove of tropical trees. Gough didn't like the trees. Even as a child he'd feared the woods. The most frightening threat in his family was to be thrown to the woods—to be "bewildered."

"Divide the brigades in two," Gough ordered. "I don't want a flank exposed to the trees."

Commands were given, and the well-trained men responded quickly, with bayonetted rifles at the ready. In the distance the walled city was perhaps two miles off.

The men proceeded carefully, awaiting a response. But there was none. Closer and closer to the walls of the city the troops advanced, in perfect formation.

Suddenly, within two hundred yards of the city walls, Manchu bannermen appeared from the water of the rice paddies.

The brigade wheeled to face the onslaught and weathered the first assault. Casualties on the front rank were high, but the second and third ranks held ground. The bannermen retreated toward the city, but Gough hesitated to follow, fearing that he would expose a flank as he advanced. Before he could consider his options a second wave of bannermen threw themselves at his troops—this time from the tall grass. The battle rapidly degenerated into hand-to-hand combat, and the superior agility of the Chinese fighters almost took the day. Finally Gough called in his cavalry, and the Chinese retreated toward the walled city.

Gough rallied his men for an attack on the walls only to have a third wave of bannermen attack, this time from the woods. This was followed quickly by a full frontal attack from the central gate of the walled city.

Neither side gave ground. No quarter was asked for or given. And when the sun finally headed toward the western horizon not a single

Chinese soldier was left standing. Not one had run. Everyone had fought to the death. Gough's superior weaponry and military tactics had finally prevailed—although without the surprise attack by Maxi's irregulars from deep in the forest the battle may well have ended British aspirations in the Middle Kingdom.

Gough took stock of his decimated troops and noted the hundreds of swooping vultures that hovered overhead. He ordered burial parties for the dead, then shouted to Richard, "Follow me."

Richard did his best to sidestep the bodies but found his boots quickly slicked with human gore. Looking toward the city he saw Maxi through the gunpowder fog and the fading light. Maxi was on the top of a western wall waving his fire-red kerchief. Gough pointed his troops toward Maxi. His men found the advantageous position that Maxi had marked and scaled the walls. Richard followed them.

Once inside the walls the troops re-formed their ranks and moved slowly toward the centre of the city.

Richard knew immediately that something was very wrong.

The city was ghostly quiet. The Chinese were a noisy people at the best of times; this silence was—it was unChinese—unAsian.

It was the first thing that had struck Richard when the family arrived in Calcutta: the noise—the constant racket. But it wasn't the noise that bothered Richard. It was the words coming from his father's mouth that he heard above the yelling and shouting of the Calcutta alley in which they lived.

"You'll see, soon the Vrassoons will honour their promise to me," he had said.

"Why will they do that, Papa?" Richard asked sharply.

"In return for a favour I did for them a long time ago, when you were just a little boy … *boychick*."

"What kind of favour could you do for the Vrassoons? You don't have anything the damnable—"

"When you're a man you'll understand the hard choices a father has to make to provide for his family. Now go play."

Richard hated his father at that moment, but rather than lash out, he wrote.

chapter twelve
From the Journals of Richard Hordoon

After two weeks of desperation, with nowhere to live and no money to buy food, the great and powerful Vrassoons deigned to let my father be a night watchman at one of their warehouses. For a night watchman's job we had trudged across desert and mountain! For a night watchman's job we had ruined our mother's health! I couldn't believe it.

With little more than a lean-to at the end of the stinking alley in which to live, Maxi and I spent our days in the open. My olive skin turned black beneath the baking sun, but Maxi's White Russian skin turned red to match his flaming hair—then shredded in long snakeskin wisps, which we quickly discovered were of real interest to the locals.

Maxi would approach a crowd and then I would announce, in Hindi, "Mera Bhai khud ki chamri cheel raha hai.—My brother is going to skin himself alive. Kuan itna himmatwala hai jo ek admi, ek larke, ko khud ko chulte huai dekhe sakta hai!—Who's brave enough to watch a man, a boy, skin himself alive? Step up and watch! Step up! Step up! How much is it worth to see this boy skin himself in front of your eyes?"

Trinkets of money tinkled into my outstretched hand. When I had as much as I could from the crowd, I would pocket the cash and step back. Maxi would then take off his shirt and pants and stand almost naked—redder than a sunset. Then slowly he would niggle an edge of skin from the top of his hairless chest and pull it slowly down his body, all the while screaming as if he were in terrible pain. Finally he'd rip off the strip and hand it to me. I would hold the length of skin aloft and call out, "Kuan lal larke ki chamri ke daam dega? Calcutta ki sabse acchi chamri—*Who'll pay for the red boy's skin? The best skin in Calcutta. Fresh skin from a red boy will cure any disease. It will bring happiness to a bad marriage. Make the weak strong, the blind see, and the limp strong like a donkey with a new mare. Eat it raw, brew it into a tea, cook it with your rice. Anyway you want, it will bring you joy.* Isse jyada kya iccha kar sakte ho? Mai kis ke boli laga raha hoon is lal larke ke chamri ki—ya jo kushhali yeh malik ko lekaraigie?—*What more could you ask? What am I bid for the red boy's skin—for the happiness it will bring the owner?*"

"You've *really picked up the lingo, brother mine,*" Maxi whispered in Farsi.

"You have *the gift of skin, me of tongues, Maxi,*" I whispered back while I continued to hold up the skin and collect bids. As I did I realized something important—how much a man would pay for happiness, even a moment of happiness, even the illusion of the slightest possibility of happiness.

Most days Maxi and I played a game we called "spy." Through the bazaars, down by the sacred river, into and out of offices and factories and private homes, we learned Calcutta by "spying."

As the weeks passed, Maxi noticed that I concentrated the "spying" on one point in the vast city.

"Here again, brother mine?"

"You don't like offices? It's where money's made."

"I'm more interested in where money is spent."

That you are, Maxi, that you are, I thought, remembering our spying in what I thought of as the "harlot district." We were not ignorant of sex, but transvestite boy whores and castrati whores were new ideas to us—and somehow fascinating to Maxi.

A well-dressed, turbaned man hurried past us. "Him!" I said. So we played spy and followed the man. He proved to be, as I had assumed, a Vrassoon courier. "See, Maxi, another one," I said.

"That makes six in two days," Maxi replied.

"Each taking the same route, you may have noticed."

"If couriers come to the Vrassoon offices, why don't we ever see them leave?"

"Because when they go to the Vrassoon offices they are carrying information—information goes through the front door. When they leave they are carrying money—money goes through the back door. Remember that, Maxi."

Around noon the next day, while Maxi "re-spied" the harlots, I decided it was finally time to see what Eliazar Vrassoon looked like. I'd never seen the great man before and somehow felt it was important. I stood amidst a crowd of beggars outside the Vrassoon offices. Two well-armed Sikhs pushed the beg-

gars to the far side of the street. That was okay with me. I wasn't there to beg a handout, I was there to watch—to see.

A carriage drawn by four large horses raced toward the entrance of the Vrassoon offices, the driver shrieking at the wave of humanity that wasn't parting fast enough for his taste. With the shrill neighing of horses and the screech of a handbrake the carriage careened to a stop at the bottom of the marble steps.

I leapt up and grabbed the stanchion of a gaslight and shinnied up. The better to see you, I thought. But before I was able to grin at my own cleverness Eliazar Vrassoon was there on the office steps, two of his four sons at his side and six Sikh guards making sure that his eminence was not touched by the rabble.

The Vrassoon Patriarch descended the steps slowly, as if out for an evening's stroll. At the bottom he looked up. He seemed to be looking straight at me. He was about to smile, when his face suddenly grew hard. He pointed a bony finger right at me. My heart fell in my chest. The hatred in the man's eyes cut through me—and I somehow remembered this man—but in a different place. In a bedroom! Whose bedroom?

A week later as the sun set, I was back at the Vrassoon company playing "spy" when I saw my father standing outside the office. I knew that he should be reporting to work in less than an hour.

Despite the heat of the evening, the men leaving the building all wore top hats and woollen suits. Finally a gaggle of young, curly-haired men left the office, followed by a richly dressed older man: Eliazar Vrassoon.

My father stepped forward and was immediately surrounded by the young men.

"Please." I heard him beg. "Please, just a word, a word, please."

Vrassoon sighed deeply. "Let him speak."

My father smiled. "Thank you. Thank you, sir."

"You have something to say, Hordoon?"

"My girl ..."

"What girl?" There was a moment of stunned silence. "I repeat, what girl? Perhaps the work I have supplied you is too taxing for you. Perhaps a younger man would be better suited—"

"No! Please, your honour, no. It was just a joke. The heat ... just the heat."

The Vrassoon Patriarch smiled, secured his hat on his rather large head, and turned to the waiting carriage. I ran home.

The next day the Vrassoons changed my father's job. They now have him working through the night lifting and moving heavy freight in their warehouse. He has become an old man. I never remember him as a young man. Maybe he never was. My mother is rotting away   sick by the time we arrived and sicker by the day. And now mad as well. Over and over she calls out for someone called Miriam. It is the last straw for Maxi and me. We're tired of begging—me of the paltry take, him of selling his skin—so we said goodbye to our parents today. Papa was too tired to protest. I'm not sure if mother in her delirium even knew what I said to her. We are heading up the Ganges to Ghazipur. But not before we stock up our larder from the Vrassoons' back door.

——

The smell of cooking fires filled the Calcutta night air. The early summer heat had not given up its hold on the vast city, so people were out on the filthy streets. A chanted melody drifted down the darkened alleyway where Maxi and Richard waited.

"Once we do this, we can't come back, Maxi," Richard said. "You understand that."

"Are you asking or telling?"

"Telling."

"No need. I know that if we steal from the Vrassoons that we'd better leave the Vrassoons' town. I think that only makes sense, don't you?" Maxi's white, toothy smile showed through the darkness, then he added, "Especially if the Vrassoon courier should happen to end up injured."

"Maxi, we're looking for seed money to get us up the Ganges to Ghazipur, not violence."

"Aye. So you've said. So you've said," Maxi repeated. "But what say you, brother mine, if by chance this Vrassoon courier isn't interested in being parted from his loot? If, say, he is as frightened of the Vrassoons as he is of us? What if he fights?"

"He won't," Richard said, ending the conversation.

"Okay, right, no violence, just theft."

"Right, Maxi, just theft. Just theft."

Four hours later Richard found himself on his knees with the Vrassoon courier's knife pressed against the back of his neck, his face crushed into the filth of the alleyway, and his eyes pleading for Maxi to do something!

And Maxi did. He hurled himself headfirst from the top of a rubbish heap directly at the courier's face. The man was shocked to see this white-and-red thing flying through space at him and released Richard to defend himself against the ghost from the darkness.

The courier's first knife slash cut straight across Maxi's chest, drawing a crimson line of pain. But before the courier could use his knife a second time, he felt Maxi's teeth sink deep into his cheek just below his left eye.

Then Maxi was on him—fists like pistons crushing his nose, smashing through orbital bones. Maxi sensed the man's resistance slacken and then he heard a low gurgle come from the man's shattered mouth. He lowered his fist slowly to his side as he sensed the stillness in the body beneath him.

He rose to face his brother, grief etched deep into the lines of his young face. "We did it your way, brother mine. 'Theft, no violence.' A little violence before theft could have saved this man's life—and mine!" Then he turned and headed back down the alley muttering, "No violence, no violence."

Richard ran to catch up to him, but before he could speak Maxi asked, "How much did we get?"

"Enough," Richard lied. "Enough."

* * *

WHEN THEY FINALLY GOT TO GHAZIPUR it was early May. The temperature was already well into the hundreds and the constant dust in the wind obscured the sun. In order to save the last of their money they hadn't eaten for three days. But their timing was fortuitous. The heat would only break three months later, when the summer monsoons swept up from the Bay of Bengal. And it was in these hot months before the monsoons that the raw opium came in from the village farms.

Opium—that which made the Vrassoons wealthy—was the fastest route to riches for the young and strong. Richard and Maxi had determined that they would learn the opium trade from the source. The village farmers around Ghazipur were at the very bottom of the trade—the source of the Nile, the beginning of the river of wealth.

Ghazipur was just up the Ganges from the more famous Benaris, but it was a world apart from that ancient city's holy sites and temples. The Government of India Alkaloid Works was the only reason that Ghazipur existed. The Works was a scattered collection of brick buildings sitting on twenty or thirty acres of parched land, surrounded by high brick walls with guard towers strategically placed. Since the river had, of late, shifted south, the Works were almost half a mile of blazing white sand from the north shore of the Ganges. If the Hordoon boys approached the Works from the river they would be shot by the guards in the towers. But if they approached the main gate, they would be granted admission to enter only if they were "of the trade."

Well, Richard and Maxi were not yet "of the trade," so they waited near the front gate until some farmers who had delivered their raw opium to the

Works left for their homes. They followed them and used the last of their stolen money to pay for a place to sleep. There they became acquainted with the base of the opium trade and the gentle people who made their meagre living growing *Papaver somniferum,* the opium poppy.

———

Ahmed, the elderly opium farmer, rose early and led the Hordoon boys to the fields. Richard translated his swiftly spoken Hindi to Maxi, who still, after all these months, barely spoke a word of the local tongue. Ahmed never went to school, but he had a formal lecture style that would have been familiar to an Oxford don. He began: "The petals of the poppy flower announce their own time of readiness. Once the leaves are at their densest orange they are about to fall. Then you must squeeze the capsule like this." And he reached down and gently but firmly squeezed the capsule between his thumb and forefinger. Then he smiled. "If it is firm like this one then you must be ready. See how it's beginning to grow a coating of white? You must check the flowers every morning. Without fail. Every morning. When the green capsule is finally completely coated with that dusty transparent whiteness it is time."

Then he reached into his pocket and produced a unique knife, called a *nashtar,* that had four slender blades held together with strands of cotton. In one deft stroke he cut the opium capsule. A thick, milk-white juice oozed from the four parallel cuts. Then he handed the *nashtar* to Richard.

Using a *nashtar* was an acquired skill. A skill Richard had yet to acquire.

"No. Your cuts are too deep. See, the resin flows back into the seeds and is lost. Try again."

And Richard did, but this time the cuts were too shallow.

"No. See, the ooze does not flow now." He shook his head and scowled. He took the *nashtar* from Richard's hand and held it out to Maxi, who quickly and accurately lanced ten capsules—just right. Ahmed smiled deeply and put a hand on Maxi's cheek.

Maxi's smile lit up that dry dusty morning.

The Hordoon brothers spent all day lancing the capsules, Richard doing more and more watching and Maxi working with ever-increasing speed, and—to Richard's profound surprise—joy.

The next morning Ahmed took the boys out to the field before sunrise and continued his lecture. "Overnight the ooze hardens into a brown gum, see?" He ran his finger across the sticky substance and held out his finger. "This is raw opium," he announced, then handed both of the boys heavy clay pots and showed them how to scoop the hardened resin into the earthen jars.

As with the *nashtar*, Richard struggled with the task while Maxi seemed to find the inherent rhythm of the process and hence real pleasure in the work.

Two days later the poppy was scored a second time and the process was repeated. A single poppy capsule would be scored up to eight times.

One night Maxi caught Richard writing in his journal.

"What are you figuring, brother mine?"

"How do you mean, figuring?"

"You sit one way when you're writing and another when you're figuring. You screw up your face, like a macaque that swallowed a bee."

Richard smiled, then showed him. Maxi eyed the figures, but they meant nothing to him. "Look, Maxi," Richard said, "the eight scorings of the opium capsule yield up to two-hundredths of an ounce of raw opium. Right?" Maxi nodded. "So Ahmed said that twenty pounds are needed per acre to turn a profit—that's about eighteen thousand poppies lanced eight times each."

Maxi nodded again, but this time he said, "So exactly what?"

"So, brother mine, although the opium poppy might be able to grow in many different countries, there are only a few places on earth where the cost of the intensive labour needed to grow the poppy is cheap enough to keep it profitable." Maxi looked at Richard blankly. "Maxi, these people hardly make any money at all, and it's that fact that allows opium to be profitable. I've checked and rechecked the figures."

"You mean they work for nothing?"

"Almost nothing."

"They work for almost nothing, but without them there is no fortune to be made in opium? Is that what you're saying?"

"Yes."

"So these people work so others can be rich?"

.. .. ..

JOURNAL ENTRY—OCTOBER 1828

I didn't answer Maxi's question. How could I? I know from my figures that these farmers are nothing more than pawns in the game where bishops and castles and queens have the real power—the money. And I know that Maxi cares for these people. Day after day he's spent more and more time with them. Of late he's even tried to learn their dances—to the delight of our hosts. And as Ahmed and his entire clan laughed at Maxi's ineptitude, a smile grew on my brother's face. But not the fierce, predatory smile he flashed in Baghdad and Calcutta. This was a smile of pure, simple contentment.

I will never forget the morning when I awakened to find Maxi staring at Ahmed and his three sons, all prostrate on mats, facing west, deep in prayer. I was tempted to make fun of the prone figures until I saw the yearning in my brother's eyes. I retreated and never spoke of it again, so shocked was I by the look on Maxi's face.

It was the hardest day of my life when I had to get Maxi to leave the opium farm. Maxi had been angry at me before—even hit me hard now and then— but never had his rage been so ferocious.

"But we have to go, Maxi," I said to him.

"Why? Why? I like it here, you know that."

It was only by inducing Maxi to chew on some of the raw opium that I calmed him enough to listen. "We are just starting, Maxi," I told him. "This is only the start of the Hordoon brothers. It is only our beginning. This place, this farm and these people, will always be here. If after—but only after—we try our luck and it doesn't work out for you, you can come back here. I'll bankroll you to come back. I promise."

"But I—"

"Maxi—"

"Brother mine, these people's lives seem to have some meaning. They are not wandering. This is their home. And their home is real. You can touch it and see it. It's in them."

I'll never forget his words. But I replied, "I know, Maxi. And they love you here too."

"They do, brother mine," Maxi said in an anguished whisper. "They really do." Then he fell into a profound silence—and I could see the tension began to rise in him once again.

chapter thirteen

Treaty Moves

Richard thought about Maxi's silence now as he confronted the unChinese silence of Chinkiang. He feared that the silence awaiting the arrival of the British Expeditionary Force in the captured city had nothing to do with love of any sort. At first Richard hoped the populace had escaped out the East Gate, but then he opened a door to an ancient courtyard—and his gorge rose in his throat. He slammed the thing shut and gasped for breath. For a moment he was desperate for a pipe, then he found his voice and called out, "Sir, over here."

Gough and his lieutenants approached. "You're white as a ..."

Richard pushed open the heavy gate and pointed into the ancient courtyard. Gough stepped in and saw a new horror. An entire family had committed suicide. Grandparents, parents, uncles, aunts, cousins, children, all on the ground—a few still writhing in pain from the knives buried hilt-deep in their chests. But no noise—not a sound.

And so it was in the rest of the city. Not a soul was left living. Not a single voice to deride or adulate the invaders. Only the silence of self-inflicted death. And as Richard watched the bodies of Chinese men, women, and children being thrown onto a pile, one upon another by the north wall of Chinkiang, he thought of the love and the vibrant life that Maxi had experienced with the peasant farmers near Ghazipur. He saw in his mind's eye Maxi dancing around the fire as Ahmed cried with laughter. He heard Maxi's hoarse cry, "I like it here, you know that!" Then Richard saw the body of a young girl roll from the top of the pile of bodies and halfway down jerk to a stop as the knife in her belly snagged on another body's belt. She dangled there like a discarded doll on a junk pile. Richard stared at her. For the first time he questioned the very reason he had come to China, all those years ago, and he knew that no amount of prayer or dovening or bowing down to Mecca would answer his question.

* * *

THE FALL OF CHINKIANG finally set off alarms in Beijing, and a High Mandarin named Kiying was enlisted to slowly and painstakingly investigate the possibility of preparing to begin to think about starting some sort of negotiations or talks or parleys with the *Fan Kuei,* the Foreign Devils.

Yangchow, the city across the river from Chinkiang, chose to pay half a million dollars in silver to be left alone. That gave the British full control of the Yangtze end of the First Emperor's Grand Canal. The British set up camp on both sides of the waterway and proceeded to raid local villages for provisions. They also commandeered junks on the river and used them as houseboats for the officers.

"From here we slowly strangle central China," Pottinger announced over a pheasant dinner on the *Cornwallis.* The officers, except for Gough, nodded their approval. McCullough proposed a toast to Pottinger, who rose to accept the adulation, wiping gravy from his chin, and said, "The Yangtze River is the throat, and as soon as we grab it and squeeze tight, the whole situation of this God-forsaken country will be determined."

There was a momentary silence as those assembled tried to decode the florid prose of their leader. The lull was broken by a tentative "Hear, hear," followed by a "Well spoken," and then many other such inane affirmatives.

From outside the Captain's cabin, Richard listened to the English congratulate themselves and get progressively more drunk.

The next morning a stifling wave of heat arrived—and stayed. A standoff followed. No junks entered or left the Grand Canal. The British didn't move from their advantageous position, but not a word came from Beijing.

And, oh yes, China began to starve.

The British suffered too. Sickness—primarily diarrhea, malaria, and dysentery—took a heavy toll on the sailors. Rats had somehow invaded every level of every ship of the entire armada. It was particularly bad on the lowest deck of the *Belleisle,* the orlop, where the soldiers lived in extremely tight quarters.

Rumblings of discontent came from the men, and the dangerous air of mutiny swept from ship to ship.

Finally Gough persuaded Pottinger that they had to do something to force the Emperor's hand. "Nanking is the key, sir. Once we have it under our control, the Emperor will have to sue for peace. Sir, if we stay here things could degenerate quickly." Pottinger's eyes opened wide and his nostrils flared, but Gough continued. "This canal can be secured with less than a third of our ships, and the rest could proceed upriver to Nanking and take her."

Pottinger rose and said, "I'll take your suggestion under advisement," then left for his cabin.

Four hours later he emerged and gave his orders. "Twenty ships are to stay and keep control of the canal. The rest are to follow me on the *Cornwallis* upriver to Nanking."

Gough, openly relieved, nodded his head and shouted orders. Shortly afterwards, fifty vessels of the British Expeditionary Force made their way upriver toward the ancient capital, Nanking.

Halfway there the British were told by a formal delegation that a Mandarin they had dealt with before over the "Hong Kong issue," Ilipu, was on his way.

"So, I see that the Emperor has finally seen the light," remarked Pottinger, scratching the non-existent stubble on his chin in a fine imitation of thought.

"So it would seem, sir," Richard said, after he had translated the last of the courier's words.

"Dismiss the heathen," Pottinger ordered.

Richard did, but in much more conciliatory terms.

As he walked the courier back to his craft he heard Pottinger announce in a loud voice, seemingly to Gough but in reality for the benefit of the sailors within earshot, "The real war on the Yangtze is about to begin. It isn't going to be fought by your soldiers or our great man o' war sailing ships, although, I admit those did their part in this tapestry. The real warriors in this conflict—and the heroes, too—will be the diplomats."

Gough stared after Pottinger's retreating figure and scowled. Richard could understand how galling it must be for a real soldier like Gough to hear a strutting popinjay like Pottinger claim the title "warrior"— "heroes" be damned. Real soldiers never believe in heroes.

* * *

ON LAND, not three miles from the ship, Ilipu sat with his superior, Kiying. Tea was brought and pickled watermelon seeds. The men sipped their chai and spat out the husks of the seeds.

"The barbarians are pleased that you are here, Ilipu," Kiying said.

"Evidently, sir."

"They also believe you to be in charge of the delegation," Kiying added.

"Only a barbarian would make such a foolish assumption, sir."

"Let them continue in this belief, Ilipu," Kiying ordered.

Ilipu nodded and poured more tea for Kiying.

Both Ilipu and Kiying assumed that, like all other barbarians who had set foot in the Celestial Kingdom, the British had come not simply to trade but rather with their sights set on plundering the heart of the Celestial Kingdom, Beijing. And both Mandarins knew that the first duty of every Manchu was to preserve the dynasty. It would be a catastrophe if Beijing fell to these round-eyed monsters. But the two Mandarins were troubled. They did not have real instructions from Beijing, except to make sure that the barbarians removed their ships from the Yangtze, and their powers to negotiate were not clear.

Both also knew that they would be either rewarded or punished based upon how successful they were in getting the *Fan Kuei*'s ships out of the waters of the Celestial Kingdom.

On May 11, 1842, the Mandarins made their first approach to the barbarians—through representatives, naturally.

* * *

RICHARD WAS CALLED to the deck of the *Cornwallis* and then quickly ushered into the Captain's cabin. There before Admiral Gough and Governor General Pottinger stood three middle-level Chinese civil servants, who delivered their message.

"So?" Pottinger demanded of Richard.

"He says that we are to cease plundering traffic on the river and prepare ourselves for a round of talks."

Pottinger spat out, "Tell these little humbugs that that is precisely what we are *not* going to do. We will continue our war on the river until such time as an acceptable treaty is signed."

Richard relayed the Governor General's message. The three men took it well, or so it seemed. Then Pottinger added, "Tell these three buffoons that they are not to return. That there will be no negotiating—none—with anyone but this Kiying and Ilipu. And that those two scoundrels needn't bother coming unless they have full plenipotentiary powers." Pottinger inexplicably giggled, then repeated in his over-educated lisp, "Potent plenipotentiary powers." An odd smile crept over his face as he added, "There will be no 'I've got no right-ee to agree-ee to' or 'I've got to bring-ee this-ee thing-ee back to my Emperor' bull thwap." He turned to Richard. Richard opened his mouth, but no words came. "Tell them, man."

Richard knew that Mandarins, even high-level Mandarins such as Kiying and Ilipu, didn't have plenipotentiary powers as they are understood in the West and had no choice but to proceed carefully in any negotiations. He was about to tell Pottinger, when he noted the man's set jaw and decided against offering unsolicited advice. Richard translated Pottinger's message. The Chinese turned ashen and hurriedly left.

Before they were even off the ship Pottinger ordered the flotilla farther upriver and said, "Gough, bombard the south side of the river as we go."

"But there's nothing there ..."

"Precisely."

"To prove a point, sir?"

"What else?" Pottinger demanded. "Bombard the south side of the river, then let's get up to Nanking. Chop chop, Gough. Chop chop."

chapter fourteen

Nanking

On Friday, August 5, 1842, the steamer *Queen* pulled the *Cornwallis* into position before the walls of Nanking. Later that day a higher-level Mandarin named Chang, under a white flag, boarded the flagship. Despite Pottinger's claim that he would not see any representative of the Beijing government that did not have full plenipotentiary powers, he surprised his officers by agreeing to meet with Chang. Again Richard was called.

Chang handed over a parchment text. Richard had only a rudimentary understanding of Chinese writing, so he offered it back to Chang and asked in Chinese, "Would you be kind enough to read the missive?"

Chang smiled, knowing full well that Richard had made this request because, like all other barbarians, he couldn't read. Some barbarians could learn to speak, but few could master the writing of the Middle Kingdom. His smile broadened as he read, "Ilipu, Mandarin and personal representative of the Celestial Emperor, requests that you not attack the sacred city of Nanking."

Richard translated quickly.

Pottinger laughed.

"Why does the chicken-faced barbarian cackle?" Chang demanded. "Does he have no manners, understanding, or sophistication?"

Richard translated every word. After a shocked moment Pottinger responded, "Tell the little monkey that Beijing, too, is not immune from the shot of our cannons."

Chang looked at Richard to be sure that he had heard the translation correctly, then drew himself to his full height and said, "You foreigners have been unopposed thus far only because of the kindness of the great Emperor, who cannot bear to kill or injure human creatures. But beware, Foreign Devil. If pushed too far the Emperor will call upon his people to rise—every man, woman, and child—every bush will be a soldier ready to kill the hideous barbarians." He turned to Richard. "Translate to the round-eyed maniac."

Richard did—word for word.

"Tell the little monkey to watch his foul mouth," Pottinger said as his face turned a vivid red.

"Enough of the maniacs and monkeys," Gough said quietly.

"What do you expect?" Chang angrily responded. "You kill people everywhere, plunder goods, and act like pirates, disgraceful, disgraceful and completely unacceptable. How can you say you are anything more than bandits? How? You alien barbarians invade our China, your insignificant country attacks our celestial court—how can you say you are anything but common thieves?" Chang slammed his fist on the table and spat at Pottinger's feet.

Gough held a hand to restrain the Governor General. "Ilipu's request is at least a beginning," he whispered.

Two days later, Ilipu sent four officials as his plenipotentiary. Pottinger rejected them outright, and the *Cornwallis*, for the first time, opened its gun ports and prepared to assault the ancient city walls of Nanking.

Quickly another embassy from Ilipu arrived promising a ransom of three million silver dollars and negotiations as soon as Kiying arrived. Pottinger's response was to order Gough to land a full regiment of Madras troops, complete with horses and artillery.

Finally, talks were arranged, but not onboard the British warship—rather, in a temple outside the town's walls. A commission was handed over by Gough. The Chinese responded that they would need time to examine the document, and that while they did the British should call off their offensive. Pottinger responded, "There has been enough dilly-dallying. The next thing you heathens will hear will be the sound of Her Majesty's cannons as they knock down the walls of Nanking."

The next morning a messenger arrived on the flagship to tell Gough that Ilipu and Kiying had read the commission and were prepared to appear for formal talks. A skeleton of the treaty was hastily drawn up in both languages and the meeting was set.

At precisely ten o'clock the next morning Kiying and Ilipu paid a ceremonial visit to the *Cornwallis*. They handed over an agreed-upon version of the treaty and were shown around the ship, offered tea and cherry brandy. It was the first opportunity for the British to see Kiying, and they liked what they saw. He had a fine, manly countenance, with a pleasant overall cast to his person. But Ilipu, with whom the British had dealt in the past, looked like a broken old man.

When the two Mandarins entered the Captain's cabin they noticed a picture of Queen Victoria. When Gough explained who she was, the Mandarins bowed.

The rest of the negotiations that day were straightforward. It was clear from the beginning that the primary concern of the two Mandarins was the immediate departure of the English fleet. "How many times do we have to tell these heathens that we're not leaving until we have a signed treaty?" Pottinger, ever the diplomat, spat out in disgust.

Negotiations over the minutiae of the treaty itself finally began.

Two days later Pottinger and Gough received a formal invitation to view Nanking. They were welcomed to the city by a crudely organized twelve-gun salute. Then, at the very end of a long working session, the real reason for the war was at long last broached—the opium trade. But the Chinese refused to talk about opium in any public forum whatsoever and adamantly rejected any official discussion of the matter.

"If I may, sir?" asked Richard.

"Go ahead," Pottinger said, with an openly bored shrug.

"Suggest to them that the subject of opium is better discussed unofficially. It is, after all, a private matter that needs quiet consideration by men of wisdom."

"More horse thwap."

"Do it," said Gough.

Richard spoke to the Mandarins, who were visibly relieved by the suggestion and quickly entered into an animated conversation. "Why do you English permit the cultivation of the opium poppy in your Indian colony?"

Pottinger offered up the stock British answer. "If we stopped its growth there it would simply move to other locales." From his "figuring" Richard knew the economics of the opium trade and knew this was not necessarily true. "Besides," Pottinger continued, "if your people are virtuous they will desist from the evil practice; and if your officers are incorruptible, and obey their orders, no opium can enter your country."

"This is no answer," said Kiying, "and as you well know neither virtue nor incorruptibility is in vast supply in any society."

"Especially in heathen worlds like yours," Pottinger muttered.

But before Pottinger's slander could be translated Gough asked, "Why not legalize it? At least then you could tax it and your government could collect money to help your people."

The Chinese refused to honour the suggestion with a response.

Richard listened and translated for days and days. In the middle of the seventh day he realized with a shock that the other issue, close to the hearts of all the British negotiators—namely, the opening of China to foreign missionaries—was not even going to be mentioned. As the official negotiations ran their course nary a word was spoken on the subjects of religion and opium! God and opium, the two major causes of the war, never entered the discussions that led to the final draft of the treaty.

The final agreement saw the Chinese paying an indemnity of twenty-one million silver dollars, six million of them earmarked to pay compensation for the twenty thousand chests of opium thrown into the sea by Canton's Commissioner Lin. More importantly for Richard, five ports were opened to trade: Canton, Amoy, Foochow, Ningpo, and of course Shanghai. The Hong trading system was abolished. Consuls were to arrive and be treated as equals, and a schedule of customs duties was to be accepted and not amended at the will of any local Mandarin.

Beijing's acceptance came before the end of the month, and the signed treaty was laid out on the Captain's table of HMS *Cornwallis*—four silk-bound copies in both English and Chinese.

chapter fifteen
The White Birds Land

Gough immediately ordered the English fleet back downstream—toward the Bend in the River—where Richard and Maxi, their obligations to the British Expeditionary Force completed, fully intended to jump ship and begin life.

The Chinese locals saw the ships heading downstream and assumed the armada had been defeated by the glorious armies of the Emperor. But it wasn't just the uninformed populace who claimed victory.

"Why are they celebrating?" Pottinger asked Richard as the *Cornwallis* passed by jeering crowds on the banks of the river.

Richard knew that the ruling Manchus believed the treaty they had signed hadn't really cost them anything. They were sure that the extremely restrictive access to Canton would simply be repeated in five other ports. Allowing consuls to come to these ports was fine with Beijing since, as far as they were concerned, *Fan Kuei* should be superintended by a *Taipan*—a business leader—of their own, who should, naturally, report to his Chinese superior. As for the other provisions the English insisted on—namely the acceptance of an English ambassador in Beijing, the demand to dismantle the Hong merchant system, and standardizing tariff rates—well, these were niceties that could be sidestepped as the Manchus deemed necessary. From the Manchu point of view nothing important had changed.

But Richard suspected the Chinese were wrong this time. Terribly wrong. He assumed the western powers wouldn't carve up China as they had Africa. They would not take over China as the English had India or the

Russians had central Asia. What they would probably do was riddle China through and through—like water carves out tunnels in limestone. Shortly, the Europeans would be able to work and live and sell their opium—and proselytize—at will. With, in fact, an absolute colonial confidence.

London's response to the treaty was less than enthusiastic. One newspaper opined, "It secures us a few round millions of dollars and no end of very refreshing tea." Another editorialized that the best thing about the treaty was that the English populace would no longer have to be bothered with reports of "sweeping away whole crowds of poor pigtailed animals with cannon or bayonet." Neither paper ran the story on the front page; both gave several more column inches to the recapture of Kabul.

The Protestant community and their press, however, were joyous. One of their more effusive newspapers stated, "Since clearly God had chosen England to chastise and humble China so He will likely employ her to introduce the blessings of Christian civilization."

The American Evangelicals were equally enthusiastic. They saw God's work as preparing the way for their imminent success.

The opium merchants on both sides of the Atlantic Ocean didn't bother expressing their pleasure with the treaty in print but simply began to plan for the full opening of China. The offices of Dent and Company in London, Oliphant and Company (also known as the House of Zion) in Philadelphia, Jardine Matheson Traders in Edinburgh, and of course the Vrassoons' British East India Company were hives of activity as they mobilized to move, en masse, into the new treaty ports.

* * *

IN PARIS a certain Madame Colombe looked at her sternly handsome Jesuit son and asked, "Are you and your order ready for a serious return to China?" He smiled, kissed his mother's hand, then took his leave.

When he was gone, Madame Colombe's other child, Suzanne, entered the room. "Are you and your girls ready for a sea voyage, *ma cherie?*"

"It is time to extend our business, Mother, and this *Shan-geh-hi* sounds ideal. Will you be joining me?"

"I'm too old for the travel, but I do envy the adventure that awaits you, my darling."

"Will my brother be doing whatever it is he does in China as well?"

Madame Colombe shrugged her shoulders and smiled. Whores and priests, priests and whores—the women in her family had given birth to both in equal numbers for generation upon generation.

* * *

IN A FAR WING of his palatial estate in Hampstead, the Vrassoon Patriarch pocketed the urgent message and took his leave of the staff of Bedlam, who were paid to carefully dress as lords and ladies for what he thought of as his mad girl's Mid-Winter Eve's Ball.

"Don't go now, Daddy!" The girl's shrill voice came all the way across the vast room. He turned and glared at the nurses dressed as duchesses at her side, then quickly crossed to her. She sat in the large chair in her expensive party dress, her eyes alive with pleasure. This was, after all, her yearly treat. The Vrassoons' Mid-Winter Eve's Ball—a falsehood within a secret—the last vestige of Eliazar Vrassoon's heart's obligation to a creature he once loved.

"Just for a minute or two, then I'll be back, dearest." He looked sternly at her nurses.

"And you'll dance with me, Daddy?"

"Of course I'll dance with you. Would a Mid-Winter Eve's Ball in your honour be complete if I didn't dance with you?" He pecked at her dusky cheek, turned, then hurried to his waiting carriage.

Forty minutes later he entered his private office in the British East India Company. There he was met by his eldest son, Ari, and his two lead China hands.

"So?" he demanded.

"It's not ready yet."

"Bollocks!" Eliazar Vrassoon shouted—no longer the Duke of Warwickshire, now simply what he truly was, a bare-knuckle street-fighter protecting his hard-earned territory. Then he turned to his son. "Where are those Baghdadi boys?" Despite the fact that Richard and Maxi were both in their thirties they would always be boys in the eyes of Eliazar Vrassoon. Dangerous boys.

An image flashed into his mind: a young boy's hand pushing open a door to reveal the madwoman as a beautiful little girl asleep in her tiny bed. He remembered exactly what he had said: "Your father has agreed, boy. Your father has agreed."

"Our ..."

"Your father ... has agreed," he had said sternly.

He shoved the memory away and looked out the window. It was the longest night of the year, but the blaze of light from the thousands of candles in the ballroom would banish the darkness. An eerie chill went through him. Some cultures thought that when you felt that, it was a cat crossing your grave. Other cultures believed that your death had found your whereabouts. But Vrassoon was from neither of these cultures. He shook off the feeling and repeated his question.

"Where are the Baghdadi boys?"

* * *

ON THE VERY LAST DAY OF 1842, Richard and Maxi shared a bottle of exquisite champagne, then completed their plans for Shanghai's upcoming concession auction.

As they did, in London, the Great Seal of England was affixed to a copy of the Treaty of Nanking at the Lord Chancellor's house on Great George Street. Six blocks away, Queen Victoria danced in the new year at Buckingham Palace.

* * *

AS HER GRACIOUS MAJESTY danced in London, Richard breathed the opium deep into his lungs and forced his mind back to how all this began. In the flickering brazier light, through the haze of opium smoke, he read his journal entries, beginning with the night after he and Maxi had left the opium farmers, over fifteen years earlier.

.. .. ..

JOURNAL ENTRY—APRIL 1828

The two small earthen jars, each packed to the brim with raw opium that Ahmed has given us in return for our three months of labour in his fields, will be our entrance fee to the world of the Works at Ghazipur and the second part of our education in opium.

The raw opium arrives at the Works in early April. It is weighed and then poured into wide stone vats in a covered warehouse. The product resembles a molasses-like tar but smells like freshly mown hay.

It smells of promise.

Opium absorbs moisture from the air quickly and needs to be thoroughly dried before it is packed for shipment. The dry, dust-rich winds of Ghazipur in late April, May, and June are perfect for the task. Once the dry weather establishes itself, small portions of the paste are taken from the storage vats and spread in shallow wooden trays on raised concrete platforms to dry.

Eventually there are hundreds of gallons of opium in the drying trays, stirred by mechanical mixers that often break down—at which point Maxi and I step in with our spades and rakes. For months Maxi and I have stirred the stuff in the stifling heat, exposing every ounce of the drug to the air.

.. .. ..

The monkeys have been our only real distraction during these long hot days. Although the animals have the run of the Works they never eat the opium from the drying trays—but they do drink from the nearby stream, and always seem a bit soused. One day, near the end of our first month, we stopped our stirring and watched a clearly dopy monkey walk on its back legs out along a tree branch that overhangs the Work's wall by some six or eight feet.

He almost got to the end of the slender limb when he let out a screech, teetered forward, and fell the thirty or so feet to the hard ground, head clunking when he hit. He lay there for a moment, then got up, smiled at us, gave a toothy chatter, took one step ... and fell over dead.

It was the first thing to put a smile on Maxi's face since we left Ahmed and the opium farm.

.. .. ..

I've learned that Maxi wasn't smiling at a drunken monkey. In the monkey's actions he'd seen thought—strategic thought in motion—and physics. As the monkey moved on the thin sections of the tree limb he reached up, grabbing a branch above him, thereby dividing his weight between the branch above and the one below.

I watched Maxi turn slowly in a full circle, taking in the entire perimeter wall of the Works. Only three trees were close enough to the wall to have branches that came into the compound. One was close to the caker's hut. It had one slender branch that stretched eight or nine feet past the glass-studded top of the wall. The branch was so thin that the guards must have ignored it since it seemed to present no means of access to the grounds.

"What do you see?" I asked him.

Maxi shielded his eyes from the scorching sun and looked above the slender branch. "Maybe twelve feet above that branch is a cluster of somewhat thicker limbs—too high for a man to reach from the lower branch, unless there was a tool of some ..."

Then he smiled as he pointed toward an unwound turban of one of the cakers stretched over the caker's roof to dry in the sun.

"Think about ways to distribute a man's weight between two or even three points—about how to divide a man's weight so a slender branch would not have to bear the full load," he said as he kept looking at the branch over the wall and the unwound caker's turban.

"It's a like a puzzle," I said.

"Aye," he smiled back, then added, "I've always loved puzzles. This one is challenging but solvable."

———

That night, as the stars ignited the southern sky and Maxi worked through the mechanics of suspending weight through triangulation, Richard finished putting into his journal all he knew about their future source of wealth, opium.

.. .. ..

Once it has dried, some of the hardened opium is moved to a shed where it is pressed into blocks wrapped in oiled Nepal paper and sold as Akbari, *which is locally consumed.* Akbari *is used mostly for medicinal purposes. It is dissolved in water or alcohol. In India* Akbari *is the poor man's malaria cure, his rejuvenator in old age, his only relief from fatigue and pain.*

"Then why don't we sell this Akbari, *brother mine? We could do that here," Maxi said.*

"So you could stay with the opium farmers, Maxi?"

"Why not? Why not just sell Akbari?*"

"Because the selling of relief from pain and fatigue is not the same as selling happiness."

"What are you ...?"

"Listen to me, Maxi. I agree that there is some money in selling a cure for pain, but not a fortune. Not a future. The real money is in selling the dream of happiness. Smoked opium, Chandra, *is where the money is. And no one in India smokes opium—that only happens in China. No, don't turn away from me, Maxi. Listen. At first the Chinese mixed the raw opium with tobacco or betel leaves in what they called* Medak. *But* Medak *only yields the smoker little dreams. Some daring smoker must have decided, 'The hell with the chaff, I'll smoke the wheat.' And he did. And the uncut opium granted him a world of dreams. An entire universe of dreams. Try to understand this, Maxi. We're in the business of selling dreams—and once the smoker has visited the dream worlds, he wants to live there. That's what we are going to supply him with, Maxi—access—access to the infinity of dreams."*

Maxi stared at me for a long moment, then returned to his "rope calculations."

.. .. ..

Maxi and I worked ourselves silly proving to the Works that we could be trusted enough to become cakers. After three months, finally, today, the monsoons arrived. With the rain there is no need for more stirring, and all the opium was hauled indoors to the caking shed. Either they are going to throw us out on our Baghdadi arses or they are going to offer us what we've been angling for—work in the caking shed.

For three months we have been stirring the muck and planning. Sewing false pockets into our britches, watching the monkeys cross over the walls on their tree branches, and digging holes near the one dark corner in the wall that can't be seen by either of the two nearby watchtowers.

So it was that we found ourselves standing in the deserted courtyard of the Works, in the rain. And it rained. And we stood. And we waited in the rain. And the Indian supervisors watched us strange boys from far away and wondered at our endurance. We stood there for two days and two nights, not moving, not eating—waiting.

Finally on the morning of the third day the head supervisor came out under an umbrella held by a lackey. "What is it that you want? Why are you still here? You have exactly one minute to answer my question, then I will have the guards shoot the two of you," he said in a furiously fast and highly accented rural Hindi.

I smiled and nodded my head. I had missed some of the first two sentences but got the gist. "Thank you for honouring us with your attentions. We want simply to stay and work for your fine firm."

"But the rainy season has come. There is no more need for stirrers."

"We thank you for the opportunity to learn the art of stirring. Now we wish to learn the art of the caker."

That clearly surprised the supervisor, and he had to think for a moment. He said, finally, "We will pay you nothing. In return we will teach you the caker's art."

"That sounds entirely fair," I replied quickly, knowing full well that the man would be pocketing our salaries. Maxi smiled.

The supervisor turned on his heel and retreated indoors, out of the rain.

I took a step forward, slipped in the muck, and fell to the ground—and lay there.

"Get up, brother mine, it's wet out here."

"Tired."

"Yes, but this is not such a good place to sleep."
"So tired."
"Your journal's getting wet."
That got me to my feet.

.. .. ..

And so we have become cakers at the Government of India Alkaloid Works in Ghazipur—and made our first serious opium trade: our labour for their product.

chapter sixteen
A Calcutta Death,
a Life at the Works

"He's dead," the warehouse manager announced bluntly. Death was hardly an unusual occurrence in the stifling heat of the Vrassoon warehouses. Although, death of a non-Indian was different—of a Vrassoon co-religionist, almost unheard of.

The Vrassoon Patriarch stood over the body and was momentarily tempted to place the point of his polished shoe against Hordoon's nose and push. But he resisted. "Leave us," he said, and the manager retreated to a far corner.

Vrassoon stared down at the dead man. "So it is over," he said in a low voice. "Our deal is finally done. That which joined us now belongs just to me and awaits me in her bed. As any good girl would. How could someone like you even know someone as precious as her?" He looked away from the body, then back at the prematurely aged man at his feet. He was tempted to say something solemn, then thought better of it and called out, "Contact the family and have them claim the body."

"I don't think there is a family to ..."

"Of course. Just get the body out of here," he muttered.

"Shall we hire someone to sit by the body until it is prepared for burial?"

Vrassoon thought about that. Then about the girl. No longer a girl, now a young woman. With sudden rages and unpredictable, sudden lusts. He thought about her docile beauty, then about being with her in London soon, and said, "No. The Ganges is good enough for the locals. It's good enough for him."

* * *

THE CAKERS SAT along both of the long sides of the dark shed with the tools of their trade lined up in front of them: brass cup about six inches in diameter, several bundles of poppy-petal sheets (made of pressed poppy petals), a pail of inferior opium called *lewah* (a semi-liquid form of the drug), and a box of crushed poppy stems and leaves called "poppy trash." Richard and Maxi watched as the caker assigned to teach them took his brass cup and lined the bottom with poppy sheets, then adhered it together with *lewah* until he had a base of about half an inch. "Give me a lump of dried opium," he ordered. Maxi did. The caker dropped the dried opium, just over three pounds in weight, on top of the poppy sheets. Then the caker fitted poppy sheets over the top and tucked them into the sides until he had a complete ball.

He held it out for the boys to see. "Do you understand?" he asked. The boys nodded. "Good." The caker dipped the ball into the *lewah* again and rolled it in the poppy trash. "The finished ball," he said, "is then moved from my brass cup to the clay drying moulds."

When the balls were finished they weighed in at just under four pounds—three of smokable opium, one of poppy trash. These were then packed into specially made mango-wood chests, two layers separated by yet more poppy trash. The chest itself, very much like a sailor's footlocker, was then sealed with pitch to keep the water out—and, theoretically, thieves away from the valuable opium within.

Richard and Maxi quickly proved themselves adept at the task. Within the week they had their own spaces against the south wall of the caking shed. And there they worked, fourteen hours a day, seven days a week, for the three months of the monsoon season.

The cool rain pelted down on the roof and often sluiced beneath the walls of the place. One morning a huge coral snake swam in with the rainwater. Maxi had a way with snakes. He was faster than a mongoose. He leapt to his feet, that damned smile on his lips, and danced toward the poisonous reptile. Then, with lightning speed, he reached down and nabbed the snake behind the head and pressed it to the ground. The serpent's body whipped back and forth in the air. The cakers screamed and raced for the doors. Maxi yanked the serpent up, holding its flat head between his thumb and index finger, and quickly bit it behind the eyes. Then, with the snake's blood on his lips, he dangled the thing from his mouth and pranced around like a clown in the bazaar. The cakers applauded wildly.

It terrified Richard.

The opium was shipped to Calcutta on a guarded train that picked up the mango-wood chests every four days once the rains came.

Maxi and Richard simply skimmed. Not a lot at a time. No need. The factory produced almost sixty-five hundred cups a day. A little patience, and the secret pockets in their britches filled by evening. Before they headed to the sleeping room they made a quick trip to their hole between the towers. After several months, Maxi and Richard Hordoon had a stake.

When the monsoon season ended, the Hordoon boys left the Works. They found a deserted alley in a nearby town and waited for a new-moon night. Then they snuck out of the alley and carefully approached the walls of the Works.

Up close the wall seemed huge. Maxi sang softly to himself as he threaded the length of turban cloth through the belt loops on his pants and then around and through his legs, cinching it together over his crotch. He flung the other end, which he had anchored with a piece of chain, over the highest branch of the tree, knotted it, and handed the end to Richard.

"This'll work?"

"Brother mine, do you have a better way of getting back into the Works and getting our opium? Maybe we should just walk up to the front gate and see if they'll understand our plight and just let us in. 'We're sorry to bother you, but we've been stealing from you for months, and now we'd like to come in and get what we've taken.' I'm sure they'll understand, Richard."

"Shut up, Maxi."

"Done. Now, you pull, slow and steady, when I signal you."

Maxi shinnied up the tree like any monkey and headed toward the slender overhanging branch. Before he did, he fixed the top end of his rope triangle on a high branch, then the apex on the trunk. He took a deep breath and signalled to Richard, who pulled—slow and steady. And Maxi's cantilever worked. As he moved along the ever-thinning branch, his weight was held less and less by the branch and more and more by the triangulation of the turban cloth.

Once across the wall he skittered down and hid in the shadows, and when he was ready he quickly raced to their hiding hole and scooped out their swag—almost sixteen pounds of *Chandra* opium. Within twenty minutes the Hordoon boys were racing along the river toward the sea—with their very first opium shipment.

They stopped in a small, dusty town almost twenty miles upriver from the Works, found a dark alley, and fell to the ground exhausted. Maxi curled in the dust and was asleep in a minute, Richard shortly thereafter.

Both awoke with a start. They were being watched.

"Where?" Richard barked.

"Right in front of us, brother mine," said Maxi as he slowly got to his feet.

Richard shook his head and, sure enough, an old man stood not three feet from them. A cloud moved and a slender beam of moonlight lit the man's ancient features. Sorrow was etched into the deep lines of his face. Then the old man sat in the dust right in front of them and remained motionless, as if he were part of the ground itself. It was only then that the Hordoon boys realized that he was almost naked.

Suddenly the man's head began to shake violently, and his voice, an echo from the depths of a vast cave, startled the boys. He pointed at them and said, "Angad and Bali."

"What's he saying, brother mine?"

Richard ignored Maxi's question and asked the man in Hindi, "Isn't Angad the god who killed his own brother, Bali?"

The old man's head stopped shaking, and his eyes welled with dark, viscous tears. "Brother will kill brother," he said, his voice a harsh whisper.

Richard knelt and, in Hindi, spoke directly into the man's face. "You see that in us?" The man did not answer. Richard repeated his question, but again the man gave no response. Finally Richard grabbed the ancient by his bony shoulders and shouted, "Do you see that in us?"

The old man's hand came up from the yellow dust of the alley. He touched Richard's forehead, then pointed at Maxi with a spindly, yellow-dusted finger.

Richard swiped his hand viciously across his forehead. Maxi noted that the yellow dust was unmoved by his brother's ministrations.

"Damn it, Richard, what's he saying?"

But the toothless man was now walking away. Suddenly he bent over double and laughter spewed out of him—the laughter of utter futility. The laughter of one who has seen the world as it is and realized that he is not important, just a tiny part of a deity's infinite jest.

"Why is the old one laughing? What did he say?" Maxi pressed as the man disappeared into the blackness at the far end of the alley.

"It was hard to translate, his accent ..."

"You're a lousy liar, brother mine. Leave that to me. So what did the old fool say?"

"Don't call him an old fool, Maxi."

"Ah, and why is that?"

Richard didn't answer. He thought of a man who would kill his own brother, then looked at Maxi and began to laugh.

"You too? What the hell are *you* laughing at?"

"Us. Look at us, Maxi. We're just kids, Maxi. Just kids."

* * *

OVER THE COURSE of the next two months, the young Hordoons made their way, with their stolen opium, to the smallish seaport of Vishakhapatnam, some six hundred miles south of Calcutta. There they found a merchant willing to buy some of their product and purchased two passages on a clipper ship to China—the Celestial Kingdom, where opium turned to gold.

Maxi loved everything about the ship. He was always above deck, learning all he could about the complex block-and-tackle systems and intricate knots that controlled the acres of canvas that drove the vessel ever eastward.

But by the third day out from port Richard had still not conquered his sea-sickness and sat by an open porthole on the steerage deck trying not to retch.

An hour earlier, desperate to overcome his nausea, he had opened one of their remaining opium packets and thrown some of the drug into his mouth. The grit was still in his teeth as he took in large gulps of sea air through the open porthole.

"Try this, me son."

Richard recoiled at the knurled brown root and the tiny, filthy hand that held it not an inch from his nose. He looked past the root and the hand and saw a very small, crippled man in a stained black cassock.

"It's ginger root, lad. Chew on't. It'll help."

"Thank you, but ..."

"It's part of God's bounty, me son. God provides for every need, all you have to do is look closely. God provides. Chew on't, lad."

Richard did, and was immediately astonished by the intense, unusual flavour. He didn't feel like retching so much, but spitting certainly gained a new appeal.

"Don't swallow it, it's nae peeled. Just chew." Then the ugly, foul-smelling little man sat right beside Richard and asked, "On which of God's quests are you, me son?"

"My brother and I are off to China," Richard managed to say.

"To do God's work," the little man said, nodding. It wasn't a question. He rested his largish head against the swaying wall of the ship. "I was much older than you the first time I landed in the Middle Kingdom."

That perked up Richard's interest. "How many times have you been there?"

"Four. God has granted his servant four lengthy stays." He nodded again and smiled. "Yes, He has been very kind to His Brother Matthew," then he added with a further tiny smile, "S.J."

"S.J.?"

His small hand touched Richard's cheek as he said in a gentle voice, "My poor benighted pagan boy, Society of Jesus." Then without prompting he added, "The *Irish* Society of Jesus."

Richard assumed he was supposed to respond so he said, "Ah."

"I doubt there's any White man alive who knows more about the Middle Kingdom than I do. I even speak what they call the Common Tongue." Then a brilliant smile crossed his face. "It's a long voyage. Learning a new language might help you pass the time."

Richard smiled back, his nausea now in retreat. He wondered if the opium had finally kicked in, or was it the magic of this tiny Irish Jesuit? He didn't care.

Brother Matthew began to speak. He had a vast knowledge of China and of everything that influenced the Chinese.

Every morning they would meet at sunrise just after Brother Matthew had completed his prayers. While Richard prepared their morning meal he had his morning chew of opium. He was aware that each day he was using just a bit more than the day before, but it calmed him and allowed him to concentrate. Besides, it wasn't *Chandu,* smokable opium, just bits of the raw product to keep the seasickness at bay.

As soon as the Jesuit finished eating, which he did forcefully and with surprising gusto for one so small, the lesson would begin. Brother Matthew was pleasantly surprised by Richard's linguistic ability, and after three weeks together they were conversing in rudimentary Mandarin.

Although Richard was pleased to learn the local tongue, he was more interested in learning what Brother Matthew knew about the Middle Kingdom—and the opium trade. And Brother Matthew was an enthusiastic teacher. When they got to a topic that he really liked he would leap to his feet and hobble back and forth in front of his ever-attentive pupil, gesturing with his tiny hands and speaking as if a large conclave had gathered to hang on his every word.

"At Calcutta, the government of India—read the government of sodding England, may the fat cow rot in Hell—sells the chests of opium at open auction to the likes of the British East India Company ..."

The bloody Vrassoons, Richard thought, catching himself already using the little man's habits of speech.

"... which holds a monopoly on all direct trade from England to China, and whose Indiaman sailing ships are the largest ocean-going vessels in the world."

That surprised Richard. So the Vrassoons had a monopoly on all direct trade from England to China. It had to have taken some real coin to line enough parliamentary pockets to keep that in place.

"There's also Dent and Company, whose English firm have been China traders since the mid-seventeenth century, as well as Jardine Matheson, the huge Scottish trading company, and the American Oliphant and Company, who claim to be in the missionary delivery business and whose ostentatious *piety*"—he said the word as if it were a ridiculous joke— "gives rise to their nickname, the House of Zion." At that he laughed aloud and repeated the name "House of Zion" eight or ten times, each time with more relish than the time before. "Apostates one and all! Bound for the fires of Hell they are. Poor misguided souls. Without Rome, what are we? I ask you that! What are we?"

Richard didn't know and said nothing. Brother Matthew happily continued. "You might note that their heretical faith and missionary zeal never got in the way of their opium trading. Wha' think you o' that?"

Again Richard didn't know what to say and was saved by the continuing monologue of his tiny teacher.

"Then there are some smaller independents."

But behind many of them had to be the money the Vrassoons made from the monopoly granted to them by Parliament, Richard thought.

Brother Matthew laughed, a high, girlish giggle. "And it's all perfectly legal—in India. But the moment the mango-wood opium chests are onboard ship, the government of India—read England, may she sink in the sea with all the bitch's sterling boys—turns its back, washes its hands like Pontius Pilate, and wonders, 'Goodness gracious, where do you think all that opium is going?'"

This last was done in a whistling, sibilant, Etonian accent that, at the time, Richard didn't recognize. Clearly the little man liked to imitate aristocrats and government officials, and Richard supposed him good at it.

"Perfectly legal opium leaves India and becomes contraband the moment it approaches its intended market—China.

"From the beginning of the process everyone knows that opium is made specifically for the Chinese market. It's totally adapted to Chinese methods and tastes." Then he giggled again and said, "It's the only commodity that the English have to trade that the Chinese want—want for their tea. Tea has, from the beginning, been the end goal for the English. Only Chinese black tea can withstand the long sea voyage and keep its potency, son. And it doesn't hurt that the import duties extracted for that potency fills Her Majesty's cunting tax coffers. All that loot must buy the bitch many a fine frock!

"So there is pressure from all sides to trade. Indian opium for Chinese tea—Chinese tea in England for pounds sterling—pounds sterling for Indian opium from the Indian government—England again. Soon the English won't even bother with pounds sterling to India, they'll make the poor Hindus buy the cotton shirts from their Manchester factories. Shirts for opium. Opium for silver. Silver for shirts. And round and round and round, like the Devil and his whore with a keg of rum."

And at every turn the Vrassoons take their cut, Richard thought.

That night Richard wrote in his journal.

.. .. ..

There is always a tremendous demand for dreams. Brother Matthew claims that a Chinese labourer, who makes twenty taels *a month, from which he needs to feed, clothe, and house his family of six, will often spend as much as ten of those* taels *for his opium.*

The little Jesuit just can't understand that.

I can.

Only under the effects of the opium is the labourer no longer just a worker living in poverty, without hope of change. Suddenly he is enjoying the luxuries that life grants only the fortunate. He is no longer poor. He is no longer a two-legged mule. He is a proud lord—for as long as the effects of the drug last.

———

The lesson continued the next morning when Brother Matthew produced a map and pointed out places and names as he spoke. "At the turn of the century the Manchu Emperor in Beijing forbade any European access to the Celestial Kingdom. Twenty years before that, we Jesuits had lost our place of esteem in Beijing and been thrown back into the hinterlands of the vast country, forbidden to approach the big cities. Many of my brethren died in anonymity. Some were martyred. Almost all of us were tortured."

Richard looked at the hobbled little man. Could his twisted body be the result of Manchu torture?

"To be honest, none of us succeeded in converting much of the population." He smiled that small smile again, then changed the topic. "Finally, in response to much British grumbling—as a nation they are snivellers and whingers—an edict was finally issued by the Beijing Emperor. It permitted the Foreign Devils, *Fan Kuei,* access to the Middle Kingdom for purposes of trading, but only through the complex river access to Canton called the Bogue." He pointed out the estuary on the map. "Westerners were not permitted to set foot on the sacred soil of China except deep up the cuts of the Bogue at one small section of Canton Harbour, just past Linten Island." Brother Matthew pointed out the location on the map.

"Is Canton large?"

"Bigger than Calcutta and London put together."

Richard had never been to London, but Calcutta was far bigger than Baghdad, so Richard was impressed.

"At Canton the Chinese divided the traders into 'factories' based on national origin. At their factories, the *Fan Kuei* are permitted to meet only with the Hong merchants who have been assigned to them by Beijing. The Hong merchants rob the fools blind, with Beijing's blessing, as a healthy percentage of the money the Hong merchants steal makes its way up the First Emperor's Grand Canal to Beijing's coffers. But the Hong merchants are both their commercial representatives and their watchdogs. Foreign Devils are never allowed to talk to the real power, the Mandarins, the *Ch'in-ch'ai.* The Hong merchants find themselves between a pillar and a post. They have to make money for Beijing and are personally responsible for the actions of all the *Fan Kuei,* and every servant, translator, cook, or labourer that they supply for the Foreign Devils."

"What?" Richard asked. "How can they be personally responsible?"

"All of China is set up that way. Everyone is someone else's responsibility. If a farmer does wrong, both the farmer and the village official who is responsible for the behaviour of his people are punished by the Mandarin. Public executions are a common sight. Millstoning or boarding is also much in use."

When he said those final words, a real darkness crossed his features. *So that's the form of torture he endured,* Richard thought. He had heard tell of this cruel punishment but didn't know the details, except that a heavy millstone or wooden board was put around an offender's neck and it stayed there for as long as the authorities saw fit.

"My son, opium strains the entirety of the Chinese system of social responsibility. Since almost everyone of power in China has his hands in the opium rice bowl, who is there to punish the supposed wrongdoer? And make no mistake, opium is the Devil's work, my son. The Devil's work."

Richard thought about that for a moment, then noticed that the little Jesuit was looking at him in a new way. "Do not do the Devil's work, Richard Hordoon. Do not do the Devil's work."

Suddenly the Hindu man's words—"Brother will kill brother"—screamed deep in Richard's mind. He heard it a second time, then a third, until his whole body vibrated with the old man's curse. He closed his eyes tight and balled up his fists—and hoped it would pass.

* * *

"ARE YOU ALL RIGHT, SIR?" the owner of the opium den asked.

Richard nodded and pushed his journal aside. Slowly he pointed a shaky finger toward the empty bowl of his pipe. The owner deposited a heated orb of opium in the centre of the bowl and then she tilted the pipe over the brazier. Smoke curled upward and Richard inhaled deeply.

Richard didn't see her deposit the third ball of opium in his pipe, but as he inhaled its sweet smoke a maniacal grin crossed his features. By the fourth ball he couldn't hold back his laughter.

"What?" Jiang, the owner of the opium den asked sweetly.

"I was just wondering."

"Wondering what, sir?"

"Wondering if anyone in England—or anywhere else in the world for that matter—has informed Her Royal Majesty, the most powerful woman in the world, Queen Victoria, that by putting her signature to the Treaty of Nanking she has become the Sister to the Manchu Emperor and ... and ..." He began to splutter, then regained control, "... and the Auntie to the Moon."

The laughter that flowed from Richard's mouth filled the den.

Jiang retreated behind a silk curtain, where the progeny of the First Emperor's Body Guard and the Confucian waited. The three listened to the hoarse laughter from Richard Hordoon, and it pleased them.

The White Birds had landed—the first part of the Ivory Compact had been completed.

part two

chapter seventeen

The Body Guard, His Brother, and His Nephew

The Village of Shanghai
1842

"You know who I am," said the tall man with the cobra tattoo on the back of his hand.

The young woman, his sister-in-law, moved her baby boy so he could suckle from her other breast, then nodded.

The tall man looked at the array of furniture and the dark, polished wood floor of this house. *They have amassed wealth,* he thought. "Where is he?"

"My son ..."

"My nephew," he interrupted her. "My nephew belongs to me, just as ..."

"... my husband could have belonged to you."

"If the time was upon us when he was younger, yes, it would have been him. It is the compact, agreed upon long ago."

The young mother held her baby tightly to her. At least this one was hers to keep, to raise, and, if necessary, to set out to revenge his brother.

"Where is the boy?" The man's voice snapped in the stillness of the room. The young mother looked up and to one side.

The boy was perched atop a tall, beautifully inlaid, lacquered armoire.

The tall man smiled. *Good,* he thought. Then he called out in a stern voice, "Here, boy."

Without hesitation, and with the elegance of an acrobat, the boy slid from his vantage point and approached the man.

The woman started toward her son.

"No, Mother, it is my destiny. As it has been the destiny of all the first-born males of this family stretching back into ancient times."

"Your father ..."

"Prepared me, Mother. Now my father's older brother will test me, and if he finds me worthy, he will finish my preparation."

"For what?" she screamed

"To kill, Mother. To kill. Am I not right, Uncle?"

The boy reached up and took the hand of the ancestor of the Body Guard. There was already strength in the boy's grip. It frightened the man with the cobra tattooed on the back of his hand—frightened him for the safety of his own son. Only one of the two boys would be entrusted with the obligation of the Ivory Compact. Only one of the two could begin the resurrection of the ancient Guild of Assassins. The other would ... he would not let himself complete the thought.

The boy's father entered the room and nodded toward his elder brother.

He saw the cobra tattoo on the back of his brother's hand. So he had finally come as the legend said he would. And, as the legend stated, his brother had insisted that his first-born go with him and challenge for the right to restart the ancient Guild.

His wife began to sob, and the baby at her breast joined her cries. Her husband ignored her entreaties. "It is our place on the Ivory."

She'd heard of the prophecy, but there had been no demand since—since forever, and now this man came and demanded her son. She protested again.

"Quiet, now. It is what I began his training for," her husband said. "It is what I was trained for by my father, and my father by his father. It is the role we must play."

His wife visibly stiffened and, holding her baby tightly to her, hissed, "And now I will have a role to play too. If my son dies, my people and I will be revenged upon all of those, I say *all of those,* who had anything to do with taking his life." Then she spat on the floor and stomped on the spittle with her left foot. "A curse into the ground will grow a branch of evil."

Her husband nodded slowly, knowing she was not wrong, then said, "As it may be. Now dry your tears and leave us." Then he turned to his brother. "I need a few moments with my son. I do not deny your right to him. I need a moment, that is all."

The Body Guard left the two—father and son—alone.

The young assassin stood by the window, feet wide apart, head held proudly. Silhouetted against the setting sun he was the most beautiful thing his father had ever seen.

His father grunted, then held out his left hand with the thumb and baby finger held apart from the three centre fingers, which were tightly bunched. The boy put his right hand over his heart and splayed his fingers.

"There will be death soon."

"I am ready, Father."

He nodded at his boy. Every morning for ten summers they had trained together before going to the fields. "Do your duty," he barked.

"I will, sir," the young assassin responded.

Then there was silence broken only by the wind outside and the breathing of the two men within.

"This pledge goes all the way back to the First Emperor's Body Guard, who is your revered ancestor, of whom you must beg a blessing. He was the beginning of all this."

The young assassin had heard the story many times. The phrase *kai shi* (beginning) had been the very first words he had spoken. It had caused a terrible stir in the village. And now, almost eleven years later, the portent of that day had come to fruition.

"Honour your weapons and they will serve you well."

"I will, my Father, as I honour you."

"Do your duty as it has been prescribed and do what you need to do to take the position and re-start the Guild of Assassins, for my brother's presence tells me that the time has come."

"I will, my Father, and help our people out of the darkness into the light."

They had spoken this litany at the end of every training session, but this time there was a quaver in his father's voice and tears were in his eyes.

The young assassin stood very still and allowed the image of his father to burn into his memory.

Then the door opened and the boy's uncle, the Body Guard, strode in. "It's time."

"He'll live with you and your family until ..."

"Until I must choose. You know this, brother."

"Can his mother and I ...?"

"Visit him? No. And you knew that as well." Then he grabbed the boy's Manchu-dictated pigtail with his cobra-tattooed hand.

"This goes first." With a single slash of his swalto blade, the hated symbol of Manchu domination fell to the polished wood floor. "Leave it there," the cobra man said to his brother. "It will stay until your son's work is done, as a reminder of him and the duty he owes his people."

chapter eighteen
The Selling of Shanghai

The Village of Shanghai
June 1843

It was hot. July in Shanghai was always hot, and humid, and mosquito-infested — no place for men in wool suits and top hats. But that was what the assembled were wearing that sultry morning of June 17, 1843, as they awaited the arrival of Queen Victoria's land auctioneer.

"Why are we dressed like this, Richard?" Maxi squawked as he scratched his thighs beneath his gabardine trousers.

"Because *they* are," Richard said, as a maniacal smile creased his handsome face. Then he broke out in an almost hysterical laugh that caused all eyes in the room to turn in his direction. Maxi gave him a sharp look. Under his breath Richard whispered, "Don't worry, I'm sober as a churchman." This last word he spoke loudly. Then he added in a whisper, "Look at us, Maxi, two kids with all these toffs!"

——

"Why are heathens allowed to bid in this auction?" asked the short, pot-bellied, bald-headed leader of the American trading firm of Oliphant and Company, out of Philadelphia. He clutched an aged family Bible to his chest. Not for nothing was the Oliphant trading house called the House of Zion by most of the other traders. Then, of course, there was also the Oliphant claim that they were in the business of spreading the word of

Christ—which they did while they sold opium to the heathens. "They're not Christians, are they?" Jedediah Oliphant asked.

"No, sir, they're Hebrews from Mesopotamia," Oliphant's elderly China hand replied.

"Mesopotamian Hebrews? Whoever heard of …?"

"The Hordoon brothers, sir."

Jedediah Oliphant paused and adjusted his spectacles. His already florid face reddened. "Those are the Hordoon brothers?"

"There are no others, sir."

"Handsome in an odd, Hebraic sort of way, I'd say."

"I've been told that some women agree with you, sir."

"Where's Rachel?" Jedediah asked quickly.

Rachel, his daughter, would have caused quite a stir at the Bend in the River. Jedediah might have been nothing much to look at himself, but his daughter, through some genetic fluke, was a true beauty. She had pale skin, a thin waist, dark auburn tresses, and startling green eyes. To the men of the opium trade, who for years had not been allowed to bring Caucasian women into their settlement at Canton, she would be a shock— a breath of pure air—a startling burst of light in their midst.

"As always, safely on board the *Water Witch*, sir."

"Hate that name. Blasphemous name. Can't we change it?"

"Not without risking a revolt amongst the crew. Sailors are superstitious, sir. The *Water Witch* has made more trans-Pacific voyages than any bark in our fleet. Not a single crewman has perished in any of the crossings, so—"

"It's through Christ's will that the ship arrives safely, not the actions of the ship's Captain or any of its—"

"I don't advise changing the name, sir. I really don't."

The head of the House of Zion looked at his China hand. The man seemed to know what he was talking about. So he simply harrumphed. "Where are the other heathens?"

"The Vrassoons?"

"Yes, those."

"Their representative will be less obvious but far more significant. After all, Vrassoon is a knighted lord of the British Empire."

"Codswallop," the head of the House of Zion announced. "Just codswallop. We should sit them down and talk to them of the Good Book. Now *there* would be a conversion!"

The China hand looked at his boss and wondered if the man realized the danger that Vrassoon and Company, with its monopoly on direct trade between China and England, posed to the Oliphants' opium assets. But he chose to say nothing.

"Codswallop, I repeat," Jedediah repeated—this time loudly enough for everyone in the room to wonder what in heaven's name a codswallop was, or did, or meant.

———

"The American looks like he's swallowed a large toad," said Percy St. John Dent, second in command at Dent and Company of London.

"Aye, or perhaps a lizard," replied Hercules MacCallum, co-owner of Jardine Matheson out of Edinburgh, as he adjusted the shoe on his left foot to relieve the pain from the gout nodule there. He and Percy had become fast friends during their years at school together on a weather-blown stretch of land on the Scottish east coast just north of Sinclair Castle—the coldest damned place in the coldest damned country in the world. Although they relished disagreeing with each other on almost every other topic, on that point they were in full agreement.

"The head of the House of Zion does sputter, doesn't he?" Percy asked rhetorically.

"It's an American trait, I believe, typical of Evangelical speech over there."

"Just Evangelical speech?"

"Aye."

"And why would that be?"

"It's my belief that it is caused by their erroneous conviction that they are the sole recipients of the Lord's final wisdom."

"And why would that make them sputter, you northern barbarian?"

"Because, my self satisfied Oxonian, it should be clear to all—even Americans—that God would not choose to bequeath His final wisdom—I do love the presumptuousness of that phrase, 'final wisdom'—well, be that as it may, God would not permit His 'final wisdom' to be housed in such a ramshackle backwater as America."

"Have you ever been, Hercules?"

"No."

"And yet you feel confident calling it a ramshackle backwater?"

"I've never been to Sweden, but I know they're all blonds."

"I rather like blonds."

"As do I, Percy—as long as they don't sputter."

"Well, that depends."

"Depends on what?"

"On whether they sputter before or after," Percy St. John Dent replied with a grin.

Hercules looked at his English counterpart and said, "And here I thought you were a God-fearing, chaste gentleman!"

"Hercules, I am a businessman not unlike yourself."

"Aye, Percy, a businessman, but not really like myself. You'll see what I mean when the auctioneer arrives."

Percy turned to Hercules. "What are you planning, you detestable Scot?"

"Wait and see, Percy, wait and see."

Percy St. John Dent shook his head but resisted laughing. He and Hercules may have enjoyed each other's friendship at their Scottish boarding school, but the two had been trained there to lead men and nations—and through their opium trade they were actively competing with each other to do just that.

A shuffle at the front of the warehouse drew their attention. The auctioneer entered, swatting mosquitoes as he did.

Vrassoon's man noted the pallor of the auctioneer's skin and leaned forward just slightly to get a good look at the man's hands—the signet ring on the middle finger of the left hand caught the light from the overhead window. *Good,* the Vrassoon man thought, *so he made it.* The Vrassoon man checked his list of properties and the double columns of figures beside each. The figures in the left-hand column were considerably lower than those in the right-hand column. He folded the paper, removing the more expensive figures from his sight. *No need to consider paying that much,* he thought.

"Gentlemen." The auctioneer cleared his throat, then coughed heavily into a linen handkerchief that had evidently received many similar deposits, since it crinkled when he folded it before replacing it in his breast pocket. "Gentlemen, I hereby open the initial land auction in the village of Shanghai."

He had just turned to a large surveyor's map affixed to the wall when over his shoulder he heard Percy St. John Dent, with his elegant accent, say, "If I may, sir? I don't mean to halt the proceedings, but since the spoils we are now about to divide were won by the actions of Queen Victoria's Expeditionary Force, I feel it only right to sing her praise before we begin." He turned to the other Englishmen and Scots, who all stood, removed their hats, and launched into a spirited rendition of "God Save the Queen."

Instantly the entire assemblage from Oliphant and Company slid back their chairs and headed toward the doors. They signalled to the other Americans to follow them. Most did, but the representative of the large trading firm Russell and Company, a man with the odd last name of Delano, remained—although he did not stand.

The Vrassoon delegation stood, but refrained from removing their hats on religious grounds.

The Hordoons had already put aside their top hats, and so they just stood. As they did, Maxi remarked, "They could sing 'Fuck Me on the Stairs, Molly' as far as I'm concerned."

"Or not sing it," replied Richard.

The assembly proceeded to sing the praise of a fat lady thousands of miles away with gusto, if not skill.

———

Jiang and the Body Guard stood in the crowd of people at the back and watched in amazement as the *Fan Kuei,* in their ludicrous dark wool suits, held their hats and seemed to scream in unison some doggerel verse they evidently all knew. Why they stood or removed their hats to say the verse neither the Body Guard nor Jiang knew or wanted to know.

The Confucian watched the proceedings from the safety and secrecy of a side chamber that he was able to use since the auction was taking place in a warehouse belonging to one of his brothers. He made a note in a small, but well-thumbed, book.

When the *Fan Kuei* screeching was over, the Americans returned. And the auctioneer turned to his map, but he was interrupted a second time by the arrival of tea that the Confucian had ordered for all the traders.

"Can we just get on with this?" bellowed Vrassoon's man.

Richard stood up and with a broad smile suggested, "We are in China and tea is our business. Surely we can pause for a moment to partake in the leaf's freshness."

Expensively gowned young Chinese men and elderly women quickly appeared and pushed beautifully made carts with inlaid mother-of-pearl tops through the room, distributing tea in translucent porcelain cups. Richard smiled as he raised his in a toast to the Vrassoon representative.

The tea was wonderful. Light, open, and refreshing. Maxi and Richard savoured the fine, delicate southern blend, just momentarily wondering why this particular tea was never available for sale. But then again, the Hordoon boys had been in China almost fifteen years, and they knew full well that even with Richard's fluency in the language and all his contacts through Chen, they had only been introduced to the thinnest upper layer of Chinese topsoil—never allowed to dig beneath the surface to find the true riches. Richard took another sip and wondered at the taste. After all, it was the appetite for tea in England and the Americas that had started the whole China trade. He took a final sip and looked around him. Richard smiled.

"What, brother mine?" Maxi asked.

"The brocades and topcoats, the waistcoats and watch fobs, the swish and bravura don't hide the scoundrels beneath."

"Save the fancy talk for your journals, the auctioneer's about ready up there."

———

The auctioneer had rehearsed his approach to the proceedings for several months with the help of the Vrassoons back in London, settling on a strategy that should put the prime pieces of Shanghai's property in the Vrassoons' hands with as little expense as possible. The first parcel of land put up for auction was a seemingly insignificant wedge with its point on the Huangpo River and its large base well to the north of the Old City. The Vrassoons were concerned about the piece since it could cut off access to the Suzu Creek. It also bisected a potentially valuable path used by traders that they called the Bubbling Spring Way. After much debate in London it was decided that this piece should be put up first and made light of.

The auctioneer cleared his throat again. "Mornin', gentlemen. Tea was very good, very good indeed. Now, I would suggest we begin with something small just to get us started." He pointed to the wedge-shaped plot on the survey map. "What do I hear for this oddly shaped little parcel?"

Maxi sensed Richard tense at this side, but before he could say anything, the auctioneer banged his gavel and stated, "We'll start the bidding at two hundred pounds. Do I hear two hundred?"

Maxi saw the Vrassoon man about to raise his hand, then he heard Richard's voice beside him, "Five thousand, five hundred pounds."

There was an audible gasp in the room. Five thousand pounds was thirty percent of a clipper's take on a successful trading run up the China coast.

"Five thousand, five hundred pounds. Very generous of you, sir. Five thousand, five hundred pounds." The auctioneer said, obviously not knowing what he should do next.

Richard shouted out, "Five thousand, five hundred pounds going once."

The auctioneer intoned, "Going once," then took a deep breath. Sweat popped out on his forehead as if he suddenly had an attack of hives. "Going twice ..."

"Six thousand pounds!" The annoyed voice belonged to Vrassoon's man.

The auctioneer smiled and turned back to Richard. "Six thousand pounds to you, sir. Do I hear six thousand, five hundred pounds?"

Maxi looked at Richard. His brother stood completely still.

"Six thousand, one hundred pounds, sir?"

Again Richard didn't move a muscle, although Maxi sensed his brother smiling.

"Six thousand and fifty pounds, sir?"

Richard's smile broadened, and Vrassoon's man suddenly shouted, "Do you want the damned wedge of property or not, man?"

Richard turned slowly to the older man, then said a single word. "Not!"

Vrassoon's man paled. Mr. Vrassoon did not care to have his money spent recklessly.

The auctioneer clearly didn't know what to do, so he went back to script. "Six thousand pounds bid from the House of Vrassoon, going once, going twice—sold, for six thousand pounds to the House of Vrassoon, excuse me, to the British East India Company."

Richard turned and walked to the back of the large room, and Maxi followed closely. "Hey! What was all that about, brother mine?"

"It's rigged, Maxi. The Vrassoons were going to get that piece no matter what—I just thought they ought to pay full share for it. The auctioneer's their man. The order of presentation is their idea. The whole thing's a fixed game."

"So aren't we going to bid on any of the land? I thought we were going to set up shop here."

"We are, Maxi, but not by the rotting Vrassoons' rules. Besides, until we pay off our debt to Barclays for those sodding steamships we lost we don't have much cash to work with. You have to trust me, Maxi. We don't need prime property now. We have Chen to act as our comprador, and he'll give us all the access to the water we need through his wharf property. Right now we need our money for other and better things. Maybe in ten years we'll buy back this expensive real estate at a shilling on the pound. Now, we conserve our funds and buy only the odd cheap property."

And as the afternoon made its way into early evening, that was exactly what Richard did. The Dents and the Oliphants bid against each other. Jardine Matheson went head to head for prime land with the Vrassoons. Even the old schoolboy ties between Dent and McCallum of Jardine Matheson didn't stop them from viciously bidding the prices up on parcels of land they coveted. And coveted was the right word for this exercise.

Just as they were ready for a dinner break, the blare of horns and then the crash of gongs and cymbals filled the warehouse. Suddenly, all the Chinese in the room threw themselves to the ground. The door opened and, to the hammering of percussion, a Mandarin, wearing a conical hat and with the tiles proclaiming his high office strung from his neck, entered the room. Of the traders, only Richard knew that his purple Chinkiang silk gown announced that he came directly from the Manchu court in Beijing. Beside him was a young, fair-faced Han Chinese man.

The Mandarin's voice was full of fury. The young man at his side did his best to translate his words into English, but his skill wasn't up to the task.

All that was clear was that the Mandarin was displeased—extremely displeased—with something.

Vrassoon's man ran over to Richard. "Explain it to His Mandarin Excellency, or whatever he calls himself, that this is a legally sanctioned auction and he has no right to interfere with—"

"You explain it to him, or have you lost your tongue? He's right over there, tell him yourself," Richard replied.

"He doesn't speak—"

"English. No. Neither does his translator, it seems. But then why should they? We're in their country, not they in ours."

"Tell him, Hordoon! Mr. Vrassoon will not be pleased with any delay."

"You'd like me to speak to His Excellency?"

"You're the only one gone native on us, mate."

"Ah." Richard smiled and then slowly approached the emissary of the Manchu court. The Mandarin's guards quickly stepped in front of their charge, their weapons drawn. Richard slowed his pace. The room had gone silent; only the street noise through the open door broke the so very unChinese quiet. A breeze picked up and whooshed into the room. Richard smelled the river and the mud flats of the Pudong across the way. Then he scented something else. Something extremely familiar. The sweet reek of opium—and it was coming from the Mandarin himself.

Richard smiled inwardly, then bowed and offered his thanks for the appearance of such an eminent man in their midst. The Mandarin stared at him and then pointed to the floor.

An air of tension cut through the room. The Mandarin was demanding a formal kowtow, something that none of the Europeans had ever agreed to do.

Richard sensed the anxiety in the room and then looked at his Christian counterparts. "It's just kneeling down," he muttered, and in quick, elegant movements he completed the complex prostrations of the full kowtow.

The Mandarin barked a command. The guards parted and the Mandarin stepped forward. "Stand!" he ordered, and remained impassive as Richard got back to his feet. Then he nodded. As he did, Richard asked in fluent Mandarin, "Will this suffice? The procedure is new to me and I need much practice. I apologize if it was not fully correct."

The Mandarin gave a dismissive grunt and stepped closer to this oddly scented, grotesquely coloured man.

When he got close enough, Richard whispered in Mandarin, "Excellency, there is more money to be made from those who refuse to kowtow than from those of us who will. If you permit me, I can show you how this can be done. As a fellow dream traveller I can show you the way."

Richard thought the man was going to order his immediate execution, but all the Mandarin said was, "And your name would be?"

Richard told him his name, and twenty minutes later, much to Richard's surprise, the Mandarin left without ever saying what had caused him to interrupt the proceedings in the first place—and the bidding continued.

The common front the traders had shown in the presence of the Mandarin disappeared the moment he left the room, and the prerogatives of business, the opium business, reasserted themselves.

* * *

LATER THAT NIGHT, the Manchu Mandarin was led by the Confucian to the door of Jiang's establishment.

Jiang bowed low and, with her eyes still averted, said, "As we agreed, my house is at your service." Jiang felt the scrape of cracked finger nails as they moved across her cheek, and she stepped back.

The Mandarin's smile had a disconcertingly easy cruelty to it.

"Excellency," she said as she stepped aside to allow the Mandarin ahead of her into the main hall, where she had arrayed her best wares. The Mandarin entered the chamber and stopped. His long fingernails came out of the sleeves of his gown as he slowly scanned Jiang's finest courtesans, posed on couches, against columns, and on leather stools. Although courtesans were used to being wooed by suitors before offering up any sort of sexual favours, for the Manchu Mandarin, the Ch'in-ch'ai, the rules were broken. The women held their poses as surely as any statue despite the pain of putting pressure on their tiny bound feet. Jiang had guessed that the Mandarin's tastes would run to the visual and the controlled, but he gave no indication that he saw anything that pleased him. Jiang nodded subtly and the women, as one, rose, turned, then repositioned themselves, the youngest, as if by accident, now in groups of two and three up front.

The Mandarin didn't move and, more troublingly, didn't speak. *Could it be that his tastes run to boys?* Jiang thought as she came up beside the man and said, gently, "Choose, it is the price we agreed upon for you to permit the auction to proceed. If there is nothing in this room that pleases ..."

"Oh, there is something in the room that greatly pleases," the Mandarin said in a hushed voice. His voice was surprisingly light, like smoke in the wind.

"I'm glad," Jiang said, "they are all most expert—"

"No doubt they are," he cut her off, "but ..." the Mandarin's eyes left the array of elaborately dressed young women and turned to Jiang, "... I doubt that any match the mastery of their mistress. It is my right. It is my right to choose a whore from this group of whores." His voice curled with a rage that somehow seemed joyous. "So I choose you," he said, touching the brocade on Jiang's dress. "You. My whore," he announced loudly. Then he smiled that cruel smile again.

The Confucian didn't know what to do. The girls were relieved but embarrassed for their "mother." The Mandarin remained silent, staring at Jiang.

Finally Jiang canted her head slightly, then announced sweetly to all assembled, "It is my pleasure to bring the clouds and rain—to such an esteemed man."

* * *

EARLY THE NEXT WEEK, Maxi came running into the leaky wooden shed that served as the Hordoons' office. "Richard. They're here!"

Richard looked up from his calculations and for a moment didn't know what had brought the blush to his red-haired brother's face. Then he understood and let out a cry of joy, grabbed his hat, and raced his brother to the docks.

There, standing side by side holding hands, were his twin four-year-old sons, both dressed in short pants, knee socks, caps, jackets, and ties. Their Malay *amah* stood behind them, her white-gloved hands holding her bag. Behind her, two Chinese men were stacking suitcases high on a long-handled wheelbarrow.

"Hello, boys," Richard said in Farsi as he stepped toward them. "Who is who?"

The *amah* started to speak, but Richard put a finger to his lips. Then he asked the same thing in Mandarin and, to his pleasure, one of the boys stepped forward and responded in kind, "I'm Milo, sir, and this is my brother, Silas."

Richard beamed. He hadn't seen the boys in three years. He put out a hand toward Milo and said, "Welcome, son."

The boy took his hand, then leapt into his arms and shouted, "Daddy."

But the other boy, Silas, stepped back behind his *amah,* and despite her best efforts he wouldn't come out from behind her skirts.

From Richard's arms Milo turned and called in English, "Come, brother mine, come to Daddy."

Maxi laughed out loud and shouted, "Brother mine! Where'd they get that?"

Richard gently put Milo down, although he held his hand tightly. Then he reached out toward Silas. "Come, son, I'm your father."

Milo crossed over, took Silas's hand, and walked him back to Richard. "Father, this is my fine brother, Silas," he said, with his surprising command of Mandarin.

Richard extended his hand. "Proud to meet you, Silas." Richard's hand hung in the air for a long, embarrassing moment, then he reached for his son. The boy hissed at him and bit his hand.

Richard let out a short shout that drew many eyes.

The boys' *amah* put her gloved hands over her mouth. Milo ran to his brother's side. "Don't be angry, Father."

Then Maxi stepped forward. "Angry? Why would he be angry at a little nip? The boy's got spunk, he does. Good lad. I've bitten your father several times myself, and enjoyed it every time. Truly." Maxi extended his hand. "I'm your Uncle Maxi, proud to make your acquaintance."

Slowly Silas reached out and shook his uncle's hand. "Myself as well, sir."

The boy's formality made them all laugh. For a moment there was a family unit, father and two sons—an idyll. Then Chen came running up with Richard's man, Patterson, who looked after his stables for him.

In furiously fast Mandarin, Chen said, "I'm sorry to interrupt, sir, but we need your signature on the waybill now or the ship won't sail on the tide. Please, sir, you must hurry."

"Patterson, take my sons back to the warehouse. Show them our horses. I'll be back as soon as I can." Richard quickly turned and ran after Chen, with Maxi at his side, toward the harbour.

The *amah* indicated the luggage, but Patterson ignored her and turned to the boys. Then, under his breath, he said, "Come, me little heathens, welcome to the monkey kingdom."

chapter nineteen
Trouble in the Opium Trade

The Village of Shanghai
August 1843

Chen's stifling warehouse, hastily erected on the docks about a mile south of the Suzu Creek, was filled to overflowing with goods, some en route to England, others intended for various locales in China. Richard, as he always did when he came to the warehouse, marvelled at Maxi's handiwork, which was evident in the building's ingenious pulley system. A series of intricate knots and pin-rails permitted items hung from the rafters to be labelled and returned to the ground with a minimum of confusion and fuss. Richard nodded as he thought, *While I was learning from the little Jesuit, Maxi was learning from the sailors.*

Teas in twelve-foot-long woven hemp bags hung from every rafter, scenting the air with a dense, exotic tang; the wooden shelves were stacked high with bolt upon bolt of silks dyed blue and red and green and opal and puce, brought from Chinkiang and Canton and secret farms farther upriver that, of the Europeans, only Richard had found. The locked wire cage area on the far side of the tall space was completely filled with mango-wood caskets crammed with India's finest opium. Even in the area outside the lockup the mango-wood chests were piled six deep almost to the ceiling.

The warehouse was stuffed with goods—but there wasn't a single worker—not one. Not a single item was being moved, or being readied to be moved, or even inventoried

Richard turned to Chen, his comprador, but before he could speak the smaller man answered the obvious question. "Because they won't work for you. They won't cross into your concession. I've tried. They won't lift or carry or load your goods, no matter how much money I offer them."

"They won't work for me?"

"No. Not for the *Fan Kuei,* not for any of you."

"Since when?"

"It was hard to get them before, but now it's impossible."

"Why now? What's happened now?"

"The Manchu Mandarin has brought in Taoist monks who tell the people they and their entire families will be cursed if they work for the *Fan Kuei.*"

Richard took that in, then looked at Chen, with whom he had worked for years. It crossed his mind that this small man might have paid a heavy personal price for his contact with the Foreign Devils. But then he cast the thought aside. He had paid Chen well, and never looked too closely at the man's books. Richard had made Chen a wealthy man, and there was always a price for wealth—Richard could attest to that.

"This is bullshit," he barked.

Chen found it humorous that Europeans made cuss words out of valuable substances. The manure of a bull was very useful, both as fertilizer and in many different medicines; in fact, there was an active market in quality bull excreta in which Chen had speculated and made a handsome profit—one of his few good bets.

Chen turned to the man whom he still thought of as Lee Char Or'oon and said, "It's bullshit, but It's the way it is."

"How much did you offer them to work for us?"

"Half a *tael* of silver every other month. And still there were no takers."

"I never authorized—"

"They think you smell bad ... and more importantly, that you bring bad luck. So they don't think, even for half a *tael* of silver, it's worth the risk."

Even knowing that Chen would exaggerate by at least fifteen percent, which he would then pocket, Richard knew that the price was still over three times what a normal worker would make in any of the menial jobs in the place Richard was beginning to think of as Shanghai.

"Have the Taoist priests been—"

"Stirring them up?" Chen smiled. "That's what priests do, stir things up."

Richard agreed with that assessment. He left the warehouse.

A dense rolling smell came from the Huangpo River. Richard saw the large tandem junks pulling a dredge net just to the north. They had probably passed where he stood about a half hour back, so the water was still roiling with its rich bounty of silt and nutrient decay. He looked across the river to the Pudong and a shiver went through him. The area was still wild in its own way. Even the Chinese were concerned the odd time they needed to access the place. If one were to believe the rumours, the Pudong was home to whores and pirates and mountebanks and ancient martial arts cults and sorcerers. Experience had taught Richard to respect the Middle Kingdom's version of rumours. Mesopotamians were fabulists. Everyone in the Middle East was a ludicrous fabulist. But the people of the Middle Kingdom were practical, very practical. When they were frightened of something—anything—it was worth taking note. Richard had had only one experience with the Pudong—and it was not something he wanted to repeat.

He turned from the river and headed east along the Suzu Creek. The creek itself was Chinese territory, not given over in the Treaty of Nanking, so it was dotted with small family junks. The odd one was larger and moored away from the houseboat junks. The creek was deep enough to float several larger vessels. One was a favourite restaurant of Maxi's, another a favourite opium den of Richard's. But it wasn't the river vessels that interested Richard as he crossed the smallest of the creek bridges and entered the American Settlement. He wanted to know if it was just him and the British that the Chinese wouldn't work for—or all non-Chinese.

Crossing the bridge, he came to a small contingent of American marines. They eyed him carefully. For a moment he thought they were going to bar his way, but they stepped aside. The American Settlement was as clear of Chinamen as the British Concession. The only overt difference was the flying of the Stars and Stripes instead of the Union Jack, but Richard didn't salute any flag so he didn't see that as very important. The streets were still little more than muddy lanes, the buildings hastily put up shacks, and the whiff of sewage wrapped itself around cooking smells—just as in the British Concession.

The Chinese referred to the area north of the Suzu Creek along the Huangpo River as Hangkow. It had traditionally been a fishing centre. Several small Chinese junks were at anchor just off the partially completed jetty. Two American clippers, owned by Russell and Company, rode the swell farther out in the river. The Americans had thrown up a dozen two-storey wooden shacks along the shore. Goods were stored on the first floor while dormitories for the White workers were on the second. In the back of the rickety buildings were rudimentary cooking and toilet facilities. As in the British Concession, wood planks sufficed for roads—where there were roads of any sort. The old Chinese cart paths were used more often than not as the demarcation of streets. Some of them even had fancy names—way too fancy for dirt paths.

As in the British Concession, there were only men—and now all of those were White. There was not a Chinese face in evidence.

Richard was about to enter the American administrative offices when he stopped cold in his tracks. At first he didn't believe what he'd seen—a woman—a White woman—a White woman here, at the Bend in the River? There had been no White women allowed in Canton for all those years. The Chinese strictly forbade it. Married men left their wives behind in Hong Kong or Malay, as Richard had. But here?

He ran quickly down the wobbly steps into the mud path, then dashed around a corner—and there she was, lifting her skirts to step over a large puddle. He stared. Deep purple outer frock, a taupe lace bonnet, white white white skin, and flashing green eyes that turned to him and held his with a kind of invitation. Then she hopped over the puddle in a graceful leap and quickly stepped up on the board sidewalk before heading down the block of rickety buildings.

Richard followed.

The woman disappeared into a particularly austere building with a small bronze plaque by the door: Oliphant and Company, Philadelphia, Pennsylvania.

Richard grinned as he recalled rumours that Papa Oliphant was such a protective father that he was unwilling to let his daughter out of his sight. "The House of Zion has a Jezebel," he said aloud.

That drew harrumphs of indignation from the frocked and top-hatted men around him who were evidently heading into Oliphant and Company (a.k.a. The House of Zion) as well.

Richard dusted off his britches and followed the crowd.

Inside the main entrance he turned to the left, and there was a modest hall in which the men all stood, hats in hands. A pump organ began to play, and the plump, bald leader of the House of Zion, Jedediah Oliphant, stepped forward. The small man wore a black woollen waistcoat and sweated profusely. He pulled at the watch chain looped across his round little tummy and pulled out a large pocket watch that he flicked open with a fleshy thumb. After a brief examination of the watch face, the head of the House of Zion said, "Open your prayer books to page two hundred and twelve and we will sing together 'Our House Is Built on His Foundation.'"

All around Richard, men turned pages and quickly raised their voices in song.

Through the heavy voices Richard heard the sweetness of a light soprano that seemed to float on the breath of the men. He stepped slightly back and there she was, the green-eyed woman. She smiled at him, and he felt his heart skip a beat—then another one.

The service or song-fest or whatever it was (Richard hadn't attended a religious ceremony of any kind in almost twenty years, and even then only when his mother had insisted) ended with a flourish and the senseless shaking of hands. Then the participants dispersed and returned, Richard assumed, to their jobs.

Richard looked for the woman at the end of the service but didn't see her, so he approached Jedediah Oliphant, as he had initially intended.

The head of Oliphant and Company knew Richard and heartily disliked him—as did all the other opium traders. But Richard had known real hate since his childhood and was not put off by mere dislike. He put out his hand as he approached.

Oliphant declined the offered handshake. "Have you come to this place to investigate the one true faith?"

For a moment Richard had no idea what he was talking about, but when it struck him, he smiled. "No, but I did enjoy the singing."

"God's songs they are, my son."

Richard let that go. "Can I have a word?"

Oliphant grudgingly led him into a hardwood-panelled room and closed the door. The board floor was carpeted with a quality Persian rug whose pattern Richard immediately identified as coming from the Takrit area. A small fireplace was embedded in one wall, and three leather wing-back chairs dominated the room. Oliphant sat in one but didn't offer Richard a place in one of the others.

"So?"

Richard ignored the slight. "I want to talk about Chinese workers."

"Do you have any?"

"No. Do you?"

Oliphant waved a chubby fist in front of his chubby red face as if smoke had somehow entered the room and bothered his nose. "No," he said slowly.

"And this is not a problem as far as you are concerned?"

"God will provide."

Richard snicked his teeth and said, "Absolutely." He turned to leave; the hypocrisy of Christian opium traders was too much for him just now. But before he could get to the door it was flung open, and the vision from the street with the soprano voice appeared. With a quick curtsey she said, "I'm sorry to interrupt, Father, but the Bible translator is waiting for you."

Richard stepped aside and she passed by, a step closer, he thought, than was absolutely necessary. A whiff of rosewater came off her. He smiled and turned back to Jedediah Oliphant. "Your daughter, here, in Shanghai?"

Gruffly the older man said, "She's a fully qualified missionary who has come to this dark place to bring the light of the Word of the Lord. Haven't you, my dear?"

The green-eyed creature smiled and retreated from the office.

"I've found her a suitable husband, a classmate of mine—two years ahead of me at the seminary, a pastor from Massachusetts. They'll be married once her missionary work here is finished. She hasn't met him yet, but they're a good match."

Richard couldn't resist asking, "And she'll be happy with you choosing a husband for her?"

"My daughter is a good girl."

Richard wondered about how long a "good girl" remained a good girl with a husband older than her father, but he didn't speak.

The silence in the room seemed to draw itself out. Finally Oliphant broke it, saying, "Rachel listens to her father."

So her name is Rachel, Richard thought, and although he'd never bothered with the Bible, he thought that perhaps he'd spend the evening figuring out exactly where in that dusty old book the name of this "good girl" originated.

* * *

RACHEL ELIZABETH OLIPHANT was not a "bad girl," but nor was she the "good girl" her father believed her to be. She had for years privately questioned her Church's teaching. Not only had she found her own urges as powerful as anything she had ever felt in prayer, but her ability to read Hebrew and Aramaic gave her access to part of the "Good Book" that flew in the face of American Evangelical thought.

She was shocked when she painstakingly translated the story of the rape of Lot by his daughters, not to mention the horrors she found in the Dinah story, or Abraham's questionable behaviour with his wife while in Egypt. But perhaps most revealing to her were two passages from the Bible at what she thought of as opposite ends of desire. The first, the openly erotic poetry of the Song of Solomon, was so surprising to her that at first she couldn't believe her translation was correct. The second challenged everything she had ever thought about faith—it was her translation of the story of Job. She had often been told the story of the good man put through horrifying tribulations to challenge his faith in his God. The way she'd always heard the story was that Job bowed down and accepted the power of God. But her translation from the original Aramaic stunned her. Nowhere did she find Job accepting the totally unjustified punishment that he was forced to endure. In fact, as far as Rachel Elizabeth Oliphant could translate, the final thing Job said to God was: "I have seen You and I am appalled."

When she realized that in its original form Job was the last book of the Hebrew Bible—not a middle book of what Christians call the Old Testament—she literally began to shake. The whole Old Testament did not lead to the arrival of the prophets that acted as precursors to the arrival of Christ, as she had been taught. It led to Job—and Job's assertion of his right to reject God's arbitrary, capricious use of power.

So, as her mother went first blind, then slowly insane while the tumour grew in her head, Rachel thought of Job's response to God, not her father's relentless platitudes about God's unfathomable plan for man.

And yet she did not openly criticize her Church or resist her father's insistence that she do missionary work. How else could a Victorian girl get to see the world—and hold off her father's impulsive desire for her to marry a man over twice her age?

She found much of Asia to her liking, although, being a woman, she had been kept away from China for almost a year, and when she finally was allowed ashore she was closely guarded by her father and his men. Yet she had still managed, often from the covered interior of a carried sedan chair, to see much. She loved the sights and sounds of the open-air markets and the street hawkers who produced delicious hot food at almost any hour of the day. She often forced her escorts to stop and, although she was seldom allowed out of the sedan chair herself, she would have her father's men buy her freshly cooked dumplings stuffed with pork and shrimp in a ginger sauce, sticky rice balls with a cooked egg yolk in the centre, or long, thick noodles in a sweet brown sauce. She was anxious to try to eat with the sticks that the locals used, but she was not allowed to try.

There were things that were less pleasing. The few women she saw—since the Chinese, like their American counterparts, kept their women behind locked doors—all waddled painfully on their bound feet. The tiny appendages were an obscenity to her.

Then she met her very first courtesan. The runners carrying Rachel's sedan chair slowed in the narrow street of the Old City as the courtesan's sedan chair approached from the opposite direction. The street was not quite wide enough to allow the two sedan chairs to pass, and as her sedan chair scraped against the wall, Rachel heard a shriek from the other chair that caused the courtesan's carriers to bump her sedan chair into Rachel's. When they did, the rungs of her privacy curtain caught on the rings of Rachel's drapery—revealing one woman to the other.

For a breathtaking few moments, beauty from the West examined beauty from the East and vice versa—and each found the other both enchanting and hideous at the same time.

The one overriding impression that Rachel came away with was that this woman who spent her time with several different men did not strike her as any less a child of God than the ostentatious virgins of her native Philadelphia.

* * *

ABOUT A MILE TO THE NORTH on the Bend in the River, in the three-storey stone headquarters of the British East India Company, heart of the Vrassoons' empire, Cyril, the Vrassoons' elder China hand, began the first of his two attacks on the Hordoon brothers.

He raised a glass of sherry to the Manchu Mandarin standing in his office and took a deep sip. The scribe by the Mandarin's side and his personal bodyguard didn't move a muscle.

Cyril's command of Mandarin was not perfect, but it was serviceable, and he had one of the very few Mandarin-English dictionaries in existence, with which he spent an hour every evening no matter how long his day had been. Ownership of the dictionary had been a result of one of the more delicate negotiations into which he had entered upon his arrival at the Bend in the River. But he wasn't thinking of that just now.

"May I congratulate you on a fine proclamation, sir. I look forward to its being made public." Cyril saluted the Mandarin a second time and once again drank alone.

The Mandarin just held his drink and waited—for the rest.

Cyril smiled. "You await *my* proclamation?"

The Mandarin didn't smile. Didn't move. Just listened.

Cyril retreated to his leather-topped partner desk and slipped a key into the lock. He pulled out the central drawer until he heard a click, then he gently pushed it forward about an inch and heard a second click—which unlocked the bottom drawer. From that drawer he withdrew a document written in English. He put it face up on the desk and resisted smiling.

The Mandarin clearly didn't speak let alone read English. He gave a quick, short shriek and the office door slammed open. Two of his armed guards entered, followed by a tall, elderly Jesuit.

Cyril noted the man's sallow pallor and the fire in his rheumy eyes. The Jesuit wheezed when he exhaled and had a pronounced limp. But he was clearly a believer. Cyril had seen such fire in the Vrassoon Patriarch's eyes when it came to matters of religion and practice. Cyril handed over the document.

The Jesuit pulled back the sleeves of his Chinese-style outer gown. Cyril had forgotten that one of the great fights between the Jesuits and the other Catholic orders in the Middle Kingdom was the willingness of the Jesuits to adopt the clothing and habits of the local population, a choice that was totally resisted by the other Catholic orders (especially the mendicant orders) and thought to be out and out blasphemy by the Protestant Evangelicals.

The Jesuit finished reading the document and turned to the Mandarin. "It is as you agreed. Once your new tariffs drive the Hebrew brothers out of business, you will be given fifty percent of all their property and opium assets."

The Mandarin nodded, then reached for the paper and with one move tore the thing in two and dropped it to the floor. "Sixty percent," he said in Mandarin.

Cyril contained his smile. He had authorization to go to seventy-five percent. He did the appropriate harrumphing and muttering, then counter-offered. They settled at fifty-eight percent, and everyone was happy. Perhaps this deal would pacify Mr. Vrassoon, although he doubted it. Cyril glanced at the calendar on his desk. Eliazar Vrassoon would shortly arrive in Calcutta, and not too long after he would no doubt make his triumphal arrival in Shanghai.

The Mandarin stepped forward and held out his long, elegant fingers. On his left pinky, the ring bearing his chop glinted in the light. He dunked it in the ink the scribe proffered and affixed his sign to the scroll. Then he turned and thought of rewarding himself for completing this unsavoury business with the *Fan Kuei*. Perhaps a session of clouds and rain with Jiang would cleanse him of the distaste.

* * *

EVEN BEFORE the Mandarin could sample the delectations of Jiang's brothel, Cyril completed his note to the Vrassoon Patriarch with the words, *"Your first plan is in place and the second about to begin. The Hordoons may soon be no more, and these new tariffs will undoubtedly raise a cry from the traders to seek extraterritoriality. As you predicted extraterritoriality may be within our grasp."* He called in his most trusted aide and gave him the handwritten note. "This is not to leave your sight, and you are to deliver it personally to Mr. Vrassoon in Calcutta. I will expect it to be in his hands by the end of the month. If I find it hasn't arrived in that time I will personally see to it that you and your family never see another penny from this fine company. Do I make myself clear?"

The young Jew nodded, took the letter, and ran to the docks—the tide was going out.

Then Cyril called the two hard men into his office and set in motion the second part of the Vrassoons' two-pronged attack on the Hordoon boys.

"So, which of you has the stomach for violence?" he asked.

The two young men looked at each other before the taller of the two stepped forward. "I'm y'r man, Guv."

Ah, our co-religionist from the hard streets of East London, Cyril thought, then added to himself as a reminder, *No matter how successful we get, we'll always need you and your muscle. You were with us at the beginning, and you'll be with us at the end.* Then he quickly amended his thought, *If there is such a thing as the end for us.*

He held out an official-looking document and said, "Do you know where the Baghdadi boys do business?"

The rough man nodded.

"Good. Take this to them, and don't leave until you can tell me exactly how they took it."

———

Well, the Hordoon brothers didn't take it well.

"The Vrassoons have bought our note from Barclays Bank and are calling in the debt," Richard told Maxi while the hard man waited for his response.

"The one from the sunken steamships?"

"The same."

"But we had years to pay off that debt."

"Not now that the Vrassoons have bought it."

"Can they do that?"

Richard's hands flew up like two doves suddenly loosed from their cage and a high-pitched laugh came from him. The formal document slipped from his hand and fluttered to the floor. "The Vrassoons, it would seem, can do whatever they damn well want to do."

"Is there an immediate demand for payment?"

"What do you think, Maxi! They want to drive us out of business. Naturally they're demanding payment."

It was then that Maxi threw himself on the Vrassoon messenger and smashed him to the floor.

"Let him go, Maxi. He's just a stupid messenger," Richard said.

"Thanks, Guv," said the man, who dusted himself off, and then in one quick move lunged at Maxi.

Richard let out a sigh. *When would they finally learn about Maxi?* he wondered as he looked away.

It took less than a minute for Maxi to rearrange the features on the man's face so that even his own mother would not recognize him.

Richard leaned over the prone, gasping man and said, "Tell your master that we received his message and you, my friend, your present condition is our response. Tell him that." Maxi yanked the bleeding man to his feet and then turned him to face Richard. "Do you understand me?"

The man nodded, and Maxi ran him out into the filthy alley. When he returned he saw Richard sitting on a wooden stool in the corner staring at nothing. Then he reached for his opium pipe.

Maxi caught Richard's hand and held it tightly. "No, brother mine, not now."

* * *

THE NEXT MORNING Richard was awakened by a loud knocking. Maxi was already on his feet, pulling on his britches, as Richard pushed aside the mosquito netting over his bed. He felt a heavy weight on his chest and pushed it off. The old Bible in which he was researching the origins of Rachel Oliphant's name fell from his chest to the plank floor with a thud. Richard took God and His Son's name in vain several times, each a slightly different, and often more colourful, variation on the basic theme.

The knocking got louder. Richard reached for the Bible and found his balance awry. More and harder knocking from the front door. "What's the time, damn it?" he called.

"At least a couple of hours before sunrise, brother mine. Maybe close to four," Maxi called back as he headed toward the barred front door of their temporary living quarters.

"Who is it, Maxi?"

Maxi withdrew the bayonet he kept hidden between the joists above the door and lit an oil lamp. The flame came up quickly, casting a sallow glow. Maxi slid open a panel and held the lamp up to it. The mirror at the end of the panel reflected the light to another mirror that brought back the image of Chen, wrapped against the morning cold, standing at their unmarked door.

"It's Chen," Maxi called back.

Richard was suddenly fully awake. Chen wouldn't venture deep into the Concession, especially at this hour of the night, unless there was an emergency.

Shanghai was a no man's land between eleven bells and sunrise. Most of the sedan-carried courtesans were safely ensconced for the night, having decided either to reward their patrons with their sexual favours or not, by that hour. With the exception of the hot-water shops almost every merchant had closed their doors. Those too poor to find housing for the night often bought the required two cups of tea in the hot-water shop and slept at their tables. It was worth the price to avoid the violence on the street, where cheap liquor was consumed by sailors, opium inhaled by the hard-muscled Chinese labourers, and the hands and mouths of lowly street whores were much in demand.

"Let him in, Maxi," said Richard, as he struggled into his clothing.

By the time Richard was dressed he found Chen and Maxi in the cookhouse, the brazier throwing heat into the dank room, the smell of brewing tea no doubt about to enter the air.

"So?" Richard demanded, looking at Maxi.

"I don't know, brother mine. It's something technical. I have marketplace Mandarin, and he has, well, about the same in English."

"After all these years, Maxi ..." Richard shook his head.

Chen held up his teacup and said in Mandarin, "*Ni de cha do hao, hao cha*—Your tea is very well brewed, very good."

"What's very good?" Maxi asked.

Richard sighed. "He says your tea is well brewed, very good. Say thank you."

"Thanks," Maxi said to Chen, who gave him a quizzical look.

"Jesus! *Shieh sheh.*"

"I know that. *Shieh sheh,*" Maxi said.

Chen stared at him, stone-faced.

"Fine, now we've got that out of the way, what are you doing here, Chen?"

The smaller man straightened his back. Richard could clearly see he wanted to say, "This is China, I am Chinese, I can go anywhere here!" But the moment passed and Chen said, "You should be prepared."

"For what?"

"The Mandarin's newest proclamation." Chen took a rice-paper scroll from his sleeve and handed it to Richard, who unfurled it and tried his best to make out the meaning of the characters. For a second he wondered at his own genius with spoken language but his almost complete inability to decipher character writing. He did recognize the characters for "all men" and "immediately" and "new," although he understood that the "new" was attached to another character that he couldn't decipher. "Would you read it to me, please, Chen?"

"Surely," Chen said, and reached for the scroll. "'The following proclamation comes into effect immediately and concerns all men in the Concession territories. New tariff rates on all goods are published below ...'"

"What?" Richard's voice bounced off the walls, "The Treaty of Nanking explicitly states that tariff rates on traded goods can only be changed after full consultation with the—"

"They consulted with the Vrassoons' representative, who agreed," Chen said, and then he went on to explain that the Vrassoons' representative had also suggested an upfront payment scheme.

Richard swore softly, and Chen saw in the flickering oil lamp light something he had never seen on the face of the *Fan Kuei* he thought of as Lee Char Or'oon—fear.

Maxi saw it too. "What? What's he saying?"

Richard explained. Maxi swore too, but not softly.

Chen watched the red-haired maniac and resisted the impulse to run. Not only was the man's violent nature clear, but he was also the ugliest thing that Chen had ever seen. Red hair, fish-belly skin, blue eyes—a devil if ever there was one.

"And the Vrassoons agreed to an upfront payment," Richard repeated.

"Explain," Maxi demanded.

"Rather than paying as items come and go from the warehouse, the Vrassoons agreed that every trading house will put up one hundred thousand silver pieces as credit from which the Hong merchant will keep accounts. When the trading company has used fifty percent, another hundred thousand is due."

"That's crazy, what kind of business deal is that?"

"The kind designed to drive us out of business, Maxi—that kind of business deal. It makes sense. The Vrassoons are the only firm in Shanghai that has enough money on hand, and they can afford to piss it away."

"But why? Why piss away money just to hurt us?"

"Because they hate us, Maxi."

"I know that, brother mine, but why? Why do they hate us?"

Richard had no answer to that, but he took the dual threats seriously. He grabbed his hat and headed toward the door.

"Where are you going?"

"To see the Vrassoons. Maxi, it took us fifteen years to get here. Fifteen years, and now it can all be taken from us. All of it, Maxi. All of it."

"Don't beg, brother mine. We've never begged. Never."

"I won't. I'll see if the Vrassoons will take our remaining clipper as partial payment of the debt."

"But what will we use to ship our goods?"

"What goods, Maxi? We have no Chinese willing to load or unload our ships. So what goods do we have? Think Maxi. Now's the time to think. Not beg. Not fight, either. We're in a box, and we need to find a way out. The Vrassoons think they have us …" He didn't speak the end of the thought, which was … *and they just might.*

Richard hurried toward the Bend in the River, where the wealthy trading houses had their ostentatious head offices. From across the road he eyed the head offices of Dent and Company. Its large Union Jack flapped in the early summer breeze while its two stone lions stood guard on either side of the large bronze doors. Richard looked to one side of the stone lions and saw Dent's real guards—men seemingly doing nothing more than lounging a few yards down the alley, smoking pre-packed cardboard Russian cigarettes and outwardly uninterested in the traffic along the river. But when a rickshaw pulled up and disgorged a portly man in a top hat, the lounging men were quickly on their guard, one with a hand inside his shirt, perhaps with the butt of a pistol in his palm.

Richard smiled at them; they didn't smile back.

Beside Dent's was a construction site whose foundation hole was only partially dug. The river water had seeped through the boarded barrier and was quickly refilling with the mud that had, no doubt, been laboriously removed. After the hole in the ground the path bent quickly to the right, so that a traveller was suddenly confronted with the imposing facade of the head offices of the Scottish trading giant, Jardine Matheson. The heavy oak doors looked as though they'd never been opened. *No doubt their major business goes through the back door,* Richard thought. *Nothing new in that.*

At the end of a series of lower buildings was, naturally enough, the tallest building in Shanghai—the British East India Company—the Vrassoons' private fiefdom.

Security was not hidden here. Four Sikhs in full regimental uniform flanked the doors and scowled as only Sikhs can. Richard walked up the steps and immediately the men stepped forward to bar his way.

"I have an appointment," Richard said in English.

They did not move.

"I have an appointment," Richard repeated, in Hindi this time.

The Sikhs didn't move, although their scowls intensified.

"Fine," Richard said in Punjabi. "I have an appointment."

Something in the smile family, perhaps the second cousin of a smirk, crossed the leader's face, and he replied in rapid-fire Punjabi, "With whom do you have this appointment?"

Richard breathed a sigh of relief. The Punjabi word for *appointment* was close to the Hindi word so he got the gist of the question. "With the chief," he said in Punjabi, knowing that *chief* wasn't the right word.

"Man in charge," the Sikh soldier corrected him.

"Thank you, the man in charge is whom I wish to see." The Sikhs didn't seem to realize that Richard had moved from having an appointment to "wishing to see" in all of thirty seconds.

The leader shouted an order to one of the others, who disappeared through the tall mahogany doors. Then the Sikh folded his arms and turned to the street. So did the other soldiers. So, eventually, did Richard.

And they waited as the day got hotter—and the Hordoon brothers, by the minute, fell further and further into debt. Finally the door opened and Richard was ushered into an office that was a perfect replica of a London men's club—unnecessarily stuffy, with the windows closed and draped. The leather of the chair stuck to his shirt the moment he sat. "God damn it!" Richard muttered.

"It is inadvisable to take the Lord's name in vain in these premises. At least swear in Yiddish if you insist on cussing."

The older man stood in the doorway, his woollen suit clinging to his skinny body, sweat visible on his pockmarked face.

"The guards say you claim you had an appointment with me. You don't, but I've been expecting you."

"Ah, you got my message?" Richard smiled.

"Our badly beaten man, that message?"

"The very one. I see he held his wits together long enough to ..." Richard suddenly stopped speaking. He found himself momentarily wobbly on his feet. "He was rude to my brother—an inadvisable thing to do."

"Really?" the Vrassoon man said, "Well, Mr. Hordoon, I've been expecting you because my employer has prepared an offer for you and your miscreant brother."

"And that would be?"

"Mr. Vrassoon is graciously prepared to cancel the debt of yours he bought from Barclays Bank in return for you and your brother handing over the paltry assets you presently hold in Shanghai and agreeing not to return to this country, either in person or in proxy, for a period of fifty years."

"Have you got a name, old man? You're not a Vrassoon, you don't have the swagger for it. And besides, you have something that no Vrassoon has ever had."

"And that would be?"

"A sense of humour. Surely you know that offer is a joke. So what's your name, friend?"

"I am not your friend, and my name is my business, not yours." His foot reached for a button on the floor. "Now you claimed to have an appointment with me. So what exactly is your business here?"

Richard noticed the silhouettes of the Sikhs behind the elderly man. Even in shadow Richard could sense their scowls.

"Perhaps a street rat like yourself has no business in the offices of the British East India Company," the elderly man suggested, with a wry smile on his face.

Richard began to nod. "Perhaps, old man, you're right. No business with the likes of you or your master. Would you tell him something for me?"

"Perhaps you'd like to write down your message for Mr. Vrassoon. If you know how to write, that is."

"Ah, a slander ... very good. No need to write it down. It's short, and I think even a dotard like yourself could remember it. So, you ready? Good, here it is. Tell Mr. Vrassoon that Richard Hordoon tells him to fuck himself up the arse with a crowbar."

The older man's face fell.

"Ah, perhaps you didn't understand my English. How's this?" Then Richard repeated his charming message in Farsi, in Hindi, in Punjabi, in Mandarin, and finally in Yiddish. By then he was face down in the dusty street, having been lifted and then thrown some fifteen feet by the Sikh guards.

As Richard spat the dust from his mouth, it occurred to him that he had eaten dirt before, and no doubt he would eat dirt again before his time on this earth was done.

———

"So how successful was your brainpower in getting the Vrassoons to change their minds about our debt or the new tariffs, brother mine?"

"Take that fuckin' smile off your face, Maxi, and get the boys."

That indeed took the smile off Maxi's face. "Why do you want to see the boys?"

"Just get them, Maxi. I'm leaving."

"What?"

"Tonight. I'm going upriver. We need workers and new markets. We have to set out in new directions. We have to get out of the box the fuckin' Vrassoons trapped us in."

"And you want to say goodbye to the boys?"

"Yes, Maxi, get them. I've got a lot to do before sundown."

———

Silas and Milo stood side by side in the shed waiting for their father, whom they heard outside giving orders to the men. The sound of horses approaching made Silas step back. Silas didn't like horses.

Patterson stuck his head in the door. "He'll be here shortly, so scrub your tears from your eyes, me little heathens."

Outside the boys heard their Uncle Maxi saying, "Not enough men, brother mine. Not enough even to carry what you need."

"I'm not carrying a lot. Just enough to prove to them that I can deliver. This is a search mission, not a trading mission."

"I wasn't talking about that. You may be able to speak their language, but you've got no fist with you—a language that everyone understands."

"I can't afford to have you come with me. I need you here to press Chen to get us workers. Press him hard. When I get back I want to see Yellow men everywhere around our warehouses. Besides, I want you to look after the boys."

Milo smiled when he heard that and turned to Silas. "Uncle Maxi to look after the boys!" he whispered.

Silas smiled. He liked his Uncle Maxi well enough, but there was something just beneath the skin that he didn't understand.

The door burst open and Richard got down on one knee and held out his arms. Milo flew across the floor into his father's grasp. Silas didn't fly, but he snuggled up to his father too.

"So, can you figure out what I'm up to?"

"You're going to find new markets," Milo said confidently. Richard ruffled his hair. "And make the House of Hordoon the greatest trading house in all of Asia."

Richard let out a laugh and then turned to Silas.

The boy resisted the impulse to pull back from his father. The strange sour odour that opium imparted was constantly on his father's skin, and it made Silas want to throw up. But he put his hands on his father's face and said, with an odd dispassion, as if he'd rehearsed what he was going to say, "Be careful, Papa."

Richard heard the distance in the boy's voice but chose to ignore it. He looked right back at his son and said, "Can't be too careful if you want to live your life. You have to take risks now and then. If you want to be a businessman you have to live with risk, Silas."

"I don't want to be a businessman, Papa."

"Do you want to live your life? Or do you just want just to be dead a long time before you stop breathing and they put you in the ground?"

Silas thought about that. He was afraid of dying, but he intrinsically understood what his father was saying. "I want to live my life, sir." The words came out stiff and formal because even at his young age Silas knew that he somehow wasn't able to "live his life" like everyone else. He backed a full step away from his father.

"Good lad. Me too. That's why I'm off upriver."

"Bring us back something spectacular, Papa," Milo demanded.

"I'll bring you back a whole new inheritance."

"I don't want an inheritance, I just want you to come back," said Silas. Although his words said concern, his tone was purely practical—cold.

Richard stared at his serious son. "I'll come back, Silas."

"Or I'll fetch him back," added Maxi, coming in the door. "Time to go, brother mine. The darkness should cover your exit." Richard looked at him. "Don't want you followed, now, do we?"

Richard turned and headed toward the door. His horse had been brought to the front of the building. He mounted quickly, then looked back through the door. Milo was holding Silas's hand and reassuring him that "Papa will be home soon." Silas nodded, but it was as if he had been told to do so.

chapter twenty
A First Foray

Richard and three of Maxi's irregulars made their way down to the Bend in the River, then headed west. As they skirted the American Settlement they turned in their saddles to look back at the beginnings of the great city of Shanghai. Then Richard pulled his cloak more tightly around him and they headed out through the west gate and passed the last of the Chinese sentries, whom Maxi had bribed only an hour before.

* * *

EARLY THAT NIGHT, after Maxi was sure the boys were comfortably asleep with their Malay *amah* curled up on her mat outside the bedroom door, he headed down toward the docks. He was usually accompanied by at least two of his irregulars, since Shanghai after dark, even for Maxi, could be a dodgy place.

Maxi passed by Jiang's ever-growing establishment and turned right into the heart of the Old City. The smell of cooking surrounded him, and many staring eyes—often angry eyes—watched his progress. On the sidewalk a street doctor applied a thick, wriggling leech to a large growth on a young man's chest. The young man turned to Maxi and sneered. He was missing both of his front teeth. It didn't surprise Maxi.

Older people sat on three-legged stools, their pant legs rolled up to expose their shins to the evening air. A woman sat calmly on the curb as a young man cut her hair. Three grizzled men shared a hand-rolled cigarette whose smoke hung in the fetid air of what the Chinese ironically referred to as the Chinese Concession. A scrawny, bearded man picked up his little girl and shook the remainder of the pee from her before sliding on her sacking pants. He didn't smile at Maxi. The girl didn't smile either. This was the Old City—Chinese didn't have to pretend to smile at the hated *Fan Kuei* here.

Maxi passed by a river stone seller who held up her very best blood stone. Maxi shook his head, then ducked into an alley. He counted four wooden doorways, then entered the fifth and quickly found himself at the south entrance to the Warrens.

He climbed down the ladder, as he had done that first time, before the British invasion of the city.

He froze. The icy fingers of fear, not something he was used to, slithered up his spine.

He breathed the fear away as he whispered, "Can't be too careful if you want to live your life." Then he retraced the steps he had taken two nights before—when he had first found his way to Rachel Oliphant's bed.

*　*　*

ON THE MORNING OF THE SECOND DAY of sailing, Richard's junk crossed to the north side of the Yangtze to a village he had used to keep the opium safe from the authorities three times in the past. Chen had made the arrangements.

Richard ordered the junk turned into the wind and headed toward shore. The villagers approached the riverside—en masse with pikes and old muskets at the ready. Just outside of musket range Richard ordered the Captain to come about.

"What, sir?"

Richard didn't answer.

"Sir?"

"Tell your men to lower a bumboat, I'm going ashore."

Twenty minutes later Richard sat in the bow of the bumboat, his arms extended to show he had no weapon. When the boat entered the shallows, strong arms grabbed Richard and dragged him through the water to the shore. He didn't resist. He kept looking for Chen's contact man in the village, but couldn't see him. The man was either no longer in the village or no longer on this earth. Richard was afraid it might be the latter.

Then Richard was thrown face down on the pebbly beach. When he turned and looked up, four pikes were aimed at his heart. He slowly got to his knees and in flawless Mandarin said, "Is this a proper greeting for an old friend? Has courtesy disappeared from the Celestial Kingdom?"

"You are no friend here."

The breathy voice belonged to a young man in full Taoist robes. From the deference offered him by the villagers, Richard realized that he was the equivalent of a mullah or a parish priest.

"Why is that? I have always been a friend to these people."

"Friends don't bring poison to friends."

"I have brought no poison. My intention is only to trade."

The young Taoist monk made a mocking sound in the back of his throat, then spat. It was at that moment that Richard heard the swoosh of boats. He turned. Dozens of swift village carracks headed toward the junk that had brought him—the junk that carried the four mango-wood chests of opium.

Soon the mango-wood chests were lying empty on the beach, the junk was sunk, and Richard and his men were set adrift in the river in the bumboat with the screamed admonition, "You and your poison are not welcome here or anywhere on the river!"

* * *

THREE DAYS LATER Richard and his men got back to the point where they'd left their horses. The horses were nowhere to be seen—so much for trusting the locals.

"Horse meat is very tasty," the Captain of the junk said, then muttered something about this being the last time he'd risk his neck or his property for the stupid Round-Eyed monsters.

Two nights later, Richard arrived back in Shanghai.

Maxi lit an oil lamp and looked at his brother. "You look awful."

"That doesn't surprise me." He told Maxi of the utter failure of the trip, then added that he'd lost four horses and owed the junk Captain for his vessel.

"He'll have to get in line. There're a lot of creditors ahead of him."

"What're we going to do, Maxi?"

Maxi had never seen Richard so utterly lost. "Now? Now we're going to sleep." He took his brother's hand and guided him toward his bed, then wrapped the sheets around him and lowered the mosquito netting.

Three hours later Maxi heard Richard rise from his bed and head toward the door. Maxi stopped him. "No opium tonight, brother mine. Sleep tonight—we have much work to do tomorrow."

* * *

THE BROTHERS WERE AWAKENED next morning by the shriek of horns and the clash of cymbals. Maxi woke the boys' *amah* and had them secreted out the back alley, then he and Richard opened the door of their Shanghai home.

There, in full regalia, was the Manchu Mandarin, his tile of office dangling from his neck, purple silk robes to announce that he was directly from Beijing, his hair braided and stacked atop his head and neatly tucked beneath his tall, conical cap. Richard remembered his first meeting with a Manchu Mandarin almost fifteen years ago. He had been tempted to laugh at the outlandish costume. Then the Mandarin, with the lifting of his hand, had had three men brought forward and executed while he washed his hands and ate sweetmeats … and smiled at Richard all the while. It took all the laughter out of the situation.

Although this was a different Mandarin and the foreigners were in theory protected by the provisions of the Treaty of Nanking, the smile on the Mandarin's face was frighteningly familiar.

Richard bowed to a middle position. Maxi at his side did the same.

The Mandarin ignored the courtesy and said in his high, nasal voice, "I have come to look at my future property." Then he tilted his head and six guards rushed forward, pushing Richard and Maxi aside. The Mandarin, like a great clipper ship under full sail, floated past the Hordoons and entered their home.

Richard sensed Maxi's growing tension. He took him by the arm and pulled him to one side.

"Are you going to just let that—?"

"*Zai xiang*, he's a *Zai xiang*, a Mandarin, Maxi."

"And he has soldiers with him?"

"That too."

Maxi looked at Richard. "What, brother mine?"

"Did you see his smile?"

Maxi nodded. "Didn't care much for it myself."

"Knowing, it was, Maxi. A bloody knowing smile. As if all this had come to pass just as he thought it would."

"I don't follow."

"As if all along he knew what would happen here at the Bend in the River. Maxi, they let us build up their village, spend our money on it and our expertise, and all along they were just waiting to take it back from us."

Maxi didn't like that, nor did he like the way the Mandarin's grossly long fingernails probed the sheets on Richard's bed.

chapter twenty-one
A Second Foray

Early the next morning Richard sat with Percy St. John Dent in the back room of Dent's formal offices by the river. Richard knew Dent was an old China hand who had worked his way up in his father's company from the very bottom. Rumour had it that his father had never lent him a penny or given him any leniency when he fell short of expectations. As well, it was common knowledge that his father had forced an unloving marriage on his son to solidify a business arrangement.

Percy St. John Dent was perhaps five years Richard's senior and still carried the sinewy muscle that hard work had built up on his long frame. The man was also a mathematical wizard, keeping massive columns of figures in his head. He was famous for his ability to spout data on a moment's notice. And now he was quoting the declining numbers of Chinese workers in the Concession and its direct effect on profits. Then, as if an afterthought, he added, "I don't actually need your clipper ship, Mr. Hordoon."

"But at the price I offered it to you, I assume it would be hard to pass up."

Percy St. John Dent nodded and turned away. He didn't like dealing with the Baghdadi Hebrew, but he had a grudging respect for the man and his maniac brother. The respect one real worker has for another. The price the man wanted for his clipper was more than fair. *So, the rumour about the Vrassoons calling in some sort of debt is true,* he thought. *Interesting. Well, no reason not to profit when the shoals shift beneath a competitor. We are businessmen, after all, and here is a substantial profit right in front of me.* He turned back to Richard and said, "What form of payment are you looking for?"

"Chinese silver or American gold coin." Richard took a breath, then said, "Now, this very moment, or I offer it to Jardine Matheson."

The mention of Dent's historic rival brought the desired effect. Two hours later Richard handed over the writ of ownership of his last clipper ship and received his compensation in Chinese silver.

"It's heavy," he said to Maxi.

"Yes, but it's not enough to pay our debt."

"No, but we should be able to buy ourselves some time by producing ten percent of the debt in currency—this is currency, Maxi."

"Fine, but it only buys us time. What are we going ...?"

Richard spun the chambers on his floor safe and opened it. "Maxi, here are the deeds for the three properties we have in the Concession. Bring them to Chen and get us buyers—Chinese buyers. Take the money and buy cheaper land, then build, Maxi, build. Keep five percent of the currency and leverage that. Call Patterson and get him to deliver the rest of the silver to the Vrassoons, and call in the boys."

"Why the boys?"

"Because I'm heading back upriver."

"Tonight?"

"Or earlier. The key to this whole thing is getting Chinese labour into the Concession. Without them, we're doomed."

"We still owe the one hundred thousand silver *taels* in tariff to the Mandarin."

"Stall. It's a language he'll understand. The money's on its way, the money got lost, the money is up your arse ... you're a Baghdadi, God damn it, so like every good Baghdadi, lie, Maxi. Make it up, just stall him—then start building. All those workers who're coming into this city need places to live."

* * *

RICHARD DIDN'T BOTHER with horses this time. He took Maxi's second-in-command, an almost silent man named Phillips, whose loyalty to Maxi was beyond question. The two of them took Maxi's much loved and much used two-man junk and sculled out into the waters of the Huangpo River. When they got to the treacherous confluence of the Yangtze they stayed on the south side of the great river.

They made sure they passed by the hostile village that had set Richard's first team adrift well before dawn on the second day. Phillips watched the shoreline warily as they passed.

At noon on the third day Richard pointed to a prosperous-looking village on the south shore.

"You sure, sir?" They were almost the only words Phillips had spoken since they had begun their journey.

"No, Phillips, this is China, what could be sure?"

But their reception was cordial, if cool. No guns, no Taoist priests, and by late afternoon two rice merchants who had done business with Richard in the past—using their good auspices and warehouses as covers for opium trade—showed up. Orders were given and the women prepared a meal. Not a feast as a show of welcome, as is customary, but a large meal.

Richard watched carefully where he was seated at the round table. Well, to be more exact, he watched carefully where the head of the fish was facing. The head of the fish always faced the guest of honour. The old woman who shambled in and placed the fish platter on the table turned it so that the head faced Richard. He gave out an audible sigh.

The food was fresh and gently seasoned with soya and ginger. The steamed buns, stuffed with pork and nuts, and a plant that the Chinese referred to as green vegetable were cooked in some sort of light, white sauce. The rice was unusual. Richard remarked on it.

"Basmati," the rice merchant answered, "best rice in the world. If the gods ate rice, they'd eat only basmati. Unfortunately, we are just beginning to grow it in the delta."

Before the meal was halfway through Richard broached the problem of the lack of Chinese workers willing to work in the *Fan Kuei* Concessions. The rice merchants pondered, or appeared to ponder, Richard's problem. Then Richard said, "Basmati may be the rice of the gods, but this," he produced a palm-leaf–wrapped ball of opium, "is the dream of the gods."

A full night of smoking later, the rice merchants had agreed to move two hundred chests of opium for Richard. They still had no solution for the lack of workers in the Concession, but Richard was happy with their commitment as a start. They also agreed to come to Shanghai and get the goods themselves when they next arrived to pick up rice shipments from the delta. This after yet another evening of fine smoke. On the third evening of smoke, Richard broached the idea of the rice merchants recruiting other rice merchants farther upriver to continue the chain of opium sales farther inland.

But Richard's timing was bad. The men wanted to smoke and dream, but Richard, feeling the need to get back to Shanghai, pushed when he shouldn't have. The presence of two courtesans in their midst and too much opium flashing through Richard's veins didn't help. When the younger of the two rice merchants suddenly retracted his offer of sale and assistance altogether, Richard lost his temper and pushed the man. He tripped over the opium brazier and let out a yelp as the hot coals fell on his foot. He hopped away and lost his balance, hitting his head hard against the stone floor—and lay very, very still.

Richard didn't remember much after that. There was some yelling and much commotion. He felt a sharp pain on his left temple—then darkness.

He awoke with the oddest sensation. He was on his knees, but his head was propped off the ground and his hands were tied to something ahead of him. It was completely dark, so he couldn't tell what had happened. He leaned to one side and found himself suddenly rolling until his face was pointed to the ceiling—or whatever was up there. His back was bent at an awkward angle and he had no choice but to stay that way, until mercifully daylight came.

There was no mercy in the light of day, however. He saw the millstone, about four and a half feet in diameter, had been, like stone stocks, clamped down around his neck, and smelled the deep reek of urine that he finally figured out was coming from him. His hands were through two holes in the millstone and chained in place. He tried to lift the thing, and it took all of his considerable strength to get it off the ground. He quickly allowed it back to the dust. It had to weigh in excess of two hundred pounds.

He turned and the damned thing rolled, putting him face up again. He gave a heave and it turned again so that he could put his knees down. He tried to control his panic. He was in the village's central square. Peasants carrying earthenware jugs to the well for the morning meal began to arrive. At first he tried to talk to them, but it soon became obvious that they would not respond to him in any way. Even his entreaties for a sip of water were ignored.

He calmed himself and took stock of the situation. The man he'd pushed in the opium den—maybe he'd died. Perhaps he himself had been sentenced while unconscious. *Not exactly due process,* he thought. Then he thought of his partner, the silent Phillips, Maxi's second-in-command. Where was he? He tried to remember if the man had been with him smoking opium. No, he hadn't been there. Richard remembered him sitting silently to one side, then leaving before the argument.

Richard knew that any punishment meted out to him would also apply to his man. By Chinese thinking, each of them was responsible for the actions of the other. Richard tried to lift the millstone to see if his comrade was in the square with him, but his knees buckled under the strain, allowing the millstone to clunk to the ground again. This thrust his head forward and drew blood from his shoulders. He took a breath and looked straight forward—east into the rising sun. He strained to look left and right but couldn't move his head enough to get a good look at whatever was or wasn't to his north and south. He didn't see Phillips. He dug in his knees and pushed to the right. The millstone rolled, allowing him to see, although upside down, to the west side of the square—no Phillips. He shifted his weight and the stone rolled, allowing him to get his knees down. He needed the stone to make a circle so he could see north and south. He took three deep breaths, arched his back, and pushed with his feet—the millstone lifted off the ground and turned about thirty degrees to the east. He allowed himself to catch his breath and looked again. No Phillips. It took him almost an hour and all of his energy to lift the mill-stone over and over again so that he completed a full circle. Phillips was nowhere to be seen in the square.

Richard allowed himself a moment of hope. Phillips was smart, resourceful, and loyal. He would have headed back to Shanghai to get help—if he wasn't already dead. Richard refused to allow himself to consider that possibility.

The heat was increasing by the minute. He needed water, and the well was almost thirty yards away. He reminded himself that in the heat, without water, a man could easily die. His shoulders ached, and the millstone continued to cut deep into them, but he needed water. He set his feet and pushed to his right. The heavy stone moved grudgingly in the dirt. He looked to his right. He wanted the line of the millstone to lead him straight to the well. He was off by a little. He regrouped and pushed again. The well was pretty much in a straight line to his right. He steadied his breath, dug in his left foot, shifted his body weight to the right, and pushed. The millstone did a complete revolution and a half and came to a stop with Richard facing the blazing sun. He shimmied his weight and the thing finally turned enough to allow his left foot to touch the ground. He pushed hard and the stone rolled, this time just a bit more than a full turn, so that his knees once again touched down. He looked to his right. He was off line. He planted his right foot in the dirt and pushed. Nothing. He tried a second time. The thing wouldn't move. He looked down. A damned pebble. A pebble stopped his progress! He planted his left foot and shifted his body weight and the thing turned a full revolution.

By this time he had generated an audience of gawking children, most of whom had never seen a White Devil, let alone a White Devil in a mill-stone. He ignored them and pushed to straighten the line of the millstone.

This time there was no rock to impede the movement of the stone. He rested for a while.

He must have slept, because when he looked up the sun was already past its zenith and the children were gone. He felt the blood on his cheek where he must have scraped it against the stone in his sleep. He looked to his right. The well was only ten yards away and, miraculously, directly in line with the trajectory of the millstone. Richard managed to roll the thing seven more revolutions in the next few hours and found himself right beside the well.

He slept for a bit to get his strength together. When he awoke he gave a mighty heave and lifted the millstone onto the ledge of the well. It almost tipped over into the abyss, but he managed to control the weight.

Now that he was there he faced an even more daunting task. How was he to lift the water to his mouth with his hands chained a full two feet away from his mouth? Even if he could pull a bucket of water up to the ledge (how he could do that he hadn't even begun to consider), how could he then get the water from the bucket to his mouth?

He felt a hand on his back and turned his head as best as he could manage. A figure was silhouetted by the sun—a small figure of a man in what Richard could only make out as a filthy black robe. A voice he thought he recognized said, "Are ye doing God's work, me son? Or the work of the Devil? Ye must nae do the Devil's work, son."

The heat was intense, and he knew he was already badly dehydrated. He could not tell if he was delirious or if somehow the dwarf Jesuit from the ship all those years ago was actually by his side, nursing water into his parched mouth and telling him that he must sleep, that he needed his strength for the challenge ahead.

Richard wanted to say thank you, but his mouth was full of water, and he swallowed it gratefully. Then he found himself on a gentle slope that allowed the weight of the millstone off his shoulders. Sleep, deep sleep, found him, and he retreated gratefully into its safety.

* * *

THE NEXT DAY Richard was pulled to his feet and marched, every part of him aching, to the local Mandarin's office. The man never looked at Richard, who swayed precariously with the weight of the millstone on his shoulders, knowing full well if he fell the Mandarin would have him executed. Finally the Mandarin pronounced his sentence, a hundred days, then called out the words "Dai nu ren shang lai, xi ling—Bring out the woman and the bells."

Quickly the Mandarin's supernumeraries attached tinkling bells to the locks of the millstone so that every movement produced a giggling burp of jingles. Then they looped a rope around Richard's waist, and a small woman, wearing a deeply cowled robe, stepped forward. On a sharp order from the Mandarin she lifted her head and pulled back her hood. Her nose and ears had been cut off. Richard had to make himself stay still. Somehow he knew he mustn't look away from this woman. She approached him and took the free end of the rope. She gave a tug and led him out of the chamber.

I'm the end of the punishment for her that began with her disfigurement, Richard thought as he staggered behind her. *I'm this poor woman's final disgrace.* He knew his very life depended on this woman. He thought long and hard before he said his first words to her. They were, "Thank you for your kindness."

She responded by screeching insults at him.

Not a bad start, Richard thought. *With other women I've done worse.*

Richard slowly learned the delicate balancing act needed for the basics of survival—like how to squat to defecate with the weight on his shoulders (like most Europeans, he didn't bother with the niceties of hygiene), how to build up a slant of dirt to allow himself to sleep without wrenching his back or having to sleep on his knees, how to find support for the weight on his neck when he stood, how to beg the woman to feed him, as he had no earthly way of getting his hands to his mouth.

It took time and effort, but Richard was able to get the woman to tell him her name, Yuan Tu, and slowly he began to read the expressions on her butchered face. By the third day he was sure that he saw concern there. Even sympathy. That night she helped him build the mound he needed for sleeping and fed him the scraps she'd collected from the village's rubbish heap.

On the fourth morning Richard found himself awakened by a strange dream. He thought his brother was there beside him telling him that everything was going to be okay. When he awoke, Maxi was nowhere to be seen—but there was a shred of rag tied to the fingers of his left hand. He strained his head to see it better and waited for the early morning light. When the first of the sun's rays cast their milkiness into the darkness, Richard allowed a smile to his lips—the bit of rag was red, flaming red.

Yuan Tu approached him with the morning's ration of food, a thin rice paste that she gently spooned into his mouth. All around him the town was coming to life. The smell of real cooking from the nearby houses almost drove him mad with hunger. To his left, three Manchu guards, who periodically checked in on him, swaggered forward. The Manchus were the only Celestials who didn't have to shave their foreheads and wear their hair in a long braid down their backs. Despite the best efforts of the Chinese to incorporate these impositions into their culture, they still stood out as the overt sign of the conquered.

One of the Manchus leaned down toward Richard and held his nose.

"No doubt you'd smell rosier in my position," Richard said.

It surprised the Manchu that Richard was willing to speak. The Foreign Devil had never spoken to them before. Then a quizzical look crossed the guard's face and he tugged the bit of red kerchief free from Richard's left hand. "What is this?" he demanded. Without waiting for Richard's response, he turned to the other soldiers and said, "Red rag for the Red Devil. The ―"

He never got out another word, as the bullet from Maxi's rifle pierced his larynx. The other guards whipped around. Richard heard a sharp slap, and six rifles snapped out from around the corner of the wall. The sun glinted off strands of silk that somehow joined the weapons. The guards looked at one another—then were almost cut in half as the six rifles fired at the same time.

Richard tugged at Yuan Tu to get behind him. She cowered into his side.

The villagers shrieked and ran for cover.

Richard heard Maxi shout something and then the sound of hooves clattering on the hard ground.

A cart pulled by two horses raced toward him and dropped its back gate to the ground. Maxi and Phillips ran to Richard and rolled him up the slanted ramp into the bed of the cart and slammed the gate shut as the horses took off at a full gallop.

"Take the woman—they'll kill her if we leave her," Richard shouted.

"Get her," Maxi yelled at Phillips, who leapt down and grabbed the woman and tossed her into the moving cart. As he did, Maxi braced himself against the side of the moving thing and pulled hard on a strand of silk in his hands. The six rifles that had magically snapped into position against the wall of the building clattered to the ground and then followed in the dirt, dragged by the cart.

Richard thought he heard more gunshots behind him but couldn't tell as the millstone rolled wildly in the back of the bouncing cart, sending him twisting and turning, slamming into the wooden sides several times, until one sharp turn sent the wheel rolling and his head smashed into the cart's iron gate. With a kind of gratitude Richard accepted the coming darkness. The last thing he remembered thinking was that he really, really wanted a pipe of opium.

———

Richard awoke to a gentle rocking motion.

"You done with the sleeping, brother mine?"

Richard looked up and Maxi was standing over him. Phillips sat silently against the port rail.

Richard went to adjust the millstone and realized it wasn't there. He almost flew to his feet, and he was lucky that Maxi was near at hand because without the excess weight he almost flung himself overboard.

"Time to sit and get your sea legs. We've a day's sailing before we're back in Shanghai."

Richard sat and stared at his brother. The horses and the cart moved slowly to the rhythm of the river. The six silk-tethered rifles leaned against the port rail of the large junk.

"What?" Maxi asked.

Pointing to the rifles, Richard asked, "Your invention?"

"A little something I'm working on."

"Well, it worked."

"This time," Maxi replied, then added with a smile, "it's never worked before." In response to Richard's grimace, Maxi asked, nonchalantly, "Is that a problem for you, brother mine? They could just as well have shot you, to be honest."

Richard said, "No, Maxi, no problem," but he was thinking about the dwarf Jesuit, about doing the Devil's work, and about the prophecy of the old Indian outside the Works in Ghazipur: "Brother will kill brother." *Well, not this time*, Richard thought, *not this time.*

The earless, noseless woman approached him and knelt by his side, keeping her disfigured face away from the eyes of Maxi Hordoon, a man she was convinced was a red-haired devil.

"What's her name, brother mine?"

"Yuan Tu are the first of her many names. But why don't you call her Lily."

* * *

"I'M SAFE BACK IN SHANGHAI, but this firm is no better off," Richard barked. His voice was still hoarse from the days with his neck in the millstone. He looked at Maxi and Phillips and the other loyal irregulars. "All we are is several days deeper in debt, gentlemen. We still have no workers and no new markets."

"Not to mention the one hundred thousand silver *taels* we owe the Mandarin, brother mine."

"Thanks, I really needed to be reminded of that. I want us all to ante up. Sell everything we have, Maxi—the horses, the food stuffs, the cooking utensils, everything. I need to go back."

"Back out there? Upriver? Are you mad, brother mine? Has that thing you wore around your neck squeezed all the reason from your silly head?"

"No, Maxi. What do you suggest we do? Sit here and let everything we've worked for all these years be taken from us? Or should we run, like Papa did?"

Maxi turned from his brother. Richard was surprised to see Maxi doing something that appeared to be calculating. "Maxi?"

"You need cover when you travel inland. A way to be there but not attract the attention of the Manchu Mandarins or the Taoist monks if they get a bee up their butts."

"I agree."

"What about travelling with the House of Zion? They're planning to Bible-thump their way into the hearts of the Middle Kingdom."

"When?"

"In three days. The expedition is already outfitted, they're just waiting for transport."

For a fleeting moment it occurred to Richard to ask Maxi how he knew all this, but the possibility of the trip so intrigued him that he let it pass. "Fine, but why would they allow me to go with them?"

"Because they need a translator, surely, if they are going to win the souls of the heathens."

"They already have a translator, Maxi, that flake McKinnon."

"Yes, but what if something should befall Mr. McKinnon that put him into the bad books of the Evangelicals at Oliphant and Company?"

Richard smiled and shook his head. "I sense a plan."

"Yes, brother mine, you're not the only Hordoon capable of planning."

"I grant that."

"Fine. Now, I would assume that Jiang's little establishment is a dire temptation to the likes of such men as Mr. McKinnon, wouldn't you think?"

Richard's smile broadened, and he clasped his brother to him—the Hordoon boys were at it again!

* * *

IT WASN'T HARD to convince the Chinese hooker to play along. Madame Jiang gave her permission, for a modest fee, and the trap was fully baited. Richard almost felt sorry for the man when he ran out into the streets without his pants or underclothes, with the hooker running after him all the way to the American Settlement … almost. But Richard had limited sympathy for hypocrites. If a religious man claims there is only one path upon which a righteous man must tread, then he had damned well better not stray from that path himself. And paying to be fellated by a whore instructed to dress as a nun would, in most circles, be considered to have strayed from the traditional path to a heavenly reward.

McKinnon's comeuppance was swift and dire. He was expelled from the House of Zion and set adrift. That left a vacancy for a translator on the Oliphants' next missionary voyage into the Celestial heartland—and translators were both vital and hard to come by. Richard, as luck would have it, was available.

Then magically a larger, better-equipped junk became available. The vessel, which Maxi had arranged already, had a crew of five men who had worked for him in the past, and the far forward section of its hold concealed forty-five mango-wood chests containing enough opium to intoxicate the population of a small city.

The sun was rising as Richard boarded the junk at the Suzu Creek wharf. He nodded slightly to two of the junk's sailors, whom he recognized, and traded simple pleasantries with a third as he awaited the arrival of the traders of the House of Zion.

Something niggled at the back of Richard's mind. The sudden availability of the junk, the sailors who were loyal to Maxi, the fact that Maxi had known of the Oliphants' imminent travels—how had Maxi …? But suddenly he didn't care, because Rachel Oliphant was climbing the gangway to the junk, and she was looking right at him.

Maxi watched the proceedings from a distance with a scowl on his face. The warmth of Rachel's smile as she boarded the junk almost matched the passion of her love making the night before. And yet Maxi knew he was somehow moving away from her—from all of them at the Bend in the River.

chapter twenty-two
Arrival of the Patriarch

Eliazar Vrassoon was in Calcutta when he received Cyril's message about extraterritoriality and within days was onboard the swiftest available British East India Company clipper ship—all sails unfurled—headed toward Shanghai. If Cyril thought extraterritoriality was possible, he wanted to be there to move the possible into the probable.

The Vrassoon Patriarch knew that extraterritoriality was the key to securing the family's fortune. His eldest son was safely ensconced in London playing nursemaid to the family's political contacts while he oversaw the textile mills in Liverpool and Manchester. His competent second son was looking after the family's operations in Calcutta, with a sharp eye kept on opium supplies out of the Works at Ghazipur. Sons three and four were heading Vrassoon operations in Paris and Vienna, protecting the family's banking interests while branching out into textile works whenever they could manage it. The market for Chinese tea, silk, and porcelain was growing exponentially, but the key remained full access to the Chinese opium smokers—something that only extraterritoriality could assure. Vrassoon opium sold in China for silver, which was used to buy tea, silk, and porcelains. These were then sold in England for more silver and cotton goods from Liverpool and Manchester, which were in turn sold for opium in Calcutta, which then went to China—a closed circle of sales, the holy grail of commerce. And round and round and round it went, generating more wealth than some nations possess. But it could all fall apart without extraterritoriality. Hence, Eliazar Vrassoon was willing to deal with almost anyone and do almost anything to secure extraterritoriality—to close the trading circle.

After a difficult and oft-delayed crossing, the Patriarch of the Vrassoon family watched the new buildings of the European trading companies slide by as his ship approached the Huangpo docks. He drew his muffler around his neck. The damp cold of a Shanghai January had penetrated his expensive clothing, but he had a smile on his face. *Things are in place,* he thought. The Vrassoons' impressive building greeted the clipper as it took the bend in the river. Vrassoon sighed. *All we need now is extraterritoriality here in Shanghai and our trading empire will be assured to last.*

By the time the great man actually set foot on the soil of the Middle Kingdom there were very few people of importance who did not know of his coming.

Cyril had arranged an elaborate greeting party for his boss that representatives from both Dent's and Jardine Matheson had agreed to attend.

The Hordoons, naturally enough, weren't invited, but they were in attendance that brisk morning nonetheless. Richard, freshly returned from his voyage upriver with the House of Zion, wouldn't have missed it for the world.

Eliazar Vrassoon stared at the ragtag group of Europeans who stood at an odd sort of attention. When Cyril stepped forward to give his speech of welcome, Eliazar held up a hand for him to stop, muttering, "What is this foolishness?"

"Just a welcome, sir, for ..."

"I'm a businessman, not a showgirl. Now put an end to this nonsense right now and take me to the company's office."

Maxi tapped Richard's shoulder and whispered in his ear, just the way he used to when they played spy back in Calcutta, "Ugly, isn't he?"

"That he is. I bet he works at it."

Suddenly Sikh guards were moving quickly through the crowd pushing open a path for the Vrassoon Patriarch.

Richard sidestepped a Sikh and planted himself right in front of Eliazar Vrassoon.

The man was nonplussed. "So we meet again, young man. What have you to bargain with this time?"

The Sikh guard pulled Richard out of the way, and by the time Maxi got to his brother, Richard was visibly shaking and, despite the cold, covered in sweat.

chapter twenty-three

Extraterritoriality

The Village of Shanghai
February 1844

Hercules MacCallum, the leader of the giant Scottish trading company Jardine Matheson, stretched his massive shoulders and cursed the cold as he propped his bare left foot on a cushion and adjusted the canvas hot-water bottle upon which he sat. *Shanghai is even colder this February than last,* he thought, then noted for the hundredth time that the Glasgow-quarried flagstones covering the floor of his office on the Bund didn't help the problem. He glanced at the massive but empty fireplace. Too many Concession buildings had burnt to the ground because of faulty chimney work, so most Europeans simply put up with the cold—and used hot-water bottles.

Hercules picked up a surprisingly dainty silver bell and gave it a ring. After a moment, a panel, made from Scottish border county oak, slid back smoothly and his personal secretary came in carrying a bronze tray upon which sat both a large tot of single malt Scottish whisky and a cloudy draught meant to combat the painful gout nodule on the big toe of Hercules's left foot.

"Have we had any responses yet, James?"

"Aye, sir. Everyone, even the Persians, has agreed to meet."

That didn't surprise him. The Hordoons were heathens, but they were nothing if not practical. He was surprised, however, that the American

145

traders had agreed. "Do we not have to undergo an Evangelical dunking in order to be honoured with the presence of the House of Zion?"

"They haven't stipulated religious conversion as a prerequisite of their attendance, sir."

"Could we suggest they leave their Bibles at home, or would they consider that ill mannered, do you suppose?" He chuckled, but it caused the gout nodule to glance against the leather of the footstool, which sent shards of pain raging up his leg.

James saw his employer's discomfort but knew better than to acknowledge it. Hercules, at forty-two, still had a body to match his name. In his earlier years the man had been a seemingly unstoppable force of nature. Women loved his physical prowess, and men followed wherever he led. And then had come the debilitating gout. James made himself smile and replied, "Perhaps, sir."

Hercules took the draught of foul-smelling stuff, then washed it down with a big gulp of the single malt whisky—and sighed. "Confirm with all of them for this hour tomorrow night."

James nodded and returned through the oak panel whence he came.

Alone in the room, Hercules stood and walked carefully toward the windows that faced the Huangpo River. He looked across to the Pudong, with its incantatory mysteries, then up the street to the House of Vrassoon, and then in the other direction to the offices of the English traders, Dent's. They could lose it all, he knew. Every one of them could lose everything. All the work. All the time. All the money could go away if they couldn't convince Chinese labourers to come into the Concessions and work.

His left foot brushed against his right shoe. Again the pain, like splinters of glass racing up his leg, took his breath from him. He waited for the agony to subside, then looked down at the small red bump on the big toe of his left foot. Such a small thing to incapacitate someone as powerful as himself. Like the little matter of Chinese workers bringing the greatest trading companies in the world to their knees. He wondered what would happen if he took a knife to the gout nodule and simply cut it out. His doctors had, in no uncertain terms, warned him against that. He took a sip of his whisky and thought that the nodule might have to stay on his foot, but this Chinese labour problem had to go away.

* * *

THE MEETING ITSELF did not start well. Hercules's proffered whisky was pronounced "spittle of the devil" by Jedediah Oliphant, who then added a few choice words that sounded like a biblical quotation. But Hercules,

who was as Bible-learned as any minister, couldn't for the life of him identify from where in the Good Book the man's vituperative admonition
against alcohol came. The food was put aside on the basis of some sort of
hocus pocus dietary restriction by the newly arrived Vrassoon Patriarch
and his skull-capped retinue. Percy St. John Dent sipped his liquor and
nibbled at the edges of his food. Only the two Persians ate and drank
heartily, the red-haired one smacking his lips loudly.

Hercules ignored these warning signs and rose from his seat at the head
of the table. "Thank you for joining me, gentlemen. Please accept my
apologies if my humble offerings have caused offence. None was intended,
of that I can assure you."

The men around the table nodded. Maxi reached for a fat turkey leg
that oozed reddish juices down his chin as he chomped down on the flesh.

"We are competitors," Hercules continued, "but we are now confronted
by a common problem." The faces around the table stared back at him. No
one spoke. The red-haired Persian set down his turkey leg and wiped his
chin. Hercules waited for someone to respond. This was clearly going to be
more difficult than he had anticipated.

"All right," he began again, "we've had years of undercutting, outdo-
ing, and outsmarting each other. We're traders, businessmen, opponents. I
acknowledge that, and I think the rest of you around this table have no
quibble with those definitions." Again, no one spoke. At least no one contradicted him, he thought. "But if we fight each other now, if we don't
come together and speak with one voice against our common enemy—"

"And who exactly would this common enemy be, in your esteemed
opinion?" asked Percy St. John Dent with an open mischievousness. Then,
with a breathless sarcasm, he asked, "Would you by any chance be referring to the British East India Company's Vrassoon family with their parliamentary monopoly on direct trade between China and England? Would
they be the common enemy, Mr. Hercules MacCallum?"

Eliazar Vrassoon spread his arms magnanimously and said, "As simple
traders, none of us here has the wisdom to question the noble actions of
Her Majesty's duly appointed Parliament. The law is the law. We are law-
abiding traders, not brigands or pirates. We all here obey the law, do we
not?"

"The law!" Maxi spat out. Richard put a hand on his brother's arm to
restrain him.

"Yes, the law," Hercules jumped in. "The law," he repeated. Then he
asked pointedly, "Why are *we* not the law here, in our own home? Why
are the Manchus the law in our Concessions? Surely our Concessions
should be ruled by our laws." He paused for a moment, then said, as if it

were nothing significant, "Why do we not work together toward extraterritoriality? Speak with one voice for it?"

Extraterritoriality was the end goal of every colonizing power. With it, the colonizers could control the laws within the bounds of their jurisdictions. No longer would the Concession be a small enclave within the mass of China. The Concession would be a piece of England—or America—a sovereign power governed by the trading houses, who would make and enforce the law as they saw fit.

"But we're *not* the law here." Jedediah Oliphant stated the obvious.

"Aye, but we could be," Hercules said, and smiled. "If we unite. Uniting is the key to gaining extraterritoriality."

Everyone agreed with that. They knew they would have to ask their respective governments to force the Manchus into granting extraterritoriality—perhaps with some substantial loss of life, and definitely with a momentary loss of tax revenue. Anti-colonial forces in both England and America were growing stronger. If they sensed any wavering in the traders' resolve they would pounce.

Maxi reached for his drumstick and took another bite. His bright, hard teeth hit bone with a clink. He looked at his brother and then reached for a second piece of turkey. But before he could get it into his mouth the discussion had degenerated into squabbling.

Richard knew the head of Jardine Matheson was right. Only if they were united could they hope to get their governments to force extraterritoriality on the Chinese. And only with extraterritoriality in place could the traders secure Chinese labourers to work for them. With extraterritoriality, they could offer the workers places to live and, most important, protection from the Manchu Mandarins' retribution. But too many years of animosity and distrust separated the men in the room, and Richard knew that Hercules wasn't the one to unite the traders. He looked at the irate faces around the table as the voices grew in both volume and anger, and his eye kept landing on the calm visage of Eliazar Vrassoon. Finally the man turned his bulbous eyes toward him, nodded, and then said in Yiddish, "Meet me tonight."

The foreign words stopped the English-speakers around the table. Quickly accusations flew against the "heathens in our midst." "English," Percy St. John Dent suggested, "is the language of this meeting."

The Vrassoon Patriarch nodded. "My apologies, gentlemen." But Richard read no apology in either the man's tone or his demeanour.

By the time Richard and Maxi finally got up to leave, the leaders of the great trading houses of Shanghai were sitting in stony, angry silence.

* * *

LATE THAT NIGHT Richard entered the very heart of enemy territory, the private study of the Patriarch of the Vrassoon clan. He stood with his cap literally in hand and waited for the older man to join him.

The room bespoke power and money—both understated, but very much in evidence. Throw rugs from the Punjab, milk-soft leather chairs to rival any found in the finest salons of Paris, delicately leaded windows overlooking the beginnings of the promenade along the Huangpo River, original oil paintings that seemed to feature the same female model at different ages, all in gilt frames, a silver menorah to one side and other telltale artifacts of Judaica.

Without fanfare or apology for making him wait, Eliazar Vrassoon entered the room followed by Cyril, his China hand. The Patriarch dismissed Cyril with the pointing of a finger, then waited until the man was out the door before he turned to Richard.

Richard eyed Vrassoon. A surge of anger raced through him, but it quickly dissipated as something else—something urgent—tugged at the sides of his memory. The head of the British East India Company extended his hand. The words *What are you doing here?* flew into Richard's mind, but he couldn't find the rest of the thought. For a moment he felt as though he were falling, somehow only a child again—and there was wetness between his legs! Then he was pointing, showing this man something. What?

Richard finally noticed Eliazar's extended hand. It felt good not to have reciprocated the courtesy.

"As you will," Vrassoon said as he returned his hand to his coat pocket. "Well, our Christian counterparts seem intent upon fighting one another," the older man said.

"Unlike us Jews, who always love and honour each other," Richard spat back sarcastically.

The older man nodded and poured himself a small glass of sherry from a crystal decanter. He didn't offer Richard a drink. "Indeed," he said, "but we at least won't squabble over religious niceties."

"Only because I have no religious niceties," Richard responded.

"No, you don't." Eliazar Vrassoon's voice was suddenly cold as ice. "No, you're not any kind of a Jew. In fact, if they didn't hate us all so much you'd have no identity whatsoever. You're only a Jew because the goyim hate you."

Richard accepted that. "I live my life by my own values."

"That assumes you have some."

"I reject your medieval darkness in favour of finding my own light."

Vrassoon shook his head slowly and then said, "You are a lonely man, Mr. Hordoon."

"Better lonely than idolatrous."

"Idolatrous!" The Vrassoon Patriarch's voice arched in a high crescendo that surprised Richard.

"Yes. Now, could you skip the preamble and tell me whatever it is …?"

Vrassoon hesitated. Did he really need this boy's assistance? Didn't he have enough power on his own? No. If it was just a man or two or three from his own company, the other traders wouldn't care. Why should they? But if it were men from two different companies, then it would imply that the next could be from their firms. It would become a real threat to their safety. Enough of a threat, Eliazar hoped, to force all the traders to speak with one voice to their governments to force extraterritoriality on the Manchus.

He looked at young Hordoon. *We are partners, you and I, and have been for a very long time,* he thought. *And only now will you begin to know it.* The Vrassoon Patriarch took a deep breath and then began.

"I hold the note on your debt to Barclays Bank."

"This is not news to me."

"Would you like an extension on the payment schedule of that note?"

Richard stopped himself from speaking. His time with the House of Zion in the countryside had shown him that he could open new markets that none of the other traders even knew existed. Those markets could generate large sums of cash. Maybe not enough to pay off the whole debt, but certainly enough to make a sizable dent in it. But it would take time to set up his networks. Time that, until this very moment, he'd had no way of finding. He made sure his voice was nonchalant when he spoke. "I'm listening."

Walking home that night Richard knew that Eliazar Vrassoon's plan was the only way to get the traders to unite. He had made as good a deal as he could, although he was shocked when, at the end of their haggling, Vrassoon had said, "You drove a harder bargain when you were younger." When Richard had pressed for the meaning of that cryptic remark the older man had just laughed and asked, "So we have a deal?" And Richard had taken the old man's hand—and the deal was sealed. He knew that he must never tell Maxi about the details. *If Maxi ever found out what I did to get the three-year extension on the debt repayment from the Vrassoons, he would kill someone. Well, many people. Eliazar Vrassoon first,* Richard thought, then added, *After that, he'd definitely come after me.*

* * *

THE VRASSOON PATRIARCH'S generous financial offer to the Manchu Mandarin assured the heathen's co-operation in this matter. The

Mandarin, in fact, seemed only too ready to write a proclamation that would call on all civic officials to "Enforce our local laws, to their full extent, on *all* the citizens of Shanghai, without exception."

* * *

MR. NORMAN VINCENT dipped his quill in the inkwell on his highboy desk and marked a bill of lading "Paid," then rubbed his hands together to revive the feeling in his fingers. The cold here in Shanghai was different from his native London, and he had been sick often since his first arrival in the Far East just over three years before. He took the locket from around his neck and opened it. The broad, honest features of his wife stared back at him. In her arms she held their baby girl. *She won't be a baby any more,* he thought. *She must be walking and talking by now.* He sighed, and his breath misted in the office.

He'd worked hard this morning and wanted to reward himself. The Old Shanghai Restaurant in the Chinese section—the Old City—was technically out of bounds for foreigners, but the food there was wonderful, and a bowl of soup, *tong,* was just the thing he needed on a cold day like today. *Maybe with those wonderful dumplings in it.* The thought made him smile as he signed out with his supervisor and, grabbing his muffler, headed out of the Vrassoons' British East India Company offices.

On the partially built raised promenade along the Huangpo River he looked across at the Pudong and gave a little shiver. He needed to control his urges and save his money, he reminded himself. That's why he was here in this far-off place—to make money. But the sexual offerings across the river were a great temptation to him. Only in the Pudong could a man get sexual satisfaction at a price a shipping clerk could afford.

He turned away from temptation and toward the rewards of the palate as he headed east along the river, then south into the heart of Old Shanghai.

Just moments after Mr. Vincent turned toward the Old Shanghai Restaurant, a fellow *Fan Kuei,* this one a bookkeeper in the employ of the Hordoons, also made his way toward the forbidden Old City. This man had a new girl, and his new girl needed a present. Something special. Only in the Old City could a bookkeeper like Charles David afford a special present—for a new girl. He whistled as he walked, his step jaunty, a smile creasing his attractive young features. It would be the last smile that would grace his countenance on this earth.

The Manchu authorities arrested both men, as had been agreed upon, strapped chains to their wrists and then threw them literally into a hole in the ground to await their fate. By entering the Old City they had, after all, broken the law, the Manchu law, and Manchu courts would decide their punishment.

Richard felt a momentary pang when he heard of the arrest of Charles David. He had put forward the names of three men in his employ, as had Vrassoon, so that neither would have directly "condemned" anyone. He comforted himself by thinking, *Someone has to make the sacrifice. At least it wasn't one of Maxi's irregulars.*

* * *

THE CONFUCIAN WAS SURPRISED when he was asked to sit as judge in the trial of the two Europeans. Usually such cases would go directly to the Manchu Mandarin, but he sensed that something was afoot in all this. He hastily sent messages to Jiang and the Body Guard. They met late that night in his study. He laid out the facts. Two Europeans had been taken into custody and charged with treason against the state for doing no more than almost all Foreign Devils had done in the past in Shanghai. The Manchu separation law had been ignored from the beginning. But now, seemingly out of nowhere, the law had been put into full force.

"Why?" asked the Body Guard

"Who cares why?" said Jiang. "There may be an opportunity here for us to advance the prophecy."

"How?"

"What is the greatest problem in the Concession?"

"What it's always been. Our people won't work for them."

"Right. So if you were in the traders' position, what would you do?"

"I'd call upon my nation's navies to force extraterritoriality—"

"So would I." Jiang cut off the Confucian. "So why haven't they done that?"

"That one I can answer," said the Body Guard. "They hate each other more than we hate them, so they can't unite themselves. They are like children unable to see what is right before them."

"True. So what can we do to unite them, to get them together, and bring in their countries' great ships?"

The Body Guard nodded. Jiang canted her head. The Confucian smiled. "Death can bring together the living."

* * *

THE TWO MEN standing before the Confucian, heads bowed, seemed piti-ful specimens of their races, but then again a full week in a dark pit had broken stronger men than these. One was on his knees begging for forgive-ness. The other stood very still and said nothing, strangely dispassionate. *These people are so short-sighted. They have no view of themselves as part of the continuum of history, as we do,* the Confucian thought as he held up his hand and the guards roughly silenced the blubbering man.

The packed court fell quiet. Maxi stood at the back and demanded a translation of the proceedings from Richard.

The Confucian rose and, allowing the old-fashioned singsong to come into his voice, pronounced his sentence on the men: "*Xuan shou shi zhong*—Death by public strangulation."

* * *

MR. NORMAN VINCENT had wet himself and couldn't control his shak-ing. The mumbled prayers of the Evangelicals only seemed to make it worse. He couldn't focus. This couldn't be happening to him. Not to him. He looked at the cracked paving tiles upon which his knees rested. Then vomit spewed from him and he voided into his britches—and he felt the bite of the rope on his neck.

Charles David caught the whiff of human excrement from the man beside him. He was strangely calm—or so the watchers felt. Some called it brave. Charles knew better. It was the normal detachment that he had been able to cloak himself in since he was a boy.

He looked up at the crowd. Every non-Asian in Shanghai had been forced to come view the strangulation. He scanned the faces, recognizing some. Then his eyes landed on the face of the young Hordoon boy named Silas. The boy was staring at him, but not with the fear and disgust that was so evident on the faces of almost all the non-Asians. The boy had a detached curiosity ... a detached curiosity that Charles recognized as akin to his own. When the rope slid around his neck he continued to stare at Silas Hordoon, and as his lungs screamed for air and his eyes bulged he stared steadily at the boy and forced his mouth to form the words, "Despite it, do great things, boy, great things."

* * *

"BARBARIC! Beyond any sense of law!" Jedediah Oliphant exclaimed, and for the first time in a very long time he envied those who could indulge in the calming effects of alcohol.

"At least demand their bodies," shouted Maxi.

Richard appreciated Maxi's sentiments, but he didn't want to deal with them now. Now, with all the traders upset and together back in the offices of Jardine Matheson, was the time to act. To rally the troops, not get bogged down in niceties like the disposition of dead bodies.

"Outrageous, beyond the bounds of civilized behaviour—well beyond it," added Percy St. John Dent as he topped up his glass with Hercules's fine whisky and took a seat.

"Never again must this be allowed to happen to our people," stated Hercules, ignoring the pain from the new nodule on the baby toe of his left foot.

The Vrassoon Patriarch stepped forward, caught Richard's eye briefly, and suggested, "Then we are agreed that we must take our fate into our own hands. That these heathens must be shown a lesson. That we will speak as one voice to be free in our lands to do as we see fit." He looked around for a moment, then lifted the glass in his hand. Slowly everyone in the room lifted theirs—even Jedediah Oliphant grabbed an empty glass and held it aloft. "To extraterritoriality, gentlemen."

The men drank to their pledge, then retreated to their offices to contact their highest government sources to begin the process that would bring on what history would call the Second Opium War.

chapter twenty-four
And Change Comes

It proved to be not much of a war, as wars go. The arrival of the six British man-o'-war and two American fighting vessels in the Shanghai harbour was remarkably effective. A slight hesitation from the Manchu authorities induced an out and out shelling of the Chinese section of the city from the ships. Before the sun set that day, the basics of an extraterritoriality agreement had been proposed by the Manchu Mandarin himself.

Richard translated, and with Hercules and Percy St. John Dent pushing the traders' points, the agreement got more and more specific. The relentless squirming and conniving of the Mandarin to make the agreement porous were resisted at every turn. Eventually, six days later, when the document was signed, it was the most inclusive, restrictive document on Chinese power that had ever been written or, more importantly, signed.

The party began that night at sunset in the British Concession and shortly thereafter in the American Concession. Oliphant tried to begin the festivities with prayer but only managed to get through an opening hymn before the revelry took over. Guns were fired into the air and liquor flowed freely as midnight—the appointed hour for the beginning of extraterritoriality—approached.

As the merriment increased, Richard retreated to the Old City and knocked at an unmarked door at the end of a dusty alley. Jiang opened the door and canted her head toward Richard. "Is the woman with you?" she asked.

Richard nodded and called for Lily. From behind packing crates in the alley, the woman without a nose or ears approached with her head down. She carried what Jiang knew were Richard's journals.

"Your usual accommodations are ready for you. Your pipe is cleaned, your dreams await," Jiang said.

* * *

SEVERAL MILES UP the Huangpo River, Maxi stood by two shallow graves. Milo and Silas were at his side. "You must honour men who fall in your command, boys, or no one will follow you." Maxi bowed his head. He didn't know prayers or care about them. He cared about lives lost for no good reason. He turned to the boys and said, "Honour these men in your thoughts. Now put your flowers on their graves."

The boys knelt and put their flowers down. Silas allowed his hand to touch the cold, sandy earth and wondered what it felt like to lie beneath the ground.

Maxi watched his nephew and sensed the boy's distance, something that he himself had been feeling more and more. And now these two senseless deaths. Two murders. He suspected they were two sacrifices but had no more than suspicion upon which to base this. He looked around at the river and the growing city behind them and knew in his heart, for the first time, that this was not his home, nor would it ever be. A strong gust of wind from the west drew his eye. The Taiping rebels were upriver. He knew that. But he wondered why that particular thought had sped through his mind as he stood on the windy hillside beside his two nephews and the two graves.

* * *

THE MIDNIGHT BELL SOUNDED and the town crier called out "Midnight Hour!" and shouts of joy came from the mouths of the non-Asians.

In the Old City, Chinese parents smelled the ozone reek of change in the air and pulled their children close to them.

The third opium ball did the trick for Richard. He opened the holes in his back and spiralled down the deep well to himself and the dark secret that lurked there.

* * *

AS HE DID a sleek sailing ship came about in the harbour. The French had arrived—with Suzanne and Pierre Colombe, madam and priest, side by side on deck.

The sounds of revelry from the land moved across the water and greeted brother and sister on the upper deck. "A party," Suzanne said with a smile. "How appropriate a welcome. You'll have to do something about that, brother. Parties aren't good for churches, are they?"

"No, my sister, they are not. Although I believe they are good for your commercial enterprise." His words were sharp.

"Nice of you to notice," Suzanne replied. Then she turned her eyes to her new home, Shanghai.

chapter twenty-five

The French

Shanghai
1846 to September 1847

Extraterritoriality immediately solved two problems facing all the traders. With the protection that it provided they were able to recruit and keep enough Chinese workers to run their businesses and households, and under the terms of the treaty the traders could avoid the one hundred thousand *taels* of silver demanded by the Manchu Mandarin. Extraterritoriality worked surprisingly well in other ways, as well. Percy St. John Dent was appointed head of the newly formed Governing Council with the understanding that the position would rotate through the four great trading houses (the Hordoons were not included) on a six-month basis. On Fridays, from sunrise to just before sundown (out of consideration for the Vrassoons), petitioners to the Council would be heard. Also, each of the trading houses (this time the Hordoons were included) was required to provide six men to act as constables. These men were to report directly to the head of Council.

It all seemed so civilized. What, in fact, this arrangement did was ensure that no trading house would have any power over the others. The "police officers," in fact, never reported to the head of Council before they had reported to the head of their own trading company.

The one notable advance was the breaking down of the border, at the Suzu Creek, between the American and British Concessions. The two sides adopted the name "the Foreign Settlement" for the merged territory.

However, the French—being French—declined to join their English-speaking Protestant counterparts and settled on the novel name "the French Concession" for their lands bordering the Chinese Old City. Shortly after, the name became simply "the Concession."

The Foreign Settlement and the Concession were divided by nothing more than an invisible line down the centre of a street, yet they had different governing bodies, different laws, different police forces—all of which made it very convenient for a felon from one side or the other to cross that invisible line and suddenly go from wanted man to free man.

Within the Concession boundaries and under the protection of the guns of the French flagship, the *Cassini*, the Colombes—Jesuit and madam—thrived. Within three months Suzanne had managed to open the House of Paris on the central road of the Concession, and Father Pierre had the foundation completed and some of the walls up for Asia's largest Christian house of worship, the Cathedral of St. Ignatius.

Much to the surprise of the English and Americans, the *Cassini* was quickly becoming a permanent fixture in the harbour. The Foreign Settlement failed to realize that the commander of the *Cassini*, Captain de Plas, was a devout Catholic who believed it was his duty to protect both the Concession and all Catholics in this "heathen hellhole," hence the positioning of his ship so that his stern port guns could reach the government building on the western edge of the Concession and the bow port guns could reach the Cathedral on the east.

It never occurred to good Captain de Plas that his guns offered as much protection to Suzanne's house of pleasure as they did to Pierre's cathedral.

* * *

FATHER PIERRE FINALLY APPROACHED the red-haired Jew who had been coming by the cathedral construction site almost every day. "Are you attracted to our house of worship? It is open to all," Father Pierre said.

For a moment Maxi thought he understood what was being asked, then he made the international signal for "I don't speak the language"—a large shoulder shrug accompanied by an ain't-I-a-fool? face.

Father Pierre nodded slowly—a Jew *and* a non-French-speaker. He couldn't decide which was more offensive. But he made himself smile and rephrased his question in torturously slowly spoken English.

Maxi began to shake his head before Pierre had even finished. "No, I don't want to come in."

"Father," the Jesuit prompted congenially.

"Excuse me?"

"You can call me Father. Father Pierre."

Maxi smiled, showing a lot of large, white teeth, and said, "I think not."

"Fine." Father Pierre's smile seemed to harden on his sharp features. "Then why are you here if not for God's word that can only be received within the walls of Mother Church?"

Maxi waved a hand, as if it were keeping smoke from his face. He wasn't going to be drawn into this sort of argument.

"What do you want here, Jew?"

Pierre's tone was one that Maxi had heard often enough in his life. In a certain way, Maxi preferred hatred out in the open. At least that way the rules were clear. "I want nothing inside your church ... Father ... just knowledge of how the building is put together."

That surprised Father Pierre. "Are you interested in building design?"

"No. I'm interested in how buildings are made." He didn't bother adding that he was actually interested in the mathematics behind the construction, and how the mathematics sometimes led him to understand the meaning of things, and that without the meaning of things Maxi felt somehow adrift. As if any day of the week or year could be any other day of the week or year. As if there was no forward motion. With Ahmed the opium farmer he hadn't felt that way; when he attended the Chinese opera he didn't feel that way. This Church, with its arbitrary rules and dogma, didn't hold out the possibility of meaning to Maxi. But the building itself, that which encased the religion, might.

Father Pierre's smile returned. He knew that every angle, every construction idea behind the building of the great cathedral had come directly from God, so he thought that the Jew's interest in the building techniques might very well lead to an interest in God, who had made the rules that governed all the principles of nature—and the building of His great churches.

Pierre called over his master builder and instructed him to answer Maxi's questions. Maxi wanted to know about the flying buttresses, their respective weights versus the weight of the section of the roof they supported, the mathematical calculation involved in finding the pivot point for the buttress, and the depth to which the buttress had to be sunk into the ground.

Father Pierre stood back and watched him soak up the proffered information. He was impressed with Maxi's quick comprehension of the information and his ability to deduce problematic issues arising from the facts he had heard.

The master builder moved on to the actual machinery used in the construction, but Maxi already knew the basic principles involved. Even the complex knotting systems used for the block and tackle were nothing new to him.

"Would you like to step inside?" Father Pierre asked. Maxi hesitated. "It is not yet consecrated. Besides, there are few walls. God's buildings require walls," he joked.

Maxi nodded and followed the Jesuit.

"Over there will be the front door of the cathedral. And where we are now is the main aisle—the nave."

Maxi looked around him. The flying buttresses on the west side were already levered against wall stanchions and holding sections of roof aloft. He could imagine the walls in place and the feeling of weightless lift given by the buttresses, which were massive outside the walls but slender inside, like the branches of the trees that fell over the walls of the Government of India Alkaloid Works at Ghazipur.

They walked side by side down the central aisle toward the high altar. About two-thirds of the way down, other aisles branched out left and right. Maxi looked at Father Pierre, who replied, "The transept. To the east," he said, pointing, "and the west, *à la* Rue des Juifs."

"Pardon me?"

"Just the name for the street outside the west transept door." Father Pierre wasn't interested in explaining that the Rue des Juifs was the only place where Jewish moneylenders were allowed to enact their savage trade. Since Mother Church seldom had enough money on hand to build the necessary buildings to glorify God, the money was often raised by borrowing it from the Jewish moneylenders just outside the west transept door. Convenient for business. And in cases where the congregation could not raise the money needed to pay back the Jews, they could be riled up on an Easter Sunday and sent to chase away those who happened to hold the debt note for the Church. No moneylender—no money lent. Very convenient.

* * *

WHILE HER BROTHER occupied himself with construction of his great cathedral, Suzanne had business of her own to attend to. She decided it was finally time to see what the local competition had to offer. Accompanied by two of her bouncers, she entered the anteroom of Jiang's establishment. Her men wore a consistent scowl, but Suzanne knew that this was just a mask. Right at that moment they couldn't have been happier, because they were about to sample the wares of Jiang's pleasure house, and Suzanne would foot the bill. Who wouldn't be smiling, especially since the bouncers were not allowed under any circumstances to touch the women in Suzanne's House of Paris?

Suzanne was impressed by the understated elegance of Jiang's establishment. Her discerning eye caught the carefully planted clues to the erotic, despite the fact that most were cloaked in a classical Chinese formality. The women wore Manchu-style robes, *hanfu,* and hair dressings, but a few ribbon ties were always left open to reveal the curve of a breast or the length of a finely defined calf muscle. All of the women had beautifully painted mouths, and tiny feet—the result of binding when they were young.

"You are troubled?" Jiang asked.

"No," Suzanne lied smoothly, then decided to be honest. "Yes. Have all their feet been bound?"

Jiang nodded. "Absolutely. It is a sign of respect from their parents. After all, who would marry a woman with unbound feet?"

"But your feet were not bound."

"Yes, but that is my family's tradition."

"Do the women in your family marry?"

"The eldest daughter, yes. She is always an artist."

"And the others?"

"One of my younger daughters will succeed me. She will not marry, but she will produce at least two daughters. It has always been thus here. So, now look at the beauty arrayed before you and choose."

To her surprise Suzanne felt an old stirring deep within her as one of the tall beauties tilted her head and gave her a lascivious smile.

Jiang's silky voice spoke a series of Mandarin words that were quickly translated into French. "Her name is Tu Yeh. She is most practised in the pleasuring of women like yourself."

Suzanne turned and looked into the high-cheekboned, flawless-skinned face of the famous Jiang. "Is she indeed?"

"She is." Jiang's round-faced translator stood behind her mistress and did her job with remarkable ease.

"Does she perform with accoutrements? Both receiving and delivering?"

Jiang needed a moment to sort through the difference in euphemisms, then understood the question. She looked closely at this *Fan Kuei* woman, allowing her eyes to examine openly the fine white skin, the petite curves, the devilish, thin-lipped smile—and tiny, very sexy ears. She knew from her many spies that this was Suzanne Colombe from the House of Paris. She leaned forward. Suzanne's delicate perfume wafted up and surrounded her. Then she kissed the woman on the neck.

Suzanne was startled by the kiss, then allowed herself to move with the touch. She reached up a hand and pulled the lovely lips from her neck. Then she looked into Jiang's unfathomably deep eyes. The women both smiled at the same time, their eyes expressing even more pleasure than their mouths.

"And how much do you cost?"

"The same as you do. Too much for paying customers."

"How about this Tu Yeh creature?"

Suzanne didn't bargain. She paid the price demanded and retreated with Tu Yeh to a back room that they accessed through a narrow hallway. On either side of the corridor, two bunks high, were pallets upon which men reclined and smoked their opium. Some were alone. A few were with partially clad girls.

Tu Yeh noticed Suzanne's interest. "Would you like to partake ... before?"

Suzanne allowed a smile up to her lips and said, "Before what?"

When Suzanne emerged from the expert ministrations of Tu Yeh she was surprised to hear a kind of high-pitched singsong colloquy of voices. She followed the sound through the main greeting chamber, through an interior courtyard, and into a high-ceilinged room with a set of raised platforms at one end. Across from the platforms sat an attentive audience on low chairs and three-legged bamboo stools. On the platforms were four Chinese men in elaborate costumes, singing. The crash of a cymbal froze them in space, and a delicate woman, wearing a costume with sleeves that draped all the way to the floor, moved quickly—it seemed to Suzanne that the woman floated on air to the centre of what was clearly a stage. A cymbal crashed and a screech came from the woman that shook the crystal chandelier. Then she threw her arms up in the air, causing her sleeves to float up like yards of silk caught by the wind. When the sleeves were at their full extension the actress struck a startling pose, the horns blared, and cymbals crashed and then crashed again. And the audience went wild. Shouts of "*Hoa!*" which Suzanne knew meant "good," rose from the room. People sprang to their feet and cheered. None louder, it seemed to Suzanne, than an attractive red-haired man whose applause led the room.

"Do you like?" It was Jiang whispering in her ear again. Suzanne didn't know if the woman was referring to the red-haired man or the performance. Before she could answer, a tall, handsome Chinese woman in her mid twenties came onstage and readjusted the actress's position, turned to the other actors, and shouted, "Again."

Quickly the actors moved offstage and the musicians rearranged themselves. The Chinese woman then counted down from three and said "*Kai shi*," which Suzanne recognized as meaning "play."

"So, I ask again, do you like?"

"It's a play?"

"My daughter's newest opera. She is thinking of calling it *Journey to the West*."

Suzanne had often had opera singers and concert violinists perform in her establishment back in Paris, so she appreciated the odd symbiosis of art and sex. "The handsome one in charge is your daughter?"

"Yes. I named her Fu Tsong."

"Fu Tsong. Very pretty."

Jiang pushed Suzanne's shoulder just a little more than gently and said, through her translator, "She's a widow, but actually she's married—married to her operas." Suzanne turned to face Jiang. The woman was smiling. "Besides, she's too good looking for an old bird like you."

Suzanne smiled back and nodded. "Absolutely too young for me. But that one over there isn't," she said, indicating the red-haired man who had returned to his seat and was watching the stage intently.

"Ah. The true Red-Haired Devil." She stopped for a moment and tried to wrap her tongue around the strange name, "Maxi Hordoon." Her pronunciation was close to perfect.

"Ah, the Jew. Is he a frequent visitor to your house?"

"Yes. He is unmarried. At first the girls were frightened of him, but once they saw his spear they changed their tune. Now he comes more often for the plays my daughter stages than for the girls. Be careful with him."

"Why careful?"

"There is violence there."

Suzanne had already seen that. But violence was also passion, and as Tu Yeh had proved to her in no uncertain terms, she needed some passion in her life just now. She also needed a partner, so she turned to Jiang. "Would you be available for tea tomorrow afternoon? I have a business proposition that might interest you."

* * *

JIANG LOOKED at the slowly lengthening shadows outside the window as she gently put the dark, hot beverage, untouched, to one side of the table. Suzanne had proudly presented it, through her translator, as a drink called coffee. Jiang had taken a sip and found it bitter. Suzanne had immediately ordered that tea be served.

When the tea arrived Jiang smiled and said, "Very considerate of you."

"My apologies. I thought the coffee might be a treat."

"Perhaps, like so many things, it is an acquired taste."

"Perhaps."

The two women drank their respective beverages in silence. Finally Suzanne said, "The men in this city have no idea how much money there is to be made in our trade."

Jiang didn't totally agree, but she nodded and said, "Let us hope they stay so blind."

"You and I both make our living off the folly of men."

Jiang didn't completely agree with that statement either, but she nodded.

"As long as men feel they are in command they can be manipulated in any manner that a smart woman   or two smart women   want."

Jiang agreed more with this statement.

"But men can also be the enemy. They can sense that we are making money and insist upon taking a portion for themselves."

"In return for their protection," Jiang said sarcastically.

"Yes. Extortion. And it never ends. And it always increases. It is the one serious downside of our business."

Jiang agreed completely with this assessment.

"What if there were a circumstance under which this extortion could be regulated? In which the government, not gangs of thugs, offered us protection? And what if the extortion money were an agreed-upon percentage of our gross income?"

Jiang looked at the long tea leaves, like tall sea grass, moving with invisible currents. She knew, as all Chinese knew, that change was a serious part of life. She allowed herself to breathe deeply. Beyond the heavy smell of the coffee and the gentle aroma of the tea she detected the unmistakable reek of ozone in the air. Change was near.

"What percentage?" Jiang asked.

"Three percent, delivered at the end of each month in cash. Never taken out in trade on our girls. Never varying. Based upon figures that we supply for them at the end of the third week of each month."

"We supply the figures upon which the percentage is based?" Jiang asked, trying to keep the excitement out of her voice.

"We do," Suzanne affirmed. "You see the advantage of this regulated system to us, I assume, over the randomness that we put up with presently."

"I do," Jiang offered carefully. "But we would need a powerful government person with whom to deal."

"Absolutely. I have a very loyal customer at the House of Paris who happens to be the head of the governing unit of the Concession—the French Concession. Do you think that would be powerful enough?"

Suzanne proceeded to outline her plan. It would work only if Jiang moved into the Concession, where the protection could be offered. Jiang could either keep her house in the Old City and open a new house in a building just down the road from the House of Paris, or she could move her entire operation into the Concession.

"I need to think about this," Jiang said.

"Absolutely. Take all the time you need. But this evening, let my house entertain you."

Jiang angled her head slightly and asked, "At what time would you like me there?"

* * *

A MERE SIX WEEKS LATER, the Foreign Settlement and the Concession were abuzz with the opening of Jiang's new house. The name was taken from ancient Chinese literature and was understood by very few. It translated as "It will happen at the Bend in the River," but the house, from its opening, was known simply as "Jiang's," the finest house of ill repute and opium den in all of Asia.

Jiang's opened on a beautiful spring evening in late April, when the wind moved softly up the Yangtze, bringing the scent of the sea into every room of the elegant house. French opera singers mingled with buccaneers who stood to have their portraits taken by a thin-faced Englishman who was showing off the newest of new inventions—the photographic camera. Two French painters mocked the newfangled thing as blasphemy, claiming that it would never replace their art.

The centrepiece of the evening was the premiere of a selection from the first act of Jiang's daughter's *Journey to the West*. Maxi was completely entranced by the singing, dancing, tumbling miracle of what would eventually be called Peking Opera. He was completely incapable of escaping the power of *Journey to the West*. Over and over he rose with the others in the audience and howled out *"Hoa!"* then whistled and shouted his pleasure.

As Maxi fell into the heart of *Journey to the West*, Richard signalled to the English photographer to follow him back to his office. He had already had an interesting conversation with the man, and there was more he wanted to know.

"Do you have the pictures you mentioned earlier?" Richard asked.

The young man reached into his leather satchel and drew out a neatly wrapped package. Untying the string knot, he folded back the brown paper and spread out the twenty photographs of which he had spoken.

"This is Eliazar Vrassoon's eldest boy?"

"Well, he's a man, sir, not a boy, but it's him."

"How did you get these?" Richard demanded.

"He paid me to take them."

"Yes, but how is it that you have them and not him?"

"He has the originals, but I have the negatives." He laughed. "He neglected to demand them from me."

Richard doubted the Vrassoon heir even knew there were negatives. "Where did you take these photographs?"

"In the anteroom of his favourite whorehouse in London."

"He let you ...?"

"Shit, yes! He wanted to pose with the little thing, but she cried and refused."

That stopped Richard for a moment. He stared at the photographer, then asked, "Little thing?"

"His whore."

"How young was she?" Richard's voice was only slightly more than a whisper. His mind was reeling with the possibilities that fate had presented him.

"Ten. Maybe twelve."

Richard spread out the photographs. Three showed the Vrassoons' eldest son without a shirt and a leg up on a stool, flexing his not inconsiderable muscles.

"Is it possible to put two pictures together?" he asked.

"You mean rip one or both and paste them together?"

"No, I mean take the subject of one photograph and include it in another photograph. So that it looks to the viewer as if the two were photographed together at the same time and in the same place."

The young photographer scratched his head. Richard was glad that nothing living crept out of the man's curls. "In theory I guess it's possible, sir, but the two photographs would have different backgrounds, so it would be obvious that the picture had been monkeyed with."

"Really?" Richard said, as he took a pair of nail scissors from his desk and proceeded to cut the figure of the eldest Vrassoon son from one of the photographs. Then he turned to the younger man and said, "What if you took a photograph of someone else and kept that person's figure on the right side of the image. Then you could paste this figure of the Vrassoon boy here on the left side of the photograph, and then re-photograph the pasted picture to get an image with both figures against the same background."

"I guess I could do that, but why would—?"

"Because I'd pay you more for that one photograph—and its negative—than you've been paid for all the photographs you've ever taken."

The younger man smiled and said, "I'm listening, Mr. Hordoon. Who's the other figure to go with the Vrassoon boy?"

Richard turned toward the large window and stared out at the wave of Chinese men and women moving past on the street outside his office. "How young was the bastard's whore?"

"Ten, maybe twelve, as I said."

Richard thought again. "And she cried?"

"I got the feeling that he hurt her, sir."

"Ah," Richard said. "The second figure will be a girl. A ten- or twelve-year-old girl. A hurt girl. A naked, hurt, Chinese girl. I'll send her to your hotel room to photograph."

The young photographer blushed. "I'll not hurt her, Mr. Hordoon."

"Nor will I. It'll be pretend. Only your photograph will make it appear real."

"But in my room, it's—"

"Improper. Certainly. This girl will have a chaperone, naturally."

"And what will you do with—"

"That's my business," Richard said. He dismissed the young man. Once alone he stood very still, sensing the world in motion all around him. He thought about revenge and then reminded himself to be patient—very patient. *It took fifteen years to get to Shanghai, what's a few years more?* But he didn't bother answering the question because he sensed there was something else, something larger than the need for patience, at play. Something more significant than revenge. Something that he could only catch a fleeting glimpse of while in the coils of the serpent smoke. Something about a young girl.

* * *

THE NEXT MORNING the young photographer was awakened by a loud knocking at his door. He opened it and stepped back in horror.

Lily was used to people being startled by her noseless, earless appearance so she ignored the young man, reached behind her, and shoved forward what looked like a ten-year-old Han Chinese girl—a beautiful ten-year-old Han Chinese girl.

When the girl stepped into the photographer's room she pulled on the ribbon tie of her robe and it fell to the ground. As Madame Jiang had instructed her, she played at being a young girl—a hurt young girl—while the flustered photographer began the complicated calculations that could produce a picture that might, if put in the "wrong hands," send the Vrassoon boy directly to hell.

That evening while Richard carefully secreted the photographic plate in his desk's hidden compartment, Maxi paid the photographer to take pictures of the boys. Dressed in Chinese silk robes, pantaloons, and slippers, Milo and Silas were photographed with huge smiles on their faces and their arms around each other. Within weeks the pictures appeared in newspapers around the world and, along with dozens of the young man's other photographs, gave the outside world its first views of the Wild West of the East—Shanghai. Silas loved the photograph of himself and Milo and wanted it framed and hung in their room. When he mentioned it to Patterson, though, the man turned on him and, ripping the photograph in half, screamed, "You're not fuckin' monkeys, heathen!"

chapter twenty-six
Opium—Dreams and Nightmares

Shanghai
1847

Rachel stood just inside the doorway, unexpectedly taken aback. Lily, instead of Richard, had opened the door to her knock.

"I'm sorry, she frightened me ... her face ..." Rachel's voice disappeared into a whisper, then was nothing more than breath.

"She's ... excuse me," Richard replied, then gently instructed Lily to leave them alone.

After a slight hesitation the woman left the room.

"Careful of her, Mr. Hordoon, I think she cares for you," Rachel said.

"Foolishness."

"Not so foolish. Take care. After all, what could be more dangerous than a woman scorned?"

Richard smiled and said, "A fallen woman, perhaps?"

"Perhaps," Rachel said with a slow smile as she thought of her time with this man's brother.

Rachel hadn't seen Maxi for over a month. And the last time they were alone he'd spent their precious time either brooding sullenly or talking excitedly about some play he had seen called *Journey to the West*. She sensed that he was trying to tell her something, something important to him, but he couldn't find the words. Then after that, nothing—not a single word for almost five weeks. She needed to see him but had no way of contacting him. She did, however, have a way of getting in touch with his brother, Richard.

They had grown close on their three-month trek upriver, but they had never been free of the ever-watchful eyes of her father and his men. When they were together they talked of books and writing. He had shown her some of his journals, and she had been helpful in editing certain passages. She also had a vast knowledge of Shakespeare, and they'd enjoyed many a lively conversation on what both agreed was the most problematic, although fascinating, of the Bard's plays, *Cymbeline*.

"And you are here now, Rachel, to …?"

"Continue my work on your journals, naturally," she lied.

Richard took her wrap, showed her to his desk, and handed her his journal. She turned to the page they'd left off at and began to read. Richard watched her from across the room and said her name, silently, over and over again.

Rachel came to an entry wherein Richard responded to Thomas De Quincy's final letter, and after reading it carefully she corrected a line.

"What have you excised?"

"Your use of several subordinate clauses back to back lacks elegance."

"Ah," Richard said as he turned down the flame in the oil lamp.

"How am I to edit without the light?" she asked, putting down her pen.

Richard couldn't take his eyes off her. Her pale skin and green eyes were somehow luminous even in the half-light. He had trouble restraining himself from reaching over and touching the strand of auburn hair that had fallen across her face. After what seemed a very long silence, he said, "And you came over here, to my home, just to edit my writing, did you, Rachel?"

"Why else would I be here, Mr. Hordoon?" She met his eyes and held them. "You are staring, Mr. Hordoon."

"It's just the light," he said, as he reached over to turn the flame up—but her hand stopped his.

"There's more than enough light now." Then she said the most extraordinary thing. "We all must live a little before we die, don't you think, Mr. Hordoon?" The light glinted in her green eyes.

"Oh, yes," Richard responded, "before we marry a man twice our age, I think it wise to live a little."

Her face took on a sudden, hard cast. She turned the light up full and stood. "I think it is time that I left."

Richard reluctantly left the room, saying, "I'll get you a carriage to take you home."

Rachel thought about that for a second and she began to laugh. No carriage could take her all the way home to Philadelphia. With Richard out of the room she took the opportunity to search for signs of Maxi—but saw none.

Richard returned shortly and walked her outside to her conveyance. He was surprised to see two of her father's men, whom he recognized from his trek upriver. As the carriage drove away the two men continued to watch Richard, who mumbled under his breath, "Shit."

Returning to his rooms, Richard sat in a corner and knocked gently on a panel. Lily came in with his ivory pipe and three balls of opium heated and ready. He arranged himself on the pillows, and Lily placed the first molten opium ball in the pipe's cup. He inhaled deeply and began his voyage.

The disfigured woman saw Richard's eyes turn back and knew he was beyond feeling, so she reached over and ran her fingers through his thick hair, leaned in close, and breathed in his maleness.

———

Richard was travelling. Alive inside the smoke. He tilted his hand up and he soared; then he breathed down and his feet touched the ground. Looking down he noted that he was wearing expensive leather shoes and that his leggings had been changed to elegant corduroy. He heard a tapping to one side and noticed that he held a pure ivory walking stick. He willed the stick up and his eyes followed. A large stone building faced him. In response to his command the end of the stick moved slowly around him in a wide arc. As the stick moved, he turned.

He was on a wide street filled with men and women and carriages and horses and large mercantile emporiums selling all the goods of the world. A sputtering sound drew his attention. A metal carriage moved slowly toward him. A man with goggles held a wheel in his hands, but there were no horses to pull the vehicle. Richard felt his face crease with a smile. "Opium folly," he said, or thought he said. He'd certainly experienced opium folly before. He turned around, pointed his stick forward, and moved down the elegant avenue. Then he recognized the old Asian oak tree that demarcated the end of his property line. He was on Bubbling Spring Road, but no longer was it a dirt path, prone to icy patches in the winter and mosquito-infested bogs in the summer. Now it was a high street to match any in London or Paris or Rome, filled with stores and fancy women and hotels.

Suddenly the thunder of horses' hooves at his back caused him to turn abruptly. And there, charging right at him, were half a dozen thoroughbred horses with men in their saddles whipping the horses into a lather. Richard held his hands in front of his face preparing for the concussion and marvelled as the horses swerved around him on all sides, leaving him completely untouched. He whooped and bent down, then sprang from his knees. And up he went. He was above a large racetrack, floating. Below him the thoroughbreds charged toward a large water jump on the back stretch of the track. The vast viewing stands were filled with people cheering. And he was there amongst them, shouting his heart out, screaming "Milo! Milo! Milo!" as his son guided his horse over the far jump.

It was a dream, he knew—but as Thomas De Quincy had implied in his early letters, sometimes the smoke dreams were precursors of the truth.

He sensed the weight of another molten orb of opium in his pipe and breathed deeply. He wanted to explore further the future that was right in front of him.

—

"Wake him up! Wake him up this very minute," Maxi shouted at Lily. But Lily spoke little English, and Maxi's marketplace Mandarin always abandoned him in a crisis. Still, they understood each other well enough—not what was said, exactly, but the intent behind the words—the safety of the dreaming man.

—

In his stupor Richard watched a man and a woman yelling at each other on the elegant, paved streets of Bubbling Spring Road. The man was White, the woman Chinese. The Chinese woman's face was covered by a large floppy hat. The White man wore a top hat that bobbed as he spoke. "No Chinese or dogs, the sign says. Can't you read?"

Richard turned in the dream to see the sign. Who would post such a thing? But he'd lost control of the smoke and he found himself racing into a huge dry goods emporium. All around him people were shopping. Dresses, hats, high lace-up women's boots, corsets, and the other paraphernalia of an expensive ladies' shop climbed the walls in leaps and bounds of colour and fabric. Suddenly he was face to face with another sign, this one on a store wall. He was too close to read it so he stepped back. Slowly the sign came into focus: "Upstairs Ladies Have Fits."

Richard began to laugh, and couldn't stop.

—

"What's he laughing about?"

The voice startled Lily. Its profound anger transcended language and made her scuttle away from the laughing man on the pillows on the floor.

"I repeat, what is the heathen laughing about?"

Lily blanched. Rachel's father and the two men from Oliphant and Company stood in the doorway. One carried a firearm, the other a massive club. Jedediah Oliphant carried no weapon, but his fury made him easily the most dangerous of the three.

"I didn't raise my daughter to end as a whore in the bed of a—"

He never got the last word out as he slumped forward and all hell broke loose in the chamber. Two gunshots sounded so loudly that Lily lost her already limited hearing, and the raw smell of gunpowder filled her nostrils. Then something red. And moving fast. A cry from a man. Another man hitting the floor with a thump, blood spurting from a third's nose as he fell to his knees.

Finally things seemed to clear and Lily saw Maxi, his red hair on end, standing alone over the three prone bodies.

"Now collect your foolish asses and don't come back here again. And if I even hear that you so much as raise your voice to your daughter I'll be there—your worst nightmare. You hear me?"

Oliphant nodded as he and his men beat a hasty retreat.

Maxi slammed the door behind them, then stepped forward and held out his hand to Lily. She took it and got up from the floor.

"It's okay, Richard is safe."

She was grateful that there was no anger in his voice. "I'm ..."

He put a finger to her lips. "It's okay. He's safe, Lily. Richard is safe."

She felt the weight of his calloused hand in hers and found herself holding on to it tightly.

* * *

THE WIDOW SEAMSTRESS looked at her son, sallow, bone-showing thin, craven-eyed—lying in a pool of his own sweat on the floor mat. His shaven forehead was thick with stubble, his Manchu-required braid ratted with dirt and what looked like bits of floor tile. She leaned in. His mouth opened and formed the word *ya pian*—opium.

She remembered that mouth clasped around her breast sucking gently and the baby who looked up into her eyes, his chubby hands kneading and kneading her soft flesh. His sweet baby smell rising to her as she stroked his head.

So long ago, she thought. *Forever ago*. She looked closely at her grown son, trying to find that child again. To find a remnant, a trace, a hint of what he had been before the smoke—so long before the smoke.

She shivered.

Crossing to the brazier she poked the embers with a stick, then noted that the coal she had bought only yesterday was almost all used up. *No, not used up*, she thought, *sold. He sold it*. He had already stolen everything else of hers that could be sold and had converted it into the dream smoke.

The sun was rising; another winter day was about to dawn. It would be the last day she dealt with the addiction of her son.

The young man moaned and the air filled with the acrid smell of his urine as it wet his pants, then found its way through the matting to the floor.

She nodded and for a moment wondered what would happen. Not here. No one would care here. But there—beyond. What would happen to her beyond?

The young man's mouth opened again and pleaded for *ya pian*.

She sighed. *Ya pian*, damnable opium. *Damnation fall upon those that brought this scourge here to the Bend in the River*.

Then she reached for the silk pillow that had been a gift from her mother on her wedding day and placed it over her son's face—and pressed with all her might.

She was surprised that he didn't struggle much. Surprised how easy it was to extinguish the life flame in an opium addict. Then, one more surprise, she began to cry. She watched as if they were someone else's tears landing on her son's very still face.

She walked over to her bed. From beneath the mattress she withdrew a Taiping pamphlet she had been given at the Bird and Fish Market almost two years ago. It was entitled *The Ways of God Explained to Man*. She folded the pamphlet carefully and put it in her belt. People had been talking about the success of the Taiping rebels from the mountains in northern Guangxi province. Talking about how they were going to rid the Middle Kingdom of the foreigners—and their damnable opium. How they needed every able-bodied person in their efforts. A woman who could kill her addict son would certainly be of use to such people.

She closed the door to her small home for the last time and took the first step on a long journey that would bring her to the attention of the largest rebellion in the history of the world—the Taiping Revolt.

* * *

SHE WAS NOT the only person at the Bend in the River who was influenced by the Taiping pamphlets. It had taken Maxi several days to get the document translated, since he didn't want to use Chen or his men, and somehow he knew not to ask Richard's help. When he finally read the translation of the Taiping pamphlet an old familiar feeling took him. A feeling he had encountered on an opium farm, years ago, in far-off India.

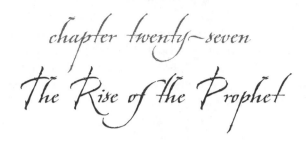

chapter twenty-seven
The Rise of the Prophet

Shanghai
Summer 1848 to Late Fall 1852

"Because I had no food for my family," the prisoner replied. Then he bowed his head, his chains rattled, and the muscles rippled across his broad back.

The Confucian had heard it over and over again in the past few years.

Just another thief, the Confucian wanted to think, but he knew differently. He'd seen too many of them lately. Strong men—men who had fed their families and been loyal to the state and paid their taxes—now out of work. Judicially he didn't really have any choice. The man would be executed. Thieves, when caught and brought to the Confucian, were always executed. He was about to pronounce his sentence when it occurred to him to ask, "What work did you do?"

"Canal work, your honour."

"On the Grand Canal?"

"Yes, the First Emperor's canal."

"And what did you do there?"

"I pulled barges. But there are no more barges." His voice began to trail off as he repeated, "No more barges."

The man is well spoken for a labourer, the Confucian thought, but all he said was, "At dawn you will journey to the Hereafter," as he had said so many times recently.

The guards hauled the condemned man to his feet and then, much to their surprise, the Confucian asked, "What's your name?" The canal worker offered up his name. The Confucian turned to the guards. "Keep him in custody. I don't want him executed, yet." Before he could be questioned, the Confucian stood and left the chamber.

* * *

IN HIS STUDY later that day he pulled the ancient journal from its hiding place and added to the knowledge there. He was deeply troubled.

The arrival of the White Birds on Water had certainly changed many things at the Bend in the River. The darkness was intensifying. In fact, the village, no, the country itself was afloat (perhaps it would be more accurate to say adrift) in opium dens, opium users, and opium addicts. But it was not just the addicts or the addiction that caused such serious problems for the Middle Kingdom. Huge sums of Chinese silver left the country to pay for the opium. With the loss of so much of China's national treasury, the Manchu powers in Beijing had begun to tax the peasants harder and mete out punishments more liberally to those who couldn't pay. Seldom did a day go by when the Confucian did not come across some poor man whose hands had been cut off, or who had been blinded, or locked into a heavy wooden board, his head and hands imprisoned through crudely cut holes. These pitiable souls were invariably led by a daughter or a wife who did her best to share the bolted and shackled weight, but to little avail.

As well, the countryside was filled with labourers who had no work. Q'in She Huang's Grand Canal, joining the mighty Yangtze River to Beijing, was virtually unused. Although Shanghai had not grown markedly, British manufactured goods, principally sold through Hong Kong and Canton, flooded almost every Chinese market, driving local producers out of business. Manchester's factory-made shirts, even after a three-thousand-mile sea voyage, were less than a third of the price of a locally milled and sewn garment. Thus thousands of strong, sometimes very strong, Grand Canal workers, used to pulling barges with their long cables for mile after mile, were now without work, without a way to feed their families.

Despite that, and the granting of extraterritoriality, not many of these workers made their way into Shanghai—just enough to run the *Fan Kuei*'s businesses. Shanghai was still little more than a large town at the Bend in the River. There were more and more *Fan Kuei* every year but few more Chinese. "Only Chinese can build the Seventy Pagodas. But there are so few of us here," the Confucian said aloud to his empty room.

The Confucian lifted his eyes from the civil service examination papers that littered his polished wood desk. Something about the paper he had just graded tweaked a memory. He allowed his mind to drift.

The White Birds have come. They brought the Europeans who built up our village at the Bend in the River. Europeans brought the beginnings of power. Without that, what possibility of rebirth is there? But bringing the Europeans must be only the first part of the plan, he thought.

He knew that on the Holy Mountain blood had opened the first window of the ancient Narwhal Tusk—but what would open the second, and further, what would make the prediction of the third window, the Seventy Pagodas, come into being? He thought again of the second window. Why was it closed to them? He knew that a previous Carver had tried to force the window open but had achieved nothing more than damaging the surface of the Tusk. Like so much else, the contents of the second window would have to wait "until the time was right." He sighed, then looked at the civil service examination paper again, and now he knew of what it reminded him a paper he had marked some ten or twelve years ago and failed outright. Then another exam four or five years after that, which he'd clearly seen was written by the same candidate. Once again he'd failed the incompetent, but this examination paper he'd kept. And now he extracted if from the hidden slot in the side of his desk and looked at it.

The calligraphy was harsh—crude—full of fury. He turned the paper so it better caught the light. The childish way that the candidate made his characters was surprising but the content of his answers was astonishing. The Confucian had been marking civil service entrance exams since he was admitted to the upper echelons of the civil service himself some twenty-eight years ago. Usually inadequate answers were filled with apologies and excuses, but the answers on the paper in his hand were nothing of the sort. They were angry—an outraged exegesis on the unfairness of the examina tion system itself. He finished reading the first two answers, then sat back in his chair. He had never heard anyone claim to be the brother of Jesus Christ before. Let alone claim such a thing on the entrance exam to the civil service. He sat very still for a moment, allowing an idea to percolate upward from his depths. He was a Confucian scholar, but he respected the promptings of his heart. Chinese people did not speak of intuition; they knew these instinctive promptings to be a truth. They knew that intuition was nothing more than knowledge in search of words.

He checked the access number on the paper and cross-referenced it with the district in which the exam had been written. He knew the proctor and no doubt, with a little money, he'd be able to find this "brother of Jesus Christ," should he want to. But why would he want to? The

Confucian remembered the ancient adage "Two thoughts in one place, like two fruits in one garden, often share a parent." But what shared parent was there between this "brother of Jesus Christ" and the Narwhal Tusk's vision of Seventy Pagodas? Seventy Pagodas would need thousands upon thousands of workers to build—many more than those presently working in the Foreign Settlement and the French Concession. Where could such a vast number of workers be found? There were legions of unemployed in the countryside. He posed himself a simple question: What could cause those peasants to leave the countryside and chance living near the *Fan Kuei?*

He put the paper down and crossed to the window of his study. The Huangpo River turned just to his right. Below him to one side a small wharf on the Bund was doing modest business. His own small warehouse, run by his youngest brother, Chen, was at the edge of his view. He took the exam paper and hurried out of his room.

Quickly crossing the dirt path down by the water he made his way northward toward the British Concession—the Foreign Settlement. Although he usually took his walks in the Old City, that day something pushed him toward the *Fan Kuei*'s territory. The streets, often little more than mud paths (at best rows of boards), were, as always, pretty much empty. He thought of signalling for one of the rickshaws that always awaited the command of the British warehouse managers but decided against it. He needed to walk. To think.

Bubbling Spring Road was hardly worth the appellation. The only traffic it had was due to the fact that it connected the British and the French Concessions to the Bend in the River. There were a few carriages closed up tight in an effort to keep the British women they carried free of malaria. *Good luck*, he thought. *Better to chance the malaria than die of the heat in one of those devices the British insist on painting black.* A few European men on horseback and several Chinese men bent beneath heavy loads passed him as he made his way.

A European riding a fine dappled mare tipped his hat to him. The Confucian bowed his head slightly. The Europeans knew him as the nominal authority of the town but had no idea that this day he was bent on figuring out how to make this town into a bustling city—bustling with thousands and thousands of Chinese workers from the country.

A Black Robe approached from an alleyway with three young Chinese men trailing behind him. The Confucian had to choke down his initial disgust with these self-righteous Christians who endlessly tried to bring their God to his country. One of the young men was wearing a filthy robe like the Jesuit. Ridiculous. Hot black sackcloth in the dead of summer heat.

What fool doesn't know to wear light cotton or silk in the depths of a Shanghai summer? These fools, evidently.

He stood still, tickling an idea forward, and allowed his imagination to generate the hundreds—no, thousands of peasants needed to complete the dream of the Seventy Pagodas.

Pieces began to fall into place. Bubbling Spring Road—Seventy Pagodas—peasants flooding in—and the fury of a young man rejected by the civil service who believed himself to be the brother of the Black Robes' God—at the very least, interesting.

That night the Confucian's wife couldn't find the right things to say or the right food to present him. She put a small bowl of sweetened rice outside his study door and headed toward her sleeping mat.

In his study the Confucian carefully reread what he was beginning to think of as "the prophet's paper." Such anger. Such incendiary rage. Many had led with much less. But before he did anything, he needed to understand the man's bizarre religious claims.

He had no real contact with the Black Robes and didn't know anyone who did but Jiang, through her connections with the French. Most of the brothels and opium dens were in their Concession. It was the French who had brought the Black Robes to Shanghai. He carefully folded the exam of "the prophet" and placed it in the interior pocket of his robe, then took his lacquered umbrella and headed out into the nighttime drizzle.

His polite knock was greeted with giggles from the women within. Then a harsh "shush" and the giggles stopped. The door opened. Jiang, the courtesan, stood with one hand on her hip and the other held high up the side of the door. Behind her the Confucian heard the muffled sounds of merriment and smatterings of a language he assumed was French.

"You can stand out in the rain if you wish or enter along with all the other clients of this establishment." Jiang's Mandarin was already becoming the strange argot that would eventually become known as Shanghainese. Her features were truly beautiful, but her smile was such that, with the movement of even the smallest muscle, it could well turn cruel.

"There is a tea house down at the end of this alley. Would you permit me to purchase you a cup of tea there?" He noted that his always precise speech was even more so when he spoke to her.

"Sure, why not?" she said, noting in turn that her language took on a whorish tinge when she addressed the Confucian.

At the tea house both refused Indian tea in favour of the dark, musky mixture grown in the south near Annam. The tall, capped cups arrived with their elegant, slender tea leaves dancing erect in the liquid, like eels in a pond.

Finally he said to Jiang, "You know the French."

"Yes. I know them. They are in business with me, as you well know."

"Indeed, but it's not that part of the French that interests me."

Jiang looked at the Confucian for a long moment. What kind of man was this? Power and distance, but no joy, no release. She had heard rumours that his family had been badly hurt by the easy availability of opium. Something about a youngest son and a wife, she remembered, but that would have been this man's mother and his brother, not his wife and his son—or maybe his grandmother and grandson. Then she took a closer look at the Confucian. Already his face was older, much older than just five years ago when he had first come into her brothel with the Mandarin from Beijing on the day of the auction.

"I have many contacts in the French community here."

"From opium and ..."

"Women. Yes, from my trade in opium and women."

"Ah," he said, clearly uncomfortable.

She reached across the table and touched his hand. He looked up and almost fell into her eyes. Then she smiled. "What can I do for you?"

"You know the French?"

"Some, yes, as I indicated."

"The whores or the priests?"

"Both."

"Ah, I had heard as much."

"And you're interested in a priest, not a whore?"

"I am."

Now it was her turn to say, "Ah." She lifted the hot tea to her lovely lips.

"A specific priest—a powerful priest—who would be willing to talk about a young Chinese man who believes himself to be the brother of Jesus Christ."

She put her teacup down and looked at him. He wasn't fooling. There never was, nor would there ever be, any jest in the Confucian. "So you have interest in the rebels?"

The Confucian was surprised by Jiang's quick surmise and nodded slowly but didn't elaborate. That was fine with Jiang. She too had interest in the rebels, some of whom frequented her house to watch the opera performances that her brilliant daughter, Fu Tsong, wrote and directed. The rebels never drank or went into the back rooms with the girls, but they seemed almost transported by the players on the stage who nightly performed their unique magic for her clientele.

"You would like to meet the powerful priest from the big church?"

"Yes."

"Why?"

"For him to explain how this Jesus, who was born so long ago, could now have a brother who lives amongst us."

* * *

"AS DOGMA it couldn't be more wrongheaded," Father Pierre said through his translator, putting the Taiping religious pamphlet that the Confucian had given him far to one side of his desk, as though it should not infect anything else of value on the teakwood surface.

The Confucian took note of that. He'd had limited dealings with what the *Fan Kuei* called "priests." He was himself, at times, treated as though he were a priest by the *Fan Kuei*. He was no priest, no fanatic Taoist monk! He was a civil administrator, a literate man versed in the classical works of the Middle Kingdom and hence a follower of the only logical system of thought and social organization in the world: Confucianism.

The Confucian picked up the pamphlet and said, "Ah."

Father Pierre rose from behind his large desk and strode to the window, his hands clasped firmly behind his back, his whole body vibrating with anger. "I thought you were a man of intelligence and learning," he said.

The Confucian was both of those but had no desire to discuss such matters with a man who wore a black wool cassock in the midst of Shanghai summer. And such an arrogant man. To be so sure of one's opinions while living in someone else's country was beyond the Confucian's comprehension. So the Confucian rose and simply repeated, "Ah."

Father Pierre turned to him. "You do realize that this is blasphemy and will not go unpunished?"

The Confucian wanted to ask, "Who will do this punishing?" but was afraid that the silly *Fan Kuei* priest would invoke some sort of deity who took words as personal insults. What kind of God could care what a human being wrote or thought about Him? What God could be so insecure in His own power that He could waste a moment of His time over such irrelevancies? Perhaps the same God that didn't seem to care that opium was destroying the lives of millions of people, or that millions were caught and in danger of losing their lives between the forces of the Taiping and the fury of the Manchus. Finally he said, "So these texts are not of your faith?"

"They are the inevitable product of those who have lost their way."

The Confucian hoped that Father Pierre wasn't going to launch into a tirade about sheep. What was it with Catholics and sheep? Sheep were particularly stupid animals. Why did Catholics insist upon calling the people who followed their faith sheep and those who led the faith shepherds—perhaps the job requiring the least amount of skill or intelligence in the entire Middle Kingdom.

"… Who have turned their backs on Rome." Father Pierre completed, or at least believed he had completed, his thought.

Ah, yet another reference to that village in the midst of one of the barbarian's insignificant countries. It had been explained to him that Rome was a city in a place called Italy. When he'd asked for further information about this fabled place he was surprised to learn that it was just a small town, that China had fifty or sixty cities that were far bigger. When he mentioned that, he was told that Rome was really a metaphor. When he inquired, "A metaphor for what?" he was given the answer that these Christians always seemed to fall back on—"For faith"—which naturally enough was then followed by the Christian catch-all, "God's ways are beyond our comprehension." The Confucian found such convenient elliptical thinking beneath contempt, so he smiled at Father Pierre and asked, "Would the Americans believe the matters discussed in this pamphlet?"

Father Pierre harrumphed. Something about Americans seemed to particularly gall him. Finally he said, "It is incomprehensible to me what American Protestants believe, if anything. They strike me as closer to Jews and pagans than to Christians."

This confused the Confucian, but what was evident to him was that Father Pierre was distressed—about something or other. So he took his leave of the man.

Two hours later, in the American Settlement west of the Suzu Creek, he stood patiently in the outer offices of Oliphant and Company, the place the other traders referred to as the House of Zion. The Confucian had asked about that reference and been told that Zion was a place called Israel that was mentioned in the pamphlet that he held in his hand. When he had asked about this Israel he had been told that, like Rome, it was small and actually just a metaphor. This time he'd decided not to ask what the metaphor stood for.

When the door opened he was surprised to see a *Fan Kuei* woman dressed in a long black dress with a bonnet of some sort that covered her head. But the effect of the bonnet was not to hide the woman's beauty so much as frame her remarkable facial features, as a fine filigree hem does a silk robe. The Confucian found most *Fan Kuei* faces almost grotesque in their size and shape—gross in both volume and composition. But this woman's features struck him as understated and pleasing. Then she smiled and the room grew a moment brighter. He smiled back, then followed her into a dark, stuffy office that had much more furniture than was necessary, and ridiculous heavy velvet curtains. The Confucian picked lightly at his silk robe to pull it away from his skin while he waited for Jedediah Oliphant, the head of the House of Oliphant, to turn from the window. *What is it about the* Fan Kuei *and their desire to look out windows?* he wondered.

When Jedediah turned to him, the man's face was awash in sweat, his colour a florid red, and his anger something to behold. "Where did you get this abomination?"

"Abomination," "blasphemy"—his religious vocabulary was increasing mightily, although he assumed these words were esoteric irrelevancies.

"It is from the Taiping. They have published much of this material and I—"

"Apostasy!"

Another interesting word. How many words did these foolish *Fan Kuei* have for …?

Then the chubby man ripped the pamphlet in two, and in two again.

The Confucian stared at him. Didn't the man understand that there were probably hundreds of thousands of that exact pamphlet in existence? What did ripping one into quarters accomplish?

The head of the House of Zion threw the pieces of the pamphlet into a bucket at the side of his desk, then said, "You do understand that you can go to Hell for reading material like this."

The Confucian had trouble not laughing about that, but he nodded, thought about leaving this fool's presence, then decided to ask his question. "Did this Taiping writing come from your religious beliefs?"

After much to ing and fro ing eventually the man acknowledged that what was written in the pamphlet had its origins in his faith. Then, without prompting, he elaborated, "It began with Reverend Edwin Stevens. He was a Yale man caught up in the great religious revival that swept through New England in the 1820s. He took a post in Canton in 1832 as the head of the American Seaman's Friends Society. He initially spent his time trying to keep English and American sailors from the temptations while on shore."

This, the Confucian thought, was a foolish way to spend one's time. These poor men had been at sea for months and months, twenty men to a room—how would you keep them from alcohol and women except by shooting them?

"But Stevens eventually realized that his real audience was the Chinese. Millions upon millions of lost souls awaited the Good Word. But getting the Book translated was not simple. The authorities blocked his every effort, until he found a Chinese Christian named Liang, who was working as a printer for a Scottish Protestant named William Milne …"

And on and on he talked. The Confucian got the basics of the story. This Liang, who had been a devout Buddhist, converted to Christianity, probably to keep his job, and produced précis of text from the American Bible, which were then brought to the Chinese. Evidently one of them must have fallen into the hands of the leader of the Taipingers, Hung Hsiu-ch'uan, and it was from this that he had extracted his unusual approach to Christianity.

The Confucian continued to listen. He didn't believe anything of this "faith" had any personal value, but he understood the need for men to escape the drudgery of their lives, to believe that there was some reason for the suffering, and in the end, relief. He couldn't help making the obvious observation that opium offered much the same rewards—escape from drudgery, a reason to work and suffer to be able to get the money to find that escape, and finally a relief from this life altogether.

The Confucian was surprised that the man was still talking. Didn't this silly little fat man realize the danger of peddling dreams? Evidently not. The Confucian thanked the American for his time and made a hasty exit.

When he emerged the sun was shining and the junks on the Suzu Creek were ready for business. He signalled to a bumboat and made his way out to one of the larger junks. He was helped onboard, then sat down to a fine dinner. As he ate the tender pork dumplings he took out another copy of the Taiping pamphlet and carefully reread it. By the time the main course of drunken shrimp—live shrimp, slightly pixilated because they had been marinating in strong Chinese wine—arrived, he had made up his mind. He tapped the side of the bowl and one of the shrimp leapt upward; he caught it between his chopsticks and watched it wriggle. "I have you," he said softly. Then he dunked the shrimp into the piquant sauce and popped it into his mouth, where he expertly snipped off its head, swallowed the body, and then spat the head and carapace to the junk's floor.

* * *

HUNG HSIU-CH'UAN smiled at his followers. Only three years ago he had been literally a voice in the wilderness. A failed scholar, seen by many as a religious fanatic. Now he was a leader.

Years ago he had received a religious tract from an American Protestant missionary. He'd put it aside as senseless rantings of White-faced barbarians. But shortly thereafter he'd suffered a serious illness during which he'd had many dreams of a heaven and a man in robes referring to him as his younger brother. In his convalescence he reread the religious tract— and was shocked to see that the man described in the tract was the man from his dreams. That he had been talked to and had talked with Jesus.

It was suddenly clear to him that he was not just another Chinese worker struggling to survive under the pressure of the Manchu Ch'ing Dynasty. He was different. Blessed. Kissed by Heaven—the younger brother of Jesus Christ himself.

His father did not find this amusing, and after Hsiu-ch'uan failed his civil service entrance exam for the second time his family disowned him. He left home and made his way back into the Hakka territory. There he found a Jesuit mission, where he related his dream and asked to be baptized. The Jesuits refused. It was the turning point in his life. He abandoned his desire to be part of any *Fan Kuei* organization and adopted a stance in rigid opposition to all of them. Amongst the dispossessed Hakka peoples he found a ready audience for his vision—to establish the Heavenly Kingdom of Great Peace, of which he was going to be the Heavenly King, with five of his followers named as Kings.

The Manchu authorities laughed. The Europeans were unimpressed. But the Confucian, in Hung Hsiu-ch'uan, believed he had found a means to an end.

* * *

JIANG ARRANGED the introductory meeting with one of Hung Hsiu-ch'uan's rebels. Not a simple thing in Shanghai. Since the revolt of the Small Knife Triad that gave the secretive Tong Society control of the city for the better part of a year and a half, security had been very tight. The British had attempted to impose a curfew, but the French refused to abide by it. They had business interests that required free movement after dark. Daylight brothels were, for obvious reasons, not all that financially successful.

The Confucian was surprised by the modest appearance of the young man whom his wife led into his study. Then he looked closer. The man had the scars of age in his eyes despite his fine, smooth skin and glossy hair. The Confucian chose to stand when the young rebel entered.

The young fighter looked at the Confucian and a snarl curled his lip. "You have words for me, old man?"

The Confucian bridled at the discourtesy but reminded himself that he had a long road to travel and it was foolish to be waylaid by insults. "Thank you for honouring me with your presence. I have a message I'd like you to carry to your leader, Hung Hsiu-ch'uan."

The younger man sat heavily. His dirt-stained smock left a slurred mark on the silk of the upholstered chair. Then he looked at the Confucian's desk and sprang to his feet.

The Confucian, confused, backed off as the young fighter kicked over the desk. "What are you—?"

"Are you an examiner, old man? Do you grade the entrance papers of those attempting to be part of the Manchu civil service? Do you work for the oppressors of our country? Are you nothing more than a foreigner dressed in our clothing, sleeping with our women and despoiling this sacred land?"

The Confucian stood his ground. "I have a message I want sent to Hung Hsiu-ch'uan, leader of the Taiping rebels."

"You mean the Heavenly King."

"Do I?"

"If you refer to Hung Hsiu-ch'uan, you do."

"Fine, for the Heavenly King."

"What is your message for the Heavenly King?"

"Please tell him that I can be of service to his cause."

"Why?"

"Excuse me?"

"Why would you wish to be of service to the Heavenly King? He will bring equality to this land. No more Mandarins. No more Confucians. Women will have equal rights. The great landowners will give up their lands and divide it amongst their serfs. Why would you support that which would rob you of your position of power and prestige? Why would you do that?"

Without missing a beat the Confucian said, "Because his cause is just, and the Manchus must be taught a lesson."

The young rebel looked at the Confucian. "Why is it that I don't believe you?"

The Confucian took a breath, then let it out slowly. "Who am I addressing?"

"Can you not guess?"

"Hung Hsiu-ch'uan?"

"The very same Hung Hsiu-ch'uan that you people refused entrance to the civil service twice."

"Perhaps we did you a favour. Rather than one scribe amongst millions you are now a man of great power." That hung in the air like something hot and volatile. The Confucian knew that his life could end momentarily if this were taken the wrong way.

Hung walked back to the podium and tilted the writing stone there. The ink dribbled down the side of the mahogany desk and dripped to the hardwood floor. "I repeat—what do you want, old man?"

"I want to support your cause."

"Why would you want that?"

"Because your victory would support my goals."

"Which are?"

"None of your business."

The rebel turned on him, his hand raised, but the Confucian did not back down.

"Think practically for a moment. You believe in your cause. I do not. But I have the means you need to help your cause succeed. Why does it matter what there is for me in this?"

The rebel allowed his hand to come down to his side. "What do you have to offer me?"

"Access to the society of the canal porters. Perhaps half a million men without work, without hope, and with very strong arms."

The Confucian wanted to smile, but he wisely chose not to as Hung Hsiu-ch'uan, the Heavenly King, took a seat and said simply, "I'm listening."

* * *

THE CONFUCIAN'S VISIT to the prison was brief. They had expected his coming since the arrival of the thief who was not to be executed. The Confucian had the man unshackled and took him by the arm and guided him out of the prison. The stunned man didn't know what to say and did his best to express his appreciation, but the Confucian stopped him.

"Can you read?"

"Some."

"Enough to read this?" the Confucian asked, handing over the Taiping pamphlet.

"I already know about ..."

"The Taipingers?"

"Yes."

"And?" The canal worker was suddenly wary. The Confucian put his hand on the man's shoulder and said simply, "The Heavenly King is expecting you and your people."

With the canal workers swelling his ranks, the Heavenly King launched his first major strike against the Manchu overlords. With his goal of a Kingdom of Heaven on earth set as firmly as frontlets between his eyes he aimed his troops toward the same vulnerable point in the Manchus' defences that the hated British had attacked in 1841—Chinkiang, the City of Suicides.

* * *

It was in the late fall of 1852 when Maxi found himself admiring the crafts-manship of a nail-free free-standing home. Perfect tongue-and-groove wooden planks fit one into the next to form a remarkably pleasing whole. Through his interpreter he asked the cost of building such a structure. Upon hearing the outrageous quote, he laughed. But he knew that even after real bargaining the price would not come down enough. He was here to create a secure depot for the Hordoon brothers' products, not a work of art like the one in front of which he now stood. Maxi changed the subject by asking, through his translator, "Where did you get the fine silk robe you're wearing?"

"A half day's journey up the river at Chinkiang. They have the finest silks in the whole of the Middle Kingdom." He paused, and a smile came to his face as he added, "I have a brother who could get you the best price for ..."

Maxi smiled back. He'd heard such offers since he was a child. This one he'd accept—and it would change his life.

A day later Maxi acknowledged the stares of the women in the streets of Chinkiang. He was happy with his purchases of fine silk robes for his nephews, Milo and Silas, and pleased that his business dealings had gone well. He was well fed and pleasantly tipsy from the strong beer brewed in the German enclave at Qintao, and the night was redolent with the prom-ise of a cool fall after a long hot summer.

He walked along the west wall of the Old City, the farthest from the Grand Canal. Torches stuck in wall niches periodically broke the darkness. He was happy to be away from the intrigues and infighting of the Foreign Settlement in Shanghai.

He looked up at the catwalk high up on the city wall and blinked him-self out of his reverie. Where were the guards? City walls were always patrolled by guards. He hurried around a squalid building that obscured his view, then down an alley to get a glimpse of the farthest section of the wall. It was empty of protectors too. He pressed himself against the alley wall and calmed his breathing. Then he heard them. The telltale clicks of feet on ladders—many feet. Then they appeared, dressed in black from head to foot with dark cloths around their faces. Their weapons must have been dulled with lard because they didn't glint in the bright moonlight. They formed up and waited in complete silence. Then a slender, taller man joined them and raised a hand high into the night air. The moonlight glinted off the large silver cross he held. The men in black all knelt in prayer, then rose ... and unearthed holy hell upon the unsuspecting citi-zenry of Chinkiang.

Although taken by surprise, the Manchus had two full regiments within the city walls and a third outside the east gate down by the Grand Canal. Maxi retreated to a rooftop and watched—watched in rapt fascination as the very first major battle of the Taiping Rebellion unfolded before him like something that had awaited his coming all these many years.

Four days later Maxi allowed the fine hair of the horse's mane to move smoothly through his grooming comb. He breathed in the earthy smell of the animal, then put his head against the horse's neck and allowed the animal's warmth to calm him.

"You're awfully quiet this evening," Richard said.

"Thinking. Just thinking."

"Of what are you thinking?"

"What I saw in Chinkiang."

"Let it go, Maxi. The Manchus put the rebels back in their place. The revolt is over."

Maxi took a coarse brush and began to work on the horse's flank. "It's not, brother mine. The Manchus had three full regiments yet they just barely won. The Taipingers fought like madmen—like men possessed. They fought for something. They fought from their hearts."

"What? Are you suggesting that the God freaks can beat the Manchu Emperor?"

"Not that they can, but that they will. I saw one of their soldiers throw himself in front of a Manchu gingall at a roadblock. The man gave up his life so the others could overwhelm the battery and escape."

"So, he was following—"

"No, brother mine, he wasn't following orders. That's the point. He gave up his life voluntarily without being ordered. Listen to me! And he wasn't the only Taipinger willing to die for their cause. That's why they're going to win. They're going to win because they believe in something. Even from that rooftop I could feel it. They're going to win because their beliefs give their lives meaning."

Richard watched Maxi turn and leave the stable. In all his years with his brother, he doubted he'd ever heard him string so many words together.

Later that night Jiang approached Maxi as he watched the actors rehearse parts of the second act of *Journey to the West*.

"You seem sad," she said.

"I'll miss this," he said.

"This? Not the girls, just the plays?"

"Just the plays. Your daughter is an artist. She touches the hearts of simple men like me."

Jiang was about to protest that he was far from simple, then she stopped herself. The monkey king character had just made an entrance, to the accompaniment of horns and cymbals, and Maxi jumped to his feet to cheer, just as any child might.

The night was late when Maxi crept down the alleyway that was the unofficial back entrance to the American section of the Foreign Settlement. Maxi had used a section of the Warrens to be sure that he wasn't followed, then exited the underground tunnels through the back courtyard of a tailor's shop before heading down the alley. As he moved through the darkness he remembered another night excursion, this time with his brother at his side as they left their parting gift to old Baghdad.

And here he was, parting again.

He had not made this circuitous trip in several months, but now he wanted to say goodbye to Rachel.

"You're leaving," she said. "I can see it in your eyes."

Maxi hung his head for a moment, then nodded.

"Why?" Her hands flew to her mouth to stop her sobs.

He gently pulled her hands down from her beautiful lips and kissed her on her forehead. "Because I need to find a place to call home before I die. Because this place is not of me. Because I yearn for something that is mine and has meaning. Real meaning. Like you find in your Bible."

"But I ..."

"I know you have your doubts about that book, but you basically believe in what it teaches, don't you?"

Now it was her turn to hang her head. After a long sigh, she said, "I do."

"That's good, Rachel. That's good. But I don't have anything like that in my life, and I need it. Everyone needs it." He put a finger under her chin and raised her face to his. "You understand that. I know you do."

"When ...?"

"Tonight."

There were tears and clutching and desperate lovemaking as they tried to remember each other's warmth. Then lips and godspeeds and parting with understanding, but no sweetness.

An hour later Maxi spotted his man Anderson with his travelling gear, gave the man the key to his private living quarters, wished him luck, and headed down the deserted streets to the west gate of the city. There he was halted by guards. He smiled at them and reached for his purse but was stopped by a familiar voice from the darkness.

"You'll have to fight to leave here."

"If necessary, brother mine. I've clubbed the daylights out of you before, and I'll do it again if need be."

"You're all geared up. Where are you heading?"

"You promised me, promised in India, that if things didn't work out you'd let me go back."

"To the opium farmers?"

"Not necessarily to them, but to something simple. You promised not to stand in my way. But here you are. Things haven't worked out for me. I want something simpler, and I know where I can find that."

"With the Taipingers."

Maxi nodded and hoisted his pack on his back.

"Nothing I can say ..."

"To stop me? No. Not a thing."

"As it must be?"

"As it must be, brother mine."

* * *

"HE WENT WHERE?" Silas demanded.

"He's gone now, son."

Milo put a hand on Silas's shoulder in warning.

"Things change in the world, boys. You change. I change. Your Uncle Maxi changed, and now he doesn't live here any more. Don't ask me where he is because I can't tell you without endangering him." He thought suddenly of the old Indian's warning: "Brother will kill brother!" Richard allowed the voice to fade away, then said to the boys, "And I won't endanger my brother. Is that clear?"

Patterson came in with a stack of waybills. Richard took them, then said, "Milo, come with me, I could use a hand."

Father and favourite son left the room.

Patterson looked at Silas. "Crying? Of course not. The young heathen doesn't know how to cry, does he? Just snivel. Oh, you're good at snivelling, you are. Well stop it! Your uncle is nothing more than a monkey-lover."

* * *

LATE THAT NIGHT Richard summoned Anderson and Patterson to his private study. The two men waited while Richard paced. Finally Richard stopped and turned to Anderson. "How goes our building?"

"Fine. We've almost filled your properties with those four-storey buildings your brother designed."

"Good. Patterson, I want an accounting of everything in our warehouses."

"Certainly, but—"

"Then sell it. Sell it all. Every last mango chest of opium, every bolt of silk, every porcelain cup, every leaf of tea. All of it, and I really don't care how much you get for it."

"And do what with the money?"

"Buy land. Cheap land anywhere in the Settlement, land for Anderson to build a hundred more of Maxi's four-storey buildings. And then a hundred more after that."

* * *

SIX WEEKS LATER, just before dawn, there was a knocking on the door of the House of Paris. An unusual time for a client, even in Shanghai. Suzanne's serving girl answered the door and didn't know what to do with the missionary woman standing on the top step.

"May I see the mistress of the house?"

It took a bit of translating, but after a few misunderstandings Rachel was led to the inner office of Suzanne Colombe, who poured coffee for the two of them.

"So if you're not here to convert me, why are you here?" Suzanne said in her accented but textbook-perfect English. Rachel hadn't touched her coffee. "Do you prefer tea?" Suzanne asked as she looked more closely at the woman's slightly sweated complexion. *Could it be?* she wondered. Then she reached to a sideboard and pushed a large platter of morning meats across to her guest, and the woman blanched. *Ah*, Suzanne thought, *ah, so that is the problem*. Then she had a second thought. *Will Maxi Hordoon come back and marry this girl or not?*

chapter twenty~eight
Meetings

Shanghai
Winter 1852, eighteen months after the start of the Taiping Rebellion

The stone thrown at his window drew Richard back from the edges of his opium dream.

Since Maxi had left he'd found that even with the serpent smoke alive in his veins he'd been unable to find rest. The deep rumble of danger kept churning in his guts. He had never been separated from his brother for more than a few weeks. Now Maxi had been gone for months and Richard had no idea if he was ever going to come back. Maxi had instructed his man Anderson in all that he was working on for the House of Hordoon, so the business didn't miss a step. But Richard found himself feeling that if he stood quickly from his bed he'd fall—as if his very equilibrium had been tampered with. Every time Richard entered a room he sensed that Maxi had just left it, that somehow Maxi was just around every corner—but he never was. Nor had there been any word from his brother.

Maxi was gone and Richard was alone, so when a second pebble struck the windowpane, he reached for his Belgian flintlock pistol and slowly peered out. There, to his surprise, was a woman, standing in the alley. When he pulled open the window the figure turned her face up to his. In the moonlight Rachel Oliphant was a luminous presence. A godly gift of beauty in this rough world.

When he opened the door she pulled her shawl tightly around her and came quickly into his drawing room.

"Rachel ..."

"Don't look at me. At my shame."

It was only then that Richard saw that she was pregnant. "Rachel."

She turned to him, her face picking up the flickering light from the oil lamp. She pushed a tendril of hair from her forehead and her beauty filled the room. Her face creased in a humble smile as she said, "Are you well, Mr. Hordoon?"

"Yes," Richard said slowly, "I am well. And you?"

She pulled aside her shawl to reveal the full extent of her belly and said, "Very well."

"You look lovely ..."

"I don't."

"You do."

Richard reached out a hand to her and she backed away. "Don't."

"I'll marry you, if that is what you want."

For a moment a quizzical look crossed her face, then she smiled. A laugh squeaked from her pursed lips and she shook her head, finally saying the single word, "No."

"I will if—"

"Where is Maxi?" her voice pleaded, and for the first time Richard understood how Maxi had known to come and save him from the attack of the Oliphants, and why the Oliphants may have attacked him in the first place. "Where's your brother, Mr. Hordoon? I need to see Maxi."

* * *

THE NIGHT was uncommonly cold, even for January. The wind howled in Jiang's face as she put a foot up onto the small plank that joined the junk bobbing on the filthy waters of the Suzu Creek to the small carrack that she had hired.

"What are you staring at, old man?" she demanded of the ancient creature who rowed the boat.

The man spat in the water and mumbled something about being paid.

"You'll be paid when you come and get me."

Again the man mumbled; this time the country word for *harlot* slid into the cold air and hung there like something dark and ugly.

Jiang ignored the insult. She'd heard far worse. What she wanted from this man was his silence. "Do you have a daughter, old man?"

The man stared at her, then slowly nodded.

"I could use a new maid. Have her appear at—"

"I know where," the old man grunted.

"Good. She'll make enough money to keep you and your wife comfortable in your ... old age." She had wanted to say "dotage" but decided against it.

"How long?"

"How long will she work for me?"

"No. How long are you here on this junk?"

She told him, and he helped her up the planking to the deck of the ship. She waited until the old man's carrack was lost in the darkness downriver before she headed below decks and found some relief from the piercing cold.

The family who owned the junk was nowhere to be seen, but the smell of their cooking brazier tainted the air. She followed the source of the smell down a narrow set of steps and into a passage. There to one side was a closed door. She opened it.

Inside, the other progeny of the Chosen Three awaited her—and of course the Carver. She noted that the Carvers seemed old even when they were young—as if they were born old men. The Body Guard never seemed to age, but the Confucian had sent his youngest son to represent his family. She nodded slightly and removed the plain woollen blanket she wore around her shoulders and as a cowl over her head—no need to advertise her beauty on the dark and dangerous streets in this part of the city. But when she shook out her long hair she didn't miss the admiring looks of the young Confucian. She had known his father, but not this young man—although both had that disconcerting way of staring as if they knew something that no one else knew.

The boat lurched momentarily and she steadied herself against an overhead timber. The Carver stepped forward and offered her a seat. She refused his offer with a curt shake of her head, then added, "I got here as quickly as I could." Before the men could comment she added evenly, "We all have our labours, gentlemen. The fact that mine bring pleasure make them no less valuable than yours—as some of your family members will attest."

"Enough," the Carver said. "The threat of the Taiping Prophet has to be understood in light of the Ivory Compact."

Jiang looked to the young Confucian. "You didn't tell him about your father and his meeting?"

The Confucian avoided Jiang's eyes and quickly gave the bare details of his father's meeting with the extraordinary young man.

"And that was how long ago?" the Body Guard asked.

"Twenty months, just before he took to his bed."

"He didn't bother consulting us?" complained the Body Guard.

"He consulted me," Jiang broke in.

"Nothing in the Compact states that all decisions must be made jointly," the Confucian said.

"Be that as it may, now we must act," the Carver said as the wide-bellied boat once again listed dangerously in the screaming wind.

Jiang steadied herself against a ship wall, as did the Carver and the Confucian. But the Body Guard's balance was such that he counteracted the motion by shifting his weight. *Like an acrobat,* Jiang thought. She looked down at the planks and thought of them as a platform that danced beneath her feet. *I think more like my daughter and her operas every day.*

The boat righted itself.

"Have you tried to open the second portal? There must be information there that we need," said the Body Guard.

"In all likelihood there is, but I've been unable to open the window," replied the Carver.

"So we work with what we have," said Jiang.

"Agreed," said the Confucian, who then turned to the Body Guard and said, "Time to stop fishing and make your selection."

"It will be done."

"Have you chosen?"

The Body Guard thought of his son—and then of his powerful young nephew, who now lived in his home. "The choice will be made soon."

"Don't hesitate, we may well need the services of a master assassin shortly," said Jiang.

A silence greeted that.

"So be it," said Jiang.

"But aren't we a little ahead of ourselves?" the Body Guard asked. "How does the rise of the Taiping Prophet fit into the prophecy of the Seventy Pagodas?"

"Simply," said the young Confucian.

"Explain," demanded the Body Guard.

"If the Long Noses declare their Foreign Settlements neutral in the struggle ..."

"... and manage to get the Prophet to agree to that neutrality," added Jiang.

"Yes, and get the Prophet to agree, then the one vital thing most missing from our village at the Bend in the River will be addressed."

"I don't follow," said the Body Guard.

"People," responded the young Confucian. "This extraterritoriality that the Long Noses received has enabled them to induce local Shanghainese to work for them. But we are still almost nothing more than a large village. We need to become a great city to build the Seventy Pagodas. Even Beijing and Canton and Nanking have nothing like that. But if Shanghai is safe while rebellion rages through the countryside, then ..."

Somehow the howling wind entered the room. Papers riffled on the table, and a tablecloth flapped. A scythe of cold cut through the room, like a warning.

"It takes many people to build seventy pagodas," agreed the Body Guard.

"Many people."

"So we must see to it that the Long Noses approach the Prophet?"

"Yes."

"And once they secure Shanghai's neutrality, we support the Prophet?"

"Yes."

There was another long silence. The slapping of the waves against the ancient timbers of the junk grew loud. They knew that there would be death—much death—and they would support it, all to fulfill a prophecy. None of the progeny in the room had ever been free of doubt about the prophecy. None had refrained from questioning and railing against the demands set upon them so long ago on the Holy Mountain. But none of them dared stand in the way of the future greatness that was promised. Much of the rest of the prophecy had come to pass: foreigners invading, foreigners sitting on the Celestial Throne but always succumbing to the luxuriance of China, the arrival of the White Birds on Water and the ensuing darkness. And here was yet more darkness—and so much death.

"What if the Prophet wins?" asked the young Confucian, although what he really wanted to ask was *What role would Confucians play in a Taiping ruled China?* No one answered his first question, so he asked another. "If he takes over all of China, won't he then turn and demand Shanghai as well?"

Jiang thought about that. Finally she said, "That mustn't happen. The Prophet is a means, not an end." She knew that the Prophet would be more inclined to burn Shanghai to the ground than to build seventy pagodas.

The Confucian recited his father's admonition: "How, once launched heavenward, can an archer be sure of the landing place of his arrow?"

Jiang, sensing something beneath the young man's words, stared at the Confucian for a long moment, then turned to the Body Guard. "That is your job. It is time to begin the Guild of Assassins so that when we need the Prophet ended—he will be ended."

The Body Guard thought again of his son and his nephew.

Jiang surprised the others when she asked, "Would your chosen assassin be able to juggle and tumble?"

"Yes, but ..."

"Good," Jiang said. "When you have selected the one to begin the Guild, send the assassin to me."

chapter twenty-nine
The Settlement and the Taipingers

Summer 1852, twenty months after the start of the Taiping Revolt

Richard watched and tried not to laugh, although he understood perfectly well that there was nothing very funny going on in this private room in the back of the famous Yu Yuan Gardens. The harmonious lines of the polished mahogany wood, the deep, still pool with its bright-orange carp and its arching bridge, as well as the peaceful orderliness of the immaculate gardens did nothing to mediate the open anger in the room. Even getting to the damned place was a challenge now that the Manchus had been defeated in the city proper by the Han Chinese Triad of the Small Knives.

It didn't matter to the traders if they dealt with the devious Manchus or the openly thuggish Triads. No one believed that the Triads would rule Shanghai for long. Already they were fighting amongst themselves.

None of the English, French, or American powers cared. The Triads would disappear back into their rat holes on their own. But these religious rebels, these Taipingers sitting across the table from the committee of opium traders, they controlled almost a third of the Middle Kingdom, including the ancient capital of Nanking, and were a significant power—and in total opposition to the use of opium by their people, all their people.

Every time one of the traders spoke, and Richard translated, the Taipingers responded with increasingly surly scowls.

The head of the Taiping delegation was not their leader, Hung Hsiu-ch'uan. This man, who sat directly across the table from the Vrassoon

Patriarch, referred to himself as the West King. There were apparently five such kings. Richard wondered which direction had two kings. But there was nothing else very humorous about the rebels. The Taipingers had come raging out of their mountain retreats just under three years ago, and although initially they had lost their battles with the Manchus, their numbers had swelled quickly, and victories followed.

Richard wondered how much his brother had to do with their military successes.

The Taipingers' particular religious approach was so stern that men and women were strictly separated and not permitted, upon penalty of death, to have sexual intercourse until the Manchus were driven from Beijing. All of their people were organized into fighting and working battalions under military commanders, who reported to captains, who eventually reported to one of the five Kings, who then reported to Hung Hsiu-ch'uan, the Heavenly King himself. The rebels quickly routed local warlords and large landowners, distributing the land and wealth to their followers, which further swelled their ranks. Then towns began to fall to them, and eventually cities. Just the year before, they had routed the Manchus and taken Nanking, which they now proclaimed as their Heavenly Capital.

Every Taipinger was required to bear arms—everyone except the very young, of which, for obvious reasons, given the separation of the sexes, there were very few. Even the old were taught to use weapons. Taken lands were divided amongst the fighters, and food was distributed to people according to their need. The Taipingers treated women as equals to men. As well, they banned foot binding in all its forms, and the Manchu-imposed long braid and shaved forehead were outlawed. It was one of the many things about the men sitting across the table from the traders that differentiated them from most other Chinese.

There was also a requirement to memorize long religious tracts from the writings of the Heavenly King. The failure to recite on command could lead to summary execution. Sabbath started on Saturday evening, when large banners were strung across the streets and all activity stopped. Attendance at church was mandatory. And of course alcohol and opium—especially opium—were forbidden upon pain of death.

The Taipinger West King put the palms of his hands on the beautifully inlaid table and stood. "We have nothing more to discuss, it seems." He shouted an order in what Richard assumed was Hakka, since he couldn't discern the meaning, then turned to leave.

"We have *much* to discuss," Eliazar Vrassoon said.

For an instant Richard thought of the doctored photograph of Vrassoon's eldest son that was so carefully hidden in his desk.

The West King turned and hissed into Vrassoon's face, "You are nothing more than thieves and pirates. You poison our people. You do not believe in the one true God."

Richard translated slowly to give the room a moment to calm down. Then Jedediah Oliphant rose to his feet and said to Richard, "Translate this accurately so the heathen will understand." Richard nodded. "Tell him that Oliphant and Company came to China for one primary reason, to spread the word of Jesus Christ and his Father, the one true God." Richard hesitated. "Tell him, man."

Richard did.

The West King turned on Oliphant. "Do you not sell opium to my people?"

Richard translated.

"We do nothing of the kind. We trade for goods, as all traders must, and spread God's Holy Word."

"Which words, exactly?" the West King demanded.

Oliphant produced his vellum-bound family Bible from an old leather case and handed it to the Taipinger. The man handed it to his translator, who flipped it open and spoke in Hakka to his King. The man smiled, then shook his head as he tossed it, like so much garbage, onto the table. "This book is not the true Word."

Oliphant's fat neck bulged out like a bullfrog's, and his bald head turned a bright red. Richard thought the man's eyes might pop out of his stupid face. Then Anderson came running into the room.

Richard signalled him over to one side. "What?"

"Their soldiers have cut off access to the Huangpo, and they are massing at the east gate."

"How many?"

"Thousands upon thousands."

Richard turned to the Taipinger, who openly smiled, evidently understanding the news that Anderson brought. "Could you excuse us for a moment, please?" Richard signalled the traders to join him in the next chamber. Once there, he quickly told them Anderson's news.

Anger immediately flared, but it was Hercules MacCallum who spoke calmly. "We don't want anything from these rebels—just to be left alone. To keep the town at the Bend in the River neutral. We can be of use to them by keeping the Manchus out of Shanghai—at least for the moment, with the Triad in control, that's no real problem. In return, we want nothing from them. Not a blessed thing. We should promise that we will trade only in the Manchu's territory and make motions toward closing our trading routes up the Yangtze. We would be protecting their eastern flank, and we also keep at least some of the Manchu navy nearby watching us, not up there fighting them."

Vrassoon nodded and Oliphant grudgingly agreed, then the traders returned to the negotiating room.

The Taipingers listened to Richard without interrupting as he laid out the deal. For a moment Richard thought he'd swayed the Taiping King, then something dark crossed the man's face. "But you would still trade opium? Do the Devil's work?"

Using the phrase the dwarf Jesuit had used all those years ago sent Richard into a moment of interior fall, vertigo, and he reached for the table to balance himself. The room was strangely quiet, he thought. Then he looked at the Taipinger and asked, "Have you met the red-haired Long Nose from the Bend in the River?"

That completely stopped the Taipinger, who slowly nodded.

"He's my brother."

Something akin to a smile crossed the Taipinger's face. "He's a very brave man."

"Is my brother all right?"

"He is by the side of the Heavenly Leader."

When that was translated, the ripple of shock amongst the traders was palpable. So that was where the maniac went. There had been rumours for months that he had gotten himself killed on a trading expedition or in a whorehouse. But now this!

Oliphant cursed under his breath. First the Jew assaulted him and his men, then he had to send Rachel back to his sister in Philadelphia to prevent a scandal, and now the red-haired crazy man was fighting for the Taiping rebels!

So the red-haired Jew is working for the God rebels, Hercules MacCallum thought. *Surely the oddest of bedfellows.* Then he looked at Richard Hordoon and the Taiping King. *Yet another unlikely pair,* he thought.

With Maxi's image secured between Richard and the Taiping King of the West, the negotiations that would eventually lead to the guarantee of neutrality for the Settlement and the French Concession began. The talks went on for two more days, at the end of which time a declaration of peace and support was signed by both sides.

With that done, Richard turned his attention to the issue of the Vrassoon. He knew he had a weapon in the doctored photograph, but he didn't know how or if he ought to use it.

chapter thirty
Neutrality and Prosperity

The Lands of the Heavenly King and Shanghai
1854

The Heavenly King allowed his fingers to trace the elegant hem of his fine Chinkiang silk robe as, from a hill, he watched the movement of his troops across the plain below. Huge banners distinguished one Taiping regiment from the next. He spotted a black line in the ground across which his troops hadn't crossed. He wondered what the cut in the ground was, but being the Heavenly King and brother of Jesus made it difficult to admit that there were things he didn't know. Then he noticed what looked like long, earth-toned silk runner carpets meeting up with the black trench. In the distance the Manchu forces of the Q'ing Dowager Empress were massed in formal battle array. Augmented by mercenaries from many countries, the Q'ing fighters were the best-trained soldiers in the whole of Asia. And they fought for personal plunder, so they really fought.

The Heavenly King turned his head and lifted a finger. His adjutant, a young man with a pockmarked face who spoke fluent Hakka, Cantonese, Mandarin, and—in this case most importantly—English, leaned in with head bowed and asked, "Majesty?"

"The red-haired *Fan Kuei?*" he demanded.

The young man pointed to a stand of trees at the extreme west side of the battlefield and held out the British-made spyglass. The Heavenly King took the instrument and panned the formation of the Beijing devil's troops, then past them to the small thicket. "The *Fan Kuei* is in the trees?" he asked.

"Yes, Majesty."

"And what is he doing in the …?" But his words ceased as, through the glass, he spotted movement in the thicket. Movement, then suddenly men on horseback broke through the treeline and headed toward the black trench on the right flank of the Q'ing formation. The black trench! Then he saw them. The earth-coloured runner carpets being pulled away by thick silk cords, revealing more black trenches beneath them. He followed the course of the darkness on the land. He hadn't noticed before that the dark path completely encircled the Manchu forces.

As the Manchus wheeled to face what they thought was an onslaught from the thicket, a single figure with a red kerchief around his neck raced from the opposite side toward the black trench. The Heavenly King gasped as he saw the red-haired *Fan Kuei* touch a lit torch to the side of the black circle. For a moment nothing happened, then the fire spirit leapt up from the ground and raced with ever-increasing speed down the length of the dark trench, encircling the Manchu forces in flame.

Maxi spoke softly to his horse to calm him in the presence of the fire, then stood on the animal's back, took off his red kerchief, and waved it. The five Taiping regiments, one composed entirely of women, swung in two wide arcs around the outside of the flaming trench.

As the disoriented and gasping Manchus leapt through the ring of flame the Taipingers opened fire—and the slaughter was appalling.

* * *

UPON HEARING of their defeat, the Q'ing authorities immediately attacked twenty villages thought by them to be Taiping centres. Men, women, and children were burned alive in the courtyards of their living compounds. Only the aged were spared, to spread the Manchus' message: *This will happen to anyone who offers food or support of any kind to the rebels.*

On the rivers, the lifeblood of China, the war was carried by the Taipingers to the Q'ing with a vigour that took the Manchus by surprise. The willingness of Taiping soldiers to offer up their lives was new in the Middle Kingdom. Then the South River pirates left their looting ways and joined the Taipingers, adding vast knowledge of the rivers and many ships to the rebel cause. And just as the British had done a decade earlier, the Taipingers began to strangle China by blockading its great rivers.

The Manchus counterattacked with particular viciousness and initially drove the Taipingers back toward their mountain aerie. But as serfs swelled their ranks, the Taipingers organized them into more and more regiments and finally drove the Manchus back toward Beijing. The viciousness of the fighting surprised both sides. There were never any prisoners taken. The soil of China was quickly drenched in the blood of its people. The initial deaths only hinted at the final death toll—some thirty million, who would lose their lives as the Heavenly King established his heaven on earth.

Those who found themselves under Taiping rule were forced to convert to the Heavenly King's particular variant of Protestantism, the one true faith, and obey strict rules about the separation of the sexes, religious observances, and military service. Not everyone found the Taipingers' way of life easy to tolerate. Meanwhile, ethnic Chinese under Manchu control were taxed unmercifully and were constantly under suspicion of being rebel sympathizers.

However, it was in the disputed zones that things were the worst. Villagers never knew if they were going to be punished by the Manchus or the Taipingers. Life quickly became unbearable. And people began to move—to safety—to the Foreign Settlement in Shanghai.

There, Richard's land purchases, crowded with four storey tenements designed by Maxi and built by Anderson, were awaiting their coming. Literally thousands of people arrived at the Bend in the River every week for almost two years—and Richard had places for them to stay. Sometimes five to a room, sometimes ten. For the wealthy from Chinkiang and Nanking he had single-family dwellings.

Finally he had more workers than he could use, and so much money in rent that he could claim the title of Asia's richest landlord.

And the first thing he did with this windfall was to hire a Pinkerton—to find out what happened to his parents back in Calcutta.

* * *

MAXI LOOKED at his pregnant Hakka wife and her two young daughters and smiled. His long day of labour in his fields had finally come to an end. Although he could have moved into Nanking and lived in luxury, closer to the Heavenly King, as a reward for his exploits in the field of battle, he didn't want that. The only things he requested were to work in the fields with all the others, and be permitted, unlike the others, to live with his wife. His requests were granted by the Heavenly King himself.

One of his adopted daughters took his big, calloused hand, and he looked down into her doe-like eyes. Then he reached for his Hakka wife and said, in Farsi, "I am finally at home." He wanted to touch her rounded belly, to feel the life within, but it was forbidden for men to touch their wives in public, just as so much else was forbidden in the lands of the Heavenly King.

* * *

"VRASSOON! Open the door to your God-forsaken house!" Richard's voice sounded foreign to him, as if it came from the other side of some great divide. He banged at the heavy door again, this time using the leather satchel he carried with him. The door opened and two well-muscled blond men stepped out. One put a bearpaw of a hand on his chest and pushed him firmly away from the door of the Vrassoons' private residence.

"Mr. Vrassoon doesn't see visitors on the Sabbath."

Richard almost laughed. His smile was enough to draw a threatening look from the second of the two. "So you're his Shabbos goys?" Richard managed.

The men looked at each other, not sure if they had been insulted or not.

"You're more like his Shabbos apes, wouldn't ya say?"

That they understood unequivocally, and the blow that landed squarely on the point of Richard's jaw sent him careening down the polished steps. Even as his face splatted against the bottom stair he wanted to yell out, *Hell's bells, these steps are marble. Marble in China! Who in fucking hell needs marble in China?* Richard found himself on his feet, blood streaming down his face. "Get Vrassoon out here. Get his slimy eminence out here. We have some business to transact. Business enough to get him away from his imitation of religiosity." The men stared at Richard. "Get him, now, you hunk of baboon turd!" It felt good to make a fuss in the lair of the Vrassoons—or even outside their lair. It felt good to muss their feathers. It felt good, but it didn't get him anywhere.

In fact it wasn't until the following Thursday that he was granted an audience with the Patriarch of the Vrassoon family.

The man's neatly trimmed beard and comfortable clothing belied the fury in his dark eyes. "You were rude at my door, and on the Sabbath. I would expect that from—"

"Yeah, yeah, but not from a Jew like me. Well, I'm a Jew like me, not a Jew like you, so can we skip that crap." Even Richard was surprised by his own insolence, but it felt good. *Why did it feel so good to abuse this man?* He thought of the doctored picture, and it was about to make him smile when an image came up in his mind. Himself as a boy giving something to this man. Not something—someone—who? He shook his head and noticed the man looking at him, through him.

"Do you need a drink? Your other vice, I'm afraid, I can't supply for you."

Richard thought about that and nodded, the irony of the world's biggest opium trader having none of his own product in his home made him smile. Richard looked at the man's clear, hard eyes. He'd never experienced the dream. He didn't even know what he was selling—yet he sold it by the ton. He shook his head, "Thanks, but I only drink with friends, and as for my other vice, I … never mind."

"Fine. What brings you here with such a heavy satchel? Another bargain you wish to strike?"

Richard hefted the satchel he had brought with him. "That's right, a bargain …" But he never completed his thought. He crumpled forward as laughter took him. It rolled up his throat and spat out into the room. Through his tears Richard saw the Vrassoon Patriarch eyeing the door of the room. "Don't leave, old man. Nah. The show's just beginning." Richard reached for the heavy satchel, unbuttoned its clasp, and dumped the equivalent of two hundred and fifty pounds sterling on Eliazar Vrassoon's desk.

The older man hadn't moved a muscle. "And this would be?" the man asked, his voice suddenly rife with sibilance.

"The remainder of the money the Hordoon boys owe you, every last fucking penny of it."

Vrassoon lifted a heavy eyebrow.

"Now give me back my debt note."

The hand Richard held out shook. Something was wrong, and he knew it. He repeated his request, but the Vrassoon Patriarch didn't move.

"You've done very well, son."

"I'm not your son," Richard shouted. "Just give me back the debt note you bought from Barclays."

"The lawyers need to look into a few things, but you should have your note by Thursday next."

Richard wanted to ask *What things?* but he was suddenly exhausted. And there was something else he felt he needed from this man—something he had given him a long time ago.

Before he could think, he found himself out on Bubbling Spring Road, his noseless, earless female companion, Lily, offering an arm to steady his walk to the opium den.

* * *

PATTERSON ANSWERED Richard's summons first thing the next morning.

"So what do you think, Patterson?" Richard asked.

"Think of what, sir?"

"Of horses," Richard said enigmatically.

Patterson resisted sighing. Was the heathen opiated again? Finally he said, "I'm quite fond of horses, sir."

"Racehorses?" Richard asked.

Patterson stared at his employer. Was he drunk? "Racehorses? I would go so far as to say that I am extremely fond of racehorses."

"Good, let's buy some."

"They can run a pretty penny, sir."

"Even better."

Patterson didn't know what to make of the skinflint actually wanting to spend money. He mentioned, "Fine idea, sir. But there's no race course in Shanghai."

"Racetrack," Richard corrected him.

"Be that as it may, a place to race horses, sir. There's no such place here."

"Aye, as you would say, Patterson, aye, that is true. Be that as it may, let's buy some racehorses, Patterson, spend a bit of our hard-earned profits."

Patterson liked the idea of spending money. Especially money that was not his. But why did the addicted heathen want to spend it here in this God-forsaken place? Why not take it home and spend it? Then again, maybe this heathen had no home except here. God help him if that was the case. But then again, spending a bit of scratch could be fun—and he liked horses. "Where will we find the animals, sir?"

"The horses? Arabia, Scotland, and Kentucky, I expect. I rather thought you'd look after that."

Patterson resisted smiling. Oh, he'd look after that all right, and skim the appropriate amount of money to buy that final parcel of land just north of Kelso in the Scottish border country, to which he was looking forward to retiring from this hellhole.

"Patterson?"

"Sir?"

"Teach young Silas about horses. Maybe that will catch his fancy."

* * *

THE HORSES DIDN'T MUCH INTEREST Silas, but they became Milo's obsession. Every new animal that arrived Milo insisted on riding—and, although Silas didn't want much to do with the animals, he was always there to cheer on his brother. Now in their middle teenage years they were closer than ever, but very different young men. Milo was much loved by his father and anxious to learn everything about the family business. Silas was often silent and withdrawn, but brilliant with languages and fascinated by the Chinese culture around him. Hearing about what many now called Peking Opera at the House of Paris, he even managed to sneak in twice to watch before being ushered out with a hand on his shoulder. The kind but firm hand belonged to Jiang, who whispered, "Soon, but not yet, my fine colt."

Richard built new stables for his racehorses, and the day they were completed he took Silas aside.

"It's time for you to become part of this family."

"I am part of this family. I'm your son."

"Yes, but this family runs a serious business, and you have to become a part of it."

"Why?"

"Because, son, a man needs expertise in this world to make a living. Time to learn the horse trade. Patterson'll show you what needs doing."

"But why me?"

Richard didn't know what to say to that and found himself suddenly shouting, "You're a Hordoon, son. One of us. Me and your Uncle Maxi, we built this business from nothing."

"And where is my uncle now?"

"Gone, Silas. Gone. But you're still here, and it's time to earn your keep."

* * *

"YE'RE AN ODD ONE, ain't ye?" Patterson asked as he handed Silas the shovel.

Silas didn't answer. It wasn't really a question anyway.

"It's called shit, lad, and that thing in yer puffy, soft hands is a shovel." Patterson laughed. "Shovel shit, me odd little heathen."

Silas turned to look at Patterson.

"Don't give me that Persian stare, boy, or whatever the fuck it is on your kiking face."

Silas hefted the shovel and slid it beneath a pile of fresh horse dung, keeping his distance from the Arabian steed who eyed him from the far side of the stall.

Silas was afraid of horses. The taut, quivering muscles in their thighs and the sidelong violence in their eyes, put together with their rock-hard hooves, terrified the young man. He was so small compared to them. Milo had assured him that as long as he didn't show fear the horse wouldn't hurt him. Often enough he'd said, "Give him a big swack on the butt, Silas, and he'll know who's the boss."

211

Patterson laughed again for some reason.

Silas wanted to turn to the man but he couldn't. It wasn't Patterson's cruel tongue or violent temper that scared Silas. It was as if the man knew his secret. His hidden shame. It was the reason Silas never said anything, even to Milo, about the way that Patterson treated him.

"The shit's on yer leg," Patterson said with a chortle.

Silas looked down and the man was right. The load had been too big for the shovel blade and some of the riper matter had slid off onto his tweed pants and come to rest in his cuffs.

"Not the perfect clothing for the job, lad."

Silas just nodded and backed out of the paddock with his shovel piled high. The manure pile was on the south side of the stables and steamed in the morning sun. Silas heaved his load onto the pile, then looked around. It was silly to carry what he thought of as horse poop, one shovel at a time, out to the pile. He grabbed a hand dolly, fitted a wooden bucket to its base, and rolled it back to the stalls.

As he passed the horses he remembered how his Uncle Maxi had fawned over his own animals. Maxi seemed, like Milo and his father, to have real affection for them. His father spent hours stroking and talking to the new Arabian pony they'd just purchased.

He'd also seen that same look on his father's face sometimes when Milo was at his side. He'd seen the look on Uncle Maxi's face when he worked out his intricate knots and inventions.

But Silas had never felt anything like that. He'd heard rumours about his father and the missionary woman, and he assumed that Uncle Maxi felt strongly for some woman—although there were few non-Chinese women in Shanghai. Silas had listened in rapt attention as Uncle Maxi told them of working on the opium farm in far-off India. How he had "loved those people, loved them through and through."

Silas had never loved anybody or anything. He knew he was incapable of it. So he pretended. But he couldn't pretend well enough to fool Patterson. Patterson knew his secret, his shame. Silas tried to make himself feel things. He cared about Milo, but he suspected that this was only because Milo had always been there for him. Some nights Silas would creep from their bed and snuggle up beside their *amah*, who slept on the mat outside their door. But even then, it was just for warmth.

Silas knew that it didn't matter to him who offered him warmth or comfort or even love—he couldn't return it. There was something wrong, and he knew it. Unfortunately, Patterson knew it as well.

chapter thirty-one
Death and Birth in the Bamboo

North of Shanghai, across the Huangpo River, in the Pudong
1854

Somehow the Body Guard knew it would end up in the bamboo thicket—
that death and decision would come in the bamboo—so he had avoided it
for as long as he could. But now they were in there, obscured from his
view—only the movement of the elegant stems in the crisp early morning
light gave a hint as to their whereabouts. And now the screams of "Help
me, Father! Help me, Father!" over and over again.

They had completed the rituals in the previous two weeks, during
which time his son and his nephew had grown even closer, as only those
who need each other to survive can. But the ancient rule of one leader for
the Guild of Assassins was firm, and he dared not break it for fear of
betraying his family's oath, sealed in the Narwhal Tusk.

"Help me, Father! Help me, Father!"

He had thought about resurrecting the Guild himself but knew he was
too old. Already the rot had set in, he could feel it, and soon every eye
would see it—as one sees a small black blotch on a peach slowly eat into
the centre and attack the pit.

"Help me, Father! Help me, Father!"

THE BODY GUARD
I wanted to put my hands to my ears to block the sound from punishing
my heart, but I couldn't allow myself that luxury.

This is my duty—as it is my son's duty, and my nephew's.

213

THE SON

"Help me, Father! Help me, Father!" The sharpened bamboo cane is sticking out of my skin just below my right shoulder. Blood is coursing down my side, but I've shallowed my breathing, as Father taught me. I realize that the pain is bearable. But I am scared, and I know that Loa Wei Fen will be in the trees, up in the bamboo—"Kill from above; always find a way above."

THE NEPHEW

My cousin fell into the pit trap I set for him. One of the sharpened bamboo stems pierced his right breast, but has not cut into the sac that holds his heart. I wish it had killed him—so that I would not have to.

THE SON

I am reaching for the swalto blade in my belt, but when I move, the pain suddenly floods me. But I need my blade to defend myself. For he will be coming. Coming soon for my heart.

THE NEPHEW

I taste the cobra skin that wraps the handle of my swalto blade as I put it between my teeth. I need both hands free to descend from the tall shoots. I've never been so high in the bamboo before, and the tassels sing to me in the morning breeze. I want to go higher to hear the clear voice of the morning's song, but below me—in a pit—lies my destiny.

THE BODY GUARD

I begin to run. The bamboo tears my clothes, cuts at my skin—one lances a deep cut just below my left eye. But I run as fast as I can to my son—my gentle son.

THE SON

A lone cloud races across the morning sky, moving a circle of darkness beneath it as it runs toward the horizon. So beautiful! So beautiful! But now I see the snake in the bamboo—my cousin, the snake.

THE NEPHEW

The swalto turns in my hand and nestles into place—as if it is a living thing—its keen edges and point a thing of immaculate purpose. Then I am moving—down, down, down the largest of the bamboo stems—my legs controlling my descent—as I move headfirst toward my destiny in the pit.

THE SON
The sun glints off the snake's swalto blade—its deadly tooth—and I look away. The blood has stopped flowing from my shoulder. The breeze is cool. It is going to be a beautiful day. A day to spend with the cormorants—my cormorants—on the water. And suddenly I am there, in the boat, the youngest cormorant in my lap. I hold up the cruel metal ring that I was supposed to tighten around my bird's neck so he couldn't swallow the fish he caught, and I look to Father sitting by the rudder and say, "Do I have to?"

THE BODY GUARD
The bamboo patch in front of me yields quickly, much to my surprise, and then I see them. My son pinned in a shallow pit and my nephew pressure gripping the bamboo stem with his knees as he descends headfirst for the kill.

THE NEPHEW
I arch my back and the cobra carved there uncoils. I feel its strength, its massive fury—and then I drop on my prey.

THE SON
"I won't do it, Father. I won't. This is a good bird. A good bird. My bird. He won't swallow the fish. He'll bring them back to the boat. I promise."

"It is the cormorant's fate to be ringed. It is its purpose. Now put the ring on his neck—and don't be gentle or it will fall off."

"But this is Kiwa—my cormorant—he loves me."

THE BODY GUARD
I thought I heard the word *love* come from my son's mouth as I approach. And it pierces my heart. "Help me, Father! Help me, Father!" My gentle son—but I look away I look away.

THE NEPHEW
Then I am there. Overtop of him, my swalto ready for the initial cut. His mouth opens and a bubble of blood comes to his lips. Then I hear him. He is saying my name.

THE SON
"Loa Wei Fen, Loa Wei Fen, help me. I cannot put the neck ring on Kiwa. I cannot."

THE BODY GUARD

I see my nephew hesitate and I shout, "Don't falter. It is your destiny, Loa Wei Fen. Either you kill him or I kill you—the choice is yours."

THE NEPHEW

Uncle is yelling at me and my cousin is pinned by the bamboo stake and the sun is rising and the cobra on my back is hissing in my ears and the swalto blade flips to the killing position in my hand—and I ...

THE SON

The cormorant bites me. He's never bitten me before. Blood is coming from my chest. From my chest? Why from my chest? Kiwa bit me on the hand.

THE BODY GUARD

Loa Wei Fen's first cut isn't deep enough. "Strike again!" I scream.

THE NEPHEW

I didn't need to be prompted. Everything in me wants the warm gush of blood to rain on me and change me and allow me to become the thing I was meant to be—an assassin.

THE SON

"Help me, Father! Help me, Father!"

THE BODY GUARD

"Strike or I will strike you!"

THE NEPHEW

All the practice, all the training—I open the cobra's hood on my back and my *chi* flows out from my centre to my arms and the swalto leaps for joy as it digs deep into my cousin's stomach, then rips up and up. Then there is a sudden stillness. Above me the bamboo sways to my *chi*'s motion and the sun turns to warm my back and the world stands very still—I can hear the smallest animals in the thickets, and the wind catches its breath and the very motion of the planet—as I cut open my cousin's chest, slice free his heart from its bonds, cut it in half, and bite deep.

THE BODY GUARD

Loa Wei Fen's face is smeared in the blood of my son as he spits the piece of heart high in the air—as the ritual demands. I can see his *chi* finally retreat into its den, and the boy turns to me—now no longer a boy.

THE NEPHEW
"We should bury your son."

THE BODY GUARD
"No. I now have no son. Leave the carcass for the jackals."

It is the final lesson I had to teach Loa Wei Fen. Pity is not part of an assassin's work—nor is honour for the dead.

THE FISHERMAN
As I hold out my hand to my blood-soaked nephew I know that something important in my life has ended. I am no longer the progeny of the First Emperor's Body Guard—and my nephew is no longer my nephew. The young man is now the founder of the Guild of Assassins, and his name, Loa Wei Fen, will be the stuff of History Tellers' tales for ages to come.

The Body Guard was now, simply, the Fisherman—a simple man who had lost a much beloved son.

part three

chapter thirty-two
The History Teller

Shanghai
1856

Jiang nodded as she listened to her tall, brilliant daughter, Fu Tsong, explain her most recent version of her opera, *Journey to the West*. Despite being impressed with her daughter's talent, her attention wandered as she thought of the communication she had received that morning from the Fisherman: "A new leader of the Guild has been chosen. He awaits your instructions."

"Then, Mother, after all the trials and tribulations, all the miles of walking and the constant danger—and the love that has grown between the Princess from the East and her manservant—they finally arrive in the palace of the King of the West. The Serving Man is shocked to see that no one is there to greet them—no banquet of welcome awaits them. Then the Princess, his Princess, is unceremoniously taken from him and, without even seeing her new husband, is sent to the house of the King of the West's concubines. They both realize that she was nothing more than a pawn in the politics of peace and war between the King of the East and the King of the West. No one cares about her or what happens to her, except the lowly Serving Man, who brought her two thousand miles across rivers, mountains, and deserts."

"It is very sad, Fu Tsong, but duty takes us all to places that we do not expect."

"Indeed, Mother. But that is not the end of the play."

"Really? What more story can there be?"

"The final image is the Serving Man. Bereft of his Princess, he turns toward the East and takes the first step on his two-thousand-mile journey back home."

Jiang smiled. Of course her daughter would see the possibility that she had not seen. She reached out and touched the strong features of her daughter's face. She was, Jiang knew, despite her mother's profession, a conservative woman. A woman whom she had helped marry into the industrious Zhong clan. A woman who had survived the sudden death of her young husband and had assumed his assigned role in the Zhong family hierarchy. A woman whom many had begun to call a History Teller.

Jiang told her so.

"History Teller?" Fu Tsong asked, puzzled.

"It's an old tradition that has faded from memory in many, but before the Manchu courts ruled in the Middle Kingdom there were always two historians in the Emperor's court. The History Chronicler gave the dates, times, and numbers of an historical event. The History Teller found the small, personal truth behind the facts of the historical event and told that story. It is rumoured that Q'in She Huang himself said, "Abide the History Chronicler for he delivers facts. But heed the History Teller for he sees and tells the truth of what really happened."

Fu Tsong was suddenly cautious and, keeping her eyes from her mother, said, "You are an endless surprise, my Mother."

Jiang smiled at that. "You are a History Teller, my daughter. It has been obvious to many of us for a long time. May I call you by that title?"

History Teller, Fu Tsong thought. *I'd be honoured to be called a History Teller.* She nodded.

"Are you and your troupe ready to travel, History Teller?"

Travel where and travel why? the History Teller wanted to ask, but she knew better than to demand answers from her mother. She also knew that her mother was never whimsical in her requests and always had the interests of Shanghai at heart. And anything that was good for Shanghai was good for her and her troupe. "This is important," she said. It was not a question.

"I wouldn't ask unless it was. You know me, History Teller."

"You honour me, Mother, with the title and your trust."

"You honour me, daughter, with your talent and loyalty. You strengthen your family. Your play is lovely, and I would not ask you to amend it in any way unless it was important. You know that."

"I do. Is there something that gives offence?"

"Nothing. Truly nothing. I only need you to include an actor in your company whom you have not used before."

"Is this an actor I would know?"

"No."

Suddenly the History Teller was afraid. "Am I permitted to ask who this actor is and why you wish ...?"

"No."

After a moment the History Teller nodded. "As you wish, my Mother. But can I ask about this actor's abilities?"

"I have no idea if he can sing or dance. But he can tumble and juggle as well or better than anyone else in your company."

"Good. He needn't sing or dance as long as he is athletic."

"Oh, he's very athletic. Very."

"Fine. May I cast him as I see fit?"

"Such decisions are yours, but I think he would make a fine Monkey King."

The History Teller's eyes opened wide. Had her mother known how displeased she had been with the present Monkey King's performance? Perhaps. "When can I meet this young athlete?"

"When you begin your journey."

"To Beijing?"

"No, to Nanking."

The History Teller paled. The Taipingers controlled the ancient capital.

"I have secured you safe passage from the Heavenly King through one of his senior generals. Someone you've met," Jiang added with a strange smile.

The History Teller wanted to ask who this man was and how her mother knew him, but Jiang kissed her on the cheek, then left.

* * *

THAT NIGHT a client at Jiang's reached for his whore. But the drunken Frenchman's aim was off target. And his hand knocked over a brazier, whose coals lit the woman's silk kimono. Which set alight the bedding in the room which torched the walls of the brothel which began a conflagration that in one night burned nearly one in ten of the buildings in Shanghai, the city at the Bend in the River, to the ground. But it was of only minor concern to the Chosen Three, who had finally launched their arrow high into the night sky.

The History Teller gathered her clan by the north bank of the Huangpo. In the distance, the eerie glow of the huge fire in Shanghai cast a further strangeness on the night. A fat pig sizzled on its spit over the coal pit. The moon was already high and the cold of the night intense, but not even the youngest had returned to the housing compound. The women, the strong women of her deceased husband's clan, the Zhong clan, stood and waited for her to speak. She poured more of the powerful Chinese wine and held up her glass. The entire clan stood and looked at her. "Drink, then spit," she ordered. They all did as she commanded. She felt the bitter liquid momentarily clench her throat.

The smell of the hundreds of pails of curing night-soil—her husband's family business—were somehow sweet on the cold air.

"And again." And they all drank, then spat a second time.

She nodded. "Good. My mother, Jiang, has insisted that we talk of great things." She laid out the basic plan of bringing the troupe to the Prophet's stronghold in Nanking. She never mentioned exactly why and quickly silenced any dissenting voices. "The Long Noses' neutrality treaty with the Prophet is in place, so we will not be held back in the city. We will not, however, trust the fates or the *Fan Kuei*'s word, so we'll leave tonight."

"Will it be safe?" her mother-in-law asked. The older woman looked at her daughter-in-law and wanted to reach over and touch her hair and tell her how proud she was to have her as a part of the Zhong clan. But there had never been outward demonstrations of affection between the two. Even in private they were subdued. The History Teller saved all of her affection for her one true love, since the death of her husband: her work on the operas.

"I don't know," she said, turning away from the question. "I just don't know." She turned toward the rest of the large clan. "You will not see me or the troupe for some time. Don't take to heart what you hear of us. I may need to gain the Prophet's trust." Then, turning to her actors, she said, "Get your things. It is time for us to leave."

The actors hesitated.

"What?" she demanded.

They looked at the crackling pig, and the History Teller smiled, then nodded. *Actors and food,* she thought, but what she said was, "There will be no meat for us for some time, so we'll await the completion of the roast—then we will leave. We will be on the river before moonset."

* * *

LATE THAT NIGHT *the History Teller hoisted the last of her bags up on the wharf railing. As she turned toward the large river junk that awaited her on the north shore of the river she was startled by the appearance, as if from the ground itself, of a young man, scarcely more than a boy. The fresh cobra tattoo on his hand stood out in the last rays of the setting moon. "I am to come with you, History Teller," the boy-man said.*

The History Teller took a breath and steadied herself. The boy-man's athleticism was obvious, but his silence was disconcerting. There was blood on the sides of his shirt. Blood newly dried.

"Did my mother send you?"

The Assassin shrugged.

"Did she?"

"My uncle gave me the order. I don't know if it came from someone else."

"And this uncle's order said?"

"To meet the History Teller by the upper bend in the river and follow what she says."

The History Teller nodded and reached for her satchel. As she pulled it off the railing the bag's handle snagged and the contents fell toward the ground. Toward, but not quite to, because the strange boy-man leapt forward, and with an unworldly speed he caught each and every article, one by one, before any of them touched the earth.

Then he looked up at the History Teller and something dark and sad crossed his face. Something the History Teller saw but made herself forget.

The History Teller indicated that the things were to be put back in the satchel. The Assassin returned the articles to the case.

Then the History Teller reached into a much larger case and threw its contents at the boy-man.

The Assassin saw the glint of metal in the moonlight. Then, as he had been taught, he shallowed his breathing, and the objects—cymbals, drums, drumsticks, horns—slowed in their twirling, spinning paths toward him.

He caught each of the seven objects, the last, a large cymbal, in his teeth. Then he stood there on one foot and awaited the History Teller's orders. They finally came.

"Pack those up and carry them onboard the junk."

chapter thirty-three

Into the Countryside

The Real Middle Kingdom
1856–57—

The heavily armed Manchu patrol boats were on their windward side.

"When did they show up?" asked the History Teller.

"While you slept," the one-eyed Captain of her junk replied as he spat into the muddy water of the Yangtze. "They'll stop us before we get to the narrows. Are your papers in order?"

"Naturally. We are on our way to Beijing to entertain the Dowager Empress. We'll use our time on board to rehearse." She nodded in the direction of a makeshift stage in the bow.

The Captain's single eye widened. He'd been paid enough money by the whore madam to get this handsome woman and her troupe of players to Chinkiang at the foot of the Grand Canal—no farther. He spat overboard a second time and said, "You are aware the Middle Kingdom is at war."

"How far are we from the narrows?"

"An hour, maybe a little more."

The History Teller nodded as she turned to her assistant, a competent but entirely boring middle-aged man. "Tell the new actor to get into makeup." Before the pedantic man could question this, the History Teller said, "I want to work on the fourth act. Maybe the morning light will bring some clarity to that mess."

The man threw up his hands and headed below decks. Waking up actors in the morning wasn't his idea of a good time.

The one-eyed Captain had been correct. In just under an hour a Manchu war junk hung a spinnaker sail and crossed their bow with gingalls openly displayed and shouted at the Captain to turn into the wind. Without hesitation the Captain pulled the long-handled tiller hard against his body. The junk's thick mast swung slowly across the deck and the ship turned smoothly and with remarkable speed into the wind—and there it stayed.

The Manchu Commander stepped onto the junk's deck after twenty of his armed men had rousted the History Teller and her players. The man strode across the deck as if he were reviewing his troops on a battle parade. He stopped in front of one of the older actors and shouted, "Remove your mask."

The older man did.

The Commander turned the actor around quickly and pulled the man's long, braided hair from beneath his robe. "It is the law for you to wear your hair out!" He turned the man around to face him and ran his hand over the man's badly shaven high forehead. Then he hit him hard across the face, drawing blood from the man's mouth. "It is the law for Han Chinese to shave their foreheads up to the line of the top of their ears. It is the law."

He didn't bother turning to the History Teller. He just held out his hands and shouted, "Papers!"

The History Teller handed over the documents her mother had supplied. She had no idea if they were good forgeries or in fact the real thing. All she knew was that they claimed the troupe was on its way up to Beijing to entertain the Dowager Empress, Tzu Hsi.

She glanced over at the boy-man. All she knew about him was that his name was Loa Wei Fen, or at least that was the name he used. She canted her head slightly in the strange young athlete's direction. Loa Wei Fen nodded and pulled the headdress from his head. He still had a hastily painted approximation of the Monkey King makeup on his face.

The History Teller heard a harrumph from the Manchu Commander, then he snarled, "Nonsense. Men are dying, and this crap is given free passage." He shoved the papers back at the History Teller, then turned to the one-eyed Captain. "Papers!"

The Captain produced the documents for both the junk and his personal passage. The Manchu Commander was not much impressed. He shouted an order that the History Teller couldn't translate, then moved back toward his own ship.

As the war junk disappeared in the rising sun, the History Teller thought of a small white bird disappearing into the past. She said the words aloud, and something deep within her resonated with them. Something old was near her, and she knew it. Something that touched her—or her mother—or both of them. Then she turned to her troupe and shouted, "Act Four is still a mess. Let's work."

They rehearsed for another hour, but it was clear the boy-man was completely lost.

"Look. It's not complicated. The storyline has to do with the Monkey King killing a family as they try to make their way through his mountain territory," the History Teller explained again.

"I just kill them?" he asked.

"Yes, Loa Wei Fen, you just kill them."

"Why?"

The History Teller turned to look at the other actors. "Already he wants to know why he's doing things."

"That shouldn't bother you, ma'am. It's what you've been asking me for years," said the actor who played the Serving Man.

"Well, you need to be asked that. He ..." She turned to Loa Wei Fen and said, "It's territorial, from your point of view, but the storyline has to do with the Princess from the West and her Serving Man. Your threat to the peasants presents a dilemma for the Serving Man. Does he leave his charge, his love, the Princess of the West, and do what is right in trying to protect the peasant family from you? Or does he ignore his duty as a human being namely, to help the helpless—and thus keep his charge, his love, safe from danger?"

"So I am no more than a dilemma to you?"

The History Teller heard something hidden behind the boy-man's words but ignored it and threw up her arms. "We are all no more than a dilemma. At least your dilemma has an interesting character and a good costume. Count yourself lucky."

Loa Wei Fen shuffled his feet a little, then said, "All right."

They started with the scene in which a family escapes the wrath of their overlord when they can't afford to pay his outrageous tax demands. The father, mother, and child make their stealthy entrance from downstage left and begin their cross to the upstage right riser. The History Teller worked with them for almost an hour trying to get the relationship between the couple clear, then the exact nature of the danger they anticipated encountering in the mountains.

She was finally happy with their performances and was about to call Loa Wei Fen to the stage when the young man leapt to the top of the high platform. His sudden presence was so unexpected, so shockingly, vibrantly alive, that every eye turned to the strange boy-man. But the History Teller just nodded slowly as a smile grew across her features, bringing an intense light to the beauty there.

The next morning the History Teller came up on deck and saw Loa Wei Fen balanced on the port bow railing without the assistance of a spar or halyard line. The boy-man effortlessly adjusted for the swell and ebb of the waves. Seeing her, he pointed upriver toward the south shore. The History Teller came over to him and shielded her eyes in an effort to see what had attracted Loa Wei Fen's attention, but it was a full fifteen minutes of sailing before the History Teller finally saw what Loa Wei Fen's keen eyes had already seen—hundreds upon hundreds of heads on pikes planted on the shoreline.

As their junk slid by the ghastly display, there was an eerie silence, broken only by the threatening caws of the carrion birds as they feasted on eyeballs and cheeks and esophageal parts. Some of the vultures perched on the heads stared at the passing junk as they dug their claws deep into the flesh beneath them.

One of the young actors broke into tears; another threw up over the side of the junk.

"It's recent," the one-eyed Captain said.

"Manchu or Taiping?" the History Teller asked.

"The victims or the attackers?"

"Who did this?" demanded the History Teller.

"Manchus. As I said before, there is war in the Middle Kingdom. Can't you smell the reek in the air? It's the smell of change. This is not Shanghai—this is the real Middle Kingdom, and the stink of change is everywhere. Write about that if you can, History Teller."

The History Teller watched as the heads stared past the birds that pecked at them and challenged those onboard the ship to avenge this outrage. For almost a half an hour they sailed past the silent cry. Then came the final outrage. On shorter pikes, as if to emphasize the offence, were the heads of children—dozens of them. The History Teller's eye was drawn to one little girl whose hair hung down all the way to the sand. The wind picked up and the girl's hair lifted from the ground. *Like a kite,* she thought. Then lines came to her:

The hair as its tail,
The head pulls at its pike bond,
To enter the sky and fly to heaven.

Later that day, from the vantage of the junk, they saw their first large group of peasants trudging east along the river's stony shore carrying the entirety of their lives' possessions on their backs.

"Where are they headed, Captain?"

"To the safety of Shanghai. You'll see many more soon. The Manchus have blocked all the roads from Nanking to just east of here. That's why these people use the riverbank. Once they get a few miles farther they'll head inland to the traders' paths. That's why you haven't seen many of them up until now, History Teller."

"And they'll walk to Shanghai?"

"Unless they are wealthy enough to own a cart or hire a horse. Some of the wealthy from Chinkiang are carried all the way to Shanghai. But not these souls."

"How many days ...?"

"Would it take to get to Shanghai from here, on foot? If they manage to avoid bandits and the roving bands of Taipingers or renegade Manchus, six, maybe eight. But many of these people travel with infants and old people. For them, longer, maybe ten days."

The History Teller looked at the man at her side and finally asked, "How did you lose your eye?"

"Looking for a story, are you?"

"Perhaps. I have a real interest in stories."

"Indeed you do."

"So?"

"In the Arab lands."

The History Teller's knowledge of geography was extremely limited. With the exception of a few travellers and merchant mariners, no one in China knew much about the lands beyond the Middle Kingdom.

The Captain hacked out a coarse laugh and said, "They tell stories there too, History Teller. Those Arabians love their stories."

"Was this far away?"

"As a story would say, far away and long ago. When I was nothing more than a boy onboard a great ocean-going junk. We had circled the world itself and seen many foreign lands. In fact, we were following the same route that our earlier mariners took, two hundred years before the Manchus came to our land."

The History Teller knew that the Manchus' Q'ing Dynasty had started in the early years of the 1600s, so the Captain was referring to a time around 1400. She'd heard rumours of great ocean-going junks circumnavigating the world even earlier than that. One story had it that the maps made by the sailors on the early junks were later sold to Arab traders who came across the Silk Road, who then sold them to the Spanish, who used them to stumble upon the Americas. The History Teller didn't know whether this was true or not, but then again her interest was not really in facts.

"So what happened?"

"A woman. No, a girl."

"So you weren't that young."

"Just old enough to want, and I was full of juice back then. Full of it." He let out a coarse chortle. "I lost my eye for a girl," he said softly.

The History Teller was willing to listen, but it quickly became clear that the one-eyed Captain was adrift in his memories and was not going to complete the story. That was fine with the History Teller. "I lost my eye for a girl" was an entire world of a story, as far as the History Teller was concerned.

That evening they stopped at the wharf of a large estate. Servants, hundreds of servants, hustled onboard to bring the actors' props, costumes, and set pieces ashore.

The History Teller was met by an elderly man wearing rich robes, with two young women at his side. "Welcome, most welcome," the old man said. As he spoke, the long wisp of hair on his chin bobbed up and down in a weird pantomime of his words. The two young women were careful to keep their eyes down and contented themselves with smoothing out the old man's garments as he moved.

The History Teller noted the angry red rash on the hands of one of the girls—then saw how carefully she kept it hidden beneath her sleeves.

"You will perform for us, I hope," the old man said.

"Indeed," she responded, "and we have a surprise for you."

"A surprise!" the old man exclaimed as his wisp beard danced up and down. "I love surprises!"

As darkness fell, torches were lit in a wide circle and chairs brought out. With the Yangtze River as their backdrop, the troupe performed the first few scenes of *Journey to the West*. The large crowd was enthusiastic, often leaping to their feet and filling the silent night with their cries of "*Hoa!*"

Loa Wei Fen was disappointed that they stopped before his section of the play, and then was surprised when the History Teller called him out onto the stage. He stepped out in his Monkey King costume and makeup and stared at the people amassed on three sides of the raised performance platform.

"Now for the special surprise that I promised," the History Teller announced to the audience. She turned to the stage and ordered, "Take a stance, Loa Wei Fen."

The young man kicked off his slippers, shallowed his breath, allowed his testicles up into his abdominal cavity, and floated his hands forward. He noted the tension increase in the audience. Then the History Teller called out, "Group one!"

Immediately six men in the audience stood and threw objects, ranging from heads of cabbages to a slender dagger, right at the young man on stage.

To the joy of the audience, Loa Wei Fen caught all the objects, including the small knife, upon which he skewered both heads of cabbage.

The old man cheered "*Hoa!*" so loudly that the History Teller thought he might collapse. Then the History Teller called out, "Group two!"

This time eight men stood and hurled objects at Loa Wei Fen. Again the young man caught all the projectiles, this time one knife behind the crook of a knee and another between an elbow and his ribcage.

Again wild cheers greeted the feat. The process was repeated twice more, ending with twelve objects thrown and caught.

The History Teller watched closely. She saw in this boy-man the results of years of training. The History Teller had an idea what the only profession was that would demand such a regimen—and it sent a slither of fear up her spine.

Three days later they approached the southern end of the Grand Canal. On the north-east shore, the city of Chinkiang—the City of Suicides—loomed up in the darkness.

The one-eyed Captain called out, "It's open," in response to the knock on his door. He swung his feet out of his hammock as the History Teller and her boring assistant entered.

The Captain lit an oil lamp and looked at the two. But he didn't speak. He waited for them to begin.

"We approach the Grand Canal," the History Teller said.

For a moment the Captain wondered why the woman never seemed to sweat or feel the cold, then he let that pass and, putting on his sternest face, said, "So what? You're bound for Beijing."

The History Teller stepped forward, laid a hand on his, and said softly, "We are not."

This came as no surprise to the Captain. Nothing about this troupe seemed likely to entertain the Manchus' Dowager Empress: the accent on Han Chinese in the play, the open criticism of power, the adulation of personal love over duty—none of this was destined to find favour in the court of the Manchus. But all he said was, "Really?"

The History Teller smiled, withdrew her hand, and nodded. "You knew."

"Perhaps." The Captain pulled on his britches and snapped the buttons on his flies, then said, "So where are you bound?"

"Nanking."

The Captain almost choked on that. "My ship goes nowhere near the Taipingers."

"We don't expect you to. Just bring us past the Grand Canal and under secrecy of night set us ashore."

The Captain's head snapped up and down like a puppet's and he spat out, "Oh, that's all? Risk the wrath of the Manchus. Perhaps you didn't see the miles and miles of heads on pikes? Well, some of those people broke fewer Manchu laws than you are asking me to break. I have no papers to land you there. And what am I to do if I am stopped and you aren't onboard? What am I to tell the damnable Manchus, that you jumped overboard?"

"No. You are to tell them that we took control of your ship and at knifepoint forced you to put us ashore."

"And they'll believe that?"

"They will after Loa Wei Fen finishes his work on you."

* * *

THE YOUNG ASSASSIN didn't like it. It wasn't what he was trained for, but after the History Teller explained their predicament he agreed.

The Captain had been sedated with strong wine and opium when Loa Wei Fen entered his cabin. With a single stroke of his swalto blade he cut away the man's robe, exposing a barrel chest and a slightly bloated belly. Loa Wei Fen put his hand on the man's chest. Instinctively the Captain's strong hand reached up and grabbed Loa Wei Fen's, but the Assassin was stronger and very skilled. He hit the man hard once just below the left ear and the man's eyes rolled back in his head. The Assassin needed the Captain to be very still. Any movement and this effort to save the man's life could cause his death.

The door opened behind him and the History Teller entered. "Bring the lamp closer," the Assassin said.

This boy is my death, too, the History Teller thought as she moved the lamp.

Loa Wei Fen reached up and pulled the lamp closer to the Captain's chest. He put the thumb and forefinger of his left hand on the man's ribs, gently forcing the skin between the ribs taut. Then he leaned in and placed his ear to the Captain's chest. He forced himself to ignore the man's heartbeat and instead listened carefully to the pull and push of his lungs. His fingers crept across the ribs to the right side of his chest. No need to enter the left side. Then he sensed it: the place where the lung expanded, and to the left, the place where the viscera moved to allow the expansion. It was not so different from the way he would have tried to find a wall beam beneath a wall covering.

Satisfied with his placement, he withdrew his swalto blade and rested the point at the exact place on the man's chest. Instantly blood welled up and began to pool. Loa Wei Fen quickly stilled his breath and made himself hear the entirety of the room. Then, with an elegant thrust, he pushed the swalto blade through the Captain's chest and retracted it instantly. He was happy, when he looked at his knife, that no hint of the bedding came back with the blade. Any foreign matter left in the wound could be fatal. Quickly he reached in his bag and crushed the healing herb into the wound, then wound it tight with silk.

"Will he...?"

"Live?" Loa Wei Fen asked. "Perhaps. Perhaps not. But if he does, he will have a very convincing wound to show the Manchus. Where are the rest of the crew?"

"They've been tied up and put in the hold."

"Who will guide the ship?"

"A man from Chinkiang who owes my mother a favour should be here shortly. He'll lead us to the horses."

＊ ＊ ＊

SIX HOURS LATER the last of the actors and their equipment were ashore several miles west of Chinkiang, and the junk was set loose to attract attention on the Yangtze. Travelling on horseback and walking, the troupe made their way through what the one-eyed Captain would no doubt have called the "real China."

And the "real China" was a place of real danger. North of the Yangtze, where they were, was disputed land. One week the Manchus controlled it, one week the Taipingers. The farmers were terrified. The large landowners had armies of their own to protect their property. Many of the merchants were the first to leave for the safety of Shanghai. The roads were not well tended, and the horses were often skittish in the foul breezes.

The first two days of travelling were relatively uneventful. The troupe stopped to admire the ancient pillars erected by villages in honour of their famous sons and the feats of engineering that allowed rice paddies to rise like stacked lily pads up the sides of sheer mountains. As well, they stopped and offered their respects at graveyards and Buddhist temples.

Twice Taoist priests stopped the troupe, but once it was established that there were no Christian missionaries, they were permitted to proceed.

Beside the mulberry trees
the women,
wrapped in scarves,
move like shadows in the dawn.

Those were the opening lines that the History Teller penned when the troupe approached the first of many silk farms on the gentle slopes of the Hua Shan. As she watched, thoughts kept moving across her mind as if imprinting themselves there like acid on a bronze plate. So unlike Shanghai. So ancient compared to the world in which she lived. But so much of who she was.

The troupe once more performed for their lodging, but this time in a large interior courtyard surrounded by wooden balustrades. This night they began with the play's fourth act, the arrival of the Monkey King in the mountain pass. The History Teller watched closely as Loa Wei Fen made his way through the moves they had practised, leading to the entrance of the Princess and the Serving Man.

The History Teller was not pleased. Although the moves were all technically correct—in fact immaculately so—they were lifeless. The young man was trying to duplicate exactly what he had been taught. There was no sense of making the leap from the notes to the music. The actual killings seemed so formal that they caused hardly a ripple in the audience watching.

The History Teller thought of the word *ripple* and wondered why that had stuck in her mind, then she mouthed the word and her head turned and there before her was a group of peasant women with their children, sitting quietly watching the play—but *rippling*. For an instant the History Teller thought it must have been a trick of the fading light, but as she looked more closely she realized that these women and their children were alive with the pupa form of the silkworm. On their clothing, beneath their clothing, in their hair, in their ears—one gently pulled a creature away from her nostril and put it back beneath her quilted coat.

The History Teller knew that the pupa stage of the silkworm was the most delicate. In that stage, the worms had to be kept warm and dry for almost three weeks before they completed the weaving of the cocoon, which was done with the silk they excreted. The only way to assure the warm and dry conditions was for the workers on the estate to each "wear" thousands of the worms.

That made the History Teller shiver—three weeks with living things on your body, day and night! But that was almost nothing compared to the women's crippled hands. The threads of silk were held together by a gummy substance. The only way to remove the substance was to submerge the pupae in boiling water. That could be done with a stick, but retrieving them from the boiling water required real delicacy and care that only a human hand could manage. As a result, not a single woman or girl could pick up a teacup without pain and tears. She wrote:

> The tears of the women
> fall on angry red hands.

But the silk was beautiful, she had to admit. And she thought of two more lines:

> Women's tears
> Bring beauty to the world.

She turned back to the stage—to the artifice she had created. And she frowned. *There needs to be more truth. This young man has to learn how to dance, not just do the steps, make art of juggling and tumbling, not just fulfill the task. He must take the art of it, the truth of it, and, like these people, put it under his clothing and in his ears.*

The next day, when the troupe finally left the silk farm, the History Teller went through her possessions and discarded any made of silk. Although the characters in her plays would continue to wear silk to represent the figures in the dramas properly, she, herself, would never again allow "the beauty that came from tears" to touch her body.

* * *

THE NEXT EVENING the Taipingers arrived, in force. They had been warned of the movements of the History Teller's troupe and were positioned and ready when the troupe turned west off the northbound trail. Quickly a second force came up behind the acting troupe so that there was no way out of the trap.

The History Teller dismounted and signalled that the rest should do the same. The Taiping soldiers looked confident, well fed but none too friendly. When the History Teller stepped forward to speak to the head of the Taiping patrol she was surprised to sense an agile movement in the tall trees to her right. She caught just the slightest glimpse of a figure scaling a tree and knew it was Loa Wei Fen. She took a deep breath and made sure not to look in the boy-man's direction.

"We come in peace," she began, but the Taiping Commander strode past her, followed closely by ten of his armed guards. They quickly but thoroughly emptied the contents from the wagons and the horses' saddle-bags.

The commander picked up a long, black wig and demanded, "What's this?"

"A king's wig."

"And this?" he asked, holding up a mask painted a bright red and black.

"A courtier's mask."

"And this?" This time he had a woman's costume with long sleeves that fell all the way to the ground, despite the fact that he held it up over his head.

"The dress of a saddened woman," the History Teller said.

That seemed to interest the Commander and he turned toward her. "Are you a saddened woman?"

The History Teller held her ground and kept her voice level, although she sensed Loa Wei Fen leaning out toward her from above in the tree. *Is the boy going to do something stupid?* she wondered. *God help me if he feels he has to protect me.* She forced her eyes away from the stand of trees and looked at the Commander. It was clear that the man was taken with her features. She allowed herself to smile. He smiled back. Finally she said, "I am not a saddened woman, Commander."

"I could make you a very sad woman indeed."

"Or a very happy woman, by bringing me to the court of the Heavenly King."

The Commander was clearly surprised that this tall, handsome woman wasn't afraid of him. He stepped quickly toward her, but she didn't retreat. She did, though, suddenly look up at the trees to his left. He was about to turn when he caught a glimpse of a red kerchief, then shortly after heard the thundering of a horse's hooves.

He stepped back from the woman, a curse rising in his throat that he quickly swallowed.

The horse entered the clearing and reared as its rider pulled hard on the reins. Then the man took the red kerchief from his neck and wiped the sweat from his face.

Maxi Hordoon smiled at the History Teller.

And the History Teller smiled back at the white-skinned, red-haired *Fan Kuei* who had sat so often in the back of her rehearsal room in her mother's brothel. Words again flew into her head:

A barbarian emerges
From the darkened woods,
Like an angel on a horse.
And the world, once more, turns.

As her smile broadened she sensed something cold near her and turned. The boy-man, Loa Wei Fen, was standing behind her looking at the red-haired *Fan Kuei*. And for an instant the History Teller thought she saw rage cross the young man's face.

More words bloomed in her mind—but these words were dark blossoms of blood and pain.

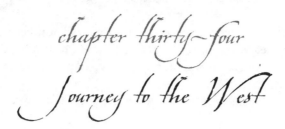

chapter thirty-four
Journey to the West

Nanking, the seat of the Heavenly Kingdom
1857

The flames from the torches within their porcelain reflectors cast a cool light in the warm spring evening. The only noise was the hum of insects moving about the interior courtyard where the Heavenly King himself, Hung Hsiu-ch'uan, sat on a raised chair. To his left, a delicately featured young girl fanned away the bugs from the lower half of his body. To his right, another fine-boned Han Chinese girl protected the upper reaches of his person. His feet had not touched the ground for more than five years—and he never waited for anything. Yet here he waited. Waited for the play, *Journey to the West,* to begin.

The other five kings of the Taiping empire were already in their assigned places with their respective retainers, concubines, and children. And they, too, waited.

Behind them were the heads of Taiping brigades, amongst them Maxi, who stood out like a dumpling on a bed of eggplant.

At last the musicians entered and bowed to the Heavenly King, then took their places downstage left.

All was still for a moment. Then, with a cymbal crash, the play began.

—

From upstage right twelve women in perfect step move effortlessly onto the stage and float in quick circles, chanting their sorrow. The patterns they make vary, then vary again, eventually revealing the figure of the small Serving Man standing very still all the way upstage. Horns sound, then more cymbals, and a long, sustained note on the two-stringed arhu follows. Then silence. Then more horns, and the Lord of the East makes his entrance with his full entourage. They come to a dramatic stop and the Lord of the East steps forward, then strikes a startling pose and sings, "Bring her here, to me, my daughter. Bring her to her father. To accept her duty to her father and her kingdom. Bring my daughter here."

But rather than the daughter, the daughter's nurse glides forward and in high-pitched wails presents the distress of the Princess. Several times the Lord of the East silences her and commands her to get his daughter. Finally the nurse relents and in a beautiful aria sings of the sorrow of duty when one is "married to the kingdom and a daughter of the state." Once more the Lord of the East commands her to get her charge. Before she does, she approaches the Lord of the East, challenging his wrath, and reminds him that his daughter is the "very jewel in your crown" and her leaving "will plant a tear in your heart."

The Lord of the East orders the nurse to get his daughter. Then he and his counsellors sing of the onerous task of bearing the weight of state on their shoulders, ending with, "Even a loved daughter is not more to us than our love of our land."

The horns give way to a chopping, snarling series of echoing notes from the arhu. In syncopation to the beat, the young Princess arrives. She wears a headdress with two tall feathers, and the sleeves of her Chinkiang silk gown are rolled up to expose her hands. She glides across the stage with such grace that the audience literally gasps. The tilt of her body shows the weight of sorrow on her back, her floating entrance her high status, and her two-feathered headdress her sensual allure. She turns as she comes to centre stage and looks out at the audience, then reaches up and pulls one long feather down into her mouth, strikes a pose on one foot, and opens her mouth—as in a scream—but all that is heard is a single sustained note from the arhu. Her sorrow is music itself.

The ensuing scene is surprisingly sweet. The daughter professes loyalty to her father, he his love to her. Then he commands her to go to the King of the West as a new wife to seal the treaty of peace between the two kingdoms. She bows. All seems well until she races downstage and throws her arms up in the air. The rolled up sleeves climb the air to the top of the stage and seem to hang there, as if waiting to be told what to do next. The horns' sorrowful moan fills the stage as the Princess of the East sings her song of parting.

———

At the end of the song there was not a dry eye in the audience. The Heavenly King, Hung Hsiu-ch'uan, shouted *"Hoa!"* which was echoed throughout the courtyard. The actress waited, collected herself, and when the cheering crested she once again stepped forward.

———

As imperious as the Manchu Dowager Empress, the Princess demands to know how she is going to be escorted to her new husband, two thousand miles away.

A cymbal crashes, then horns sound in discord, and the small Serving Man at the back of the stage steps forward. He doesn't dance, or glide, or juggle, or tumble—he simply steps forward, and bows low.

The Princess shoots a look at her father and throws her sleeves out toward him. But the Lord of the East is unmoved. "Trust him, daughter. For I trust him, with your life."

The stage erupts in motion as the entire court moves in a scatter pattern about the stage. Forty bodies in seemingly random patterns, which are anything but random, producing the effect of a whirlwind, blowing the beloved daughter away from her father.

———

Maxi held his breath. He'd watched the History Teller work on this section for hour after hour. Rehearsing, changing, retrying—searching for the pattern of bodily motion that was random but exquisite, like the woman herself. And Maxi saw the beauty and stood to holler *"Hoa!"* Every eye in the audience turned to him. Stunned. Few had ever heard him speak a single word of the Common Tongue in public. They shouted *"Hoa!"* back at him, this time cheering his use of Mandarin as well as the performance. But Maxi didn't care. He saw the beauty of the History Teller's work and hollered *"Hoa!"* again—for both her art and her person.

———

The next scene is a tearful goodbye with the nurse, whose attendants are all there to strew the way with rose petals for the departing Princess.

The journey of the Princess and the Serving Man does not begin well. She is not pleased to be going, not pleased to be virtually unescorted, and furious that her only companion is a peasant. Silence, so rare in Peking Opera, dominates the opening dance between the two—and indeed it is both a physical and emotional dance that ends with the Princess pointing toward the floor and the Serving Man kowtowing to her.

Then the journey begins in earnest. By taking a small bamboo shoot with cornsilk attached to it in her right hand, she indicates that she is riding—while the Serving Man walks. They venture across rivers, over mountains, through open plains and blistering deserts—all without the use of scenery, just the adjustment of the body position of the actors and the music—and the dance and the juggling and the tumbling—and the magic of Peking Opera. They encounter rogue soldiers that they fight off, merchants with whom they bargain for water and food, other nobles who refuse to meet their eyes, Taoist monks who bless their travels, mad-eyed mullahs who attack the travellers, and other pilgrims who join them on their march to the West. The companions change, the dangers increase—the closeness between the Princess and the Serving Man grows.

Finally, in crossing a swift stream, the Princess is saved from falling by the Serving Man, who in turn is hurled down the river where he smashes into a large rock. It breaks his leg cleanly between hip and knee. The Princess dismounts and insists that he ride. When he is unable to bear the pain any more they make camp and the Princess nurses him. That night (in a scene that brought the entire audience to its feet) the Serving Man cries out in pain in his sleep and the Princess crosses over and lies beside him while she sings to the haunting strains of the arhu.

Then the action returns to the court of the Lord of the East, who misses his daughter and needs help dealing with the new intrigues of the court.

———

The History Teller hated it. It was so obvious that the only reason the scene was there was to allow time for the audience to believe that the Serving Man had recuperated from his injury enough to continue the journey. She watched and tried to contain her irritation. She knew the audience needed a break from the story of the Serving Man and the Princess, but she wasn't sure about returning to the Lord of the East. She knew that the reason she chose it was that the audience already knew the Lord of the

East so he didn't have to be reintroduced. She wondered, though, if she could jump ahead in the story and bring on the Lord of the West. She had never seen a story jump ahead in its time sequence. She wondered how that would work. How would she get back to the chronological story after she did that? For a moment she was outside the event, looking down on it, as one would at a raw piece of ivory that awaited the sculptor's chisel.

———

The performance was now in its fifth hour but was only reaching the climax of its fourth of seven acts, in which the family who has joined the Princess and the Serving Man in their travels is threatened by the Monkey King in the high mountain passes. The Serving Man must choose between his duty to defend the Princess and his duty as a fellow human being to confront the Monkey King to save the helpless family. The interior conflict of the Serving Man is explored in a most extraordinary feat of juggling with throwing clubs that the actor performs while he sings his dilemma.

———

The next scene once again brought the audience to its feet, but this time not to cheer or cry—but in fear. Loa Wei Fen had arrived.

This audience had never seen the likes of Loa Wei Fen's performance as the Monkey King; no audience in the Middle Kingdom had ever seen its like. From his leaping entrance, to his tumbling run across the stage to grab the child, to his race with the wife up to the highest point of the mountain—it was completely unique. At the exact place where reality and art meet.

The History Teller watched in awe. Loa Wei Fen had made the leap from form to feeling, but what he was doing was not really acting. There was no distance between performer and performance. The danger seemed real because it was real. For the hundredth time, the History Teller wished she had demanded more information about the strange boy-man when her mother had insisted she take him into her troupe. The performance was startling, grotesque but beautiful. To add to the shock of it, the History Teller had removed all the dialogue. Loa Wei Fen as the Monkey King never made a sound, but the music and the physical reality of his performance lifted the entirety of the event to another plane. A dangerous plane that both tantalized and appalled the History Teller.

The History Teller leaned back against the post to watch the climactic ending of the scene. Not only was the violence unexpected, but it came on what the History Teller thought of as the "offbeat," so that just as the audience relaxed, the Monkey King made a sudden, fatal lunge.

The Heavenly King clambered back up onto his raised throne, amazed that he, in response to the Monkey King, had actually leapt out of his seat. His feet had landed on the mud ground! The young girl in charge of the lower half of his body quickly knelt and swept up any part of the dirt that may have touched her lord's foot. The moon was now high overhead and the stars were in their early summer brilliance. The "brother of Jesus" readjusted his robes and returned his attention to the stage performance.

—

The final days of walking in the scorching desert challenge the Princess's and the Serving Man's endurance. Twice they come upon oases that are dry. In the intense cold of the desert night they huddle together for warmth—but also because they have now become lovers.

—

The History Teller was most pleased with this sequence. She had layered in physical clues throughout the play to lead up to their joining—and it was done simply, almost casually, as if their coming together was no more unusual than a man holding a door open for a lady.

—

As they approach the end of the act they begin to stagger, thinking they cannot go farther. They think of simply lying down side by side in the sand and allowing the carrion birds to find them, but the Princess's sense of duty to her father forces them back to their feet.

Shortly thereafter the clamour of horns and cymbals announces the arrival of the Lord of the West's cavalry. All forty of the actors, dressed as soldiers with the small bamboo switches in their hands to indicate they are riding horses, enter the stage, and once again an intricate dance of seeming randomness ensues that ends with the reveal of the interior of the court of the Lord of the West.

The Princess bows. "My Lord and husband, may I introduce the man who guided me all the way from the court of my father?"

"Enough!" shouts the Lord of the West. He is unconcerned with her and orders her brought to the house of his concubines. But as she is hurried out, she tries to get one final look at the Serving Man.

In the last scene the entire stage goes into tableau, forty actors perfectly still—a single note of the arhu sounds and the Princess floats out from upstage. She stands behind the Serving Man and reaches up. She grabs the feathers from her headdress and pulls them down into her mouth, arches her back, and lets out a cry that is a perfect third above the note of the arhu. The arhu moves up to her note and she pitches her cry up to the fifth. The arhu moves to the fifth and she moves to the tonic. The arhu moves to the tonic and she to the third, and on and on for what seems like a suspended moment in time. As if her broken heart has torn through the fabric of time itself—and they fall—and the audience falls with them.

—

The crowd rose as one and howled its approval.

—

Then the cymbals sound and the Princess steps in front of the Serving Man. "What will you do now?" she sings. He doesn't look at her as he responds, "I will walk back to the lands of the East. Alone." The tableau breaks and the Princess is swept away into the anonymity of the house of concubines, no more important to the Lord of the West than a new horse for his stables, while the Serving Man takes his initial step on his two-thousand-mile journey back to the East—with only the memory of the Princess who loved him as company.

* * *

LATER THAT NIGHT Nanking was thrown open—a true oddity for the Taipingers—to celebrate the first complete performance of *Journey to the West*. But it was a strange kind of celebration. Men and women on the whole were kept apart, and there was no alcohol, as it was against one of the Heavenly King's God-inspired edicts. But, nonetheless, the city celebrated. Perhaps it would be more accurate to say that the city "released." There was something that approached dancing in the streets, music where there had been little before, and people chanced offending the authorities by shouting their joy to the night skies.

After the acting troupe had been introduced to the Heavenly King and his consorts they were allowed to join the revels—such as they were.

That evening the History Teller wandered the streets of this alien city—a city strewn with banners. Some exhorted the people to work harder for the good of Jesus' brother, the Heavenly King; others warned the people of dire consequences should they break the laws of the Heavenly Kingdom, especially the laws segregating men from women; other large banners spoke of the requirement of prayer and the rules against breaking the Sabbath; but the largest banners were devoted to the prohibition against the use of alcohol and opium—special emphasis was put upon this final prohibition.

Yet the people seemed to be happy. There was evidently enough money to go around. Unlike in Shanghai, there were no beggars on the streets of Nanking. Nor were there women with bound feet. Women also didn't seem to be subservient to the men, and many of them led both military and work units. All dressed modestly and were covered from the neck down, despite the warmth of the evening. All businesses inside the city walls were run by the Taiping government, although there were several private businesses outside the walls, often using the city wall as the back wall of the shop.

It was in one of these private businesses, a restaurant, that the History Teller looked up from her excellent noodles and found herself staring, across the room, into the deep pools of Maxi Hordoon's eyes.

The red-haired *Fan Kuei* nodded.

The History Teller pointed to the empty seat across from her.

Maxi walked across the restaurant. At her table she pointed to the empty chair again and smiled. He sat. A young *Fan Kuei* soldier stepped forward and offered to translate for Maxi. Maxi knew the man as one of the mercenaries hired by the Taiping Kings. Maxi found the idea of being paid to fight distasteful but was grateful for the man's service.

"You have found a fine restaurant, History Teller," Maxi said through the translator.

"By accident, I assure you."

"I doubt that. The food inside the city walls is not very good."

"True." The History Teller smiled. "I left two government restaurants whose food was literally hard to swallow."

Maxi smiled, then asked, "Do you have a name?"

"I used to, Mr. Hordoon, but now people call me the History Teller."

"And that's what you want me to call you?"

"No."

"Then what?"

"I don't know yet, but I'll let you know, when I know."

* * *

LOA WEI FEN WATCHED the History Teller leave the small restaurant with the red-haired *Fan Kuei*. The actors in the troupe didn't feel comfortable in his presence, and that was okay with him. He didn't feel all that comfortable with them, and when one suggested that there had to be "some real fun in this town" he left their company and began to wander the streets of the ancient capital.

Once he left the wealth and beauty of the compound of the Heavenly King things changed quickly. The old city was drab and grey; the people seemed drab and grey too. There were no bright lights here, no bustle, no outward joy of being alive, and very, very few *Fan Kuei*. He quickly realized that he was being followed, and it almost made him laugh, although Loa Wei Fen seldom laughed. He made a sharp turn down an alley and in a single step was running at full speed. A wall scaled, a window climbed up to—and his followers were gone.

But of course now it was him following—following the History Teller and the red-haired *Fan Kuei* out into the countryside. The inky blackness of the night made his task simple. As they walked he often came within ten yards of them. With his keen eyesight he matched their footfalls and inhalations. They never sensed his presence—although he was acutely aware of them, of everything about them: their steps in perfect pace, her height equal to his, their hands touching, seemingly inadvertently, from time to time.

At the small but neatly kept farmhouse, the *Fan Kuei* and the History Teller removed their shoes, and Loa Wei Fen circled the building. Finding an open door to a dank cellar, he entered and stood very still. He heard them above. He felt his way in the darkness and found a ladder that led to a door in the floor, which he opened an inch. Through the crack he saw Maxi pour wine for the History Teller and a Hakka woman bring out a newborn and two young girls. It was obvious from the way that the red-haired *Fan Kuei* held the baby that the child was his own. The two young girls held their mother's hands, but when they were called over to be introduced to the History Teller they were happy to be with the red-haired *Fan Kuei. These must be stepchildren,* Loa Wei Fen thought.

After their wine and a sticky rice pastry that the History Teller proclaimed to be the finest she'd ever tasted, she and the *Fan Kuei* went out into the fields. Loa Wei Fen retraced his steps and followed them. The fields smelled of newly laid fertilizer, probably night-soil. But the sky was clear and the wind blew gently. Loa Wei Fen climbed a small tree and watched the two of them walk side by side through the rows of sorghum and soya and then enter the dense field of tall bamboo canes. Something about their body language made Loa Wei Fen's heart ache. It was clear to him that these two, despite the *Fan Kuei's* Hakka wife and children, were destined to discover something Loa Wei Fen had never had—love.

That night the History Teller slept in the open room on fresh mats laid on the floor by the Hakka woman. But she was not alone. Up above her, stretched out on a rafter beam, was Loa Wei Fen, watching, protecting the woman for whom his heart ached, the History Teller.

chapter thirty-five

Deal with a Devil, Deal with an Angel

Various locales in the Celestial Kingdom
1860

The Dowager Empress, Tzu Hsi—also known as "Old Buddha"—looked at her beautiful feet and smiled. They were her pride, now that the glitter in her eyes had dulled and the skin of her face had spotted brown. Her feet remained her final claim to the great beauty of her youth. Ah, she had been a very great beauty—a famous beauty—and had taken full advantage of her exquisiteness to satisfy her gargantuan sexual appetites. Even the memory made her glow and waters move where they had not moved in quite some time. Was it the danger that quickened her, loosed her interior streams—gave her access to the lava flow? She didn't know, but she enjoyed the motion, the life within that even further curled her tiny toes beneath her perfectly arched foot.

"Majesty?"

She'd forgotten that the ugly man was standing at attention waiting for her to answer some question or other. She didn't know which. She'd almost forgotten that she was at a war council that she herself had ordered into session. These were ugly men, though, of that she was sure. The ugliest she had seen in some time. Still, they were better warriors than the pretty ones she had appointed at the beginning of this noisome rebellion.

"Majesty?"

"Report," she said with a curt nod. That was always a good thing to say.

"Yes, Majesty. The rebels approached our Shanghai positions in force. They were led by General Li Xiucheng."

Another cow-faced man, she thought. *This one I'll have boiled in oil when they catch the insolent pup.*

"Majesty, they sent letters in advance to the heads of each of the *Fan Kuei* groups guaranteeing the safety of their persons and property. All they wanted from the Round Eyes was a continuation of their neutrality while they attacked our positions."

But the Fan Kuei *did not remain neutral,* she thought. Her spies had already told her that the Taiping assault on the Chinese section of Shanghai had been repulsed by the guns from the *Fan Kuei* ships. But why? She stood, and the men in the room leapt to their feet. She smiled, inside this time. Her smile was not for the consumption of these ugly men. She walked with the oh-so-desirable hip-swivelling gait that was the natural result of the binding of her feet as a little girl. It had hurt terribly, but she'd never cried, never showed the world the cost of attaining beauty—great beauty—celestial beauty.

When she came to a stop two servants rushed to place a satin stool behind her. Without looking down the Dowager Empress of China plopped her rump on the padded seat. As she did, she remarked, "Perhaps it is time to approach the Foreign Devils—perhaps it is finally time for them to join us in ridding the Celestial Kingdom of these heavenly fools." Then she thought of the ugliness of the Foreign Devils and momentarily the sweetmeats she had consumed an hour before threatened to move up her throat and out her mouth. She let out a breath that picked up the scent of the anise flower that she kept in her left cheek and listened to her stomach flip one last time. Perhaps it was better just to poison the *Fan Kuei*'s water supply and be done with them. She smiled at the thought—to rid the world of so many ugly people at one time pleased her. She glanced at her tiny feet in her tiny satin shoes and thought, *Beautiful. Truly beautiful.*

She looked up at her ugly generals and said, "Offer the *Fan Kuei* trading access to Beijing if they commit their forces to join ours to rid China of these Taiping fools." She looked away. How long could she bear to look at these unsightly men? Then she thought, *First the* Fan Kuei *will help us eradicate the rebels, and then I will eradicate them.*

* * *

MAXI REACHED UP and touched the tunnel struts beneath the Taiping stronghold. He gave one a yank and it didn't budge. He shook his head.

The three Taipingers with him hadn't seen their strange red-haired *Fan Kuei* behave like this before. His translator, a Hakka man whom Maxi called Cupid, asked, "Is something wrong, sir?"

Maxi called the man Cupid because he couldn't begin to pronounce the man's Hakka name, and the man also had a bizarrely tiny, bow-shaped mouth. But Maxi had also been to battle with Cupid and knew him to be a man with a warrior's heart, and because of that he trusted him, not something Maxi did often or easily.

"They're getting better," Maxi said.

"The Manchus?"

"Yes, the Manchus, unless someone else built this tunnel," Maxi, uncharacteristically, snapped. Maxi had successfully defended several of the Taipingers' walled cities against Manchu attack. His strategy wasn't complicated. Once he was sure the city's walls were sound—and many of the walls were very sound—then he knew the attack would have to come from underground. That being the case he sent out spies to try to establish where dirt piles were accumulating. Then he drew what amounted to a straight line from the dirt pile to the nearest section of the city's walls. That was where the tunnel would be. In the night he'd instruct his men to dig down and intersect the Manchu tunnel.

Initially he'd simply diverted sewage from the town into the tunnels and allowed the townspeople to laugh at their filth-covered enemy as they emerged. Naturally the laughing citizens were safely behind their yards-thick walls. Then he'd begun to undermine the tunnels themselves, strategically removing solid struts and replacing them with hollow pieces of timber filled with blasting charges. When his spies told him that the Manchus had entered their tunnels he would set off the charges and the tunnel would collapse on them. The strategy had worked for quite some time, but this tunnel was different. It was built by a craftsman. Maxi, despite himself, admired the workmanship. Then he said, "Blow it up," and returned to the surface.

Once back above ground he turned to Cupid and said, "I want to go up." Cupid hollered a series of orders and a horse was brought. Maxi leapt on its back and cantered down the rickety streets to the hill on the west side of the city centre. Standing on the back of his horse he reached for a rope harness that hung from a sturdy, tall pole and fitted it about his waist—just as he had done years ago in India, when he had retrieved the Hordoon brothers' first opium supply. With one end of the rope dangling he grabbed the other and hoisted himself into the air. As he did, he admired the lightness and strength of the silk ropes and the efficiency of the knots he had learned onboard the ship that had first brought him and his brother to China. He had since sat with several Taiping craftsmen, and they'd made porcelain block-and-tackle devices to direct the ropes, so that now he could hoist himself high in the air, and then switch harnesses and pull himself along an adjoining guide wire across the top of the crowded city.

The children ran beneath him trying to keep up, but this was no game. This city had been under siege for almost three months and the system he had developed allowed him to see the oncoming armies of the Manchus—the seemingly endless oncoming armies—armies that were getting better at their craft. The glint of light on the ground in the west fulfilled his worst fears—the Manchus were building a moat. They had made real advances in their ability to guide the course of rivers, and now they'd ushered the water into their moat, from which they would guide it toward the walls. Walls were nothing more than two stacks of bricks or stone filled with dried mud between the masonry. If the Manchus were able to channel their moat water toward the walls, the dried mud would soak up the water and make the walls themselves unstable. And there was nothing Maxi could do about it.

The Manchus had finally found a way to besiege the Taiping cities. Maxi let himself down slowly. A grim smile was on his face.

"What?" asked Cupid.

"Nothing," Maxi answered, but he knew that the Taipingers couldn't win, and this brave man would undoubtedly die for a doomed cause.

It never occurred to Maxi to worry about his own safety. He was responsible for the safety of others, and that was all that concerned him.

* * *

ELIAZAR VRASSOON SQUIRMED uncomfortably. It was quickly approaching sundown and it was Friday. But the two men standing in front of him seemed to be in no hurry to complete their business. If this had been opium business or silk business or rubber business or silver business, then Vrassoon would have put up his hands and called a stop to the proceedings. He had religious obligations that, unlike business negotiations, could not wait. But these men in front of him were not traders. They were emissaries sent directly from Tzu Hsi, the Dowager Empress of China. And they were proposing a most interesting arrangement—a deal to allow the traders full access to the very heart of China, to Beijing and its surrounds.

The interior of China had remained entirely off limits to the traders. They had entered the Yangtze and traded with varying degrees of success upriver until the Taipingers took over Nanking, but never up the Grand

Canal to Beijing itself. Few Whites had ever seen the interior of China's capital city. None had entered the Empress's Forbidden City. Despite the specific agreements in the Treaty of Nanking, the Chinese had always refused to allow any foreigner into their capital, let alone permit *Fan Kuei* to trade freely in Beijing.

Vrassoon glanced out the window. The sun had not yet set—but it would shortly. He stood quickly and the Manchu Mandarins were shocked into silence. "Tell Her Majesty in Beijing that I am very interested in her proposition and will present it to the other traders. Now, as you can see, the sun is going down, and I have religious obligations that call upon my time."

The translator stumbled over this last, since religious obligations linked to sunset were the result of ancient desert thinking—not the thinking of the Middle Kingdom that joins Heaven and Earth. Eventually he conveyed Vrassoon's basic meaning.

The Mandarins both raised an eyebrow, creating a humorous picture of Oriental confusion—where in fact none existed. Both men had been fully briefed concerning the odd "religious obligations" of the Vrassoon Patriarch and had purposefully extended their meeting to back up against the setting of the sun. Both men then bowed slightly and canted their heads to one side—perfect bookends again. But Eliazar Vrassoon didn't notice. He had already left the room and was heading toward the Beth Tzedic Synagogue—a place he had built and that he found very good for the contemplation of both religious and strategic problems. If his mind had been so inclined he might have seen the similarities between the two—but the Vrassoon Patriarch's mind was not so inclined.

After sunset of the next day Eliazar Vrassoon presented the Dowager's offer to the heads of Dents, Oliphant, and Jardine Matheson—he felt no need to contact the Baghdadi boy. The men listened in what Hercules thought of as a perfunctory silence. Then the Scot broke that silence with a single word: "Why?"

"Indeed," Percy St. John Dent added, "why bother? The rebellion has been a boon to our little town. Without it we'd still be lifting and toting our own goods and living without servants or retainers. Now, thanks to the violence in the countryside, Shanghai prospers—we prosper. Why endanger that on the promise of a Celestial? We all know how much such promises are worth. They still haven't lived up to their side of the Treaty of Nanking, and it's been more than fifteen years."

He didn't bother mentioning that the traders hadn't lived up to their side of the treaty either, but that wasn't the issue as far as Percy St. John Dent, now the head of Dent and Company of London, was concerned.

Vrassoon thought this all a bit short-sighted and said as much. But the traders were making money—lots of money—and were unwilling to risk the opium markets they had for those that they might get.

* * *

WHEN SHE WAS TOLD of the *Fan Kuei*'s refusal of her offer, the Dowager Empress gripped the arms of her golden chair so hard that she snapped the long nail on the middle finger of her left hand. She looked at the stub of the nail that remained. The blunt end was deeply yellowed. She knew that fungus was alive in the tissue and that it could not be eradicated. She hated the idea that something was growing in her. Something foreign. But then again, something infinitely foreign was growing in her country. Two foreign things! The damnable *Fan Kuei* in Shanghai and elsewhere, and the Taiping religious fanatics in Nanking. *One at a time,* she told herself, *deal with them one at a time.*

She looked up at the waiting men. "Bring him in," she said simply.

A low ranking officer turned and left the chamber. Moments later he returned, followed by an officer whose right eye drooped from its socket. He had been in charge of securing all the territories that the Manchu armies had wrested from the Taipingers. It was a hard job, since the filthy peasants and thieving merchants would turn around and sell their mothers for a bolt of cloth or a bucket of rice. And the Taipingers always returned, and by coercion or force or both often regained the support of the locals. Without local support there was no way to secure territory, and without secured territory there could be no reliable base from which to mount the final assault on Nanking. It had been a serious problem until the man who stood before her, the man she'd heard them speak of as the Droopy-Eyed General, had taken control. The man's viciousness was the stuff of legend. His willingness to tie hundreds of men to piles of brush and then set them alight had changed the loyalties of many a peasant—and every merchant.

He had also conducted several successful sieges against Taiping-held cities by diverting water to undermine the defensive walls. The details of such things were both shadowy and of no concern to Tzu Hsi, Dowager Empress of China.

She looked more closely at the man. A tear had formed in the droopy eye and it was about to fall to his cheek when his hand viciously swiped it aside.

Good, she thought, *he is furious with any sign of weakness. I can use such a man.*

* * *

MAXI HELD THE BABY in his arms and looked at the deep, dark pools that were her eyes. *Mine*, he thought, *mine*. His Hakka wife held the hands of her two children as they all, as a family, walked through the tall canes in his bamboo stand. The wind blew gently through the stalks, making them sway. And Maxi's family was in their midst so they swayed too—no different from the canes, all part of one great, moving thing, just as Maxi had felt all those years ago in India when he and Richard had worked with the opium farmers.

Then he saw them standing on the far hill—waiting for him. His wife saw them a moment later and grabbed at his hand and begged him not to go to them. But there was no real argument. These men were from the Heavenly King—no doubt this new general they called the Droopy-Eyed One had taken the field to the east of Nanking.

Maxi held the baby close to him and rubbed his rough chin against her silky cheeks. The baby laughed. Maxi knew that he would have to defeat the Manchu General if he were ever to hear that laugh again.

——

If Maxi had known his Bible stories he might have been aware of the parallels between him facing the Droopy-Eyed General and David facing Goliath—but Maxi neither knew nor cared about such desert-inspired fairy tales. He appreciated them as stories, just as he appreciated the Shakespeare stories that Richard used to tell him, but he never saw Bible stories as morality tales, let alone stories with any portent.

The Droopy-Eyed General was backed by five times the number of troops that Maxi commanded—fine. *Just one factor in deciding the outcome of the day,* Maxi thought. He looked toward the rising sun and for a moment wondered what Richard was doing at that precise moment. He hadn't thought of his brother in a long time. Then he thought of the History Teller and a pang threaded through his heart, so sharp but so sweet that for an instant he wobbled on his feet. Finally he took the red kerchief from his pocket and wound it round his head—the signal for his left flank to charge the siege forces of the Droopy-Eyed General.

——

"What?" the Droopy-Eyed General shouted as he turned in the saddle of his desert pony.

The adjutant repeated the message from their right flank. They were under attack and requesting orders.

"Tell them to fall back slowly, and send me the commander of our centre."

The man arrived quickly and the Droopy-Eyed General told him of the slow pull back of their right flank. "Should we wheel on the rebels as they chase our troops?" he asked.

The Droopy-Eyed General stared at the man. Finally he spoke. "Why else would I have let our men fall back? Rouse yourself. The day is upon us."

—

Maxi's men advanced quickly against the enemy's right flank, and much to his surprise the Manchus didn't stand their ground but gave way under the attack. His adjutants were joyful, but Maxi was unsure. He galloped to the highest hill and once again hauled himself up by a rope-and-pulley system—and what he saw terrified him. As his men advanced, the whole centre of the Droopy-Eyed General's army wheeled right and were setting up to attack Maxi's exposed flank. He hollered an order to his adjutant then loosed himself down onto the back of his horse and galloped at full speed to catch up to his left flank.

He managed just in time to get to the flag-bearers in the rearguard to signal a retreat—and not a moment too soon. Twenty minutes later and his forces would have been devoured by the massive power of the Droopy-Eyed General's centre.

—

"What?" screamed the Droopy-Eyed General as he was given the report of the escape of Maxi's left flank. "Bring that general here with his men."

A half hour later, the general of the Manchu right flank knelt before the Droopy-Eyed General, who looked past him and addressed the assembled troops.

"This man," he said as he ripped the general's silk robe, "failed you. He failed me as well." The Droopy-Eyed General drew his sword and with a scything motion cut at the man's neck. Much to his consternation his cut did not go all the way through. A tear built in his malformed eye, but before it came to his cheek he swung a second and then a third time, until the man's head fell from his shoulders. Then the Droopy-Eyed General swiped the tear aside with his sleeve and shouted at his men, "We are not here to fail. Is that clear?"

He leapt onto his horse and rode to the battle front. As he approached, the bannermen lifted their flags and horns sounded. As much from fear as from loyalty, the Manchus cheered their leader.

* * *

"HE'S VAIN," Maxi said through his translator to his assembled captains.

"And ugly," one of the younger captains quipped.

Maxi knew that the two sometimes went together, the physical deformity causing the overweening pride. He thought about that and the new tunnel structures he'd been finding. Pride. He had met many prideful men. Then he smiled. Prideful men often thought themselves excessively smart. He ordered his men to go on shifts to mark their way through the night. To Cupid he said, "Assemble the generals. We need a plan." To himself he added, *A complex plan for a vain man who thinks he's smarter than the rest of us.*

With the generals assembled, Maxi began.

"My brother used to read me stories when we were young. One, a play called *Cymbeline*, had a lot to say about deception and vanity. Vanity is all about appearance, and this Manchu General needs to be shown he is important because in his heart, and maybe this time in his eye, he knows he's not.

"So let's give him the tribute he wants, that Manchus have always wanted since they invaded the Middle Kingdom all those years ago. I think a huge trunk filled to the brim with silver and gold—and two of our most beautiful women should suffice."

The Taiping generals balked at that. Sex was an entirely forbidden subject in the Heavenly Kingdom. Maxi saw the resistance and said, "We all make sacrifices for the Heavenly King—some with our lives—these two but with their modesty." Maxi gave the generals only a moment to object. Then he went on. "Go tell the History Teller what we want. She'll know how to dress the women."

"How big should the trunk be?"

"I'll have designs for our artisans by evening. I want only our best craftsmen to work on this—and only men we trust."

"And the gold and silver?"

"Get it for me. If things work out properly it will just be a loan."

"But how does giving this monster money and women help us defeat him?"

"As in that play I mentioned, there will be something other than money and women in the trunk—on this, trust me."

The Taiping artisans stared at the crude design Maxi had presented them but did not speak. Finally Maxi asked, "Can you make this?"

"Do you have permission for us to make something like this?" the head artisan asked, pointing to the coitally entwined figures of a nude man atop a nude woman on the lid of the six-and-a-half-foot-long trunk. The man's face was buried in the woman's neck, his arms lost beneath her back, while the woman's face was turned out, her eyes open, looking outward while her left arm reached with her fingers splayed.

"I give you permission," Maxi assured them.

There was a lengthy silence that finally the head artisan broke. "And the man's figure is to be solid but the woman's hollow?"

"Yes."

"The woman's figure is rather large ... for a woman."

"Yes, it is," Maxi replied, "and the floor of the trunk should be four inches thick, made of mahogany."

The artisan nodded. He knew that no knife could penetrate a hard wood to that depth. "What about the lid beneath the woman's hollow figure?"

Maxi thought for a moment, then said, "No. No extra depth there."

"So there is no protection from below for whoever is inside the hollowed out woman's figure?" the man asked.

"Either the deception works or it doesn't," Maxi said.

The artisan nodded slowly, then asked, "How long will the person have to be inside the hollowed figure?"

"A while." Maxi sighed. "Just tell me if it can be done."

The artisan looked quickly to the other craftsmen, then shrugged as he said, "It can be built." The man hesitated.

"What?" Maxi demanded.

"How will the hidden figure get to the latch to release himself?"

Maxi thought about that. Then his toothy smile lit up his face. "Put a silk ribbon in the woman's hair and thread it into the cavity."

The artisan nodded, then asked, "But how shall it be tied?"

Maxi nodded, an old memory from onboard a ship sailing from India to China filled his head, and he said, "Leave the tying of the knots to me."

* * *

AT NOON the following day, emissaries were sent to the Droopy-Eyed General with a proclamation that did not surrender the city but requested: "The right to present to the most honoured General a token of our esteem for his greatness."

Although two of the emissaries were kept as hostages, the third returned with a note outlining exactly how and where the "token" was to be delivered. Maxi was not surprised by the demand for much pomp and ceremony to accompany the delivery of the Taipingers' gift.

At the appointed hour Cupid led the small but stately group, who presented the massive carved chest filled with gold and silver, along with the two girls, to the Droopy-Eyed General. The Manchu was much impressed with both the gold and silver and the girls—or so Maxi was later told.

Maxi felt the trunk lid being flung open, and he assumed the Manchu was examining the wealth. Then Maxi felt a heavy shock race through the wood. It set his ears to ringing. As his hearing slowly returned it occurred to him that the Manchu must have thrust a knife, or more likely a spear, into the thick bottom of the chest.

Then Maxi felt the lid slam shut and the whole chest being lifted. Maxi couldn't determine how long he was carried, but the thump upon landing momentarily snapped his head up and then down, almost causing him to black out. After that he didn't remember much. The two hollow reeds in his mouth were slowly disintegrating from his spittle, and he was worried that he wouldn't be able to get enough air from the tiny air holes without them. As well, his muscles had cramped badly, especially the muscles of his left arm that reached out toward the front of the chest. And he had a terrible need to urinate.

He held on as long as he could, then he pulled on the silk ribbon that controlled the interior latch and pushed.

In his weakened condition the lid felt as though it weighed hundreds of pounds. But it opened smoothly and soundlessly as the artisans had promised.

The luxuriance of what he assumed was the Droopy-Eyed General's tent surprised him. In the dying light from the brazier he saw a pair of feet extended past the end of the silk-swathed sleeping pallet. Maxi assumed the two Taiping girls were somewhere in the tent.

He hoped the Manchu had not hurt them. But that was all he could do for them—hope.

He slid his knife from his pant leg and allowed himself down from the large, carved chest. He thought about closing the lid, then decided against it. He looked around the Manchu's tent and tried to discern exactly who was there. But all he could do was guess. Hope the girls were not hurt. Guess that the Manchu General preferred his sex in private. Too many variables, and he knew it.

———

The Manchu General saw the white-skinned ghost rise from the chest and smiled. Gold, silver, dead girls—and killing a *Fan Kuei*. A fine day.

On his raised bed the two dead girls lay in each other's arms. His little game of *show me yours and then I kill you* had been a great success as far as he was concerned.

And then the ghost took out a knife.

——

Maxi whipped around and stared at the feet hanging off the end of the pallet bed. The feet had the slightest glint of nail polish. He spun quickly and threw himself to the floor.

The Manchu's knife sailed over Maxi's prone body.

The Manchu rose to call for his guards, but he never got out a word as Maxi's fists crashed into his face and broke his nose. The droopy eye was no longer the most deformed part of the man's face.

Maxi grabbed the man's ceremonial sword from his sash. And as the General's droopy eye opened, Maxi raised the curved sword. The man turned his head to face his executioner and smiled.

Maxi's blow bisected the smile, and the man's life leapt from his skull like a canary finally released.

Then Maxi waited. Shortly he heard it—the sound of shouting and the sound of gunfire, as he had ordered. Crouching in the recesses of the tent he watched the guards race in and discover the humiliation of their General.

As Maxi had hoped, word of the Manchu's death loosed chaos in the ranks, and as the Manchus tried to restore order in their midst, Maxi made his escape.

chapter thirty-six
Shanghai Prospers

The City of Shanghai
May 1860

Richard couldn't help smiling. He was selling units in his new four-storey apartment buildings faster than he could get them built. And they were being built with incredible speed. Bamboo scaffolds sprang from the ground in leaps and bounds. Peasants carried the world on their backs up the bamboo ladders to the masons and carpenters and framers above. And all of them—all the Chinese workers—now fought to work for the Foreign Devils. There were almost seventy thousand Chinese living in the Foreign Settlement, and many more awaited housing there. Richard almost laughed out loud when he remembered how he'd nearly lost everything he'd worked for because he couldn't find workers. Finding workers was no longer a problem.

He felt a tug at his sleeve and looked into Lily's brutalized face. The ear holes, all that remained after her ears had been cut off by the Manchus, were carefully covered with her hair, but there was nothing she could do about the absent nose—the dark blotch in the middle of her face. She indicated the metal thermos bottle in her hand. He nodded, and she poured dark musky tea into an almost translucent porcelain cup, then covered it with an equally translucent porcelain lid and handed it to him. The skin of the underside of her baby finger just grazed his palm and she smiled— inwardly.

He took the lid from the tea and drank deeply. The dense flavour, once so foreign to him, was now comforting. He looked at Lily and smiled as he remembered her help in the village where he was millstoned. And she had been with him ever since. Always there. Never demanding anything from him except the odd smile. He smiled again, and she seemed to smile back. It was hard to tell with her features.

She tightened the cap on the thermos bottle and retreated a few steps—and awaited another opportunity to help the man she loved.

* * *

"GONNA BE A FIGHT, a real big fight, and the Brits are going to help the Johnny Rebs to get back at the Yanks, and the Yanks are going to invade the Johnny Rebs, and the cotton's going to burn or be blockaded and Europeans are going to wear scratchy wool for the foreseeable future. You gonna finish that beer, son, or wha?"

Silas passed his half-finished mug of beer over to the man who he assumed was an American, although he hardly seemed religious, which most Americans, in Silas's experience, were. How religious could he be sitting in the whorehouse waiting his turn?

"First time, lad?"

Silas wasn't interested in answering the man's question and was pleasantly surprised when a hand landed on his shoulder and a lilting, French-accented voice said, "Don't bother with the fool's questions. Your brother tells me that he is buying you a birthday present."

Silas nodded, intoxicated by Suzanne Colombe's perfume. He said, "Yes. It's my birthday," then added quickly for some reason, "my twenty-first birthday."

"Milo told me," Suzanne said, then added with a smile, "he celebrated his birthday a few days early."

"Did he? Why? We were born on the same day." Then Silas added, stupidly, "We're twins."

Suzanne smiled and said sardonically, "Really, I would never have guessed."

"Is Milo here?"

"Usually, but not tonight." She thought of telling Silas that his brother was in one of her opium dens but decided against it. She was enjoying speaking English. "Milo told me that you have never experienced the clouds and the rain?"

Silas didn't catch the reference and asked for it in Mandarin, which Suzanne supplied. He shook his head quickly, "No." Then he added, "Not yet."

Suzanne put an arm through his and walked him into the next room. The slightest trace of opium smoke scented the air. But Silas didn't notice. His eyes and senses were filled with the array of women sitting, lounging, laughing, playing cards.

Suzanne prodded him in the ribs with her elbow. "Is there anything here that you like?"

Silas had seen her the moment he walked into the room. Tiny compared to the French and English women, the Han Chinese girl sat quietly to one side. Her flawless skin drawn tight across her cheekbones, her beautiful tapered fingers arranging the cascade of her jet-black hair.

"Ah," Suzanne said, "I see."

———

The girl's skin was cool to the touch and her tongue a lightness almost indistinguishable from the air itself. But alive. Her mouth a warmth and her hands in motion, unbuttoning, caressing, pulling ... then she stopped and stepped away from him.

Silas stood there, his pants and undergarments around his knees, not knowing what to do.

She pointed at his member.

For an instant he forgot how to speak Mandarin, then finally found his words. "Is something wrong?"

Still pointing, she asked, "Did it hurt when you lost it?"

He tried to smile, never having spoken of his circumcised member before, let alone to a girl who was pointing at it. "No."

"Ah," she said, and placed her hand, light as a feather, on its cap. Then she guided him between her thighs and put her arms around his neck. With her tongue deep in his mouth she gently put him on his back and then placed his hands on her small breasts and murmured, "We'll bring the clouds and rain, together."

And her nimble body moved on his and heat came from her—and Silas felt all this happening to someone else—not him.

* * *

PATTERSON'S REPORT of Silas's twenty-first birthday celebration began with the charming phrase, "And there were all sorts of White whores and he chose the one Chinee twat in the place."

Richard ignored him, wanting to talk about how to keep their work sites safe, but Patterson insisted on continuing, "It reflects on me too, sir. What young Silas does reflects on all of us in the Foreign Settlement, it does."

Richard needed Patterson. The man knew building, and his willingness to mix it up with the Chinese contractors had saved Richard a small fortune. And although Richard never really trusted him, he paid him well enough that he expected some honesty from him. "So, my son's behaviour reflects badly on you, does it?"

Patterson drew himself up to his full height and said, "On all of us. All of us. We are as good as occupying their country, sir. And there are millions of them Chinee and only a few of us. How are we going to control them if we treat them like equals? They are not our equals. They are not Whites, and we are. Simple as that." He looked away from Richard, whom he didn't consider a White at all but rather some kind of murky brown, then he muttered, "There are enough Chinee hotheads out there without shoving a hot poker up their butts by sleeping with their women. We need them to do what we say. We need them to work for us. We need them to accept our occupation. Your son doesn't seem to understand that."

Richard didn't completely disagree. He'd heard the rumblings before, and he was aware that it was a delicate matter to appease the upper-echelon Chinese so that they would continue to help keep the lower orders—well, in order. "Go find him and send him to me."

———

Milo entered with Silas. "I would like to stay, Father," he said.

"That might be, son, but this is between myself and your brother."

"But if it concerns him it concerns me, Father."

"Sometimes, Milo, but not this time." Richard pointed toward the door of his office, then made a "scat" gesture.

Milo turned to Silas, who shrugged his shoulders. "Go, brother mine," Silas said in Yiddish.

"What?" Milo asked in the Common Tongue.

"Go," Silas replied.

Milo left, and Richard made sure the door was firmly shut, then he turned to his son. Before he could speak, Silas challenged him in Farsi, "You wanted to see me, Father?"

"I did." Richard met the challenge in Farsi.

"Why?" Silas asked, switching to English.

"Because we have much to talk about," Richard replied in the Queen's tongue.

"Such as?" Silas asked in Mandarin.

"Don't question me, Silas," Richard replied in Mandarin.

"Well then, perhaps you need to question me, Father," Silas said in Cantonese.

"Enough of the games!" Richard snapped in Shanghainese.

Silas corrected Richard's use of the idiom, then said, "Fine," naturally, in Shanghainese. They had at least agreed upon the language of the argument. "What is troubling you, Father? I have done what you asked. I now spend time in the stables shovelling horse droppings, which was what you wanted."

"I want to understand what is going on with you."

That stopped Silas. For a brief moment he thought about telling his father his dark secret, but then he shrugged his shoulders and said, "Nothing is going on with me." Then he corrected Richard's word choice for the idiom "going on."

"Stop that. You know what I meant." Richard took a small cigar from a teakwood box on his desk and lit it. "You're not a boy any more." A smile crossed his face. "How did you like your twenty-first birthday present from your brother and me?"

That surprised Silas. So his father had contributed to his night at the House of Paris. "It was a very thoughtful gift, Father. Thank you."

Silas's formality brought a laugh to Richard's lips, but he suppressed it. "Why with her? Come on, son, answer my question. With all the French and English girls there, why choose the Chinese girl?"

Because I was trying to find someone who could make me feel something, he wanted to shout, but couldn't. It would just sound stupid. So he said, "Did Mademoiselle Colombe report my choice?"

"In English or Mandarin. I don't speak French."

"Sorry. Did Miss Colombe tattle on me?"

"No. An American who was there told Patterson and he—"

"The drunk who claimed that every European would be wearing scratchy shirts soon?"

Richard stopped and put down his cigar. "What's that about scratchy shirts?"

Silas told him of the man's claim of an oncoming civil war between the North and South in America and the inevitable blockade that would stop the cotton trade out of the Americas to Europe.

Richard picked up his cigar and allowed the smoke to float up through his fingers. Then he said, "Tell me that again, but slower, and any detail you can think of, no matter how small, I want to hear it." He reached to the buzzer on his desk and pressed it. Instantly a secretary from the front office opened the door.

"Describe the man," Richard ordered Silas.

The boy did.

Richard turned to the secretary. "Find him. Bring him here. Take as many men as you need. Kidnap him if necessary. My bet is a bottle of whisky should do the trick. And bring me any other American you can find who has arrived recently."

The secretary nodded and left.

Richard turned to Silas. For the first time in Silas's life he felt that his father actually wanted to hear him speak. It was possible that his father was actually smiling at him as he laced his hands behind his head and said, "Now tell me again about this drunken American."

* * *

AFTER TWO DAYS of interviewing Americans, Richard was ready—no eager.

He barged into Eliazar Vrassoon's private office and announced, "You win. I'm willing to leave the property game to you and your den of thieves." He recalled Milo advising him to stay abusive to avoid suspicion. That's why he was reeking of opium, despite the fact that he was stone-cold sober.

Then Richard threw the deeds to all of his properties on Vrassoon's desk. Just as he and Milo had planned it.

"Get out," the Patriarch said, with a steely cold that penetrated Richard's bones, and suddenly he wasn't sure he could pull it off, or that he wanted to pull it off. But he had lived his whole life walking on the edges of cliffs, going where others refused to go, and besides, he was there—actually in Vrassoon's office—so he charged on.

"What? Is it Shavuos? Sukkott, then? Damn, I never remember when ... or is it Simchas Torah   fuck, I always miss Simchas Torah."

"Get out!" the Patriarch repeated, but Richard noticed that the man's eyes were devouring the property deeds on the huge mahogany desktop.

"Maybe you're right," Richard said, reaching forward and collecting the deeds together in a drunkard's pile. Then he felt a deeper coldness enter him as the old man's hand rested on top of his—the land deeds beneath both.

"How much do you want for these marginal properties? I'm willing to be generous, but there is a glut of property now on the market and ..."

Richard slid his hand out from beneath the Patriarch's and, with what to Vrassoon was surprising dexterity, stacked the deeds and put them back in two large manila envelopes. "I think not. Perhaps I'd be better off with Hercules, or maybe even Dent's. I understand that both are angry that they didn't buy land when they could—that they left the field to us Yids."

The guards at the door made a move toward Richard, but Vrassoon signalled them to back off. "How many properties are we talking about, son?"

Richard resisted saying, *I'm not your son!* and managed to smile as he enumerated the number, location, and potential revenue of each of his one hundred and seven properties without ever referring to the deeds.

The rest was just dickering. Since Richard knew exactly how much he needed, he refused to sell when the offer was too low and accepted when the offer rose to his needs. The whole process took less than three hours— substantially less time than it had taken him to buy up the entire cotton crop from the Shanghai delta lands—the cheapest fine cotton available in the world outside of Egypt and of course the southern states of the United States of America, which just that morning had declared themselves independent from their federal government in Washington.

* * *

"HOW LONG should it take, Father?" Milo asked as he went over the last of the warehouse contracts that he had settled with Chen.

"For what, Milo?"

"For the price of our cotton to go through the ceiling, naturally."

Richard lit a cigar and leaned back in his chair. Lily immediately came forward and supplied a fresh ashtray. Richard blew the blue-grey smoke into the evening air and shrugged his shoulders.

Milo stopped what he was doing with the warehouse contracts and stared at his father. "You don't know? Hell's bells, you don't know!"

"We're traders, son, not mystics. We invest and hope. Sometimes we win, sometimes we lose."

"And if we lose this time?"

"We lose it all. Warehouses, trading routes, steamships, even the house we're standing in."

"You mortgaged our house?"

"There's no point in having only *some* of the Shanghai delta cotton."

"You bought the whole crop?"

"And optioned the next two years', as well. I think the Americans will be fighting with themselves for a long time."

"Over slaves?"

Richard shook his head. "That war has nothing to do with slaves. It's got to be about money, control, and, you can bet your last *tael,* religion.

Both sides claim to be doing God's will. And when religious nuts fight they fight for a long time. Usually until a new generation comes along and tells the old bearded zealots to put their guns up their own arses, that no one cares whose God or gods are right or wrong. That it's time to recognize the obvious, that the world is clearly a place of random occurrences and whim. If there is a God up there, son, he's bored silly with us and awakens only periodically to tinker with our hearts and destroy our lives." Milo stared at his father. "Worried about my immortal soul, are we?"

"No, Father, I don't give a damn about your immortal soul."

"Good, because I *have* no immortal soul, nor do you, nor do any of them."

"As you will."

"Fine, but what is it that is worrying you, then?"

"You cashed in everything that the Hordoons own, didn't you? Everything. If this goes bad we lose everything."

"Not true, son. Absolutely not true."

"Then you didn't sell everything we own?"

"Oh, that I did, son, that I did, every last item that had our names on it has been sold."

"Then I'm right, we could lose everything."

"Wrong."

"How am I wrong, Father?"

Richard began to laugh so hard that he had to take the cigar out of his mouth. He sputtered with laughter. He rocked with laughter. He giggled and guffawed and roared with laughter. And Milo couldn't help himself and joined his father—and Lily thought the two had gone mad, quite mad.

Finally Milo got control of himself and pulled his father to his feet by the lapels of his waistcoat. "So, Father, if you are wrong we end up with nothing."

His eyes streaming with tears of laughter, Richard shook his head. "Absolutely not you'll have seventeen warehouses full of cotton!"

* * *

WITHIN SIX MONTHS—six harrowing months in which Richard laid off his entire house staff, closed down all of his operations, and sold off the last of his ocean-going clippers—Richard's cotton gamble proved to be the single most successful commodities play the Middle Kingdom had ever seen. The cost of cotton doubled, then trebled, then doubled that—until finally Richard agreed to sell some of the only available cotton in the world—his Shanghai delta cotton—to keep the shirt factories of

Manchester and the textile factories of Lyon and the clothing factories of Bremen afloat.

And money the likes of which had never been seen—more even than the wealth of the Kadooris' rubber monopoly in Siam—flowed into the coffers of Shanghai's Hordoon and Sons.

"Why aren't you happy, Father? We won!" Milo asked.

Richard was still groggy from last evening's opium dreams. Groggy and haggard. He felt the snakes of opium trails in his blood, their slow, sinuous dance lingering where they were no longer wanted. He lunged toward the porcelain bowl in the water closet and doused his face with cold water, then looked in the mirror. The deep lines on his face surprised him. Behind him, in the mirror, his handsome son Milo stood waiting for him to answer his question. How handsome this boy was. How competent this boy was. How this boy loved him—how he loved this boy. He turned to face his adored son.

"Ask me again."

Milo did. "Why aren't you happy, Father?"

Richard thought of the report he recently received from the Pinkerton he had hired. The report informing him that his father had died in one of Vrassoon's warehouses and that the great man had thrown his father in the Ganges like so much rotten fruit. He thought of the simple two lines about his mother: "No definitive answers. But it is most likely she starved to death long ago." He sighed deeply, knowing that even that was not the reason for his unhappiness. *Because I'm haunted by whispers of a memory,* he wanted to say, but instead he put his hand on Milo's soft cheek and said, "The Vrassoons. The Vrassoons keep happiness from me."

"And me, Father."

"Good. Now let us finally do something about that damnable family. Look, Milo, the source of much of the Vrassoons' power is the English parliamentary decree that grants them the sole right to sail ships directly from England to China. Everyone else has to figure out elaborate trade and counter-trade provisions at the various stops—Malay, India, Singapore, Ceylon, India, and finally the Azores before they land in England. This costs time and money and opens the vessels to danger from the pirates in the China Sea and the Straits of Malacca, and from other enemy vessels. Ships that need to make that many stops must also be lighter in weight so they can run before the wind and hence carry only limited cannon."

"I know all this, Father, but—"

Richard charged on, "Not so the great Vrassoon boats of "the Company." Sometimes twice the size of ours and always armed to the teeth—the Company's ships are seldom the subject of attack. Their huge

Indiaman sailing ships load in the safety of Plymouth and land in the equal safety of Shanghai, stopping in the six-month voyage only for food and fresh water. It's a tremendous—and vastly unfair—advantage over us and all the other traders. And why do they have this advantage? Are they better businessmen than us? Do they work harder? Do they risk more? No and no and no." He reached into the top drawer of his desk, slid a finger under the hidden panel there, drew out the doctored photograph of Vrassoon's eldest son with the little girl, and tossed it on the desk. "And why can a Vrassoon do this to a little girl and ...?" That memory again tickled the back of his mind. But what slight chance he had of retrieving it had been forever forfeited by his nightly opium voyages. "Why?" he demanded.

"Because they have the British Parliament behind them, Father. This is nothing new."

"No, not new, but wrong, Milo. Wrong."

Milo reached across and looked at the photograph. He stared at the eldest Vrassoon son standing over the partially clothed Han Chinese girl with the flawless skin—maybe ten, maybe twelve years old—naked and bloody on the bed. The blood from between her legs had evidently sunk deep into the feather mattress.

Milo thought for a moment, then tossed aside the photograph. "Okay, what do you need to get back at these bastards, Father?"

"A way into the British House of Lords. Someone who knows those people. Someone who will do our bidding there."

Milo thought about that, and then about Mademoiselle Suzanne and all the people she knew. "Leave this with me, Father. I think I know where to start looking for just such a man."

* * *

HIS FATHER HAD CALLED HIM, in his calmer moments, Lord Snivel. *Well, maybe I am,* thought the Third Earl of Cheselwich, Lyndon Barrymore Bartlett Manheim by name, as he looked at the young, naked boy asleep on the bed. *Such fine skin. Fine brown skin,* he thought as he ran his hand along the boy's back. He'd like to pay this fine Chinese boy for the excellent services he'd so nimbly and obligingly rendered, but the Third Earl of Cheselwich had a problem. He was broke. Again.

The boy stirred, turned over, and stretched. Suddenly the boy was on his feet, seemingly not a boy any more—and the knife in his left hand was no child's toy.

The boy's right palm was open and the chunky sounds coming from his mouth, the Third Earl of Cheselwich assumed, were a demand for payment.

He'd heard that demand in many different languages since he had taken his father's unasked for advice and headed for "parts East to seek whatever fortune you can manage." His father had been right that he could play upon his title, and with the assistance of the three letters of introduction from his father's friends who were members of the British House of Lords many doors would open for him.

He straightened out his linen shirt and said, "Put down the knife. Don't be a silly bugger."

"*Gei qian!*"

"Ah, am I to assume you are demanding a payment for services rendered?"

"That's what he's asking for."

The Third Earl of Cheselwich spun around, his pudgy paw of a left hand flying to his puffy-lipped mouth, to find the source of the new voice in the room. After a brief squint his eyes discerned a dark-complexioned young man standing in the doorway. The young man, without so much as a by-your-leave, walked past him to the boy and said, "*Duo qian?*"— Mandarin for "How much?"

The Third Earl of Cheselwich saw the boy's eyes narrow and shrink to small black marbles. Then he spat out, "*Wu shi gang bi!*"

The dark young man laughed a hearty chortle and replied, "*Wu shi gang bi?* Fifty Hong Kong dollars is pretty steep."

The boy whore shrieked a high-pitched wail that hurt the delicate eardrums of the Third Earl of Cheselwich. Then the boy whore proceeded to pull at his own hair with such force that literally a hunk of the thick black stuff came out in his hand. As he did his knife swung wildly, often close to his face, and he shouted in English, "No, no, no!"

"I comprehended his response. Perhaps my language skills are increasing," said the Third Earl of Cheselwich with a smile.

"I sincerely doubt that," said the dark young man, who then threw up his hands and continued in English, "If he is as he is, and this circumstance is evidently as it is, then I leave you to each other." With that he turned to the door and headed out.

The Third Earl of Cheselwich lunged to follow the dark young man, but the boy whore shouted words that were clearly a warning.

"I don't think he wants you to leave before you pay him," said the dark young man, known to most of Shanghai's Foreign Settlement as one Milo Hordoon.

"My boy, I'd be in a state of unrelenting happiness if I had sufficient funds to cover the aforementioned expenses."

"Is that English you're speaking?"

"The Queen's own, and pure, I might add. The voice of Milton and Shakespeare, the ebb and flow of oral commerce, the tongue of the Sceptered Isle itself."

"Fine. But is it English, yes or no?"

"Put that way—English, yes."

"Fine. Did you agree on a price with the boy before you began?"

"Of course not. I'm a gentleman."

"And it would be too crude for ..."

"... a gentleman to barter for intimacy as a fishmonger does with a peasant woman or a simple shopkeeper would with a kitchen wench. Matters of the heart are beyond financial recompense."

Milo stared at the Third Earl of Cheselwich and smiled. His father would be pleased, very pleased, but he couldn't resist a bit more fun before he paid the fool's bill and brought him back to see the head of the Hordoon clan.

"What did he do for you?"

"Do? Do? We, he and I, partook in ..."

"Did you fuck him? Did he fuck you? Did you suck him off? Did he suck you off? Or did you just use your hands?" Milo wished that Silas were at his side to see this.

"My good lad!"

"No. Two mistakes. I'm not your lad and I'm certainly not good." He couldn't wait to tell Silas about that retort. "So, exactly where was your prick in all this, or his prick both of your pricks, where were they exactly?"

"Really!"

"This is China, sir. You may be in the House of Paris but make no mistake this is the Middle Kingdom and we here in the Middle Kingdom are not squeamish about pillow matters."

"How barbaric!"

"Not paying for contracted services is barbaric."

"Why, I've never in all my life ..."

"Cut it out or I'll leave you here with him and his very sharp, pointy knife."

After a moment the Third Earl of Cheselwich said, "Please don't."

Milo looked at the pathetic man. Probably closer to forty than thirty, pear-shaped and with a sickly pinky-white skin. The man's handcrafted leather shoes had clearly not been polished in some time, and his expensive linen shirt hung limp on his frame, as if it had been left out in the rain. Milo looked carefully but saw none of the telltale signs of cholera. If this clown was sick he wasn't coming anywhere near the Hordoon household, no matter what level of nobility he came from.

"So what did you do with the boy?" Milo asked as nonchalantly as he could manage.

To Milo's surprise the older man leaned over and whispered into his ear a litany of sexual acts and positions of some considerable length and variety.

When the surprisingly long recitation finished, Milo took a step away and said, "And how long did all this take?"

"Just under fifteen minutes, I expect."

"Really, under fifteen minutes for all of that?"

"I would appreciate your confidence in these matters, as one gentleman to another."

Milo stuck out his hand. "Milo Hordoon."

The Third Earl of Cheselwich took the proffered hand limply in his and mumbled his name and title. Milo asked for it a second time, and this time it was delivered with a bit more enthusiasm.

"So what can I do for you, your Earlship?"

"Your Lordship ... and I seem to be in a slight financial predicament."

"Ah, you'd like me to pay the boy for his no doubt expert ministrations."

"If that were possible I would be forever in your debt."

Milo peeled off a series of bills and handed them to the boy as he said to the Third Earl of Cheselwich, "Yes, you will be in my debt."

———

Richard looked at the almost nude body of the Third Earl of Cheselwich as he collected the cards from the table and said, "I thought you were a gambler, sir."

"I was ... I've been trying to ... could I have some of my clothing back? It's chilly."

"No, I'm sorry, but you lost your clothing to me in this fine game of whist."

"But I have nothing ..."

"You have those three letters."

"But sir, they are introductions from family friends."

"Powerful friends?"

"I guess they are powerful, yes."

Richard got up and went to his desk drawer and removed the doctored picture of the eldest Vrassoon son with the bleeding girl. He caught sight of Milo out of the corner of his eye. The boy nodded. Richard sat and threw the photograph on the tabletop. "Recognize him?"

"He's that Jew!"

"Careful. I asked you if you recognized him."

"I do ... what's he doing with—"

"I can arrange it that you have an income of seven hundred pounds sterling per annum from this day forward until you finally pass away. Would that interest you?"

"Well, yes, it would, but what ...?"

"Would you have to do?" Richard pushed the picture into his hands. "Deliver that and several copies of it to your family's powerful friends. And your financial future is assured."

* * *

THE BRITISH HOUSE OF LORDS might not have been the most exclusive club in the world, but it certainly pretended it was. And like all would-be important institutions, it could be stirred to defend its supposedly untarnished reputation with the same avidity that a lioness shows in defending her favourite cub from attack. But action was not the métier of the House of Lords. Slow, considered discussion and then assignment to committee were the normal patterns of this august body. Never starting a session before ten-thirty in the morning and seldom sitting past teatime, the House of Lords was a luxurious, courteous debating society for the indolently privileged. But when Richard's photograph of the eldest son of one of its members circulated in their private clubs and drinking dens, a strange thing began to happen. Outrage stirred these old souls to the most unusual of things in the House of Lords—action.

Naturally, taking action was easier when the offending member was not really one of their own. "These Vrassoons are Hebrews, aren't they?" A Hebrew was never really a part of British nobility. A Jew was not one of them. A kike should watch his p's and q's—and those of his eldest son. The fact that many owed money to the Vrassoons simply added a certain zest to their enterprise.

Eliazar Vrassoon had responded to a cryptic message received from his head man in London by sailing on the first clipper from Shanghai to Britain. He had been back just over a month when he found himself sitting in the deep leather Windsor chair and resisting putting his head in his hands. He'd been shown the photograph that evening. The man addressing him was a younger member of the House of Lords, from the standards and procedures committee or some such thing, but it was clear to Vrassoon that the man had the full support of the House. The photograph explained the sidelong glances he'd received since his return to London, and why people left his club the moment he arrived. Even at Bedlam there seemed to be a peculiar distance.

"Have you shown this to …?"

"Some of us in the House of Lords have seen it."

"How many?"

"More than enough!"

Vrassoon couldn't believe it. Members had seen, and no one had contacted him. Not one of these creatures whom he had bailed out of financial straits of their own making, not one of them had had the decency to at least warn him.

The image of the little girl on the farm blossomed in his mind and the thunderous reality that this was God's punishment for his sins fell on him. His hands flew up and then just stayed there. Around him he noticed other men peering in his direction. Men he had thought were his friends.

The man was speaking, but Vrassoon was having trouble focusing. Finally he heard a snippet, "We are considering asking the Queen to revoke your seat in the House of Lords."

"Can you do that?" he said before he could stop himself. The smile that came to the little man's face was one that Eliazar Vrassoon—that all Jews—recognized. So it was about that, too. Finally he said, "What do these noble lords want?"

"Excuse me?"

"Has a sudden deafness taken you? You heard me. You came for something. What? These honourable members would like the world to believe that they are above bartering, but they are not! So, what do they want from me to keep this picture secret?"

After only the slightest pause the little man said, "They want you to renounce your monopoly on trade from England to China, so that the companies with which they are associated can receive the same benefits that you and yours do."

It stunned the Vrassoon Patriarch. Was that the reason? Why now? But he couldn't think about it. "And if I refuse to renounce what is mine?"

"The photograph will go to Her Majesty and then be given to the press. Many of whom would be only too glad to publish it."

"They wouldn't dare."

The young man stood. "Are you sure of that? Would you really be willing to risk the reputation of your entire family on the honourable intentions of our Fleet Street press? Are you willing to risk a pogrom in London?" He withdrew a formal document with a royal seal on the bottom and the imprimatur of Britain's House of Lords emblazoned across the top.

Eliazar Vrassoon scanned the document—"fully renounce"—"as of the signing of"—"all title to and assumption of"—words. Words that would bring him to heel, like a disobedient dog who was finally muzzled tight enough that he could be whipped.

"Sign it, Jew."

The young man was enjoying himself.

The Vrassoon Patriarch looked at the document and forced his mind to race through the possibilities. Then took the proffered fountain pen from the young man and signed away the source of his greatest wealth in a single pen stroke.

———

Two hours later the eldest Vrassoon son stared down at the rail tracks beneath the bridge. He felt strangely calm. Almost light-headed. He'd taken this very train several times to Paddington Station and from there ... He decided not to think of where he went from Paddington.

The rain had finally stopped and there was an inkling that the sun might come out. *Come out and bless the day,* he thought. Then he heard the Paddington-bound commuter train in the distance. He looked at his watch. *Right on time.* The sound of the approaching train grew louder behind him. He climbed up to the railing of the bridge and balanced himself against a strut. He looked up. *I will know, presently,* he thought. The train whistle sounded shrilly as it charged toward his bridge. He thought, just before he jumped, that he heard a young girl call his name. But he may have been mistaken.

* * *

IN SHANGHAI, news of the Vrassoons' loss of their monopoly set off one of the biggest parties that even this town, very used to big parties, had ever seen. Jiang and Suzanne marked the occasion by cutting the rates on their wares, and the clear, cool evening was ideal for an all-night drunk. All of Shanghai participated. Those who had never been in the Foreign Settlement or the French Concession came with their whole families. Fortune tellers set up shop on every corner, and there were no constables to be seen. Store owners stacked bales of hay in front of their stores for protection from the inevitable window-breaking and looting, then joined the party. The whole city sang and staggered and drank and danced.

As the old clock in Richard's room clanged three bells, Lily knelt and lit the opium ball she'd prepared for him. It was the fourth Richard had inhaled that evening. Outside there was the sound of revelry the odd

275

gunshot and the subsequent sound of sirens. Richard propped himself up on an elbow to inhale the sweet smoke and muttered to Lily, "Sirens outside, sirens inside, it's all one, Lily, it's all one."

Later that night the Shanghai *Star Standard* dropped its stack of morning papers on the corner of Nanking and Henan Lu. The crowds were still out and the drink was still flowing, so no one noticed the banner headline: "TAIPINGERS THREATEN TO ERADICATE OPIUM FROM THEIR TERRITORY." The subhead read "TAIPINGERS CLOSE DOWN OPIUM DENS AND ARREST TRADERS."

chapter thirty-seven

Final Journey

The City of Nanking and the City of Shanghai
1863–64

No one ever claimed that the Taipingers were sparing in their use of the rod, or that the Taiping Kingdom of Heaven, Nanking, was a place of peace and tranquility. But even the hardest of the hard hearts of the Taiping faithful were shocked by the display that awaited them when they reported for work on the cold morning of April 21, 1863. Despite the horror, they stood and gawked without saying a word, knowing that any show of sympathy or revulsion would be taken as an act of sedition against the state of the Heavenly King. So there was just a profound silence in the ancient city—a silence broken only by a periodic whimper of pain from one of the seven hundred men who had been crucified upside down on wooden crosses and were now on public display in the central square of the city. The seven hundred men now awaited, with various degrees of patience, the balm of death that was still several days and nights away.

Hung from the feet of each of the inverted, crucified men was a placard proclaiming the victim's involvement with the *Fan Kuei*'s Devil drug, opium.

None of the shocked spectators doubted that the men, now impaled through their feet and hands and dripping blood from their ears and eyes, were involved with the opium trade. In fact many of the onlookers began to make plans to escape Nanking and Taiping control, since they themselves were either storing, supplying, importing, or using the *Fan Kuei*'s tar-like bringer of dreams.

But these crucifixions were only the beginning of the Taiping campaign against opium. These crucifixions were literally for local consumption. The ones that followed were unapologetic threats—threats to the entire *Fan Kuei* community.

* * *

HERCULES'S GOUT HAD RETURNED with a vengeance after his night of drinking. *Damn,* he thought, *a little pleasure, a tiny little pleasure, and He takes his revenge.* Hercules was in such pain that he almost missed the commotion on the Bund Promenade down below him. He carefully placed his gout-afflicted foot on the cold flagstones of the floor and made his way over to the large, leaded window that overlooked the Bend in the River. Pushing open the large pane, he was at first unsure what it was that he saw—then he recoiled in horror, and in so doing slammed the gout nodule on his foot against the wall. But he was in too much shock to feel the pain.

———

Percy St. John Dent was returning from a night at the House of Paris when he first saw them, and before he knew it he had thrown up his entire extravagant dinner into the murky waters of the Huangpo River.

———

Jedediah Oliphant, head of the House of Zion, called to his assistants to get horses. They galloped past the American guards at the crossing point of the Suzu Creek and down to the Bund river-promenade, where a huge crowd had formed. Jedediah at first couldn't discern why he found this particular large crowd so disconcerting, then he figured it out. There were literally thousands of souls here, but there was total silence. There was never silence in Shanghai! Then he heard a moan from the river and looked at the six ships there—and froze.

———

Jiang had been the first to see them and had immediately sent for the Fisherman and the Confucian—and there they stood at the far end of the promenade at the Bend in the River and stared at the six ships, their tall masts denuded of sails, slowly swaying—like a stately matron at a lavish ball who had consumed one too many glasses of fine champagne and was somehow disoriented in her own home. But these ships were not matrons at a ball. They were warnings—graphic warnings etched in the blood and the pain of the hundreds of men who hung, head down, nailed to the masts of the boats in mockery of the Crucifixion. Even from a distance their cries for help could be heard when the wind blew shoreward. Then the wind would shift, throwing their voices away from the shore toward the Pudong, and the onlookers would have the odd sensation that the pain had suddenly ceased and that the men were somehow just acrobats holding unusual positions on the tall masts. Then, just as unexpectedly, the wind would blow shoreward and the cries of pain would fill every ear.

Just as mysterious as the arrival of the boats was the seemingly magical and very sudden appearance of thousands of pamphlets in the crowd of onlookers.

Jiang grabbed one of the poorly printed things from the rickshaw boy beside her and read it quickly. "Behold what befalls those who have traffic in the Devil's drug. See and take warning what happens to those who do the Devil's work in the Heavenly Kingdom." It was signed by the Heavenly King.

The Confucian looked at Jiang and said, "We'll meet tonight in the Warrens. Inform the Carver."

———

"Not exactly an understated message, that," remarked Percy St. John Dent as he poured himself a healthy glass of Hercules's very fine sherry.

"Well, no one ever claimed that the Taipingers were fond of any form of subtlety," replied Hercules from his high-backed chair.

Percy took a tiny sip of the sherry and said, "Oh, very good, Hercules, very good indeed. So what exactly was the message meant to say, gentlemen?"

"Can't your interpreter read the pamphlet for you?" asked the Vrassoon Patriarch from behind his steepled fingers.

"Oh, that part of the message was clear enough. It's the other part of the message that bothers me," said Richard abruptly reminding the others that he was in the room.

"What other part?"

"The unwritten part. The part that says that they can come and go whenever and wherever they please. That they have only left us alone up until now because they wanted to, not because they had to. That they live amongst us. They cook for us, clean our houses, move our goods, look after our children. That we are in their country not they in ours."

What followed was a silence unlike any that the traders could remember. Their meetings were complicated, bombastic affairs, not contemplative meetings of minds, which suddenly this conclave had become.

Finally Oliphant asked, "Whose ships were they?"

"What does it matter?" asked Vrassoon. "The message they carried was evident and clear."

"Perhaps, but if we knew …"

"Are you suggesting that we track down the shipowners and see who's doing business with the Taipingers? Look around you, here. We are all doing business with them. If we didn't, we couldn't exist," said Hercules.

"This is mad. This is the act of a madman," Percy said.

"Of a madman who thinks he is the brother of Jesus Christ," scoffed Oliphant.

"Not a madman, just a religious man, like several of you in this room," said Richard flatly. Then with a smile he added, "So madness is to be taken for granted."

Oliphant immediately rose to the bait, but Vrassoon signalled him to sit down and turned to Richard. "We have had our differences in the past."

"Really? What differences?"

"Fine, even had we been friends of the heart for years it makes no difference. We are both now facing a real danger to ourselves and our families and our businesses."

"I am in the cotton business."

"Ah, yes, the cotton business. A safe business. But what is to stop the Taipingers from next suggesting that all trade from the Middle Kingdom is to be done only by Chinamen? What's to stop them from doing that? Then what happens to your brilliant speculation and your tons of cotton? Do you think your Chinese workers would defend your cotton against the Taipingers? Would they risk being nailed to posts for your cotton?"

Richard reluctantly nodded agreement.

"Good," said Eliazar Vrassoon, "then you'll contact your crazy brother? He's a man of some power and suasion in Taiping circles, I'm told. Go to him. Talk some sense into him."

Richard looked out the window at the gathering clouds, then finally nodded again and said, "I'll set out tonight."

———

"Why does Milo get to go and I have to stay?" complained Silas as he backed into a paddock to allow a large black horse past him.

Richard patted the animal's shining flank, then stroked the boy's hair and said, "Next time I'll take you."

"But I want to see Uncle Maxi. It may be the last time—"

"It won't be!" Richard's voice was hard as granite. Then he softened as he said, "Don't worry. Your Uncle Maxi is indestructible. He'll be around for a long time yet. Patterson, are the supplies waiting for us?"

"They're all aboard, sir. Are you going to take horses too?"

"Just these two."

"Done, sir."

"Good. Come on, Silas, cheer up. With Milo and me gone, you're the head of the House of Hordoon, that's got to be worth something." The boy tried to smile but managed only a rough approximation. His father grabbed him to his chest in a bear hug, then turned on his heel and left Silas alone with Patterson.

"Why couldn't I go too?" Silas whined as he kicked at the hay in the stables.

"Probably because monkey-lovers aren't wanted on the voyage," Patterson said smoothly as he picked up the shovel and tossed it to Silas, with a simple command that made it perfectly clear who was in charge of the House of Hordoon while Richard was away. "Muck up, monkey-lover."

* * *

RICHARD'S TRIP WITH MILO to Nanking was closely monitored by the Manchus. Their patrol boats, which controlled the lower stretches of the Yangtze, accompanied Richard's large junk right up to the disputed waters just west of the Grand Canal across from Chinkiang. Thereafter, for twelve hours, the junk sailed without escort. But on the following morning Taiping ships came up on either side of their boat and silently stayed to starboard and port all the way to Nanking, the seat of the Heavenly King.

To Richard's surprise the welcome in Nanking, although not effusive, was openly friendly. A modest banquet was set for him, followed by a performance of the History Teller's Peking Opera company's final act of *Journey to the West*. The entirety of the piece's seven acts took almost nine hours to perform, so usually only sections of it were acted at any given time. The section they showed this evening was the end, entitled "Partings."

As the sun set, the presentation ended with the Serving Man turning away from the falling sun and striding off—back to his home in the East. The crowd was on its feet applauding the elegantly understated sorrow. As Richard leapt to his feet the actors stepped forward, turned, and applauded to their right. And there, to Richard's shock, was his brother Maxi—that damned red kerchief around his neck—stepping forward to accept the applause of both actors and audience as the patron of the company.

———

"So, I assume you are here to talk some sense into your wild, red-haired sibling, is't so, brother mine?"

"Aye."

"Well, that could be something in the doing," Maxi said, showing his full mouth of large, white teeth.

And then, suddenly, they were in each other's arms, hugging each other with an ardour that surprised them both. Then, just as suddenly an odd embarrassment came upon them and they each took a step back. An awkward silence followed, which Maxi finally broke.

"Milo looks a fine young man."

"He is. Strong like you, and wild like you."

"And Silas, why'd you not bring him too?"

Richard looked away. He really didn't know why he hadn't brought Silas with him, just a feeling. At last he said, "Someone has to look after the shop while I'm gone."

"So you finally turned him into a businessman?" Maxi asked with open astonishment.

"Not really," Richard replied. "He's a fine linguist, though, and could be of real use to us."

"To you. There is no *us* any longer, brother mine."

"But Maxi ..."

"Do I have to set you on your keister in front of your son to prove my point? 'Cause I will, if that's necessary. You promised me that I could go back if I didn't find what I wanted in our new business. Well I didn't find it, brother mine, so I moved back, to here." He indicated his ripening fields of sorghum and soya beans and his large stand of bamboo. "And I'm happy here. Happier than I've been since we left India."

"I see," Richard said.

"I don't think you do. Look at this place. Look at my crops, and my wife, and our child. Look—allow yourself to really see, brother mine. This is the kind of place that could rid you of the opium addiction that rules you. I could help you. We could all help you here—and love you here, brother mine."

———

SHANGHAI

His final night in Nanking, Richard dreamt of the old Hindu man who had surprised them in the alley of the town outside the Works at Ghazipur—and the man's curse of one brother murdering another rang in his ears until he forced himself from sleep and watched for hours as the sun rose over another dangerous day. He longed for the escape that only opium could offer him. But it was not only the opium he wanted. He felt somehow incomplete—was it Maxi he missed? Perhaps. But more likely it was the constant, silent presence of Lily for which he longed.

———

Maxi kissed Milo on the cheek, then said to him, "Tell your brother I look forward to meeting him, now that he is a man like you." He turned to Richard and said, "There is still time for you to decide to stay with us here."

"There is still time for you to convince these people to stop this madness."

"Stopping the selling of a drug that kills people is madness in your way of thinking? Opium is the Devil's drug."

"You've been with these fanatics too long."

"Perhaps. But you've also been with your fanatics too long too, brother mine."

———

The History Teller watched the parting of the two White men on the south Nanking docks. As their leave-taking proceeded, words flew into her head:

On a dock, in sallow light,
Brothers say final goodbyes,
As men do to the world
From their death beds.

———

The Assassin watched the History Teller watching the two *Fan Kuei,* and for the first time in a long time he felt blood fill the hood of the cobra that had been carved into his back. The snake arched up, and the Assassin's head snapped back as his arms pulled tight to his sides. To his surprise his right hand came forward holding the swalto blade that glinted in the fading light. The only word that came to him as he looked at the killing

283

instrument in his hand was "hunger." Yes, the snake on his back and the knife in his hand were hungry—hungry for blood.

———

Richard and Milo travelled back to Shanghai in almost total silence. A silence that was broken only by the few words needed between father and son to allow a day to proceed. Both felt the heavy weight of failure on their shoulders and the ominous movement of history. Milo even smelled the reek of ozone.

When they finally docked in the Pudong, Richard took a bumboat to the Bund and reported his failure to the traders gathered there. His report was greeted by another kind of silence. He stood there waiting for their comments. None was forthcoming. Finally he turned on his heel and left. No one moved to stop his going.

* * *

"WHAT DOES IT MATTER?" the Vrassoon Patriarch said to Hercules and Percy St. John Dent. "We will still need the Royal Navy—actually, we deserve the Royal Navy's support in this little matter. Her Majesty makes a fortune by taxing the tea we sell in England, tea that can only be bought from the Chinese with the money we make by selling them opium. And that tea tax accounts for just under thirty-two percent of Her Majesty's annual taxation revenues."

"That much?"

"Perhaps more. And that tax money pays for roads and schools and hospitals and orphanages and more ships for the Royal Navy. It pays for England itself. England is paid for with the proceeds from the opium that we sell to the Chinese. Make no mistake about that. And now it is time for England to do its fair share in this joint enterprise."

"But with the Royal Navy?"

"Why not? What else are they doing at anchor in Hong Kong and Macao? It's time to show these rebels that it is one thing to defeat the Manchus but quite another to take on the forces of the British Empire."

Percy smiled, and then added, "Perhaps a Sikh regiment would be a useful addition. I understand that they hate Celestials with a passion—something to do with religious differences."

"Perhaps," Vrassoon said, "perhaps Sikhs would be the ideal people to show these rebels what violence really looks like." He paused and then added, "They might be of use should our dear Queen decide that the Manchu Empress needs a lesson as well."

* * *

WHEN THE ROYAL NAVY began to arrive in force at the Bend in the River, Richard headed down to the Shanghai docks. He was pleased to find Admiral Gough was in charge of the military side of the mission. He was even more pleased when the Admiral remembered him and willingly took him onboard as an extra translator, and then insisted that he wear the uniform of a British lieutenant.

As Gough turned to more pressing business, Richard took the opportunity to explore the ship. There had been definite advancements from the vessel upon which he had sailed upriver in 1841. But the intent was the same—to terrorize. Every available space on the great sailing ship was devoted to armaments—every space except the forward hold, where, much to Richard's surprise, there were four billiards tables stacked one on top of another.

"The men need to be entertained, Mr. Hordoon," said Gough from behind him.

"Sorry, sir," Richard said. "I didn't know you were there."

"Well I am." He hesitated for a moment, then asked, "Is it true that your wild brother is a commander with the Taipingers?"

"So it would seem, sir."

"Ah," the Admiral said. "Well, a siege can be a very long process, and the greatest impediment to success can be boredom amongst the troops. Hence these billiards tables."

"I see." Richard smiled, then mused, "The click of billiards balls give dreadful note of preparation."

The Admiral smiled and responded, "The country cocks do crow, the clocks do toll ..."

"... and the third hour of drowsy morning name. Proud of their numbers and secure in soul, the confident and over-lusty English do the low-rated Taipingers play at billiards."

"Very good, Mr. Hordoon. You know your Shakespeare."

"Some. A certain Thomas De Quincy suggested it as an antidote to a bad habit of mine."

"Interesting, Mr. Hordoon." It was evident that the Admiral wanted to pursue the topic but decided, out of decency—one gentleman to another—to let it go. "We'll take Nanking, Mr. Hordoon, of that you may be sure. It's just a matter of time. But during that time there's only so much building and toting to be done. Basically a siege is a matter of starvation. And a big city like Nanking can take many months to starve."

Richard thought about another conversation on a similar ship about starvation. But that seemed a lifetime ago.

"These are also very helpful in passing the time," the Admiral said, holding up a broad cricket bat. At first Richard assumed that the Admiral was referring to the bat as an enforcer of discipline, then he realized that the man was talking about entertaining the troops again.

Richard looked at the Admiral holding the cricket bat and said, "Is this a party or a war, sir? Surely the Taipingers will mount a counterattack against your positions both on land and sea."

The Admiral smiled. "I doubt that."

"Excuse me, sir?"

"Do you know what those are?" he said, pointing to several large cannon-like weapons that had eight narrow barrels attached together and a crank behind them. "They're called Gatling guns, and they'll change everything. A single man can now fire hundreds of rounds a minute by turning that handle. These guns will protect our heavy cannon batteries so no force on earth can get to them. With these Gatling guns as protectors, our cannon can fire day and night without fear of assault—even from that crazy brother of yours. Think of it, Mr. Hordoon: One man can kill hundreds in a few minutes. Forget about sallies from Nanking. They may try it once, but certainly not a second time."

Richard stared at the awful thing.

"Things change, Mr. Hordoon. Things change."

Richard found himself breathing deeply—and for the first time smelling something acrid in the air.

* * *

TWO WEEKS LATER Maxi found himself roused from his bed by Cupid, and the look on the man's bow-shaped mouth was grim.

"British," he said, clearly. "Many British."

Maxi threw aside his blanket and kissed his wife goodbye. Then he went to the children's room. His wife's two little girls slept in one bed, entwined, thin limbs around and through and about each other, loosed hair a combined tangle of dark beauty. He touched each of their faces, then moved to the small bed of his daughter. To his surprise, her eyes were wide open despite the early hour. When he went to kiss her she turned her head aside. Her mane of red-tinged black hair fell across her face. Her mouth that never smiled opened and closed but said nothing.

"Say goodbye to your papa."

She turned, tears in her eyes, and said, "Come back, Papa, come back to me."

Two hours later Maxi walked the south walls of Nanking with Cupid and three of his most experienced commanders at his side. There, arrayed like lines on a canvas, were six brigades of British troops. In their centre was a regiment of Sikhs in full battle dress. The entire assembly stood stock-still while behind them four British men-o'-war came about and positioned themselves to shell the walls of the ancient city.

"*Ta men ma shang jiu kai shi wa jue ma, xian sheng?*" asked one of his commanders.

Maxi's translator said, "Commander Wu asks if they will start digging soon."

Maxi shook his head. Suddenly he was pleased that six weeks earlier he had ordered the building of an underground trench system attached to an oil reservoir. Only he knew that it would be the city's last line of defence.

"*Na hao, mei shi me hao pa de. Wo men de cheng qiang jian bu ke cui.*"

"He says then there is nothing to fear, as the walls of our city are strong. Unassailable."

Maxi let out a long, low sigh. "Tell him that's not true. Look over there," he said, pointing to the west. There the Manchu bannermen were planting stakes in the ground. "How many?" he asked.

"I count fourteen banners, sir."

"Fourteen Manchu legions, four British men-o'-war, and at least six brigades of British troops—our walls have never been challenged by such a force."

"But—"

"Open the evacuation tunnels out of the city for the women and children."

Cupid took a step aside, and Maxi said, "What?"

"I already looked, sir. They've all been blocked in the night. No one in the city is leaving. Besides, the Heavenly King wouldn't permit retreat from the seat of the Heavenly Kingdom, would he?"

Maxi ignored the comment about the Taiping King, who no doubt had his own way out of the city. But it shocked him that the attackers had bothered to block routes that were clearly to be used by women, children, and elders. Maxi had made sure that the routes were narrow so that any attacker would know that they were not exit or egress routes for soldiers and armaments. They were just wide enough for a person carrying a load on his back.

"Are you sure?" Maxi asked.

"About the escape routes? Yes, sir. Two were blasted closed in the middle of the night, three others have cannon stationed facing them. They seem to have a new weapon, sir?" He pointed to the crest of a nearby hill and handed Maxi a spyglass.

Maxi looked through the glass and saw a large mounted gun with several barrels and a crank on it. He panned down to the mechanism and gasped. His keen mechanical mind quickly saw how the rotation mechanism worked the rifle barrels. He panned across the field and spotted six more of these instruments of death. Each of them was set between Nanking and the batteries of heavy cannon that were aimed at the city walls.

He was about to ask if anyone had seen these weapons work when the first of the British batteries on the north side of the city loosed a barrage of cannonballs aimed at the walls, and scrap metal aimed high over the walls to lacerate and slice and terrorize the inhabitants of the seat of the Heavenly Kingdom.

Maxi turned to see the damage caused by the first barrage and was amazed to see fires spring to life in the city. A turret on the south wall was leaning dangerously as its supporting brickwork caved in under the onslaught.

Maxi turned to Cupid and said, "Is your family safe?"

Cupid shrugged his shoulders. "Is yours?"

Maxi turned his head away from the man. Then the four men-o'-war fired all ninety-six cannons at once—and the terror grew.

For three days the English batteries thundered without let-up. The destruction in the city was manageable, but it would undoubtedly get worse with time. What took the most serious toll on the city was the lack of sleep. Through his spyglass Maxi saw the head gunners looking at pocket watches before signalling their men to fire. Maxi surmised that some inventive person had organized it so that the cannons didn't fire in any sort of regular, repeating pattern. Instead they fired intensely, then stopped, then fired sporadically, then stopped altogether, then fired intensely again. Maxi timed the intervals and they were never the same. Someone understood that people could adapt to noise so long as it occurred in some sort of regular pattern, but random loud blasts robbed the city of Nanking of sleep. After three days without sleep, the fabric of discipline a city needed to survive a siege was already beginning to fray.

In the early evening of the fourth night of the siege Maxi gathered his most trusted men. Men with whom he'd been to war. Men who had trusted his decisions. Men who had followed him and, under his leadership, had defeated the best units of the Manchu bannermen.

Maxi tried to smile, but he was troubled. He hadn't seen those strange guns work so he didn't know exactly how to attack them. He'd sent out several small decoy parties, but none had been able to draw fire from the things. As well, most were placed far enough from the city walls that the Taiping cannon couldn't reach them.

"Sir?" It was Cupid. He was holding out Maxi's red kerchief.

"Thanks," Maxi said, as he took the thing and put it around his neck. Then he turned to his men and said, "One more time, gentlemen—and I use the term loosely."

A cheer went up—and Maxi finally smiled.

Maxi and his men emerged from the sewage drain and assembled along the side of the stinking cesspool. Cupid touched Maxi on the shoulder and pointed at the sky. A large, dark cloud was moving slowly across the new moon. Maxi nodded and the word was passed. When the cloud obscured the moon they would charge the British southern battery, which continued its barrage of the city.

Maxi looked up. The edge of the cloud tipped across the point of the new moon. He tapped Cupid's shoulder and the men emerged from the tall reeds of the cesspool and crept toward the southern battery with the strange gun in front of it.

Then they were running.

Maxi felt the wind on his face, and his blood surged. His senses moved forward to his skin and his eyes became bright. A fight! He'd always loved a fight.

Four hundred yards and still no resistance.

The large black cloud completely obscured the slender moon. The lanterns from the British tents in the far distance were the only points of light in the pitchy dark.

Three hundred yards and the British hadn't spotted them. They increased their pace to an all-out sprint.

Suddenly light.

A trench of oil on his left sprang to life.

Maxi looked. *That can't be right. The trench should be in front of the battery to protect it. Not to one side. What was the point of having it to one side?*

Then something spat bullets—hundreds of them pinging off rocks, whizzing past his ears, thudding sickeningly into the flesh of his men. Cupid whirled around and crashed into Maxi, his right arm almost severed from his body, a bloody blotch where his left eye should have been. Maxi held him. He took the red kerchief from his neck and wrapped it tightly around Cupid's face, trying to staunch the bleeding from the empty eye socket. Another bullet had hit a vein, and blood was raining down.

Cupid's hot blood quickly coated Maxi's face. Through the blood he stared ahead at the thing spitting bullets. A single man stood there cranking something that fired the bullets. Behind him British officers drank beer. Some carried pool cues. All of them cheered.

Maxi looked to the fire trench and he understood why it was there to one side, not in front of the gun battery. It was there to light the scene! As though it were a play. The fire wasn't for protection, it was for illumination. His men were dying to provide entertainment for the British!

Three more slugs hit Cupid hard in the back and yanked him from Maxi's arms.

Maxi took a quick look at his old friend, then yelled to the others, "*Che! Che!*—Back! Back!" It was one of the few Mandarin words he knew, and he'd never had occasion to use it on a battlefield. But with this new weapon he had no choice.

Of his just under two hundred men, only seventeen made it back to the sewage drain. As they gathered, the dark cloud cleared the new moon, and in the thin moonlight the men saw their comrades littering the field while the British toasted the man who had cranked the strange new weapon.

Maxi felt liquid on his face. At first he thought it must be Cupid's blood, but then he realized he was wrong. It was his own tears.

———

Richard witnessed the appalling slaughter. He never saw Maxi, although after the firing stopped he ran out on the battlefield and spotted a red kerchief on one of the dead Taipingers.

And then he heard them and looked up. Vultures. Their dark forms filled the sky, obliterating the stars. Battlefield dead always attracted carrion birds, but somehow this carnage, this open field charnel house, drew more of them than Richard had ever seen. More and bigger. It disgusted him that the British returned to their games of billiards as the great birds tore lobes of grey livers and purple strings of intestines from the dead and dying.

He reached down and retrieved the red kerchief from the body, which had been badly mutilated by the Gatling gun's large-calibre bullets. As he folded it carefully he began to think of how to get into Nanking and save his brother and his family from the inevitable bloodletting that was about to befall the capital of the Heavenly Kingdom.

Richard stood at the crest of the hill looking over the farmland to the south of the city, where Maxi's farm ... had been. All that remained were the burned stubs of field crops and the lonely hearthstones of burned out farmhouses. It took Richard a while to orient himself so that he could find what remained of Maxi's farm.

Roving Manchu warriors were everywhere. On occasion a woman's cry would cut through the sound of burning. Rape was never a silent activity, and in war it was often a spectator sport. Oddly, the screams of the victims seemed to intensify the fury of the Manchus.

Richard was challenged by Manchus several times, but with his British officer's uniform and his command of Mandarin he talked himself past every checkpoint.

It wasn't until dawn that he picked up a trail from talking with two terrified farm women. They pointed to a hill to the west.

It took Richard two days to find Maxi's wife. One of her daughters had been dragged from her arms by Manchu soldiers and she hadn't been seen since; the other had been viciously raped and now hid behind her mother's skirts. Maxi's wife held their little girl in her arms as if frightened to let the child out of her grasp. But the girl just stared, seemingly unafraid, into Richard's eyes.

Maxi's wife suddenly drew in a sharp breath and pointed at Richard. It was only then Richard realized that he was wearing Maxi's kerchief around his neck. "No. No, don't think that. I didn't find his body. If anyone can stay alive in this hell it's my brother Maxi."

He gave her the red kerchief and she clutched it to her breast. Then he gave her all the money he carried, although he wondered if currency was of any value in a war zone. He questioned her about Nanking. About exits and entrances. About refugee routes. About where she should meet up with him and her husband. They agreed on a place. She asked, "When?"

Richard didn't know what to say, then it occurred to him. "Watch the Manchu banners in the field. When they head toward the city you go to that place to meet us. Once the Manchus are in the city it's all but over."

But the siege wore on and on. Dogs and cats were the first obvious victims in the ancient capital. They simply disappeared. Then the plants and grass were gone. Eventually even the weeds disappeared from the park lands. Stomachs distended. Envy caused fights to break out everywhere. And finally the most unwelcome, although most common, of guests came to visit the terrorized, weakened citizenry of Nanking—cholera.

And yet the city did not fall. The walls were punctured during the day and repaired at night. Fires roared through the city from incendiary bombardments but were put out by organized, although depleted, teams of Taipingers.

A strange, unofficially sanctioned kind of trade began between those under siege and those doing the sieging. At first it was just the trading of creature comforts from the homes of the Nanking residents for food from the soldiers. Then began a brisk trade in antiquities for food. Finally, anything of any value in the city was traded for food. It was under this rubric that the History Teller's troupe was traded to the Manchu Commander for two fat sows.

———

"Welcome," the Manchu Commander said to the History Teller as he openly admired her beauty.

"Are you a follower of the arts, Commander?"

"If they are your arts, I am sure that I am a follower."

"Then shall we perform this evening?"

"Indeed."

The troupe performed that night, literally for their dinner—and every other night the Commander felt like being entertained by a troupe of Peking Opera performers.

* * *

IN THE FOURTH MONTH of the siege, rumour spread through the city that the Heavenly King had left with his son, and finally the inevitable revolt of the dispossessed and exhausted brought the city to the brink of surrender.

Maxi pleaded, through his interpreter, that to open the gates was to allow in destruction. "The Manchus will be let loose to avenge themselves on you. The British already have what they want. They've broken our prohibition on opium. All that remains is the slaughter. You open the gates and that is what will happen."

Three days later, the front gates of Nanking, China's ancient capital, were flung open and a committee of twelve officials, all dressed in white silk robes, strode out in the time-honoured fashion, to surrender the city. The Manchus beheaded them and raced toward the open gate.

From the hills, Maxi's wife saw the Manchu banners begin to move, and she knew the end was near. She picked up the toddler and held her other daughter's hand as they made their way carefully to the meeting place she had agreed upon with Richard.

Richard raced into the city with the first wave of Manchus. There were screams everywhere. Limbs literally littered the streets, and old men were nailed to the doors of their ancestral homes. The Manchus were drunk on revenge. For over a decade they had fought the rebels and lost. Now was their time to get back at those who had shamed them.

But the Taipingers were not finished. They fought for every street, every alley, every building of the capital of the Heavenly Kingdom. They held back the Manchus for four full days and nights—then they could hold out no longer.

Maxi's Hakka wife waited at the assigned meeting place, with their little girl and her daughter, for a day and a night. The frozen dawn of the second day presented her with stern choices. What little food she'd managed to buy with Richard's money was quickly running out, and she didn't know when or where she could find more. As well, Manchu soldiers—drunken Manchu soldiers—had begun to frequent the hill. They dragged girls there. Raped them. Then slit their throats.

By noon of that second day Maxi's wife was forced to make a choice. She had very little food. Soldiers were everywhere. This place wasn't safe—and her daughter cried all the time.

She took one last glance at Nanking below them, then tied the red kerchief on the toddler's head and laid her gently on a bed of ferns as far back in the stand of trees as she could go. Then she took her traumatized daughter by the hand and began down the far side of the hill. They got only half a mile before the taunting calls of three Manchu soldiers stopped them—once and for all.

—

Richard saw the last line of the Taiping defence sunder and run—and he knew the end had finally come. He looked desperately for the high ground of the city. Finally he spotted silk overhead lines and ran furiously, following them until they brought him to an open clearing in a park in the north end of the city. And there, sure enough, Maxi was organizing a group of wounded men for one final stand. He held a flaming bamboo torch in his hand.

"It's no use, Maxi. The Manchus are in total control of the city. If you fight on it will be suicide."

"If we don't fight it's suicide, brother mine."

"There is an alternative."

"What? To run?"

"No. To see your family. To protect them. You've given years of your life to this cause. Now at least offer something to your family."

Maxi opened his mouth, but no words came. He slowly dropped the burning torch. It gave off an angry hiss as it hit the wet pavement—within inches of an access point to the large oil reservoir hidden below. Richard put his hand on his brother's shoulder and said, "Now it's time for me to save you, brother mine."

———

Two hours later, Richard found the History Teller helping the actor who played the Serving Man redesign his makeup. They were deep in discussion about the performance they had just given. The History Teller noticed Richard and stepped aside to address him.

"The Manchus let you into their camp, Mr. Hordoon?"

"I'm a resourceful man."

"So it would seem."

"I need your help. Actually, my brother and his family need your help."

The History Teller allowed her breath out slowly, then turned away from Richard. Finally she asked, "Where is your brother?"

"Getting his family from their hiding place."

The History Teller lowered her lovely head and tried to still her heart, but she did not speak. For all her time in Nanking she'd been careful, after that first night, not to get too close to the red-haired *Fan Kuei,* and now here was his brother asking her to hide Maxi and his family.

"They need your help."

"So you've said. What would you like me to do to help your brother and his family?"

She listened closely as Richard outlined his plan. Unbeknownst to Richard and the History Teller, however, someone else was listening as well. Someone with extraordinarily acute hearing and a cobra carved into his back.

———

Maxi raced to the assigned meeting place but found no one. Following tracks he eventually came upon a clearing in the woods—jackals had eaten away what little flesh had been left on his wife's and her daughter's bodies. But where was his daughter?

He retraced his steps and searched the area carefully. Nothing. He sank to his knees in the middle of the clearing, then something, something out of place, caught his eye. A spot of red amidst the greenery in the copse of trees. He stood and walked cautiously toward the patch of colour.

He found his little girl playing quietly with two sticks while lying on her back on the bed of ferns.

She touched the red kerchief on her forehead, then looked at her father—but she did not smile.

* * *

THE SACKING, PILLAGING, AND RAPING of Nanking took almost a week. Well before it was over, the British had left Nanking behind and headed back to their bases in Hong Kong and Macao. Eventually sated, the Manchus reorganized their troops and headed out into the countryside to rid the rest of China of the "scourge of the Taipingers."

One morning, unceremoniously, the History Teller was called to the Manchu Commander's tent.

"Sir?"

"It is time for you and your troupe to go."

"Go where?" she asked.

The Manchu just laughed. "Go wherever you can. But watch your pretty head, History Teller. There are bandits everywhere, and roving bands of Manchu bannermen who are hunting down the last of the Taipingers. Both the Heavenly King and his son are still at large. And of course the red-haired *Fan Kuei* general. Until they are all caught and executed, the rebels are dangerous. There are bounties on all of their heads. Should you see them, you might consider what that kind of money could do for your little company of players." The Manchu Commander turned to leave, then stooped to lace his boot. As he did he mentioned, "Stay away from the river. Any boat that does not belong to the Manchus will be boarded, and the people onboard put to the sword."

"Really?"

"A word to the wise."

"Why do you tell me all this?"

An odd smile crossed the man's hard features. "Because I enjoyed your performances. They touched me." He stood. "But be careful, History Teller, or your beautiful head will end up on the end of a pike. What kind of history could you tell from that vantage point? Not much, I'd guess."

The History Teller gathered her people, and—along with Maxi and his daughter—they started the dangerous journey back to Shanghai.

* * *

THAT VERY NIGHT the Chosen Three met with the Carver in the deepest section of the Warrens beneath the Chinese section of Shanghai. The

Confucian already looked twice his age, and something was definitely wrong with the Fisherman, the uncle of the Assassin. The young Carver had taken over from his ancient father but carried himself with the dignity that all representatives of the Carvers managed to display.

Jiang was unsettled by the distant stare of the Fisherman. "What draws your eye so far away, old friend?" she asked.

"Just my age," he said unconvincingly.

"We all age, Fisherman, but some of us have bad dreams as we near our end. Do you call out in your sleep these days?"

The Fisherman had no idea how Jiang knew that, and he was appalled that his privacy had been so breached.

"Are they dreams of your son whom the Assassin dispatched?"

The Fisherman slowly nodded. His whole life had collapsed since the passing of his gentle son. The birds refused to fish for him. His wife had contracted the palsy and died amidst howls of pain. Now he was alone in his bed—alone with the nightly pleading of his beautiful boy: *Help me, Father, help me.*

The Confucian stepped forward and put a hand on the Fisherman's shoulder. "We have all sacrificed for the future of our people. For the Seventy Pagodas."

Again the Fisherman nodded, although he kept his eyes down.

"The Three of us carry a heavy burden," the Confucian continued, "and that burden takes many forms. My grandmother—"

"We are not here to bemoan our present state," shot back Jiang, viciously. "We have a duty to carry out, and at this time a momentous decision to make. My people tell me that the Heavenly King is trying to contact the red-haired *Fan Kuei,* and that the people in the countryside are so enraged by the treatment they have received at the hands of the Manchus that if those two were able to unite, the rebellion could well start again."

"Do we want that?" asked the Fisherman.

"That's why we're here, to decide if defeating the Taipingers will complete the prophecy of the White Birds on Water, or if supporting the Taipingers will complete the prophecy."

"What does it matter what we think? We have no control over the Heavenly King or the red-haired *Fan Kuei.*"

"Not over the Heavenly King, true. But over the red-haired *Fan Kuei*— yes, we have something to say about his life and death." The others looked at Jiang as if she were speaking in riddles. She sighed and said, "The red-haired *Fan Kuei* is being kept safe by my daughter, the History Teller, hidden by makeup and costume in her troupe."

"And my nephew the Assassin is in the same troupe?"

"The very same," Jiang said. "So you see, gentlemen, we have a choice. The Heavenly King is nothing without the red-haired *Fan Kuei*. If the *Fan Kuei* lives, he will no doubt rejoin the Heavenly King, and the rebellion will swell once more. However, if our Assassin rids the world of the red-haired *Fan Kuei* ..." Jiang allowed her voice to trail off as the others felt the weight of their choice in the still air of the deepest cavern of the Warrens.

But the Carver wasn't listening. He was staring at the Narwhal Tusk—at the still-closed second window of the Ivory Compact.

* * *

THE HISTORY TELLER'S TROUPE made its way slowly eastward, performing when they could to raise enough money to feed themselves. Several nights they slept in the open air without having eaten that day. But despite that, they rehearsed a new, centre section of *Journey to the West*, adding a scene for a new comic actor and his unsmiling little girl. They rehearsed that section so often that some of the actors stayed in makeup and wigs almost all the time—especially the new comic actor playing the Lost Peasant, an actor that only the History Teller knew was the red-haired *Fan Kuei* general who had led the defence of Nanking for the Taipingers.

After a long nighttime rehearsal, the History Teller sent the company back to their beds, then said, "But not you."

Maxi stopped in his tracks.

"You have made some progress with this role, but you have a much longer road to travel before you have any mastery of it."

Maxi didn't doubt that, but he chose to say, "Your English is very good."

"You are generous. It is only good because your Mandarin is execrable."

"*Execrable*'s a serious word for a new English-speaker."

"*Execrable* sounds like what it is—sluicy, loose shit."

Maxi nodded. "Never thought of it that way. Don't actually think I've ever heard the word *execrable* used in a proper sentence."

"Do you miss your wife?"

The question surprised Maxi. He'd managed not to think about her. "I was unable to keep her safe."

"Yes. That's true, but it's not what I asked. Do you miss your wife?"

Maxi thought about that for a moment, then said, "Have you been married?"

The History Teller nodded as a sadness crossed her lovely features. "A long time ago, and only briefly. Typhoid took him from me."

"I am sorry to hear that."

The History Teller shrugged her slender shoulders. "So, do you miss your wife?"

"We were very different. She never learned any English or me very much Hakka. We communicated ..."

"With touch?" the History Teller suggested.

Maxi nodded. "Yes. She was a good woman. Honest and hard-working, and she loved the children." He paused for a second, then added, "She was assigned to me by the second King of Heaven. The King of the West."

"Ah, Jesus' other younger brother."

Maxi nodded.

"And why do you think you were assigned this wife, while most Taipingers were kept strictly away from the opposite sex?"

He looked at the History Teller. At her strong features. The elegant way she held herself. Her full lips.

"Answer my question, please."

Something deep inside Maxi opened and a long sigh escaped his lips. He knew the answer to her question, had known it from the beginning, but had never admitted it, even to himself. But here, with this beautiful, mature woman sitting before him, he said simply, "To report what I was doing to the authorities."

The History Teller nodded. "So you don't really miss her in your heart?" Maxi didn't answer. He didn't have to. Suddenly tears came to his eyes. "Don't," she said, "your makeup will run, and you don't know how to put it back on yourself."

"How long do you think I can get away with this charade?" Maxi demanded.

"That, my friend, depends on how well you learn your part. Play your part well and no one will guess that the man beneath the hideous makeup of the Lost Peasant is in fact the second most wanted man in the Middle Kingdom."

* * *

THE ASSASSIN had been expecting an order since the night, two days back, when he had seen a man in the front row of the audience stand on his entrance and signal with his fingers the same way his father had taught him all those years ago. Loa Wei Fen had waited for an order—longed for it. And there it was, on the underside of his writing stone, etched by an unknown hand but with his uncle's chop affixed to it to lend it credence: "The Lost Peasant is the red-haired *Fan Kuei*—he and his daughter are to die—but it must be a very public death so the rebellion will never reform and terrorize the people of China again."

The cobra on his back uncoiled slowly as he took his swalto blade into his right hand and slid it slowly across the writing. Thin, even sheets of soapstone came away, and with them the message, until all that was left was his uncle's chop, and the yearning to fulfill his destiny.

At the end of the week the troupe approached Chinkiang. Sitting on the north-east bank of the Grand Canal and the Yangtze, the strategically placed city had been handed over back and forth between the Manchus and the Taipingers. It was now a highly fortified city, fully in Manchu control.

When the troupe approached the west gate they were ordered to stop and lie face down on the side of the road. The company—and Maxi, who, like about half the company, was in full makeup and costume—did as they were ordered. The springtime sun became slowly hotter and hotter as the day progressed, and still they were left face down by the roadside. Maxi was afraid that his makeup had sweated away and hesitated when, after a Manchu officer's shouted order, the troupe slowly got to their feet.

Maxi carefully moved behind the tallest of the actors and bowed his head.

"So, History Teller, we meet again!" The voice belonged to the Commander of the Manchus to whom the troupe had been traded for two sows at Nanking. "And I see your pretty head has avoided finding its way to the end of a Manchu pike. My congratulations. Welcome to my new posting as Commander of the Empress's Manchu forces here, in Chinkiang. Well, enough of that. What are you going to do for your .... ah, I know," he said with an odd tilt of his head. "I command a performance—a full performance of your masterpiece."

"It is a very long play."

"The people of Chinkiang need something to take their minds off their misery. What better than the misery of the characters in your play? Right?"

"When would you like this performance?"

"Tomorrow, starting at midday and going for as long as it takes." The Commander of the Manchu forces turned to leave, then stopped and turned back to the History Teller.

"Yes, Commander?"

"Just this, History Teller—welcome to Chinkiang, City of Suicides."

———

"When will you learn how to put on your own makeup?"

"Maxi, my name's Maxi."

"I know your name," the History Teller said. "I've known your name since you first arrived to watch a rehearsal in my mother's establishment."

"Brothel. Your mother's brothel."

The History Teller bobbed her head in acknowledgment, then took the small metal trowel and scooped out the white paste and began to apply the base to the *Fan Kuei*'s face. As she continued to work the makeup deep into his skin, she looked down and saw Maxi staring up at her."

"Why do you stare?" she asked.

"You're very beautiful."

He said it so simply that it took her by surprise. To cover her embarrassment she said, "Your Mandarin is awful."

"You ought to hear my Hakka, if you think my Mandarin is awful. How's your English today?"

"Eloquent, erudite, and acute," she responded in highly accented English. A smile creased her face.

"Sounds like English, but I've never heard those words before. What do they mean?"

"You are staring again. It's impolite."

"I don't care, unless it bothers you."

"It doesn't."

The simplicity of her response caught him off guard.

"I've been staring at you since the first time I walked into your rehearsal, what was it, nine or ten years ago?"

"Nine years and two months. On the second day of the month of the Rat." She tilted his head back so she could apply the dark eye makeup. "Look over my shoulder."

"Can't."

"What?"

"Can't stop looking at you." Then he slid a hand up her thigh, and she pivoted her hip to allow his hand access to her as she squeezed her legs on either side of his knee and allowed herself to be moved as the world is moved—by the restless winds of a lonely heart.

"What's your name?"

"I'm the History Teller."

"I know that, but what's your name? Or perhaps you don't know your name."

"Oh, *I* know my name—it's you, Maxi, who doesn't know my name."

———

The audience was crammed into every available space as the play, under the blazing sun, began. The excellence of the company's performance brought the audience to its feet over and over again. The play continued as dinner was served to the Manchu nobles. Others had brought their own repasts, but the crowd was quiet. A true rarity for a Chinese audience.

———

The History Teller sometimes did her best writing in the presence of her own work. And it was so that day, as *Journey to the West* began its meandering but inescapable voyage toward heartbreak. She allowed the sights and sounds of the play to move past her, and forced the enthusiastic crowd response into the background. And there she stood, apart from both the play and the audience, facing her new project, a story that she'd been tinkering with for months—that of an arhu player whose music is so rapturous that those who listen fall in love. The musician is surrounded by love—but he himself is utterly and totally alone. He is called to the homes of the great and powerful, to the deathbeds of the lowly, to the arranged weddings of merchants. And everywhere he plays, love flowers.

The History Teller didn't have to be told how close this was to her own life.

———

At the beginning of the fourth hour the Monkey King made his first entrance, and every person in the audience knew that something serious about the evening had changed. Even the actors, who were used to the odd energy of the private boy-man who played the Monkey King, were startled by the height of his tumbling and the energy that seemed to flow from him.

By the sixth hour the Serving Man was approaching a high mountain stream with his Princess of the West in tow, and he was met by the Lost Peasant, his wife, and little girl.

Maxi was having trouble in his costume. The costume mistress had changed one of the straps, and it restricted the mobility of his left arm—

his sword arm. The plump actress playing his wife followed him onstage carrying Maxi's daughter in her arms. She stopped and threw her sleeves high in the air to signal her distress. Maxi executed the moves he'd learned, and the crowd howled with laughter. Maxi was always surprised by that. He thought he was doing exactly what the History Teller had taught him, but the audience immediately pegged him as the comic relief. Fine, just so long as they didn't peg him as the red-haired *Fan Kuei!*

———

The History Teller had outlined the basic scenes of her new play about the arhu player, and several had already been committed to paper. But she knew her own process, and she knew that she was stuck. She also knew that the way forward was to find the very centre of the idea, the cry of the heart that propelled everything else—and that cry would become the title.

She knew the final song of the musician as he tossed aside his ancient arhu and left the realm of men and women. She knew the lyric of the chorus was:

> *The raindrops fall*
> *One, then another*
> *On the hard ground*
> *Until finally wisdom,*
> *The true gift of the gods,*
> *Blooms.*

She also knew that although this lyric was close to the very centre of the idea of the evening, it was flawed—fell somehow short of what she wanted to say. She repeated the lyric in her mind as she allowed her attention to return to the performance.

———

Maxi opened his arms, as he had been taught to do, to indicate that the Lost Peasant's wife and child should follow him. Suddenly the crowd stood as one and pointed toward upstage left. Maxi turned to see what had taken the audience from him, and there he saw the boy-man who played the Monkey King in full makeup, hanging from an overhead beam by one hand as his other hand reached inside his tunic.

———

The swalto blade turned in the Assassin's hand and found its purchase. The boy felt his head swivel on his neck and heard the *click click click* of his vertebrae, one at a time, twisting past their previous locked positions. Then the sharp tang of the acid from the snakeskin on the swalto's handle filled his mouth. His tongue traced the length of the smooth snakeskin handle as his testicles retracted into his body—ready.

———

"Papa!"

Maxi spun around and saw that his little girl was crying, reaching for him, and calling his name loudly. He took one step toward her, then heard the sharp whine of wood yanked clear of its nails. He looked up.

———

"*Always attack from above. Always from above,*" the voice of his father, who for all those mornings had taught him the skills of an assassin, whispered in his ear. He felt his father's hand on his shoulder. "*Do your duty for China,*" the voice said, as it had at the end of every morning's training session. But this time the boy heard not only the words, but also the loneliness in the voice and a desire to reach out and touch.

"I will, Father. I will do my duty," he said aloud.

———

The History Teller rose from her seat at the back of the audience and shouted, "No!" and pushed her way through the thick crowd that separated her from the stage.

———

Maxi saw it happening right in front of him but somehow in unnatural slowness, in the way that shadows emerge from deep caves. The boy-man Monkey King had a knife in his teeth as he dropped from the beam. In mid-air he turned his body in a full somersault and fell face first toward him—the knife a shard of death pointed at his heart.

———

Joy surged through the boy. He felt his own elegance. He was a thing of inestimable beauty. A god falling to himself. Something worth the love of the History Teller!

———

Maxi felt a weight in his arms, and time snapped back to the frenetic present. His daughter was in his hands. How had she gotten there? The girl wasn't looking at him, but at the knife plunging toward her.

———

The History Teller climbed over three people who wouldn't let her through and flung herself toward the front of the stage.

———

Maxi lifted his left arm to defend the girl from the blow, but his arm snagged on the newly fitted costume. He tugged, and the new tie snapped free just in time for him to slide his daughter to safety before he fell to his knees on the hard stage floor.

———

The red-haired Fan Kuei's sudden fall caused the Assassin's perfectly aimed dagger to miss its target and slice cleanly through Maxi's shoulder and upper arm. Then it cut straight down the outside of the man's leg and lodged several inches deep in the stage planking.

The Assassin touched down with his left hand, then somersaulted and began a tumbling run across the stage.

The audience cheered wildly.

At the end of his tumbling run he snatched the red-haired *Fan Kuei*'s little girl from the stage floor and then, holding the girl in one hand, cartwheeled off the other. When he once again stood erect, the swalto was magically back in his hand.

He turned to the audience and struck a pose, the girl in one hand and the knife in the other.

The musicians awoke from their stunned silence and cymbals smashed and horns blared.

The audience shrieked its approval.

Then Loa Wei Fen stuck his knife deep into the chest of the girl. And time stopped.

———

Maxi threw himself at the Monkey King. The wig covering his red hair fell to the stage floor as he smashed into the blood-covered Assassin.

———

The History Teller leapt onto the front of the stage and ran toward the Monkey King. Maxi saw her and shouted, "No!" But the Monkey King spun and his swalto sliced cleanly across the History Teller's neck.

Words flew into her head:

Crimson line,
Across my soul
Invites flights of angels.

For an instant she saw the Monkey King's face and, through the miracle of Peking Opera makeup, finally saw, saw so clearly, the boy's longing for her—and she at last knew the title of her new opera:

The Tears of Time.

Then she heard whistling—from beneath her nose, beneath her chin—air, whistling out of her.

———

Maxi saw the History Teller's face take on a strange expression, as if something were suddenly clear to her. Then her head fell from her neck, hit once on her shoulder, and landed on the stage and stayed there, staring at him.

———

The Monkey King spun to face Maxi, his love gone. All that was left was his *chi* screaming to be set loose upon this *Fan Kuei.*

Maxi did not move. He'd seen a lot of death in his life. He'd caused much of it. But his own death was something that he'd not prepared himself for. He looked at his dead little girl, then at his dead love. He was partially aware that people were screaming, that the audience was running—but it didn't matter. He saw the terrifying keenness of the swalto blade.

The boy-man turned from him and slowly removed his silk costume. The cobra on his back, its hood gorged with blood and its eyes a flat black, spoke of endings. All Maxi remembered was thinking, *Such anger. So much rage*. Then he was back in India, the gentle opium farmer's hand on his, guiding the knife across the casement of the opium plant.

"See, it oozes, it's life."

"Like me, Father," Maxi said.

"Indeed," the opium farmer said, "indeed, like you, my son."

———

The cobra leapt from him and his swalto cut deep into the *Fan Kuei*'s chest, but the man's eyes were strangely calm. The Assassin jerked the knife up and heard the breastbone crack beneath its pressure. Then he cut down and ripped the man's ribcage open.

He turned. He knew that the audience must be screaming, but he couldn't hear them as he cut the red-haired *Fan Kuei*'s heart from his chest, slit it in two, and bit deeply into one half. And then he heard it. Faintly at first but then stronger, the voice of his friend, his cousin: *Don't kill me, Loa Wei Fen, don't kill me*.

The Assassin turned toward the stunned audience and raised his hands—he made no attempt to catch the objects hurled at him and felt only relief when the bullets thudded into his body and threw him to the stage floor like a discarded child's toy.

chapter thirty-eight
A Prophecy

Virginia, U.S.A., and Shanghai
1864–65

On the same day that Richard was told about Maxi's death, in a small church several thousand miles away, in a place called Virginia, an ostracized but unbowed woman named Rachel Oliphant walked beside her white-skinned, red-haired boy up the aisle of a small Episcopal church to receive his First Communion. Later that day Rachel sat down with her son, Malachi, and told him of his father, a wild, red-haired Jew named Maxi.

"My father's name is Maxi," Malachi said without a hint of comment. "Maxi," he repeated, "is a fine name – a fine name for a man."

Rachel smiled at her red-haired son, whose rugged Hordoon features were clearly underlying her own, more delicate looks.

"Yes, he was a very fine man."

"Is he dead, Mother?"

With a surprising certainty she said softly, "Of that, Malachi, I'm sure."

—

Silas felt a cold breeze move across his face, and he thought someone had called his name. He looked up into the high ceiling of the sixth floor of the Hordoons' massive new department store on Bubbling Spring Road, which his father had built directly across from the Vrassoons' newest emporium.

307

"Did you say something?" Silas asked the accountant with whom he was setting up the store's books.

"No, young sir," the man said.

"It's cold in here, isn't it?"

"I don't think it's cold, sir. Perhaps you have a chill."

Then Silas saw Milo at the far end of the aisle, his face a mask of pain, tears streaming down his cheeks—and Silas knew, just as surely as Rachel had known, that the force of nature that had condescended to take the human form of Maxi Hordoon was no more.

Silas looked out the window and for a moment thought he saw the silhouette of a man dancing on the roof of the Vrassoons' department store, a silhouette of a man that somehow wore a red kerchief around its neck.

—

Richard rejected all offers of sympathy and was especially harsh when the Vrassoons offered to sit shiva for Maxi. Although he had the body brought from Chinkiang to Shanghai he refused any religious rituals, Jewish or otherwise, and had Maxi's body buried in a simple pine box, beside the graves of the two White men who had been strangled to death by the Manchus all those years ago when the traders needed a sacrifice to force them into a united front.

The day of his burial was clear and cool. All anyone said that day was, "Maxi would have approved of the weather."

That night Richard sat alone in his office and stared out the window at the Huangpo River and remembered. Remembered the boy who had allowed Teacher to sodomize him so as to save Richard; the boy who had danced and laughed around the bonfire at the opium farm; the young man who had donned the red kerchief and led his irregulars into battle after battle; the grown man who had saved him with a trick of guns attached somehow by silk threads; and finally the man who had tried to convince him to stay with the Taipingers, saying, "This is the kind of place that could rid you of the opium addiction that rules you. I could help you. We could all help you here—and love you, brother mine."

Richard reached out and pulled the drapes together. In the darkness of the room only one thought offered Richard any solace: at least he had not been the cause of Maxi's death. The old Indian's prophecy that brother would kill brother had not come to pass.

* * *

308

WHILE THE HORDOONS went into mourning, Shanghai celebrated the end of the dreaded Taipingers. The country was open for business once again, and opium began to flow upriver as it had never flowed before.

Stores opened, and new streets were built. The city expanded south and west. People from the four corners of China, and then from the four corners of the world, flocked to the economic miracle that was Shanghai.

The Confucian's eldest son now joined his father at the meetings of the Chosen Three. It was clear he would soon take over his ailing father's place in the Compact. Jiang knew him by sight but had never conversed with him before. *The Fisherman is not long for this world either*, Jiang thought.

The Carver flipped the latches on the cabinet that protected the Narwhal Tusk, and they leaned down to look at the image of the Seventy Pagodas in the third "pane."

"We prosper," said the Fisherman.

"Indeed," replied the Carver, enigmatically.

"But are we near the Age of the Seventy Pagodas?" asked the young Confucian.

Jiang couldn't tell if the young man was being sarcastic or not. Finally she said, "We have all given up much to bring and then intensify the darkness of the Age of White Birds on Water—much," she added, thinking of the last time she'd seen her beloved daughter, the History Teller. She'd been offered her daughter's body, but she had declined to have it transported to Shanghai. She'd simply instructed them to follow the rituals, then scatter her ashes. "I'll see her soon enough," she'd said.

The Fisherman was deep in thought about his lost son and worried who, now that his nephew was gone, would lead the Guild of Assassins. He had another son, and perhaps he had the years left in him to complete the boy's training.

The Confucian thought of his father's bent frame and the book of ancient writings he'd been given. All the weight of the family's addiction to opium had been carried on his father's back as surely as a coolie carries water on his carrying poles. Heavy, painful—always there.

"I doubt it is so simple," the Carver said.

No one had to ask to what he was referring—the city at the Bend of the River was becoming large and powerful. But it was a large and powerful European creation. Europeans built cock-proud buildings on the Bund, but not pagodas—pagodas were light and tall, they were Chinese buildings. The Age of the Seventy Pagodas was not yet upon them.

"No doubt we need to discover how to open the second window before any pagodas can be built."

No one argued with the Carver's statement.

* * *

FOR JUST UNDER A YEAR Richard saw almost no one. He handled his business dealings almost exclusively through Patterson.

Silas threw himself into his Chinese language studies, and Milo threw himself at as many women as he could find—and being a handsome young man, as well as the wealthiest potential husband in all of Shanghai, he had many takers.

A year after Maxi's death, Richard called his sons to have dinner with him in the big house. Lily sat to one side—she was the only other person in a room that was designed to sit forty comfortably for dinner.

"It's been a year, now," Richard began.

"It was a year yesterday, Father," Silas corrected him.

"What does that matter?" Milo asked.

"If it's a year or a year and a day—it's enough. It's time for the House of Hordoon to re-emerge. To come back to life."

"I agree," said Milo.

"I didn't notice that you had particularly retreated from life's delectations, Milo," Richard said.

"Well, one of us has to continue to fly the flag."

"Enough. What have you got in mind, Father?" asked Silas.

Richard reached beneath the table and withdrew a large set of blueprints and spread them out on the table, then said simply, "The Shanghai Racetrack."

"So that's why you never built on ..."

"I don't know why I did it, Milo, but it seems to make sense to me."

"A way to honour Uncle Maxi that Uncle Maxi would approve of," said Silas.

"Are we agreed, then?" Richard asked.

They mulled over the blueprints well into the night. Only as the light began to dawn through the windows did the three settled upon the last details, and Milo said, "How shall we open Uncle Maxi's race course?"

"With the biggest, richest horse race in all of Asia, naturally."

"A single race. One horse from each of the great houses. Each house puts up fifty thousand pounds sterling and one horse. Winning horse takes all."

Only in Shanghai, with its access to literally thousands upon thousands of workers, could a racetrack have gone up with such astonishing speed, and the talk around the town grew from excited to ecstatic as the date of the opening race approached.

A month before the scheduled opening, Silas waited for his father at breakfast.

"Silas? To what do I owe the ...?"

"I have to speak to you, Father."

"Speak, but pass me the porridge first."

Silas ladled some into a fine crystal bowl for his father and handed it over. "I have an idea, Father, but I don't think you'll like it."

"About the race?"

"Yes."

"You don't want us to race?"

"No, Father, I want the race to go on as much as you do."

"So what is it?"

"We are Shanghainese."

"Absolutely, we are. This is our home."

"Right, not rotting Shanghailanders who just come here to rape—"

"Your point, Silas? The day's upon us."

"Make the race open to everyone."

Richard looked at his son for a moment, then said, "But it is. The French, the British, the Americans, the Germans ..."

"The Chinese?"

"Now you know better than that, Silas," he said, throwing aside his serviette and rising.

"Better than what, sir?" Silas stood to meet his father's wrath.

"Listen to me, Silas. You can spend as much of your time as you like with them. I've never said a word about that."

"Do you not approve, Father, of me spending time with—?"

"It's not for me to approve or not. That's not that point! We cannot allow ourselves to socialize with ..."

"Monkeys. The word you're looking for, Father, is monkeys."

"Aye, monkeys, damned monkeys I say, lad!"

Silas whirled around and stared into the florid face of Patterson, who had somehow gotten into the room without Silas noticing. "I'll not ride in front of monkeys and neither will any of the other riders. If you want a race, your damned monkeys had better not be there."

Richard put a hand on Silas's shoulder. "See, son, even if I wanted to, my hands are tied on this matter. What kind of race would it be without riders?"

Silas remembered standing for what seemed like hours with his father's hand on his shoulder. He didn't remember leaving the room—or when the rage came upon him.

———

The night before the race, Silas slipped into the Hordoon stables and moved to the stall of the family's prize mare. The animal eyed Silas with a barely concealed menace, but Silas walked into the paddock and slapped the horse hard on the rump. The animal hesitated, then shuffled aside.

"Good," Silas said, careful to keep his voice down and his tone stern. He walked to the back of the stall where the hard tack was kept and pulled out the hand-carved leather saddle that Patterson loved so dearly. Then, using a small, sharp knife, he carefully cut several striations at various points of the saddle's cinch strap, which was meant to secure the saddle to the horse's belly. He held the thing to the light, and his rage abated. Without the tension that the strap would experience once around the horse's midsection, his cuts could not be seen, even if someone was look-ing for them. Replacing the saddle in the hard tack box he said, "A little treat for you, Mr. Patterson, from your 'lad'—and his monkeys."

* * *

THE DAY OF THE RACE dawned crisp and clear, with a breeze from the east that brought the smell of the ocean to the thriving small city at the Bend in the River. The celebration began early with champagne breakfasts all over the Foreign Settlement and the French Concession. Suzanne was surprised to see customers arrive just after breakfast. *A little something before the race,* she thought. Jiang made ready for early customers, know-ing that many Chinese, despite the fact that they were not allowed to attend, had wagered heavily on the race and were trying to guarantee their success with an early morning session of clouds and rain.

The racetrack itself threw open its doors at ten o'clock and the *crème de la crème* of the English, American, French, German, and even Russian com-munities pushed their way into the lavish facility. They oohed and aahed at the luxury all around them and quickly made their way to the betting windows.

By ten-thirty, over a quarter of a million British pounds had been shoved through the windows. But the real betting was on the side. Richard had taken bets from both Percy St. John Dent and Hercules MacCallum, but they were minor compared to the bet with the Vrassoons. And their bet was unique. It had nothing to do with which horse won the race. It had only to do with which of their two horses outdid the other—a grudge match.

By eleven o'clock the few bars that had closed the night before had opened, and the excitement in the city ratcheted up as whisky added its own unique acceleration to human joy.

At noon the horses were finally walked out on the track to take their pre-race workouts, and a hush fell over the gathering crowd. Shanghai was used to superlatives—the best wines, the sheerest silks—but the horseflesh on the track in the bright morning sunshine was the finest collection of Thoroughbreds that hundreds of years of careful breeding could produce.

The Vrassoon rider walked beside the large, almost pure-white stallion and offered up sugar cubes as they promenaded around the track. The stallion stood a full two hands taller than any of the other horses on the track. The Vrassoons had kept their animal in a secret paddock all the way downriver at Woosung, so that no one knew much about the stallion. But everything necessary to know was openly on display as the powerful animal pulled hard at the reins, clearly anxious to race.

The Dent's rider noted the muscle of the Vrassoon stallion and then looked at his fine grey gelding, as the Jardine Matheson colt pranced by with its jockey holding the reins tight on his Orkney-bred steed.

The American horse was technically the entrant of Russell and Company, but as Russell's representative, a Mr. Delano, later confessed, "We at Russell's were just a front. Jedediah Oliphant was the money behind our entry. Because of his religious convictions he is opposed to gambling in all of its forms, but he would have killed himself if he'd been left out of the race, so he contacted us, and, for a modest fee, Mr. Roosevelt and I fronted his Kentucky pony." And the animal was a marvel—sleek and light of foot and probably the most beautiful animal on the track.

The Hordoons' mare was the last to make its entrance, surprisingly late, and the chocolate-coloured animal seemed to shy away from its rider to the point that the man dismounted and tried to coax it into walking by his side.

At twelve-thirty the bar at the racetrack opened, serving champagne on ice to all comers—and it did a brisk business—as did the betting windows, which by that time had taken in more than three-quarters of a million British pounds.

Then the first set of betting odds were posted, and the lines in front of the betting wickets doubled.

The Vrassoon horse was almost even money, followed by the American horse, then farther down the other three horses.

Side betting came out in the open as the water trap jump was filled and the three hedge jumps were pulled into position. The horses left the track for their final preparations.

The day grew hot, but no one even thought of leaving as the clock clicked slowly toward race time: one o'clock.

———

Silas noted that he was the only non-Chinese on the Bund Promenade that day. Across the water, the challenge of the Pudong stared back at him. He'd never been there, but there were stories, such stories about that bit of Shanghai! He approached a five-spice egg seller and purchased one of her products. The old seller was pleasantly surprised with Silas's fluent Mandarin and told him as much. He balanced the hot thing between the tips of his fingers as he took a bite out of the top. His teeth scraped just the edge of the hardened yolk, as he had been taught to, allowing the flavoured white of the egg to mix with the dense taste of the yolk. He smiled as he heard the chatter around him. And he took it all in: the peasants squatting on their haunches, planning the next moves in their complicated lives; the rickshaw boys sitting in the shade of their conveyances; the old man on the ground surrounded by the heels of women's shoes while he cobbled an ancient shoe back into use; the four elderly men moving like shadows across the pavement as they performed the moves of their Tai Chi exercises in perfect unison; the man selling delicate wrens and hummingbirds in bamboo cages; the two young men playing Go on a board drawn on the pavement itself, surrounded by other men offering unsolicited advice; a woman carrying a large wreath of flowers destined to be draped across the doorway of a new business for good luck; men, their backs stacked high with parcels or furniture or equipment or cages of live animals or garbage pails or water on poles—men carrying the world itself on their backs. And Silas took it in and it made him smile. Shanghai—his Shanghai—his home.

He turned toward the Pudong and a shiver went up his spine. Instantly he turned back toward the city and heard the roar of hundreds of voices from the direction of the racetrack. He ran to the nearest rickshaw and in rapid Shanghainese shouted, "To the racetrack, as fast as you can!"

———

A loud gunshot started the race. As soon as the horses hit stride, the Vrassoon rider pulled hard on his stallion's left rein, forcing him to cross in front of the Hordoons' mare. The smaller animal veered, then shied away toward the rail. For a moment the mare lost her gait, then she sorted herself out and headed after the pack of horses that was now several lengths ahead of her.

The other three horses wisely moved away from the big white stallion and raced toward the first of the three hedge fences, with the American horse the first to reach the low hedge.

Oliphant was cheering so loudly that the other members of the House of Zion were taken aback. But he turned to them and screamed, "God's horse! Cheer on God's horse, for God's sake!" The fact that, through Mr. Delano, he had placed what he called "a modest, truly modest wager" on his horse—some seventy thousand British pounds—had nothing whatever to do with his enthusiasm.

The low hedge posed no problem for the American pony, which leaped over the obstruction as simply as a child skips a step while running down stairs. The Vrassoon stallion seemed to gain as he left his feet to clear the obstruction, followed closely by the horse from Dent's and then the Orkney pony of Jardine Matheson, which cut toward the rail as soon as it cleared the hedge and quickly passed the Dent's horse. Then, five full lengths back, the Hordoon mare approached the hedge.

Hercules managed to step on his own gout-afflicted foot when his rider did as he had ordered and passed the Dent's pony on the rail. "Ride," he shouted, "ride for Scotland!"

The Hordoon jockey felt his mare find her stride on the far side of the first of the three hedges and smiled as he thought back to the day's events in the Hordoon stable. Then he whooped a characteristic whoop and grabbed a handful of the mare's mane and shouted, "That'a girl. Good girl, Rachel."

———

The second hedge, about twice the height of the first, was in the jockey's line of sight as Silas threw money at his rickshaw boy and ran toward the entrance of the Hordoons' racetrack.

———

The American horse was the first to the hedge and just cleared it, with the top of the obstruction rubbing across the animal's belly. The American

315

rider adjusted to the change in mid-air and the horse landed perfectly bal-anced and shot forward toward the third obstruction—the water jump.

The Vrassoon stallion sailed over the second hedge, its powerful flanks providing more than enough lift to clear the barrier. His front hooves hit ground only half a length behind the American pony.

Quickly after the Vrassoon stallion, the Jardine Matheson Orkney pony raced toward the barrier, then suddenly ducked its head, throwing the rider into the hedge. The hooves of the Dent's horse just missed the fallen rider's head, and when the Dent's rider looked back he was surprised that the Hordoon mare had passed him in mid-air—and raced after the two front-runners.

The third obstacle, the water jump, was approaching quickly, and much to everyone's surprise, while the American pony was in mid-air clearing the water, the Vrassoon stallion made no effort whatsoever to jump and instead raced through the pool, which the Vrassoons had made sure was only six inches deep rather than the traditional three feet. Seeing the Vrassoon stallion, the Hordoon rider let out his reins and urged his mare on through the water.

They were now on the far side of the track beginning the long turn toward home. Only the large hedge remained. The Vrassoon stallion led by two lengths, but the Hordoon mare was closing fast.

———

Silas spotted his father and ran up the aisle to him. With all the noise, Silas couldn't hear the words his father was shouting. Then he looked past his father and saw Patterson. Patterson! Silas whipped around to face the track, and over his shoulder he heard his father's voice shouting, "Milo! Yes, Milo! Catch him Milo! Ride that mare, Milo!"

And Silas's heart sank as the horses made the last wide turn, Milo now only a length behind the Vrassoon horse as they headed toward the large hedge.

Milo, no, not Milo.

———

Milo sensed it. He didn't know what, but something was different. Some odd smell in the air. Then he dismissed it—it was the anticipation of the race. All the planning, all the excitement. Each of the great trading houses backing a horse, and the mammoth purse that his father had put up and all the betting and all the people—it must be that, just that. Then he smelled it again, and so did the Hordoons' prize mare in her stall.

"Easy, Rachel," Milo said, but the powerful animal's eyes were wild and she reared, kicking out with her front legs against the wooden slats of the paddock. "Easy," Milo cooed to the animal. Suddenly the horse turned in the stall and slammed her powerful back hooves against the stall's gate. "No, Rachel, no," he shouted. Then he smelled it again. A dry, musky, acidic smell in the air.

Had Milo asked a Chinese peasant, he would have been told what the reek was—the smell of change. But there were no Chinese workers in the Hordoons' stables. All the work there was done by the Hordoons, some of Maxi's old irregulars, and of course Patterson, who even now came running down the centre aisle of the stable, shouting, "Leave that animal alone, boy."

Milo took a step back from the mare. Patterson opened the gate and swacked the horse hard across the nose. "No, me lovely, we'll none of that." Then he moved past the horse and got his prized saddle out of the hard tack box.

"Trouble, gentlemen?" Richard said as he came into the stable.

"No, sir, no trouble."

"I hope not. It's race day. Race day," he repeated happily. "Where's your brother, Milo?"

"I don't know, Father."

The mare shied away from Richard. "Easy Rachel, easy," he said as he put his hand on the animal's smooth flank. As he did, he continued to speak softly to the animal and run his hands along her back. Then he slipped the bit into her mouth and tossed the reins over her neck. "What's gotten into her?"

"She smells something," said Milo.

"Nonsense," snarled Patterson. "What does an animal smell, do you suppose, lad? She's just excited about racing, like me." Patterson hoisted the saddle up on the mare's back.

Milo looked to his father and was about to ask, "Don't you smell it, Father?" when the mare reared suddenly and kicked out. Her right fore hoof caught Patterson beneath the chin and the man crumpled to the ground like a puppet whose strings had been cut.

Milo grabbed the reins and yanked hard, turning the powerful animal's eyes to his. The mare immediately calmed. Milo ran his hand up the horse's muzzle.

Richard pulled Patterson to his feet. The man had a hard noggin, and, unlike those whom he called monkeys, his bulldog Scottish body was built to take a fall. But the blow to his head had left him woozy and disoriented, so, over the man's vociferous objections, Richard sent him back to his home and turned to his son.

"Be honest, you wanted to ride for the family all along, didn't you?"

"I always did, Father," Milo said as a smile bloomed on his handsome face.

"Well, now it's not a matter of wanting." Richard straightened Patterson's leather saddle on the mare's back and said, "Cinch her tight, son, then mount up. We'll walk her slowly to the track."

Milo reached under the animal's belly, grabbed the cinch strap, and pulled it tightly through the catch. Then he swung up into the saddle. From his perch on the fine animal he looked down at his father, who was looking up at him with a peculiar smile on his face.

"What?"

Richard wanted to say, *What a wonderful son you are,* but he didn't. He just chuckled and said, "Son, ride like the wind."

"I'll make you proud, Father."

Richard smiled and said softly, "You already have, son, you already have." He thought for the briefest moment of his promise to Milo's mother and vowed that he would, at long last, write something about Milo—just for her.

———

"Ride, Milo! Ride, son!"

Silas strained to see his brother as Rachel pulled even with the Vrassoon stallion just before the large hedge.

———

Milo pulled back, then loosed the reins on Rachel and she flew—flew over the large hedge and landed at the exact same time as the massive Vrassoon stallion.

Milo heard the crowds screaming as he leaned into the final turn in the track's back stretch, Rachel neck and neck with the larger Vrassoon stallion. Then stride for stride, just waiting to break out of the turn and into the home stretch. Milo knew that Rachel could outrun the heavier animal on the straightaway, all he needed to do was stay even on the curve. Just a few more yards!

He leaned hard in the saddle—and felt something—shift. Had Rachel missed a stride? He leaned forward to settle her when he felt the saddle move. Then he heard it—something snapping—something metal hit him—and he fell.

As his limber body hurtled toward the track he smelled it again. That dry, musky reek. Then he saw them only inches from his face—hooves— the massive hooves of the Vrassoon stallion.

* * *

THERE WAS NO FUNERAL. No rites. Just a simple pine box and an unmarked grave over which stood a beaten man and a guilty son.

Silas never told his father what he had done to the cinch strap of the saddle that had loosed his brother to his death. Never admitted his guilt. But he knew that he had fulfilled the prophecy that Richard and Maxi had heard from the mouth of the ancient Indian man in the alley in the town near Ghazipur: *Brother will kill brother.* Knew it, and didn't know how he was going to live with it.

———

Richard actively retreated from the world. Even his writing, which always brought him peace, was a torment. He never was able to complete the journal entry about Milo. He refused to see anyone but Lily, then one night he awoke with a start. There was someone in his room. He lit the oil lamp by his bed and was shocked to see Eliazar Vrassoon in the flickering light of the lamp.

Richard had no idea how the old man had gotten into his bedroom, but there he was—the Vrassoon Patriarch—at one time the most powerful man in all of Shanghai, now a bent thing leaning on a walking stick. But evidently the man was not so powerless because he had gotten into his bedroom, unannounced and definitely uninvited.

The old man coughed. Something red flecked his lips. Then he smiled.

"What are you doing ...?"

"In your bedroom? Well you might ask, but I've been in your bedroom before. In one way of thinking, I've been in your bedroom every night of your life."

Richard swung his legs over the side of the bed and grabbed a silk bathrobe which he wound around himself.

"The other time I was in your room you wore only dirty under-clothes—but perhaps you don't remember."

"Remember what, you—"

"Careful. No need to insult the dying. Whatever reward awaits is already prepared in a manner unforeseen on this earth."

"More gobbledygook!"

"Really?" Eliazar Vrassoon said under his breath.

"So you're dying?" Richard remarked brightly.

"So it would seem. Then again, we are all dying, my boy."

"I am not a boy. I am not your boy!"

"You've been my boy since the first night we met. In another bedroom a long time ago—in Baghdad."

Suddenly Richard knew what kept beckoning him in his opium dreams. The door that always awaited his coming. Not the door, but what was behind the door. Not what, but who.

"You took my sister?"

The Vrassoon Patriarch seemed to sway for a moment, then, through a coughing fit, asked, "Took your sister? You think I took your sister, Miriam? You believe I stole her?"

"What else could you call it?" Richard screamed at him.

"You are shouting, boy. Why are you shouting, boy?"

"I killed your son," Richard announced triumphantly.

Eliazar Vrassoon nodded slowly. "With the picture?"

"Yes."

Vrassoon continued to nod. "By that token you could say I killed your father. But neither claim would be true. My son threw himself from a bridge. You may think you caused it with your photographic invention, but my son was so filled with remorse for his sins that his jumping was just the final act in his tragic life. Just as your father's death was no more than the final act in his comic existence." Eliazar Vrassoon shuffled his feet, then turned to Richard and in a loud voice said, "Come with me, boy. Your father has agreed."

Richard felt himself falling. As if the world were suddenly upside down. "What?"

"You heard me, boy. Your father has agreed, and you are the price. Grab your trousers and come with me. Now, boy!"

Richard breathed deeply. The smell of spicy chickpeas was in the room. The cry of the muezzin calling the faithful to morning prayers entered from the window. But how? This was Shanghai, not ... the sound of a peacock shrilly screaming a warning ... and he was back. Back in Baghdad in his room as a four-year-old boy, and this big man was in his room saying, "Your father has agreed, boy."

Richard staggered two steps closer and smelled the odour deep in the man's gabardine coat. He looked up into the man's eyes and the Patriarch was young. Powerful. Full of fury. "Your father has agreed. Now come, boy."

Richard heard his knees hit the floor but felt no pain. He looked up at the old man leaning on the cane. "You were in my room in Baghdad."

"Yes."

"You had come for my sister, Miriam."

"No."

Richard felt his insides fall again and suddenly he was tumbling, plummeting down an ancient well, backwards, on a moonless night—falling.

"No, boy. I came for you. As your father had agreed. You were to be my apprentice, in return for which I was to make sure your family survived and got safely out of Baghdad. I came for you, boy. For you."

Richard nodded slowly and looked up at the old man. "But I was afraid and I pointed toward my sister's bed."

"You were afraid, perhaps. But you didn't point toward your sister's bed."

"I did—toward her bed."

"No."

"I did!" Richard was screaming again.

"No. What Jewish family would put two sons in the same room with a daughter?"

The truth of that pierced Richard's heart. Something was falling away. His skin? His bones? His heart?

"You took my hand, walked me to her door, and opened it for me. Then you traded, boy. You traded your sister, Miriam, to me so that I wouldn't take you. You even offered me your brother, Maxi, as part of the deal. You traded like any stinking kike of a Jew boy. You made a deal. You sold her to me. Four years old and already swinging deals. What a Jew you are!"

"Go to hell," Richard managed to say weakly.

"That's not really your decision to make, now, is it? Besides, you don't believe in a heaven or a hell. Be that as it may, boy, wherever I go, I'm sure you'll shortly follow. Oh, by the way, you seem to have pissed your trousers, boy." Then he laughed and made a motion with his hand as though tipping his top hat. "Good night, Richard Hordoon. I'm sure we'll meet again in another bedroom another time—of that I have no doubt."

After that night Richard seldom chanced sleeping. And with an ever-increasing frequency he turned to opium for relief from his waking dreams of opening a door and pointing at his baby sister and begging, "Take her. Take her, not me."

And opium, Richard Hordoon's true love, opened her arms to him and he succumbed to her—completely.

book two

A Man with a Book

Wherein the interlocking lives of
three great Shanghainese
families—the Hordoons, the Soongs,
and the Tus—are revealed.
The book also relates the strange
history of the removal of the
Narwhal Tusk from Shanghai.

chapter one

Silas Hordoon

December 31, 1889

Silas was shocked when he realized where his nightly wandering had brought him. As the growing city prepared to celebrate the new year—the new decade—he had walked aimlessly, allowing Shanghai itself to dictate the direction of his steps. Since he'd murdered his brother Milo, he'd walked every night, regardless of the weather, and through his evening ramblings he had found the concealed entrances and exits to every alley; every tiny store and stall on the innumerable side streets; all the secret entrances to the Warrens; the main routes into and, more importantly, out of the still wild Pudong; and, of course, every inch of the Foreign Settlement and the French Concession—every part of his home at the Bend in the River.

Home, he thought. *That which has finally opened my heart.*

Silas felt the subtle motion of change within. The city—his city—had worked its ancient alchemy on him, turning cold stone to soft gold. Just as opium had opened doors in his father's soul, so had Shanghai opened cracks in Silas's defences and sent down roots to break the adamantine granite surrounding his heart. One day he passed by a street doctor and for the first time he knew exactly where the next acupuncture needle would be inserted; another day he spotted the finest river stone in the stone seller's collection, despite the fact that the crone had cleverly hidden it beneath two entirely nondescript rocks; another day he allowed his hand to touch the hip of a courtesan and for the first time felt the pulse beneath the skin. Shanghai had awakened Silas Hordoon. At first he had thought it was just the death of his father—as though the removal of such an enormous shadow had simply allowed the sun to reach the son. But whatever the reason, Silas Hordoon's heart was opening, and the most eligible of bachelors in the city at the Bend in the River smelled, beneath the heady aroma of the late-night incinerators, the reek of ozone, and was ready for change.

Two lovers had found the most elusive of all commodities for the poor in Shanghai—privacy. In the mouth of a darkened alley their bodies enmeshed as one lithe thing. Silas was about to smile when he saw where the city had led him ... to this place. This place that he had not seen for ten years. But even as he pushed open the low door he knew who he would find. Who would always be there between the floating layers of opium smoke, the harsh smell of the braziers, and the musk of sex. His father, dead these ten years, had died in this place but would always be here—always—waiting, waiting for his one remaining son to visit.

———

"So you found me, Silas," Richard had croaked out from his straw mat on the floor. Behind him in the corner, hidden in the gloom, was Lily—Lily was always there too, always at his father's side. The disfigured peasant woman had been an even more constant presence at his father's side since Milo's death.

"Lily," Silas said, and took off his hat.

Lily ducked her head into her sloping shoulders as acknowledgment, then knelt to help Richard readjust himself on his pillows. She picked up the ancient ivory pipe from his chest, placed it carefully on the floor beside the mat, and then retreated a few steps into the darkness.

"So you found me, lad," Richard said.

"I did, sir," Silas said, anxious not to look at his father's rotted teeth or the spittle crusting at the creased corners of his mouth.

"Lily," Richard said, leaning over and picking up his pipe.

Lily crept forward with a molten ball of opium on a tray. She skewered the opium with a long needle and placed it into the bowl of the pipe. Richard breathed deeply, then let out a long line of acrid smoke and a sigh.

Silas coughed as he drew some of smoke into his lungs.

"Sorry, son," Richard said.

"Don't be. It's your one true love, sir." *Why can you not resist hurting this man?* Silas demanded of himself. But he had no answer.

"Aye, that and your brother," Richard said, knowing full well the barb would sink deep into Silas's heart.

Silas had never admitted to his father that he had cut the cinch strap on the horse that had thrown Milo to his death, all those years ago. But he knew that Richard knew. He also knew that his father knew all his other secrets.

"Do you know your Bible, son?"

That surprised Silas. "No, not much, sir."

"I do. I committed much of it to memory in Farsi, a long time ago now."

"And you remember it?"

"More than I care to admit. Some of it comes back to haunt ..." Richard's voice trailed off, then he said loudly, "... haunt me. Haunts me still."

Silas had heard his father go off on tangents before, rants that seemed to have no direction but somehow erupted from the man's conscience. Over and over Silas had heard him howl, "Don't do the Devil's work, mustn't do the Devil's work." Silas had assumed these were just the ravings of an opium addict—oh, yes, his father had been a substantial opium addict for years—but of late the ravings had taken on a bizarre consistency. Themes kept emerging from the babble over and over again, like a harbour buoy swallowed by the waves that always bobs back to the surface.

Richard patted the side of the mat and Silas knelt down. Suddenly the old man's hands were on his lapels, pulling him in close enough that the sour smell of opium, which always nauseated Silas, now filled his nostrils.

"Don't do the Devil's work son, don't ..." Richard's once powerful grip slipped from Silas and his lips muttered, "don't don't don't—do the Devil's work." Then he lay very still, the pipe resting at his side.

Silas reached over and touched his father's chest. His breath was shallow but present.

"Not gone yet, Silas," Richard said, as a smile creased his now thin lips. "The time has come, the Walrus said, to talk of many things."

Silas recognized the quotation as coming from the strange book of children's stories that his father so treasured. "Such as, Father?"

"Something something and ceiling wax and something something and kings, I believe. Although such things don't interest you, Silas."

"Not much, sir."

Richard sighed. "Ah, *sir*. You were always the one who called me sir. Your brother ..." Richard's voice retreated to a whisper. Lily lifted the pipe to his lips. He breathed deeply, and when he exhaled, the sour smoke wrapped around Silas, in a constrictor's embrace, before it fled to the safety of the far corners of the ceiling.

"Your mother was a fine woman, Silas."

Silas was shocked. He'd never heard his father speak of his mother before.

"A good woman. But so angry at the end. I held the both of you in my arms and leaned over her to show the two of you to her. 'Boys, Sarah, boys,' I said, but all she did was grab at me and scream, 'What have you done, Richard?' Oh, how a single question can follow you your entire life. 'What have you done?' I often wondered how she knew, but in truth I never spent much time on that, just got on with it. With living." He laughed hoarsely. "How did she know that old man Vrassoon came into my room, do you think?"

Silas sat very still. He'd never heard any of this before. "Into your room, Papa?"

"In Baghdad."

Silas knew that his father and Uncle Maxi had left Baghdad with their parents before they were teenagers. "In Baghdad ... when?"

"I was scared." Silas had never heard that word come from his father's lips before. And now his father's voice was so thin, like morning mist on the Yangtze.

"What were you afraid of, Papa?"

"I pointed ... pointed to her door." Then his father did the strangest thing—he giggled.

"Her door? Whose door?" Silas demanded.

Richard's eyes danced, but he kept his mouth shut. Then he began to cry. Silas looked at the remains of what had been his powerful father. He reached over and put his hand on his father's forehead.

"Keep your hands to yourself, boy!" His father's voice was remarkably strong, and his message direct and unmistakable. "Make yourself useful for once in your life and hand me my pipe."

Silas reached for the ancient, carved ivory thing and handed it to his father. Richard grabbed the pipe from him and inhaled the dregs of the opium in the pipe's bowl, then grinned as he said, "Don't listen to an old man's carpings." And he swung his head violently away from his son and muttered something. Silas leaned forward and thought he heard his father say, "It matters not, as it's all one. All one."

Suddenly his father turned on him and grabbed the sides of his face, his jagged nails cutting into his cheeks. "Haul your arse out of here. Nice boys don't belong in places like this." He threw Silas back with surprising strength as he pointed to a stack of journals. "Take them, lad. I bequeath them to you. No. Please take them. I promised your mother I'd write them. At least that promise I kept." Then Richard held out a formal-looking document covered with flowing Farsi script and said, "Take this too."

Silas quickly scanned the words. It was a deed of ownership for property in Baghdad. "And this would be?"

"The Vrassoons' Baghdad home. I came into possession of it." A sly smile pursed his cracked lips. "I own it. Now you own it." Then his father laughed a throaty chortle before he drew deeply on his pipe yet again. The spittle in the stem gurgled.

Silas took his father's precious journals and the deed and left the opium den. He never spoke to his father again.

———

That was exactly ten years ago, on the evening of December 31, 1880. And now, on the eve of the turn of the decade, Silas Hordoon left the same subterranean establishment and was greeted by the very first of the fireworks exploding across the river, over the Bund. *In a few hours it will be a new year,* he thought, *the beginning of the last decade of this century.*

* * *

LI TIAN IGNORED the other master fireworks makers' stares and taunts. They didn't believe in the stories of his artistry and were annoyed that his work had been given pride of place—at the very end of the evening's "explosive" entertainment. Li Tian didn't care what they thought or said—or did, for that matter. His fireworks would be the last because they would be the very best. And this night would literally bring his artistry to light in a brand new way. He had been the first to create a circle of fire in the sky. The first to make the "stars" burst in a clockwise sequence. *Tonight will dwarf that achievement,* he thought as he carefully removed his charcoal mixture from a wooden case and arranged sixteen star clusters on the sand.

Then he began.

chapter two
Arise the Assassin

December 31, 1889

Wang Jun stood naked astride the grave of the man he thought of as his noble ancestor—the First Assassin, Loa Wei Fen—and grimaced as his aged father carved the first line of the cobra on his back. He watched the shadow of the moonset as it crept along the Bend in the River, casting deep shadows on the elaborate gargoyles and gewgaws on the facades of the European buildings across the river on the Bund.

The second cut was longer and wider than the first, demarcating the outer line of the fully spread hood of the serpent. He knew the third and fourth cuts would be small but very deep—the eyes of the cobra's hood were the heart of its fury.

His blood ran in narrow, viscous streams down his back and pooled momentarily on the rise of his backside before it sought the eternity of the earth whence it came.

His father picked up dirt from Loa Wei Fen's grave and worked it deep into the cuts on his son's back. He had taught his son well, as his father, the Fisherman, had taught him after his gentle brother was put to death in the bamboo canes. He forced more dirt into the cuts. The dirt would cause the wounds to welt upon healing—or cause infection and death—either way, his son would fulfill his destiny. But he knew in his heart that his son would not die from the wounds. And his son would outshine even the First Assassin. His son would revive the ancient Guild of Assassins and help his people to the Seventy Pagodas. He was proud to have such a son.

A son who did not cry out at the pain he caused as he dug deep into his flesh to carve out the first eye on the cobra's hood.

The left eye, Wang Jun thought as he resisted the impulse to pull away from the knife in the flesh of his back. He watched a trail of blood curl around his hip and proceed down the front of his left leg, then around the knob of his ankle, and finally between his toes onto the sacred ground of the grave of Loa Wei Fen. It was for this ceremony that he'd had the First Assassin's remains brought from Chinkiang to this side of the Bend in the River—the wild side—the Pudong.

The first of the new year's fireworks lit the newly darkened sky and shadows seemed to leap briefly from the dense forest.

The final cuts were quick and shallow, following the ancient design first seen on the wrist of Q'in She Huang's Body Guard on the sacred mountain, the Hua Shan. He heard his father sigh deeply and sensed the last of the older man's *chi* enter him as the knife fell to the ground of Loa Wei Fen's grave.

"It is done," his father said in a hoarse whisper.

"As it is decreed," Wang Jun replied. He hugged his father, surprised by the man's sudden frailty. It was as if he had aged twenty years in a day.

As he walked his father to the small boat that would take him back to the Shanghai side of the Huangpo River, he wondered if he'd ever see him again. This stern, strong, righteous man who had taught him the art of the assassin.

"Do you know the sign ...?"

"For the Chosen to meet? Yes, Father, we meet this very night. It was all arranged before we came to the Pudong. Now, Father, forget me—as you have taught."

"Will I never see you again?" the man asked, his voice cracking.

"No. Wang Jun is no more. But you will hear of me. You will hear of your son, Loa Wei Fen."

His father looked at him closely. Suddenly a brightness came back into his eyes. "You have taken his name, the First Assassin's name?"

"Yes, Father, as befits one who will revive the ancient Guild of Assassins."

* * *

LI TIAN IGNORED THE FIREWORKS going off overhead and concentrated on his own creation. He carefully sealed the four-foot-long paper tubing and attached it to a six-foot bamboo stake that he had sunk deep into the hard ground. He gingerly placed two measures of his potassium nitrate, sulfur, and charcoal mixture into the base of the tube. "That will gain us the height we need," he said aloud.

Then he wedged in a paper divider, through which he inserted a two-foot-long fuse, and adhered it to the side of the tube using a small brush to spread the egg yolk paste.

chapter three

Shanghai, City at the Bend in the River

December 31, 1889

Silas continued his walk in his city, the sixth-largest port in the world. He allowed the rhythm of the place and the irregular shocks of light from the fireworks to lead him. It guided him past its luxurious nightclubs, past the exclusive four-storey Shanghai Club, where at this very moment men were proving their worth by buying whole cases of champagne "for the bar"; its race course, where his brother died; its fabulous shops on Bubbling Spring Road, which many now called Nanking Road; its world-famous homosexual bars; its twenty-one cock-proud European buildings on the Bund, its wide avenues running perpendicular to the Bund named after great Chinese cities, and those running parallel to the Bund named after the provinces; its selective brothels for boys, girls … and others; its vast network of opium dens. It took him past Good Food Street, with its all-night outdoor food stalls; its rickshaws and carriages and traps and carts pulled by swift Mongolian ponies; its quick-trotting coolies loading and unloading goods from the greasy piers; its brokers rushing, even on this night, in sedan chairs with the latest rates for cotton or silk from New York or London; its warlords, known as Tuchons, carried in high style by silk-dressed servants; its lesser Caucasians in Norwich cars or broughams; its emporiums stocked with edible delicacies from every part of the world—no trouble finding jams or scones from Fortnum and Mason or peanut butter or Saratoga Mineral Water from Crosse and Blackwell—its liquor shops stacked tall with the world's finest wines; its florid-complexioned fat Taipans demanding attention for their mercantile success. He passed an elegant Tudor-style house deep in the French Concession and heard the sounds of an orchestra playing the latest dances. No doubt phalanxes of houseboys, cooks, laundresses, stable hands, *amahs*, gardeners, table boys, and porters were in constant attendance to "Missy" to allow the ball to proceed smoothly. On Beijing Lu, Silas passed the modest storefront of a sensationally wealthy comprador and recalled Commodore Perry's confusion, then anger, at the financial success of these "blue-robed Slants." Turning onto Julu Lu, Silas saw the central offices of the American Evangelical Society. It was rumoured that Shanghai had the biggest evangelical army in Christendom. *But they don't seem to have put a stop to the joy-hunting in our modern-day Sodom and Gomorrah,* he thought.

With the song of a street hawker and a sudden profusion of overhead booms, the city tilted Silas away from the bright lights. Turning into a *shikumen* alley, Huile Li, he spotted a pear syrup candy seller whose song—"*Wuya wuli kuangya, liya ligaotang ya*—Grandpa eats my pear syrup"—had drawn him. He bought a dollop of the sweet confection that he had so loved as a child. As it dissolved on his tongue, an exhausted peasant woman shambled into the alley, two rattan buckets dangling from her shoulder pole. In each basket sat a wide-eyed, oddly silent child, dressed in rags. Behind her Silas saw a street food seller, his portable kitchen carried on his shoulder pole. Silas ordered fried bean curd, which the man expertly produced, flipping the bean curd over and over in the hot oil until it was an even golden brown. Then the street food seller plucked the deep-fried treat from the oil and strung it on two clean, fresh stalks of straw. Silas paid the man, then gave the bean curd to the peasant woman with the two children, saying, "Be careful that they don't burn their tongues." The woman grunted a thanks in a language that even the multi-tongued Silas Hordoon didn't recognize. As he contemplated the origin of the peasant's dialect, the city spun him again and sent him through one of the newer shantytowns, then through the east gate of the Old City and along Fang Bang Lu. Outside each doorway the circular, red-painted night-soil bucket awaited the dawn arrival of the night-soil collector, the least respected but best paid labour in Shanghai.

The hour approached midnight. Fireworks cascaded overhead, and the people of Shanghai—yellow, white, red, black, and brown—surged out into the streets. Silas stood very still and marvelled—people, people, everywhere people. *His* people—a people and a city that he knew could not have come into existence without his father's willingness to "do the Devil's work."

* * *

"THAT WILL GIVE ME the needed delay," Li Tian said, then he inserted a series of small bamboo ladders, each with eight rungs. He carefully picked up eight of the stars that he had made by pasting blasting powder to a central stone and rolling it in iron filings. After that he'd rolled them in more blasting powder, more iron filings. The stars, like giant sparklers, were each about two inches in diameter and perfectly round. The first of the stars he placed carefully on the first rung of the first ladder inside the tube, then the second star on the second rung of the second ladder, and so on until each of the eight ladders supported a different star. He aligned the ladders with great care so that the distance between each was exactly the same. Then he filled in the rest of the cavity with more of his explosive mixture. When he had the cavity exactly halfway filled he inserted a second paper disk, through which he threaded another fuse.

chapter four
Gangster Tu

December 31, 1889

Another man—a Chinese man with extraordinarily large ears, Tu Yueh-sen—looked at the tumult of Shanghai that New Year's Eve, and as the fireworks lit the sky of the dawning decade, he withdrew a blade from his belt and silently renewed the promise he had made to his dying grandmother. He thought again about the best way to punish the *Fan Kuei*—by hurting them in the only way that they could be hurt, in the marketplace, in money—and in Shanghai, the only vast swell of money was in opium.

He twirled his knife as his man came out of the Old Shanghai Restaurant to tell him that the leader of the Tong of the Righteous Hand (the *Shan Chu*; the Mountain Master) was fattening his gut on noodles in a private room at the back of the old eatery.

The Tong of the Righteous Hand was once an underground anti-Manchu movement, but it was now just another criminal gang that controlled a small although growing part of the opium trade—the only Chinese part. Tu Yueh-sen planned to take over the Chinese section of the opium trade, then use that as a base to mount his all-out attack against the *Fan Kuei* traders.

Several Tong foot soldiers came out of an alley and ran up the wide staircase leading to the main entrance of the Old Shanghai Restaurant. Tu readied himself. He knew that the time for change had come. He could smell it in the air. In other men there might have been a quickening of the pulse, a slither of excitement moving up the spine, perhaps a cooling of the skin—but not with Tu. He simply took a step farther back into the alley and signalled for his men to be calm.

The Tong foot soldiers disappeared into the restaurant, then the Tong's head bodyguard stepped out, followed by ten Tong lieutenants, *Hung Kwan* (Red Poles). The lieutenants quickly cleared the steps of Chinese couples and families waiting to get into the popular eating spot and took up positions on either side of the staircase as they scanned the street and nearby buildings. They were shortly joined by the foot soldiers.

Their boss, the Mountain Master, will come out first and spoil our plan, Tu thought. But he was wrong. The Tong's tall, thin Incense Master, who was in charge of the Tong's secret rites and ceremonies, stepped out into the cool night air and belched loudly, and then a second time.

It was the agreed-upon signal.

Tu Yueh-sen smiled. *So they are off a-whoring. Good,* he thought. He turned to his men and whispered, "Follow them from in front."

"Not possible to follow them when we're ahead of them."

"Very possible if you know where they're going."

"Do we know that?"

"*We* don't," Tu said slowly, noting that he would enjoy this one's death, "*I* do. To Jiang's …" He turned to his men and quickly relayed the information.

A runner immediately sprinted toward the French Concession to alert Tu's men who were already in position there. The plan they had practised for almost two months in the dirty shantytowns where they lived was now to be put into action.

Moments later the Tong boss stepped out of the restaurant. He was closely followed by his head sycophant, known in Tong lore as a "White Paper Fan," who opened a gold cigarette case and offered a Snake Charmer to his rotund boss. The cigarette almost disappeared into the man's chubby cheeks.

So, you are going to get fucked, are you, fat man? Tu thought. Tu had been with his share of women but seldom found it satisfying—in fact he often felt a profound disgust when he was finished, especially if the girl continued to writhe beneath him—astride him—before him—her eyes rolled back in her head searching—searching for something. *No doubt the same thing this pudgy Mountain Master is in search of,* Tu thought. Then the chubby Tong boss strode down the steps of the restaurant like a great conqueror returning to his people.

Tu spat. His saliva glistened in the reflected glow from the fireworks that lit the northern heavens. Then he stepped on the spit, as his grandmother had taught him, "to send the curse deep into the ground." He took out his knife and allowed its keen edge to cut lightly into his palm, as he had when just an urchin boy in the trash-filled alleys, where his friends looked to him to lead them to a better life. And he had, by unleashing unheard of levels of violence. The violence had led to power and the power to better food, better homes, and, as he grew—better women. His life had been so consistently involved with violence that he simply saw it as the way the world functioned. He didn't think of things in terms of right and wrong. Rather, he thought of violence as nothing more than the most direct means to an end. Although he found no joy in inflicting pain, on occasions he saw the beauty of it. The elongation of time when the blade entered a living thing always thrilled him. And, oh yes, his realm of violence had much to do with sharp things—knives. But although he owned a sacred swalto blade he chose not to use it. His reading of the *I Ching* had convinced him that he must respect the sacred. That as long as his killing was in the arena of the profane, he would continue to progress toward his goal the end of *Fan Kuei* power. But if he cut into the sphere of the hallowed, "disaster that way lay." His work and the sacred must not mix. He lit joss sticks most mornings at the Long Hua Temple after he read from the *I Ching*, always taking time to admire the carved lions on the narrow struts at the roofs' edges. His rage was not against the gods. His rage was against the *Fan Kuei*. The fires of his rage had been stoked long ago by his grandmother. And it was her voice he heard in his ears whispering for him to "wreak revenge on them, on all of them." Whose owl-claw hands grasped him by the throat from her deathbed and screamed at him that it was "Your duty to use your strength to punish them. To punish the *Fan Kuei*. To take back all that they have taken from this family!" Tu had heard often enough the story of the family's wealth and position being stolen by the *Fan Kuei*. How the family had fallen all the way down to the shantytown that, as a boy, he had called home. But now his targets were in his sites. First take over the Tong of the Righteous Hand's opium assets, then use them as a base to mount an assault on the *Fan Kuei* traders.

Tu Yueh-sen, he who would soon be called Gangster Tu, looked again at the rotund Mountain Master of the Tong of the Righteous Hand. The man waddled down the restaurant steps looking at his feet. "Look up, fat man," Tu whispered, then added, "See how these fireworks rise, explode in light, then fall to earth? Well, my fat friend, your fire has already been extinguished, and now it is time for you to fall all the way to Hell."

* * *

LI TIAN REPEATED the process with his other eight bamboo ladders and eight more sparkler stars, but this time the ladders were closer to the centre—a tighter circle than the one below.

Then he filled that cavity with his blasting mixture. He sealed the top of the firework, sat back, and lit a cigarette. It may have been the *Fan Kuei*'s New Year's Eve, but it was his night to shine—like no one had ever shone before.

chapter five
The Chosen Three

December 31, 1889

Even as the Mountain Master of the Tong of the Righteous Hand made his leisurely way to Jiang's, Jiang herself, the Carver, and the Confucian waited in the deep, secret cavern of the Warrens for the arrival of the new member of the Chosen Three.

The sound of the Huangpo River could be heard on the other side of the stone wall. The winter dampness had entered Jiang's bones, and she shivered as she wondered how the old Body Guard's son would accept the duties of the Ivory Compact he had inherited from his father. She nodded briefly as she remembered how her mother had given her the initial instructions about the family's obligation to the First Emperor's prophetic relic. Her mother had taken her aside only a few hours before she would attend her first meeting of the Chosen Three and told her all that she needed to know about the Compact. Then the old woman had kissed her hard on the forehead and said, "Now your name is Jiang, and what was mine is yours. Do me and your much-honoured older sister, the History Teller, proud. Make them revere you the way they did her."

"And you, Mother, the way they revere you still."

"For that praise, I thank you."

Mother and daughter embraced. Then her mother said, "Now get out of here. Even a whore, no, fuck that, *especially* a whore, has a right to die in some privacy."

Those words had echoed in her mind as she sat through her first meeting in the secret chamber of the Warrens. That was almost twenty-five years ago, and soon she would have to assign the name Jiang to one of her two younger daughters—and then tell her to "get out of here," because—and on this she totally agreed with her mother—after a life as a whore, she had the right to privacy at the end.

On that long-ago night she had returned from her first meeting of the Ivory Compact to find her mother's delicate features twisted in pain and her face bloated black from the poison that she had swallowed. A poison not so different from the one that Jiang herself, standing in the cold of the Warrens on that decadal evening, carried in a hidden pocket of her silk robe. Although there was a time when she'd doubted that she could ever take her own life, life itself had taught her many lessons, not the least of which was that only if you were willing to take your own life were you in control of your life. And control had been a major tenet of hers during her almost quarter of a century in control of the Chinese demimonde of Shanghai.

The Confucian was younger than Jiang by probably ten years, and the two had known each other for several years but not intimately. The Confucian was a very private man. His father had passed on his responsibilities in the Ivory Compact in the opening pages of a lengthy diary, the entries of which—every one by Confucians in the Ivory Compact—stretched all the way back to the time of the First Emperor. The young man had found the extraordinary document beneath his father's ancient writing stone two days after his passing.

He would never forget the first meeting of the Chosen Three he attended. He had thought it nothing but foolishness, but quickly changed his mind when he peered into the first portal of the Narwhal Tusk. That night he read the entirety of the diary and made his first written contribution to the Confucian legacy. That was just over twenty years and hundreds of diary entries ago.

"He's late," the Carver said. Despite the fact that the Carver was easily the youngest in the room he assumed a senior position to the others—as the Carver always had, from the very beginning on the Holy Mountain.

They heard a loud thump from the south corridor and Jiang looked to the men. Both quickly ran down the length of the hidden corridor and found the Body Guard's son slumped against a wall just past an overhanging ledge that was a little known marker for an access to the hidden corridor from the south. They helped him into the chamber. The man's clothes were soaked through with the blood of his initiation, but once he was in the chamber he stood erect. Jiang noted the signs of great age in his eyes—something closer to the many years of his grandfather the Fisherman.

The Confucian was aware of something very different about this young man. Upon Loa Wei Fen's death on the stage in Chinkiang, the Fisherman's younger son had become the Body Guard. He had now passed the torch to his son. But this young man was not a bodyguard. He was clearly an Assassin. Bodyguards used their exceptional martial arts skills in a purely defensive posture. Assassins used those same skills to take steps to advance the prophecy of the Ivory, the most serious of which was the re-formation of the ancient Guild of Assassins.

For the very first time in the Ivory Compact the Body Guard had been replaced by an Assassin—potentially the head of the Guild of Assassins. A serious change to the constituency of the Compact. But they all knew the time was right for a man of action to be part of their conspiracy.

"Are you weak from your wounds?" Jiang asked.

"No. They make me strong," the Assassin responded.

The Confucian nodded. A particularly loud series of fireworks sent dull, concussive thuds through the underground chamber.

Loa Wei Fen held his hands over his ears until the sound dissipated.

Jiang watched him closely. "Does the sound hurt you?"

"No. Not the sound. The fact that the sound is theirs, not ours. Their new year, not ours. Their new decade, not ours." He looked at the others of the Ivory Compact and stated the obvious. "Theirs, the *Fan Kuei*, not ours." As the sound of the waves of the Huangpo River outside the walls of the Warrens chamber slowly pushed aside the din of the fireworks, a calm descended on him. The sound of the Huangpo River was the sound of their river. A Chinese river.

In the light thrown by the torches, the Carver nodded and unlatched the side catches of the beautiful mahogany box that stood on the two jade pedestals, exposing the relic. The Chosen Three looked in the first portal at the image of hundreds of Han Chinese men, their long braided queues flying behind them as the thin reeds in their mouths bent against their bizarre dance.

Everyone now knew what those reeds were—and what the dance was too.

"Has it been changed?" Jiang asked.

"What?" asked the Carver.

"Bring the torch closer," Jiang ordered as she peered into the hollow cavern in the Narwhal Tusk. "Now move it to your left." The Carver did. Loa Wei Fen and the Confucian adjusted their positions to get a better look. "There," Jiang said. "Have you seen the two women at the back before?"

The Carver moved the torch but did not answer the question.

"I've never seen them," said the Confucian.

"Has someone tampered with—?"

"Not at all." The Carver's voice was pulled back in his throat but clear in the still air of the chamber.

"So how did those two women come into view?" demanded Jiang.

"They may have been there before but …"

Jiang gave the Confucian a look that silenced him quickly, then added, "We are not fools here. We do not 'overlook' things. Those figures have somehow moved forward."

"How do you mean, moved forward?" the Carver asked slowly.

"Not physically moved forward, but somehow they've come into focus."

"Indeed," the Carver said as he stepped up to the Tusk. "Look." He ran his hand over the top of the sacred object. Inside the cavern, the shadow of his hand moved across the ivory figures.

"Why …?"

"It's rotting," said the Carver, "as all things must, and as it rots some sections of its surface are becoming translucent."

"Allowing in light where there was not light before," said Loa Wei Fen.

"So the women's figures have always been in the background," Jiang said, then added, "I always looked for the role of women in the destiny within the window, and for all those years all I could see were shadows, near the very back of the tableau. Now, with the decay of the Tusk, these two women have assumed light and focus."

"But I don't understand," said the Confucian.

"Understand what?" asked the Carver, as he moved his hand over the top surface of the Tusk again.

"This Tusk is a duplication of an earlier Tusk that in itself was a duplication of an earlier one—going all the way back to the original Narwhal Tusk delivered by the First Emperor to our ancestors on the Holy Mountain."

The Carver didn't say anything, nor did he nod agreement.

"Isn't it?" pressed the Confucian.

The room instantly filled with tension. The Assassin involuntarily placed his hand on his swalto blade. Jiang sprang to her feet. Slowly the Carver said, "There have never been copies made of the Tusk. We were always prepared to make duplications of the relic—but it was never duplicated. It wasn't necessary."

In a tiny, awed voice, Jiang said, "Then this Tusk is the original that was given by the First Emperor to our ancestors all those years ago on the Holy Mountain?"

"Yes." The Carver's voice was little more than a whisper. He looked at the relic and took a long breath. A silence, deep and seemingly solid, filled the chamber. Finally the Carver spoke. "This secret has been the greatest burden that my family has carried all these years."

"Why would you keep it from us?" Jiang demanded.

"All of us in this room have secrets. It is part of the strength of the Compact. This secret we have always felt was handed to us directly from the First Emperor and our patron, Chesu Hoi."

"But how ...?" the Confucian began.

The Carver shrugged. "The ancients had their ways, which died with them. Some sort of preservative, one must assume. But exactly what pre-servative is another mystery of the relic. Until lately there has been almost no decaying of the ivory at all. As I said, each successive Carver prepared himself to duplicate the Tusk—but it has been unnecessary, as you can see."

"The Tusk in front of us is the original?" asked the Confucian, still unable to come to grips with the startling truth.

"Yes," the Carver acknowledged.

"So is it wrong to assume that what we are seeing in front of us now is what the First Emperor, over two thousand years ago, wanted us to see as the Tusk rotted?" asked Jiang.

"It is a very logical conclusion, perhaps the only possible conclusion," replied the Carver.

Everyone in the deep cavern in the Warrens allowed that surprising fact to find a place in their hearts. No longer was this a clever replica that con-fronted them, now it was the original message from the Holy Mountain—and the relic, as it decayed, was changing its focus, bringing new things literally to light ... talking to them.

"It's guiding us," Jiang said. "First there are the two women ..."

"And they're oddly dressed," the Confucian said.

That had escaped the others. Jiang pulled back from the Narwhal Tusk as a shock of recognition rocked her. "Look at their feet," she said.

Only one had the tiny, bound feet of a high-born woman, and her cloth-ing was clearly Beijing style—Manchu aristocracy. The other woman wore a courtesan's robes with the large, wide central sash of a brothel madam—a belt not dissimilar from the one that Jiang now carefully moved beneath her cloak.

"What does all this mean?" the Assassin asked.

"That it is women's turn to step forward," Jiang said as she knelt again to get a closer look at the Tusk. Then she turned away from the portal and looked at the Carver. "Is the Tusk being carefully guarded?"

This surprised everyone in the room.

"Why do you ask?" demanded the Carver.

"Because the Beijing Manchu woman has a sword in her hand."

* * *

THE DOWAGER EMPRESS LEANED on her ceremonial sword as the mid-winter midnight procession passed by offering tributes. *So hollow,* she thought, remembering when, as a young girl, she had received the tributes for the first time. Then, they had been offered not only in supplication but also in fear. When the Q'ing Dynasty was a great power in the world, not a desiccated skeleton picked dry by the European carrion birds. She nodded as the delegation from Annam placed several large ivory tusks on the dais in front of her. She acknowledged the tribute with the slightest wave of her bejewelled fingers. Then the representative from Bengal stepped forward and presented a large, beautifully engraved box. He flipped open the beaten copper latches and turned the box toward the Dowager. Three large rubies sat on a velvet mound. The Dowager had always loved rubies, but her eyes, much to her surprise, were drawn back to the tusks from Annam. She lifted the ceremonial sword in her hand and allowed its point to rest on the widest part of one of the ivory tusks. The sword's tip penetrated the ivory. A synapsal flash triggered a memory in her ancient mind and the word *carved* came out of her mouth in a throaty burp. Instantly her assistants were there to inquire, "Excuse me, Highness?" "Is there something you wish, Your Majesty?" and a hundred other little requests that tried to justify their continued employment in the Forbidden City. She turned from the fools and called for her Head Eunuch.

"Madam?" Chesu Hoi asked.

She pointed at the tusk with her sword and once more allowed the tip to cut into the surface.

Again her Head Eunuch asked, "Madam?" then added cautiously, "Is there something with which I can be of assistance?"

She thought about that for a moment, then responded, "Not assistance."

"Ah, then what, Madam?"

She looked at the man. He was almost as old as she. He was the only old person she allowed near her person. "What would a History Teller make of an ivory tusk, do you suppose?"

Chesu Hoi thought momentarily of contacting the Carver in Shanghai but discarded the precaution and said, "I am not trained as a History Teller. In matters of history, I am closer to the History Chronicler of old, as you well know, Madam."

She did know. "Are there any History Tellers left? A History Chronicler is of no earthly use when it comes to legends."

"Legends, Madam?"

"Yes, legends. Legends of carvings in tusks."

* * *

"DO THE TWO WOMEN CHANGE our position in the prophecy?" the Assassin asked.

It was the question on all of their minds. They all knew that the White Birds on Water had landed and that the darkness they brought with them had intensified for years, but it was also clear that there was a step, still hidden behind the closed second portal—or perhaps several steps—missing between the White Birds landing and the building of the Seventy Pagodas.

Shanghai had become a booming commercial centre under the rule of the *Fan Kuei,* and immigration into the city from all over China had increased every time there was chaos in the countryside—which was an ever more frequent occurrence. The city now had more than enough labourers to build the Seventy Pagodas, but no pagodas had been built. The massive statements of European and American power had been erected along the Huangpo, but these were not pagodas. In fact, although Chinese sweat built Shanghai, the Chinese owned few of the buildings outside of the walls of the Old City. Shanghai's second most profitable business was real estate, which, just like its first business, opium, was almost entirely controlled by the *Fan Kuei.* True, wealthy immigrants from Ningpo and Canton had begun a housing style of their own by building traditional interior courtyards with frontage on streets. They called them *shikumen,* or "stone portals," referring to the carved stone structures over top of the entrance door. Newer, often less expensive homes, built with access to alleys rather than streets, were called *lilong,* and a few had such extravagances as sanitary fixtures and electricity. But the majority of the Chinese in Shanghai could never dream of owning *shikumen* or even *lilong.* They were poor people from the country who had come by boat down the Grand Canal and then along the Yangtze. They ended up anchored in the murky waters of the Suzu Creek. New arrivals lived on their boats. When the boats began to rot, either from natural causes or the creek's vile pollutants, the family pulled the boat ashore and lived in it on land. When the boats collapsed, the peasants used the materials from the boat, especially the reeds from the roof, to build a hut in which to live. The Shanghainese, with their cruel sense of irony, named these structures *gundilong,* or "rolling earth dragons," the joke being that the word for dragon, *long*, is the same as the word for cage. Few of these people ever managed to move from their "rolling earth cages." Only the very talented and the very fortunate moved past straw shacks to the stone buildings of the *lilong* or *shikumen*.

Money was being made by the fistful in Shanghai—but not by the Chinese.

All about them was the darkness caused by opium, but how were they to get to the promised light that was the Seventy Pagodas?

"Will there be more figures revealed?" asked the Assassin.

"Who can tell?" replied the Carver. "It's likely that there are more figures ready to come to light."

"More prophecies," Jiang said. "The Tusk must be kept safe. Should it fall into the wrong hands ..."

"The Tusk is as safe as it's always been," said the Carver.

"Not good enough now," spat out Jiang. "Now we must assure its safety. Assure it!"

The Carver nodded but said nothing. The newly revealed figures were interesting, but the mysterious central, closed portal was surely more important, and he, unlike most of the previous Carvers, had a scientific bent—a mind that led him to want to experiment on the portal that Q'in She Huang, the First Emperor, had said could be opened only "by people in the darkness of the Age of White Birds on Water."

A heavy series of concussive sounds, yet more fireworks over the Huangpo River, filled the cavern.

* * *

LI TIAN IGNORED what he thought of as senseless banging and readied his rocket.

chapter six
Tu's Attack

December 31, 1889

Jiang had left orders to set aside the south wing of her French Concession house for the Tong members. She didn't like them, but thanks to her family's deal with the Colombe family, at least her protection money was paid to the French authorities, not to the likes of these thugs. There was a special price charged for the girls' services at Jiang's to Tong members—double what everyone else paid.

Jiang was considering doubling even that as she arrived back from the warrens. Then she saw the large-eared young man—and his knife. *Where are my guards?* she wondered. Then there were more men like the one with the knife. One knocked over a Go board, sending the pieces skittering across the floor and garnering a loud protest from an old player. Before Jiang could calm the Go player she noticed a young man carrying a pearl-handled pistol she recognized as one belonging to her private bodyguard. She watched as the "the knife's" men filtered through the crowd in her reception chamber in choreographed patterns that bespoke both youth and savagery. Then she felt him at her side. His body was pressed up tight against her hip—his taut sinew against her soft curves—but she felt no tumescence between his legs.

"Evening, Miss Jiang," Tu's surprisingly light, slightly lisped voice murmured.

"Good …"

But that was all she managed before his hand pushed through the slit in her dress and covered her sex. "Do you smell it, Miss Jiang?"

"What?"

"The reek of change."

Then she heard the fat Mountain Master's wild cry from the far corridor.

Moments later, the man, his head bodyguard, and both of his syco-phants, known as the White Paper Fan and the Straw Sandal, came run-ning out of the back rooms and stumbled to a stop in the centre of the large reception room. All were completely naked.

Jiang noted with a start that the "knife man" wasn't by her side—and then the chubby Tong boss screamed and the crowd parted, everyone doing their best to get as far away from the naked howling man as they could.

Tu's first knife had gone easily through the Tong boss's hand and buried itself almost four inches deep in the ornate table upon which it rested. Then Tu's second knife went through the Mountain Master's left foot and sank almost three inches into the mahogany boards of the brothel's floor.

"Don't even think of touching those knives or I'll put knives through your other hand and foot," the young man said. He calmly crossed to the Tong's head bodyguard and said, loudly enough for everyone in the room to hear, "Put your hands on your head."

Slowly the bodyguard moved his large hands from his grey pubic hair, exposing his smallish member. Without taking his eyes from Tu he put his hands on his bald scalp.

"Don't scowl, old man," Tu commanded. "You wouldn't want to lose a hand as well as your dick."

"My ..."

But he got out no more words before his crotch blossomed red and a hunk of aged flesh fell to the floor.

Immediately there was a charge to the exit, but the young man's voice cut through the uproar. "Death awaits anyone who makes it through that door."

The crowd stopped.

"Now turn, all of you, and watch." Then he added, ominously, "It is important that you see what is going to happen here."

Slowly, as one confused thing, the crowd turned to the young man with the blooded knife.

"Good," he said. And he wheeled on the remaining Tong members.

———

Outside the brothel, Tu's carefully positioned men and vehicles encircled the majority of the Tong's foot soldiers and some of the lieutenants, while the rest of Tu's men, by the light of the fireworks, attacked the remaining lieutenants, disarming some, killing others.

———

Inside Jiang's the operation was nearing its climax. The head bodyguard had blacked out from loss of blood. The Mountain Master was pinned to the floor and table with Tu's knives, too frightened to move or call out. The lieutenants left outside the brothel were frogmarched into the reception chamber by Tu's men. The wealthy clients of Jiang's prestigious establishment, most importantly, were wide-eyed and attentive.

Tu leaped on a table and called out, "Incense Master!" The tall, thin man who had given the signal belches on the steps of the Old Shanghai Restaurant not forty-five minutes before now made his way through the crowd and stood before Tu. The young man nodded. The Incense Master smiled broadly, bowed, and began the first of the nine prostrations of the formal kowtow.

Tu's blade slid into the back of his neck exactly where the spinal cord entered the skull. The Incense Master jerked spasmodically for ten seconds, then stilled. Tu turned the knife. The man's arms and legs all shot out at once, like a puppet whose master had yanked on the wrong strings. Tu pulled up on the knife and held the man several inches off the floor, watching him twitch. Then he yanked the knife out of the man's dead body and it dropped to the floor like so many potatoes in a sack.

"Traitors are like virgins. They can only claim the title once."

The Incense Master's body lay on the floor, limbs in all directions, knees and elbows at angles not inherent in the evolutionary plan for the human body.

Then Tu said, "Bring me the Tong's sycophants." The two men were shoved forward, whimpering. Tu showed them absolutely no mercy.

When the second was dispatched, Tu looked to the six remaining lieutenants of the Tong of the Righteous Hand. "I offer you six Red Poles the opportunity to swear loyalty to me as the new head of the Tong of the Righteous Hand. You!" Tu said pointing at the eldest of the men.

The man's face darkened, but before he could move, Tu was on him and had his chest open with a single slash of his knife. With his hands inside the man's chest cavity, Tu turned to the others and said, "Does anyone else have a problem with the new order?"

No one did.

News of Tu's savagery quickly took on the air of legend in the teeming streets of the city at the Bend in the River. And later, as Jiang took him to her bed, Tu heard his grandmother's pleading words over and over again in his head: *"Yueh-sen, give me my revenge. My revenge against the* Fan Kuei, *the Foreign Devils."*

* * *

THE FINALE OF THE FIREWORKS momentarily turned night to bright day—then darkness and silence, that rarest of entities in Shanghai, followed. Silas Hordoon stood, almost alone, on the Bund Promenade, staring at the still wild Pudong across the Huangpo River. The rest of Shanghai had grown, prospered, matured. Shanghai had already expanded rapidly to the west and south, but there was no footprint of Shanghai on the Pudong. The other side of the Bend in the River was still true to its nature, a challenge to the *Fan Kuei* and their compradors and their nightclubs and department stores on Bubbling Spring Road. Silas shivered involuntarily. The Huangpo was not a wide river—that untamed land so close to his home made his heart race—and the word *danger* crept up from the bottom of his consciousness and fell from his mouth in the cold dawn of the first day of the last decade of the nineteenth century.

* * *

THEN LI TIAN LIT his firework.

It whistled loudly as it ascended in an arc of flame that drew every eye. An enormous bang assaulted every ear, followed quickly by an elegant ring of eight shimmering stars in a perfect circle. Then a second bang threw out a second ring of eight stars in a circle within the larger first circle. To the amazement of every watcher, the outside ring exploded one star at a time in a clockwise circle while the inner ring, in exact synchronization, exploded counter-clockwise. Finally, as if on some godly cue, the exploding stars began to change colour and shape. Red began to dominate and the sparks falling earthward formed tears. Red tears filled the night sky, then plunged from the heavens to the earth below—and Li Tian smiled. He could smell the change in the air. And the tears this time would not be Chinese tears.

The blood tears were the last that anyone saw or heard of Li Tian. He simply packed his materials into his plain wooden box, affixed the box to his bamboo shoulder carrier, and disappeared into the dense forest of the

Pudong. He ignored the applause all around him and the looks of awe and wonder; he ignored the questions and the requests to learn from him. He simply disappeared and was never seen again in or around Shanghai.

But he didn't disappear from history. He was a muse to many a Chinese dreamer. Here was a Chinese man of real genius. A unique Chinese genius. One of the many inspirational figures that would, almost sixty years later, be foremost in the mind of a seasoned revolutionary leader as he entered Shanghai at the head of a great army.

chapter seven

And in Far-Off America

On that same night in another port city, but this one far from the Bend in the River, a twelve-year-old Chinese boy ducked just in time to avoid the beer tankard that had been thrown at his head. The heavy thing thudded against the wall of the basement tavern and splattered its liquid in a fireworks pattern. It was hardly the first projectile that the boy, Charles Soon, had avoided in his three years of working at the Ploughman's Pune in the Southey section of Boston, Massachusetts. At least he didn't have to service these Irish pigs, like the two young girls did. All he had to do was take their abuse and clean up their mess. Then try to get the smell of their urine and their foul beer out of his hair before he returned home to his sick father, who had brought him, shortly after his mother died, to the Golden Mountain. That was almost nine years ago.

The two young Negro boys who also worked at the Ploughman had befriended him early on and shown him how to stay out of trouble. They were the closest thing to friends he had in that cold place. One had taught him how to read English, while the other had a truly wicked sense of humour that made many a hard night's work bearable for Charles. "Catholics live to get drunk," he had said, "and they get drunk to live." Charles remembered that as he swept the floor with his hand and came up with the dented tankard. He knew he'd have to fix it before the end of his shift or he would have the cost of a new tankard taken out of his paltry wages. The Irishmen were singing again. They were always singing. He looked to his Black friends, and their eyes were smiling. *There they go, singing again,* their eyes seemed to be saying.

Charles recalled one terrific night when another group of Irishmen, this time wearing orange-coloured clothing, had come in singing something that enflamed these particular Irishmen, and the vicious fight that had ensued was the best thing that had happened in the Ploughman's Pune, as far as Charles Soon was concerned. He'd even joined his two Black co-workers in cheering on the pugilists.

"Hey, you fuckin' Celestial, clean the puke from my table before I make you lick it up." This supposed witticism drew raucous laughter from the other louts in the man's company, and Charles rushed over to the table. He didn't take such threats lightly. Drunken Irishmen were not to be contradicted or reasoned with. That had been the other Chinese boy's advice to him on his first day working in the bar. Charles didn't know where the boy was now. He simply hadn't shown up one night. And no one in the bar, or in Boston's small Chinese community, talked about it. He had just vanished. Charles hoped he hadn't ended up stuffed in a hole in the ground—or worse. He prayed that the boy had somehow just disappeared. He prayed that the boy was happy and had escaped. Like he was going to do this very evening, once this shift was over.

He also prayed that his father had been sincere when he'd said, "There is no future for you here, son. This place hates us. Go, escape if you can, and I will see you in the next life."

This New Year's Eve the whole city was drunk. Hopefully he could sneak onboard a ship that would take him—at the beginning of this final decade of the nineteenth century—to a new life.

———

The smell of the Irishman's vomit was on his hands. The bits of smoked bacon and other undercooked meats he had eaten added a kind of acid to the bile in the man's stomach, the odour of which had moved from Charles's rag to his hands. So he stuffed them deep into his pockets as he looked up at the brutally cold Boston night sky. The sounds of drunken revelry were all around him as he carefully made his way down Blackstone Street. He ducked into a darkened storefront as a horse-drawn police wagon turned onto the street. It made its way slowly down the roadway, swinging its lantern, from one side of the street to the other. The edge of the light crossed Charles's shoes, but the wagon didn't stop. Shortly it picked up speed and moved farther down the street.

Charles let out a slow breath, then turned, startled. He wasn't alone. There was someone else in the safety of the darkness. He looked but couldn't see anything. Then he saw the whites of eyes in blue-black skin. He staggered back and fell. When he scrambled to his feet again those large white eyes were close to his face. Charles could see that the eyes were milky, frightened.

"You have some food for Edward?"

It was the voice of a child like himself. Charles stepped out into the street and was surprised when a tall, large African man stepped out of the darkness and approached him. This was a grown Black man, not like his two friends in the bar who had helped him survive at the Ploughman.

"You understand English?" the man demanded.

Charles reached inside his thin cloth jacket and pulled out some of the food he'd taken from the Ploughman's Pune. He cracked a loaf of stale bread and gave half of it to the African, who ate it greedily, stuffing the thing into his mouth so fast that he choked on it and almost vomited it up on the street cobbles. Charles was happy he hadn't—he'd seen enough barf for one day.

Then the Black man looked at Charles. "Where are you going?"

Charles noted the slow speech, the broad, flat forehead, and the wide space between the man's nose and upper lip. This African was an idiot.

"Take Edward with you."

"I'm not going anywhere."

"Then I'll not go anywhere too."

Across the street, men were pouring out of a saloon. Charles took the African by the arm and guided him back into the darkness of the doorway. No need attracting attention. Then he gave him more of his bread and said, "You can't come with me, where I'm going."

"Why Edward can't ...?"

Exasperated, Charles shouted, "Because you're a fool." Then he grabbed his small satchel, darted across the street, and ran down the alley as fast as his short legs would take him, his breath a mist before his face. He turned north and headed toward the cargo port.

Not twenty minutes later the road dead-ended into a large square with a private park surrounded by a high metal fence. Four cobbled streets entered the square from four different directions. He was shaking from the cold and was confused as to which way was north.

Then he heard them. The kind of racial taunts he had lived with his whole life. But it was dark here and he was alone in a part of the city dangerous for a Chinese boy. He heard the snowball smack into the wall just over his shoulder before he spotted the boys gathered by the gated park.

He smiled—just boys. Then he turned and looked at the snowball one of them had thrown at him. It had hit the brick wall full force and not broken apart. He picked it up. It was a large stone covered with just a sprinkling of snow.

Then a second whizzed by his head—and a third and fourth. He saw the pack of boys coming at him from two sides. The lead boy in each group carried a large stick. This was no fun snowball fight.

"Hey, Chinky!"

The insult seemed to float on the cold air, enter Charles's ears, and crash into his heart.

Then a chorus of "Chinky, Chinky, Chinky!"

Charles looked quickly to his left. They were coming that way. Then back to his right, the other group was coming at him from there. He took a breath and sprinted toward the fenced-in park in the middle of the square.

And they raced after him.

Charles ran straight at the iron gate and leaped up as high as he could manage. His hand found purchase on a metal post but seemed to stick to the iron. He ripped it free, leaving some of his palm attached to the frozen metal, and scrambled up and over the fence … but so did most of the boys chasing him.

Charles ran to the fountain in the centre of the small park, desperate to find a place to make a stand. And he waited. And waited. But no boys followed him. He strained to hear. But there were no more chants of "Chinky, Chinky"—although there were thuds, several thuds as things fell to the ground.

Charles peered into the darkness and he saw motion. He readied himself to fight, then, as a cloud moved past the moon, he saw the large, dark figure of Edward coming toward him. His face was bloodied and his hands a mess. His coat had a large rip in it, but there was a huge smile on his face. "Can Edward come with you now?" the man asked.

Charles ran past Edward and saw almost a dozen boys lying on the ground in various degrees of distress. Charles turned back to Edward and said, "Sure."

They made their way quickly out of the park, but once again Charles couldn't figure out the way to the docks. He'd gotten all turned around and couldn't determine which way was north.

"Can Edward help?" the African asked patiently.

"Only if you know where the docks are."

"What direction are they?"

"North," Charles said, almost crying since the night was passing and he knew that only on New Year's did he stand a chance of getting past the sentries of the heavily guarded docks. Everyone at the Ploughman's Pune talked about New Year's being the only night that the owners didn't care if the sailors got roaring drunk.

Then Charles looked at the large Black man. He was pointing.

"North?" Charles asked.

Edward pointed up at a bright star and said, "North toward that star, always, my grandma told me."

And Edward was right.

Less than an hour later they were at the cargo docks. And twenty minutes after that they had snuck past two sleeping sentries and stowed away on a cargo ship.

chapter eight
Stowaway

January 1890

The darkness was complete. Above them, Charles and Edward heard the footfalls of the sailors. On occasion they heard a gruff order and a surly response. But shortly there was only silence in their hiding place onboard the ship—silence and darkness.

Then the rats came.

"Buggy bite my foot," Edward whimpered.

"What?" Charles whispered.

"Oh, no, oh, no, oh, no!"

"Shh! Come on, Edward, you have to ..." Then Charles felt something furry scamper over his hand, up his arm, and past his cheek.

"Buggy bite my foot! Buggy bite my foot!"

Edward's voice was rising in both pitch and volume.

"Ouch! Help Edward!" the poor man called out. "Edward needs help!"

"Edward, Edward, it's just mice. Just little mice. Little tiny mice. A big fellow like you can't be afraid of little mice, Edward." Charles heard the Black man's breath loud in the closed space. He reached for Edward's hand and grabbed hold of it. "Hold my hand, Edward, just hold my hand. We have to get out of harbour before they catch us, otherwise they'll put us back in Boston." Charles had an idea. "Does Edward want to be put back in Boston?"

"No, Edward doesn't like Boston."

Charles thought, *It's more likely that Boston doesn't like Edward. Sure as shootin' Boston doesn't like Charles.* But all he said was, "That's right. Now just ignore the little mice and this nice ship will take us to a much better place."

Something seemed to catch in Edward's throat as he said, "This ship goes to the better place? This ship goes there?"

Charles didn't understand Edward's excitement but was pleased that Edward was quieting down, and he said, "Yes, a better place. A better place than Boston."

Edward shifted his position, rubbing hard against Charles. The man's odour was hard for Charles to ignore. Charles's house was not fancy, but they were conscientious about cleanliness there. Being Chinese, they knew the connection between sanitation and disease—knew it all too well from the family's experience.

"Move over, Edward," he said.

Edward moved his large body to one side, then reached out for Charles, inadvertently smacking him hard in the face with the heel of his meaty hand. "You promise Edward this boat is going to the better place? You promise? If you lie to Edward there be a curse on you."

Charles was confused by Edward's response, but before he could answer he heard the African's hoarse whisper, "Buggy bite my foot!"

———

It's far better than whaling, Malachi thought as he watched the last of the cargo placed in the hold and the hatches being secured. Although, for religious reasons, he wasn't pleased with his present cargo—strong Irish whisky from Boston to New York—he was pleased with the rest of his routing. Small appliances, soft manufactured goods, household items, and decorative blown glass from New York to Norfolk, Virginia, and Wilmington, North Carolina, where he'd pick up cotton to bring back to Boston to feed the textile mills of New England. His offload and reload schedule in Wilmington would give him enough time to visit the seminary there—for years a place of peace for him after all the killing of his whaling time. This particular sojourn at the seminary would also allow him to contemplate his imminent fatherhood. He and his wife had already agreed that if the baby was a boy they would name him after the father that Malachi's mother, Rachel, had told him so much about. He was going to be a father—the Hordoon line was going to continue.

He ran his fingers through his thick red hair and then applied more of the salve to his severely sunburned nose. All those years ago his mother had warned him about exposing his white skin to the sun—even the winter sun.

"Tide's begun to turn, Captain."

Malachi nodded. "Just check the seals on the forward hatch and be sure the longshoremen haven't decided to join us on our voyage. Breeze is up, so once we've cleared Peachey Head, set a top and gallant."

"Aye, sir."

Although this was a merchant ship, these seamen had survived several close calls at sea because of the bravery and seamanship of their red-headed Captain, so they treated him with military courtesy, a true rarity in their hard and rancorous world.

Malachi took the Bible his mother had given him on the day he was confirmed—the day she'd told him who his father was—and opened it at random. The verses of the Book of Ruth presented themselves to him, and he scanned the elegant seventeenth-century words with an old, familiar pleasure. *Old friends, they are,* he thought as he allowed the tips of his fingers to glide across the beautiful tissue-thin paper.

He'd found the Bible his mother had packed in his sea trunk a real sanctuary in his whaling days. The horror of the kill zone, the screaming of the wounded mammals, the night ocean red beneath the swaying of the oil lanterns, and everywhere the smell of death and the screech of carrion birds—while the sharks circled endlessly. Only the beautiful Bible poetry could lift the revulsion from his heart. And then there were his mother's elegantly penned words on the inside of the cover leaf: "Read and spread only the best of the Words herein. Think kindly of me, when you are far away, and remember that men's hearts are the object of your quest, not their minds. Your Mother, Rachel."

The tide was heading out quickly now, as it often did near the full moon in Boston Harbor. His sleek bark caught the wind and headed seaward.

———

"We're moving, Edward. Can you feel it?"

"Edward is on the boat to the better place." The African's voice was resonant and calm.

"Right. Now just relax. Ignore the mice and try to get some sleep."

"Edward isn't afraid of the mice because he's going to the better place."

* * *

ON THE THIRD DAY at sea, Charles awoke to the kick of a hard boot and the order, "Stand up! Stand up, I say!"

He and Edward emerged from their hiding place and were roughly walked up on deck, where they squinted in the early morning January sun. Two strong seamen held them against the port rail. Charles tried to compose his thoughts. It was possible they would throw the two of them overboard. Very possible. He hadn't thought of that before. Then a red-haired man came forward and said, "And what have we here?"

"Stowaways, sir. An African and a Celestial. A dinner for the sharks, sir?"

The red-haired man signalled that the two should be separated. Charles was walked forward while the red-haired man, who Charles assumed was the Captain, went to talk to Edward. The African had a wide grin on his face, as if he were about to meet an angel.

After five minutes of talking to Edward, the red-haired man approached Charles. "Let him stand on his own," he ordered the sailor. "Do you speak English, boy?"

"I do, sir," Charles said, unhappy that his voice quavered.

"You realize that this is a private sea vessel and that I am its Captain?"

Charles nodded.

"And that your crime is punishable in any manner that I see fit?"

Charles hadn't known that, but he nodded again.

"Why are you here, boy?"

Charles didn't know what to say.

"Do you think our ship is going to the better place, like your dark friend?"

"Any place would be better than Boston, sir."

"Perhaps, but not *the* better place?"

"I don't know what Edward meant by that, sir."

The man looked at Charles closely and finally asked, "Can you read, lad?"

Charles nodded and blurted out, "Yes, sir. English and Mandarin."

"Really."

"Yes, sir."

The red-haired man turned away from Charles and looked toward the horizon. He pointed at a series of towering clouds to the west and scowled. "There'll be a storm, lad. When it's done, you are to tell me which of the two of you is to be thrown overboard. Either you or your African friend is not long for this world."

The storm seemed to last for hours and hours. The forward privy in which they had locked Edward and Charles was foul-smelling, but the tossing of the waves left them little time to be offended by the odour. Quickly they were thrown from one wall to the other, and ocean water

360

squeezed between the loose planking. But through it all Edward was calm. Almost serene. Charles finally held on to the massive man for support and was surprised to finally awaken in Edward's lap, with the man's huge hands smoothing the hair from his face.

The door of the privy slammed open. Overhead, winter stars pierced the black of the sky like some sort of jewels. As Charles was marched toward the stern of the ship he saw the Dipper standing out so starkly that it almost made him laugh—as if God had put one constellation up there that any jerk could find.

The sailor opened the door to the Captain's quarters and shoved Charles in. The boy stumbled, then caught himself at the corner of the man's desk. A leather-bound book was on the desktop. The red-haired man came in and took a seat at the desk.

"You claim you can read, lad." The man picked up the book and handed it to Charles. "Read aloud."

Charles read where the man pointed. It was a story. It began with two women coming to a king with one baby that each woman claimed to be her own. The king questioned each woman, but both maintained their claim. Finally the king took the baby and threatened to kill it. Charles went to turn the page to read on but the red-haired man said, "Fine," and took back the book. "Now it is time to decide. Who shall go overboard in these cold seas, you or your slow-thinking African friend?"

Charles couldn't think. All that was in his head was the story from the book, where the king wanted to kill the child to determine who was the real mother. Finally he blurted out, "You can't kill him. He doesn't know what's happening to him. It wouldn't be fair. If you must, throw me overboard."

Then Charles began to shake and tears streamed down his cheeks.

When the red-haired man's hand landed on his shoulder he was sure the man was going to lift him up and march him to the rail. But the hand rested on his shoulder, then gently brushed away his tears. "Very brave, lad. Very brave. Sit. You read well. Do you understand what it is that you read?"

It was Charles Soon's very first Bible lesson.

By the time they were halfway to Wilmington, Charles had read much of Genesis aloud, and looked forward to discussing it with the kind red-haired Captain after dinner each night. When they finally arrived in Wilmington it was agreed that he would enter the seminary there.

And Charles Soon and Edward spent the next seven years of their lives in Wilmington, Edward learning to be a cook and Charles Soon training to be a Southern Methodist missionary.

chapter nine
The Second Portal

In the flickering light cast by the taper, the Carver stared at the Narwhal Tusk. He had been drawn to the relic that night, just as he had been drawn to the sacred object over and over again in the past month, since the dreams had begun. Dreams of the Tusk alive with maggots and spiders and scorpions. He would awake in a sweat, slip from his bed, careful not to rouse his wife and sons, and race to the relic's hiding place in the depths of the Warrens. There he would light a taper, then release the Tusk from its mahogany casket.

Like the Carvers before him, he was fully versed in the lore of Q'in She Huang's Ivory Compact and knew in great detail the history of the revealing of the first and third windows to the Chosen Three. But unlike many of his ancestors, the Carver had a real interest in what caused things to happen in the natural world, something not always present in accomplished artists. The Carver, from the very first time his father had shown him the object, had been curious about the sealant that must have been used all those years ago on the Holy Mountain to preserve the ivory and its carvings—both hidden and revealed.

He put his hand on the relic, knowing that the cool surface beneath his palm had been touched by his honoured ancestral patron, the Eunuch Chesu Hoi, and by the First Emperor himself.

The Carver knelt and peered in at the vision of the Age of White Birds on Water. He knew that this portal had been opened by blood. He also knew that the third portal, the Age of the Seventy Pagodas, had been opened on the Holy Mountain by the First Emperor himself. As well, he knew that "only those in the darkness of the Age of White Birds on Water" would be able to open the sealed second portal.

He stood and moved his taper closer to the surface over the closed portal. There was filigree there, as on the rest of the Tusk's surface, but it appeared to be no more than decorative etching.

He returned his attention to the first portal—all those whirling Han Chinese men that they now knew were not sucking on reeds but rather on opium pipes. Opium had ushered in the darkness of the Age of White Birds on Water. Momentarily he peered into the third portal, at the vista of Seventy Pagodas. Then he looked back at the closed second portal.

He stood again and took two steps back from the relic. He knew there had to be something in the sealant of the second portal that had stopped the First Emperor from opening it for the Chosen Three on the Holy Mountain. "Something that was not present in that time on the Holy Mountain but is now—in the Age of White Birds on Water—present," he whispered.

The Carver felt a tingle at the base of his spine. He began to speak aloud again, but slowly. "Q'in She Huang opened the first window with blood. The First Emperor's uniting of China was an exercise in blood. His armies viciously suppressed all opposition to uniting China, to building the Grand Canal, and to standardizing the character writing of our people." He stopped. He knew he was close to something important. He knew that anyone who had resisted Q'in She Huang could expect a bloody response. The First Emperor's uniting of China had drenched the soil of the Middle Kingdom in its people's blood.

The Carver slowed his breathing and forced himself to concentrate. "Blood was the essence of the First Emperor's time." He smiled and spoke aloud again. "Blood was the essence of that time, so blood opened the first portal." He paused and tried to get the words from his brain to his tongue. Something—hundreds and hundreds of years—was resisting him giving voice to his thought. But he finally got words to his throat, then out into the emptiness of the cavern. "Blood was the essence then—opium is the essence now."

It took him several days of trials, but on the fourth day he pulled back the banana leaf that covered a ball of raw opium and, after brushing aside the remaining *lewah* and the poppy trash, took a small quantity of the sticky stuff and applied it directly to the closed second portal. In short order a crack appeared in the solid surface of the ivory, then a second, and finally the outline of two large panels. The Carver gently inserted a slender chisel into one of the cracks and applied the slightest pressure—and immediately the two panels fell to the floor, revealing a small scene of Han

Chinese men, without shaved foreheads or long Manchu-imposed braided queues, in a cave, bent over a table, staring at something on the table's surface. What exactly they were staring at he could not make out. As his eyes adjusted he saw, behind them, three women in what the Shanghainese would now call modern dress.

He stepped back from the Tusk. Both the first and last of the portals had inscriptions overtop of them: "The Age of White Birds on Water" and "The Age of the Seventy Pagodas." But there was no inscription over the middle portal.

He knew that couldn't be right, and he began to experiment further with the opium.

On the following night he blew opium smoke directly into the second portal, with the vision of the men around a table in a cave, and the three women standing behind them. To his surprise, the surface above the portal cracked, realigning the filigree design on its surface. He ran his fingers over the repositioned etching and it felt as though the lines were no longer flowing and fluid but had formed themselves into the basic square formations of classical Chinese characters. He took a tiny amount of the opium tar and spread it over the etched lines, then carefully removed the excess resin from the surface, leaving only the resin that had entered the filigree tracks. And there it was. In bold, old-style Chinese characters: "A Man with a Book Will Come and a Woman Will Guide His Steps."

* * *

TWO NIGHTS LATER, the Carver revealed the second portal, to the amazement of the Chosen Three. Even Jiang didn't know exactly what to say. A silence descended on the chamber, then deepened. After more than two millennia, the second portal had finally revealed the step between the arrival of the White Birds on Water and the goal of the Seventy Pagodas.

Loa Wei Fen broke the silence. "Has this changed our task?"

"What do you mean?" Jiang asked.

"The second portal—"

"Is just an interim step," interrupted the Confucian. "The goal is still the Seventy Pagodas. So our task has not changed."

"How does the Man with the Book or the Woman fit into the building of the Seventy Pagodas?"

"As we ushered in the darkness of the Age of White Birds on Water, so we now must find and assist the Man with the Book and the Woman to end the darkness."

"I agree," said the Carver.

"But how are we to know which man—which woman?" demanded the Assassin.

There was a further long moment of silence, broken this time by Jiang. "He'll be the one most likely to bring the end of the Age of White Birds on Water. That age began with the arrival in force of the *Fan Kuei*'s ships. It would only make sense that the beginning of the end of that age will have to do with the *Fan Kuei* leaving the city at the Bend in the River."

"So we let the *Fan Kuei* in, with their darkness, to build the village at the Bend in the River into the powerful city of Shanghai of today?"

"Yes. We let them in. But now they have fulfilled their role here," Jiang said.

"Role?"

"Yes," the Confucian agreed. "That was their role. But they must be replaced by the Black-Haired people now. Only we can build the Seventy Pagodas."

"And the Man with the Book and the Woman?" asked the Assassin.

"They'll be powerful enough to rid Shanghai of the *Fan Kuei*," Jiang restated. "He'll give the city they made—back to us."

The silence in the hidden section of the Warrens was complete. No one moved. They all sensed the gravity of the task ahead—and the danger if they supported the wrong Man with the Book or the wrong Woman.

The *Fan Kuei* had to be bested. On that the Chosen Three agreed. But who would lead the charge against the powerful foreigners? Jiang kept thinking back to the five women in the Narwhal Tusk's first two portals: the Beijing woman, who she assumed was the Dowager Empress, and the figure representing her from the first portal, and now these three women wearing western dress in the second portal. She could see how the Dowager might influence events at the Bend in the River, and, as a member of the Ivory Compact, she certainly had a role to play ... but who were the three western-dressed women?

"Who are the potential strong men? Chinese strong men?" asked the Assassin.

"Gangster Tu," replied Jiang reluctantly.

"Do we want to back him?" demanded the Confucian.

"He certainly is a Man with a Book. It's said that no one refers to the *I Ching* more than him—no one living outside a monastery, that is."

"True," the Confucian said, "but remember, once an arrow is launched skyward, even the best archer cannot be sure of where exactly it will land."

"True, but a cruel hand can be put to good use," Jiang responded.

Heads nodded.

"Who else?"

"There are several compradors whose growth is worth watching."

"Watching, yes, but not pursuing. And which among them can even read, let alone be called a Man with a Book?" demanded the Confucian.

Jiang nodded. She was thinking, *And none of them has three daughters. Chinese girls who wear western clothes and whose feet have not been bound.*

"Why not back several different possibilities?" asked the Carver.

There was a general agreement to this, accompanied by the usual platitudes about not putting all one's rice in one bowl, all one's savings in one hiding place, and on and on. Everyone in the room knew that they were approaching a crossing point.

The Confucian spoke first. "At this time, Tu Yueh-sen is our only serious candidate." Then he turned away from the others and assumed what Jiang thought of as his "teacherly attitude"—which she hated—and said, "Perhaps our best way of helping Gangster Tu is to gain him a temporary *Fan Kuei* ally. Is it possible, for example, to get one of the *Fan Kuei* families to back Tu against the other *Fan Kuei* families? The *Fan Kuei* hate each other more than they do us. Perhaps we can use them against each other."

Jiang nodded. Not a bad suggestion. "Who amongst you can get to Gangster Tu?"

The Carver spoke up. "I think I may be able to. He's ordered pieces from me."

"Ah," Jiang said. "Be careful, Carver, this is a violent man."

"So if you can speak to Tu, which one of the *Fan Kuei* trading houses do we have access to?" asked the Confucian.

"I deal with the Vrassoons, as well," said the Carver, much to everyone's surprise. "They pay exorbitant amounts for cast-off pieces."

"Good," Jiang said. "Get them together—it's a start."

———

Jiang's family and the Assassin's had often worked in concert in the past. Both knew well the story of the placement of the original Loa Wei Fen in the History Teller's troupe, so it did not surprise Jiang when a gentle tapping on her third-floor bedroom window interrupted her sleep later that night.

She unlatched the window. The Assassin leaped from his perch on the outside wall to the rug in Jiang's private chamber with no more difficulty than a normal man has standing from a chair.

They did not bother with the niceties of tea but started right in.

"The Carver's introduction of Tu to the Vrassoons is a good beginning, but only a beginning."

"True," the Assassin said. "We need to gain Gangster Tu's confidence if we are to get close to him. Otherwise there is no way to keep track of a man like Tu Yueh-sen."

"I'm already close to him," Jiang said. An odd pride had crept into her voice.

"Pillow close," Loa Wei Fen responded, "but not close to his heart. His heart is in his business. I must get close to him that way."

"Men tell tales in bedrooms that they'd never tell in other places. Tu wants revenge against the *Fan Kuei* and believes that the only way to do it is to beat them at the opium trade—and I'll encourage him in that thinking."

Loa Wei Fen nodded. He agreed with that assessment—everyone in Shanghai agreed with that assessment.

Then Jiang shocked him. "I will arrange it that the only way he can get his stake in the opium business is to attack one of their great ships."

Loa Wei Fen was astounded. No one had ever attacked an Indiaman sailing ship. "How will ...?"

"That is my business. Yours is to be ready. To follow him. And when he attacks the ship, make yourself invaluable to him. Only if the danger is high and the stakes enormous will a man like Tu Yueh-sen take the chance of allowing someone like you close to him. He is no fool. You are clearly no ordinary thug. Only if he is distracted and desperate can we expect him to accept you. And that is what we need—for him to accept you, Loa Wei Fen, as a Red Pole in his Tong of the Righteous Hand."

Just as the History Teller accepted my namesake, he thought.

By morning they had coordinated their plan to set up Gangster Tu. Loa Wei Fen then asked, "Do you wish to share the rest of your plans?"

"What makes you think I have more plans?"

His head was shaking before she finished her lies, and with a smile he said, "It is dangerous to underestimate the head of the Guild of Assassins."

She stopped mid-sentence and nodded. "True. We both use our weapons, Loa Wei Fen. You your skill and your swalto—me my guile and my daughters." She looked at the powerful man, then asked, "Tea?"

He canted his head and said, "Please."

chapter ten
A Game of Raft

April 1893

Gangster Tu's Red Poles sat with him around the large, round table in Jiang's private dining room and cheered as the madam's youngest daughter, Yin Bao, removed her petite, silk-embroidered shoe—no more than three inches long—to reveal her tiny left foot, her "Golden Lotus." With great show the young courtesan placed the slipper in the centre of the circular table and then put a slender crystal champagne glass in it. "A game of Raft, perhaps, gentlemen?" she suggested, with a startling naïveté.

Raucous shouts from the men greeted her suggestion. Shortly the shouts turned into a bizarre chant of "Raft! Raft! Raft!"

Yin Bao acted appropriately shocked as she bent her knees so that her clothing covered the nakedness of her exposed foot. Then, with a sly grin, she snuck her hands beneath her skirts and pulled out the second shoe and swung it by its ribbon laces around her head as she dead-eyed the men— just as she did when she was on her knees before a wealthy customer. She stood and put the slipper in a large glass bowl set conveniently by her side. Then she allowed an openly lascivious leer to cross her slightly parted lips.

"So, you would like to play Raft, would you?"

The men couldn't take their eyes off her exposed feet. Yin Bao allowed them a quick peek, then bent her knees again to cover the object of their desires. The girl's control was impressive. Her effortless shift from embarrassed virgin, shocked that she even had Golden Lotuses, to practised courtesan, openly teasing the men with the nakedness of her sensual feet, was part of the reason for her growing fame in Shanghai's Flower World.

The rest of the fame that Jiang's youngest daughter had garnered came from the extraordinary dexterity of her toes when her two Golden Lotuses enwrapped a man's jade spear.

"So, we are ready to begin our game?" she asked innocently as she stood … exposing both of her tiny feet. The men's intake of breath was gratifying. *Power is always gratifying,* she thought as she minced around the table, carrying the second shoe in the large glass bowl at arm's length.

The men bent over to gawk at her feet. For two of the more powerful guests she stopped and lifted a foot into their laps. The men then fondled it as she allowed her mouth to go slack with supposed pleasure. Each of the men took his eyes off the girl's delicious feet just long enough to toss lotus seeds at the shoe in the bowl—the raft. If the lotus seed missed the shoe, Yin Bao would, to the ecstatic howls of the men, assign punishments. Drinking between one and five glasses of wine from the glass in her other shoe in the centre of the table was the usual penalty.

The men gladly drank their "punishments" since it gave them an opportunity to stroke the tiny silk slipper and sniff the heady aroma of the courtesan's perfumed foot that still lingered there.

For most men in Shanghai, courtesans were the only women with whom they felt comfortable enough to joke and play. Only in the presence of a courtesan were the traditional separations between men and women ignored. Men relaxed and gave themselves over to the charm, and more importantly the power, of women.

The winner of the gangsters' Raft game was, as always, Tu Yueh-sen, the *Shan Chu*, the Mountain Master of the Tong of the Righteous Hand. But Gangster Tu was not interested in Yin Bao. His affection, or what he had that approximated affection, was for another family member. He chose one of his Red Poles to have the young courtesan. The Red Pole grinned widely and then took Yin Bao into a room just off the dining hall, where the girl's tortured, deformed feet—her Golden Lotuses—would be his to do with as he pleased.

Moments after the game of Raft ended, the Carver knocked on the private dining room door and presented Tu with a carving he had commissioned—an exquisite jade sculpture depicting a warrior on a rearing horse. Beneath the horse's left front hoof was a large snake that was rising up, mouth open and fangs exposed. The warrior was leaning over to cut the snake in half to save both himself and his glorious mount.

Tu held the small thing in one hand and turned it around on his palm. "Magnificent. And all from one piece of stone?"

"As you requested," the Carver said.

"Superb."

"I am pleased that you are pleased, Tu Yueh-sen."

"I am."

The Carver took a breath, then said, as if it were a natural part of their conversation, "I have done lesser works for the *Fan Kuei*. They can't tell the difference between good and bad, so they buy anything."

"And you, no doubt, charge them appropriately?"

"About three times what I would charge a Black-Haired person." Then he added nonchalantly, "Four times when I sell to the Vrassoons."

Tu put the sculpture down and asked, "You know the Vrassoons?"

Then, as he had planned with the Confucian, the Carver said, "Know? No. I do business with them." Then, again as if it were nothing, he asked, "Would you like an introduction to them?"

* * *

TU DISMISSED THE CARVER, as if meeting with the Vrassoons were a ridiculous idea, but later he considered the possibilities such a meeting might offer. The one thing he knew from heading the Tong of the Righteous Hand's opium business was that the Tong was just a bit player. Surprisingly small. They didn't have enough basic product to leverage anything from the *Fan Kuei* traders. What he had thought would be a point of entry to the lucrative opium trade had proven to be little more than a taste of the riches—a limited taste at that. And supply was the problem. *Chandra*, smokable opium, came only from India—British India—a fact that was reinforced once again that night in conversation with his bed-mate, when Jiang pointed out, "No opium supply—no opium trade, dear."

The next day he made a decision and set a plan into motion. Then he waited for reports. Waited longer than he was used to waiting.

Finally, just past the end of the month, three bespectacled scholars whom he had hired on Jiang's advice stood in his warehouse office in front of his desk with folios of paper and scrolls in their hands. They had just completed a summary of their report—and Tu was not pleased.

Tu tried to control his fury as the rain pelted down on the corrugated tin roof of the old building that had once been the Hordoons' warehouse—the very one that their Hong merchant, Chen, had run for them all those years ago. The men's reports outlined all the reasons why Tu could not—why no Chinese person could, for that matter—possibly become part of the great Shanghai opium trade. The crux of the matter was supply—the lack of access to supply, to be exact.

Tu shoved the reports aside and grunted, "India?" A slash of lightning lit the large windows facing the Suzu Creek.

The three men in front of Gangster Tu nodded, as if someone had pulled a string and all of them were attached to the same strand.

"Why can't opium be grown here in the Delta?" Tu's voice arced dangerously as the wind picked up, slapping the large late-autumn raindrops against the windowpanes.

The eldest of the three men produced a long, beautifully penned scroll from his sleeve and put it down in front of Tu.

Tu shoved it aside and leaped to his feet. "More and more documents. Always documents! Just tell me!"

"Poppies could be grown here, sir, but the infrastructure necessary to make opium could take several years to put into place."

"Several years!"

The man spoke quickly, running different ideas together. "The plants can take as many as three years to mature, and many of the fields presently devoted to rice or soya would have to be switched over to poppy production, which would cause food shortages and hence would be opposed by many powers in the city, and then the opium would have to be cured and our hot humid weather is not appropriate." He was going to re-emphasize the probably violent resistance there would be to taking fields that fed people out of production and putting them into a product that only fed their dreams, then thought better of it as Gangster Tu turned almost beet red with anger.

"So what you're saying, after all your study and all your intelligence and all your documents and all this time wasted, is that we can't grow our own poppies?"

"Or manufacture—"

"I understand." Tu's voice cut through the chilly fall air as he stepped to the window of the office and looked toward the docks. Ships of several nations were loading and unloading cargo. Although he couldn't see the mango-wood chests stuffed with Indian opium, he knew they were there. He also knew that if the opium were not there, none of the other trade would be there either. The whole thing—the whole city—floated on a river of opium, and the money it generated made the White men in the tall towers on the Bund wealthy and powerful.

Although over the past years he had secured his place in the Chinese underworld, he had made precious few inroads into the real source of wealth all around him. True, he'd recently "convinced" the French administration to leave the brothel-protection business to him—a move that, unbeknownst to Tu, had been engineered by Jiang. But Tu knew that losing the protection money from the brothels wouldn't really hurt the *Fan Kuei*. He allowed his eyes to glance over at the harbour and that idea dawned again—or had it been suggested by Jiang? He couldn't remember.

"So we can't make opium of our own?" he finally said, as if to the air.

"Not at least for—"

"But there is opium in India, and opium onboard all the fine sailing vessels in our harbour—just sitting in our harbour."

"Yes ..."

"Has anyone ever robbed an Indiaman sailing ship?"

The men looked at each other. The Indiaman sailing ships were the largest ocean-going vessels in the world, and they were defended by British mariners and large numbers of their own guns. They loaded in the safety of India's ports under the guard of armed British and Sikh regiments and didn't stop, except to pick up fresh water, until they arrived in Shanghai, where once again they were protected by the Queen's troops. It was one thing to steal from Chinese, but quite another to steal from the *Fan Kuei*—especially from a *Fan Kuei* Indiaman sailing ship!

"Get my Red Poles. I want all ten of my lieutenants here." Then he looked at the three scholars. He'd almost forgotten they were still in the room. "Your services are no longer required. Change is brought by action, not reports." He swept the documents from his desk and they fluttered to the floor.

Tu turned from the men and walked to the windows. Fork lightning lit up the darkened sky, silhouetting their Mountain Master in the windowpane. The scholars got out of the office as quickly as they could.

Two of the three made the wise choice of leaving Shanghai that very night, as Jiang had suggested, never to be seen in the city at the Bend in the River again. The third one's body was found later that night when the storm had finally blown out its fury, plugging up a newly laid section of sewers that emptied into the Suzu Creek.

* * *

EARLY THE NEXT MORNING Jiang extricated herself from Tu's arms and legs. *The man seems to be all arms and legs,* Jiang thought as she looked at herself in the mirror. She'd listened to his rant about the impossibility of growing opium and suggested, yet again, that there was lots of opium just sitting in the harbour. And as the evening had progressed she'd noted that he got quieter and quieter. *Good,* she thought, *my seed has taken root.*

During the night she'd noted several times that he had left her bed, and she'd heard through the door hushed discussions between Tu and his Red

Poles. Around three in the morning she'd heard the sound of many men running, and she'd known that Tu was ready to move.

She finished her toilette and soundlessly let herself out of the room. But before she shut the door she looked back at the sleeping gangster—he had his thumb in his mouth.

She passed by Tu's bodyguards and noted that four Red Poles sat, wide-eyed, to one side. Lounging in the anteroom were forty or fifty other Tong soldiers.

Jiang signalled to her head bouncer that she wanted a rickshaw.

As she stepped outside she saw a dark figure huddled in a doorway and nodded subtly in his direction. The dark figure didn't move—although the hood of the cobra carved onto his back filled with blood and his swalto blade felt hot in his hand.

A boy pulling a leather-upholstered rickshaw came running up. The bouncer offered her a hand but she ignored it and hopped into the seat. Curtly she told the boy where she was going, then sat back to watch the sun take the day.

It is a whore's time of peace, she thought. She liked these hours.

They passed by the Cathedral of St. Ignatius. Chinese women were already out cleaning the steps with straw brooms and wet rags. Jiang hoped the Black Robes paid the women well for their hard labours, although she doubted the poor women were paid enough to buy a five-spice egg.

"Here!" she shouted. "Left."

The rickshaw boy came to a stop, backed up a pace or two, then turned into the alley. Two hundred paces down the lane was an innocuous red door to a *lilong*. She told the boy to stop the rickshaw.

She tipped the boy handsomely. The reward for her generosity was a leer. She immediately reached into his still-open palm and took back half of the tip.

"What …?"

"To teach you to respect your betters."

"You're …" But the boy swallowed the rest of the thought and said, "Want me to wait for you, ma'am?"

"No. Scat!"

Jiang waited until the rickshaw had left the alley, then tapped lightly on the red door. A truly beautiful White man, dressed and coiffed immaculately, opened it. He stared at Jiang but made no motion to step aside.

From behind him Jiang heard a female voice say, *"Qui est là, Julien?"*

"It is I, Mademoiselle Colombe," Jiang said.

Anais Colombe, Suzanne's only granddaughter, stepped forward and tapped the handsome man on his shoulder. "It's early, Jiang," she said.

"It's a whore's time of rest," Jiang replied.

Anais laughed softly, then said, "My grandmother used to say that."

"So my grandmother told me, Anais."

"Coffee, Jiang?"

Jiang hesitated for a moment, but she resisted looking back over her shoulder. She had no reason to doubt that Tu had successfully followed her.

Jiang sat at the table, the hot coffee cup between her hands, and informed Anais Colombe that the French administration was no longer willing to provide protection for their brothels, and that Gangster Tu would now provide that "service."

Anais Colombe nodded, then said, "Surely you know that I knew that."

"I do, Anais. What you didn't know, but would no doubt find out, is that I am the cause of this change."

Anais's eyes opened wide, but before she could speak Jiang produced a promissory note personally guaranteeing all of Anais's potential losses under the new protection arrangement with Tu.

Anais looked at the note, then at Jiang. "Do you care so much for your young gangster lover that you are willing to pay this much for his approval?"

Jiang smiled. She knew that Anais would never believe that any young lover was worth the small fortune she had promised to pay the Colombe family.

"So?" Anais pried one more time.

"So," Jiang said, "sometimes one must give in order to get." To prove a point. To prove to Tu Yueh-sen that her word could be trusted, that her advice was good. She had promised him control of the brothel-protection rackets in the French Concession, and he now had it—and now it was time for him to take her more important advice and attack the Vrassoons' ship in the harbour. Circles within circles and schemes within schemes, she thought, and all leading back to her obligation to the Ivory Compact. If Tu Yueh-sen was the Man with a Book who could bring on the Age of the Seventy Pagodas, one of the Chosen Three had to get close to him. She had his "pillow attentions," but it wasn't enough. She wanted Loa Wei Fen to be part of Tu's inner circle. She needed it to fulfill her obligation to the First Emperor's vision.

She suddenly noticed Anais Colombe staring at her. Had she been speaking aloud? "What?" she blurted out.

"You drank your coffee, Jiang. You never drink the coffee I offer you."

———

Tu took a step back from the edge of the tile roof. He nodded as he said to his second in command, his head Red Pole, "Good. We'll let the hookers discuss the new order in their businesses. Jiang will be telling the French whore that they both have to deal with me now that the French administration has withdrawn its protection."

"How did you …?"

"Manage that?" Tu asked with a smile on his lips. "I found that French men are particularly frightened of knives, sharp knives. A few well-placed cuts—not fatal cuts—changed minds over there." But he wasn't completely sure of that. There was something wrong. The French had given up a lot of money with barely a fight—as Jiang had told him they would.

"So the women will pay us?" the head Red Pole asked.

"Of that I have no doubt. They're just chattering now to save a little face."

"Fine. So that's done?"

"Yes, it is," Tu responded, although it was clear his mind was elsewhere.

"My congratulations, sir."

Tu nodded. He scented the air and thought he detected the subtle reek of ozone—the smell of change. Finally he said, "One small victory prepares the way for a greater one." He bit at the cuticle around his thumb and drew blood. "Are our men in position?"

"Yes, sir, they await your orders," his head Red Pole said, clearly relishing what was about to happen.

Tu hesitated. It was a big step from protection rackets to raiding a Vrassoon opium ship. He recalled his *I Ching* reading from the previous night, then said, "To the docks."

———

Loa Wei Fen loosened his grip on the gutter just inches below where Gangster Tu had stood and slid down the drainpipe to the street. Magically the swalto was in his hand, ready—ready to prove his worth to Tu Yuehsen, Mountain Master of the Tong of the Righteous Hand, when he exposed himself by attacking the Vrassoons' Indiaman sailing ship—as Jiang had planned.

* * *

THE SHANGHAI HARBOUR was considered one of the most secure harbours in all of Asia. There had been mutinies and fires, but never a theft. Until that day, April 11, 1893.

The captain of the Vrassoons' ship was lighting his first cigarette of the morning. He'd just brought the ship to harbour the night before after almost three months at sea. His men were anxious to get ashore, but he'd released only a third of them because his ship was packed to the tops of its holds with chest upon chest of India's finest *Chandra* opium.

The captain scanned the activity in the harbour—hundreds of boats of all sizes moved between the large vessels and the warehouses. He put his cigarette on the rail. He was an experienced ship's captain and could read wind and currents as easily as most men read their morning paper. He also had a second sense for the approach of danger. And looking at the sudden proliferation of small junks approaching his ship, that was exactly what he sensed—just before the expertly thrown knife entered the left side of his throat, severing his carotid artery and fountaining blood onto his polished black leather boots.

Tu's assault on the Vrassoons' Indiaman sailing ship proceeded without drawing attention from the other ships at anchor in the busy harbour.

No one saw anything out of the ordinary—just Chinese men carrying mango-wood chests of opium from the great ship onto the decks of their small junks. It wasn't until much later that it occurred to a watch on a nearby ship that the junks weren't heading to the Bund wharves or the Suzu Creek docks, but rather were making their way across the Bend in the River to the Pudong.

Gangster Tu watched his plan in action. His junks were already nearing the Pudong, and the deck of the ship was littered with dead and dying European sailors and marines.

His head Red Pole stepped forward and in a confident voice announced, "The ship is completely secured. You can do with it what you please, sir."

Tu nodded to the man as a second fleet of his hired junks approached the ship and began to offload the last of the opium cargo.

The day was going to be cool but clear. Gangster Tu took a deep breath, then strode across the deck and stood over the body of the dead *Fan Kuei* captain whose life his blade had taken. His grandmother's words came back to him. He whispered, "It begins, Grandmother. Your real revenge begins this very day." He pushed the corpse with his foot and it rolled over. This was the first *Fan Kuei* he had killed. And he liked the feeling of it. The taste of it in his mouth.

He heard a cry from overhead and stepped aside just in time to avoid the body of a falling *Fan Kuei* sailor, who although dead still clutched his flintlock pistol in his right hand.

Tu looked up and saw to his surprise an agile man swinging down to the deck from a gallant crow's nest, gripping a halyard. Tu's hand immediately went to his knife, and he was ready to attack when the agile Han Chinese man stepped nimbly onto the deck.

"Who are you?" Tu demanded.

"No one important," the man said, keeping his hands in plain view. "I just need to retrieve my blade."

Tu saw the ropey sinews of the man's arms and the rock-hard shine of his eyes—then he traced the man's eyes to the swalto blade protruding from the dead European sailor's chest. "Yours?" Tu asked.

Loa Wei Fen nodded, then said, "I'll retrieve my knife and leave you to your business here." He reached down and drew out the blade with a simple tug.

Tu stepped forward, his knife extended. "Who are you?" he asked a second time.

Loa Wei Fen sheathed his swalto blade and said softly, with a small bow of his head, "Just a man to whom you owe your life, Tu Yueh-sen." Then, referring to the body, he added, "If you climb to the gallant crow's nest you'll see he had enough weapons to spoil whatever your plans were on this ship, and no doubt both the angle and the height necessary for a clean shot at you standing where you are now. And since he's a master gunner I assume he wouldn't have missed. Nor would the four others I killed up there."

Tu glanced aloft. He could just make out a few arms draped over the side of the topgallant crow's nest. He turned back to Loa Wei Fen. "One more time I ask, who are you?"

"A competent soldier looking for employment and willing to prove his worth."

"Really?" Tu snapped.

Tu's head Red Pole, who only moments before had informed him that the ship was completely secured, leaped forward and put his knife to Loa Wei Fen's throat. "Don't trust him, boss," he said.

Tu said nothing.

The Red Pole's eyes bulged as he pressed harder at the side of Loa Wei Fen's neck, drawing a steady flow of blood.

Tu smiled, then said, "Kill him."

Loa Wei Fen sensed the depth of the cut on his throat—not too deep. More importantly, although he hadn't seen the blade, he could tell that it was not a swalto but rather a single-sided knife. It had an ugly scrration to it, but the point was not made for killing. So Loa Wei Fen knew that the head Red Pole with the bulging eyes would either cut straight back to sever his windpipe or swipe to the side to cut the artery there. Then he sensed something else—a hesitation—and he acted. With devastating speed he arched his back and bit down on the blade of the knife with his teeth before the Red Pole could move—and the rest was child's play for a fully trained assassin. Only moments later he held the Red Pole by the hair. He turned the man's face to Gangster Tu and asked, "Shall I kill him, sir?"

Tu Yueh-sen smiled and said, "No, but you can have his position." Then he slapped the Red Pole across the face and demoted him then and there. "Let him go," Tu ordered Loa Wei Fen.

Loa Wei Fen released his grip on the man and watched him move away, aware that he had made a life enemy—someone whom he would eventually have to kill before the man killed him.

Tu said, "Follow me, you have work to do."

Tu watched as Loa Wei Fen butchered the few still-living members of the crew, then helped Tu set the great ship ablaze.

Later that night, after overseeing the initiation rites for Loa Wei Fen, Tu sent a message to the Carver. It read simply, "I am fully prepared for a meeting with the *Fan Kuei* Vrassoon. Set it up quickly."

It was not the only message sent that night. Loa Wei Fen sent a simple, four-word message to Jiang. It read: "I am in place."

* * *

AFTER SOME CONSIDERABLE NEGOTIATING, a meeting between Tu and the Vrassoons was arranged through a series of third parties. Initially Tu had refused to go to the *Fan Kuei*'s office and insisted that the *Fan Kuei* come to him. This impasse was sidestepped by the suggestion that there be two meetings. The first meeting would be no more than a way to get to know each other, and the second meeting would be a real business meeting. The first meeting would be in the Vrassoon offices; the second would take place in Tu's offices by the Suzu Creek. After yet more negotiating, mostly to do with protocol, the meeting at the Vrassoons' was set for late on the following Thursday afternoon.

The Vrassoon in charge of the family business, Meyer, was the youngest of the Patriarch's sons. He ran the Paris office for years, and although he was not emotionally close to his late father, he understood the old man's business acumen and shared his religious beliefs. He was a handsome man with sharp, swarthy features and a quick temper. His personal life was just that—completely personal. Few people had ever seen his wife, who wore a veil whenever she left the family estate. All that was known about her was that she was surprisingly plump, and of course wore a wig.

Meyer had enjoyed his time in Paris and had a grudging respect for the French and their culture. He loved their opera. But here in the Middle

Kingdom he found no such solace. He quickly learned to hate the Orient, its smells, its sights, and its people—although he did admire Asian furniture, especially the Mosul carpet that covered a large portion of the centre of his office floor.

From the first, things did not go well between Vrassoon and Tu. Even gestures intended to be conciliatory were quickly taken as insults. The fact that the young Vrassoon didn't speak any of the local dialects made things worse. Both sides had brought translators, but they could not agree on exactly what was said by whom and to whom and with what intent. Both parties were quick to anger, and salacious slanders quickly filled the room, leading to dangerous silences. Tu dismissed his own translator with a wave of his hand.

The silence was uncomfortable for all present, but no one was more uncomfortable than the Vrassoon translator, who stood rigidly, still hoping to get some sort of inclination of how to proceed. Both the *Fan Kuei* and the gangster had said the most awful things to each other, and it was his job to translate the slanders honestly but somehow make them palatable. He smiled, then spoke. He did his best, but neither man was a fool and both quickly picked up on the fact that their words were being manipulated.

Gangster Tu bolted to his feet and shouted at the translator, "Tell this stupid Round-Eye that I am not to be fooled with. That I am a man to be respected."

Before the poor translator could even open his mouth, the young head of the Vrassoon family brought his hand crashing down on his mahogany desk and snarled, "Tell this big-eared Slant that the house of Vrassoon has no need for him or his criminal friends."

The translator turned to Gangster Tu and, after clearing his throat a few times, said, "The foolish Round-Eye wishes you to know that he has his reservations about doing business with a man with so much honour in his background as yourself." Then he turned to Vrassoon and said, "This unfortunately immature Celestial doesn't seem to understand the nature of your position in the honourable Foreign Settlement."

Both men thought about the translations they had been given and then ignored the translator and tried to communicate directly with each other in pidgin, the strange polyglot language that had developed in Shanghai over the years. But pidgin's extremely limited vocabulary was not designed for the races to communicate on any sort of sophisticated level. It was there to give orders and acknowledge receipt of such, and nothing else. There was only one adverb in the language, the frequently heard "Chop chop— fast, fast."

Vrassoon threw up his arms and shouted, "Enough," to the translator. He reached beneath his desk and pressed a button. Immediately four brawny men entered from hidden panels behind him. Two were Sikhs who rushed in with weapons drawn.

Tu didn't back off a step. He put two fingers in his mouth and produced an ear-splitting whistle. For a breath nothing happened, then all twenty of the floor-to-ceiling windows of the large room exploded inward as Tu's men, led by Loa Wei Fen, broke into the room with weapons aimed and ready.

"How dare you?" shouted Vrassoon.

The translator translated that accurately.

"I dare because I am Tu Yueh-sen, the Mountain Master, the *Shan Chu* of the Tong of the Righteous Hand, and I am not a man to be insulted by a foolish, ugly Round-Eye."

The translator translated that accurately, except for the very end, where he replaced "Round-Eye" with "Foreign Devil," feeling somehow that was less offensive.

Tu screamed an order. The front door of the Vrassoons' office was flung open and two large dollies carrying many mango-wood chests full of opium were wheeled into the room.

"What is the meaning of this?" Vrassoon demanded.

"Look at the markings on the chests, foolish man," Tu said, pointing to the stamped ownership on the bills of lading attached to the chests: "Property of the British East India Company."

Vrassoon gasped, "Are you …?"

Tu looked to the translator, who did his best to translate and fill in the end of Vrassoon's thought without accusing Tu of any wrongdoing.

Tu laughed and spat out, "It was me who assaulted your ship in the harbour. And I can do it over and over again, and there is nothing that you or your British friends can do about it. Now, do you want your property back or not?"

The translator put that into simple, extremely accurate English.

Vrassoon surprised everyone by sitting back behind his desk and ordering his men away. Then he waited.

Tu smiled, nodded to Loa Wei Fen, and then ordered his men to leave as well. The men retreated, leaving only the echoes of crunched glass in the room.

Finally the room was empty except for Vrassoon, Gangster Tu, and the translator—and of course the swirling winter wind that blew through the broken windows and lofted the heavy curtains like sails that had been cut from their riggings.

The men quickly dropped the insults and moved to ground that both understood: bargaining. This was business at its starkest. The threat of immediate violence sat on Tu's right hand, the threat of the British Navy sat on Vrassoon's left—and between the two sat the possibility of control of the great opium trade of Shanghai, which had slipped from the Vrassoons' hands by the late 1870s. Since the death of the Vrassoon Patriarch the family had consolidated its assets and now was more invested in real estate and the large mercantile emporiums that would eventually be called department stores. But neither enterprise had the consistent staying power or the virtually guaranteed profits of the old opium trade.

From Tu's perspective, he needed a backer. A powerful backer to move from thief to master of the opium trade—a necessary half-step for him to have the power base to fulfill his promise to his grandmother to punish the *Fan Kuei*.

Vrassoon knew he needed muscle and daring to re-enter as a major player in the opium game. Ever since the Vrassoons had lost their monopoly on direct trade from England to China, the family's share in the opium trade had dwindled. Was this Chink thug what he needed to regain supremacy in the *Chandra* trade?

The men approached each other warily and began to make progress, until Vrassoon suddenly went silent. He looked at the photograph of his father on the desk—his father's desk. The Vrassoons had never had a Chinese partner. His father's strict prohibition against dealing with anyone who was not "of the faith" had not really been lessened after his death. "They are our consumers, not our partners," the old Patriarch had told him on his deathbed. "Their religion makes them weak, so they succumb to the lures of *Chandra*. They were made to lift and tote and smoke themselves into oblivion. Remember that, son."

"Is there a problem?" Tu asked, and the translator conveyed the question to Vrassoon.

Vrassoon thought about his father's words a second time, then abruptly stood. Tu was shocked at such impoliteness. Vrassoon turned to the translator and said, "Tell him that he has thirty seconds to get his Slant eyes out of my home, and that I expect restitution for the damage done here and the full return of the property that belongs to the British East India Company." Then he turned on his heel and exited.

"What did the stupid smelly man say?" Tu demanded.

The translator hemmed and hawed in both languages.

"Fine," Tu said, then added, "if you value your life, or that of your idiot wife and rat children, tell me exactly what the *Fan Kuei* said."

The translator did so, word for word.

Tu allowed the anger to make its way through his body, then said, "Find him and tell him this—exactly. He will never get back his opium. I will never give him money to fix his ridiculous house, and he had better not appear without guards on all sides of him if he wishes to breathe the air of the city at the Bend in the River beyond the end of the week."

With that, Tu turned and headed toward the door. Halfway there he stopped, opened his flies, and let loose a long, arcing stream of urine that quickly soaked into the fabulously expensive Mosul carpet.

chapter eleven
The Revolutionary

Ru Chou, the hot-water store owner, checked in on his sleeping daughters, then made his way in the pre-dawn light down the stairs to the small courtyard in the back of his *lilong* that fronted on the alley. Six years ago he had converted the living room of his home into his now quite popular hot-water store and teashop. Earlier that morning he'd heard the rumble of the night-soil cart, and he was happy to see that his family's "honeypot" had been not only emptied but also well scrubbed. He lifted the round, red-painted wooden bucket by its brass handles and placed it by the back door—far enough away from the kitchen, but close enough that the curtain hung there could be pulled to offer a person some privacy as they did their daily ablutions.

Before he put down the night-soil bucket he heard the song of the newspaper seller, followed shortly by the pleasant song of the flower seller. He bought a paper from one and purple winter irises from the other, which he placed in a vase on a small table beneath the circular wall mirror. Then he opened his store just as his usual first customer of the day—a poor labourer—approached his shop. It was another fine, cold day. Ru Chou's business was progressing, and he was happy with the simple repetition of his daily rituals. It reassured him. It made him feel part of this great growing thing called Shanghai. He pocketed the poor man's single coin, pulled off three sheets of toilet paper, and handed them over. The man tugged on each sheet to be sure that it was solid, then handed over a second coin. Ru Chou gave him two cigarettes. The poor labourer turned and headed toward the public outhouse. It had been thus with this man for several years, and with luck, Ru Chou thought, would be for many, many more.

The poor labourer was not the only one who used Ru Chou's hot-water store for assistance in getting the day started.

Outside, in the alley, two barbers were setting up their stools. Because one was new to the sidewalk, Ru Chou assumed there would be trouble. Rich people fought over money and prestige and women; poor people fought over space. Barbers always had to be near hot-water stores to get the necessary heated water for shaving, so this scenario was not new to Ru Chou.

Ru Chou saw frost on the north-facing window, so he knew that it would be a busy day. He stoked the fire beneath the great cauldron with bean sprout stems and other wood refuse. He'd thought about using coal but had decided against it. Instead he had taken the money he saved and bought two fine tables. Now he had a brisk business in serving tea at those tables, made from the same hot water boiling away in the great cauldron, which would also be used for those interested in public bathing in the back.

He began to fill hot-water bottles. For the poor they were the only relief from the severe cold of a Shanghai February.

As he did, a housemaid entered and beckoned to him. She opened her apron and displayed the remains of a broken opium pipe and two small tin containers filled with the opium dregs she'd scraped out of pipes and off trays and from the tips of piercing needles. Ru Chou smelled the materials and slipped three coins onto the table. The maid gladly picked them up and left the shop. Ru Chou took the pipe and the dregs behind the counter and added them to the other dregs he had bought over the past few days. A dealer would be around later in the day, and Ru Chou would sell his stock of dregs to the man. The dealer would then, in turn, clean the pipes and other leavings of opium smokers into a large bowl, add water, and put it over a flame. The mixture would take on the various properties of opium in a tea-like form that he would then sell to labourers far too poor to avail themselves of the Indian opium smoked by the wealthy. Everyone gained. The wealthy woman's maid earned a few coppers she would not normally have, Ru Chou benefited from his markup, the seller of opium dregs gained when he sold the opium tea, and the workers gained when they finally found some affordable relief from the pain and drudgery of their lives. Thus was Shanghai.

Ru Chou noted a lean, hungry-looking young man with a purple birthmark covering much of his face eyeing him through the front window of his store. Ru Chou's family slept above the store, and people in the *lilong* complex all looked out for one another, but he assumed that none of them had seen this particular hungry boy—no, this was no boy, it was a young man, and from the way he carried himself and the clothes he wore, an arrogant, literate young man.

Suddenly the door opened and the young man entered the shop. "May I help you?" Ru Chou asked.

"May I help you?" the young man mocked back.

"Is there something wrong?" Ru Chou asked, quickly scanning the street to see if there was anyone around—there wasn't. Where had the barbers gone?

"Wrong? Why should there be something wrong? This is Shanghai, everything is wonderful in soulless Shanghai. You make money, everyone makes money, but there is no soul here. No advancement of the human mind. Just money! Endless grubbing for money."

Ru Chou slid behind the counter and allowed his fingers to touch the two hot-water bottles sitting there. They were not much of a weapon, but they were something.

"What say you to that, merchant Ru Chou? What say you?"

"I say that people come to Shanghai to have a better way of life, and that many have found that here. Me and my family came here with almost nothing, and now we have a home and a shop, and my daughter is to be married."

The young man scratched at the large raspberry birthmark on his face, then nodded his head. Finally he said, "But at what cost?"

"No cost," Ru Chou replied, gaining confidence that this young man was not a robber. "No cost except the sweat from our brows and the calluses on our hands. If you work, you eat in Shanghai, not like in the country."

"And the educated, do they eat in Shanghai?"

"If they work."

"What about their work learning the classic literature of our people?"

"Stupidity. A waste of time and good paper," Ru Chou said, then laughed.

The young man with the wine stain on his face didn't laugh. Instead, he pointed directly at Ru Chou's heart and made the sound of a gunshot.

Two men from the alley arrived with soap and towels and paid Ru Chou to use two of the six tightly packed tubs on the far side of his cauldron. The men pulled the privacy curtain, disrobed, and held their clothes out to Ru Chou, who slipped them onto hangers and then, with the assistance of a twelve-foot bamboo pole, hung the garments on a very high bar suspended from the ceiling.

"So that thieves will not steal the clothes of the fat merchants," snarled the young man.

"Exactly, but you may have noticed that neither of the men is fat, and for your information, both work in the sugar factory."

"For the *Fan Kuei!*"

"Yes, this is the Foreign Settlement, so—"

"Shameful!" the young man spat out. "Shameful!" Then he calmly took a small-calibre pistol from a pocket of his long robe and shot Ru Chou through the heart. The merchant fell instantly to the floor beside the cauldron.

Suddenly the young man sensed someone watching him. He whirled to his right only to see his own countenance reflected back at him from the circular wall mirror. The purple blotch on his face was almost the same colour as the winter irises in the vase beneath the mirror. He turned quickly from the mirror. Then, without rushing, he stepped up to Ru Chou's body and drew two characters on the hot-water store owner's forehead: "Murdered Collaborator."

chapter twelve
The Go Player's Secret

Jiang watched the Go players. The older man she had known for many years; the younger one had only recently begun to frequent her brothel. Years ago the old man had been considered quite a goat in the bedroom, his prowess known to many of the girls. His exertions were often just on the edge of cruelty and had not gone unnoted. But now he was just an old man who was lucky enough to have the wherewithal to spend his days in Jiang's house, much as older men without money spent their days sitting and chatting with the street barber or the street cobbler. In Jiang's house he was charged a minimal fee that he paid at the end of every fourth month. In return he could come and go as he pleased, be served middle- to low-ranking tea, and play Go to his heart's content.

The old man's knurled fingers slipped into the porcelain cup that held his black stones. The board was almost two-thirds filled with his pieces and the younger man's white ones. The outcome of the game looked to be still in doubt—or so the casual viewer would have believed. But Jiang had never seen the old man lose a game, even though he often gave his opponent substantial handicaps, sometimes as much as four or even six pieces. However, judging by the considerable amount of money bet on the contest, money that now sat on one side of the board, Jiang doubted that the old man had given his younger opponent much of an edge.

Jiang's practised eyes counted the money and quickly calculated the twelve and a half percent that would be paid to her house no matter who won the game. She considered raising the house's percentage, then thought of her last conversation with her French counterpart, Anais Colombe. Business was falling off in both of their houses. The novelty of European whores had worn off long ago for the established Chinese comprador class, and Jiang knew that although the European community—who often frequented her houses—continued to grow, there were still not enough of them to make up for the escalating costs she faced. First-rank courtesans were becoming rare, and they were demanding finer clothes, personal servants, and private carriages. Gas fixtures and indoor plumbing were also far from cheap. But it was the protection money demanded by Gangster Tu, now that Jiang had arranged for the French authorities to stop "protecting" them, that was driving Jiang's need to generate new business.

Jiang knew that immigrants to Shanghai were not preponderantly European or American or Japanese any more—they were Chinese, often educated Chinese.

She knew that this was a vital new source of income for her house, and she needed to figure out how to lure more of them away from the French houses and into hers. She accepted the curiosity of Chinese men that drove them to sleep with Caucasian women. But she also knew and understood why that curiosity often ended after the first or second visit. Jiang had just as many Caucasian men fulfilling their curiosity with her girls, so that was not a problem. The problem was how to entice the newly arrived and educated Chinese men into her houses after their initial fling with the *Fan Kuei*—and then keep them coming back week after week, and then year after year.

A gasp from the crowd watching the Go match snapped her back to the present. The old man had, with three quick moves, completely upended the balance of the game. Turning to his younger opponent, he asked magnanimously, "Is there any reason to play out the last of the pieces?"

The younger man stared at the board, openly shocked. "I was winning ..."

"You thought you were winning," the older Go player corrected him.

"But I was ..."

"I allowed you to play the role of the conqueror, which you played very well. So well you saw the movements on the board through the haze of the image of yourself."

Suddenly the younger man slashed his arm across the board and the pieces tinkled to the hardwood floor. "You speak nonsense, old man!"

"Perhaps, perhaps," the old Go player said, ignoring the younger man's outburst as he reached for the money on the side of the table and counted out Jiang's share.

Usually Jiang would have sent one of the girls over to get the money, it being beneath her dignity to be seen handling cash, but this time she signalled for the old Go player to follow her into a private room.

Upon entering Jiang's private quarters, the old man said, with a chuckle, "I'm too old for you to use sex to coerce me. Your percentage is twelve and a half and that is that. Not a jot more will I hand over to you, even if you put both your hands upon my jade spear."

Jiang chuckled back, "Now be honest, grandfather, what would that do?"

"Nothing. The twelve and a half percent is yours, and not a jot more," he repeated, then added, "even if you should use your tongue or your jade gate."

"Now, now, grandfather, would I do something as coarse as that simply to get more money from my favourite Go player?"

The old man thought for a moment, then said, "Absolutely."

"Absolutely not."

The two smiled at each other and Jiang poured some tea for him. He took a sip and sighed. "Annam tea, how kind of you."

Jiang moved to a wall hanging depicting several Peking Opera characters—one the Princess of the East from her famous aunt's *Journey to the West* and straightened its seam. Then she turned to him.

He saw the quizzical look on her face and chose to ignore it. Instead he swallowed the rest of the tea and, as if Jiang were his servant, held out the cup for more. Jiang, much to her surprise, immediately fell into the role he had assigned her and began to fill his cup. Then she stopped herself. She was no serving girl! She was about to say as much when the old man reached forward and grabbed some paper off her desk and began to read as he leaned back in his chair. He continued to ignore Jiang, although he did look into his half-filled cup and harrumphed. Again Jiang had the impulse to fill his cup. Then she understood something

She took the teapot and tapped the old Go player lightly on the forehead with the hot thing.

"Ouch," he said, and turned to her.

Immediately he returned to being just an old Go player and she to being a madam of a great and powerful house. Order had been restored. She looked at him. "Hold out your cup, old man," she said. She filled it, this time as Jiang, the madam, not Jiang, the servant. "What exactly did you mean when you said to that young man that you 'allowed him to play the role of the conqueror'?"

"Ah," the old Go player said. "You want my secrets, hence the good tea and fine surroundings. But they will cost you far more than that. I have earned my secrets one painful mistake at a time, and now you wish me to give them away like a peasant girl offers up her virginity for twenty *taels*? I think my secrets are worth more than a country girl's knot." He smiled. He was missing two teeth on the left side of his mouth. "Don't you?"

Jiang readily paid for prime girls, for music lessons for the best of her girls, for clothing for the girls, for the cleaning of her houses, but paying for this old man's secrets—that was something she'd never considered.

The old Go player finished his tea and stood. "Thank you for your hospitality." He put down the cup and headed toward the door.

"I'll forgo your charges in my house for a year."

The old Go player stopped. "No girls?"

"Absolutely no girls."

"This is not a good bargain for me since I can easily pay the charges. Yet you wish me to give you something of great value, my life's secrets."

Jiang balked at this, then said, "Two years—no girls."

"Still makes no sense to me, since the fees you charge me are both fair and easily within my financial reach. But my life's secrets—that's something else."

"Name your price, old man."

The old Go player smiled, and he and Jiang sat down to serious bargaining.

The price they arrived at was high by any system of valuation and consisted of free access to the house and "use" of one of the young girls once a month. Jiang knew that the old man wouldn't have sex with the girl and would probably just want her warmth beside him in the bed. Jiang also knew that the old Go player would probably be asleep by ten at night, at which time the girl could slip out of the bed and return to her duties.

"Fine," Jiang said, "I agree to your terms. Now tell me how you beat that young man. Was he a good player?"

"Very good, a better player than I am. He has more knowledge of the game, and his mathematical calculations are first-rate, and usually that would be enough to win at a simple game like Go."

"Go is simple?" Jiang asked.

"Extremely simple. Each player has the same number of stones and can place them anywhere he wants on the board. My turn, his turn, my turn, his turn. Until one of us captures more space than the other. Very few rules. Every piece has the same value. No luck whatsoever. A completely even playing field. A very simple game."

"But you beat him."

"I slaughtered him." The old man chuckled.

"How?"

"I have already told you. I made him play the role of the conqueror so that he saw the world, or the game in this case, through the eyes of one who had already won."

"You made him play a role?"

"I induced him into playing a role."

"I see that, but how did you do that?"

"We all have dreams for ourselves. I simply grease the hinges of the door to their dreams. Oftentimes all a person needs is to be pointed toward the door. On rare occasions he needs a push, but as I said, not often. Find the dream image the person has of himself, the person he wants to be, the thing he thinks he should have become—a great warrior, a great lover, a great scholar—and the person can be manipulated. But only by those who do not enter a dream themselves."

Jiang understood this. The best of lovers never entered what Suzanne Colombe used to call the *folie à deux*—the dream of being loved. The best lover keeps a cool dispassion, to allow herself to service the one in the folly—in the role of being loved.

Jiang thanked the old man and walked him to the door of her office, her arm through his. As she did, she noticed him fall into the role of the new lover of the house madam, a role she allowed him to play for only the first five or six seconds out of her private quarters.

* * *

A WEEK LATER, as was now her custom, Jiang was promenading with her finest courtesans (by name Yin Bao and Mai Bao, her daughters), and she bought a copy of the newest edition of Yao Xie's one hundred and eight poems, called *Travelling in the Bitter Sea*. The poems were a guide to Shanghai's world of prostitution. After the usual warnings about lust and its attendant evils, the book laid out the basic rules for those wishing to avail themselves of the services of the women of the Flower World. It was in direct competition with two classics that dealt with the same issues, *Miscellaneous Notes on Shanghai Flowers* and *He Who Gives Directions to Those Who Don't Know Their Way Around*. Jiang ignored the latter and paid the bookseller for the former. As she did, she noted a large stack of a newly printed version of an old favourite of hers, *The Dream of the Red Chamber*. Before she could reach for a copy, two clearly wealthy young men bought copies of the book. Jiang looked at the bookseller and asked, "*The Dream* is selling again?"

"I can't keep enough copies. Every morning I demand more and more, and by evening they are gone."

"Could I have one, please?"

The bookseller took one from the bottom of the pile and held it out to Jiang.

That night Jiang sat in her private study with her eldest daughter.

"Have you read this?" she asked, holding up her new copy of *The Dream of the Red Chamber*.

Her daughter nodded.

Jiang looked at her already married daughter and wondered if she would present her with a grandchild before too long. As was the custom in her family, the eldest daughter did not work in the business or enter the Ivory Compact but rather married into the strong Zhong family and made her living from one of the arts. This daughter was not a History Teller but an accomplished seamstress—the girl could do anything with cloth. Jiang's two younger daughters, Yin Bao and Mai Bao, were already practised courtesans and were waiting—one patiently and one impatiently—in the next room as their mother had requested. For a moment Jiang thought of them. Upon which would she bestow the name Jiang, give ownership of her businesses, and force the obligation of the Ivory Compact? She hadn't decided yet.

The younger of the two, Yin Bao, had taken the extraordinary step of having her feet bound when she was twelve. She was extremely popular with men and could have conducted herself in almost any way she wanted, but she chose to be extremely modern, making herself available to anyone with enough money to pay for her services. Jiang's middle daughter, Mai Bao, was much more traditional. She met with men only when she had been properly introduced and appropriate gifts had been exchanged. Then, and only then, would she accept invitations to dinner. Her suitor would provide banquets for upwards of twenty of his friends, and she would deign to arrive and stay for sometimes as little as ten minutes. She often attended eight such parties in an evening. She had sex with very few of her suitors, and even then only after exhaustive efforts were made on his part. Often it would take over two years for the liaison to come to its culmination. While this was proceeding, just as in the old days, Mai Bao followed the ancient tradition of giving her heart to a lowly scholar—in this case, a young man with an unsightly wine-stain birthmark on his face.

Jiang respected the choices of both as to how to live their courtesan lives. One because she followed the old ways, one because she had so fully adapted to the new. Which daughter should be given the name Jiang and inducted into the Ivory Compact? Time was moving, she could feel it, and she had to make a decision while she was in full control of her faculties.

She shrugged off that thought. None of her three daughters could out-think her yet.

"Mother?" her eldest prompted.

"Yes, sorry. What is your opinion of this book? This *Dream of the Red Chamber*?"

"I think it's brilliant."

"Yes. But can you see why it is now so popular?"

"Because it posits a way of behaving that is ancient, formal, and respected."

Jiang nodded, wondered what the word *posit* meant, then asked, "But it's a book about sex?"

"Absolutely—and power and money and honour—very old ideas. But very deep in our culture, Mother."

A dream idea, Jiang thought. *A vision that is common to many. Not a hard dream to induce men into.* "Would you reread the book for me, daughter?"

"Surely, Mother."

"And design some clothing for the girls of our house to wear that would make them seem as though they are playing parts in the book?"

"Surely. I would enjoy that."

"Good."

Jiang's eldest was about to leave when the two younger daughters came into the room.

"I asked you ..." Jiang began.

"Yes, Mother," the youngest, Yin Bao, said, "but we lost patience. Isn't that awful of us?"

"I am sorry, Mother," said Mai Bao, the middle daughter, "but I couldn't stop her."

"You both heard our discussion, I assume?" Jiang asked innocently.

The eldest smiled and shook her head. "No need to play-act, Mother. You wanted them to overhear our conversation. That's fine with me."

"Make us really beautiful things, sister," said Yin Bao, "really beautiful."

"What about clothing for the customers as well as for us?" asked Mai Bao.

Jiang looked at her middle daughter and was, as always, struck by her simple, classic beauty. "Explain, please."

"We dress as characters from the book, and so do they."

"We play characters and they play characters," Yin Bao added. "Our customers don't want to be passively entertained, like watching a courtesan play the arhu—boring, boring, boring—or listening to stories." She put her finger in her mouth and made a most unladylike vomiting sound.

"They want to *be* the stories." Then she added with a lascivious smile, "And do all the naughty things the characters in the book do."

"Perhaps," Mai Bao snapped.

"For certain," Yin Bao retorted.

Mai Bao took a small step back and said demurely, "What they really want is to be part of the dream we create."

"Nonsense! They want to have sex in other people's clothes."

"Because," Mai Bao's voice arced dangerously, "it allows them into the Flower World that we have so carefully built."

Jiang nodded. "Very good, Mai Bao." *Perhaps you will be the next Jiang, my dear,* she thought. Although she didn't really approve of the girl's latest companion, the penniless member of the literati with the ghastly purple mark on his face. Jiang had seen them together many times holding hands and talking softly to each other. Despite the young man, her daughter still attended to her courtesan duties, entertained at parties, and on rare occasions offered sex to the most ardent of her pursuers. Jiang wondered briefly how the young scholar felt about that, then dismissed her concern. Penniless scholars and whores were the stuff of stories—ancient stories. Although Jiang could not recall a single scholar from a story who had a raspberry mark on his face.

Her other daughter, Yin Bao, was not tradition-bound. She didn't attend dinners and wait to be paid twice a year. She didn't wait to be wooed. She was a modern girl and slept with any customer who could afford her services. She charged such exorbitant rates that only merchants and gangsters—and *Fan Kuei*—could avail themselves of her attentions.

Two such different girls. But only one could become Jiang and join the Ivory Compact.

"I like your idea about costumes for the customers," Jiang said, then asked, "Any comments from you, Yin Bao?"

The girl threw a practised whorish grin and replied, "The garments should come off simply."

"Yes, of course," Jiang said, then asked her eldest, "Is this possible?"

"Mother, it's just cloth. In my hands cloth can be made to do almost anything."

Jiang nodded, then looked sternly at her two younger daughters. Both of them knew that only one of them would inherit her fortune and her title. Both also knew that they would have to produce at least two daughters if they were to be eligible to become Jiang. But then again, both were young—there was time to produce daughters—or so they thought.

chapter thirteen

Three Graves, Three Memories

In some ways, the most surprising of all the changes at the Bend in the River may well have been the transformation that took place in Silas Hordoon. Through the magic of Shanghai and the arrival of a certain woman from a small Hereford farming community, the most unexpected thing happened to Silas—love bloomed where before there had been only stone.

Then, as quickly as love had flowered—it withered, and died.

Silas stood above the graves and looked out at the mighty Yangtze River as it turned away from the Huangpo and headed toward the sea. Three marked mounds and a small rise were at his feet. Three souls that had touched him and one that he'd never known.

His father had been cremated as he had requested, and Silas had scattered his ashes across the western reach of the Huangpo where Richard and his brother Maxi had first landed at the Bend in the River. He couldn't think where else to spread his father's remains. It had briefly occurred to him to dust them through the opium dens that had been his father's real final resting place. He'd ultimately discarded the idea, although it held a perverse appeal.

But these mounds before him were graves, and the rise in the land overlooking the powerful river was his choice as a final resting place to honour those he had loved and those who had loved him.

He knelt beside the first grave and placed three sprigs of bamboo in a narrow-necked vase near the small headstone. He felt the bamboo's slender leaves and sensed their life within. His *amah* had never said much to him, but he had spent many nights as a boy nestled into the warmth of her back, and whenever he'd smelled the deep musky odour of her body it had brought on a feeling of safety. Silas knew her but never knew her. There had been a mention of her having children of her own back in Malaya, but he had never met them, nor was there ever an effort to bring the children to their mother. She was just a constant presence in his young life, a presence that was willing to protect him when others were not—and yet, he knew almost nothing about her. Even her real name was a jealously guarded secret. Like many in her position she was referred to simply as *amah*. She cleaned him and had access to his body in a way that no other female ever had. He remembered standing naked and covered with mosquito bites as she applied ointment to each red spot. He had touched her hair as she worked on a knee that had four bites, one on top of another, and she had looked up at him. Her large brown eyes opened wide and she smiled. He hadn't seen her smile very often so he remembered that. Then she laughed and said, "Put on your clothes, Silas."

"Put on your clothes, Silas," he said aloud. The wind picked the words from his lips and flung them along the river and out to the sea. He noted that the bamboo had already begun to align itself to the sun.

The second grave was Milo's. His father had demanded an elaborate funeral for Milo, then had smoked so much opium that he wasn't able to attend. After the public ceremony, Silas had been left alone at the graveside with the coffin awaiting its descent into the pit. He simply turned to the four gravediggers and gave them all the money he had in his pockets to take the coffin to this hill overlooking the Yangtze. And here, beside their *amah,* Milo had rested ever since—although it was hard for Silas to think of his handsome brother at rest. Milo was like the wind and the rain. Like laughter in the darkness and joyous as he gorged on life itself. Silas stifled a swell of tears as a bubble of pain rose in his throat. He put a single stem of orchids on the grave and said only four words, "I am so sorry." He'd said the words so often that they had taken on the weight of a prayer. They were all that he could find to say. What do you say to a brother you murdered? Now Milo was just one of the ghosts Silas carried on his back. There were times when he could swear that Milo was at his side as he walked around Shanghai—pointing out the fabulous women, the new bars, the prancing ponies. Silas hadn't ridden a horse since his brother's death, and after Richard's death he had sold every horse in the Hordoon stables. But it wasn't enough to expiate his sin, to gain forgiveness. That had been done by the person in the third grave.

For a moment he looked away, unsure whether he could bear the sight of the grave or its small accompanying mound. But he forced himself to sit beside the simple stone that read: "Here lies my heart."

Silas remembered reading Chaucer's dream allegories as a young man. He had been stunned by what he thought of as the insensitivity of the young knight who finds a lord crying in the woods. The knight asks the lord why he's crying. The lord immediately replies that his wife has died. The knight seems not to have heard and asks about the dead woman and leads the lord through how he met the woman, fell in love with her, married her, and then how she eventually died. The poem ends with the sounds of the "chase of the hart," and the lord rises, brushes away his tears, and rejoins the hunt. Rejoins life. Silas had been trying without success to "rejoin life" for several years. He vowed that he would follow Chaucer's example this day and lead himself through the entirety of the sad tale of his life with Miranda—to perhaps allow him to rejoin the "chase of the hart."

———

It had started on a particularly hard day at the office. He had never been good about enforcing rules, let alone firing workers, but that morning he'd had to face dismissing five men for stealing from the firm. The meeting had quickly escalated into threats, then accusations against the two Chinese men by the three Whites. Silas waited out the accusations, then addressed the two Han Chinese males in Shanghainese. The men answered his questions, and it quickly became clear to Silas that the two Chinese men had been extorted into joining the three Whites. He thanked them and sent them from his office. Then he called for the police. "Be thankful we're in the Concession," he told the three men remaining. "The Manchus have a particularly ugly way of dealing with theft."

After the police hauled away the three White men, Silas looked out his office window down onto the Bund. As always, he marvelled at the swell of humanity on the street below. Then he saw her. Looking up at his window. He stepped back from the window, then carefully snuck a second look. The woman wasn't wearing a chapeau, and her red hair tumbled in curls down her back. Her pale white skin made the red hair even more startling. She turned and spoke to a pastor as she pointed up at his window. She spoke in an English accent that Silas was never able to identify.

When he returned from his lunch she was sitting in his outer office.

Their romance was quick and conducted in secret—as much as things can be secret in a town like Shanghai. But they were able to keep things at least somewhat to themselves, since neither needed any entertainment except the other. They spent all their free time together, mostly in Silas's private rooms. He was amazed how comfortable he was with her, how familiar.

For the first time in his life it didn't matter to Silas that he couldn't fully feel what he believed others felt. He was happy just making her happy. Happier than he'd ever been.

Their only excursions were to gardens. Miranda—her name was Miranda—loved flowers and the ornate ornamental trees sold in the Bird and Fish Market. She turned the earth in the area behind Silas's house, and every morning when he went to work she went to her garden. Things grew for her that seldom grew in Shanghai. They grew as if they knew that Miranda loved them.

Then, on the Sunday morning when she announced that she was carrying his child, his happiness increased exponentially. In a private service they were married by a Justice of the Peace, and they prepared to give their child a fine home. Silas gloried in shopping for the baby to come, but early on Miranda's pregnancy gave signs of trouble.

"Miranda, are you all right?" he cried out when he realized that she wasn't in the bed beside him.

But when he went toward the water closet she insisted that she was fine and that he wasn't to come in. For weeks she barely ate, and Silas called in the company's doctor, who gave him a sly smile and said, "Women's problems. Don't worry about it. If it gets really bad, give her some of this." With that he handed Silas a bottle of Mother's Cordial—an opium product widely used by European women with "women's problems."

Silas pocketed the medicine and headed out on the street. Somehow he knew that giving opium to a pregnant woman wasn't the soundest advice. He walked north on the Bund, then headed up Beijing Lu. The sides of the street were lined with all kinds of tradesmen—one of whom was a doctor whom Silas had used several times to help him find an escape from his chronic insomnia. He waited patiently as the doctor dealt with a woman ahead of him. The woman had a large growth on her neck, and the doctor pondered the tumour before he inserted two sharp needles beneath her left arm, then told the woman to sit and wait.

Then he turned to Silas. "You are having trouble with sleep again?"

Silas smiled. This was probably the only Chinese man in all of Shanghai who didn't use the word *sir* when speaking to him. Silas liked that. He liked the man's gruff honesty and his refusal to see one human being as any different from another. Silas laid out the basics of the problem, then the doctor asked the obvious question. "Why are you here and not her?"

How could Silas tell him that it was one thing for people to gawk at him talking to a Chinese street doctor, but quite another for his wife to be seen there with the man? The woman with the tumour on her neck began to moan softly, and the doctor went to her. He readjusted one of the needles, placed six more, then returned to Silas. "Tell me more. Tell me everything you know about this woman."

"You mean about her illness?"

"Is your Shanghainese failing you? I said tell me everything you know about this woman."

Silas did as he was ordered and was surprised how little he actually knew about Miranda's personal history. The street doctor's face grew darker and darker. Finally he said, "Bring her to see me. You can come very early in the morning. I'm here before the sunrise. But I'm not sure I can help you, or her."

"And the baby?"

"I said nothing about a baby," the doctor snapped.

The next morning, when Silas brought Miranda to the street doctor, the meeting was cordial but brief. At the end he spoke briefly to Miranda, then pulled Silas aside. "Get the best midwives you can. I can suggest two if you wish. Don't allow her to take the opium, things are bad enough as they are."

Despite Silas's questions, the doctor refused to be drawn out on the meaning of his ominous statement. Then he took Miranda aside.

Walking home, Silas asked, "Miranda, what did he say to you?"

Miranda smiled wanly, then replied, "That I should enjoy the rest of my pregnancy."

A shiver of fear etched its way up Silas's spine as he grabbed hold of her hand and held it tight.

For the remainder of her pregnancy he was hardly ever from her side. He had delegated much of the Hordoon Company's business and simply put entire projects on hold. Then her waters broke, and Silas sent for the two midwives the street doctor had recommended.

Both arrived with surprising speed, as if they'd expected the summons that morning somehow, and they ushered him out of the room. But before they closed the door he saw the darkness on their faces and heard one say to the other, "This will be very bad."

Sixteen hours later one of the women came from the room and touched Silas gently on the shoulder. He jolted into waking. "Must come, fast now. Be brave."

Silas followed the midwife into the room. Miranda was propped up on the pillows, her red hair a sunburst on the white linen, her pale ivory skin glistening with sweat. Something small, entirely encased in sheeting, sat on the foot of the bed. The moment Silas entered, a midwife grabbed the thing from the bed. Silas saw blood on the linen. "The baby …"

"No baby. No baby here."

"But …"

"No baby here!"

Suddenly he was on her and throwing off the sheeting. The thing that the morning light revealed was more vegetable than human. Some parts were identifiable. Many were not. The shape itself was almost like a ball. He looked up. "What …?"

"Not a baby. Not live. Dead. Not a baby. Give back, give back. And look to your wife, sir. Look to your wife."

Silas didn't remember the thing being taken from his hands, but the strength of Miranda's grip on his lower arm surprised him. "Promise me," she said.

"Anything."

"Promise me you'll build a garden. A garden to honour things that grow."

"I promise, Miranda, and when you're feeling—"

"And find my mother's grave. Her name was Miriam."

"Miriam, yes … but where …?"

Suddenly Miranda's eyes flared wide and she gasped.

"Miranda, what?"

She turned slowly to him and said simply, "Why?" and then exhaled one long breath—and did not take in another—ever again.

—

Silas weeded the small garden he had made at the foot of her grave, then turned to the small mound beside her. The "not baby" he had buried at his wife's side. At first he had resented the thing that had taken Miranda from him, then he'd managed to move past that.

He put his hand on the small mound. Thoughts flew into his mind—but only one word came from his lips: "Why?"

And even as he said that word he looked up and a great Indiaman sailing ship—a white bird on water—took the far reach of the river and headed to the port of Shanghai. On deck was a young, enthusiastic Southern Methodist missionary named Charles Soon—another Man with a Book.

chapter fourteen

Silas's Inheritance

That night, after his return from the three graves, Silas tried to induce sleep with brandy and only managed to make himself sick. So as the depth of the night crept upon him and the dark minutes took hours to pass, he roamed his house, sensing Miranda in every room—every room except his private study, which he entered precisely as the grandfather clock in the front foyer struck the first bell of three. It was the hour the Bard of Avon had called "the very witching time of night, when churchyards yawn and Hell itself breathes out contagion to this world." Silas wouldn't have put it that way, since Shakespeare was not on his list of favoured authors. The Bard of Avon definitely was one of his father's most loved, though. Silas recalled as a boy his father quoting Shakespeare to his Uncle Maxi, who would always nod sagely. Then, after asking, "What does that mean in English?" he would demand that Richard tell the story of the play from which the quotation came. Silas remembered his father often putting aside whatever work was at hand and sitting to tell Maxi about Hamlet or Macbeth or Cymbeline. Silas would listen carefully, but it was the joy on his Uncle Maxi's face that was his real reward. How his Uncle Maxi enjoyed things! No, loved things! What joy he found in his life! *How unlike me,* Silas thought.

"How unlike me," he said in a whisper aloud, then laughed softly. But as the last echo of the last chime of the grandfather clock faded to silence, Silas suddenly sensed someone else's presence in his study. He spun around, somehow expecting to see Uncle Maxi, but found himself staring up at the top shelf of one of the many bookcases. To be precise, staring at the overhanging edges of the unruly pile of journals his father, the famous opium trader and opium addict, had bequeathed to him at their last meeting.

Silas hadn't thought much about the stack of personal journals his father had given him. He'd put them on the back of the uppermost shelf in his private study beneath the elementary Mandarin books he'd used as a child to learn the language, the oldest version of which was the original Mandarin-English dictionary from which Vrassoon's head China hand, Cyril, had so assiduously studied.

Silas needed to stand on his tiptoes and reach as high as he could to take down the uppermost journal. He turned on the green baize lamp on his desk and began to read of the great crumbling palaces of Calcutta, the failure of the grandfather Silas had never met, Maxi and Richard's time at the Government of India Alkaloid Works at Ghazipur, and finally of the prophecy that a brother would kill a brother.

For a moment Silas thought that the light in the lamp had failed, but he quickly realized it was his tears that made the words swim on the page. Brother would kill brother—he had killed Milo. He, Silas Hordoon, was a murderer—a fratricidal murderer. It was why Miranda was taken from him, of that he had no doubt. He shuddered and pushed his father's journal aside.

The grandfather clock chimed the fourth hour of the night. He opened the window and the dense aroma released by the sweet olive trees entered the study. "It's quiet," he said aloud, "only at this hour is the Bend in the River quiet." The great city seemed to breathe a sigh of relief. The last of the night carousers was safely abed, and the morning chores of the nightsoil collectors had not yet begun. A moment of peace was on the land. Then he felt Miranda's hand on his shoulder and almost turned to see her—but he didn't. He knew that she was just another of the ghosts that he would have to carry. His brother, his father, his uncle, and now his beloved. Stacked like cordwood on a coolie's back. High and heavy.

He bowed his head and looked down. In the plate glass of the window he saw the lamp's reflection and his father's journal open on his desk.

A dry wind, all the way from the Gobi Desert, whooshed through the window, swirled past Silas, and flipped the pages of the journal. Silas knew the Chinese warnings about the dry wind—the madness wind—and respected them, as he had found over and over again that when a practical people like the Chinese feared something, there was always a reason for concern.

He walked slowly to the desk and looked down at the page the wind had exposed. And there was his father's story of meeting the dwarf Jesuit,

Brother Matthew, and the man's pleading imprecation, "Do not do the Devil's work."

Silas looked up and took in the many markers of his own wealth in the room—the fabulous carpets from Tikrit, the Ming Dynasty vases, the hand-painted leaded glass windows, the polished mahogany floor, the large roll-top desk—and wondered if he had, all this time, been doing the Devil's work.

"Nonsense," he muttered, and shoved the book aside. It fell from the desktop onto the floor. Silas heard the old binding crack. He hefted himself out of the chair to retrieve it.

The book had landed open and the spine had fractured. The surprisingly cheap thing had loosed several of its pages onto the hardwood floor. Silas cursed silently. His father hadn't numbered the leaves so it was going to be hard to figure out exactly which page went where. When he picked up the loose sheets from the floor he was taken aback to see that in this part of the journals each entry was a different, completed entity with a date at the top and the word *Finis* at the bottom. Each was penned in his father's unique hand, but in a script so tiny that it filled every inch of the page. Without close examination one could believe that there was no writing on the pages at all—that they were just ink-filled leaves.

Silas smoothed out the first of the pages on the floor and brought down the lamp from his desk. He sat cross-legged on the floor, something he hadn't done since he was a child, and read the first of the opium voyages his father had so meticulously committed to paper.

.. .. ..

I knew it from the very first. Knew it but couldn't express it. But now I know—or believe I know, that we were somehow expected. All those eyes on the banks of the Yangtze somehow knew we were coming. And although like every occupier we were hated, they knew that they needed us—needed to use us, somehow.

As I stood on the deck of HMS Cornwallis *with Maxi at my side I felt them. I even said as much to him, but my brother was not inclined to such nuances. I was. I always had been, and it was part of what drove me to ... to the serpent smoke.*

In the smoke I often see their eyes watching, expecting us. I have written several times to Thomas De Quincy of my insights, and he has responded with warnings. Warnings that "while riding the serpent's back it is hard to discern true from false, what is to come from what has already been, and what we wish to meet us with what is in fact awaiting our coming." True. Just before his death Mr. De Quincy sent me a manuscript of a young writer he thought I should read. The man had "unusual insights that seem to match up to yours." Mr. De Quincy suggested I acquaint myself with this promising young writer, a certain Mr. Rudyard Kipling.

———

Silas jotted down the name, then continued reading.

.. .. ..

The short story he sent me was untitled. It postulated how fear first came to the jungle. According to the story, the jungle had assumed a kind of hierarchical order developed over many centuries, and although there were those who bridled at the "law of the jungle," none broke its basic precepts, and there was peace. Then a limping tiger, unable to track and bring down his usual prey, left the jungle and was the first to kill a human.

And of course men replied by invading the jungle and bringing fear where there had been no fear before.

When I put down the story I noted the perspiration on my hands and thudding of my heart in my ears.

It will happen here at the Bend in the River. Of that I am sure. There have been Europeans killed in Shanghai but never in a manner that was outside the understanding of the order of our occupation of their country. But it will happen. A "limping tiger" will assault our power and kill as many of us as they can. Look for its coming and the inevitable "bringing of fear" from us—then ultimately their response to our terror and the oncoming of the end of our time at the Bend in the River.

———

Silas looked up from the manuscript and thought of the rumours now racing through the city of a murderer killing those he labelled "collaborators." *A limping tiger, perhaps,* he thought as he turned the page.

.. .. ..

For all of its religious mumbo-jumbo, the Taiping Rebellion was really just an expression of the destitution of the huge number of poor people in this massive country. The more wealth we bring, the more we egg on the poor. The more we support those Chinese who continue to suppress the poor, the more we enrage them. Despite the huge number of deaths in the Rebellion, their movement has not ended. Cannot be ended. There is not enough wealth in the entire world to raise up the poor of this vast country, and they will not remain content in their poverty with our wealth constantly there for them to see. But the poor are not the only potential source of rebellion in the Middle Kingdom. The Manchu government has been fatally wounded by our presence. Every day that we continue to prosper we turn the knife in the wound we have inflicted upon them. As they lose power, their institutions sunder. Some of them may well have outlived their time. But those institutions brought order to the millions upon millions of people in the Middle Kingdom—an ordered hierarchy to their jungle. Should that order ever break down, the first object of the anger of the Chinese will be us. And they may well be led by those who have been cast out by the decline of their system. Namely, their literati. These people have devoted their lives to the learning of an ancient literature that we no longer value. They will fall from their elevated status very quickly, and because they have histor ically had power, they may well be able to rally others to their anger against those whom they perceive as having brought them low—us, again.

But that is not the greatest danger.

The greatest danger will come when these two disaffected groups—the poor and the literati—join. Then our time here is within breaths of being over.

Can this be stopped? Not while every Fan Kuei's only interest is in the making of as much money as quickly as possible.

Should this be stopped?

Perhaps not. Perhaps what all those eyes watching us on the deck of HMS Cornwallis gliding up the mighty Yangtze knew on that day in 1842 was that we were only visitors—unwelcome, but necessary visitors—only here to lift them to the next level of their glory.

Watch their eyes as they watch us and try to understand the hate that lives there. And beware the limping tiger.

———

Silas gathered together the pages and sorted them carefully. Then he stacked the journals and got to his feet. He took two steps toward the bookshelf before he stopped himself. He once more rose on tiptoe and took what he believed were the rest of his father's writings in hand. He didn't want these journals with his other books. These were special. They were his. He looked at the journals in his hands, but he didn't see journals—he saw one great thing—one book.

He left the study and returned to his bedroom—his and Miranda's bedroom before, but now just his. There he opened the delicately inlaid table beside the bed and slid Richard Hordoon's journals—his book—into the waiting drawer. Then he closed it, and for the first time since Miranda's death he fell into a deep and restful sleep.

And as he slept the dust in his study sifted down from the ceiling and set a thin layer of impediment between any reader and the three final pages of Richard Hordoon's testament, which his son, Silas, had inadvertently left on the uppermost shelf of his bookcase. The three pages bore a simple title: "Doing the Devil's Work."

———

And as the sun crested the horizon, a second barber took his place on the sidewalk on Julu Lu. He stared at the barber who was already set up, then the two nodded—and a young scholar with a wine stain on his cheek entered the shop of another "collaborator."

chapter fifteeen
The Progress of Charles Soon

1894–97

Charles Soon's return to his native China was not all that he had hoped for. The Chinese treated him as if he were a yellow-skinned *Fan Kuei,* while his *Fan Kuei* fellow Southern Methodist missionaries treated him as if he were a barely literate Celestial who had somehow weaseled a degree out of Wesleyan College. Charles, although he had not stood first in his class, had earned respectable grades at school, and although the only Asian in his class, he was well liked. Under the guidance of Captain Malachi and an American industrialist who had taken him in as a ward, he had blossomed into a fine young man. He was highly regarded by both his church and his peers and invited to all the best events of Wilmington society—although he was careful never to be alone in the company of any of the fine young American ladies of the town.

But here, in Shanghai, where his entire life had clearly been leading him, he found himself for the first time alone and friendless. Then without so much as a word of explanation his superiors shipped him out of the Foreign Settlement to a small village two hundred miles to the north.

In the depths of rural China he was even further at a loss. His cultured Mandarin speech was barely understood by the people of the village, and the crude living conditions were like nothing he had experienced before. There wasn't even running water, let alone a proper toilet, in the whole village. He wrote many letters pleading with his Bishop in Shanghai to increase his allowance so that he could purchase some basic amenities, but he was always curtly rebuffed—in the way a *Fan Kuei* might rebuff a stupid Hakka servant.

He resisted the temptation to use his only two possessions of value—a watch given him by Captain Malachi and a small pouch of gold coins given to him on his leaving by his industrialist benefactor—to better his living conditions, believing that these two gifts were to be saved for more important things.

The squat, windowless hovel that was his church was alive with scorpions and stank of mould. His first two services were attended by a single old lady who slept until it was time for Communion, when she promptly got to her feet and downed the wafer and wine with a nod and a burp.

Charles had never been so low.

It was at the beginning of his second month in the village that he answered a knock at the ill-fitting planking that passed for a door to his hut to find a peddler selling, of all things, a single page of a novel.

"What would I do with a single page?" he asked.

"Read it, of course, assuming you can read," the peddler replied.

"Trust me, I can read."

"Good. So pay me, then read the page, and then read it to others in the village and charge them. I'll be back in a week with another page, and you can buy that one from me and read that one to them—and charge them, of course."

"It could take years to read a whole book that way."

"True, but that's not a problem with this kind of book. They'll be waiting for every new page, now, you trust me," the peddler said with a wink.

Charles took the page and read the first two lines. To his shock, the thing was set in a courtesan's boudoir. He was about to throw the page back at the peddler, but something told him not to. He looked at the man carefully. Then at the man's cart. The thing was piled high with finely made cooking utensils, including a dozen or so hand-beaten woks, many bolts of fine Chinkiang silk and Persian cloth, along with the usual array of pins, needles, thread, ribbons, and other sundries that were common to peddlers the world over. Most impressively, he also had a fine, strong horse. This man was making good money!

"Are books popular?"

"Books?"

"This kind of book? Are they popular?"

"Very," the man said with a cackle.

"How much per page?"

The figure quoted was small, but when Charles calculated the per-page cost of a three-hundred-page book against the modest cost to buy it, he was surprised by the profit. No, he was impressed—very impressed.

Two months later he was granted his first leave, and he immediately headed toward Shanghai and its French Concession—not to the brothels and opium dens common in the alleys there, but to the bookshops. There he saw shelf upon shelf of books, many in translation, and in one corner a single badly bound magazine. On a whim he bought the magazine and read the inept articles. Then he turned to the front leaf and sought out the printing credits. The printer's address was displayed prominently. It was on Hua Hai Lu. Charles Soon headed in that direction.

Crossing Bubbling Spring Road, he was almost run down by a fast-moving horse-drawn carriage. Then, much to his shock, another carriage, pulled by a fine white horse, darted out from an alley, and the two headed directly for each other. A loud thud was followed by the ear-piercing neighs of horses that were in turn drowned out by angry female shrieks.

Along with everyone else, Charles Soon ran toward the tumult and was amazed when he got there to see two very beautiful young Han Chinese women, exquisitely dressed, standing in their respective carriages and screaming insults of the most salacious nature at each other. As the women hurled their scurrilous epithets the crowd doubled, then doubled again. It finally occurred to Charles that these young women were courtesans and that this huge and growing crowd was fascinated by everything these ornate creatures said—or did.

He got close enough to hear one call the other a "cunt faced loon!"

That brought squeals of joy from the crowd—especially from the older women. Then the other shouted back that at least she kept her feet in her own shoes—a reference that really thrilled the crowd, although Charles didn't completely understand what the tiny shoes that held bound feet had to do with the sex act.

Finally the police arrived. When they did, one of the watchers slipped back into the crowd, the raspberry blotch on his face turning yet a deeper crimson with fury. After much complaint the officers sent the two courtesans on their ways.

Charles watched the crowd slowly disperse. As they did they chattered loudly about the incident and argued with real intensity as to which of the two courtesans had won the verbal battle. It was clear to Charles that they had had an exceedingly entertaining time.

Charles looked down. His sweaty palms had adhered to the pages of the magazine and the cheap ink had run onto his hands. He looked in the direction that the courtesans' carriages had gone, then once more down at the mangled magazine in his hot hand, and headed toward the print shop.

At the end of a long alley close to the west wall of the Old City, he spotted the printer's address. Entering under a stone portal he found himself taking a stairway down into a sub-sub-basement where dozens of men were hunched over tables busily picking out single character tiles from racks that held thousands. The tiles were set into precise brackets that would eventually be run through a printing press that would produce pages of print that would tell the news to the people of Shanghai or entertain the indolent wealthy of the city at the Bend in the River.

The speed with which the men worked was astonishing. A chubby Japanese man with glasses approached him and asked, "Do you have an order for me?" His Mandarin was word-perfect, but his accent was as foreign to Shanghai as was Charles's. "Well?" he demanded.

Charles hemmed and hawed, then managed, "I need a few more details about your operation before I am willing to offer up the kind of large contract I have in mind."

"Fine," the chubby man said, "ask me whatever you like." He took out a Snake Charmer cigarette and lit it as he scraped ink off his hands onto his blue apron.

"I am anticipating placing a very large order," Charles said.

"Good," the chubby Japanese printer said as he let out a long line of smoke. "The bigger the better."

Charles smiled inwardly—he was good at this. All those years of telling the truth at the seminary must have masked an innate skill at prevarication.

Charles quickly established that handwritten material was brought to this print house, where these men supplied the enamel tile characters that went into the tight brackets that went to the printer, and that the place could reproduce documents at a rapid rate and for what Charles thought of as a remarkably cheap price. Then the man added, "And of course we can handle the new lithograph technique. We were the first ones in Shanghai who could take a photograph or drawing and reproduce it in a book."

"Or magazine?" Charles was surprised to realize that he'd been holding his breath.

"Sure. Magazine, book, scroll, or a whore's ass. Anything that fits into a printing press."

———

That evening Charles Soon sat in an inexpensive wine store down by the Suzu Creek with a glass of strong Chinese wine on the table in front of him.

He was going to spend the night in the shop, sleeping in the hard chair, hopefully not having to buy more than the one glass of wine.

"Is that wine poisoned or something? Wine's for drinking, not staring at, Padre."

Charles looked up into the face of a young, inebriated Han Chinese man. Then at the long blue robe of the literati that he wore. He couldn't help noticing the robe was filthy and torn.

"Excuse me?"

"You've been staring at that glass of wine for almost an hour. If you're not going to drink it, I'll take it off your hands."

"Oh, will you?"

"I'm not asking for charity. I'll recite a poem for you. My fine poem for your cheap glass of wine? A fair trade."

Charles was intrigued and replied, "Okay."

The young, impoverished scholar then stood and recited for the better part of twenty minutes the opening of one of the classic poems of the early Ming Dynasty. When he finished Charles applauded, truly impressed. "Where did you learn that?"

"A sip of your wine, your honour, and I'll tell you."

Charles pushed the glass across the table. The man drank greedily, but Charles reached over and tilted the cup away from his mouth. "Tell me where you learned that."

The young man spread his arms wide and wailed out, "I am an educated man. I am a literate man—a scholar. But here in this city where only businessmen matter, I am nothing."

"Did you write the civil service exams?"

"Stood third in my whole prefecture. Third!" The man held up his three end fingers to emphasize his point. Then he reached for the wine again.

Charles stopped his hand before it got to the glass. "Then why don't you have a job with the Doatai?"

"Because, friend, Padre, whatever you are, this is the *Fan Kuei's* Concession and they run things their way here, and they don't need literate men, writers, real writers, like me."

"Okay. But why not work in the Chinese section of …?"

He didn't get out any more before the man's laughter drowned out his question. "Because, my stupid friend, there is no money to be made there, almost no one lives there. Everyone lives in the Foreign Settlements. They have all the money. All the power … and they don't give a dumpling's squirt about whether a Slant like me can read or not."

Charles pushed the cup across to the man. "Can you really write?"

The man nodded. "Read, write, recite, you name it."

"And do you have other friends who can write?"

"Dozens."

Charles took one of the coins from his benefactor's pouch and ordered the man another cup of wine. When the wine arrived he told the young scholar about the shouting match he had seen on the street between the two courtesans. "Could you write about women like that?"

"Sure, why not? Until recently courtesans saved their special favours for scholars. They only really fell in love with scholars. Now they just fuck merchants and scream at each other in public. What was that, that one called the other?"

"A cunt-faced loon," Charles said, amazed that he was able to say the words without blushing.

"That's good. Very good. It even scans. 'Cunt-faced loon' is very good."

"Yes. But could you write stories about these kinds of women?"

"Those kinds of women? Absolutely." Then a slyness came into his face as he added, "If you paid me for it."

"Waiter. Bring this man writing implements and a bottle of wine." The waiter nodded when he saw a second coin from Charles's pouch appear and headed back behind a cheap curtain. Charles turned to his tablemate and asked, "And you have friends who are also able to write?"

"I have friends who ...?"

"Are unemployed like you and can write stories?"

"Yes. But let's leave the unemployed part out, because if you hire them then they won't be unemployed, will they?"

"But can they write stories about courtesans?"

"Sure. Yes."

"For wine they'll write stories?"

"Wine and a little food should be enough for a story."

By midnight Charles Soon had the first story for the first edition of Shanghai's newest magazine, *Chronicles from the Flower World*. He bought the scholar another bottle of wine and gave him a few small coins. The drunken scholar was pleased. He had a bottle of wine to warm him through the cold night ahead, and he had finally made some money in Shanghai. Charles was pleased. He had the beginnings of an enterprise that could make him enough money to get out of the poverty of missionary work.

The scholar took the bottle from the table and rose.

"Tomorrow, here, at the same hour," Charles said, "and for each writer friend you bring I will give you ten percent of what I pay them."

The scholar tried to calculate that but he was too drunk to make the figures align themselves, so he stuck out his hand and Charles shook it—like two old friends.

"What's your name?" Charles asked.

"Tzu Rong Zi" the writer replied.

They shook hands a second time and slapped each other on the back.

But before they parted they argued. The poet was outraged that Charles wanted to name the magazine *Chronicles from the Flower World*. The scholar was adamant that the only true name would be *The Cunt-Faced Loonicles*. But he was too drunk to really argue so he clutched his bottle to his chest and headed toward the door, chanting "The Cunt-Faced Loonicles" several times before he looked skyward and said to the gods of poetry, "It even scans."

* * *

THE FIRST PRINTING of *Chronicles from the Flower World* cost Charles the watch that Captain Malachi had given him, but the run sold out within a day. Charles immediately took ninety percent of his profits and bought a second, and then a third, and then a fourth printing of the magazine. With the other ten percent he commissioned twenty stories from Tzu Rong Zi and the two scholars he brought to work. Charles locked them in a room he had rented with three of the coins from his benefactor's pouch. He provided six bottles of wine and would not let them leave until they had completed seven stories apiece.

The second, third, and fourth runs of the first edition of *Chronicles from the Flower World* had already sold out by the time the second issue of the magazine was in the kiosks, stores, and tea houses. The second issue sold out in a day, and fights were reported on several street corners as people jostled to get a copy.

Charles still had six coins left from his benefactor and had made enough money to buy back Captain Malachi's watch—although it annoyed him that it cost him twice as much to buy back the watch as he had made selling it. But it was a good lesson—one he never forgot.

Charles sent a one-line resignation letter to the Bishop of the Southern Methodist Missionary League and signed it "Charles Soong." Adding a *g* to the end of his family name made it sound more Chinese. Charles had big plans—dynastic plans—and Chinese dynasties all ended with the letter *g*: Ming, Ching, Soon(g).

Charles rented four rooms at the very foot of Bubbling Spring Road and ensconced Tzu Rong Zi and his writing staff—now six strong—there. He had them supplied with all the food and drink they wanted so long as they each produced two stories a day—and not a word less.

After the seventh issue of *Chronicles from the Flower World* he bought out the chubby Japanese printer, then took him on as a partner. Two months later they were putting out three different magazines every week, each detailing the exploits of the women of the Flower World.

Charles bought a large house in the French Concession and began the long, protracted process of finding a wife—beginning with finding a matchmaker.

While the process proceeded, Charles continued to add to his empire. He translated and then printed extracts from the Bible and sold them at tremendous profit to the various Evangelical societies in Shanghai. Then he had several English language classics translated and printed. These sold briskly. But his real money and his central concern was the Flower World. At the beginning of his third year he hit upon an ingenious idea: Flower World contests, to name the best courtesan. To ensure fairness the winner was selected on the basis of the number of people who sent in their votes to his publications. The contests were run twice a year, and whole issues were devoted to each of the contestants. Circulation soared, and there was demand for his weekly magazines from Nanking and Canton and Beijing—and even San Francisco. Letters poured in extolling the virtues of various courtesans.

The courtesan contests were, in fact, the very first democratic exercises in the Middle Kingdom—and Charles knew it—as did the Manchu rulers in Beijing, who were not amused. But the courtesans responded enthusiastically to what was for them completely free publicity. Many of the winners garnered fine marriages to wealthy men. The magazines would cover the marriages and the babies and the fights—and often the courtesans' return to the Flower World. By 1897 Charles Soon(g)—lowly Boston busboy; studious seminary student; ignored missionary—had become one of Shanghai's wealthiest Chinese men, and an ardent opponent of the Manchu Dynasty.

* * *

JIANG CAREFULLY WATCHED Charles Soong's growth and remarked aloud, "Now here's a Man with a Book … a Man with a Book who needs a wife."

chapter sixteen
Jiang's Choice

December 1897

Jiang knew that the time to choose between her daughters, Yin Bao and Mai Bao, was approaching. Although she felt as strong as a dragon, the last time she had summoned her doctor the old man had lingered over a series of moles on her back. His sharp intakes of breath and little gasps did not bode well for a comfortable or long old age. Jiang was all right with that. She had no desire to live forever, but she had an obligation to supply a daughter to the Ivory Compact, and she was troubled by the options presented to her by her two youngest.

"Sit," she commanded them.

Yin Bao, the younger of the two, moved with surprising grace and speed, despite her bound feet, and slid into Jiang's favourite brocade chair, then crossed her almost totally exposed legs. The middle daughter, Mai Bao, shook her head and said simply, "I'll stand, Mother."

"As you will," Jiang said as she turned from them and allowed her fingers to stroke the edge of the painted silk hanging beside the window. It was a classic Ming country scene, complete with a frozen highland lake and peasants running to their eel pen. In one corner there was a shocking slash of red across a white ice floe. Although Jiang didn't realize it, the painting portrayed scenes from the day of the First Emperor's death. The events of that day on the Holy Mountain had made their way into the very heart of the culture of the Black-Haired people. But even if Jiang had known, the connection to the Holy Mountain could not have made her more fond of the painting. The painting had been given to her by the man who was Yin Bao's father, perhaps the only man Jiang had ever loved.

She turned and looked out the tall window. There the reflections of her two daughters awaited her, as if caught in the depths of the glass. She studied their images: Yin Bao so round and full of life, Mai Bao so erect and stern, although blessed with great beauty. Both women serviced men, just as she had done for so many years, and yet in completely different ways. The youngest was as modern as Shanghai itself. She never bothered to learn classical dancing or storytelling, or even how to play the arhu. With three simple sentences she had dismissed the entire idea: "Dress-up and play-acting is fine if it brings in more customers. But the entertainment we provide is sex, Mother—not ancient frippery. Sex for money, and in my case very good money for very good sex."

Yin Bao's take was substantial. She slept only with clients who could afford to pay the outrageous prices that she demanded, and she often had more than one customer a night. As well, she was popular in the press, although she refused to enter the Flower Contests run by Charles Soong's magazine. Men now wrote poems to her beauty that were published in the newspapers, and many travelled for days just to catch a glimpse of her. She was better known in Shanghai than the most famous of opera singers, and she paraded in public in an open carriage drawn by two white horses, from which she had been known to shout at other "less worthy" courtesans who blocked her way. In fact it was Yin Bao's use of the phrase "cunt-faced loon" that had in a way launched Charles Soong's publishing career. She dressed in only the most exquisite of clothes and took full advantage, and a secret delight, in playing roles from the novel *The Dream of the Red Chamber*. She loved dressing in the elaborate period costumes that her eldest sister recreated for her. She played many roles from the book for her patrons, including that of Lady Chao, the powerful concubine who is on "good terms" with the nun Miao-yu, a role enacted by her maid for foolish men who thought that one woman could not possibly satisfy their needs. But her most popular role was that of Hsia Chin-kuei, the pretty but treacherous daughter of a royal merchant. Hsia is a shrew. She mistreats the concubine Hsiang-ling and, at one point, plots to poison her, but poisons herself by mistake. Her extraordinary sexual prowess allowed Yin Bao to actually act out her own mistaken poisoning at the exact moment she brought on the clouds and rain for her client.

The newspapers caught wind of this astonishing feat and outdid themselves trying to create euphemisms to describe, within the bounds of decency, the "action" to their breathless readers. The girl took real delight in collecting the coded references in the papers to her auto-erotic asphyxiation and could be heard late into the night regaling the other girls with the latest phrases she'd found in the press.

Both daughters knew that only one of them would be granted the name Jiang, and the new Jiang would become the undisputed owner of the entirety of their mother's three brothels and many opium dens, with the power to deal with all the employees of the establishments, including her other sisters, in any manner that she deemed appropriate. Jiang knew there was no love lost between these two daughters and had no doubt that whoever was passed over in her decision would not long have a place of employment—no matter what provisos she put into her will.

Jiang thought about the responsibility under the Ivory Compact that the new Jiang would have to assume, as she turned from the window to look at her aloof middle daughter, Mai Bao. The girl had classic, long lines in her legs and torso, and her flawless skin was a wonder to behold. She carried herself like the finest of thoroughbreds and had all the haughtiness of those exquisite creatures. Mai Bao enjoyed playing characters from *The Dream of the Red Chamber* as well—although different characters from her younger sister. She loved to portray Hsueh Pao-chai (Precious Virtue), Chia Pao-yu's wife—a devoted daughter and a faithful consort.

The first time Mai Bao played Precious Virtue, Yin Bao slid over to her mother and snarked, "I thought that men came to us to get away from wives like Precious Virtue."

Jiang smiled and said, "Men come here for many reasons, dear. Remember that."

To that Yin Bao probed, "Why exactly, Mother, should I remember that?" She smiled the smile that only a young woman in full bloom could smile, then leaned down and kissed her mother full on the mouth. For the first time Jiang noticed that Yin Bao's lips felt just like her father's had all those years ago. Jiang patted her daughter's hands but thought, *Not so fast do you become the queen and enter the Ivory Compact.*

Mai Bao also loved playing Shih Hsiang-yun (River Mist), an almost nondescript girl who is little else but pretty and vapid. Her younger sister's response to this performance was terse: "Big sister has a great talent at portraying boringly an extremely boring person. Now we know everything there is to know about someone we really wish hadn't existed. How very clever of her."

Jiang responded by saying, "What is boring to one man may well be exciting to another."

"Yes, Mother, but a honeypot is a honeypot to one and all."

The middle daughter's favourite was playing Yuan-yang, Lady Dowager's personal maid, who refuses Chia Sheh's proposal to be his concubine, and when Lady Dowager dies, she hangs herself in an act of devotion.

Yin Bao's only response to this performance was to mutter, "I could have lived without the opening—although the end, big sister hanging herself, is very satisfying."

Jiang just stared at her. Was she really so coarse? Could she really leave all the responsibility of the Ivory Compact in this one's hands?

"No comment, Mother, about one man's hanging being another man's sex, or something like that?"

"No, dear. No such comment."

"Too bad. I would have thought that a man well hung was well worth comment." The girl's raucous laughter disappointed her mother.

Although the two sisters never spoke of it, both knew what was at stake in being named Jiang upon their mother's passing. Neither daughter knew of the Narwhal Tusk or the responsibilities of being a member of the Chosen Three, but both had watched their mother for many years and understood that Jiang was special. Being Buddhists, the Catholic idea of "being blessed" was foreign to them, but they both knew that their mother was a marvel—one of nature's true gifts.

It was Yin Bao who picked up on the strange relationship between her mother and the Confucian. "Does he prefer boys, Mother?" she asked.

Jiang was caught off guard, being unaware that anyone had taken note of the time she spent with the Confucian. She managed to say, "I have no idea where his sexual preferences lie."

"Well, what's he doing in a whorehouse?"

Yin Bao was one of very few persons who referred to Jiang's as a whorehouse.

"Perhaps you're overlooking the obvious, Mother."

"And that would be?"

"That he is one of those who prefers old women like yourself?"

There was not another person in all of Shanghai from whom Jiang would allow such rudeness, but the girl reminded her of the man who had sired her, and it melted her heart. She cared deeply for her youngest—and brashest—daughter. She worried how this one would fare if she named the middle daughter Jiang. Then she dismissed the thought. It had been thus with her and her older sister. Once Jiang surrendered her name to one of the girls she surrendered her power—in return for which, Jiang needlessly reminded herself, the daughter named would also have to assume the full responsibilities of the Jiang family in the Ivory Compact.

And those responsibilities seemed to be finding a focus. It was now clear to Jiang that there were already three strong candidates for the Man with a

Book. There were many, many men with books in Shanghai, but very few with enough power to enact change at the Bend in the River. Gangster Tu, Charles Soong, and strangely enough the *Fan Kuei* Silas Hordoon. Years ago she had seen Richard Hordoon, night after night, writing his strange opium journals, and when she was told they had been passed on to his son Silas, he became a candidate for the Man with a Book. One of those men might well become the responsibility of the daughter who was given the name Jiang. Responsibility to do what, exactly, Jiang was unsure.

She took Mai Bao's hand and looked her up and down. She saw in her strong features the well of time from which their entire clan had come. This girl, unlike her younger sister, was not modern. Although she embraced *The Dream of the Red Chamber* costumes, she was devoted to the old ways. She shunned newspaper reporters and never spent her time with merchants. She was a fine classical dancer and storyteller, and her arhu playing was famous. Mai Bao offered men an access to the "other world," the Flower World, and was a denizen of that profound place. And like all true denizens of the Chinese demi-monde her true love—just as in the classic literature—was a poor scholar or poet. In this case the penniless scholar had a large wine stain birth mark covering much of his left cheek.

The scholar made Jiang feel uneasy. "Why him, particularly, dear?" Jiang demanded.

The girl hung her head in the classic pose used by great painters to depict women of royalty in mourning and murmured, "Love is the gift we offer and only seldom receive."

Jiang could recite the rest of that poem by heart. She had heard it many times from foolish girls in her employ who had at first risked, then thrown away, all their prospects for the idle dream of the love of a penniless and often shiftless scholar.

"It's just books you're responding to, Mai Bao," Jiang claimed.

"No, Mother, he is my heart's completion. Together we are whole."

Jiang stared at her tall, smart daughter. The girl's scholar pauper was probably waiting for her, even now, in the inner courtyard beneath the sweet olive trees. Jiang sighed.

"Don't be sad for me, Mother. He makes me happy."

"And what does he think of your life here?"

"He understands that if I am named, I will stay here."

"And what will he do then?"

"As scholars have always done, love me in the quiet hours, alone and in peace."

Jiang wondered about that. About exactly how that would work. Her great love, Yin Bao's father, could not bear the idea that anyone else could be with her. Even before he'd asked her to marry him, she knew, because of the Ivory Compact, that she could not leave her post as the head of the most prosperous brothel in all of Shanghai. So they had met late at night and always in the fury of passion. They had coupled and re-coupled and awoken often adhered to each other by the sweat of their ardour. But she knew it could not last. And it did not last. And one night she waited until sunrise for him—and he did not come. In the dawning light she acknowledged that it was not him "not arriving" that ended their love affair—it was her "not leaving" that had driven him away.

At least he left me with a child, she thought. She turned to Mai Bao. "And what about children? Does this man believe in children, or are children too pedestrian for his lofty tastes?"

The girl looked away. Her lover talked of revolution, not children. In fact he railed against having children, saying, "Once you have a family it is impossible to remain a revolutionary. Impossible to bring down this stinking old regime. Impossible to bring justice to the peasants. Children should be outlawed until the revolution is complete and the world is scourged of its tyrants. Until there is real justice in this world I want nothing to do with bringing children into it."

"Mai Bao, she who is named Jiang must produce at least two daughters—one to eventually become Jiang and the other to marry into the Zhong clan. You understand that, surely?"

Mai Bao nodded, for the first time wondering whether she cared for her scholar just because of books she had read. She didn't know for sure, but she suspected her mother might be right.

"Then fool him, girl. You are more than smart enough to do that. Get pregnant, or all you see around you will belong to your younger sister before the *Fan Kuei*'s millennium comes."

It was December of 1897 by the *Fan Kuei*'s counting. That left her just over two years to bear a child—a girl. Two years to claim her rightful heritage from her frivolous younger sister.

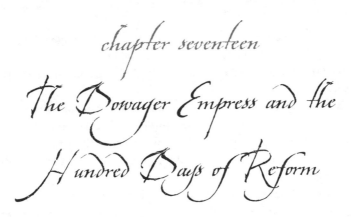

chapter seventeen

The Dowager Empress and the Hundred Days of Reform

1898

It occurred to Tzu Hsi, the Dowager Empress of China, that she had been very old for a very long time. She was perfectly aware that many of her retainers referred to her now as "the old Buddha." As well she knew that a British general had reported to his superiors that she was the only real man he had met in all his time in the Middle Kingdom.

She was born sixty-three years ago, in 1835. Although she was the daughter of a lowly Manchu official, by sixteen her striking beauty had brought her to the attention of the court, and Emperor Hsien Feng had chosen her as a concubine, third class. Whether by luck, as popular belief would have it—or trickery, a fact known to only a few—she was the first of the concubines to bear the Emperor a son, and so was immediately promoted to the rank of concubine, first class, second only to the Empress herself.

She easily outlived Hsien Feng, the man she openly referred to as "her First Emperor," who died when he was twenty-six. After his death she manoeuvred the court into naming her Regent until her son, Tung Chih, was of age to take the throne. In 1873, Tung Chih became Emperor, but despite his best efforts to take control of the court, all official business of the Middle Kingdom continued to go directly to his mother. The Dowager Empress governed without so much as a nod of approval from her son, the Emperor. In 1875, two years after Tung Chih became Emperor, the young man suddenly, after a particularly spectacular sexual debauch, came down with a virulent case of smallpox and quickly died.

My only son died, she mused. Then she added a second thought, *Though who really noticed?*

By then the Dowager Empress dominated everything and everybody in the Forbidden City, so she found it simple to have her three-month-old nephew, Kwang Hsu, named as her son's successor to the Heavenly Throne. That allowed her to reign uncontested for another sixteen years—until the boy came of age.

When the boy turned sixteen and took the throne it didn't concern the Dowager Empress even a bit—but then he began to challenge her authority. And now, in 1898, there was this nonsense the young whelp had proclaimed: "A Hundred Days of Reform." He wanted to include western studies in all Chinese education, adopt a public school system, have elected local assemblies leading to a national parliament, remove the Civil Service examination system and replace it with a western-style bureaucracy, and some nonsense about reforming the army—and a thousand other ridiculous plans.

"Where did he come up with these strange ideas?" she demanded of her Head Eunuch, Chesu Hoi.

"Perhaps the newspapers, Your Grace."

"I never permitted him newspapers!" she exclaimed. "Can he read?"

"Indeed, ma'am, and he is both inquisitive and resourceful."

She harrumphed. "Never should have allowed those tutors to get access to him. Why did you permit such silliness?"

Chesu Hoi bowed his head slightly. He had not allowed any such silliness. The Dowager Empress had been deep in one of her periodic bouts with opium and had signed permissions that had been sent directly to her by the young Emperor.

"A hundred days of *de*-form is more like it," she snapped. "What's wrong with the old ways? I ask you that?"

Chesu Hoi knew better than to answer rhetorical questions, so he simply smiled.

"Well, what are we going to do about this inanity?"

"What you already requested we do, Your Majesty—undermine, subvert, avoid, and malign all One Hundred Days of Reform."

She looked at him closely. She didn't remember ordering such a thing, although maybe she had. She'd certainly meant to. "Good," she said, "very good." She paused for a moment to scratch the side of her nose. "And how does our plan proceed?" she asked, anxious to sound in control but having trouble finding the right words. Was the opium serpent still in her blood? Finally she resorted to an old, reliable standby command and shouted, "Report!"

"Excellently, Your Majesty. Just as you had predicted, the Mandarin class has refused every suggestion." Chesu Hoi was hardly surprised by this, since the young Emperor's very first reform was to close down the entire civil service examination system and replace it with a western-style system based upon skill, not the knowledge of literary classics.

The other reforms, having to do with taxing persons of wealth, redistribution of land to peasants from absentee landlords, and taking away the privileges of Mandarins, were easily subverted by the Manchu authorities at every turn. Rumours of anarchists behind the proposed changes—rumours that Chesu Hoi had slipped into his trusty gossip channels in the Forbidden City—simply helped sell the reason for the cancellation of the entire program.

As Chesu Hoi completed his report to the Dowager Empress, she sat back in her satin chair and smiled. She wondered when her next pipe would arrive. Then she thought of her nephew and swore one simple oath: "He will not outlive me. He will *not*."

Then she looked at her Head Eunuch. He was still talking. He had nice lips. She watched them part and round as they formed words. She liked eunuchs' lips—she always had.

Then she said, "Have you found it yet?"

Chesu Hoi averted his eyes.

"Have you?" she screamed.

He'd hoped she had forgotten about the Narwhal Tusk, as she had about so many other things.

"If you wish to keep what little manhood you have left, I would suggest you find the Tusk before the year is out."

chapter eighteen

Mai Bao,
Jiang's Middle Daughter

"And you haven't seen him for how long?"

Mai Bao stared at the police officer. *He must be in his late thirties or early forties*, she thought. *And tallish for a Han Chinese—and clearly attracted to me.* It was his third visit, and she suspected there was more to his questions than seeking information about her ex-lover, the scholar.

"Almost seven months," she answered.

"And was there anyone with him?"

"Besides myself?"

"Yes, besides you. Were there tradesmen with him?"

"No. We met in private."

"And was he acting oddly at the time?"

Mai Bao nodded but did not answer. She remembered her last meeting with her scholar.

She had rolled off her birth-marked lover and was sitting on the side of the bed. His interest in actual intercourse had lessened over the years, and now it was almost of no interest to him at all. He would accept other forms of bringing on the clouds and rain from her, but he showed no interest in bringing her to the clouds and rain—and naturally these kinds of love-making precluded any possibility of producing a child, let alone the two daughters that she needed.

But Mai Bao was a strong-willed woman, and she was not going to be easily denied her mother's full legacy.

Mai Bao's young scholar rolled over on the bed and stretched a lank arm over her hip. She gently but firmly pushed his arm aside and said, "Sleep." Without much protest he turned over, hiding his wine-stained cheek from her, and shortly she heard his breath slow and the soft whisper of slumber slip from his lips. For a moment she wondered what had happened to the young, romantic lover he had been. Where his violence had come from. Why he seemed to want to hurt her as she brought on the clouds and rain.

She turned to the police officer and said, "He once mumbled in his sleep, 'Where are the two barbers?'"

"Two barbers?" the detective asked.

"Yes, that's what he said, Officer, and I haven't seen him since."

"The man's a fool to have left you."

Mai Bao looked up into the haunted eyes of the man in front of her. "Would you like some tea?" she asked.

That interview was six weeks ago, and now he was her new lover—hopefully the father of her baby girl—and he awaited her in the back of the Yipin Lou Storytelling Theatre on Shanxi Lu.

As she descended the two steps of her carriage, Mai Bao noted the newspaper headlines on a nearby street kiosk. Another Chinese merchant, the sixth in a month, had been murdered found in his shop with the characters for "Murdered Collaborator" inked on his forehead. Mao Bao shivered.

She waited for him in a private backstage room of the theatre. She presumed that his lateness—so unlike him—was due to the new murder. He had led the Chinese investigations of all the previous murders, so she assumed this would be his responsibility as well.

It was well after midnight when he finally arrived, and immediately Mai Bao knew he had been at the crime scene. The darkness in his face and the far-away look in his eyes were not new to her.

"Was it awful?" she asked.

He didn't respond for a moment, then asked, "Do you have your arhu?"

She nodded toward her maid, who handed over the instrument.

"Good. Play me something that will make me forget, Mai Bao, something that will cleanse my dreams."

Her maid turned off the lights and lit a single candle.

Mai Bao knelt, carefully arranging her skirts about her, and positioned her arhu. As she did, her police inspector leaned forward and buried his head in his hands. Mai Bao plucked a single note from the arhu—then, as it began to dissolve in the still air, she plucked a second note a perfect third above the first—then a third note a perfect third beneath the initial note. Then she strummed a chord and began to sing.

She sang of a Holy Mountain far back in Anhui Province, where an ancient priest saw the world gather its forces and give birth to a dazzling city.

Mai Bao's lover looked up, and she saw tears in his eyes. Inwardly she smiled. She knew that a crying man most often sired girl babies. Perhaps twin girls. *That would put an end to all this foolishness,* she thought.

By the end of the song her lover had regained his composure and demanded wine from Mai Bao's maid. But when the maid returned, Mai Bao sent her away and poured a glass that she held out to him.

He drank deeply.

She leaned forward and tasted the wine on his lips.

He poured her a glass and she smiled. She took a sip and leaned forward again. When she parted her lips he tasted the liquor on her slender tongue. She smiled inside his kiss and he reached for the sash at her waist. Her clothing parted as she positioned her hips.

Another glass was poured, but it stood untouched on the small lacquered table, refracting the light from the single candle into arching rainbows across their bodies as they rocked in the simple motion of bringing on the clouds and rain—clouds and rain that Mai Bao knew would give her at least the first of the daughters she needed to ascend to the title of Jiang.

—

Without ceremony Mai Bao left the city at the Bend in the River. There were rumours that she had retreated to a monastery. Others that she was on a pilgrimage to northern India to learn the great Sutras. The newspapers had never had much access to her, since she refused to be photographed and never answered reporters' questions when she was in her carriage on her way to parties thrown in her honour. And needless to say, she never participated in the newspapers' Flower Contests. But her sudden absence from Jiang's fascinated the press—and annoyed her sister, Yin Bao, who went on record as saying her sister had retreated to work with a master so she could play "her silly instrument in such a way that she can finally seduce men with her music, since clearly she can't manage it with her charms."

Mai Bao gave birth to twin girls and left them in the fine care of a peasant couple who were only too happy to have her money in return for raising her children and keeping their mouths shut.

She returned to her mother's house entirely without fanfare and was ensconced in her rooms for over two weeks before her younger sister even knew that she was there.

Jiang, of course, was informed immediately upon Mai Bao's return. She did the simple mathematics of pregnancy, and nodded. "Enough time to have one daughter only," she said.

"Enough time for twin girls, Mother," Mai Bao responded.

Jiang smiled. Her spies had already told her. "Indeed," she said as she lit the joss sticks at her small altar and offered a momentary thanks before donning her sheerest cottons to entertain the evening's guests. Her daughter was sitting on her bed, a small book in her hand. Jiang, with a flip of her wrist, motioned the girl to stand. She did. Jiang's practised eye saw the reassuring telltales. Mai Bao's exquisitely tailored dress fell from her shoulders with just the subtlest of a fold, where there was no fold intended by the seamstress's hand.

"Welcome home, daughter."

"Thank you, Mother."

Both nodded. Both knew that the other knew. There were no kind words or tender caresses—just a new knowledge between two powerful women.

chapter nineteen

Newspapers and Whores— A Marriage Made in Heaven

"Because they need us as much as we need them," Charles explained slowly to the two young Chinese Christians sitting in his office. They both had concerned smiles on their faces. *Only Christians could have concerned smiles,* Charles thought.

"But it's sinful."

Charles resisted smiling, concerned or otherwise. He certainly recognized the theological thinking behind the young man's comments. But Charles had, of late, also realized that such thinking belonged to desert people. People who had never seen or even heard of the Middle Kingdom. And besides, the Good Book was filled with stories of men, respected men, who owned concubines and slaves, and instances of "acceptable" incest and "permissible" rape. Somehow it was only when people not of their colour or ethnic background enjoyed the company of courtesans that it was a sin.

Charles had had his fill of the hypocrisy of the Good Book—especially the interpretation of the Good Book by White people, those whom he had finally begun to refer to, with an unconcealed joy, as *Fan Kuei*. He still considered himself a Christian, but no longer a hypocritical Christian. Now he thought of himself as an honest Christian, a Chinese Christian, and he would insist that any woman he married adopt his faith and agree to raise his children as honest Christians.

"I see," Charles said, then added, "Thank you for your input. Now I have work to do."

The two young Chinese Christians said thank you, and one left a pamphlet on Charles's desk. Once the door had closed behind them, Charles looked at the pamphlet and smiled. He'd both translated and published the thing.

He called in his head printer. The chubby old Japanese man hadn't changed much. Despite the fact that he now managed the six printing facilities used by the Charles Soong Corporation and never touched either ink or paper, he still looked as though he had been up all night turning the printing press himself. Charles loved that about him.

"Sit," he said, and then slid behind his desk to face the man.

"So?" the Japanese printer asked.

"I want your opinion."

"Sure." The man scratched his crotch. Charles wished he wouldn't do that. The man shifted in his chair and scratched again—this time even more vigorously.

"We already publish a lot of articles about courtesans," Charles began.

"Hookers."

"Yes. But I think there are more ways for us to interconnect with the Flower World."

The Japanese looked at him oddly, then finally asked, "Interconnect? Is that a word? If it is, what does it mean?"

Charles smiled. "What else can we write about courtesans?"

The printer smiled back and said, "Favourite positions, secrets of the trade, most men serviced in one night ..."

"No. Not that sort of thing. What else happens to courtesans?"

"You mean besides ..." He allowed his hands to make an odd circular motion.

"Yes, besides that."

"Well, dumb stuff. You know, we write about how their hearts are broken by faithless lovers, how they sometimes end up penniless and alone, and even how sometimes they get sick. Personally I don't read any of those stories. I think they're morbid."

"That might well be, but no, I'm not talking about things like that. Just normal things in their lives. I mean, besides sex. What happens to them that doesn't happen to you and me?"

"Well, they move a lot."

"Excuse me?"

"They move a lot. A house madam has had enough of them and they move. Someone doesn't pay his bills, so they can't afford to pay the rent, so they move. A building goes up and takes away their sunlight, and they move. Their shit suddenly doesn't smell like roses, and they leave."

Charles sat for a moment, then said, "And when they leave, their clientele has no way of knowing where their favourite courtesan has gone."

The Japanese man smiled. "Unless they take out an advertisement in your newspaper to announce their new address. A *gaobai*—in this case, a change of address announcement."

"Good," Charles said, "very good. I bet we can market that. But you said something earlier about debts?"

"Yeah, well, clients often stiff them for the money they owe the hookers."

"Stiff them?"

"Yeah, courtesans don't charge before they service their clients. Don't ask me why—a really dumb tradition, if you ask me—but they don't. In fact, they keep records, and every four months they demand payment. But lots of clients, especially those who don't want to go back to the same whore—I mean, why pay for food if you've already eaten and don't want to go back to the restaurant ...?"

"Right," Charles said, and chuckled.

"That's a dirty laugh, Mr. Soong."

"Yes, I guess it is. But what would happen if we permitted the courtesans to publish their complaints against clients who ... 'stiff them'? We could publish their complaints complete with accusations, names and addresses, dates and times. Then we could allow the client to respond."

"It would fill lots of column inches."

"And bring in lots of readers. What's better than a fight in the press to sell newspapers?"

Two months later courtesans' words filled Charles' newspapers and readers lined up to buy copies "hot off the presses." Some were innocuous announcements, *gaobai*, such as: "Chenjing Jinlan at Xiao Jiuan has moved her residence to the luxury of Baoshu Lane" or "Wen Yuanyuan, who resides in Tongan Lane, is changing her name to Wen Yuyun for the pleasure of her clients and is moving to Huihui Lane for more privacy." Some were anything but innocuous, such as this exchange between a courtesan and one of her suitors.

"Here in this public place I proclaim that the courtesan Miaxi is nothing but a detestable prostitute! She did not appear when I had arranged an elaborate banquet for her, and my friends and I lost much face because of the actions of this loathsome creature. Take care that you do not involve yourself with this unsanitary whore."

In the very next edition of the paper, Miaxi responded, "He has no compassion for the labours of my profession. I was overbooked that night. Besides, his so-called banquet was little more than a cold bowl of rice, which is pretty much what he has both between his ears and between his legs!"

The paper then published learned opinions about these opinions, and then further forays by both the client and the courtesan. The papers were in such demand that people lined up all night to be the first to read the newest slanders.

———

Charles put aside the final article for the next edition, looked at the writers gathered around the table, and said, "Very good, oh, yes, very good."

"And very profitable," said Tzu Rong Zi, the drunken scholar who had written the very first story for Charles. "Lots of dough!"

Charles looked at Tzu Rong Zi and wanted to ask him how much he'd already had to drink at this early hour. His drinking had gotten very bad of late. There was a time when Charles would have brought the man to church to cure him of his addiction, but Charles no longer believed in church that way. *At least it isn't opium,* Charles thought. Tzu Rong Zi hadn't written anything worth publishing for almost a year, but Charles couldn't find it in his heart to fire him—after all, he'd been with him at the beginning of Charles's sensational good fortune. So Charles just ignored the writer and looked at the others around the table—all of whom were well scrubbed and anxious to participate in the financial glories of Charles Soong's publishing empire.

"All right, I'm prepared to entertain new initiatives for the paper," he said.

Suggestions were put forward for new ventures, and a few were seriously discussed. Several writers wanted to add a crime column to the paper. That was amended to a crime "section" that could be launched with a detailed report on the twenty-seven unsolved murders of the merchants, all of whom had "Murdered Collaborators" printed on their foreheads.

"I'll consider the idea," Charles said, although he knew it was much too dangerous. The Manchu authorities were watching his every move. There was no point antagonizing them by suggesting that there was a murderer out there that their incompetent police force couldn't catch.

Through his spies, Charles knew that the Manchus were aware that it was his money that allowed Dr. Sun Yat-sen to spend so much time in Europe and America looking at their governmental systems. The good doctor had returned to China with what he called his "Three Principles." The first was the Principle of Nationalism, which postulated the need for the Chinese people to throw off the "yoke of Manchu rule" and live in peace with the minorities within their borders, and with other nations of the world. The second principle was the Principle of Democracy, which basically stated that the people were the power in the country, not the Emperor, and that all people were equal. The third of his principles, the Principle of Social Welfare, was a sometimes watered down, sometimes hard-line version of socialism that gave most land to the state.

Charles was a supporter of the first two principles but had his doubts about the third.

"Sir," a young writer said, "can I propose something different? A brand new approach we might consider in covering the Flower World contests?"

"All right," Charles said, returning his attention to the room.

"Hold them at the racetrack, boss."

Charles would never get used to being called "boss," especially since the word the man used was not the Mandarin *shang si*, or even the more colloquial *lao ban*, but rather the pidgin *boss*. He had strictly outlawed the use of pidgin in his four offices and amongst his seventy employees, but he was appalled that the hideous language of degradation was becoming fashionable amongst young, literate Han Chinese. Many a time he'd heard a writer yell at a copy boy, "Chop chop!"

He checked his watch—he didn't have much more time. He had to prepare to meet the first of the girls the matchmaker had arranged for him as a prospective wife. He was twenty-four and single. He was a man of great wealth. It was time to start a family.

"Sir?" the young reporter prompted.

Charles looked at the avid faces around the large table. It didn't surprise him that Tzu Rong Zi was the only one who had not made a single suggestion for the editorial meeting. His old Japanese printer was snoring quietly, hands folded across his expansive belly. *Enjoy your rest, old friend,* he thought. Then he looked at the eager young man who had first spoken and asked, "You have a plan in mind for the racetrack?"

"I do, sir. We have had great success with our Flower World contests."

"I know that."

"But we can do even better, sir."

"How?"

"By coordinating the contests with the beginning of each of the two horse racing seasons."

There was a momentary hush around the table. Each of the men knew that the young man had spotted something obvious—as rare but as obvious as a shrimp making a surprise appearance in a shrimp dumpling in a Shanghai restaurant. The spring and fall openings of the Shanghai Race Course were the most avidly attended events in the entire social calendar of this extremely social city, and among the only times that *Fan Kuei* and Chinese mixed freely. Most importantly, hundreds of the city's almost two thousand courtesans were always in attendance, wearing their newest and most expensive finery. If Charles Soong's newspaper could arrange to have the Flower World contest take place at the racetrack before the first race, the coverage would be extraordinary. Interest in the contest would go through the roof—and newspaper sales would follow quickly. *Perhaps an English-language edition is called for,* he thought, but then dismissed the idea. *If they want to follow our sport they'll have to do it in our language.* For weeks, perhaps months, after the beginning of the Flower World contest the newspapers would be able to feed off the copy they got from such an event. Then, of course, the thousands of letters and follow-up stories that would be published as they approached the crowning of the Flower World Princess would increase the audience tenfold, and then perhaps tenfold again.

Charles smiled as he thought how well this dovetailed with the meeting he had convened last night in his private quarters. Dr. Sun Yat-sen, whom he had been bankrolling for almost four years now, had encouraged him to use the power of his newspapers to attack the Manchu Dynasty.

"There are already subtle jabs at Beijing in most of the articles in my newspapers," he had protested.

"Subtle, Charles, too subtle to do any good. Only those in the know understand what you are saying."

Charles thought, *And that's how it should be. If I am ever accused of sedition, all I have worked for will be taken from me in one swift and sure Manchu reprisal.*

Charles's coverage of the Flower World was ribboned with comments that any intelligent reader knew were jibes at the creaky old dynasty. His use of an ancient Manchu name for a fictitious, ugly, old courtesan was as blatant as he was willing to get. He just prayed he never had to produce such a courtesan to prove that his stories were not fictions. With the failure of the Hundred Days of Reform in 1898, politics had become an extremely dangerous game.

Perhaps the most inherent and damning criticism of the present regime was the very way that the winner of the Flower World contest was named—by the counting of public votes submitted to the newspapers. Charles knew that this was actually the very first democratic exercise ever undertaken in the Middle Kingdom, and his guests at last night's meeting had roundly applauded him for it. All but a surly man named Chiang Kai Shek, whose whole bald head seemed to scowl as he said, "What would commoners know of great beauty or talent in the Flower World?"

Charles heard the unmistakable sound of privilege at work. The sense of entitlement. That somehow this man's eyes were the only ones able to see true beauty, his ears the only ones that could hear sweet melody, and his jade spear the only one allowed to contemplate entering the jade gate of a great courtesan. And beneath it all, Charles heard a cruelty that he didn't understand. A cruelty that the courtesans of whom he wrote knew all too well. Sexual cruelty had its own music, its own smell, its own place in the hearts of men like Chiang Kai Shek.

The man was soundly put down by the others around the table, although Dr. Sun Yat-sen had suggested that "everyone here has the right to an opinion." Charles doubted the wisdom of that statement when it was applied to creatures like Chiang Kai Shek. Not for the first or last time, he wondered about the judgment of the good doctor, whom the others looked to as the leader who would dethrone the corrupt old Manchu Dynasty.

It troubled Charles that the man was a doctor but was always penniless. It was Charles's money that allowed the Doctor to travel to America and Japan to organize his "revolution."

"Sir? Thoughts on this?" the young man asked.

Charles's thoughts returned to the present with a clunk. "I think the racetrack is a fine idea, and, like the rest of the men around the table, I wonder why I didn't think of it first." Laughter greeted the comment.

The old Japanese printer awakened with, "What's so funny?"

"Nothing," Charles said. He saw some of the men collecting their papers, hoping to end the meeting. Charles knew that most of them were anxious to have a cigarette. Charles had strictly forbidden smoking in his presence. In lieu of tobacco, he always provided the most expensive of Annam teas, served in tall porcelain mugs fitted with lids to keep the liquid hot. Charles removed the lid from his mug. The long, slender Anamm tea leaves seemed to dance in the hot liquid that they so delicately flavoured. He blew gently into the liquid and his glasses fogged. Ignoring that he said, "Although, clearly, there is a problem with your plan."

"And that would be, boss?"

He controlled the knee-jerk bridle at being called "boss" in pidgin and then said simply, "The racetrack belongs to Silas Hordoon. Nothing can go on there that he doesn't agree to. Now, who amongst you has contacts strong enough with that *Fan Kuei* to arrange a meeting?"

Charles knew the answer before he asked the question. None of them. How could they? The paper was filled to overflowing with open criticism of almost every aspect of *Fan Kuei* life in the city at the Bend in the River. The sense of deflation in the room was palpable. It made Charles smile. He cleaned the lenses of his glasses and finished his tea. "Ah," he said resignedly, then got to his feet and headed toward the door.

Behind him he heard the rustle of papers and the sliding of chairs away from the table. He turned back to the assemblage in the room. The noise stopped. He said, "I guess I will have to mention it during my lunch with the great man, tomorrow."

chapter twenty
Silas and Charles

Although neither man moved from his chair, both were aware that they were circling each other, not unlike two fighting cocks before one delivers the first blow.

Silas had done his due diligence and knew much about the wealthy young Chinese man who sat across from him. Although he didn't know exactly how, he knew that Charles Soong had begun his extraordinary rise to wealth and power from the position of a lowly busboy in a tavern somewhere in the wasteland of America. He knew that somewhere in the process of his meteoric rise to wealth he had added the *g* to the end of his name. So that it would sound more Chinese? More dynastic, perhaps? Silas had been given bank statements that proved the young man had substantial wealth, although Silas couldn't see how anyone could make all that money solely from publishing—even publishing about the Flower World. Silas had tried to figure out if there was a connection to Gangster Tu or any of the other Triads in the city but had found only hints—sometimes tantalizing—of association with the underworld figures. The one connection he had managed to unearth was with the pugnacious Chiang Kai Shek. Silas assumed that some of Charles's money was behind part of the revolutionary foment that periodically swirled through the Chinese living in the Foreign Settlement. But then again, almost every successful Chinese businessman donated to the cause of dethroning the old Manchu Dynasty.

Silas knew that there was something not open to public view about this unusually successful young man. It was just that he couldn't say exactly what that something was.

When the request came through a mutual Hong merchant friend for a meeting, several potential meeting spots were suggested, with the usual Middle Kingdom wariness, and then rejected. Runners carried personal letters between the two men's representatives for weeks until finally this place—the Old Shanghai Restaurant—was agreed upon. And now here they sat at a private table, ignoring the waiters, who kept approaching and suggesting that they order, and staring at each other in a stony silence.

The restaurant owner finally came over and stood still as a statue, waiting for instructions. When, after several minutes, none were forthcoming, he made a strategic decision and returned to the kitchen.

—

In the kitchen, the head chef looked up from a wok filled with boiling oil into which he was gently slipping a large, breaded river perch and demanded in a surly tone of voice, "What?"

The owner had always hated cooks. If only he could run a restaurant without a cook, he would be the happiest Han Chinese man south of the Yellow River. But no—here was yet another cook scowling at him. He had found that cooks have only two facial expressions: drunken oblivion and scowls. Right now the owner couldn't figure out which he would prefer—although the cook's scowl was making that choice easier to make, by the second.

"Speak! What do they want to eat? Why not give them deep-fried sheepshit smothered in brown sauce?"

There it was again. The owner never knew if cooks were fooling or not. From his experience with this cook, he believed it very possible that more than one of his valued customers had eaten large portions of various animal fecal material deep-fried and smothered with the cook's ubiquitous brown sauce.

"No. They should begin with shark-fin soup. I bought the shark fin yesterday and gave it to you myself."

The cook stared back at him with a markedly blank expression on his face.

The owner gathered his courage and asked, "Do we still have the shark fin I purchased?"

The cook deigned to nod, then produced the incredibly expensive item.

The owner breathed a sigh of relief and, although he saw clearly that a prime piece of the fin had been cut off and probably sold by the cook, he decided to smile and say, "Good. But no brown sauce in the shark-fin soup, huh?"

The cook turned to the owner and smiled. "There are so many kinds of liquids I could add to the soup that maybe you'd prefer I add brown sauce—at least you'd know what the colour in the soup was." Then without waiting for a response he said, "Now get out of my kitchen before I chop off some of you and put it into the broth—just for a little snivel flavour."

———

Back at the table, Charles picked up the menu, written in Mandarin, and said in English, "Time to order. Or would you prefer an English-language menu?"

Silas reached across, took the menu from the younger man's hands, and asked in fluent Mandarin in the Shanghai dialect, "How would you like to begin our dinner?"

Before Charles could answer, the shark-fin soup arrived—but neither man touched it. The restaurant owner didn't know what to do, so he just stood there, his eyes moving slowly back and forth between the *Fan Kuei* who was born and raised in Asia and the Han Chinese man who was raised in America. Finally he said, "Is there something wrong, gentlemen? I assure you, this is the finest shark-fin soup in all of the Middle Kingdom."

And neither Charles nor Silas doubted that. But that wasn't the point. Both had eaten shark-fin soup. Both could afford to eat this extremely expensive delicacy. But this wasn't about eating—it was about challenging.

"There's nothing wrong with the soup," Charles said, "but I think Mr. Hordoon ought to have something—oh, more exotic." He smiled.

Silas smiled back and said, "Absolutely, the more—exotic—the better."

"Good," Charles said. Never taking his eyes from Silas he continued, "Bring us hot and sour soup. Very hot and very sour—with congealed pig's blood in mine."

"And mine," Silas responded, then added, "and bird's nest soup—real bird's nest soup."

The owner nodded and took out a pad of paper and pen. Few people actually wanted real bird's nest soup, since it was made from the spittle-soaked straw and twigs that form the nest of a small bird in southeast China called a swiftlet.

"And chicken hearts on a skewer with a side of minnows in peanut sauce," Charles said with a shrug.

"And squid jerky with stinky tofu and durian slices—I think that would go well, don't you?" Silas asked with a smile.

Charles acknowledged the challenge and said, "And for main courses?"

"Dog in brown sauce with pig intestines?" Silas suggested innocently.

"Absolutely," Charles agreed, "with jellyfish."

"Naturally. I always have dog with jellyfish."

"Good," Charles said. "And to drink?"

"Green pumpkin," Silas said, his stomach taking a lurch.

"With the fried chicken feet or after them?" Charles asked.

"Well, after the snake-and-turtle stir-fry would be better, don't you think?"

"Yes, I do, but I think we have to add antler velvet to that."

"Absolutely, or the turtle would be tasteless."

"Agreed."

"But I think we're a little short."

"How's about thousand-year-old eggs?"

"Good, as long as they are on a bed of raw sea cucumber."

There was a pause, and only the scratch of the owner's pen filled the silence. Then he stopped writing and said, "No cobra hearts?"

Both Silas and Charles had seen the extraordinary delicacy before and had passed on the opportunity. A live cobra was brought to the table and stretched to its fullest length by its handler and an assistant. Then the handler slit the belly of the serpent open and cut out the tiny heart, which was popped into the customer's mouth ... still beating.

Silas considered it.

Charles considered it.

Then both at once said, "Maybe next time."

"And rice?" the owner asked.

Both men shook their heads.

———

It took them just under three hours to eat their "exotic" dinner. When it was finally finished, both men pushed back from the table, and at last Silas asked, "Okay, now that we've stuffed ourselves silly, what is it that you wanted to speak to me about?"

Quickly Charles laid out his desire to stage the Flower World contests at Silas's racetrack.

"That's it?" Silas asked, clearly amazed.

"Yes."

"You mean we made absolute pigs of ourselves, and will no doubt be sick for weeks, because you wanted to ask me that?"

"Yes."

"Just that?"

"Yes."

Silas sighed. He wished he could belch. Oh, how he wished he could belch. But all that came from his lips when he opened them were the words "Sure, why not?"

chapter twenty-one
Leaf Contests

"Does anyone know who placed this notice in last week's paper?" Charles asked as he entered the room reserved for the writers.

The writers looked up and glanced at the full-page advertisement offering "To Buy Any and All Very Large Antique Ivory Pieces." But none of them knew.

Charles turned to go, then stopped and said, as nonchalantly as he could manage, "Our Flower World contests are all set for the racetrack. I convinced the great Mr. Hordoon that it would be to our mutual benefit—and he agreed."

The room erupted in applause. Then Charles added, "I think we should add Leaf competitions to our Flower contests."

The looks on the men's faces changed to the very definition of nonplussed. One lit a Snake Charmer cigarette. Tzu Rong Zi stubbed one out in a large, standup, crystal ashtray, then spat on the floor. This was the writers' room; they could do as they wished.

"Leaf competitions to augment our Flower Competitions," Charles explained. "Flower competitions for the courtesans, and Leaf competitions for their maids."

Faces brightened. Although courtesans were beyond the financial wherewithal of most newspaper writers, the attentions of the courtesans' maids were within striking distance, and the Leaf competitions would be the perfect time to meet and impress these young women— not always an easy thing for newspapermen to do. Besides, courtesans' maids periodically became courtesans. The maids were the only chance that these men might have to couple with an actual courtesan.

"We could call the contests *Yebang,*" the youngest writer suggested. The idea was met with smiles all around.

"*Yebang,*" Charles said, savouring the name as he spoke it. "Why not add *Wubang* and *Yibang* as well?" he suggested.

Once again the faces turned nonplussed. None of them liked to acknowledge that they didn't know what in heaven's name Charles was talking about. So he explained, "Contests for courtesan singing and courtesan instrument playing."

"Ahs" of various sorts greeted Charles's suggestion. Then the "ahs" turned to open agreement when it occurred to the writers around the table that if these contests were held twice a year, like the Flower contest, then there would be a contest almost every six weeks, each of which would generate follow-up stories and letters sent to the paper. With any luck, they wouldn't have to do any honest reporting whatsoever for the entire year. As that thought circulated, support for the idea grew and grew in all the writers—as Charles knew it would. The only exception was Tzu Rong Zi, who seemed to be in the throes of a particularly angry hangover.

* * *

THE CHICKEN-FACED MATCHMAKER put Yin Bao's photograph down on Charles's office desk. Charles immediately rose and stepped away. "This is a courtesan," he protested.

"Yes," said the matchmaker, "but she, unlike the others who you rejected, is young and very beautiful, don't you think?" The woman actually seemed to cluck as she spoke.

Charles agreed with the crone's assessment but was loath to say as much, although he snuck a second look at the beguiling smile of Jiang's youngest daughter.

The matchmaker bowed her head and smiled inwardly. She had known, since first being approached by Jiang, that Yin Bao was the perfect solution to Charles Soong's bachelorhood. The crone recalled how much money she had extorted from Jiang in order to present "your compromised daughter to this fine gentleman," and she wanted to smack her lips and rub her palms together—or perhaps peck at nonexistent grain husks on the office floor—but she refrained from both displays of glee.

"Maybe," Charles said softly, "a discrete meeting could be arranged."

The matchmaker bobbed her head slightly, then smiled a toothless smile as she responded, "Perhaps such could be arranged, although it is not a simple matter to ..."

"How much would it cost to arrange such a meeting?" Charles asked icily.

The matchmaker posed an outrageous figure, at which Charles would usually have balked, but his eyes were glued to Yin Bao's picture, so he simply nodded agreement.

The matchmaker asked, "Would next Wednesday be convenient?"

Charles nodded again.

"Good. The details will follow in a missive from my second." She was having fun; only with effort did she stop herself from crowing aloud. "Employing a second person is an additional expense ..."

"Pay her what you need and bill me for it," Charles said, then turned on his heel. "I suggest care in this matter. If my confidentiality is breached, I will refuse to pay you a single *yuan*."

"Naturally, sir, your confidentiality is foremost in our concern," she said as she considered to which of her gossips she'd first tell this juicy news. Then a new idea occurred to her, and she bowed her way out of the room.

Two hours later she was in Jiang's private office, apologizing that she was "completely unable to get Mr. Soong to even consider your daughter as a possibility. He's a Christian, you know, and as such has standards that are incomprehensible to those of us native to the Celestial Kingdom."

Jiang smiled, then said, "Scat!" and waved her hand in the air. She knew that Charles Soong wanted a Christian wife, but she thought it just a minor hurdle over which Yin Bao would have to jump, because twenty minutes before, she had been informed by her spy in the Soong offices that Charles Soong had pocketed Yin Bao's picture and cancelled all his meetings for the day.

Ah, men and photographs—a combination made in heaven, she thought.

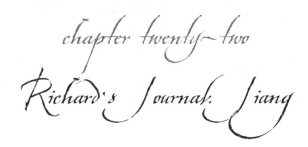

chapter twenty-two

Richard's Journal: Jiang

I first saw her on Bubbling Spring Road two days after the land auction. I retrieved her parasol from the mud. A pure white parasol in the thick muck of Shanghai—I'll never forget it. And now she is by me again—but this time in the smoke.

Bubbling Spring Road—so many of my dreams lead me to Bubbling Spring Road. In the light of day it is nothing more than a mule path leading from the Huangpo docks to the canal system in the west. But not in my serpent dreams. No. Here, Bubbling Spring Road is a wide avenue of stores and emporiums and carriages and women in fine dresses and Chinese eyes watching—always watching. Right from the start they were watching as if they knew something that we did not. Like this woman Jiang is watching me now through the serpent smoke. I know it is her. Once Lily is asleep, it is she who brings me opium—but she only appears after I am deep in the coils of the smoke. I know it is her hand that wipes the sweat from my brow then. It is this Jiang woman. She is there. Has always been there. Was there when we first landed at the Bend in the River. She is something ancient and both seductive and terrifying—like the Middle Kingdom itself.

The smoke yanks me away and I am soaring. This night's voyage is toward the sky, not the holes in my back.

Boys, I've done the Devil's work! I've done the Devil's work! Don't do the Devil's work. Don't do ...

She's standing there at the door, the light behind her. She steps past Lily's sleeping body and sits on the pallet at my side, her cool hand on my hot chest. "Tell me," she says, "tell me of your sons." I try to speak but I breathe out statues, not words. A statue of Milo on a horse. A statue of Silas. Blood on Silas's hand! "Tell me of your boys?" And I try. Milo so strong, so beautiful. Silas and his studies—then a thundering of horse hooves and blood on Silas's hands. So much blood. But her hand wipes away the blood and says, simply, "Tell me of Silas, the quiet one—your son Silas."

"Do you speak English, madam?"

"I am teaching."

"Learning, I think you mean."

"Yes. I do mean 'learning,' thank you."

"Silas has been to your ..."

"My establishment, yes. You and Milo paid for his first visit to a brothel."

"Yes. It was a present."

"Very thoughtful," Jiang said with a smile.

That was my first time in all my years in China that the word inscrutable actually fit the situation. I really could not tell whether she was mocking me or congratulating me. Then she shocked me.

"You were angry that he went with a Han Chinese girl."

"Not angry ..."

"Disappointed, then? I heard that you were angry."

How did she know this?

"Your anger disappoints me, Richard Hardoon. We honoured your brother, despite his Taiping activities. He honoured us. It appears that you do not. How very disappointing."

And then she was there beside me, filling the pipe in my hands. Her cool lips on my forehead, the fourth opium ball opening me, tumbling me to my centre. My arm/wings are spread and I am searching, searching. Then I hear a laugh and force my eyes open and there is Jiang, as ancient and beautiful and eternal as China itself. She is standing over me, her lips moving, producing round bubbles of sound, "Search, if you must, Richard. Search."

My lids are too heavy to keep open, but the moment the darkness is upon me again I find myself in front of a familiar door. Where do I know this from? I thrust up my hand, then turn it. I am facing the other way. Maxi is asleep in his bed. A little boy! I hear a deep voice say, in Farsi, "You drive a hard bargain, boy." I turn and push open a door. Then I hear my own voice say, "Here. Here she is, sir."

She laughs. Jiang laughs. I turn to her and reach for her. "Who are you?" Then she says the oddest thing. "You know who I am. I am Jiang, but I am also my daughter and my granddaughter and my mother and her mother *before her—I am and have always been waiting, watching—attending." Then she touches my chest with her left hand while she looses her blouse with her right. "Now help me do what you no doubt would call the Devil's work."*

———

Silas reread the end of his father's journal entry and said aloud to the empty room, "Why did you hide yourself from me, Father?" His soft words bounced off the walls of his study and flowed out the window, where they were plucked by the wind and carried east along the mighty Yangtze River to the sea.

But some of his words also sifted the collected dust on the three pages of his father's journals that he had inadvertently left on the topmost shelf of his bookcase—only seven feet away from where he sat and cried for a father now dead that he had never really known.

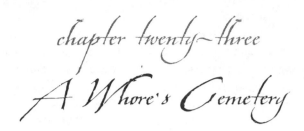

chapter twenty—three

A Whore's Cemetery

Just over a month after she returned to Shanghai, Mai Bao was shocked to see her mother crying quietly in her office. Mai Bao had seen her mother in many moods, but never had she seen tears on Jiang's beautiful cheeks.

"Mother?" she asked cautiously.

Jiang raised her head, and another look that Mai Bao had never seen on her mother's face crossed her comely features   shock.

Jiang looked away from her daughter and grabbed a cloth, which she quickly dipped in rosewater and applied to her face. "Close the door." Mai Bao did as her mother ordered. "I'm sorry you had to see that, and there's no reason for the girls to see me like this."

Carefully Mai Bao asked, "What has happened?"

"They dug her up."

"Dug up? Who did they dig up?"

Jiang named an old friend of hers who had passed away several years ago.

"They dug up her dead body? Who would do that?"

"The French from Siming Gongsuo Cemetery."

Mai Bao knew that Siming Gongsuo was a cemetery exclusively for women from the Flower World. Jiang had given the seed money for the cemetery years ago. Many other courtesans eventually offered up money to complete the project. It hadn't been easy to organize, since competition between the courtesans was intense and constantly being whipped into a frenzy by the newspapers. But now this outrage.

"Why would the French do that?" Mai Bao asked.

"Because they claim we bury our dead in temporary coffins and that it is illegal in the French Concession to bury anyone except in a permanent coffin."

Mai Bao looked at her mother, stunned. Finally she said, "A permanent coffin? That's ridiculous. No coffin is permanent. And even if there were such a thing, why would one want a permanent coffin of any sort?"

Jiang nodded. Every Chinese person knew that the earth always reclaimed that which came from it.

"Besides, what the French claim are permanent coffins are ludicrously expensive, Mother. And for what?"

Jiang's composure had returned, and now she was just angry. "It makes me furious, this stupidity of spending good money to put someone in an expensive box into the ground and then cover it over with dirt. Ridiculous!" she said, then mumbled, "The *Fan Kuei* are ridiculous."

Mai Bao agreed. "It makes no sense what they want."

"None," Jiang agreed. "When will they finally learn to be practical?"

Which was exactly what Mai Bao was now being. She began to think of how exactly to go about starting a new courtesans' cemetery. She already had a name: The New Hundred Flowers Cemetery. Her incisive mind quickly ordered the issues that faced her, and then she laid out the basics of a plan to buy the land outside the French Concession that she'd need.

"Mother, I'll sell my famous orchid paintings, and hopefully by the end of the month other courtesans will donate enough money—and perhaps the newspapers will also contribute—so that I can make a down payment on a land purchase."

Jiang admired the basics of the plan but kept a sad look on her face until Mai Bao had finished and left her chambers. Then Jiang smiled. Producing tears was the hardest thing she'd had to do in years. The ointment the doctor had given her to force the tears still stung. But it was worth it to get Mai Bao on a track that would inevitably bring her to the attention of the largest land owner in all of Shanghai and the city's most eligible *Fan Kuei* bachelor—one Silas Hordoon, a Man with a Book.

For a moment she wondered if it was necessary to trick Mai Bao into this course of action. She had, after all, always been an obedient daughter. But marrying a *Fan Kuei*—well, that was different, and not the kind of order even Mai Bao would readily obey.

Jiang allowed a moment to pass as the pain in her intestines shifted slightly. Her doctor had told her that she might not live long enough to see the first snow. She sighed. Although she sensed destiny's portal approaching, she knew that she had several years left. As her mother had said to her, "It takes more than a cancer to kill a Jiang, dear ... much more."

She thought of Mai Bao's two girls out in the country, and then of Yin Bao. Perhaps Yin Bao would give birth to a girl before too long. Perhaps not. In either case, each of her youngest daughters was, in her own way, pursuing contact with a potential Man with a Book.

chapter twenty-four
Silas Finds a New Wife

Mai Bao appreciated Silas's formal deference in dealing with her. She was also impressed with his beautifully spoken Shanghainese, and complimented him on it.

"I have always found great beauty in Shanghainese—roughness, but great beauty."

She nodded and replied, "Like the city at the Bend in the River itself."

Silas Hordoon nodded in turn, then gestured for her to sit. He noted the grace with which she manipulated her formal attire and the simple elegance of her movement into the chair. Then she smoothed the outer sash of her garment with long, tapered fingers.

He felt clunky and thick in her presence and found himself pulling in his stomach as he sat.

It surprised him—she surprised him. "Miss Mai Bao, what is it that I can do for you?"

Mai Bao heard the soft underside of his words and took her fan from her sleeve. With a gentle snap she opened it and stirred the air in such a way that he received as much of the relief as she did. Finally she said, "We in the Flower World have suffered a great loss."

Silas wondered if Mai Bao's famous mother had finally passed away, although he thought it unlikely since there had been no mention in the Chinese press of her passing—and Jiang's death would have filled the pages of those papers for days. Suddenly he found himself flooded by the odd warnings from his father's opium diaries and a sweat sprang to his forehead.

He reached in his pocket for his handkerchief only to find that Mai Bao was holding out a delicate square of Chinkiang silk. He took her proffered kerchief and, without thinking, breathed in its scent before saying, "I wouldn't think of soiling so fine a piece of cloth, but thank you." Nevertheless, he held on to the silk longer than was necessary—and she saw it.

Mai Bao had dealt with many *Fan Kuei*, although she had never permitted a *Fan Kuei* into her bedchamber. However, unlike most Han Chinese women, she didn't find them particularly repulsive. She had long ago trained herself to ignore the odd growths of hair that so many Chinese found abhorrent, and she was not offended by the largeness of their features. She did still find the smell of their skin odd and couldn't fathom their desire to drink milk or eat cheese, although she liked the smell of tobacco that encircled many of them. Being tall, she was often the first of the courtesans that attracted foreigners' eyes. But she was discrete and old-fashioned so she seldom had to deal with their advances. The closest they came to her was when she performed. Chinese men valued her arhu playing and her singing, but it was her experience that *Fan Kuei* were both puzzled and often put off by her artistry.

"I've seen you play," Silas said.

That surprised her. "Where, if I may ask?"

"The Dangui Theatre a few times," he said, putting the handkerchief down on the desk between the two of them.

"Was this recently?"

"No. Several years ago."

She smiled and said, "I am not that old that you could have seen me several years ago, Mr. Hordoon."

"True," he said, then quickly added, "I meant no slander."

"None was received. But you say it was several years ago?"

He sighed heavily and looked away from this extraordinary creature. He had a terrible desire to tell her his history, or at least the history of the death of his wife and unborn child.

She looked at this strange man and read the distress as it raced across his features. Like everyone else in Shanghai she knew the story of Silas's first marriage and his wife's death in what some might call childbirth. Could that be what was on his mind? She folded her hands in her lap, then said, "Death creases time and turns it on itself so that what took but a day can feel as if it happened over the course of a year or more." She held her breath waiting for his response, but there was none. He just stared past her. "Was it your wife's passing that brought you to the Dangui Theatre?"

He looked at this strong, handsome woman and said, "Only your playing stopped the pain. I lied to you about coming to see you play."

"I am sorry, I don't understand. About what did you lie?"

"I didn't go to listen to you three or four times. I was there every night for months on end. Every time you played I was there." His hands seemed to fly up like doves suddenly loosed from their cages, and unexpected tears flooded his eyes. "Your music allowed sleep back into my life."

Mai Bao was astonished. She'd had no idea. When she performed, the limelight was often in her eyes, which she usually kept closed. But why had no one told her? Here was a man to whom she had been speaking with her music for all that time—and she hadn't even known!

"Where did you learn those songs? You're the only person who sings them."

"They were written by my great-aunt, the History Teller."

"Did she write the song you call 'The Tears of Time'?"

Mai Bao nodded, although she had in fact written the song after reading her great-aunt's notes on an unfinished play about an arhu player who induces love in others but is without love himself. The actual title "Tears of Time" she intuited from her great-aunt's musings, although it did not appear in the History Teller's notes.

Silas rose and turned away from her. She noted that he wasn't as big as many of the successful *Fan Kuei* were. Somehow the fools felt that getting fat was a sign of true success. This man in front of her was certainly not fat, although he had the thickness that attended late middle age. There was a surprising grace to his step and at times a clarity in his eye that she found interesting. He turned back to her.

"I apologize for being personal," he said.

She bowed her head slightly.

"Your note said that there was a business matter that you wished to discuss with me. Your mother's business is well known to me. Please send her my best wishes."

"I will, Mr. Hordoon," she said with a smile as she recalled stories of Silas as a young man at Jiang's.

"Good. Now, what can I do for you, Miss Mai Bao?"

"Do you know of the Siming Gongsuo Cemetery?"

Silas knew of the desecration of the courtesans' graves and had fought unsuccessfully to convince the French authorities that their actions were dangerous for the safety of the entire Foreign Settlement. He hadn't bothered adding that they were also stupid and offensive. But the French had ignored him, pawning off his comments as those of a heathen butting his fat nose into church business.

"Yes, I'm sorry about the French actions in this case."

Mai Bao tilted her head forward to accept his apology for the actions of other *Fan Kuei*, and then she lifted her face.

Now it was his turn to be surprised that tears streaked the flawless skin of her cheeks.

"My mother is nearing her end, and with Siming Gongsuo Cemetery closed I will have no place to lay her remains. We who are of the Flower World need a place to bury our dead, and I had hoped that you would help me find an appropriate piece of property within the confines of the Foreign Settlement for us to open a new cemetery. A place not controlled by the Catholic French and their foolish rules about permanent coffins."

Silas momentarily recoiled. Was he being conned? Despite all his efforts, Silas had become a hard-nosed businessman and knew a pitch when he heard one. He stared at Mai Bao and finally asked, "Are you asking me to donate land that I own?"

She heard the voice of the scholar, her one time lover, shouting in her ear, *They think they own land here. They think this land is theirs. This land is ours and will always be ours!* but she ignored the angry voice and said, "No, Mr. Hordoon, I come to purchase land. We in the Flower World are neither beggars nor penniless. We pay our way and have always done so."

He breathed a sigh of relief. "Would you like me to show you prospective sites for your cemetery?"

"Very much," she said, rising.

He offered her his arm and she took it, resting her hand lightly on his forearm, as they walked toward the door. Once there he stopped and turned to her. She was only an inch or two shorter than him. Her perfume rose up and surrounded him. He found himself tilting toward her, and for the first time since he'd buried Miranda on the high hill overlooking the Yangtze he felt an ancient stirring—a calling—a plea for him to live his life, to rejoin the "chase of the hart."

"What do you propose to call the cemetery?"

She smiled and said, "The New Hundred Flowers Cemetery."

———

As they left his office, eyes followed them. Many eyes—one pair of which belonged to a young man with a wine stain on his face and rage in his heart.

———

Jiang listened to her spy in the Hordoon household as the woman described in minute detail the leaving of Mai Bao with Silas and the private carriage they took to the various possible cemetery sites.

Jiang thought of Silas's father and all the nights her mother had spent in the man's presence once the disfigured woman had gone to sleep. Several times her mother had called her into the room and spoken to her of this man. Then one late night, Jiang had called her to see Richard Hordoon asleep in the grip of the opium snake. She'd told her, "We have expected them. We knew they were coming. They will bring on the darkness, but it is your obligation to bring on the light."

And now the second portal had been opened. Finding the Man with a Book was the next step. She had seen the diary that Richard Hordoon kept by his side in his opium stupors. And she knew that book had been given to his son, Silas. That was why she had set Mai Bao on her path toward Silas Hordoon. *Perhaps they brought the darkness, and one of their own will bring on the light,* she was thinking as her spy from the Hordoon house said, "They stopped for tea at the Yu Yuan Gardens."

Jiang raised a single eyebrow. "And did they talk there?"

"Indeed, Madame Jiang. They talked of gardens—and children."

Jiang nodded. She felt a movement in her gut and knew that the pain would begin again shortly, so she dismissed her spy with thanks and a handsome reward. Afterwards she retreated to her chamber and soothed her pain with the tincture of opium her doctor had given her, but soon the pain returned, and only her feather pillow could smother her cries.

———

As Jiang screamed into her pillow, Silas stood silently in the back of the Dangui Theatre and waited for Mai Bao to play. The audience had grown steadily in anticipation of Mai Bao's arrival, now a rarity. When she walked out on the raised stage a hush fell over the large crowd and people strained to get a look at the famous classic courtesan.

This time Mai Bao sensed Silas in the back of the theatre, although she could not see him. She took her arhu from its silken case and positioned it on her lap.

Silence entered the large room like a welcomed guest at last arrived.

Mai Bao closed her eyes and began.

Silas shifted his weight and leaned forward, unwilling to miss a single sound from either Mai Bao or the arhu. Then they came, as one welling thing, voice and strings entwined about one another as they stirred the still air of the theatre with a new song of a ship's captain who in his travels loses an eye for love.

chapter twenty-five

A Meeting of Minds

The meeting hall was hot. The open windows did little to alleviate the situation, although they did allow in thousands of mosquitoes, midges, moths, and various other night-fliers attracted to the newly installed electric lighting in the cavernous room.

Silas was not surprised to see the large turnout, or the clear division between the tiny group of European Shanghainese like himself (although he was technically Persian, he was considered part of the European contingent at the Bend in the River), who considered Shanghai their home, and the much larger group of Europeans who called themselves Shanghailanders. These people were simply expatriates out to make as much money from China as quickly as they could and then escape to the sanctuary of wherever they came from. This even though some had lived in Shanghai for years.

The assembled represented the few thousand families who ruled Shanghai, and they were very picky about who they included in their ranks. The Europeans were principally British, French, and German, although almost every other European country had some representatives in this grouping. Americans, Canadians, Brazilians, Argentinians, and Cubans were also counted as Europeans, since the designation really meant "White." Interestingly, Portuguese and Polish families were not considered to be Europeans but rather were segregated into a lesser grouping called Polyglots, along with Filipinos, Egyptians, and Afghans. Perhaps the strangest bit of categorization was for Russians, who were not included in either group and hence always tried to pass as Poles.

One of those who had been counted as a European, a puffy-faced Englishman, had the floor and was gesticulating with his arms as if he were a flywheel that had come lose of its moorings.

"I say no to this," he repeated for the third time, as if somehow repetition increased meaning. "I didn't come here to buy sewers and electric street lights for Slants." The crowd stirred. Silas did his best to keep his anger from his face. "I am a businessman, plain and simple. I'm not a charity for heathens. I leave that to the churchmen. I'm here, like most of the rest of you, to make money. There's no law against that. And the money I make is for my expenditure, not to be given away willy-nilly. I work hard for my money, and my money is *my money*—not the damned Chinks'." Silas had heard the pejoratives for Chinese people all his life but he still found himself deeply angered by the inherent disrespect of the terms—all the terms. "So I cast my ballot against. Against! They can shit in their pots in the dark for all I care."

There were hardy cheers from much of the room, led by Meyer Vrassoon and the newly arrived leader of Britain's Dent and Company, William Dent.

William Dent was the tallest man in all of Shanghai—perhaps in all of Asia. Settling in at just a nick short of six feet and ten inches, he had a unique view of the world—and of the opium traders' position in Shanghai. He was of the belief that the traders were to be wary of any of their kind who "went native." He believed in the glory of King and Country and was pleased to be a stalwart part of the British Empire, upon which the sun never set. His mother had died at an early age and his father was a wastrel, and it had been left to him to care for his brothers and sisters and to reinvigorate the family fortune—which was what had brought him to Shanghai, and to this meeting.

Silas wasn't surprised by the Shanghailander's speech, although he was interested to see that Heyward Matheson, the leader of the Scottish trading house Jardine Matheson, assiduously sat on his hands. Well before the meeting Silas's spies had briefed him on this unusual man—and potential ally. Silas knew that Heyward Matheson had been born and raised in China, and that he was the grandson of the famous Hercules MacCallum. Matheson both knew and loved China, and in some ways the Chinese, but he was a careful man when it came to politics. He had been brought up as a strict Scottish Catholic, and he looked on an early case of gonorrhea as a justifiable punishment for his sexual misdeeds. For years he had put up with the torture of what were euphemistically called mercury baths, but they'd only barely kept the disease in check. Finally he'd appealed to the company's Chinese doctor, and within a week of the doctor's treatments

Heyward had gained a kind of relief that he had not experienced for years. As he'd memorably said one morning, "The glory of pissing without pain cannot be overstated."

The elderly leader of Oliphant and Company out of Philadelphia spoke next. Silas didn't listen as the man rattled on about electric light bringing on God's light, or maybe God's light *was* electric light, or perhaps who needs electric light with God's light ...? It was one of those; Silas neither knew nor cared which. He found the Oliphants and their like so stupid that every time one of them spoke his teeth hurt.

The debate continued. Tea was served. Hard liquor was consumed in ever-escalating quantities. Flies were shooed away. Sweaty necks were bitten by various forms of Asian bugs, and the Europeans and the Polyglots kept their wallets firmly in their pockets. Without money, the large and densely populated Chinese areas of the Foreign Settlement would go without electricity and indoor plumbing. In the absence of electric street lights, the resulting nightly violence would no doubt continue, and without proper sanitation, diseases like malaria and typhoid and leprosy would persist in taking their devastating toll in human lives. And it was totally up to the assembled *Fan Kuei* as to whether the situation would be changed or simply allowed to go on as is.

Silas knew that the Shanghailanders—those who would never think of Shanghai as their home—lived lives more privileged than many a king in his castle. They seldom rose before the sun, often in one of the Vrassoon luxury apartments that could run to twenty or thirty rooms. Number-one boy would bring the master tea in bed while number-two boy organized the servants for the day's chores. There were, at the very least, two cooks (always males), a house coolie, an *amah* for the lady of the house, a wash and sew-sew *amah*, a carriage man, and a foreign governess for the children. Breakfast was strictly national in origin: cornflakes, eggs, and coffee for Americans; cold toast, bitter marmalade, and overcooked tomatoes for the English; chicory and croissants for the French. As they ate, they read the English-language *North China Daily News* or the American *Shanghai Evening Post and Mercury,* which included such relevant items to daily life in Shanghai as a crossword puzzle, Dorothy Dix, and Ripley's Believe It or Not. No Shanghailander read any of Charles Soong's publications, or any of the other Chinese newspapers. Few of the Shanghailanders spoke enough Mandarin to even order a meal in a restaurant. Almost none could read the character writing of the Black-Haired people.

With breakfast done, the portly Shanghailander would descend to street level only to hop immediately into his private carriage, in which he would be driven through streets thick with peasants carrying the world on their shoulders. The streets were filled with thousands of different sorts of man-pushed or -pulled conveyances, running the gamut from simple wheelbarrows to elaborate wagons designed for up to twenty people, thousands of water-spider–like rickshaws, hundreds of thousands of pedestrians, the odd other private carriage belonging to another Shanghailander Taipan, trolley cars on tracks, and a few Sikh police officers trying in vain to control traffic. Horns honked, peasants shouted—the whole city was one great cacophony of squealing and blaring. Above the roads, colourful Chinese banners announced the opening of new shops and not-to-be-missed sales. They competed for the sky with the infinitely proper signage advertising such European niceties as "Postal Savings."

After the adventure of the road, the Shanghailander would arrive at his completely westernized office and be greeted by his overly good-looking secretary, who was probably American or British—or at the very least a Portuguese who had come over to work in Macao and then moved on to the richer fields of Shanghai. The Portuguese were the city's bookkeepers, clerks, typists, cashiers, and secretaries. They were paid less than "White" people, but far more than the Chinese.

Once the Shanghailander's coat had been helped off by the secretary, he would head for his private office and pick up the cables from his home office that were laid out on his desk. They would all be in code, so their instructions would have to be first decoded and then followed—to the letter. Home office directives were the word of God to Shanghailanders. Once the cables were dealt with, the Shanghailander would turn his attention to the stock quotations, especially silver quotes. Then it would be time to trade: Pelfrees of London traded anything and everything, from cotton to toilet seats; Butterfield and Swire, sugar and shipping; British-American Tobacco Co., buying and selling of their nasty product; Gibb, Livingstone and Company, silk, tea, and piece goods; Standard-Vacuum Oil Company imported and distributed oil before its Chinese competitor, Kwang Wha Petroleum, could beat them to the punch. But these were really just merchants. The real traders—Dents of London, Jardine Matheson of Scotland, Russell and Company of Delaware, Oliphant and Company of Philadelphia, the Vrassoons late of London and Baghdad, and of course the Hordoons—quietly went about their business, the opium trade.

Before noon the bulk of a Shanghailander's work would be done and he would make his way—once again by private carriage—to his private club for a lunch that began with at least two cocktails. The most exclusive of these clubs was the gloomy Shanghai Club, which was exclusively British. There, over lunch, the economic geniuses of Shanghai—most of whom lost their shirts on rubber speculation—pontificated on their own business brilliance. After a heavy lunch the Shanghailander would retreat to the second-floor library, where he would plop his expansive rear end onto one of the large leather chairs and take a well-deserved nap.

The American Club, with its brick facade, was not much different, except that every person was greeted with a hearty handshake, even by men they had never met before. The furniture was maple colonial and the bar always filled to overflowing.

There were, of course, other famous clubs: the Shanghai Bowling Club, the Race Club, the Husi Country Club, the Yacht Club, and the Cercle Sportif Français.

Eventually these masters of the universe rose from their torpor and returned to their offices, but by four o'clock at the latest they would book out for the day and head toward the Shanghai Golf Club or the Hungjao Golf Club for a round. The experience was not much different from playing eighteen holes at the Winchester Country Club outside Manhattan, except that the attendants in Shanghai all wore white robes.

Their wives had equally untaxing days. With servants to do any and all work around the home, they attended ladies' clubs, drama clubs, and endless tea parties. Sometimes there was an attractive young man from one of the consulates to bring news of home ... and the possibility of lurid moments in darkened halls. Correct wines were served by white-gloved servants, month-old magazines read as clouds of gossip filled the air, and the afternoon somehow whiled itself away.

Then it was dinnertime.

After a full five-course dinner, liqueurs and cigars were served. Then the master and mistress of the house headed out for dancing at one of the many private dance halls, or the grand ballroom of one of the hotels. The frivolity paused only momentarily at eleven o'clock when the stockbrokers had to race to their offices to get the opening quotes from the New York Stock Exchange. But after half an hour (or at most forty-five minutes) they had placed their trades and returned to their Shanghailander social life—often after a very quick visit to a Russian émigré whore.

Silas knew many of these men and counted none of them as friends. He stood up.

The tension in the room increased exponentially when Shanghai's richest bachelor and, more importantly, Shanghai's wealthiest European Shanghainese made his way to the speaker's podium.

The Shanghailanders braced themselves.

"Gentlemen," he began, "and I use the term loosely." A small pocket of laughter greeted the comment. Silas noticed Heyward Matheson smile. "My father and uncle first set foot in the Middle Kingdom almost eighty years ago. They were traders, not unlike many of you assembled here. And they came here to make their fortunes, like all of us here. My father made a great deal of money, but he died alone—a foreigner in the land he should have called home."

A moment of silence greeted that statement.

From somewhere in the back a voice called out, "And your uncle?"

Silas took a deep breath, then said simply, "My uncle died fighting for what he believed in, something that surely most of you in this room understand. My Uncle Maxi was no different than most of you. Just braver, and more convinced that there are different ways to live one's life than simply making money."

Again a moment of silence. Respect amongst the Europeans was rare, but Silas held a special place. He was of them, but a foreigner—a Jew. And his business success was the envy of every person in the room.

The same voice in the back of the room called out, "And your brother, how did he die?"

The silence that followed this question was different. This one was filled with anticipation—and fear. Rumours of the cause of Milo's death had been rife at the time of his demise and had continued to be a source of gossip in this most gossip-filled of towns.

It was as if the entire room held its breath.

Then Meyer Vrassoon, the handsome, swarthy head of the Vrassoon house, stepped forward and repeated the question, this time in a louder, more openly accusatory voice. "And your brother, how did he die?"

"Beneath the hooves of a Vrassoon racehorse, face up, staring at the glorious sun, whose light and power he resembled more than any man I've ever known."

As one, the attendant crowd exhaled and a cheer slowly swelled from them.

Silas smiled and then said, "We must not remain strangers in our homes. We must not be separate from the owners of this place. Yes, the Chinese own this place." For a moment he thought of his father's cautionary opium dream—"*They were expecting us. Expecting us to do something— something for them.*" Silas shook the thought from his head and repeated, "We must not, I emphasize, *must not* reap the benefits of this country and then bring that money back whence we came. Shanghai is my home, and I will invest my earnings—*all* my earnings—*from* this place *in* this place."

A few men rose to applaud. Many others sat in stony silence.

Silas looked around. Every face was watching him. He said simply, "I vote for the proposal and put up ten thousand English pounds to begin the process." An audible gasp came from the crowd. Silas was envied for his wealth but hardly noted for his philanthropy. In fact, most of the men in the room thought philanthropy to be a kind of insanity visited upon aged men who tried to buy their way into Heaven after years of doing as much evil as they could manage. Then they noted something truly odd. Silas Hordoon was laughing. Giggling, really. Quite out of control. Finally he stopped himself with a strange spluttering sound and said, "While I have your full attention, I have an announcement of a personal nature to make."

This was truly unique. Something personal from the famously private Silas Hordoon?

"Yes, personal. I invite you all to my wedding."

A cheer came from the crowd, although the head of the Vrassoon household thought it odd that a man of Silas's years should remarry—not unlike Sarah giving birth to Abraham's child at the age of one hundred. Then it struck Vrassoon, and he shouted furiously, "Who's the bride?"

Silas took a breath and relished the moment. Then he let all hell loose in the room by simply saying, "Mai Bao, Jiang's middle daughter."

chapter twenty-six
Yin Bao Meets a Feminist

"You could be of great value to us," Ch'iu Chin said to Yin Bao.

"Us?"

"Those of our sex," Ch'iu Chin replied as she reached across the table and took a small handful of pickled watermelon seeds from the delicate porcelain bowl. Then she flipped one into her mouth. She was having fun. Her boss, Charles Soong, had given her a free hand in "finding out what you can about this Yin Bao. Push her. Challenge her." Ch'iu Chin bit down and swallowed the tasty seed almost at the same time as she spat the shells to the floor—like a man, a working man.

Yin Bao was taken aback.

Ch'iu Chin noticed. "You are offended! The whore is offended!"

Yin Bao sprang to her feet and opened her mouth to speak, but Ch'iu Chin spoke first. "There is no real difference between men and women."

Yin Bao's mouth opened even farther, but now there were no words there to answer what she thought of as the most extraordinary comment she had ever heard.

"We're all the same, just different plumbing," Ch'iu Chin said as she nonchalantly spat a stream of watermelon seed shells to the floor, then said, "These are pretty good. Not the best I've ever tasted, but good. Not as good as I thought they would be, though, considering how much they are charging you."

Yin Bao found that she had sat down but didn't remember doing so. Nor did she remember why she had allowed this—person—to sit at her table. Yin Bao never paid for the food or drink she consumed. The client always paid. Always. She reached out and pulled the bowl of pickled watermelon seeds away from this strange women and said, "I am not paying for you. You are paying for me."

"I think not, Yin Bao. I'm not a client. Is that what you call the men you charge to fuck you?"

"If you are not a client, what are you?"

Ch'iu Chin smiled. "I don't find you attractive. You're only famous because you're famous, and that's why I'm here."

"I still don't understand. What are you?"

"A fighter for women's rights." Ch'iu Chin handed a pamphlet to Yin Bao. "Can you read?"

Yin Bao put the pamphlet aside. "Of course I can read."

"Good, then read this," Ch'iu Chin said as she got to her feet, "and I'll be back to chat with you about it."

"Just a moment."

"Yes?"

"Men and women are not the same. How can you claim such a thing?"

"Because you are going to prove that I am right. You are going to do something that up until now only men could do."

"Stand up to pee?"

"No, I'm sure that you are supple enough to do that already."

"Then what?"

"Choose the person you're going to marry—and I'm going to help."

"You?"

"Yes, I'm quite well thought of in the newspaper world. Perhaps you know my boss. His name is Charles Soong."

———

The "accidental" meeting of Yin Bao with Charles Soong was not an accident by any definition of the term. It had cost Jiang a fortune to get Charles's matchmaker to introduce the "next fine, young, and eligible marriage prospect." Covering Yin Bao's courtesan background was impossible, but not completely necessary. Jiang's spies had told her of Ch'iu Chin's dinner with Yin Bao and assumed that the woman had reported back to her boss. The remaining stumbling block Jiang saw was Charles's demand that his wife be a Christian.

"A what?" Yin Bao had demanded.

"A Christian," Jiang said sweetly.

"Do I have to wear a smelly old black robe?" Yin Bao asked in real distress.

"No, those are Jesuits, and I believe only men are permitted—"

"Jesuits? Aren't they Christians?"

"Yes, but Charles Soong is another kind of Christian."

"What kind?" Yin Bao asked without a hint of sarcasm.

"The kind that could well get you named Jiang—that kind of Christian," Jiang said, and kissed her daughter on the forehead. Then she added, "It's time you thought of children. Remember, as Jiang you would be responsible for producing at least two females."

Yin Bao wanted to say, "Who could forget?" but she chose to smile in a manner she thought of as demure. It caused Jiang to laugh.

"What, Mother?"

"That smile needs some practice."

"Then I'll practise," Yin Bao said, and turned from her mother.

And Jiang knew that she would practise as much as was necessary to get what she wanted. In all her years of dealing with girls she had never experienced a more strong-willed woman than her daughter Yin Bao. When, on her twelfth birthday, Jiang had asked Yin Bao what she wanted as a gift, the girl had astonished her by saying, "I want my feet bound to complete my undeniable beauty." Jiang had protested vigorously, but the girl had simply threatened to have it done without her mother's permission.

"But the pain will be terrible," Jiang had finally said.

Yin Bao had just shrugged and said, "What of value comes without pain?"

Jiang had finally relented, although she did insist that her doctor do the operation and then oversee the recovery.

———

The initial operations took place the following week. Jiang stood by her daughter's side as the doctor inserted over thirty acupuncture needles into Yin Bao's torso and legs. The girl never winced. Jiang looked to the doctor, who responded by raising his shoulders.

Before they had begun Jiang had asked the doctor, "Will she feel pain during the procedure?"

He'd looked at her as if she'd asked him if there was water in the ocean, then said, "I'll be breaking bones in each of her feet, then forcing her toes under toward her heel. I may have to cut through muscles, and I'll definitely have to cut at least two major tendons. Wouldn't you assume that would cause some pain?"

Jiang nodded. The doctor picked up his bag and headed toward the room that had been prepared for the operation when Jiang stopped him.

"Could she die?"

The doctor put down his bag and shrugged his shoulders. "We all can die. It is our nature."

"Yes, but can this operation …"

"Kill her? Certainly. The acupuncture needles should be able to block the paths of pain, but the body is wise. It knows when it is being invaded and it seeks ways to warn the brain of the threat. Pain is the body's way of warning the mind that it is in danger. So, although my acupuncture needles will fend off the initial pain, the body will find new tracks to the mind to warn it."

"And when that happens?"

"If she's not strong enough she'll go into shock … from which she may never recover."

The breaking of the tiny bones was awful. Each let out a cracking sound like the wishbone of a chicken when it is snapped. But Yin Bao remained very still and kept her eyes shut. She held her mother's hand. Then the doctor made the first incision to cut a tendon and blood fountained up, splashing on Yin Bao's thighs. Her eyes snapped open and Jiang held her breath.

"Mother!"

"What, Yin Bao? Close your eyes."

"No, Mother."

"What do you want me to do? Do you want me to stop this?"

"No. Cover my dress, Mother. It's made of purest Chinkiang silk. You know how hard it is to get blood out of silk."

Jiang looked from Yin Bao to the doctor, who smiled as he cut through the tough tendon.

Jiang found herself studying her daughter's face during the surgery. She was appalled by Yin Bao's insistence on wearing silk. It was forbidden for any Jiang to wear silk because it was made from the tears of women. The girl stifled a cry of pain and Jiang thought, *You are willing to endure this but unwilling to give up your silk dresses!*

Yin Bao's recovery was slow, and she kept herself scrupulously out of public view, allowing only her maid to see her. The girl redressed her wounds, then wound the long, strong bandage around her broken feet tighter and tighter every day. Yin Bao took her food in her private room and didn't leave. Despite Jiang's pleading, she refused to allow her mother to see her. Rumours of her demise began to spread, and the newspapers leaped on the possibility that the great Jiang had lost her youngest daughter.

Weeks became months. Every morning the maid entered Yin Bao's room with a hundred-foot length of clean white cloth and a half hour later emerged with a blooded, smelly length of cloth of a similar size. Jiang would send each of these cloths to her doctor, along with Yin Bao's night-soil. Each evening the doctor would sit over tea with Jiang and give her his report on both the dirty cloth and the night-soil. Finally, by the end of the third month, the doctor's reports stopped using terms like "we may be all right" or "this is troubling."

Near the end of the sixth month Yin Bao's maid approached Jiang and said that Yin Bao would like to see a dressmaker.

"Her eldest sister?"

"No, sorry, madam, she was insistent that it not be anyone of her family. She would like it to be a man."

—

Chen was noted for two things: his expertise with needle and thread, and the pronounced ugliness of his features. He had come from the country as a child. The rumour was that he had been abandoned by his parents once they had seen that his features weren't going to change. Be that as it may, he was a lonely but talented man who worked out of a small shop whose back wall was the wall of the Old City itself. When the renowned courtesan Jiang flung open the door to his workshop, he fell to his knees to hide his face from this celebrated beauty.

Chen listened to the courtesan's request without getting up from his knees or lifting his head. He even bargained the price from that position.

"Will you be standing when you come to my daughter or will you be crawling like a crab?" Jiang asked, honestly not knowing the answer to her question.

"With your permission, I will walk," he said.

"Fine. I grant you permission to walk. Now stand up."

He did.

Jiang had seen a lot of deformity in her life. Often men with physical deformity could find sex partners only when they paid for it. But there was something else in this man's face. Something that made her want to say awful things to him. Something that seemed to say "hurt me." She resisted, but didn't speak for fear of what would come from her mouth. She just put her payment on the table, turned, and left.

Chen came to Yin Bao's room on the following day. When he entered he was happy to see that the draperies had been drawn and that the light was dim. The woman on the divan, facing away from him, didn't rise, but signalled with her hand that he was to approach.

He did.

Again he was pleased that the light source was behind him so that his face was in shadow. But the light graced the beauty of this girl's face. He noted that her feet were covered with a tightly wound silk cloth. She wore a beautifully embroidered robe that was slightly open to expose much of her leg and a patch of her thigh, and loosely enough tied that he could see the swell of her small breasts.

"Don't be afraid," she said.

Her voice was surprisingly deep. He stepped closer, being careful to keep the light directly behind him.

"Closer," she said.

He felt his heart jump in his chest.

"You will make me the most beautiful dresses that anyone has ever seen," she said as her left hand came up and pivoted, then, to his shock, settled on his thigh.

He went to turn to hide the imminent swelling of his sex but she said sternly, "Don't." He turned back to her, his shame beginning to tent his trousers. "Ah," she said, as her fingers slid across the bulge. "Ah," she repeated as she applied pressure with her hand. He opened his mouth as if to let out a moan, but she stopped him with a sharp "No!" Then she expertly unbuttoned him and, without taking her eyes from his, touched him, then brought the clouds and rain as she murmured, "The most beautiful dresses that any courtesan has ever worn—no—has ever dreamed of wearing."

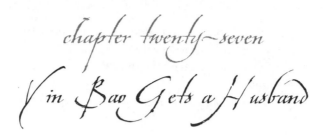

chapter twenty-seven
Yin Bao Gets a Husband

After endless negotiations, Yin Bao finally decided to take matters into her own hands. She barged into her mother's private office and shouted, "Enough, Mother! This Charles Soon or Charles Soong—whatever his name is—is just a man, after all, so what could be so hard?"

Jiang feigned offence, but she had secretly been waiting for Yin Bao to declare her real intentions by taking action. She smiled simply and said, "I see."

Yin Bao rang for her maid.

The girl appeared quickly and asked, "Ma'am?"

"Enter my name in the next Flower Contest that takes place at the race course."

The maid was shocked. Yin Bao had always made herself available to the press but she'd shunned the Flower Contests that Charles Soong's newspapers sponsored. Often the maid had heard her mistress make fun of the "Four Diamond Cutters," the name assigned to the first four winners of the Flower Contests by the newspapers. The most salacious of Yin Bao's comments about the Four Diamond Cutters had become famous in the Flower World. "I have no wish to be a damned Diamond Cutter," she'd said. "I only wish my lovers to have jade swords as hard as diamond cutters!"

"Scat!" Yin Bao said to the maid.

Jiang smiled at that. *Yin Bao sounds like my mother,* Jiang thought.

"You are smiling, Mother. What did I say to amuse you?"

"Scat—you said scat." But before Yin Bao could question her, Jiang added, "I'm sure that the famous Yin Bao's entry into the Flower Contest will be front-page news for several days to come—never a bad thing for my business. Tea?" she asked.

"Please, Mother."

As Jiang poured she asked, "Are you sure you'll win, Yin Bao?"

To Jiang's surprise, Yin Bao did not snap back with a sarcastic reply; rather, her baby girl didn't answer at all. Instead she drank slowly from her teacup and cracked the pointed big toe of her right foot inside its tiny satin slipper.

Then the girl winced.

Jiang had noticed her daughter's steps of late becoming smaller and more careful. "Are you in pain, Yin Bao?" she asked.

"Always, Mother. I am always in pain."

"But is it more now than ...?"

"Enough! Pain is the price I pay for my great beauty."

Jiang nodded, happy to see the fire return to her daughter's eyes. "You will win, then?"

"Absolutely, Mother. I will win and be crowned Flower Princess by the great Charles Soong himself. But first I must have new clothing. Send for my dressmaker," she said imperiously. Then, seeing her mother's face, she added the all-important, "Please, Mother."

After a pause Jiang asked, "The ugly one?"

"Yes. The only one who can make silk into gold."

———

Five days later, Chen sat with his head bowed carefully to keep his face out of the lamplight and spread three exquisitely painted sketches on the table in Yin Bao's bedroom. The woman sat catty-corner to him at the square, black table, her knees almost touching his, her right hand hanging limply at her side, but a few inches from his leg.

Then she put her left hand on the table and with a painted fingernail flicked the topmost of the striking sketches to the floor. "A dress for a whore, not a courtesan," she said.

Chen swallowed and tried to speak, but his mouth was too dry to form words. He couldn't take his eyes off her right hand so close to his leg.

"Do you agree?" she snapped.

He nodded. It was all he was able to do.

Her right hand landed on his leg just above the knee. "Then again," she said, sliding her hand farther up his leg, "perhaps it is the perfect thing to catch a Chinese Christian husband." She leaned over and picked up the sketch from the floor with her left hand while she withdrew her right hand from his thigh.

He sat back in his chair, inadvertently allowing the lamp to light his features.

She put the drawing back on the table and said, "Make me this. Make me the most beautiful dress that Shanghai has ever seen ... and I'll give you a special reward." She allowed her right hand to land on the table, then she splayed her fingers.

Chen grabbed the sketches and held them strategically over his middle, then spun on his heel and left the room.

Yin Bao smiled. *Funny,* she thought, *he doesn't seem as ugly the second time you meet him.*

———

The Flower Contest drew a huge crowd and almost a hundred contestants. But from the moment Yin Bao descended the steps of her two-horse carriage wearing Chen's dress, the result was a foregone conclusion. When Yin Bao crossed the stage in her seductive, mincing steps, her hips swivelling, a cheer erupted from the Chinese in the crowd. The *Fan Kuei* in attendance were shocked by the response.

She nodded politely to the audience and then bowed her head demurely—something that had cost her considerable study and patience to master.

And the crowd went wild!

As she heard the swelling roar she recalled something else that had taken even more patience—sitting still for two hours as the doctor had carefully extracted the nail from the big toe of her left foot three days earlier.

"Must the nail be removed?" she had demanded.

"Yes," the doctor had replied.

"Are you sure?" she'd pressed.

"Yes, the fungal infection has rotted the nail. But it's not the nail that concerns me. It's the toe. If the fungus pierces the skin and sets into the bone, I'll have to cut off your toe as well."

Thinking of it now made Yin Bao shiver. What was a golden lotus without its protruding pistil?

———

When Charles Soong saw Yin Bao in the flesh, all his years of shame for desiring the company of White women that he had kept strictly under wraps during his time in America—especially at the seminary in North Carolina—vanished in an instant. Here, before him, was true beauty. Not fish-belly–white skin and round eyes, but real beauty—Asian beauty—a Princess of the Flower World. And within three months she would be his bride.

chapter twenty-eight
A Carver's Son

The years between 1899 and 1902 brought important change in Shanghai.

Charles and Yin Bao set about creating three daughters in almost record time. Silas and Mai Bao began to build their private world—a garden, as Silas had promised Miranda, surrounded by tall walls to keep both the world out and their twenty adopted street children in. Two of the children were Mai Bao's, retrieved from the peasants who had sheltered them. Never had a race track been put to a better use.

Jiang's precarious health continued to confound the doctor's predictions of her imminent demise—as did that of another powerful woman, this one in far-off Beijing, who continued her quest to find the Sacred Tusk. She sent her spies out to contact the most powerful of the Tongs. And to the one who found the Tusk, she offered a reward "worthy of a Manchu Emperor."

The Soong daughters, even as children, showed remarkable differences one to the next. They would before too long be known to all of China as "She Who Loves Wealth," "She Who Loves Power," and "She Who Loves China." As they grew, their father continued to supply the money necessary for Dr. Sun Yat-sen's efforts—often foolish efforts—to overthrow the Manchus. As the Doctor proved himself over and over again to be incapable of organizing the required revolt, his right-hand man, Chiang Kai Shek, grew more and more powerful—and Charles grew more and more wary of the man and his obvious violence.

But there was another man, a powerful figure in Shanghai, a man known behind his back as Big-Eared Tu, who was not frightened by

Chiang Kai Shek's violence. This man was waiting for an opportunity to take control of the city at the Bend in the River and as he had promised his grandmother, finally wreak revenge upon the *Fan Kuei*. And at long last, an opportunity dropped into his lap. All he needed to do was claim the reward "worthy of a Manchu Emperor."

* * *

I HATE IT when Father does that.

In front of everyone. In front of the other workers. In front of baby brother. Come to think of it, Father never has any criticism of baby brother's work— only of mine. And then I went and split the jade block when I was only sup- posed to score it for Father. And soon Father will know. But it was, after all, only a second-rank piece of jade. Yes, but it was large enough and perfectly shaped to make a standing Manchu bannerman. So I'm not good at this. So what? I've never been good at this. My hands are too big and my mind wan- ders and I can never figure out which tool to … damn it to hell. If Father is going to keep secrets from me, what does the old man expect? Father and baby brother—always huddling in the corner and whispering. Father showing carvers' secrets to the baby but not the eldest! Who ever heard of such behav- iour? Then the sneaking off in the night. Oh, they think they are so clever. They thought that I wouldn't notice. Well, I noticed—and tonight I followed. All the way down into the tunnels.

The shudder that followed brought an end to the monologue that seemed to be constantly running in his head. The tunnels—the Warrens—had shocked him. Well, not the tunnels but what he had seen there. What, until that very moment, he, like the rest of Shanghai, had believed to be a fable. A silly children's story. In the flickering light before the others arrived he had seen his father open a mahogany case and show a Narwhal Tusk to his baby brother.

He had been around things of great beauty all his life, but this was a thing of wonder. It seemed to call out to him. And he had just barely avoided detection, first by the famous courtesan Jiang, and then by the sil- houetted men already waiting in the back of the cavern, one of whom seemed young, while the other he'd have guessed was older.

He had taken one final peek, then carefully retraced his steps to the entrance against the south wall of the Old City.

That night he drank in the fanciest bar he could find. No more buying cheap liquor and drinking in a filthy alley. He had broken into his father's room and taken a handful of cash, and now he was spending it. Buying drinks for the bar, being treated properly—like someone worthy of respect.

People listened to his complaints and nodded their heads in sympathy.

Hands slapped him on the back, people laughed at his jokes, and it seemed to him that the whole bar—every patron—at last knew that he was an important man. A man to be listened to and respected. An artist. Even if his father couldn't see it that way.

Just past midnight he ordered a third round of drinks for the bar, and to his chagrin realized that he didn't have enough money to pay for it. He started to apologize to the bar owner, to whom he had already paid hefty sums of money for the previous two rounds, and was amazed that the man called him names and threatened to tell his father.

"You wouldn't dare!"

"You owe me money. You owe me money, now!"

"I'll get you your money, I will. Just give me an hour."

The bar owner took every *yuan* the young carver had left and one of his shoes to guarantee that he would return with the cash he owed.

As the young carver walked out of the bar with as much dignity as a one-shoed man could muster, a looming figure at the back of the room—a man who had not been drinking—got to his feet and followed him. People who could buy three rounds of drinks for a crowded bar always interested the disgraced Red Pole who used to be Gangster Tu's number-one lieutenant until Loa Wei Fen's arrival.

When the young man opened the door to the famous carver's workshop the disgraced Red Pole's interest grew. He knew that his Mountain Master, Gangster Tu, bought sculpted pieces from this famous carver—and here was the carver's son clearly stealing from him. How to use this bit of knowledge was the question.

The young carver shortly re-emerged from the darkness of the workshop and started back toward the bar—one shoe on, one shoe off.

The Red Pole followed him at a distance, and after the young carver had paid off his debt to the bar owner the Red Pole stepped forward and demanded, "Aren't you going to give this fine young man a list of the drinks he's purchased?"

The bar owner stiffened and was about to respond when he noticed the angled Triad tattoo on the man's neck over his jugular and held his tongue.

The Red Pole nodded and smiled.

The bar owner shuffled a bit, then said quite loudly, "I seem to have made an error on your bill, young sir. Let me just …" The man slapped several rows of beads along his abacus, made a face that was supposed to show concern, then shook the thing and started again.

The Red Pole reached over and grabbed the abacus from the bar owner's hands. "Enough. You charged him twice as much as you should have, didn't you?"

The bar owner blanched but didn't speak.

"Didn't you?" the Red Pole demanded.

"Yes, I guess I did, I'm terribly sorry that—"

"So pay him three times what you owe him and we'll call it fair." The Red Pole smiled.

The young carver looked from one man to the other, then back again, and then, to his amazement, the bar owner counted out a large stack of *yuan* bills and handed them over to him with a grunt that might well have been an apology.

"Good," said the Red Pole. Then he added, "Always ask for an accounting, young sir."

"Yes, very good. Yes, and thank you. Can I buy you a drink?" the young carver asked.

"No," the Triad member responded, "but I'll buy you one. What are you drinking?"

And so began a friendship that the young carver felt he desperately needed. Here was someone to tell his problems to. And, damn it to hell, his father was bound to find out about the broken jade tomorrow

"And what will he do then?"

"Throw a fit. Cut me into pieces and throw me in the wok. Whatever he wants he can do."

The night continued that way, and the Red Pole was beginning to think that this was nothing more than a stupid boy who hated his father, when all of a sudden, just before the blue light of morning slid in the window, the boy said, "I know his secret. I know it."

And what exactly would that secret be? the Red Pole wondered. But he did not ask. He knew that someone who offers to tell a secret once will always offer a second time.

As the two men got up from the table in the dawning light, another man watched carefully from the shadows. This man had a cobra carved into his back, the hood of which was now filling with blood. The Assassin had been a trusted member of Tu's personal bodyguard since he'd murdered the *Fan Kuei* on the great Indiaman sailing ship, and he had learned much in that time. But nothing he had learned concerned him so deeply as the approach of Gangster Tu's disgraced Red Pole to the Carver's eldest son.

chapter twenty-nine
The Assassin and His Wife

She thought he looked terrible. She'd noticed his decline more in the past few years, now that she was able to see him only every other new moon— and he had missed several of their assigned meetings. She knew little of what he did, but whatever it was it had taken its toll on him. He had also grown increasingly critical of the martial arts progress of his eldest son, to the point that the boy dreaded the arrival home of his father. And she'd noticed her husband being more and more encouraging to their younger son. The older boy hadn't begun his training until his sixth year, but her husband had started their younger son on his third birthday. And the younger boy was clearly more adept than his older brother.

But it was her husband that most concerned her. One time he'd returned with a barely healed cut across his chest. Another he had lost a finger on his right hand. His response to her queries about both was to slough off her concern with a scowl—clearly a warning for her to probe no deeper. And she didn't probe.

When they were finally alone, on their sleeping platform above the goats, he was an almost indifferent lover; he performed, but without much zeal. And there was the calling out in his sleep after they brought on the clouds and rain. Not shrieks or cries, but clear calls. Calls to various men to do various things. She never asked exactly who the men were or what they were meant to do.

In the mornings he was always up before her and out in the marsh with the two boys. Often he returned angry with the older boy. Once he hit him. The younger boy he praised and often took out near sunset for a second session.

"I hate him!" her older son shouted at her.

"Say no such things. He is your father."

"He hates me."

"No. No, he is your father and he wants you to succeed so you can follow in his footsteps."

"Doing what? Murdering collaborators?"

She was silent. It had crossed her mind that her husband could well be the murderer loose on the streets of Shanghai. He certainly had the skills necessary to avoid the police for all that time.

"Or, Mother, is he just a stupid gangster?"

She quickly crossed to him and put her hand over his mouth. There were tears in her eyes as she said, "Your father is a great man on a great and honourable mission. You must not—"

"If he's not a murderer or a gangster, then what is he?" She actually didn't know the answer to that question. She knew he was a master martial artist, and the cobra carved on his back was surely a sign that he was important in some organization. For a long time she had thought him a Triad member, but when she'd accused him he had corrected her sternly.

"Never. Never would I use my skill for fools like that. You have to trust me. I have a great obligation to the Middle Kingdom, to the city at the Bend in the River, that makes me associate with these evil men. But I am not one of them."

She paraphrased that to her older son, whose response was, understandably, "And you believe him?"

She put her arms around him and drew him to her breast as she said, "I do," while in her mind she continued the thought with, *What else can I do?*

———

Loa Wei Fen laughed as his younger son split the piece of wood cleanly with a simple heel kick. The boy was talented and loved the work. He took a stance and Loa Wei Fen took a defensive posture in opposition to him. Then the boy challenged, "Hit me, Father."
Loa Wei Fen smiled and lashed out.

The boy sidestepped the blow and came back at his father's legs.

Loa Wei Fen parried his son's attack, then somersaulted over the boy. But the moment he landed his son was on him—only Loa Wei Fen's superior strength stopped the boy's attack.

The boy squealed with delight as his father lifted him high in the air, then threw him over his shoulder like a bag of rice and ran toward home.

———

Later that night he spoke to two of the men he had trained previously and outlined exactly what he wanted them to teach the boys in his absence. Then he went to the boys' mattress and talked softly to his sons about their duty to the Black-Haired people and how much he loved them, and also that he had to leave the next day.

The older boy turned away from his father, but the younger one crawled into his lap and showed him his left hand. The hand was bloody and scabbed.

"What is this?"

"I've carved a cobra on my hand like you have on your back."

Loa Wei Fen reached out and cleaned away the scabs. He was surprised that the boy didn't wince. Then he wiped away the blood with his sleeve—and there, although not elegant, was clearly a coiled cobra, its hood spread and mouth open, ready to strike.

Loa Wei Fen patted the boy on the head, then turned him over and said, "Sleep." He didn't bother saying the rest of what was in his mind: *An assassin must take rest when he can find it.*

That night he slept with his wife but refrained from ejaculating since he was now convinced that he had sired a successor to his obligation in the Ivory Compact. She noticed, and at first thought he no longer cared for her, and when she said as much he denied it vehemently.

"Then what?"

"Our youngest will follow me."

"And our oldest son?"

"He will have to make his own way, but I will not have him trained any further. There is no need. And if he learns more I will have to choose between the two, as my ancestor did to start our line as the Head of the Guild of Assassins. I won't take his life to make way for his brother. But he must accept. He must—and you must make him—or his death will be on your head. Now, help me collect my clothing. I leave before the moon sets."

And even as the moon set the young Assassin-to-be had the most extraordinary dream. He was in a great city, but not Shanghai. And there was terror all around him. Chinese everywhere, slaughtered. And he slept with his eyes open, while his men awaited his orders. Even in his sleep, he took a deep breath and readied himself for the terrible task ahead.

chapter thirty
Tu and the Tusk

The opening of the door at the far end of the former stable drew Gangster Tu's attention. To his surprise, the Red Pole he had disgraced onboard the Indiaman sailing ship strode into the gloom of the barn followed closely by two of his bodyguards, who threw the man to his knees.

Tu stood, as imperial as a Manchu Emperor standing on his throne dais. The disgraced Red Pole responded accordingly by performing the full prescribed kowtow.

Tu allowed him to finish the entire ritual and then stay in the prostrate position at the end of the formality for over a minute before he shouted, "What?"

The man kept his head on the ground and began to tell of a young man he had met two weeks before at a bar.

Tu was about to tell the guards to get him out of his presence when the words *carver* and *tusk* slid from the man's mouth.

Tu quickly shouted, "Enough," then sent the guards away with a curt wave of his hand and an order that no one was to interrupt his discussion with his "wayward Red Pole."

Once the guards were gone, Tu crossed to a side table inlaid with designs in mother-of-pearl that sat against a near wall. With a key he opened the panels of the cabinet to reveal a display of fine European liquors to rival any such array anywhere in the world. "A drink, perhaps?" he suggested. He turned and was surprised to see that the man still had his eyes to the ground and his forehead pressed hard against the cold floor.

Tu shrugged his shoulders, thinking that perhaps he would leave the man there permanently. Then he decided against it. "You may rise," he said.

The man stood slowly but kept his eyes averted.

Tu poured himself a measure of fine Irish whisky, then said, "You were saying something about a carver's son and a tusk?" After a few minutes Tu had the basics and told the man, "Bring this boy to me this evening."

"Here?" the Red Pole asked.

"No. Not here. To my home."

"Yes, sir. But it might be late. He doesn't leave the workshop until after sundown."

"Fine. I'll be in my home from sundown onward, and I'll expect you to bring the boy to me there."

"Yes, sir."

"Without fail!" Tu shouted, just to remind the Red Pole that there were more disastrous things that could happen to a member of the Tong of the Righteous Hand than to be publicly disgraced.

——

Later that night the young carver followed his new friend, the Red Pole, down the dark streets of the Old City. They crossed Fang Bang Lu near the Temple of the City God, then headed toward the old waterfront. He was surprised when his friend tightened his grip around his shoulder and said, in a harsher voice than the younger man had heard from him before, "I have someone who is anxious to meet you and hear your stories."

When they entered the large house off the alley in the north end of the Old City the young carver was amazed by the luxury, both European and Chinese, that suddenly surrounded him. As he was walked deeper into the large house, however, the decoration became more and more exclusively Chinese. He recognized a jade sculpture of a warrior on horseback slashing at a snake rising from the ground and a shiver went through him. He had helped polish that figure, and his father had grabbed it away from him with a sharp remark to the effect that at least he hadn't broken it … yet.

The young carver's friend opened a large door and then motioned that he should enter. The older man would not meet his eyes. The young carver took a step into the room and was surprised to hear the door slam shut behind him.

He stood alone in the room and waited, not knowing what he was waiting for.

Then a hidden panel behind the large desk opened and a grotesque-looking man stepped into the room. The young carver had never seen him before, but he knew that he was in the presence of Big-Eared Tu, Gangster Tu, perhaps the second most powerful Asian in all of Shanghai—certainly the most dangerous.

He didn't know what to do, so he did nothing.

The gangster took a few steps toward him, then smiled. His teeth were surprisingly small and pointy.

"I ..." the young carver tried to begin, indicating the closed door behind him.

"You what?" replied the gangster, his voice a sibilant whisper.

"Nothing, sir." He felt as though he should bow, or something, but didn't know if that was appropriate. Then suddenly he didn't care if it was appropriate or not, and fell to his knees and placed his forehead against the ground.

He heard something scrape against the polished hardwood boards of the floor and slowly realized that the gangster was pulling a chair up beside him. He opened his eyes and saw the bottom of one of the legs of a peasant's three-legged bamboo stool just at the edge of his vision. The common stool seemed out of place amidst the luxury of the room.

"My Red Pole tells me that you know a great deal about carving. True?"

"Some, your honour."

"You make trinkets for the wealthy Round Eyes, then?"

"Never, never for them."

"You never work for them?"

"No."

"Why should I believe you?"

"There is no reason, sir."

"Do you know who I am?" Tu asked.

"Yes, sir." The boy's voice was barely a whisper. Then the boy had an inspiration. A way to get back at his father. "I want to work for you, sir."

Tu smiled. "What can you do for me?" he asked.

"Whatever is necessary."

"Are you a fighter? Can you build munitions? Can you blow up a train?"

"No, but my father has something that may be very powerful."

"Ah, and what does your father have?" he asked, careful that his words not betray his excitement.

"The secret to the future of Shanghai, I think," the boy blurted out.

"Your father carves the secret to the future of Shanghai?" Tu asked as simply as he could manage.

"No. But I think he has the First Emperor's Narwhal Tusk. No, it's true, I saw it. I thought, like everyone else, that it was just a fairy tale. A myth. But I think it's true. I think my father has the First Emperor's Narwhal Tusk."

Tu reached down and put a cold finger on the back of the young man's neck. He felt the warmth of the young carver's blood only a moment beneath the silky skin. He lifted his finger and asked, "And where would this Tusk be at this moment?"

The boy raised his head and found himself looking into the coal-black eyes of Tu Yueh-sen—and quickly he told of the Narwhal Tusk's hiding place in the depths of the Warrens.

———

After the boy was safely stowed away, Gangster Tu sat at his desk and carefully thought through the options available to him. How exactly could he use this new knowledge against the *Fan Kuei?* He thought about the Dowager Empress in Beijing.

The Old Buddha was still immensely powerful. Tu couldn't even recall the present Emperor's name, the fool who had tried to pass the Hundred Days of Reform. No one paid him any mind. It was the Dowager Empress who ran things. And she had promised to pay a reward "worthy of a Manchu Emperor" for the First Emperor's Tusk. Tu knew exactly what reward he'd demand for the relic. He smiled and tapped his jagged fingernails on the desktop. He drummed out the rhythm of the rain, and it brought him slowly back to his grandmother and her claw hands on the sides of his face, and her insistence that he wreak revenge upon the *Fan Kuei.* He once again questioned why his grandmother's revenge was so important to him. The rain continued. His fingers drummed and slowly his thoughts coalesced—then hardened. Revenge gave him focus for his rage. In a purposeless world it gave him reason. Like the *I Ching,* it gave form to the formless.

"Drive them out of Shanghai, then out of China. All of them, Yueh-sen, out of the Middle Kingdom until nothing but the Black-Haired people remain in our land." Then she'd spat and ground her spittle deep into the earth, saying, "My curse upon you, boy, if you fail me in this."

He shook his head to clear it of his grandmother's angry voice. Now he needed a clear head—and a powerful ally, like the Dowager Empress—and her promised reward "worthy of a Manchu Emperor." But first he had to figure out how to get to the old slut. That would take some doing.

He flipped open his *I Ching* and read the advice there, and a smile creased his thin lips.

He pressed a button on his desk and his Incense Master slid into the room, silently. "Sir?"

"Who do we know who has access to the great court of the Manchus?"

chapter thirty-one
A Deal for the Tusk

After months of intermediaries going back and forth between Shanghai and Beijing, and dozens of offers and counter-offers, Gangster Tu finally found himself in the Dowager's meeting chamber deep in the labyrinthine Forbidden City. He had come to claim the "Reward worthy of a Manchu Emperor."

As he waited, Tu Yueh-sen did his best not to marvel at the wealth in obvious display all around him. He had been waiting for almost four hours but had been informed by his spies that this was to be expected. He sat on a satin-pillowed chair and for a moment wanted to lift his feet and put them on the nearby onyx table. He resisted the impulse. He was not there to make an enemy, he was there to enlist a powerful ally—the most powerful in all of China. For an instant he wondered if the Old Buddha knew that he was "playing footsie" with men like Chiang Kai Shek, who were, at least on paper, dedicated to her overthrow. He doubted it, although he didn't put it past the Dowager to realize that keeping your enemies close was a good strategy. And the Dowager had been in power for a very long time.

Tu got to his feet and began yet another slow circumnavigation of the room. He paced past the floor-to-ceiling windows overlooking a fine inner courtyard garden; past a large hanging scroll painting of a country scene, with a mountain in the distance, done on some sort of sheer linen that almost covered an entire wall; past several Manchu ornamental lions; then past long, low, reddish lacquered furnishings. The whole room had a pleasing feel to it. Large, but human in dimension. Thoughtful, tasteful, and utile—yet screaming of money.

Trumpets sounded and he turned. The large gold-plated doors opened and a phalanx of purple-robed men, led by a tall slender man Tu knew to be the court's Head Eunuch, Chesu Hoi, entered.

Tu looked at the half-man—the silky soft skin of his cheek, his lightly rouged full lips, his impossibly long fingernails, his elaborate hairstyle partially hidden beneath a square black board worn at an acute angle, the cold calculation in his eyes.

The Eunuch bowed slightly in his direction and indicated a chair at the oval table in the centre of the room.

Tu sat in the indicated seat. Quickly some of the Eunuch's men moved to either side of him and positioned their writing tablets. Chesu Hoi did not sit but rather moved toward the large scroll painting and bowed his head.

"So you *do* have big ears, as they said."

Tu looked in amazement at the Eunuch, but the man's head stayed bowed and his lips had clearly not moved. Besides, the voice had been an old female's, not a de-sexed male's.

"You are lucky they don't call you Ugly Big-Eared Tu—that would be more accurate."

Tu finally understood that the voice belonged to Tzu Hsi, the Old Buddha, the Dowager Empress of China. She had been watching all this time from behind the wall hanging, which explained the gossamer-thin linen upon which the artist had committed his vision.

A light came on behind the painting, outlining, in silhouette on the linen, the figure of an ancient seated woman leaning on what Tu assumed was some sort of cane—no, sword. For an instant he was happy that he hadn't put his feet on the table.

He belatedly noted that the other men had all leaped to their feet on the first words uttered from behind the wall hanging. He slowly got to his feet. He smiled.

"Please don't. You are repulsive enough with your big ears and your mouth closed. Please don't smile in my presence. Don't."

Tu noted that the men in the Eunuch's party had drawn weapons. Two had swalto blades. He removed the smile from his face.

"So, ugly giant-eared man, do you have the First Emperor's Narwhal Tusk?"

Tu nodded. He told her of the carver's son and the Tusk in the Warrens.

The Dowager Empress of China listened and allowed her anger to slither up from her ancient heart. *So it is true,* she thought. *All these years of rumours of an ivory tusk. All these years of claims and counter-claims of a plot to control the future of the Middle Kingdom—my kingdom. All the efforts to locate it! All the expense!*

"What reward do you want for the trinket?" she asked.

"I want nothing but what would most benefit the Sister of the Moon."

"Yes, well, don't we all," she muttered. "Would one thousand silver *taels* suffice?"

"No," Tu said in a cold, flat voice. "No, it would not be a reward worthy of a Manchu Emperor—as you promised."

"Did I ever make such a promise? Surely not!" She shifted slightly in her seat, and servants appeared from hidden alcoves and moved quickly to reposition her pillows, careful not to touch her—especially her gingerroot-like feet. She swatted them away and shooed them out of the room.

Although the Europeans had robbed her of much power with their insistence on legal extraterritoriality and their damnable land grabs, she still had a vast system of spies. And knowledge came to her from many sources, from people who didn't even know that they were spying for her. She knew what this intensely ugly man wanted for the Tusk.

"You want an ally, don't you?" she asked bluntly. "The most powerful ally in all of China. I will be that ally if you bring me the Tusk. You want revenge against the *Fan Kuei* for some reason. Fine—revenge against the *Fan Kuei* is fine. Who cares about the reason?" Then she chortled a quick laugh that sounded ominously like a death rattle.

Chesu Hoi's mind was flooded with fear. *At least the Chosen Three thought ahead and have Loa Wei Fen in position. I must contact him. Should I tell the Carver to move the Tusk now? No, that might endanger the Tusk even more. No. Wait until the attack is imminent. Prepare, but wait.*

Suddenly the Dowager Empress screamed inside her head, *We must have the Tusk! I must have the Tusk!* She began to fret, scratching her long nails against the delicate skin of her palms, drawing blood. She wanted to scream, *Get it for me. If you love me, get me the relic!* But she held her peace. She'd waited for years—she could wait a little longer. But not too long. She knew that there were other parties in the Middle Kingdom anxious to claim legitimacy, and they would literally kill to get the Tusk to prove to the people that they should rule.

She controlled her voice and said, "How kind of you to have my concerns paramount. So bring me the Narwhal Tusk, like an obedient servant of the Celestial Kingdom." She coughed a throaty chortle.

Tu noted the anxious stares of the men in the room. The coughing continued. The silhouetted figure swayed ever so slightly. Then suddenly the coughing stopped and a single word followed. "Now!"

The force with which the word came from the obviously frail body was impressive, and much to Tu's surprise, he felt a desire to obey the command. But he resisted the impulse and sat.

A stunned silence entered the room. Chesu Hoi signalled his men to step back.

Then Tu put his feet up on the table.

Tu Yueh-sen found the squeal from behind the wall hanging gratifying. Before it crested he said, "I want your detailed promise in writing before I bring you the Narwhal Tusk."

Tu sensed the men in the room preparing to attack.

"If I do not return to Shanghai, my men have strict orders to destroy the Tusk."

Another, even more gratifying squeal came from behind the curtain. Tu sensed the men in the room in motion and found himself on his knees with a knife pressed against either kidney and a swalto blade across his throat, so keen that its touch drew blood.

Tu allowed his breathing to steady. He did not resist. He did not move. He waited. He knew where the Tusk was   she did not. He didn't need the Tusk—she did. So, despite his present physical predicament, he knew that he had the power in the room. He watched the blood drip from his neck onto the intricate pattern of the tiled floor. Watched it find paths as it entered the hatching marks on the tiles. And he waited—waited for the world to change.

And it did.

Within the hour he was on his way back to the city at the Bend in the River with a written promise from the Old Buddha, the Dowager Empress of China: "If you deliver to me the First Emperor's Narwhal Tusk, then you may have your way in Shanghai. My troops will not interfere. They will encircle the city at a distance of forty *li* and not allow anyone in or out. What goes on within the circle of my troops, within both the Old City and the Foreign Settlements, is strictly your business."

—

Shortly after the ugly man left the meeting chamber, the Dowager Empress called in Chesu Hoi. The two walked side by side—very slowly—through the most interior and most beautiful of gardens in the Forbidden City.

Chesu Hoi had already written his warning to the old Carver and had seen his most trusted servant on his way with the warning, "Spare no speed. China itself is in the balance. Deliver my message personally to the Carver, then disappear." He had handed the man a small pouch of gold and said, "And don't allow me or anyone from the court to ever find you again."

Chesu Hoi turned slowly back to the Dowager.

"Do you approve?" she asked.

The Eunuch put his hands behind his back and assumed the classic pose of the scholar. "Of your decision?" he asked, knowing full well the answer.

"Obviously, of my decision."

"Gangster Tu could become a dangerous power in Shanghai."

"He could, but his hatred of the *Fan Kuei* is beyond all bounds. He will attack them, and they will fight back. Perhaps, if there is any justice under the heavens, they will mortally wound each other. If not, my troops will go in and finish the job that this ugly man began."

Chesu Hoi doubted that, but kept his counsel to himself.

The Empress nodded her head and put a hand on the Eunuch's cheek. "Do you understand why we need that Tusk?"

He did. It offered her a legitimacy that no other action or object under the heavens could grant her. A direct line back to the First Emperor. A way to defuse the ever growing wave of anti-Manchu anger in the country.

He nodded.

"Good," she said, then she reached up and kissed him full on the mouth. His lips were warm and firm. Soft. She sighed, then said, "I've always wanted to do that."

Chesu Hoi didn't move a muscle. He knew that he was in as dangerous a position as he had ever been. If he were to make a wrong move, either physically or emotionally, he wouldn't live to see the sunrise.

The Dowager nodded and smiled. "Good," she said. Then, with a dismissive wave of her hand, she added, "But if you ever bring a man as ugly as that into my presence again I will have what little of your manhood remains deep-fried and fed to you as your last meal on this earth."

chapter thirty-two

A War Council

Before Chesu Hoi's messenger could get to Shanghai, Loa Wei Fen was summoned to a most unusual meeting. He had never seen anything like it in his time as a ranking Red Pole in the Tong of the Righteous Hand. It was a war council. He had been party to raids and executions—thefts and strong-arm work—but this was different. Even the constituency of the meeting was different. Besides the usual inner circle, there was a builder, a map-maker, a river pirate, and a strange young man whose eyes kept rolling back in his head. On the central table was spread out a huge map of the Foreign Settlement and the Chinese Old City leading down to the water.

"The Warrens?" Tu said, pointing out a series of dotted lines on the map.

"Yes, but the marks on the map might not be completely accurate. The Warrens are constantly changing."

"Why is that?"

The builder took a deep breath, then said, "Sometimes from cave-ins—the river is, needless to say, very close, so some of the tunnels are under pressure. As well, some passages get used for years and years and then are closed up. Even the access points to the Warrens keep on changing. Some of the entrances are in the basements of buildings or houses. When a property changes hands, an entrance can be lost. Many of the entrances are tightly held secrets."

Tu didn't need to be told that. He knew of a secret entrance to the Warrens about which he had not told a soul.

"What about the Manchus?" asked Loa Wei Fen. "Don't they have access to the Warrens?"

Tu's answer—"That's been taken care of"—startled the Assassin. Then Tu allowed a crooked smile to his face. He was recalling his final negotiations with the Old Buddha. He turned slowly to the strange young man and said, "I don't think any of these problems are important, since we know exactly where in the Warrens we're going, don't we?"

The Carver's son nodded very slowly as his eyes settled for a moment in their sockets. He shuffled over to the large map.

Loa Wei Fen looked at the young man's hand and noted the cuts and scrapes and the hint of dust ground into the creases—he was a carver!

Then the young carver's fingers traced a route on the map and stopped precisely at the secret chamber within which the Narwhal Tusk lay, as if in state. He said simply, "It's there. That is where it is."

Loa Wei Fen was shocked.

The rest of the meeting went by quickly. Loa Wei Fen, despite all his training, was having trouble concentrating. His mind was racing.

Tu Yueh-sen opened his leather-bound, well-thumbed copy of the *I Ching* and quoted a verse. It dealt with the uncovering and executing of an unbeliever. As he read, he looked right at Loa Wei Fen.

Then another shock.

The man Loa Wei Fen had replaced, the disgraced Red Pole, entered the room and stood beside Tu, and the Mountain Master put his arm around the man's shoulder. The Red Pole looked right at Loa Wei Fen, and his smile bespoke a profound rage. A rage carefully fed for years.

chapter thirty-three
Loa Wei Fen's Warning

Jiang felt dizzy, and Loa Wei Fen grabbed her by the arm moments before she would have fallen to the deck of the Suzu Creek junk. The Chosen Three had not met there for years but the Assassin had insisted and insisted that they meet immediately.

Once they had sheltered from the howling wind on the lower deck, Loa Wei Fen told them of the meeting with Tu.

They questioned him, but he silenced their queries with a simple statement. "Are you willing to risk the Tusk?"

"We mustn't. The Tusk hasn't finished revealing its secrets," Jiang said, thinking back to the five women who had been last revealed. She knew the two women in the first portal were herself and the Dowager Empress, and she was beginning to suspect that she knew who would grow up to be the three women in the second portal.

"Who ..." the Confucian began, but he stopped short when he saw the fury in Loa Wei Fen's face.

Jiang completed the question. "Who broke the Ivory Compact? Who betrayed our trust?"

The Assassin softened his features and said, "None of the Chosen Three." There was an audible sigh of relief, but then slowly all faces turned to the Carver, who was not technically one of the Chosen Three and was the only other person who knew the whereabouts of the Tusk.

"My eldest son," the Carver said, his voice aching, "betrayed us all. It is my shame. My shame."

"How do you know?" demanded the Assassin.

"The Dowager Empress's Eunuch, Chesu Hoi, contacted me."

"Why would he do that?"

"The Head Eunuch of the Emperor's court has always been the Carvers' patron."

"And you never thought to tell us?" Jiang demanded.

The Carver spoke slowly. "Our Assassin was positioned. When Loa Wei Fen was called by Gangster Tu then we would have to act. Acting earlier might have endangered the Tusk."

The Confucian turned toward Loa Wei Fen and said, "This Tu Yueh-sen has lived long enough."

"No," the Carver said, "he may still be the Man with a Book." He turned to Loa Wei Fen and asked, "Did he consult the *I Ching* before he set his plans?"

Loa Wei Fen nodded. *Boxes within boxes,* he thought. Then he cast aside the thought and said, "We must act now. We must move and hide the Tusk."

"How?"

"Indeed how—and where?" demanded the Confucian.

Jiang stepped forward and said simply, "With a diversion, and to my place."

Shanghai was a place of many eyes. Secrecy was its most elusive and often most expensive commodity. Spies were everywhere, reporting on everything—every new face in a neighbourhood, every person who suddenly changed their order in a water shop, every carriage and rickshaw that passed, every large item carried or toted. Almost every faction in the city paid for such information—paid handsomely enough that thousands upon thousands of eyes watched and reported what they had seen. And no doubt soon there would be an unusually large reward offered for anyone reporting a large, heavy object about six feet long being carried on foot, in a rickshaw—in any way. The spies would enlist their children, who would then enlist their friends. The thousands of eyes would become hundreds of thousands of eyes—and the Chosen Three knew it.

"So what sort of diversion do we need to move the Tusk?" the Confucian asked.

"Something major," Jiang said.

There was a long silence in the belly of the junk as the foul-smelling waters of the Suzu Creek slapped against the ancient hull. Everyone there knew that there was one sure diversion, but it could cost lives.

Finally, it was the Assassin who mentioned the unmentionable. "Fire."

The blaze was reminiscent of the great fire that had swept through the city at the Bend in the River the night before the History Teller started on her epic journey upriver some forty years before. Once again, the conflagration began in a whorehouse and spread quickly through the makeshift out-buildings, then to the buildings on either side of the alley. The wind picked up the flames and tossed them across streets, igniting rooftops—and screams followed, screams of the injured and dying.

As a secondary diversion the Carver and the Confucian carried the large mahogany box that had once contained the Tusk through the southern exit of the Warrens. As they did, Jiang emerged from a western exit yelling at a strangely dressed porter who carried a large, stiff carpet on his shoulder.

"Hurry, you slug! And watch my carpet! If it burns, you burn with it!" Jiang was gratified to see that the chaos caused by the fire had drawn every eye. She whispered, "Hurry, a storm is coming."

The Assassin shifted the carpet on his shoulders. He kept his head bowed, but his eyes scanned the street as he followed Jiang to her estab-lishment, the Sacred Tusk safely rolled inside the carpet.

———

Tu smelled the smoke before the others in the room and leaped to his feet. He moved quickly to the tall windows of his warehouse office that over-looked the Suzu Creek. For a moment he couldn't see the smoke, then he saw a tall, thin line seemingly cross the full moon hung low on the eastern horizon.

"Fire, boss?"

Tu thought about that. Fire was not uncommon in the city at the Bend in the River, but he was suspicious.

"Call our lieutenants. We move tonight."

———

The Assassin secreted the Tusk in the velvet-covered box bench that Jiang had prepared in the front room of her brothel, then turned to her.

"He's not a fool."

"Your boss? Is that to whom you refer?"

"Why do you mock me? I serve the Compact as you do."

"I meant no harm," said Jiang, thinking that she "served" the Compact in an even more intimate way with his boss. "So what do you mean by Big-Eared Tu not being a fool?"

"He might find the fire suspicious—its timing, anyway. He might attack the Warrens sooner than he'd planned."

Fine, Jiang thought, *the Tusk is not there.* Then it occurred to her that she could prepare a surprise for Big-Eared Tu's men. Tu might be the Man with a Book, but his men were not. Robbing Tu Yueh-sen of at least some of his thugs struck Jiang as a good idea, and an opportunity for a bit of revenge for the pain and financial losses he had inflicted on her. She dismissed Loa Wei Fen and sent for Mai Bao.

An hour later her handsome middle daughter bobbed a bow and said, "Mother, you sent for me?"

"I did. I need your help." Quickly Jiang asked her daughter to contact the police officer with whom she'd had an affair.

Mai Bao's hand flew to the neck of her robe as if she had exposed herself, but all she managed to say was, "Mother!"

Jiang swatted the complaint aside. "Tell him that Big-Eared Tu's men will shortly invade the Warrens. His men should be ready."

———

Mai Bao summoned her covered carriage and hopped into the back seat as four coolies pulled the thing into motion. The inside of the carriage was dark and it took a moment for her eyes to adjust. When they did, she was shocked to see her ex-lover, the Revolutionary, sitting across from her. The wine stain on his face seemed to pulse with the blood captured there.

"Riding with coolies pulling you, like any empress." He momentarily looked out the window and then snapped the covering shut. He looked her full in the face and screamed, "Men are not beasts!" Before she knew it he had a clump of her hair in his hand and was twisting it downward as hard as he could. She fell to her knees before him, and he reached down and yanked her face up to see his. "Open your eyes, whore."

Slowly Mai Bao opened her eyes. She was shocked to see the hatred in the Revolutionary's face. "What do you want with me?"

"So are you bringing the clouds and rain to the fat White man now?"

She went to move her head away, but his fingers dug deep into her face; a nail cut her cheek, sending a single ribbon of blood over his hand and down her neck.

"First they take our country, then our women."

Mai Bao remembered his violence in pillow matters. His disdain for children, his angry refusal of intercourse in favour of more rudimentary forms of pleasure. Then she saw the glint of a knife in his free hand. With supreme effort she calmed her racing heart, then reached a hand forward toward his centre and rested it there. The rage didn't diminish in his eyes, but she felt him swell beneath her fingers.

Then he threw her hand aside and demanded, "Where are you going, and in such haste?"

Relieved that it seemed he didn't want sex in any form, she told him about going to the police to get them into the Warrens to ambush Gangster Tu.

"What is Gangster Tu doing in the Warrens?"

For a beat she didn't know what to say, then she said simply, "Stealing something hidden there, I assume."

The moment her words were out of her mouth a smile crossed her ex-lover's face. He flung open the door, ordered the coolies to stop, and jumped down. While holding the door open he turned back to Mai Bao and then casually spat in her face.

"Thanks, whore. You may have served your people in spite of yourself."

———

"I'm not sure I like the new bench," the ancient Go player said as Jiang entered the reception hall of her brothel.

"Why would that be, old man?"

"I noticed that in the games I've played since sitting on this new bench my thinking has been somehow slowed."

"Is the bench uncomfortable for your bony bottom?"

"No. And thank you for mentioning my bottom. It has been many years since a courtesan deigned to discuss my posterior."

"My pleasure, I think," Jiang said, anxious to end the conversation about the newly arrived, velvet-covered, six-foot-long box bench.

"What happened to my old stool?" the ancient Go player asked.

"We're having it bronzed and a plaque affixed to it."

"And this plaque says?" the Go player inquired with a smile.

"*Upon this simple stool, a Go player's rump did sit.*"

"Poetic, but I think it's missing something."

"And that would be?" Jiang asked cautiously.

"The words *brilliant* and *much desired*, as in: Upon this simple stool, a brilliant Go player's much desired rump did sit."

"Fine. A fine correction. I will be sure to get that to the engraver."

"Do so quickly, please. I will not live forever."

Jiang thought, *Perhaps not forever, but you have already lived for the better part of forever*. Then she noticed his keen eyes and, not for the first time, wondered if he had guessed what lay inside his newly acquired but evidently uncomfortable box bench.

She ordered him sweetmeats and a glass of wine, then sat down opposite him.

"A game?" he suggested, clearly surprised.

"No. I have no need to be shown how talented you are at the board." She paused, looked around her, then said, "We have known each other for a long time."

"Known each other only the once, and that was for a long time, but a long time ago." He smiled his crooked smile and said, "So what is in the box upon which my bony bottom sits?"

chapter thirty-four
Attack on the Warrens

Mai Bao's message to her ex-lover the detective was received at eleven-thirty that night. By dawn the police had established seven major traps for Gangster Tu and his men throughout the vast tunnel complex of the Warrens.

By nine that morning the Revolutionary had his six cadres positioned and ready to move.

By noon the fire was under control.

By three o'clock the Dowager Empress's troops had completed their encirclement of the city at the Bend in the River, as she had promised Tu.

At four o'clock precisely, the Revolutionary's six cadres, in a daring raid, overpowered a lightly guarded city arsenal and, for the first time in their existence, had the means in hand to foment the bloody revolution of which they had been dreaming for almost a decade.

As the sun set, Tu Yueh-sen's Incense Master started the blood ceremonies that always preceded a major Triad battle action. The slaughtered calf's blood ran down the corners of the mouths of the ninety or so initiates as they completed the most ancient of Triad rites on the wild side of the Huangpo River, the Pudong.

The initiates had to pass through three specially constructed arches. Above the first, between crossed swords, were carved the characters *On Entering the Door, Do Not Proceed Further If You Are Not Loyal.* Above the second arch was written *Before the Gate of Loyalty and Righteousness All Men Are Equal.* After passing through this arch, the initiates were required to pay a fee—a fee so high it would have been prohibitive to all but the rich and the larcenous. The third arch, The Gate of Heaven and Earth Circle, was inscribed with the words *Through the Heaven and Earth Circle Are Born the Hung Heroes*. It was only after passing through this final gate that the initiates would be tested and then symbolically reborn as Triad members. They washed their faces, removed their clothing, donned white robes and straw sandals—their old lives washed away. Then they were moved to the altar.

Once more the Incense Master took control of the ceremony. Thirty-six oaths were sworn by each initiate, who was then offered a knife that he used to seal his oaths in blood. A chicken was killed and its blood dripped into a large bowl of wine. A sheaf of yellow paper was burned and the ashes added to the bowl. Each of the initiates drank deeply, and afterwards the bowl was broken to illustrate what happens to those who break their oath.

The *Fan Kuei*'s spies had been screaming warnings at their European and American masters for almost twenty-four hours, but what exactly they were concerned about remained a mystery. They spoke of smelling change in the air, then ranted on about an ancient prophetic relic, and finally they spoke of death and change and what every Chinese person feared most in the world—chaos.

Many of the newly arrived *Fan Kuei* traders dismissed these reports as mere "Chink superstition," but the older trading houses were not so sure. They had learned, often at great cost, that the Chinese were a practical people. The simple fact of their huge population and the incumbent need of feeding so many mouths made the Chinese decision-making process both basic and practical. Chinese history seldom produced ranting mad-men. There were very few Chinese Ezekiels or Elijiahs or John the Baptists. Those were desert creations able to exist only where there was more space than people—and way too much time to contemplate the world rather than live in it. Despite his religious babble, even Hung Hsiu-ch'uan, the leader of the Taiping Rebellion, had proved to be more the leader of an agrarian poverty revolt than a prophet.

So when the spies reported to their *Fan Kuei* bosses at Dent and Company and Jardine Matheson and to Silas Hordoon, the respective Taipans of these great old mercantile empires metaphorically and literally circled the wagons. Runners were sent to the family homes of the major employees and family members. Quickly they put into effect an emergency plan that had been developed many years before. Hansom carriages with armed guards arrived at every *Fan Kuei* family home, and within three hours the major employees and their families were safely inside their respective headquarters either on the Bund or on Bubbling Spring Road. In either case, the fortress-like structures were quickly surrounded by several rings of armed troops, both Sikh and British, bayonets at the ready and with orders to shoot to kill anyone who approached the great trading houses of Shanghai.

At midnight the initiates of the Tong of the Righteous Hand, led by the Incense Master, poured through the open door of a hot water shop, down the hidden basement steps, and into the most southerly entrance of the Warrens.

Moments later the disgraced Red Pole led over a hundred seasoned Tong fighters through the well-known western entrance. Once underground they fanned out into the dozens of ancillary tunnels that splayed out like the fingers of the Yangtze as it approached the China Sea.

As they did, Loa Wei Fen led the third of Tu's raiding parties into the Warrens from the east.

It was a massive pincer movement intended to prevent any egress of the Tusk or its keepers. The north end of the Warrens was bounded by the Huangpo River, and the Carver's son had identified the Tusk's hidden chamber in the north central section of the Warrens.

The moment that Loa Wei Fen slid down the ancient rope ladder to the lowest level of the Warrens he knew that something was wrong—very wrong. There were traces of too many people in the underground tunnels! He smelled their fear—the fear of many more men than Gangster Tu had ordered into the Warrens that morning. Then he heard the echo of gunfire in the enclosed underground tunnels—to him a new and truly terrifying sound.

The battle was a grudge match for the police. For years they'd lived in fear of the Triads, maligned by the *Fan Kuei* and disrespected by their own people. Their leaders took bribes and betrayed them, and they were constantly accused of cowardice in the face of Triad violence. But it was time to prove they were men. Under the leadership of Mai Bao's ex-lover, they would, unlike so many times in the past, fight for their honour. Surprise was on their side this time, and they had every intention of taking full advantage of that ... advantage.

And they did.

First in the south tunnels, where they slaughtered almost all of the Tong of the Righteous Hand initiates within the first twenty minutes. Only the Incense Master and six of his men escaped, as the Incense Master had chosen to lead from behind. Some managed to backtrack and reach street level, but the police pursued them, shooting many in the back.

Then the police began to fall in a hail of bullets.

Much to everyone's surprise, young Chinese men were shooting at the police who worked for the *Fan Kuei*. Shooting and killing many. Then these young Chinese men, the Revolutionary's men, turned their rifles toward the *Fan Kuei's* buildings and began to hunt the Foreign Devils in their midst.

The first *Fan Kuei* to die was a clerk in the service of Dent and Company, who had only a day earlier arrived from his posting in Cape Town. He literally took a wrong turn looking for an outhouse, and a bullet caught him in the shoulder. Before he fell to the ground he was surrounded by a group of screaming young Chinese men, two of whom held him against a wall while a third raised a remarkably sharp knife that removed his head from his neck in three quick strokes.

For what seemed forever the body staggered as if somehow still alive before it fell forward to the cracked pavement.

And Shanghai held its breath.

With the police busy fending off the Revolutionary's cadres while at the same time manning traps in the depths of the Warrens, *Fan Kuei* Shanghai lay basically unprotected. The Triads had no quarrel with the Revolutionary's cadres, nor did the hundreds of eyes that watched in fascination as *Fan Kuei* power seemed to disappear like a bad dream with the coming of the dawn. Weapons appeared in the hands of men who had never shown their weapons in public. Women strode forward with cleavers. Children stood by their parents as they set out to settle old scores with the hated *Fan Kuei*.

———

While the revenge began on the streets, below street level, in the Warrens, another war proceeded toward a conclusion and its prize.

In the absolute darkness of the Warrens' tunnels two questions raced through Loa Wei Fen's mind. The angry young carver must have somehow followed his father to the Tusk, but had he seen any of the Chosen Three? More particularly, had he seen him? The Assassin's second question was even more pressing: where in the Warrens' darkness was the Red Pole he had disgraced to get into the good graces of Tu Yueh-sen?

Loa Wei Fen led his men directly toward the Tusk's hidden chamber. The quicker they could prove the absence of the Tusk to Gangster Tu, the quicker he could get out of the darkness of the Warrens. The combination of the physical restriction of the narrow tunnels and the darkness nullified the advantage of his years of training. In the dark, narrow tunnels, a stupid man with a stupid gun could defeat a skilled assassin—and Loa Wei Fen knew it.

Loa Wei Fen put his ear to the wet southern wall of the tunnel. It took him a moment to adjust to the natural sounds of the river in the rock. Once he recognized the rhythm of the water he began to hear other rhythms deep in the stone. From the north he heard the disorganized scuffing of boots on rock—policemen? From the south, stealthy, quick movements that might have been the Incense Master's southern advance. Loa Wei Fen was surprised by a slight scraping sound that seemed to come from above, far along the tunnel, maybe halfway between where he and his men crouched and the chamber in which the Tusk had been successfully hidden for all those years. Hidden until about this time yesterday, when he had delivered it in the midst of the great fire to Jiang's.

Loa Wei Fen split his men into three groups. One group was to stay and control the tunnel and guard his back. The second group he sent south at the fork just ahead of them, while he led the third group due north toward the strange scraping that he heard yet again.

———

The Red Pole adjusted the metal belt buckle he had taken from the body of the dead police officer. Shanghai police officers were so proud of those belts and buckles. Well, now it was a trophy he would give his Mountain Master, Tu Yueh-sen.

The Red Pole sent his men south, then headed toward a hiding place he had found as a boy. It was a low-ceilinged ledge running above the route he knew the hated Loa Wei Fen would take. The hiding place was a lot tighter now than it had been when he was a boy, and he heard his belt buckle scrape against the low ceiling of the shelf as he turned to take up the position of his ambush.

He readied his new pistol. A single shot from the dark would end his disgrace and humble the mighty Loa Wei Fen, who had taken his place in the hierarchy of the Tong of the Righteous Hand.

———

Loa Wei Fen passed the niche that contained the heavy ancient statue of Chesu Hoi that the carvers venerated. He was within three hundred yards of the hidden entrance to the Tusk's chamber when he saw a lit torch in the crevice of the south wall.

Then he heard the scraping rasp in the rock again, this time much closer and higher up. Was there a hidden shelf above?

A distinctive metal *clack*. A gun being cocked? He quickly reached for the torch and doused it against the wall. As he did, he rolled across the smooth tunnel floor—and heard the unmistakable *ting* of a bullet first ricocheting off a wall, then hitting the barrel of his gun, throwing it far into the darkness. A second shot skipped off the wall and ripped most of his left ear from his head. Reaching for his ear he stumbled forward and kicked his weapon sharply into the darkness.

Loa Wei Fen lay flat. When he heard the thud of sandalled feet ahead of him on the stone floor of the tunnel he rolled and scrambled to his feet. He thought of trying to find his gun in the darkness, then discarded that idea and raced down the tunnel, bouncing off the walls as he ran. A third bullet, then a fourth pinged past him.

Loa Wei Fen ignored the blood flowing down his neck and ran with his hand out against the wall on his left, trying to find the niche that contained the statue of the First Emperor's Eunuch, the original Chesu Hoi. Then a bullet tore through his left shoulder and flung him full force into the very crevice that contained the heavy ancient statue of the Carvers' patron.

———

The Red Pole was convinced that he had hit Loa Wei Fen. He was amazed that the man hadn't fired back. Assuming the man must have dropped his weapon, he raced down the tunnel firing as he went, thinking that it was only a matter of time before he came across his enemy's dead body.

He felt something hard crack into his side and he staggered against the far wall.

Then another thing he knew was a heel of an open palm slammed into the tip of his nose with such force that it drove the bridge into the frontal lobe of his brain.

———

Loa Wei Fen stuffed the Red Pole's body into the crevice, then forced the statue of Chesu Hoi back into place to hide the body.

He was gasping for breath and weak from loss of blood, but he knew that his wounds would heal—that he knew—and at least now he also knew the answer to one of his two questions.

———

An hour later they were all gathered in the secret chamber. No one said a word. Loa Wei Fen thought that the deep chamber somehow echoed with its own silence. Then he saw the young carver staring at him, and he thought he knew the unfortunate answer to his other question. But before the young carver could approach Tu Yueh-sen, the Mountain Master of the Tong of the Righteous Hand screamed a profanity and kicked the jade stands that had, until yesterday, held the First Emperor's prophetic Tusk.

Then he turned to the young carver and with one slashing motion of his blade solved the Assassin's dilemma. Tu Yueh-sen turned to his men in the sacred cavern and shouted, "Clear the tunnels of the *Fan Kuei*'s police, then the streets of the *Fan Kuei*. Every day they walk upon our land they sin against the sacred soil of the Middle Kingdom."

———

And so they first made the tunnels of the Warrens run with blood of the *Fan Kuei*'s lackeys, then they emerged from the tunnels and went after those who controlled the police—the *Fan Kuei*.

And on the streets they were gleefully joined by the six armed cadres of the Revolutionary, already drunk on blood, as well as many, many ordinary Chinese who had simply had enough of *Fan Kuei* rules. Three men pried loose the sign on the Bund Promenade that said "No Dogs or Chinese Allowed" and tossed it far out into the Huangpo.

Then the city exhaled all at once and the slaughter of the *Fan Kuei* began. The years of pent-up pain born of disrespect and hate were finally loosed—and for the first time in *Fan Kuei* history at the Bend in the River they were no longer the rulers. No, they were the hunted.

When dawn finally broke, *Fan Kuei* corpses were hoisted on poles and the news spread. Canton erupted in rage at the *Fan Kuei* overlords, and then Beijing exploded, aided by the Dowager Empress, who publicly pronounced that it was time to rid the Middle Kingdom, her Celestial Kingdom, of every Foreign Devil—now!

———

Father Pierre had been an old man for a very long time. He had outlived his madam sister and pulled the appropriate Jesuitical strings to have her body buried in hallowed ground. He had returned to Paris twice in his sixty years at the Bend in the River. And both his cathedral, the Cathedral of St. Ignatius, and diocese had continued to grow, even after he lost his sight sometime in the late 1880s. He didn't remember exactly when. Many of his memories were mixed up now. He'd been having a lot of conversations lately with the red-haired Jew who died fighting for the Taipingers. Yes, many long talks lately—communions. He'd begun to look forward to those times. In fact, he was pretty sure it was that Maxi character who had just opened the door to the east transept of his cathedral. That door squeaked differently than the other doors. And naturally the Jew would use that door; after all, the east transept door led to La Rue des Juifs. Although this Jew was certainly a warrior, not a moneylender.

Father Pierre turned his sightless eyes toward the opening east transept door.

—

The Revolutionary saw him first. There on his damned knees, like the other Black Robes he and his men had just finished murdering. But he wasn't mumbling ridiculous verses like the other fools, he was smiling and signalling him to come—to approach—to take his hand.

—

Father Pierre sensed his old friend's approach and waggled his fingers in Maxi's direction. Of late he'd liked having his hands held. He was cold, always cold now. "Take my hand, old friend," he said.

—

The Revolutionary heard the man call out in his direction in some foreign language. He assumed it was French. He didn't care which foul *Fan Kuei* language it was. He just wanted it to stop. Wanted the foreigners gone from his home. He screamed at the kneeling fool, "Shut up, old man!"

—

"Maxi, you're very loud today. I'm blind, not deaf." Father Pierre laughed at his own joke. "Come take my hand, old friend." He held his hand out farther but didn't still feel Maxi's hand. Finally he said, "Okay, don't, if that pleases you."

—

The man's hand stopped waving in his direction and it made a gesture that the Revolutionary understood to mean "okay." So the Revolutionary drew his sword and cut the hand cleanly from the wrist.

A shock of pain raced through Father Pierre's arm and he vaulted to his feet and then threw himself backward, away from the pain.

The Revolutionary was surprised by the man's reaction. Before the man's severed hand hit the floor, the man's body landed in the midst of a large floral display.

———

"Easy there, old fellow, you'll hurt yourself," Maxi said as he gently put Father Pierre back on his feet. "And you'll be needing this where you're going," he added as he gave the old priest back his severed hand.

"Where am I going?" Father Pierre asked.

———

The Revolutionary was shocked to see the old priest get up from the floral display, cross the aisle, and pick up his severed hand.

———

"Come now," Maxi said.

"No. Where am I going?"

"You know the answer to that," Maxi said with a smile. "You're the priest, after all, aren't you?"

"I am. Yes, friend, I am."

———

The Revolutionary watched in horror as Father Pierre Colombe of Paris, France, lately of Shanghai, took twenty-six steps and then laid his head on the high altar, and once there moved his head a single time as if to hear some final words—from his God.

———

"Good, very good." Maxi's voice was very near to Father Pierre's ear. "You work and work and when you cannot work any more—you rest. Come, old friend. You've worked enough."

———

The Revolutionary heard a sigh come from the old priest. Then his eyes opened wide, and the Revolutionary knew the blind man had, in the last moment of his life, seen … something that he would never see, no matter how long he lived or how keen his sight grew.

* * *

THE KILLING OF FATHER PIERRE and the subsequent torching of the Cathedral of St. Ignatius emboldened still more Chinese with grievances against the *Fan Kuei,* and what could have been a controlled moment of racial viciousness became the beginning of an all-out race war that history would eventually call the Boxer Rebellion.

Rickshaw drivers stopped pulling in deserted alleys and murdered their riders. Cooks who had worked their entire lives in great *Fan Kuei* kitchens poisoned their finest dishes. Writers assassinated their publishers. Chambermaids attacked their mistresses while they slept. Even the wealthy Hong merchants and compradors, scenting a change in the air, supplied food, arms, and succor to the Boxer rebels.

The city at the Bend in the River—the sixth-largest trading port in the world, the place where White men made fortunes—shook at its centre and seemed about to throw those who lived at its very peak into the depths.

The Dowager Empress, ignoring the protests of her nephew, the Emperor, pressed her advantage, opening Manchu armories to the rebels and offering a cash payment for every *Fan Kuei* head. At the same time she kept increasing the pressure on Gangster Tu. She was certain that he had the relic, and that he was either going to try to start a dynasty of his own with it, or at the very least extort huge sums of money from her for the prophetic Tusk. She did not for a moment believe the note she received from the gangster claiming that the Tusk had not been where he had been told it was.

She ordered the troops she had surrounding Shanghai into the city to aid the rebels and called on them to "Bring me the head of the big-eared gangster!"

———

For the first time in his life Tu Yueh-sen felt fear. He knew that someone had betrayed him, and although at first he thought it was the carver's angry son, he changed his mind when the disgraced Red Pole's body was found crushed behind the ancient statue in the Warrens.

And then there was the price put on his head by the Manchus—and Manchu bannermen entering his city.

First things first, he thought. *Find the betrayer, then get him to reveal the Tusk's hiding place, then present the Tusk to the Empress, and that solves that problem.*

But who was the betrayer in their midst? The disgraced Red Pole and the carver's angry son were dead. The only other people who had known enough to betray him were his Incense Master, his head sycophant, and his first lieutenant, Loa Wei Fen.

As the war raged on the streets he did what the head of any large business concern would do. He called a meeting.

* * *

THE WARRENS WERE NO LONGER a safe place to meet, and the streets were dangerous both day and night, but the Chosen Three had to meet to decide the Tusk's future.

"In plain sight," the Confucian's note to the others suggested. They considered the Temple of the City God after morning prayers, but eventually settled on the ancient Long Hua Temple at the end of the Buddhist festival scheduled, despite the violence, for the following day.

———

Mai Bao was surprised to get the summons from her mother and hoped that nothing was wrong. She gave Silas an excuse that she knew he didn't completely believe, then left the wall-encircled gardens she'd begun to love and the houses she now thought of as home. Before leaving, she tiptoed into the girls' sleeping quarters and pressed her beautiful lips to the foreheads of the two youngest girls in their tiny beds.

"Take the carriage," Silas said. "MacMillan will drive you."

"I would prefer not," she said, then added, "I need you to trust me on this. I'll be safe. I have many people looking out for my well-being."

Silas looked at the tall, handsome woman who now shared both his bed and his life, and he first silently thanked the gods for her, then wondered at how little of her he really knew. She was attentive to his needs and wants and always at his side when he wished, but there were dark shadows in her that he, in his late middle age, knew he would never understand, and was perhaps not entitled to understand. Did she love another?

Had there been a great love in her life before him that she couldn't forget? He didn't know, and he knew he would never know.

———

Mai Bao spotted her mother on her knees, four lit incense sticks perfuming the fetid air as she rolled them slowly between her palms in solemn prayer. On the far side of the narrow hall, before the towering gold-plated Buddha, was the man she recognized as her mother's strange confidant, the Confucian. Beside him was a man with an arm in a sling and a bloody poultice wrapped around his head over his left ear.

"You're late," Jiang snapped.

"The streets are full of madness."

"True, daughter, but for meetings of the Ivory Compact you are never again to be late." Then, right there on their knees, with incense sticks rolling in rhythm between their palms, mother told daughter of the history of the ancient Ivory Compact—of the obligation to bring on the darkness of the Age of White Birds on Water, then to find the Man with a Book who would lead them to the revival of the Age of the Seventy Pagodas.

Mai Bao, like most Shanghainese, had heard stories of an old prophetic whale bone or some such, but had noted, then ignored them as superstitious hocus-pocus, probably generated by the Taoist priests to frighten the populace.

"So it is true, Mother?"

"It is the truest thing in my life. Even truer than you and your sisters. And to you I pass on this truth, this obligation in the Ivory Compact, all my worldly possessions, and my name, Jiang. But only if you accept the obligation of the Ivory Compact by getting the First Emperor's Narwhal Tusk to safety."

"But how can I better manage that than you or anyone else?"

"Because your husband has the wherewithal to manage this task. All you need do is use what you learned as a courtesan and ask this favour of him."

Mai Bao starred at her mother. So many pieces of her own life fell into place at that moment. Little mysteries were resolved. Suddenly she wondered if it had been an accident that she had come upon her mother crying in her private rooms over the removal of her friend's body from the Flower World's cemetery. Had her mother set all that in motion once she had given birth to her daughters, so that she would meet and marry Silas Hordoon? Her husband was certainly a Man with a Book—Richard Hordoon's opium dream diary—and someone who would have the wherewithal to move the First Emperor's Tusk to safety.

Then, as quickly as her suspicions came up, Mai Bao dismissed them. She was honoured to represent her family in the Ivory Compact and, after a quick introduction to the Confucian and the Assassin, promised to provide safe sanctuary for the most powerful relic beneath the heavens.

"Where is the Tusk now, Mother?"

"Nearby, easily accessible. Provide me with your plan and I will show you the Tusk's location."

"Do you not trust me, Mother?"

"I trust you, or I would not have revealed my greatest secret, bestowed my greatest gift. But should you fail to develop a plan to my liking I will have you removed by Loa Wei Fen and offer your place to your younger sister. This is not a beauty contest or a singing competition. The Tusk's safety is crucial to the future of the Black-Haired people. We will, as the First Emperor said, 'Either rise as a great nation or be picked apart by carrion birds.' My obligation to the Ivory Compact far supersedes my obligation to any of my daughters. Do you understand that, Mai Bao?"

"I do, Mother. As my obligation to the Compact will supersede my obligation to my two daughters."

Jiang smiled and touched Mai Bao's strong features in what, in a Christian country, would have been called a mother's blessing. Finally she withdrew her hand and said, "How are my granddaughters?"

"They prosper. One looks exactly like you, Mother."

"And are they happy inside your racetrack garden walls?"

"They are, Mother."

"I would like to see them before I die."

"I will arrange it. I promise. But since I managed to include them both as two of our ten street children, you will have to come and visit all the children, not just them."

"Fine. I'm sure I can pick out which two are my grandchildren."

"I have no doubt."

"And when will you tell them, Mai Bao, who they really are?"

"On the day you pass on from this world, leaving us all behind, Mother."

Jiang nodded. Suddenly she was so tired that she could hardly stand. "Good. Yes. Very good, Mai Bao. Shortly thereafter you'll have to begin to test them."

"As you did me, Mother."

"Yes, as I did you. For only one daughter can succeed you in the Ivory Compact."

Mai Bao nodded and touched her fingers to her mother's beautiful lips, and for the first time in her life she saw her mother cry and had absolutely no doubt that the tears were real.

* * *

AS GANGSTER TU'S MEETING BEGAN, Loa Wei Fen, for the hundredth time, considered killing Tu, as he was sure that the man's search for the betrayer was narrowing quickly to him. But he reminded himself that under his obligation to the Ivory Compact he could not, since it was possible that Tu Yueh-sen was the Man with a Book, and even in these desperate times Tu's power was considerable, although reduced by the Manchu price on his head.

As was usual in Big-Eared Tu's meetings, he and his sycophant, the Straw Sandal, did most of the talking. In this meeting the Incense Master punctuated many of the Straw Sandal's remarks with harsh throat clearings and the odd well-timed spit.

Loa Wei Fen did not speak as accusations flew all around him.

Tu took a single step toward the Assassin and commanded, "Surrender your swalto blade!"

The cobra carved on his back uncoiled and its hood filled with blood. Giving up the swalto was like defanging the serpent. Loa Wei Fen reached for his swalto and the handle of the blade turned in his hand, found purchase, ready to act at his slightest command.

Then Loa Wei Fen flipped the swalto over, catching the blade in his open hand, and extended the handle to Gangster Tu.

Tu took the swalto and in one motion plunged the blade into the Incense Master's heart. He yanked the knife free of the man's chest and shoved the already dead body aside.

Loa Wei Fen accepted the return of his knife and asked, "Why kill him?"

"Because it is important to keep one's friends close but one's enemies closer—isn't it?" Gangster Tu said, staring into Loa Wei Fen's eyes. "And that is that. I must consult the *I Ching* to see what I should do next. Come," he ordered the Straw Sandal.

Left alone with the body of the Incense Master, Loa Wei Fen carefully cleaned his swalto on the man's elaborate silk robe, then hoisted him on his shoulder—much as he had hoisted the Tusk in the rug less than a week before. He noted that the man was much lighter than the First Emperor's Narwhal Tusk—destiny weighs more heavily on man than life itself.

Then he thought of Gangster Tu's threat about keeping enemies close, and his devotion to the *I Ching*, and the Straw Sandal who claimed to interpret it. Loa Wei Fen was sure that Tu was not the looked-for Man with a Book in the second window of the Tusk, but Tu was his charge, and he would not betray his obligation to the Ivory Compact. He felt something in his hand and looked down. His swalto blade was ready—ready to defend him.

———

Tu Yueh-sen was a Han Chinese male, and as such was by nature practical. However, the *I Ching*—the ancient book of changes—appeared to offer him a new way of interpreting events. The *I Ching*, one of China's oldest texts, contained a symbol system designed to identify order in what seem like chance events. From randomness it discerned patterns. Its philosophy centred on the ideas of the dynamic balance of opposites, the evolution of events as a process, and acceptance of the inevitability of change. The Chinese people believed in change and the fact that deep within events that seemed chaotic there was often a progression. The *I Ching* taught a system for understanding the hidden patterns. Besides, Tu Yueh-sen liked the air of spiritual authority that citing the old book gave his orders. And on more occasions than one he had changed his plans after consulting the ancient text, and through its insights saw the hidden layer of logic beneath what seemed like whimsical, unrelated events.

It was, in fact, on the advice of the hidden pattern the *I Ching* had revealed to him that he had spared Loa Wei Fen's life, following the instruction to "suppress your first impulse but follow your second promptings even to a death." Tu also knew that if Loa Wei Fen was the traitor he would never admit it, let alone tell him where the Tusk was hidden, no matter what form of torture was used on him. Perhaps threatening his boys would do something. But Tu was cautious about crossing that line. So for now he would keep the man close and use him as the most accomplished bodyguard in Shanghai—a role, unbeknownst to Gangster Tu, that Loa Wei Fen's ancient ancestor had played for the First Emperor, Q'in She Huang himself.

And so it was that Loa Wei Fen found himself accompanying Gangster Tu to Jiang's the next evening, where the man, to the Assassin's horror, decided to challenge the ancient Go player, whose bony backside sat upon the new bench inside of which was hidden the First Emperor's prophetic Narwhal Tusk.

Sitting opposite the old man, Tu said, "Throwing my *I Ching* this morning revealed an interesting piece of advice."

"And that would be?" asked the Go player as he scratched his grizzled chin.

"That 'beneath a game, truth lies.'"

The old Go player nodded for several excruciating seconds, then said, "You want to play black or white?"

"White, old man, so you go first."

"A wager could increase the interest in ..."

"If you win, I'll buy you the services of any courtesan in the place."

"For an entire night?"

"For as long as you stay awake."

The ancient Go player chuckled and rubbed his swollen knuckles, knowing he had enough money to buy a fine strong tortoise. He would have its neck pulled out as far as it could go, then he would bite into it, swallowing as much of the animal's adrenalin-rich blood as possible, so as to swell his member for the evening's revels.

"And in the unlikely circumstance that you win, Tu Yueh-sen, what forfeit do I owe you?"

"The truth beneath the game—as the *I Ching* foretold."

The Go player shifted his bony bottom along the top of the new bench and longed for his old chair. "White goes first," he said, and placed an initial stone in the upper quadrant of the board, already anticipating the joys of his night to come.

Loa Wei Fen caught Jiang's eye as the Go player continued to fidget on his new bench while the game quickly progressed.

"Sit still, old man!" Gangster Tu said as he failed to complete the necessary double eye to keep his white pieces safe from the black encirclement.

"As you wish," the Go player said, secure in the fact that the whole north-west quadrant of the board was in his control and the south-east quadrant was going to be a draw. All he needed to do was move carefully, one counter of his for each of the gangster's counters, and he would force a draw on the two remaining quadrants, giving him a free, tortoise-adrenalin-assisted night with the courtesan of his choice. Perhaps the very young one—the new one. Or maybe it was time to try a *Fan Kuei* ... no, the young, new one, for sure.

He allowed himself to smile about that, although he was not pleased that he felt almost no motion in his jade spear. The pace of the play picked up. Only one quadrant remained. Six moves—seven—and even the fool across the table from him saw that it was useless. The old man had defeated one of the most powerful men in Shanghai at a game whose outcome was the direct result of skill alone. Luck had nothing to do with determining the winner of a game of Go.

Tu in one swipe knocked the pieces from the board. They tinkled to the floor and bounced about. Then the gangster smiled at the old Go player. "You win."

"I do," the Go player said, trying hard to keep the joy out of his voice as he looked at the man he thought of as Elephant-Eared Tu.

* * *

THE REBELLION QUICKLY SPREAD and picked up ferocity. No *Fan Kuei* was safe on the streets of the cities of the Middle Kingdom. During the day police would try to reassert their power despite ever-increasing desertions from their ranks, but as soon as the sun set the rebels were back in full control of the streets.

The Revolutionary's troops had swelled almost a hundredfold. His initial six cadres were now the vanguard of a People's Army. Manchu raiders were in the streets of the city at the Bend in the River looking for Gangster Tu. Gangster Tu's men were under orders to search for the Tusk and kill any *Fan Kuei* who stood in their way, and thousands upon thousands of unaligned Chinese took full advantage of the breakdown in order either to settle old scores or to simply rob and plunder.

Fan Kuei women, if caught, were gang-raped; men were beheaded. China's first race war was picking up steam. Every major Shanghai building was festooned with red banners proclaiming revolutionary slogans, and most large walls were covered in revolutionary posters that were whitewashed over during the day only to re-emerge in the morning with slashes of violent colour and statements of open racial hatred.

———

Heyward Matheson, the leader of Jardine Matheson, stood before a full-length portrait of old Hercules MacCallum in the company's offices. The Hercules in the painting had broad shoulders and smouldering eyes, which never betrayed the fact that his gout had spread as he aged. He had finally died in agony, which only his personal bravery allowed him to keep from all but his closest associates.

"They've had their fun," Matheson said. "Now it's time this nonsense was ended."

The American trading houses quickly agreed.

Even the French, after Father Pierre's murder, were willing to join the other traders—a first in the history of Shanghai.

Only Silas Hordoon deferred comment as he recalled the Kipling story of how fear had come to the jungle.

"Be thee with us, Mr. Hordoon?" Heyward Matheson asked, his brogue broadening as he spoke.

Silas thought of the "eyes watching" that his father's opium diaries often mentioned. Finally he asked, "What exactly do you propose?"

"To teach these heathens a lesson," said the head of Oliphant and Company.

"Exactly to which heathens do you refer, Mr. Oliphant?" Silas asked softly.

Recognizing his faux pas, the Oliphant man spluttered, "The murderous ones, naturally."

"You wouldn't, then, be including me, as a Jew, amongst the heathens you'd teach a lesson, or our Papist French allies, or perhaps my Chinese wife?"

Chastised, the head of the House of Zion said, "Not them," although it was evident that he'd love to include "those heathens" too.

After an hour more of contemplation, and a stern warning from William Dent that no company was to gain financially from the coming military action, the traders returned to their offices under tight security and contacted their political masters in their respective countries of origin. They had little doubt they would be successful in their request for military support, since taxes on the imports of their goods from China made up as much as a quarter of all government revenues. In fact, most European countries would have gone bankrupt without the tax revenue generated by the import of Chinese goods.

Only Silas didn't make such contact. Instead he sent a message to Charles Soong, his brother-in-law: "This madness must stop."

———

Charles knew that Silas was right, but he felt powerless to stop the carnage. He couldn't even control the men he employed, some of whom he suspected of being part of the rebellion. His papers all preached against the Boxers, although Charles noticed a definite softening of the stance from many of his younger writers—and one of his older ones.

Charles put aside Silas's note and reviewed his meeting of the previous night with Dr. Sun Yat-sen and the man he was now referring to as his "Generalissimo," Chiang Kai Shek. He remembered their heated argument as to whether the Boxer Rebellion furthered their cause of dethroning the Manchus or not. "Our revolution must be in two parts," he had argued. "First, dethrone the Q'ing Dynasty, and then displace the *Fan Kuei* gradually. If the *Fan Kuei* leave suddenly, businesses everywhere in the Middle Kingdom will fail. People will starve, and that will allow the Manchus to reassert control. Their regime will just continue on as if nothing has changed."

Chiang Kai Shek had retorted, "Any action is good action. Stir the pot," he'd said. "It can't be worse than now." Then he had added, in what Charles thought of as typical to his way of thinking, "They're fucking our women. Look at your sister-in-law."

Charles tried to remember the last comment from Chiang Kai Shek that hadn't included some reference to "his" women. He looked to Dr. Sun Yat-sen and couldn't get over the feeling that the good doctor hadn't been able to follow the basic arguments being put forward.

"And that thing with the children! Disgusting!" the Generalissimo added.

Charles sighed. Despite himself, he liked the Persian Jew, even though it had hurt his Flower Contests when Silas closed down the Shanghai Race Course, then encircled it with high walls within which he built vast gardens and many homes. Silas's and Mai Bao's taking in of twenty street children and raising them as their own—ten Chinese and ten of mixed race—had made the front page of every paper. Charles himself wrote the lead articles that were picked up and run in newspapers as far away as San Francisco. Later he had tried to establish exactly who the fortunate ten Chinese street children were but had come up against considerable resistance. One tantalizing lead suggested that two of the girls were actually Mai Bao's children that she had given birth to a few years back when she had suddenly disappeared from the Bund in the River. He had cornered his wife, Mai Bao's younger sister, about this, but she had remained evasive. Then she had laughed it off. "My sister is a virgin courtesan, husband. She couldn't have given birth to children, unless the neck of her arhu accidentally impregnated her." Then she laughed again, a sound he found irresistible, and added slyly, "Her silk curtain is still drawn across her jade gate."

Charles nodded. He loved his wife, but the jealousy that she exhibited toward her sister made her opinions on that subject unreliable. He was enticed by the rumour that Mai Bao had had a child with the head police officer who died in the Warrens, and that that child was one of the ten Chinese children taken to grow up in what was quickly becoming known in Shanghai simply as "the Garden."

"Why adopt children? Why not just have children of your own?" he said aloud to Silas's note. Then the answer occurred to him—she wouldn't have it—Mai Bao would not bear mixed-blood children. But why?

The sound of shouting from the streets drew his attention. The Boxers were at it again. He closed his window, then his eyes, and was tempted to pray for the violence to stop.

* * *

WITHIN A MONTH any action that Silas or Charles might have taken was rendered academic. American Marines landed on the Chinese coast just south of Beijing, and within three weeks had ransacked the Dowager Empress's summer residence, packed up and sent back to America for sale all of its furnishings, paintings, and even the Empress's bed, and charged her a personal indemnity of several million dollars. Never had a Chinese ruler been so humbled.

The Boxer Rebellion died as quickly as it had started. Business returned to the Middle Kingdom, and the city at the Bend in the River continued to prosper—but not before the victors punished the vanquished.

chapter thirty-five
Victors and Vanquished:
Mai Bao and Her Revolutionary

"Why are you here? Why is Mai Bao, the famous courtesan and *Fan Kuei* whore, in my cell? Are you a guest of the Shanghai police as well?" The Revolutionary's voice whistled slightly as his breath moved through his shattered teeth. His left arm hung useless at his side, and the swelling of his left cheek, which oddly stretched his wine stain, had almost closed his left eye. "Damn it, I asked why you were here."

"To try and remember," Mai Bao said without inflection.

"Remember what?" the Revolutionary demanded.

"If I loved you." Again Mai Bao's response was simple and to the point.

"Oh, you thought you loved me," the Revolutionary said with a coarse laugh.

Mai Bao allowed herself to look at the dank cell. The hard walls were covered with thin lines, many she feared made by the scraping of human fingernails. Only Silas's vast power had enabled her to get access to her former lover.

"What are you thinking, whore?" he demanded.

Mai Bao allowed his curse to enter her, then dissipate in her heart. "I'm thinking that you think I only thought I loved you."

He shifted on the hard bench and clenched his broken teeth to stifle the pain. "You loved the image of what I represented. The lowly scholar and the courtesan—it's as old as our entire race."

"But it's just an image?"

"Just a foolish old image. Did they tell you it was me who was murdering the Chinese who were *Fan Kuei* collaborators?"

She nodded.

"Good," he said.

"The lead investigator left notes about you."

"You mean your other lover?" he spat out.

"Yes," she said, not bothering to mention that he was also the father of her twin girls.

"And how did he know it was me?"

"Something about barbers. You mumbled something about barbers in your sleep—and I told him."

"And he found them, and they betrayed me?"

She shrugged.

"And where is this genius of yours now?" the Revolutionary asked with a twisted grin.

"He died in the Warrens."

"That's good. Very, very good." He shifted again, and this time couldn't stop the cry of pain. "You wouldn't have a cigarette, would you?"

She had brought a pack of Snake Charmers, which she knew were his favourites. She handed one to him. He took it in his right hand, but it fell through his fingers to the floor. She bent over and picked it up. She put it in her mouth and lit it. Then she placed it between the Revolutionary's scarred lips. He dragged deeply.

"I suppose I should say thank you," he said between the layers of smoke.

"Only if you mean it," she said.

"Bourgeois nonsense."

"Fine," she said. For a moment she wanted just to get out of that awful place, then she gathered her courage and said, "And you never loved me?"

He smirked through the smoke. "I loved hurting you. Loved pulling down your image of what we were doing. Pulling it through the dust and scraping it off the heel of my shoe like dog shit from the street."

She momentarily wavered under his attack, then allowed herself to hear the feelings between the words, just as she heard the notes between the notes on her arhu—and there it was—longing, desperate longing.

"You are going to die," she said.

"Better death than this hateful life."

"Perhaps," she said, but she didn't believe him. She put a hand on his arm and his face softened. The cigarette drooped in his mouth. She took it from his lips and breathed in the harsh smoke. Then she said, "Open your mouth."

He did.

She blew the smoke from her mouth into his mouth and down into his lungs.

Tears filled his eyes.

"Are you frightened of dying?"

He didn't answer. He didn't have to.

She took a deep breath and put the cigarette aside. "Do you still want me?"

He couldn't find his words.

So, wordlessly, she brought on the clouds and rain only hours before he left this earthly plane.

———

That night, when she returned to the safety of her home inside the high walls of the Garden, she walked straight into Silas's private study and took him by the hand and pulled him to their bedroom. She undressed him quickly and then herself. Then she said, "Love me, and make me forget."

And he did.

chapter thirty-six
Victors and Vanquished:
Charles Soong and His Writer

Charles had never been inside a prison—or close to a gallows, like the one that he could see outside the barred window of the tiny cell. Snow was drifting on the cross-arm of the gibbet and piling up on the platform of the scaffold. *Snow in Shanghai?* he thought. *Not unheard of, but unusual. Appropriate weather for a hanging.* Charles pulled his coat tightly about himself and stamped his feet on the stone floor.

He heard the sound of chains rattling and turned to the metal door. It swung open, revealing a beaten figure that used to be Tzu Rong Zi, the writer who wrote the very first story for his very first publication. The man who started him on the road to wealth, marriage, and three children—a fourth on the way. He owed this man something—but what? And how could this old friend have been working with the Boxers? How?

Tzu Rong Zi shuffled toward the table in the centre of the small cell, then stopped. He looked at Charles and said, "Help me sit, will ya?"

Charles quickly stepped forward and offered the man his arm. The writer winced as he bent his knees to sit down. Then he looked up. "You look sad, boss."

Charles sidestepped his knee-jerk reaction to the term "boss" and forced a smile to his face. "How's that? I look sad?"

"Looks like you need a drink, boss, which I could really use. You have any on you?"

Charles shook his head.

"Too bad. A man needs a drink before they put a rope around his neck and yank hard."

There was a lengthy silence. Finally Charles asked, "How could you be part of that? A rioter? A murderer?"

"Or a patriot, boss. Scratch that. I don't give a shit about patriotism."

"Then why were you part of that?"

"Why weren't *you* part of that? That's a better question. Did all your money make you a *Fan Kuei*? Is that it? How does that work?"

Charles stood and looked toward the cell door. Then he turned back. Outside, over Tzu Rong Zi's shoulder, a man was being walked up the steps of the gallows. No, not walked, dragged, pleading.

"A charming way to go, don't you think, boss?"

"An earned way, if he was a murderer."

"Still believe that Protestant eye-for-an-eye crap?"

"Don't you?"

"Not really. If I did, I would have demanded long ago that the *Fan Kuei* kill one of their intellectuals, because they killed that in me." Then he snapped, "Listen to me! I was something before they came. I could sense the long line of scholars going all the way back to the First Emperor. I walked in their footsteps, breathed the air they breathed, and added to the knowledge they had added to. Then the *Fan Kuei* came ..."

"And you became another kind of writer. That's all."

"No. I became a commoner. A pornographer. The lowest form of writer there is. They stole what I was from me."

"Maybe I stole that from you," Charles said.

"Nonsense. It was the *Fan Kuei*, so when ..." There was another long silence in the room. "So do you hate me, boss?"

Charles didn't hate him. He understood him. In his own way he had been working for change too. But not through violence. The old Manchu Dynasty was tottering. It would fall of its own idiocy. He said as much to the writer.

The man shook his head, causing himself to wince. But he managed to speak through the pain. "No. No, boss. You don't understand. The Manchus are too stupid to be real enemies. It's the *Fan Kuei*. The Taipingers had it right. We were just the children of the Taipingers, and our children will carry on their fight. There can be no peace when so many are excluded. None."

"So you are not sorry for what you have done?" Charles asked.

The writer was about to respond when the jarring sound of the trap door in the scaffold slamming open stopped him.

Both men looked out at the man hanging from the thick rope. His neck had not snapped, and he fought against the rope. His legs jerked and kicked. His face turned blue, eyes bulged, blood came from his ears and nose—then finally, blessedly, he stopped struggling—and stood still in the air as snow gathered on his shoulders.

"You sure you didn't bring a drink, boss? A man about to be hanged can really use a drink."

chapter thirty-seven
Time Passes

And life returned, with startling speed, to what people who lived at the Bend in the River thought of as normal.

After the hangings came a brief but severe crackdown by the authorities. Some newspapers considered to be subversive were closed down—none of Charles Soong's publications missed a single edition—public gatherings were limited, and law and order became the watchword. A thousand police officers were hired to replace the four hundred who had been dismissed as rebel sympathizers.

The Cathedral of St. Ignatius was washed clean of its scorch markings and there were plans for a brand-new interior. New stained-glass windows were commissioned, and the high altar upon which Father Pierre died was roped off and viewed as a martyr's site.

Hong merchants mended fences with their *Fan Kuei* overlords and recommenced the business of doing business. The Manchu legions returned to safe barracks upriver or went back to Beijing.

And the Tusk remained in its box bench in the reception room of Jiang's in the French Concession south of Fang Bang Lu in the Old City.

Yin Bao popped out two boys to add to her three girls in, once again, record time. Charles was very pleased with his new sons, and continued to publish his papers during the day and take meetings in private with Dr. Sun Yat-sen and Generalissimo Chiang Kai Shek at night.

Gangster Tu re-emerged and could often be seen dining at the Old Shanghai Restaurant in the company of several young courtesans and his omnipresent bodyguard, Loa Wei Fen. He was constantly on the watch for assassins sent from the Manchu court, as he had never satisfied the Dowager Empress with his explanation that "the Tusk must have been moved from its hiding place in the Warrens before we could get to it." He continued to offer a huge reward to anyone who led him to the Sacred Relic, but there were no takers. He considered his position and decided there might be other ways to attack the *Fan Kuei* than through Beijing. He began to court the Generalissimo, Chiang Kai Shek.

The Generalissimo had a background as cloaked in mystery as any man in China. His family had historic Triad ties, and he'd grown up the pampered son of the wealthy. He'd bought his commission on his twenty-first birthday and found his way to the "good doctor" shortly thereafter. Quickly he'd made himself indispensable to Sun Yat-sen, since he was the only one of the conspirators who had legitimate military training.

Their first meeting at Tu's office did not go well.

As the tiny Generalissimo (Tu thought only a tiny man would need such a long title) ranted on, Tu recalled a cook who, in an effort to please him, had stuffed a shrimp dumpling inside a delicately spiced slice of eggplant that was then stuffed inside a cured duck breast that was in turn stuffed inside a flattened and rolled chicken—all, naturally, lightly breaded and deep fried and then covered with a thin, brown tamarind sauce. Unfortunately for the cook, a small piece of the duck's wishbone had got into his concoction, and Tu had momentarily choked on the bone, which resulted in the cook being thrown down a well. But the cook's death wasn't what was on Tu's mind as he stared at the wasp-waisted, almost bald little man across the table from him. It was the idea of one thing stuffed inside another that was then stuffed inside another and so on and so on— like Shanghai, he thought. Spies embedded by one group inside another, then leaders of one faction going inside another and forming alliances that were unknown to their supposed allies—things stuffed within other things. In such circumstances there was always the chance of serious error, a wishbone to choke on.

Chiang Kai Shek was still talking. The man clearly liked to hear himself speak. Tu knew that this poncey man had family connections with a powerful Triad from the south, and that he was now Dr. Sun Yat-sen's right-hand man. But what really interested him was a piece of information that his spies had told him: the fact that Charles Soong did not allow this man to handle any of the money that he forwarded to "the cause." Interesting. Very interesting.

Tu knew of the man's prodigious sexual appetites from his business connections in the Flower World. He also knew of the man's willingness to hurt the women with whom he brought on the clouds and rain. Cruelty against women struck Tu as the action of a coward, and for a moment he had the impulse to reach into his desk and throw the dagger hidden there into the man's heart—or perhaps into his eye.

But Tu also knew that cowards can be useful, sometimes more useful than brave men. Brave men simply fight—cowards plot. *So what are you plotting?* he thought, as the Generalissimo was completing some complicated idea or other.

Tu stood. Chiang Kai Shek stopped mid-sentence, a look of open anger crossing his hard features. "Did I interrupt something important," Gangster Tu asked, "or just more of your self-congratulatory yapping?"

Chiang leaped out of his chair.

"I would suggest you sit, Mr. Chiang, if you want to be able to sit ever again." Chiang slowly sank back in his chair. "Good. That's a good boy."

Chiang's face turned a bright red.

"No!" Tu shouted at him. "No anger when I tell you what to do. No resistance. No desire to strike out—or your life will be ended shortly—very shortly. Is that clear, Mr. Chiang?"

Slowly Chiang Kai Shek nodded.

"Good. We will try that again. All right?"

Chiang nodded slowly once more.

"Good. That's a good boy." He crossed to the man and patted him with an open hand on the cheek. Then hit him, hard. "Good boy."

Tu saw the flush on the man's cheek begin and then retreat. *Okay,* he thought, *the beginnings of a dog brought to heel.* But he knew that this was a mad dog, and mad dogs were never really brought to heel—they just came to heel periodically when they saw no other way to get what they wanted. "Fine. Now, why are you here?" Tu asked.

"You requested my presence."

"Try again. I requested your presence but you agreed to come. So why are you here?"

Chiang Kai Shek drew himself up to his full diminutive height in the chair and said, "I think we have much with which we can help each other."

"Really?" Tu asked innocently.

"Yes!" Chiang replied, clearly having trouble keeping his temper in check. "We both want change."

Tu nodded but did not deign to offer words of agreement.

"We both want the Manchu—"

"I have no concern with the Manchu government in Beijing," Tu interrupted. "As long as they stay north of the river I have no quarrel with them. I leave them be, and they leave me be." It wasn't completely true, but true enough for this preening fool.

"Fine," Chiang said, rallying his forces and trying for another means of access. "We both hate the *Fan Kuei*."

Tu thought, *Who amongst the Black-Haired people does not hate the Fan Kuei?* He wondered how well this imp of a man understood the depth of his hatred of the Round Eyes. Whether he knew about his pledge to his grandmother to rid the country of the hated occupiers. Likely he knew some of that, since there was every probability that this man received reports from his no doubt well-placed spies. Spies were unavoidable in the city at the Bend in the River. Just stuff within stuff.

Tu stared at the man, an act of open disrespect among Han Chinese men. Was there a way to use this peacock of a man? Was it possible that this man had the Tusk? No. If he did, he would have boasted about it. Even this idiot would have been able to see the value of owning the First Emperor's Narwhal Tusk. But the man was talking again—this time about Dr. Sun Yat-sen, and the man's incompetence. Slowly Tu began to understand that this popinjay was here to enlist his support against the good doctor. Tu wanted to laugh. He didn't care who led the revolt against the Manchus, just as long as they waited until the Dowager unleashed whatever attacks she had planned against the *Fan Kuei*. After that, they could war all they wanted. He needed the *Fan Kuei* weakened if he was ever to really control Shanghai.

Tu allowed the man to talk for a few more minutes but didn't hear a word. He just watched the man's lizard lips open and shut. For a moment he allowed himself to be astonished by the foolhardiness of the man, then he quickly bemoaned the time he had already wasted in this moron's company. Abruptly he said, "Enough," and before the Generalissimo could get a word in he continued, "I have had more than enough of you." And he was out of the room, Loa Wei Fen covering his back.

———

As the years passed, Silas watched his adopted children grow in the Garden. He brought both Buddhist and Jewish scholars to look after their religious education, although he made it clear that he wanted his children to "understand religious thought, not think like religious people." On a whim he set up a department store right across from the Vrassoons' largest emporium on Bubbling Spring Road. It pleased him to continue his father's antagonism toward their ancient enemy.

And—oh, yes—he bought a motorcar, the very first horseless carriage in Shanghai.

chapter thirty-eight
Silas and Automobiles

1902

From the moment Silas had first read his father's journal entry documenting the opium voyage that brought him to Bubbling Spring Road, he had begun to search for the horseless carriage that had almost run over his father in that dream. His search quickly yielded answers. And although Silas hated horses, he had an instant love affair with the horseless carriage.

He investigated the first automobiles that Karl Benz made in Germany. He even drove a Benz Velo in Frankfurt in 1895, but he didn't buy one. Later he read with great interest about Horatio Nelson Jackson's transcontinental drive across the United States, and assuming this was quite a feat, although he had no idea how big the United States really was, he put in a bid for the car but his bid was refused. So when he was sent material on a new, as yet unproduced automobile from Italy, a Bugatti, he bought the thing, sight unseen, several years before the first Bugatti hit the streets of Rome. And so it was that on the morning of June 2, 1902, Silas Hordoon amazed the fine citizenry of Shanghai by driving his newly polished Bugatti out of what had been his father's stables and then down Bubbling Spring Road all the way to the Bund.

People stopped whatever they were doing and stared, mouths agape, fencepost teeth on clear display. A few women fainted. Some peasants screamed. Silas couldn't recall a more gratifying series of responses in his life. He reached for the large, round rubber bulb of the horn and gave it a good squeeze. A blaring honk came from the brass enunciator. Silas smiled even more broadly and honked the honker a second time. In fact, Silas's behaviour on this, the very first automobile ride in Shanghai, set a pattern for all subsequent automobile rides in the city at the Bend in the River: turn on your automobile, honk your horn loudly, then honk it again whenever possible in the course of your journey.

The fifth or sixth horn blast brought Gangster Tu to his feet and then to his warehouse window. From his vantage point he could see Silas Hordoon, whom he thought of as a frog of a *Fan Kuei,* sitting on his shiny red leather seat in the open carriage of the Bugatti like an emperor returning after having conquered the vast itself. The horn sounded again just as Tu was about to speak. He closed his mouth, then opened it again and said quickly, before another blast could drown out his words, "I want one."

Immediately six men leaped to his side and began to jot down notes on the automobile.

"The same one, or different, sir?"

"The same but bigger, with more brass and more ..." Not knowing the word for the automobile equivalent of house gewgaws he stuttered his hands through the air alternately pointing at the automobile, the sky, the road, and then in frustration at the men themselves.

Knowing their Mountain Master as they did, the men immediately sprang into action. They tapped their contacts, especially in the press, and within the month Shanghai's second automobile had arrived—another custom-made Bugatti, but this one a full foot longer than Silas's, and much redder, and more chrome-encrusted. Tu Yueh-sen loved it like a glutton loves a mound of peanut noodles. It made him happy just to look at all the chrome and polished leather. The very smell of the thing made him happy. Everything about it sent jolts of real pleasure through him. Like the first time he'd put a blade into a living thing.

"Get in," Tu said to Loa Wei Fen one day as he folded back the leather roof and then hopped up onto the red-leather–upholstered bench seat. He gripped the polished wooden steering wheel in both hands, then stuck his right hand out and squeezed the horn. The blaring honk made him smile again. It always did, and it was just as well, because the way he drove he had need of the horn quite often.

He was thrilled that his automobile had an electric ignition system so he could start it with the flick of a switch, while the *Fan Kuei* had to insert a metal turning device into the engine block and crank his engine into life. Tu remarked to himself that it was the first time he had ever seen Silas Hordoon do any manual labour whatsoever.

Tu's only complaint about his new automobile was that it had only three speeds: very slow, pretty slow, and not so fast. He set his men to work on that, and within ten days his Bugatti could go fast enough to scatter peasants in the streets, outrace a trotting horse, and, if he so desired, smash into and through carts that were in his way on the road.

Gangster Tu was a happy man.

Meyer Vrassoon, not to be outdone, but being of conservative tastes, ignored the fancy Italian cars and purchased four Meredith tonneau cars from the Abingdon Automotive Works of Birmingham, England.

Charles Soong shortly followed suit, buying two cars built in France under licence from Armand Peugeot. Soong's vehicles used a Daimler engine with a pedal-operated clutch, a chain transmission leading to a change-speed gearbox, and, perhaps most astonishing, an engine mounted in the front. And they could really gain speed, especially if started in a downhill position.

The House of Zion, ever patriotic, bought their automobile from America, a Curved Dash Oldsmobile built by Ransome Eli Olds.

William Dent bought the actual automobile that won the Peking to Paris automobile race, an Italia. While Heyward Matheson, in prudent Scottish style, awaited the more reasonably priced machine that eventually came off the world's very first assembly line, the Ford Model T.

And these Taipans drove their horseless carriages on the streets of Shanghai with a conceit that matched the cocksure buildings they had erected on the Bund, and an indifference to the safety and well-being of their fellow citizens that, with the exception of Silas and Heyward Matheson, mirrored their basic attitude toward the unfortunate need for other people to inhabit their town, prepare their meals, be converted to their faith, and, most importantly, pay for their opium.

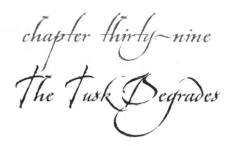

chapter thirty-nine
The Tusk Degrades

The Chosen Three and the Carver scanned the front room of Jiang's carefully. The dawn was moments away. They'd had to wait for hours until the room was finally clear of its clientele. An hour earlier Jiang had woken the old Go player and helped him to a rickshaw that would take him home. One of Tu's men had gotten so drunk that he'd had trouble finding his way out, and one of Jiang's girls had found that she was pregnant and needed to talk with Jiang about her future.

During all this, Loa Wei Fen had been forced to wait in a small anteroom lest Tu's man see him.

And now the sun was about to rise.

Mai Bao took her mother's arm as she painfully moved toward the velvet-covered box bench. The Confucian closed the front door, and Loa Wei Fen carefully shut and locked the door leading to the interior rooms. The Carver loosed the curtains from their sashes and pulled the shutters to. Then Jiang turned on a single light and said, "Open the box."

The Confucian and Loa Wei Fen lifted the heavy thing onto a couch, then unfastened the hidden latch on the back. It flopped open, revealing the Tusk.

"Take it out and hold it by the light," Jiang ordered. The men did as she requested. When the Tusk was near her, Jiang tilted the light toward the relic and said, "Look, it's talking to us again."

Mai Bao turned to her mother. Using fanciful phrases like "talking to us" were not like her. Mai Bao smelled the gentle sweetness of rot about her mother and noted the deep yellow of her eyes. She was about to say something when her mother ordered, in a surprisingly strong voice, "Look!"

And they did—and what they saw shocked them. The relic was deteriorating at a much quicker pace. Several open cracks were now evident in the upper surface, and in each of the three windows new figures were emerging as the "roofs" of the tableaux rotted away.

"Change is coming," Jiang said. "Can't you smell it?"

chapter forty
Typhoon

And the dance that was Shanghai continued at the Bend in the River, but not without missteps—dangerous missteps.

In 1905 the Japanese defeated the Russian army, marking the first time in modern history that an Asian army had bested a European army. Victory celebrations broke out all over Asia, especially in the Middle Kingdom. But before the celebrations ended, the American Congress extended the Chinese Exclusion Acts, which forbade any person of Chinese origin from entering the United States. Immediately the victory celebrations turned into riots on the streets of Nanking and Canton. Denying access to the Golden Mountain to the Chinese fuelled a hatred that had not ended with the failure of the Boxer or Taiping rebellions.

Then, in the middle of a moonless night, a massive typhoon slammed into the island of Hong Kong.

It smashed into the coast with such ferocity and speed that the shore-line districts were instantly swamped, and thousands of poor Chinese who lived there were dragged out to sea in an icy embrace that would be the last thing they felt on this earth. In the darkness, women lost children and old people were left abandoned as they slept. Only the fortunate found a strong enough boulder behind which to escape the ocean's surge, although many of them were crushed between the water's pull and the adamantine rocks.

Cries of pain and fear filled the darkness as the living and the dying begged for the light of dawn to come quickly.

The typhoon headed out to sea without swooping up the mountain to the homes of the *Fan Kuei*.

When the dawn finally came, thousands of sodden, terrified Chinese made their way up the mountainside to ask for help from the wealthy *Fan Kuei*. They were met with rifle fire and Sikh police officers who beat them unmercifully.

Hundreds of them died on the first day, and thousands on the second. The guards were instructed to stop "any Chink bastard trying to get onto our property!"

Without shelter and food, thousands more lost their lives, but still the European powers that ran Hong Kong refused to lift a finger to help the destitute Chinese.

It was only when Mai Bao came to her husband and told him of the catastrophe—"And they shot them like snakes. Thousands died in the storm. Tens of thousands died of starvation waiting for the *Fan Kuei* to help them. Our people beg for what is ours in our own country!"—that any heed was taken.

She had never challenged her husband this way before. But Silas was not upset. Rather, he called in MacMillan, his chief aide, and ordered, "I want the head of every major trading house in Shanghai that has a branch office in Hong Kong to be here, in the Garden, at this time tomorrow—no exceptions."

Silas Hordoon knew very well that the only major trading house in Shanghai without a branch office in Hong Kong was his own company. He also knew that the response of the Hong Kong *Fan Kuei* to the typhoon could endanger the *Fan Kuei* throughout the Middle Kingdom. He was only too aware that Chinese anger toward the Foreign Devils had not diminished, only gone dormant. He looked at his strong Chinese wife and nodded to her. "I will do my best to deal with this, Mai Bao."

"Thank you, husband."

"No need to thank me. An unattended fire in an outbuilding can easily burn down the entire mansion."

She smiled. Her husband's Shanghainese was perfect, but his use of the ancient idiom was not quite correct. The bit of Taoist knowledge he was trying to quote was more accurately stated as "A rot in a building's foundation, if not treated, can bring down the entire structure." Fire connoted an act of nature or an accident. Since all things under the heavens, even stones, eventually rotted, rot suggested something more profound—a neglect of the inevitable, an act of stupidity and hubris.

Most of the traders had never been inside the walls of the Garden, and although they were men used to luxury and all the trappings of great wealth, they were openly impressed by the magnificence of the ten homes, two schools, the once fabulous stables, elegant Buddhist temple, the simple Jewish synagogue, and the various gardens and outbuildings of Silas's famous walled-in world. As well, they were impressed by the appearance and courteous behaviour of the twenty street children who greeted them by name upon their arrival.

Although it was against Silas's better judgment, Mai Bao insisted that she not make an appearance before the traders. "We want to enlist the support of these men for the Chinese of Hong Kong, husband, not to enrage them because you married a Celestial."

Silas disagreed but, as in so many important decisions in the Garden, he gave way to his wife's finely tuned practical approach to the world beyond the Garden's high walls.

The meeting started as all powerful business meetings did in the Middle Kingdom, with fine oolong tea and delicately prepared dumplings of various sorts. The traders ate, and some drank from the well-stocked bar. Most smoked cigars, which Silas found distasteful, although he made himself smile as he fanned away the dense smoke.

Finally he indicated the large, oval table and the men took their places. As they did, Silas signalled his serving people that they were to leave the room. This was to be as private a meeting as could be had in the spy-rich world at the Bend in the River.

Silas took a final sip of his tea, replaced the lid on his porcelain cup, and pushed it to one side. The green baize lamps on the table gave an odd funereal air to the room. He briefly repeated a thanks for the attendance of his guests, then, looking at the heads of Jardine Matheson, Dent, and Oliphant, launched right in.

"I believe that your offices and people in Hong Kong have made a serious mistake—a mistake that will have an impact upon our lives and livelihoods here in Shanghai."

Zachariah Oliphant, the new leader of the House of Zion, asked simply, "And what mistake would that be?"

Silas quickly reviewed, not that any of the traders at the table didn't already know, the facts of the typhoon and its aftermath on Hong Kong. Then, surprising even himself, he banged a heavy fist on the table and said, "Foolishness. Dangerous foolishness."

"Easy for you to say, Mr. Hordoon, since you have no business interests on that rocky little island," William Dent said.

Before Silas could reply that Dent's statement missed the point, Zachariah Oliphant added, "There are times when the Almighty insists upon teaching these heathens a lesson, Mr. Hordoon. Read your Bible, Mr. Hordoon. God's revenge often comes from the sea."

Naturally, Silas thought, it would be the Oliphant man who would play the religious card! He resisted telling the fellow what he thought of his specious statement and turned instead to Heyward Matheson, the head of Jardine Matheson, the old-line Scottish trading firm first established in the Middle Kingdom by Hercules MacCallum. "Do you share Mr. Oliphant's opinion, sir?"

Heyward Matheson did not, but Silas Hordoon was a competitor, not an ally, and until he heard more from those around the table he was unwilling to pick a side in the dispute. His firm had major offices on Hong Kong, rivalling their Shanghai operations. But unlike the Shanghai operations, where employees actually moved their whole families to the city at the Bend in the River, in Hong Kong, corporate officers were rotated in and out on a three-year schedule. The head of operations there was about the only employee who called the craggy island his home. Heyward Matheson took a sip of the excellent sherry that Silas had supplied and said, "There are tangled webs here, Mr. Hordoon, that need to be further unwound and discussed."

That brought other traders into the discussion.

Silas resisted speaking again until after lunch had been served. Then, over their port, he said, "Gentlemen, not meaning to be abrupt, but I think that the last two hours have been a serious waste of everyone's time. The facts here are simple. They are the same facts my father dealt with when he first arrived here in 1842. We are foreigners in a foreign land. There are few of us and many of them. If we do not find an accommodation with the people of the Middle Kingdom, then we will not be permitted to live here amongst them."

"I don't want to live amongst them," interrupted a new trader from Boston. "I want to trade with them, that's all."

"Fine, sir," said Silas, rising to the challenge, "but they need not allow you to do even that."

"There's always opium. They need our opium."

"Do they?" Silas challenged. "They have begun to grow their own poppy crops upriver. It is only the fact that the Manchu officials make so much more money from the sale of your opium that it is still permitted. You all have them on your payroll. But the Manchus are in decline. It's obvious. You can see the signs everywhere. And whoever takes over from the Manchus may not view us *Fan Kuei* with the same benign neglect that the Manchus have. There have already been two major revolts."

"Oh, not that business about the Taiping again," shouted one of the other new traders, this one from Bristol.

Silas took a breath to control his temper. "I think, for those of us who live amongst the Han Chinese, it is not hard to understand that the forces that pushed the Taiping Revolt and the Boxer Rebellion were the same."

"I thought the Taiping was run by some guy who said he was Jesus Christ himself—God, these people!"

"He claimed to be the brother of Christ, not Christ. And it was not that claim that gained him followers. It was his promise to redistribute land from the wealthy to the landless. To provide care for the poor. To stop the suffering caused by the opium trade. In fact, I think it obvious that the only thing that kept the Taipingers from total victory was their foolish religious dictums, which eventually punished their own followers so much that they caused the movement to weaken."

"Even if your interpretation of the Taiping Revolt is true, which I don't totally grant, how do you see the Boxers as an outgrowth of that?" challenged Zachariah Oliphant.

Silas took a look at these men. On the whole, bright men. Not all educated, but all worldly. "How long can the few—us—keep power and wealth from the many—them? The Boxers tapped into the ever-festering anger of the Chinese. It is a deep well of hate that we must not tempt by foolishness like the response on Hong Kong. It would have cost so little to show compassion to the dispossessed there. And we would have gained so much. Think, gentlemen. I am not asking for charity. I am not asking for generosity. I am asking you to make an investment in your businesses and all of our futures."

It took several more hours, and Silas offering to match each and every offer, dollar for dollar, to convince the traders to ante up the money that Silas quickly moved, through Mai Bao, to the destitute on Hong Kong.

The delay in the arrival of the money was noted by the Chinese. Although they were grateful for the assistance, they also understood that it was really given only to pacify them—and they were only momentarily pacified.

chapter forty-one
Change—Death of a Dowager

1908

Chesu Hoi thought that he had heard every conceivable kind of cruel request from the Dowager Empress, but this new and perhaps final request of her long, evil life shocked even him. He read it a second time to be sure that he had not been mistaken. But there it was, in her unmistakable hand: *"Kill the Emperor. I won't have him outlive me. I won't have it!"*

Chesu Hoi held the silken parchment over the candle on his desk and watched it curl as flame took it. As the Forbidden City's Head Eunuch, he was fully aware of much of the happenings within the ancient complex. He had arranged the arrival of the famous beauty Tzu Hsi while she was just a pretty country girl. He had watched her connive to produce a son for her Emperor and thus rise to the role of Emperor Consort above the forty other women in the Emperor's stable trying to produce male children for their ruler.

He had been at the gate when the boy child was handed over in exchange for the girl Tzu Hsi had delivered. It was their first meeting, and one that neither would forget.

He had been listening to the report from the midwife who oversaw Tzu Hsi's delivery and was astonished to hear that the woman didn't know the baby's sex, since Tzu Hsi had grabbed the baby the moment it had appeared and pulled it to her breast under the blankets. "She almost wouldn't let us cut the cord. It was the strangest thing I've ever seen in a

537

birthing room. She just grabbed the thing and got to her feet. I was amazed she was able to stand. She'd just expelled the afterbirth and …"

But Chesu Hoi didn't listen to any more details. He knew more about the birth of babies than almost any male alive. It was the job assigned to him by the Head Eunuch of those days—to ensure that royal children were birthed and registered properly. So far he had registered seven girls. The Emperor was furious. He needed a son to secure his dynasty. Now this— Tzu, still weak and bloody between her legs, lurching on her tiny bound feet down the corridor.

He left the midwife and followed Tzu Hsi. Despite her bleeding, and what Chesu Hoi assumed was her exhaustion from having just given birth, she was trying to run. She turned into a side room, and he quickly followed. For a moment after entering the room, he thought that he had lost her. The room was empty. Then he noticed a slight trail of blood on the polished hardwood floor. It led directly to a fine country scene painting of the Hua Shan, the Holy Mountain. He walked slowly toward the painting, then looked down at the floor. His feet were in blood—her blood. He pulled the wall hanging aside and there, to his shock, was a beautifully concealed door whose frame lines matched exactly the design on the wall. If he hadn't been sure that there was an exit he would never have seen the door, so well did it blend into the masonry of the wall. He reached forward and the door swung outward in a silent, graceful motion, revealing a dark circular staircase. He quickly followed it, down three flights, until his feet touched cold stone. To his right he saw a figure moving quickly toward a slender opening in the solid rock. He followed.

Out the portal was a view that took his breath from him. The pure mountain across the way was unexpected. The beauty flooded him, and for a moment he couldn't breathe in its presence.

Then he saw Tzu Hsi take her baby from its royal blanket and hand it to a peasant woman who somehow was waiting for her. The peasant gave her a baby that she quickly wrapped in the royal cloth.

The peasant turned and ran away as Tzu Hsi turned back toward the staircase—only to see Chesu Hoi standing there. He canted his head slightly in an effort to avoid the hate in Tzu Hsi's eyes.

"Are you following me, you despicable creature?" she shouted.

"Only doing my duty, madam," he said. She was not royalty yet, so deserved no further title.

"Away!" she commanded.

Her voice was so compelling that he almost obeyed. Then he thought better and held out his arms. "Shall I carry the Emperor's first son back to the safety of the inner world, Majesty?" He saw the effect of calling her that. "You may lean on my arm, Majesty, as you must be tired from your labours."

For a moment Tzu Hsi didn't move. She glanced back over her shoulder.

Chesu Hoi thought, *If she has a knife, now's the time she'll use it on me.* But she had no knife. Only guile—and ambition.

So they made their first of many deals that day. He would keep her secret. She would secure his position at court for the remainder of his years.

And it was a good deal for both of them. He watched her back and she his. In her youth he brought her enough young, handsome men to satisfy her gargantuan sexual appetites. He also supplied the infected towels necessary to remove lovers who were no longer of interest to Tzu Hsi. He helped her through the death of the first Emperor and the subsequent placing of her son on the throne while Tzu Hsi ruled as regent. Of course he had assisted her in undermining her ridiculous nephew Kwang Hsu's Hundred Days of Reform, and there had even been a time when his elegant fingers had proved adequate for her needs.

But now this. A request to kill the present Emperor so that she should not be outlived by the little snot.

He approached her chamber and waved both her doctors and young "chamber men" aside. He wanted to speak to her alone, and no one at court dared risk his wrath so they obeyed him.

"Majesty?"

Her yellow, glaucoma-clouded eyes turned toward the sound of his voice.

He repeated himself.

Her twisted, swollen, arthritic hand moved slowly along the silk sheet and touched his leg—up by the thigh. She applied a bit of pressure and something resembling a smile came to her lips as she said, "Eunuch."

He sighed. So she'd be rude to the end. "Yes, Majesty, your faithful eunuch—if you must."

She opened her mouth but no words came. He leaned forward and placed his ear close to her lips. Her breath was foul. "My note. Did you get my note?"

"Yes, Majesty."

"And?"

"And it will be done, Majesty. Rest now. Be assured, the young Emperor will not outlive his Dowager."

She smiled. It was an awful thing to see. Several teeth were missing. Those that remained were clearly rotted. Her gums were almost black.

Then she surprised him by kicking one foot free of the silk sheet, exposing an ancient bound foot to the air. Her lips moved, but once again no sound entered the still air of the bedroom. Then she tried a second time, and this time a whistle of sound came from her.

"Kiss my foot."

* * *

CHESU HOI MADE SHORT WORK of the Emperor. He was a silly boy, and the girl the Head Eunuch had secured for him was riddled with smallpox. So the race to death was on, and everyone in the Forbidden City knew it. There were bets being placed at the highest and lowest levels of Manchu society. Even kitchen help placed wagers. The betting odds were that the Old Buddha would outlive her Emperor—and they proved to be right, by some twenty-six hours.

Unnoticed by the betting audience in the Forbidden City was another death in their midst. Less than an hour after Tzu Hsi finally died, Chesu Hoi, her faithful Head Eunuch, slipped into a little-used room down a long corridor and approached a beautiful wall hanging depicting the Hua Shan, the Holy Mountain upon which the First Emperor had given up his life. Pulling the wall hanging aside, he—for the second time in his long life—faced the beautifully concealed door. He reached into the pocket of his purple robe and took out the last communication he had received from his oldest friend, the Carver. It said simply, "We work and we work and when we can no longer work—we rest, old friend." Chesu Hoi smiled at that thought, then he pushed the door. It slid smoothly open and he passed through it and down the long spiral staircase.

At the base of the staircase he walked toward the slender entrance. The sun was setting over the far mountain. He stood and watched the clouds move in the fading light. Then he leaned back against the cool wall and took the poison from his sleeve. He had lived long enough—and it was so beautiful here, a fine place to die.

He had somehow taken the poison, he didn't remember if it was before or after he thought how beautiful this place was. Then he thought, why should that matter? Then he thought no more as the beautiful vista in front of him seemed to enter him and he became part of it—or it part of him, he didn't know which. His last thought was, *What would the Carver do with such a vision? How would he capture it?* Then the answer came to him, and it calmed him. *In ivory, naturally. Narwhal would be best.*

chapter forty-two
Change—Death of a Courtesan

1908

Even as the Dowager Empress was breathing her last breaths, Jiang shooed the doctor away. "Enough. It's enough, old friend."

The doctor, who had attended to her health for almost forty years, bowed slightly and left her alone with her three daughters. Her girls helped her into a beautiful white robe that her eldest daughter had made for her. Following the Jiang tradition, it was not made of silk, since, as the History Teller told, "silk comes from women's tears." As Jiang lay on her bed and spread out the pure cotton robe, she remarked, "We've all had enough of women's tears now, haven't we?"

Her eldest daughter took it as a kind of rebuke for the tears in her eyes, but Jiang shook her head and said gently, "No, my dear, you honour me with both the elegance of the robe and your sorrow. You do me much honour, daughter." She kissed her eldest on the forehead, then sent her away.

Next she turned to her youngest, Yin Bao, now a mother five times over but still a sassy girl with a lewd smile. Jiang held out a hand to her. The girl minced her way over on her bound feet.

"Silly, those," Jiang said, pointing to Yin Bao's tiny, deformed feet.

"Perhaps, Mother, but much adored. Much adored."

"Yes, yes," Jiang said, "but I don't want any of my granddaughters to follow this foolishness."

"They won't, Mother. My feet are of the past—my girls will be China's future."

Jiang nodded. She had no doubt that with Yin Bao as their mother and the immensely wealthy Charles Soong as their father, these girls, whom she had first seen in the back of the Tusk's second portal, would have a serious role to play in Shanghai's future. Perhaps a crucial role.

"Five children is more than enough," Jiang said.

"Perhaps, Mother. Perhaps."

There was a silence between them as each recognized herself in the other. There were no tears between mother and daughter this time.

"Lives end," Jiang said.

"Then others take their place," Yin Bao answered.

For a moment Jiang felt slighted by the didactic nature of this thinking, then she chastised herself for such foolishness. "Go now."

As Yin Bao left the room, Jiang's elegant middle daughter stepped forward and bowed low in the old fashion. She was aging with extraordinary grace. Still thin and erect, her graceful carriage seemed to add a sense of history to her every step.

"Does your husband treat you well?"

"You know he does, Mother."

"And are you happy with him?"

"He is a good husband. Thank you, Mother."

Neither woman spoke, then Jiang said, "Your two daughters are lovely. They will make it hard for you to choose which should assume my name and enter the Ivory Compact."

"No doubt, Mother, as Yin Bao made it complicated for you to choose."

Jiang smiled briefly. It had ultimately not been a hard decision. "But answer my question, Mai Bao. Are you happy with your husband?"

"Happy? Yes."

"But not in love, as you were with your scholar?"

"We were young, Mother."

"Ah, yes, young," Jiang said wistfully, and glanced at the wall hanging Yin Bao's father had given her, when she was young. Then she grimaced as the pain swelled in her belly.

"Mother?"

"Just pain, Mai Bao, just pain."

"Can I get you something?"

"Soon. But not yet. First we need to talk. You have one great task left to do."

"For the Compact?"

"For the Black-Haired people. The Sacred Tusk must be moved to safety once and for all. As the Manchus falter, people will be anxious to have some sign that they have been chosen by the heavens to rule. There are many parties competing to replace the Q'ing Dynasty, but none of them in their own right are strong enough. None of them have the support of the people of the Middle Kingdom. But if one of those groups were to have the Narwhal Tusk, it could claim direct descent from the First Emperor and demand the right to rule. This must not happen! It must not. Gangster Tu is still in search of the Tusk, and we know that Tu has already met with Generalissimo Chiang Kai Shek. Yin Bao's husband bankrolls Dr. Sun Yat-sen, the foolish man. All would value the Tusk. None must be allowed to possess it."

"Agreed, Mother."

"The Tusk must leave Shanghai. It must be taken far away."

"How? There are eyes everywhere in Shanghai. It's so large—how could we move it without drawing attention?"

"As we did last time, with a diversion. Use your husband, Mai Bao. He is a powerful man—with a book."

Mai Bao nodded slowly, then asked, "Where is the relic, Mother?"

Jiang told her daughter and the younger woman smiled. All those games of Go she had watched as the old man squirmed uncomfortably on the box bench, and it had never occurred to her.

"How soon should this be done, Mother?"

"Within three moons of my passing."

"That won't be for years."

Now it was Jiang's turn to smile. She touched Mai Bao's face gently and said, "Nonsense. Now take the stopper from that small flask on the table for me, please."

Mai Bao did.

"Now give it to me."

Mai Bao hesitated, then stepped forward and handed it to her mother.

"Now leave me. Even a whore has a right to a little privacy at the end—remember your promise to get the Tusk to safety."

"I will remember, Mother."

"Don't cry. It's time for me to go." She tilted the viscous contents of the bottle into her mouth. Then she began to laugh.

"What could possibly be funny, Mother?"

"I said, 'Even a whore has a right to a little privacy at the end.' I should have said, '*Especially* a whore has the right to a little privacy at the end.' Now leave me, Mai Bao. It is my time."

Mai Bao joined her sisters in the anteroom. The eldest daughter was sitting on the box bench beside the ancient Go player. They rocked gently together. Then Yin Bao came and put her arm around Mai Bao and they too began to rock—and as they did, the poison took Jiang—and the world changed.

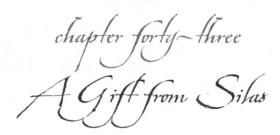

chapter forty-three
A Gift from Silas

Mai Bao insisted that Silas not attend the final rituals of her mother's elaborate funeral. "I must do this alone, husband," she said as she put on her white mourning robes.

"Why?" he asked.

"Because my mother was special. Her passing has been noted by everyone of importance in our city. There has been no privacy. My mother was, in the end, a private woman. And she would not wish you to be at my side, attracting the attention of yet more newspapermen. Do this for me, husband. Go to the synagogue you had built here and pray for her. But do not appear at the New Hundred Flowers Cemetery at my side."

He agreed to the latter but not the former. Since he'd had the synagogue built in the Garden he had never entered the building. Like his father, he felt a deep revulsion for what Richard referred to in his journals as the "ancient desert thinking" that drove all three of the major western religions. Silas remembered his father saying, "If the men who wrote those books could have thrown a pit from a plum onto the ground and in a short time had a plum tree, they would not have thought the way they thought. Toss a plum pit in the Yangtze and a plum tree will grow downriver. China is fecund. Even with its enormous population it is not an importer of food. The ground is rich. The people are practical. They are not fools lost in deserts."

While Mai Bao attended the final interment rites for Jiang, Silas retreated to his study and took out the journals his father had penned so many years before. If he had looked up and to his left he might have seen the corners of the final three pages peeking over the edge of the uppermost bookshelf. But he did not look in that direction. Instead he opened the earliest of the journals and reread the first entry of a twelve-year-old Baghdadi boy upon arriving in the great city of Calcutta. Silas was once again surprised by the intelligence of the writing, but it was its lyricism that amazed him. His father had a way with words, and although Silas's Farsi was rusty, he was enchanted by his father's use of the flowing language and his insights into the crumbling majesty of Calcutta.

Silas flipped through the entries about his father and Maxi in the opium works. Silas had moved his company completely out of the opium business but still found it complicated to believe that the fortune he had inherited owed much to the intoxicating drug.

The newest Hordoon enterprise was banking, and because of Shanghai's questionable international reputation Silas had decided to name his bank after both Shanghai and another Chinese city. He was still pondering which one and was presently thinking of calling the business The Shanghai Macao Bank.

He flipped forward and reread his father's account of his trip to China and meeting the dwarf Jesuit, Brother Matthew. When he finished reading the section he was struck by something else.

He pulled out the other journals and searched through them. Naturally there was no index, and Silas had never bothered to annotate the texts since his memory was so good, but he thought he remembered another mention of Brother Matthew in his father's writings. It took him several hours, but he finally found it. In his father's recollection of being millstoned there was the unusual mention of a dark dwarf figure offering him water in his agony.

Silas put down the journal and had a strong impulse to shove it aside, but he resisted it. He knew that he was in the presence of something important. His father, Richard Hordoon, as profoundly agnostic as any man Silas had ever met, had been "visited" twice by the squat figure of Brother Matthew. Silas realized that his father had probably been delusional with pain and dehydration while being millstoned, but nonetheless, the dwarf Jesuit made two appearances in his father's journals—and neither was during his opium voyages.

Silas took his noon meal in his study after a brief conference with his right-hand man, MacMillan. When he dismissed the large-boned Scot, he recalled his own problems with another Scot, his father's right-hand man. Now Silas understood why such men were valuable—no, *necessary*—for the running of a large business. They got things done. They were not particularly interested in the niceties of interracial or even interhuman relations, so they bulled their way through problems that would have stopped most others in their tracks. They would have stopped him, Silas knew. Stopped him cold. These men were bulldozers, they moved the earth itself to get projects finished. For the briefest moment Silas wondered if there would be a time when men like MacMillan might be unnecessary to men like him. Then he sighed and put the thought aside. He lived in China. He thought like a Chinese man, a practical man, and every practical man knew that the Silas Hordoons of the world would always need the Evan MacMillans of the world.

———

That night Silas was surprised to be awakened by the feel of Mai Bao at his side. She often slept in her own chamber. His snoring kept her awake. But she was at his side, her slender body curled into him, her fingers interlacing with his.

Silas wanted to ask if everything at her mother's funeral had been all right, but he didn't know a proper way to ask the question so he just returned the pressure of Mai Bao's hand and hoped she understood that he was thinking about her in her time of need.

"My mother made a final request," she said softly.

For a moment Silas wasn't sure if he had heard her correctly. "A request?"

"Yes," Mai Bao said. "You do not owe me this favour. You have done nothing to bring this obligation upon you."

"Except love you," Silas said.

They both realized that it was one of the few times either of them had talked about love. She knew that this was not the kind of love she had had with the Revolutionary, or the kind of love that she felt for her mother or for her two growing daughters. But he was right, what existed between the two of them was love. And she repeated the word in Mandarin, "*Ai.*"

Silas kissed her fingers. His night beard tickled her hand. "Do but ask and the favour is yours," he said in archaic Farsi, then laughed aloud.

"What?" she asked.

"Nothing, just reading brought back old ideas." He propped himself up on an elbow and reached for her long hair. Its silk always amazed him. "Ask, and if it is within my power I will give you whatever favour you wish."

Mai Bao turned on the electric light at the side of the bed and began to talk. She spoke of an obligation and the need to protect the future of the city at the Bend in the River.

Finally he stopped her and said, "If you cannot tell me details, then don't. But ask your favour."

She took a deep breath; her chest rose and fell. "I need a large, curved object moved out of the city to a place of safety, and no one must know what the object is or where it has gone to."

Silas put on a robe and sat on the side of their bed. He asked about the dimensions of the object and was surprised to hear it was over six feet long and at its widest just under a foot.

Then he asked, "Is it fragile?"

"More so with every passing day."

"And are people watching for this object?"

"There is a huge reward for it, and thousands upon thousands of eyes watch for it."

"Where is it now?"

"I cannot tell you that, husband, until you agree to move it to safety."

He nodded. He realized that was a fair precaution on Mai Bao's part, although he found it insulting and said as much.

"I owe you a great obligation, but I owe this object even more than I owe you."

He stared at her. Was it a relic of some sort? But that hardly fit with the practical woman he knew as Mai Bao, the woman who would soon be known throughout Shanghai as Jiang. He shoved that concern aside and asked for more details. How heavy was it, could it endure cold and heat, would wetness hurt the object, how long did the object have to be hidden for? The answer to that last surprised him.

"Maybe forever, husband."

Then he asked how soon this had to be accomplished, and she replied, "Within two months. Before the decade ends."

He got up and opened the curtains. On the other side of the high garden wall he knew the city was coming to rumbling life. *It seldom sleeps,* he thought. Then he corrected himself. *It never really sleeps.* There were eyes awake and watching at all hours at the Bend in the River.

He turned back to Mai Bao and said, "I can't move an object of that size without people seeing me or my men do it, unless ..." His voice trailed off and he heard shouts, cheers—no, the echoes of cheers.

Somehow he was down on the Bund, only a youth, and he heard cheering so loud that it caught his ear a full mile away—away from the racetrack—the racetrack where he had murdered his brother. He looked back out the window. He had carefully designed the gardens of his walled sanctuary so that the largest and most beautiful would be at the exact spot where Milo had fallen from his horse—right outside the window of his bedroom. *How do you get past killing your brother?* he thought. *By taking a pilgrimage—like the desert people used to.*

He looked at Mai Bao and opened his arms. She walked over to him, the growing light of morning gracing her elegant features, and he thought *I know where I can take the object. Now all I have to do is find a diversion to attract the eyes of the people.* He was hearing the cheering again. Then he heard a loud car honk from just outside his garden wall—and he knew exactly what diversion he could use.

chapter forty-four
A Diversion

The next day, Silas retreated to his office on Bubbling Spring Road and spent the night. He weighed and re-weighed options, but every time he thought he had the basics of a plan in place he cast it aside. He was overlooking something important, and he knew it. Something vital was eluding him.

As the dawn's light came through his office window it finally occurred to him. Although he considered himself a native of the Middle Kingdom, although he spoke the language as well as any true-born Celestial, although he had married a Chinese woman and now raised ten Chinese children, he had never been close to the birthing myth of this great place, the vulnerable wellspring of the strength of the Black-Haired people. And never before had he felt that his actions could influence the destiny of his adopted country. Never before was it so important to think like them—like a man of the Middle Kingdom.

"Practical!" he said aloud to the empty room. Then to himself he whispered, "Think like them—think practically."

He began to pace, biting hard at the skin around the cuticle of his left thumb. Then he stopped. Who was the one to fear most? Who had the most eyes and ears on the streets of Shanghai? Who threatened to find out and stop him from moving the object?

An image of Gangster Tu driving his automobile with the number-one licence plate came to his mind. Just in the past month the city had begun to issue licence plates, and although Silas's Bugatti had been the very first automobile in Shanghai, Gangster Tu had received the licence plate with the number one proudly displayed. For a time it had been a source of much gossip in the press, especially since Silas had been given the number-two plate. Silas shivered. His last meeting with Gangster Tu had been distinctly unpleasant. Silas had seen Tu screaming and honking his horn at a poor woman whose skirt had got stuck in the grille of his automobile as he bulled his way through a crowd. Silas had raced out of a meeting to come to the woman's rescue, much to the shock of the Chinese crowd and the fury of the gangster.

He thought about Tu for a moment, then the others who collected information through spies. Each of the great trading houses had its spies. So did his brother-in-law, Charles Soong. No doubt the Republican movement led by Dr. Sun Yat-sen had some sort of spy network of its own. And then, of course, there were the Manchus—although now that the Dowager was gone he doubted they were much of a force.

He put on his coat and headed toward the door. He felt he had to know exactly what the object was, and its significance, so that he could know who the opposition might be and plan properly. But halfway down the front steps he stopped himself. Mai Bao had made it clear that she would not tell him any more than the object's dimensions and the desperate need to get it to safety—and he doubted she would offer up any more information now. He returned to his office and ate his breakfast of thin Shanghainese gruel at his desk.

The word *diversion* kept circulating in his mind, and slowly a multistage plan came into focus. He began to jot down notes. He rewrote them several times, and when he finally looked up it was almost eleven o'clock. He read the notes one more time. *Excellent,* he thought as he reached for the talking piece on his desk. It was immediately answered by a secretary. "Send in Mr. MacMillan."

Despite the fact that Silas hated cigars he lit one and puffed heavily on it. Men like MacMillan expected it of him.

Moments later Evan MacMillan, his hard-hearted but reliable Scot, pushed open the door and entered the room from which Silas ran his vast empire.

"So, did you check into that little matter of the licence plate for my Bugatti, MacMillan?"

MacMillan was surprised. That had been almost four weeks ago—and a frivolous complaint. "Aye, Captain."

Silas never knew if MacMillan was mocking him with that "Captain" stuff. Jews weren't captains—at least not captains the way MacMillan was talking about.

"So?"

"It's true, Captain. Tu must have bribed the officials to get that licence. No other way it could have happened."

"Damn!" Silas was on his feet, his cigar half chomped through. "Damn and damn again. I won't have this. I won't. MacMillan, do you hear me, man? I won't have this."

MacMillan had seen the kike angry before, but never quite like this.

It had been bad when the little heathen had insisted on marrying his Chinese whore, but at least that was understandable. Even to MacMillan's eye she was an A-one piece of beef. Not that he'd marry any of the local Slants, but she was a catch. Then he'd thrown a fit when he'd had to defend himself against his critics for taking in those twenty brats with their constantly shitty bottoms. But even that didn't have the intensity of this. He'd never understand these heathens.

"At the time, you talked about me bombing the offending vehicle, Captain?"

Silas stopped in his tracks. "You could do this?"

It always amazed MacMillan. The Mesopotamian was so savvy about so many things but so stupid when it came to the simplest forms of combat. "Aye—a bomb will do the job, if that's what you still want."

"It is! Damn it to hell, it is! But MacMillan, no one is to get hurt. Just that damn automobile of Tu's is to be bombed. Bombed to a better world. To Automobile Heaven, if there is such a place."

"Mr. Hordoon, let me be sure I understand you clearly. You want Gangster Tu's automobile blasted to smithereens, but you don't want anyone hurt when I do it—is that the ticket?"

"As you would say, MacMillan, 'Aye!'"

"And you want the little runt's automobile bombed because it has a licence plate on it that is one number shorter than yours. Is that right, Captain?"

"Who had the first automobile in this city, MacMillan?"

"You did, Captain."

"Then why does that gangster, Tu, have the number-one licence plate and I have the number-two? Answer me that?"

MacMillan thought, *Because Tu is Chinese, you little Mesopotamian heathen, and he bribed officials, and this is China, and besides, who cares about things like that?* But he said, "Sounds unfair to me, Captain."

"So you'll do it, then?"

"Fire-bomb Mr. Tu's automobile. Perhaps you'd like me to take the number-one licence plate off his automobile before I blow it to kingdom come?"

Silas thought about that for a moment, then said offhandedly, "If that wouldn't be too much to ask. As well, take off the number-two plate from my automobile and leave it prominently displayed near his ... wreckage."

MacMillan protested. "Switch his licence for yours? But then he'll know who bombed his automobile!"

Silas just smiled.

MacMillan was about to say something about foolish heathens, but instead he said, "What the hell, the automobile's not mine."

"No, it's not, Mr. MacMillan."

"Fine. Not a problem. I should have the plate for you by morning. Anything else?"

"No, MacMillan—you're a good man—good man."

MacMillan left the office and headed toward the old Chinese section of the city. As he did, Silas looked down at the thick traffic on Bubbling Spring Road. Bicycles and rickshaws and Hansom cabs and wagons and carriages and people—everywhere, in every crevice, people.

He had no doubt that Big-Eared Tu would respond in kind to MacMillan's little blast. He picked up his pen and wrote a note to Charles Soong, suggesting that his paper make space for a certain story or two that was bound to "explode" into the public's perception in the next three or four days.

He gave the note to his secretary, who hailed one of the six runners who were always at Silas's beck and call and gave the boy the note.

Silas sat back. He assumed that MacMillan would manage the deed that evening or the next. Then Tu would retaliate, and the press would have a field day. And everyone at the Bend in the River would begin to think about automobiles. That was the first step in the diversion—get everyone to think about how they worked, how to blow them up, why someone would want to blow one up, how to protect them—and eventually how to race them.

Silas smiled. Then he called in his secretary a second time. Holding the ashtray with his partially smoked cigar in it toward her, he said, "Throw this disgusting thing out."

Silas turned and looked down at the street. *So many eyes,* he thought. *So many eyes that need to be distracted if I am ever to get Mai Bao's large, curved object safely from the city at the Bend in the River.*

Silas glanced down at the open newspaper on his table. It was one of Charles Soong's oldest and most popular publications. Its undemanding Shanghainese prose was designed to appeal to the simplest of tastes. *The widest of the very wide base of the vast Chinese population,* Silas thought. He turned a page and noted a letter of bitter complaint from a courtesan. Silas stared at the courtesan's letter—he didn't read it. He didn't care if she was complaining of a madam or a client or the noise of streetcars. What he cared about was the fact that the courtesan's letter could be read by more than six million people, who might well tell twenty million more about it. That was a lot of eyes turned from the problems of the day to the problems, or supposed problems, of a courtesan.

He picked up the phone on his desk and ordered his automobile with the number-two licence plate put out on the street. "Yes," he said, "in an open place," then he added, "and far away from where people may be." He hung up before he added the thought, *Far enough away that when the thing blows up no one will get hurt.*

Silas headed home, then, and summoned Mai Bao, who appeared quickly, with a quizzical look on her face.

"Who do you know who writes for the newspapers?" She started to protest, but he stopped her. "I know that there was a time in your life when you were very ..." for a moment he hesitated, "... very close with writers. Do you still know any who would appreciate a news exclusive?"

"Is this about my request?" she asked.

"Certainly. Now just answer my question, Mai Bao."

After a little more cajoling Mai Bao acknowledged that she knew several newspaper writers, "From the old days." "Good," Silas said. "Tell them that if they want a good story they should loiter outside the warehouse where Gangster Tu keeps his automobile with the number-one licence plate."

"And they will know where this place is?"

"If they are real newspapermen, they will know."

———

MacMillan's explosion threw several of Gangster Tu's men, who slept in the loft above the garage, from their beds. The building itself seemed to ripple with the concussion of the blast. And when Tu finally made his way down to the stables where he kept his prized automobile, he was shocked to see that his pride and joy was little more than a smoking, blackened, twisted piece of useless metal—with a melted rubber bubble of a horn.

"What ...?" Tu was about to shout some elaborate profanity when he saw, much to his surprise, a completely clean, downright polished, licence plate with the single number two on it, nailed to the wall. He bent down to see if his number-one licence plate was still on his automobile. It was not.

Gangster Tu pulled the unscathed number-two plate off the wall and screamed, "Find me the automobile that this rightfully belongs to. Now!"

———

"HORSELESS CARRIAGE BLOWN UP!" screamed the local papers, which flew off the kiosk stands even faster than when a new Flower World Princess was crowned.

When, two days later, Silas's automobile—now bearing a licence plate with the number one—was blown to smithereens, the newspapers had an even better story: "HORSELESS CARRIAGE WAR!" The papers neglected to mention the dumpling seller who had happened by just as the bomb tore through Silas's prized Bugatti.

When Silas was told about the man he put his head in his hands and wept. Mai Bao had never seen him like this.

"It was not your fault. The man wandered there by mistake. It was a mistake. His mistake."

Silas looked up at his powerful, smart wife and said simply, "I carry too many souls on my back already. They bend me over like an old peasant beneath his firewood."

For a moment she thought that he was finally going to tell her about his brother Milo, but the moment passed, and Silas's business face returned. "What was the dumpling seller's name? Find it for me, Mai Bao, please. I want to pay for his funeral, and if he had a family I want them moved into the Garden."

Mai Bao did as he ordered.

Later that night, after he had been assured that the dumpling seller's family had been moved into the small house on the south side of the Garden, Silas Hordoon went over to see the man's widow and two small children. And in an act seldom, if ever, seen in the Middle Kingdom, a *Fan Kuei* Taipan knelt down before a Chinese peasant woman and her two small children and begged their forgiveness.

———

Two days later Silas's office desk was covered with newspapers. The city was following the "Horseless Carriage Wars" like an opium smoker follows the approach of his pipe. Silas had seen it before—a single idea taking control of the entire city. As a boy, Silas had seen Shanghai swept up in the thrill of the first theatre with women performing in public. Manchu law strictly forbade such female performances, but the theatres were in the

Foreign Settlement and thus protected from Beijing's edicts. For months you couldn't get a ticket—even *Fan Kuei* couldn't get seats. Several years after that, some merchant had introduced white cotton gloves as a fashion statement, and overnight everyone had to have a pair. No matter how hot or cold, every self-respecting Shanghainese wore their white gloves. Their clothes could be filthy, but those damned white gloves were always pristine. And of course there was the madness caused by his father's famous horse race. Silas stared out the window at the exact spot where Milo's saddle had shifted and his head had hit the ground. Roses and hydrangeas threw splashes of red across the dark earth. Silas always insisted that there be red in that flowerbed. It was the only request he had ever made for the dozens of beds throughout the Garden.

Silas knew that his father's famous race had been as much about mass hysteria as the running of horses. And that was exactly what he needed now, mass hysteria. Hysteria about automobiles, so that all those eyes would be watching automobiles and not a six-foot-long object being moved through the streets of the city at the Bend in the River by a middle-aged Jew. But how exactly he was going to move the large, curved object was a problem still awaiting a solution.

He thought about simply jumping to the ultimate part of the diversion, then decided that the diversion would work better with a buildup—just as an aria needs to be introduced by a recitative, and a fine main course by hors d'oeuvres and a cocktail.

He said the words aloud—"Hors d'oeuvres and cocktails." Then he smiled and called for Mai Bao. He told her what he wanted, and after a quick smile she bobbed a bow and headed out.

———

The next day's newspapers were filled with letters from courtesans about the glory of being chauffeured in automobiles to assignations, and the "preferability" of this means of transport over the covered palanquin. Others extolled the wisdom of accepting a month's use of a client's automobile as payment for particularly fine service. And finally, there was a wonderfully scandalous letter in which the courtesan implied that she had brought on the clouds and rain for a special client not just *in* an automobile but *as* he drove along the Bund with the European buildings on one side and the river on the other. Mai Bao had penned the letter herself and was proud of her achievement.

As these courtesan letters and the letters in response kept the city's focus on automobiles, Silas fanned the fire by offering the very latest

Italian Bugatti automobile to the winner of the next Flower Contest. And then, on the stage, as he handed over the keys to the winning courtesan with thousands upon thousands of cheering people watching, he announced, "In exactly a month I will race my automobile against anyone else's automobile on the streets of our city. The winner will take home one hundred thousand pounds sterling." Then he added, to the astonishment of the *Fan Kuei* community but to the open glee of the Chinese, "The race is open to one and all. Any resident of Shanghai—any resident of any race of Shanghai who can put up the entrance fee—is welcome to enter the Fabulous Shanghai Road Race."

The race to the race was on—and, as Silas had hoped, mass hysteria began to set in. Eyes turned from spying on the streets of Shanghai and narrowed their focus in anticipation of the racing of automobiles through the few paved streets of the city at the Bend in the River. And this being Shanghai, the betting began, even before the contestants were known.

chapter forty-five

A Long, Curved Object

Silas had never lost his temper with Mai Bao, but this night, as they sat over their simple evening meal, he pushed aside the prawns and said, "Not good enough, Mai Bao."

"It's as good as I am able to manage at this time, husband."

Silas sighed deeply. He still had no answer as to how to safely move the object, and his failure to solve the problem was making him both concerned and angry—not usual for him. He took a deep breath to calm himself, then asked, "This is important to you?"

"The most important thing in my life. I have said as much several times—several times." Her answer came back angry as well. For the first time in their marriage there was a tense silence between them.

"Fine, then tell me more about this object that I am supposed to spirit out of Shanghai."

"It is a—"

"Long, curved object, that you've told me. But surely you can tell me more. I am trying to help you but I have so little information that I might do damage to this 'long, curved' object." He paused for a moment, then said, "Help me to help you, Mai Bao."

Mai Bao stood and carefully closed the sliding doors of their dining room, then said, "Ask me questions, and I'll try to answer as honestly as I can."

Silas was tempted to get up and leave but resisted the impulse. He reminded himself that Mai Bao was not frivolous, had never been so.

"Is it delicate?"

"More so with every passing day."

"But it's also heavy?"

"Yes."

Silas waited for more information, but Mai Bao shook her head.

"Will water or cold or heat damage it?"

"They all could damage it, as I have said, but I don't think slight exposure to those elements would do any serious harm."

"And it's about six feet long?"

"And curved, husband," she snapped.

"And heavy but delicate," he snapped right back, then threw his hands up in frustration.

"Yes, husband, as I have said." Her voice was little more than a whisper.

They ate the rest of their dinner in silence. When they finished she crossed over to his side of the table and knelt with her head in his lap. "I am sorry."

He reached down and stroked the silk of her hair and thought, *I am not. Whatever this is, it is a gift to me, as you were a gift to me—a way to lighten the load I carry on my shoulders.*

chapter forty-six
The Racing Cars Arrive

Then the race cars began to arrive, each one redesigned for as much speed as it could muster. Mechanics were flown in from the United States and England and Italy and France to look after the temperamental machines. And the owners kept their new toys hidden away, just as the Vrassoons had kept their prized stallion a secret before the race that took Milo Hordoon's life.

The newspapers were paying huge sums of money for any information about the vehicles and would latch on to any tidbit they could find and blow it up into a front-page story. News about the teetering final gasps of the Manchu Dynasty never bumped information about Silas's "Fabulous Shanghai Road Race" off the front page.

Tu Yueh-sen was the first to display his entry, along with his twenty thousand pounds sterling entry fee. Although he had urged his Japanese contacts to get their manufacturers to produce a motorcar for the race, none was forthcoming. He desperately wanted to enter an Asian car but, unable to find one, settled on what was, to his mind, the next best thing— an Italian car. He bought the newest and best Italian automobile made by Anonima Lombarda Fabbrica Automobili. The car was better known by the company's acronym, ALFA, and because the firm was taken over by a Mr. Nicola Romeo, the car quickly became known as an ALFA-ROMEO. Tu demonstrated an unexpected flare for the dramatic by revealing his extraordinary racing car at Shanghai's Chinese New Year celebrations, nearly causing a riot. Following the great dragon that ended the huge parade came the very loud honking of a very powerful horn. Every eye turned to see Gangster Tu, wearing a long leather coat and goggles, standing on the front seat of his race car with his Japanese driver behind the wheel. Then Tu Yueh-sen began to throw silver dollars to the crowd—the effect was both impressive and complete.

The next day, William Dent presented a cheque for his company's fee and showed off a true oddity of a car—a Stanley Steam Automobile, whose engine, as the name suggested, ran on the steam generated from a boiler that was powered by coal. The car was remarkably sturdy and solid on the road, but it was carrying a tub of boiling water—a hazard on a train, let alone on a car jostling for position on a race course.

Heyward Matheson entered a remarkable British vehicle called a Simplex Racing Car, which was one of the few two-seater cars in the race. Although unproven on a racetrack, the car was smaller and faster than any of the competition.

Zachariah Oliphant wanted the actual Rambler 55 driven by President William Howard Taft, but, much to his surprise, the President of the United States refused to part with his beloved vehicle. When the Rambler Company heard of this they offered Oliphant any model they made—free of charge. But Oliphant refused, still evidently confused as to why the President of the United States would not contribute his automobile to the noble cause of showing the heathens of Shanghai what real engineering from a God-fearing country could do. He eventually settled on an Oldsmobile Model M Palace Touring Car—and a fine thing it was.

Meyer Vrassoon struck a secret deal with the Rolls Royce Company for the use of their inaugural Silver Ghost, which had already won its first three races. Part of the deal gave the Vrassoons exclusive rights to sell the Silver Ghost line once it went into full production.

Silas entered an exact replica of his beloved Bugatti, sacrificed in the Horseless Carriage Wars, and hired three technicians to increase the speed of the car.

Charles Soong fretted and fretted. Like Gangster Tu, he had wanted to enter an Asian car, but none was up to the competition. He finally settled on an Italian Zust, one of only three cars to complete the New York to Chicago race of 1908. It had four cylinders, a chain drive, and could attain a remarkable sixty miles per hour. Charles's only problem was that his wife and three daughters thought the car was "dowdy." As with so many comments from his wife and daughters, Charles really did not understand their complaint.

The French team (partially bankrolled by the Colombe family) bought all three major brands from their native land—Motobloc, Sizaire, and De

Dion Bouton—then began to mix and match the parts, with varying degrees of success. When beauty is the prime mover in decision making, sometimes things don't move so well.

—

MacMillan was shocked when he heard what Silas wanted done with the Bugatti. "Take off the top, Captain?"

"Yes, with a wrench, I guess."

A blowtorch, perhaps, or cutting shears, but certainly not a wrench, MacMillan thought. "Why?" he demanded.

"For speed," Silas said. Then he added, "And is there a way to affix a bar that goes over the top?"

"For what?"

"Safety," Silas said, adding then, as casually as he could manage, "should the automobile roll over."

"Whose safety?" MacMillan demanded.

"Yours." Silas's voice had dropped to a whisper. "Yours, Mr. MacMillan, should you agree to drive the automobile and should the Bugatti roll over."

MacMillan was thrilled. "I'd be happy to drive your car, Captain."

"Good," Silas said, "but I want that bar installed." He thought, *I will not have another death on my conscience.* He noticed MacMillan preparing to argue about the roll bar again and quickly said, "Install the bar for me, MacMillan, please, just do it."

—

It was an interesting day when the representatives of each of the eight race car teams got together in the meeting house in the Garden to decide upon a route for the race. Gangster Tu had sent a representative who stood silently to one side. The French had sent their driver and a translator— neither spoke much. And Charles Soong stood by himself with an odd smile on his face.

"It needs to be long enough to be a real test for the automobiles," William Dent said.

Silas noted that the lanky Mr. Dent had a slower but reliable car in the Stanley Steam Automobile, so that made sense from his point of view.

"With lots of curves and turns for excitement," Heyward Matheson chimed in.

Naturally, Silas thought, *since you have the smallest and lightest of the cars in the Simplex Racer.* But he responded, "I agree. This is an entertainment for the good citizens of Shanghai, and as such, as many twists and turns as we can manage would be just fine."

They eventually agreed upon a route that started on the long straight-away of the Bund, ran along the water, and then swung in the sharpest turn on the course inland along Bubbling Spring Road. After that it took a wide, gentle turn eastward and through the Old City along Fang Bang Lu, then back toward the river—and round and round.

"How many times?" Zachariah Oliphant asked.

Silas looked at the route. He had driven and timed approximations of the route himself only the previous night. It took just under ten minutes to complete the circuit. He calculated that he needed at least two hours to be safely out of Shanghai with the "long, curved object," so he said, "A round number, let's say fifty times."

A chorus of anguish rose up from the men, as Silas knew it would, but it was finally agreed that thirty laps was a fair and challenging test of both car and driver.

Thirty laps would give Silas three hundred minutes, five hours. It would be enough time—especially if he could figure out how exactly to make his own car roll.

chapter forty-seven
The Blessed Virgin

"The Bund's too narrow," MacMillan announced, only moments after barging into Silas's office.

"Too narrow for what?" Silas demanded.

"For the race, for eight cars to line up for the start of the race—it's too narrow. How're we going to start the race? It's only a week away, and we haven't even figured out how to start the damned thing."

"I'm afraid I'm not following, MacMillan. The problem with the Bund is what, exactly?"

"Width."

"The width of the Bund is a problem for the race?"

"Aye! It's twenty-one feet across, and each car averages a width of five feet, and there are eight cars!"

"And the problem with this is what?"

MacMillan stared at Silas. It always amazed him that certain kinds of problems, often those involved with simple mathematics, completely stymied the little heathen. Somehow the man couldn't envision the issue. Yet he ran a vast mercantile empire that produced millions of pounds of profits every year, and his new banking venture was rumoured to be generating more profit than all the rest of his assets combined. MacMillan illustrated the problem on a sheet of paper on Silas's desk.

Silas laughed. "Ah, I see, well, put four cars in the first row and four in the second and the problem is solved."

"No it's not, Captain. How can we explain to the owners which cars get to go in the first row and which cars are relegated to the second?"

"Ah, I see your point. How do other races handle this problem?"

That momentarily stumped MacMillan. He hadn't thought of using previous races as examples. "Well, most races are over long distances, like Paris to Peking, so it doesn't matter who starts first or second."

"But we're not racing over a long distance, we're racing round and round a circuit of roads, so who starts first or second does make a difference, am I correct?"

"Aye, Captain, that's the problem."

Silas shrugged. "Have there been other road-circuit races?"

"Yes."

"Good. So find out how they handled the problem, and I'll expect you back in this office at this time tomorrow with the answer to the question."

Silas turned from MacMillan and his mind returned to the problem of moving a "large, curved object" out of Shanghai without prying eyes seeing it. Moments later he looked back and was surprised to see MacMillan still standing in his office.

"Go. And close the door behind you."

———

The next morning, an ecstatic MacMillan was waiting for Silas when he arrived at his office.

"Morning, Mr. MacMillan."

"Aye, it's a very good morning, Captain. That it is," he said, waving what looked like a large lithographic reproduction of a photograph in Silas's face.

"Is that for me?"

"Aye, it solves our problem, Captain."

Silas had spent another long night trying to devise a plan to solve his own problem. Just before sunrise he had retreated to his bed, pleased to find Mai Bao there. He'd curled up against her back and slept for two hours before rising and coming to the office—his problem still unresolved. Now he glanced at the photograph in MacMillan's hand and said, "Well, good, come in."

MacMillan almost ran to Silas's desk and plunked down the large lithograph with the Scottish version of "ta-dah." Silas removed his coat and moved to the desk. The lithographic reproduction was of a photograph that must have been taken from high above. It showed ten or twelve race cars parked at an angle on one side of a road while several men, who Silas assumed were their drivers, ran across the broad avenue toward their respective cars.

"See?" MacMillan announced proudly. "We park the cars on the river side of the Bund, while we keep the drivers on the far side. On the sound of the starting pistol they race across the Bund, start their cars, back up, and take off. First to get going is first to start the race. Simple. Aye, simple, Captain."

Silas nodded, but his eyes were not on the parked race cars or the running drivers in the photograph, but rather on a car, clearly not a racing car, that had a large sculpture of a figure—Silas assumed it was a saint—with its arms outstretched for some reason, standing in the passenger's seat.

"What's that?" he asked.

MacMillan couldn't believe the heathen's question but saw no way of avoiding answering. "It's the Blessed Virgin."

"Ah," Silas said, raising his eyebrows to acknowledge that he had asked something foolish. But he pressed on. "Yes, but what is it, or She, doing standing on the front seat of that car?"

"The photograph's from the Rome road race, so it's probably blessing the course from the lead car."

Silas finally sat, and motioned for MacMillan to do the same. Then he asked, "Do all races have lead cars?"

"No, Captain."

"But if there is a lead car, explain what it does in a race."

"It goes around the track once, sometimes twice, just before the race begins."

"While the Virgin blesses the route?"

"Aye."

"Are we going to have a lead car, MacMillan?"

"I thought you didn't believe in that sort of thing, Captain."

Silas heard the nasty edge to MacMillan's query but ignored it. "That's not the point. I think we should follow Rome's example."

"Aye, that's the stuff. So all eight race cars will be parked at an angle facing the river, and on the sound of the starting gunshot the drivers run to their cars."

"Yes, MacMillan, but only after the lead car drives the course and the statue blesses the route."

MacMillan stared at Silas. What was the little man up to? But all he said was, "These Chinks don't believe in saints, Captain."

"You're right, MacMillan. It won't be a Catholic saint blessing the course."

"Then what?"

"A Buddha, naturally. A great big laughing Buddha should do the trick, don't you think?"

chapter forty-eight
A Laughing Buddha

Silas stared at the old man in front of him. Mai Bao had introduced the man as a master carver—and a reliable man who could keep a secret. Silas couldn't get over the feeling that he had seen this man before.

"Have we met, sir?" he asked, proffering a cup of the finest oolong tea.

The man took the delicate porcelain cup in his hands and smiled. "I think not, Mr. Hordoon."

But Silas couldn't shake the feeling that they had some sort of connection. "But you know my wife?"

"Yes, sir, through her deceased mother."

Silas nodded but was still troubled. What or when or how was he connected to this man? He shook his head.

"Sir?" the old Carver asked.

"Nothing, just a foolish feeling." But Silas had lived in the Middle Kingdom long enough to know that such feelings were not foolish. They were indications of insights yet to be understood. Impulses awaiting words. The Carver knew that too. The old man knew the connection that was trying to burble up into Silas's consciousness. The Carver was well acquainted with the story of this man's uncle requesting a carving, not so different from the one that he knew Silas was going to ask for. Back then the hidden object had been a red-haired man, rather than the Sacred Relic.

"How can I be of service, sir?" the Carver pressed.

Isn't that something, Silas said to himself. Then he put aside the strange feelings and explained in great detail what he wanted the man to produce.

To keep up the illusion of innocence, the Carver asked for details about the "large, curved" object that was to be secreted inside the Laughing Buddha. Silas promptly told him the little that he knew.

The Carver nodded, then asked, "And this Laughing Buddha is to be in an automobile?"

For an instant the Carver held his breath. Would Silas notice that he'd mentioned this detail, despite the fact that Silas had not mentioned anything about the statue riding in a car?

"Yes," Silas said, "I'd almost forgotten that."

The Carver allowed his breath to return to normal as Silas showed him the lithograph of the Rome road race's lead car.

The Carver asked, "May I see the automobile that will carry the Laughing Buddha?"

"Surely."

Silas walked the Carver down to where an older-model car sat, with a number-one licence plate on its front bumper. He put down the folding roof and indicated the front passenger seat.

"And you will drive?" the Carver asked.

"Yes."

"Good."

"Anything else you need, sir?"

"No." The Carver smiled and said, "I have all I need. The Laughing Buddha will be ready the day before your race. Will that suffice?"

"Yes." Again Silas stared at the elderly man.

"What is it, sir?"

"Just this feeling that I have been here before."

The Carver smiled, knowing full well that China's history was folding in on itself yet again. What this man's Uncle Maxi had done all those years ago was about to be repeated, but this time with a different kind of hiding place, and a very different hidden treasure.

chapter forty-nine
Rolling a Racing Car

It was the moment of pause in the great city—when it held its breath and allowed its head to loll forward on its chest ... and rest. It was just past three in the morning. The night soil collectors would begin their morning visitations in about ninety minutes. But now, silence reigned at the Bend in the River. And Silas was counting. Counting steps from the Bund, along the alley, and down to the wharf. He had previously measured the width of the alley and been grateful to find that at least some of it was wide enough for clearance. But now it was the length of the alley after it narrowed that worried him. So he walked slowly and counted his steps. Every five steps he turned back toward the Bund. "So once I am twenty yards into the alley, no one can see me from the Bund," he said aloud.

At the end of the alley he drew another deep breath and began to count his steps again as he made his way toward the large iron cleat screwed into the heavy timbers of the wharf. He walked backward, facing the city. Sixteen paces away from the mouth of the alley he would be clearly visible to anyone looking from the turn in the Bund where it intersected with Bubbling Spring Road. He turned toward the wharf and continued to count his paces. And his anxiety rose. It was almost two hundred yards to the iron cleat on the wharf. And during all that time he would be in clear view of whoever happened to glance back over their shoulder from the intersection of the Bund and Bubbling Spring Road.

Then he looked across the river. The Pudong stared back at him a challenge to everything civilized that the *Fan Kuei* had made at the Bend in the River.

"Don't worry, the Pudong's on its side and we're on ours."

Silas stilled the sudden thudding of his heart and looked at the beggar who had evidently curled up on the wharf for a night's rest.

"You're right, sir," Silas replied.

"It's prayer that keeps it over there and us over here," the old man said.

"Really?" Silas asked in earnest.

"Yes. Prayer does it, sir." Then the man drew back a blanket and pulled out an ancient arhu. In a moment he had the instrument's strings tuned and he began to play.

As he did, Silas said the first prayer he'd uttered since he was a boy: "Please keep MacMillan safe. Please."

The arhu player looked at him and said, "This music is prayer."

And Silas relaxed. He recognized the song. It was one that Mai Bao had played, "Tears of Time." Silas slowly sat down beside the old man and the two listened to the arhu's prayer and watched the dense woods of the Pudong across the Huangpo River as the sun slowly snuck above the eastern horizon.

———

Silas ordered the workmen to make the wall higher, "Much higher."

"It's not necessary," MacMillan protested for the tenth time.

"I say it is, Mr. MacMillan." MacMillan flushed with anger as Silas turned from him and addressed the workmen in fluent Shanghainese. "Please, I need this wall built higher and the curve continued farther up."

The workers nodded, then turned to MacMillan for their specific orders.

"Chop chop! You hear, mister? Chop chop!" Then he turned back to Silas, but Silas was gone.

Silas had no desire to discuss with MacMillan his decision to build a twelve-foot, concave wall at the point of the sharpest turn on the race course, where the cars would leave the straightaway of the Bund and head inland along Bubbling Spring Road. He had hoped that his explanation— "For the safety of the crowd that is watching the race"—would suffice. But MacMillan had simply replied, "The Chinks'll just climb up it for a better view."

Silas knew that MacMillan might be right, but still he had insisted on the wall. It was a vital part of his getaway plan—that, and the roll bar he had ordered MacMillan to weld to the Bugatti. He needed an accident to attract eyes away from the dock, but he wanted no repeat of Milo's demise. He made a mental note that MacMillan was to wear a seat harness.

The final piece of his plan had come into focus when MacMillan's mechanic explained the need to gear down as a driver spun the steering wheel to allow for a tight turn in a race when taking the turn "at speed."

"And there is no other time when the steering wheel would turn rapidly at the same time as the car gears down?" Silas had asked.

"Not that I can think of, Guv," the cockney mechanic had said.

"Fine. Very interesting, sir, very interesting," Silas had said as he left the man to ponder what, exactly, this conversation had been about.

That night Silas spread out the mechanical drawings of his race car's innards on his office desktop. Each corner of the large drafting sheets was held down by a piece of rough-cut jade. Silas's hand glided over the intricately etched drawings. It had served him well over the years to plead ignorance of any and all matters mechanical—but he was far from ignorant of such matters. Although not as adept as his Uncle Maxi had been, Silas had always been fascinated by what made things work.

And now he saw quite clearly what the car's moving parts would look like if the steering wheel were turned hard to the left just as the vehicle was geared down from third to second to first.

The slight crossing of the two sets of pulleyed wires offered him all the opportunity he needed.

———

The following night he was alone with the car raised on a hoist. He nicked his hands several times as he connected the two sets of guide wires to the sides of the pivot that would, when the car was geared down sharply while the steering wheel was spun hard counterclockwise, turn the steel blade to which it was attached in such a way that it would slash the right front tire. The car would roll up the curved wall—then, hopefully, safely back down—attracting every eye to the track and away from the wharf long enough for him to cover the exposed, two hundred-odd yards to the cleat on the wharf to which the junk would be moored.

The initial wires he had brought to do the work were too brittle and kept breaking when the gearshift clunked into place. For an instant he thought that all was lost. Then an ancient voice in his head whispered the word *silk*—and he laughed. He was in China, and silk was the cord of choice here. As he made the knots to join the gearshift wire to the point of the turning axel base, and then to the pivoting knife, he once again felt, as he had with the Carver, that he had been in this precise spot before.

Silas was using the exact same silken knots that his Uncle Maxi had used to affix the rifles that saved Richard from the millstoning.

———

Silas recognized the smell. He had smelled it so often when his father was alive, and it had always nauseated him. But now the smell was coming not from his father's clothes or hair or hands, but from himself. The smell of serpent smoke. Opium in his mouth and in his bowels and wrapping its constrictor self around his heart—and pulling tight.

Silas opened his mouth to scream and red hydrangeas flew from his mouth toward the startlingly white ceiling. As each flower soared upward it struck the ceiling, leaving a blood splatter in its place. Then the blood began to drip onto him, to coat him from his forehead to his somehow naked belly to his feet. Boots of blood formed on him. He reached toward his feet and felt the wind strike him hard in his face.

Then he heard it.

Cheers. Cheers of *Milo! Milo! Milo!*

He looked to his right and the thousands of faces in the grandstands of his father's racetrack were moving past so quickly he didn't recognize a single one.

Then he felt it. A stinging across his back. He looked to his left. The Vrassoons' jockey on the huge white stallion had struck him across the back with his whip. The man raised his whip. Silas saw the blood dripping from it and noticed the open wounds on the stallion's side.

Then the whip fell a second time on Silas's arm, jerking the reins free from his grasp. He lurched forward and grabbed handfuls of the horse's mane and shouted, "Run!"

And the horse beneath him, as if lifted by a great wave, moved like a majestic Indiaman sailing ship with God's pure wind at its back, taking the far reach of the Yangtze and entering the Huangpo … heading home.

Silas leaned into the upcoming turn and felt the distance open between himself and the Vrassoons' great stallion. He was ahead. He was winning. On the other side of the turn he saw the finish line. He leaned harder into the turn, shouting encouragement to his horse.

Then he sensed it.

Something moved.

Had his horse missed a stride?

Then he heard it. The sound of the hemp of the cinch strap ripping.

He felt the saddle move beneath him and saw the ground racing toward him. The heavy metal of the right stirrup slammed into his face and gouged out his left eye in a blinding flash of pain. His back slammed into the ground and he heard a bone snap, then another. He found himself somehow in a sitting position looking back up the track. The Vrassoons' great stallion was going to pass him by on the rail side. Then he saw the jockey pull on the right rein and the horse headed directly at him.

Everything slowed, and he saw the stallion's huge right fore hoof rise up and land on his pelvis, snapping it cleanly and rolling him to his back. Then his single good eye filled with dirt and he felt a terrible weight on his back as, he guessed, the stallion's huge left fore hoof stomped down hard … on his spine.

———

Silas awoke in a mound of pillows and sheets on the floor beside his bed. His eyes streamed with tears. The smell of opium was gone, but somehow it lingered in the corners of the room   waiting for the next time he let his guard down.

He threw open the window of his room and turned on the light. And there, as it had always been, was the very spot where his brother Milo had met his death. A death that he, Silas Hordoon, had caused. The square of light from his window lit the spot. To Silas's shock the hydrangeas had all bent so that their blossoms touched the ground—great red tears about to fall.

He promised himself that he would make MacMillan wear that seat harness, if it was the last thing he ever did.

———

The morning was raw. Cold wind swept up the Yangtze all the way from the sea and found Silas standing at the three graves and one mound on the rise of the north reach of the Huangpo. After his awful night, despite the cold, the slowly dawning light was reassuring.

He knelt by his brother's grave and laid his hands upon the wet earth. "I am so sorry, Milo. So very sorry." The wind answered him in swirling gusts—angry howls. Silas dug his fingers into the soil of the grave and then found himself flinging back clods of earth. The exertion felt good. Somehow Milo felt closer. Then his left hand felt something moist and very cold.

For a moment he felt the sucking grip of the earth and images of Milo, long buried, grasping his hand and pulling him into the grave filled his mind—then they were gone, and the sun came out from behind a cloud. The wind abated, and the warmth of dawn crept into his bones and his mind. It was a new day. A day when he would take the first steps in paying for the sins of his past.

He sat back on his haunches and looked at Milo's grave. Then slowly, meticulously, lovingly, he reformed the ground over his dead brother's body and patted it into firmness. He rose and looked for the briefest moment at the other graves, realizing that if his plan succeeded he would not see them for quite some time. But time, he knew, was part of the penalty you paid for doing the Devil's work.

chapter fifty
Race Day

People came from all over the Middle Kingdom to see the Fabulous Shanghai Road Race. Manchu court officials snuck away from their duties and made their way south. They came from the Macao and Hong Kong trading houses, finding business that just had to be done in Shanghai on that particular day. From Nanking and Canton and all places in between, the wealthy and the not-so-wealthy made their way to the Bend in the River. They arrived on carts and on foot, in palanquin carriages and on horseback. Some were driven in cars—but not many. Boats travelling in both directions on the Yangtze were stuffed to overflowing with passengers literally holding on for dear life to ropes slung to boats that they towed. But those who were drawn to the spectacle were not just from China. They came from abroad as well, from France and Italy, England and Scotland, and the Americas. And those who came from across the water came with their entourages—their mistresses, their bodyguards, their drivers, their masseuses, their sommeliers, and their cooks. One of whom, a tall, broad-shouldered Black man, had been rescued, as a boy, from Boston and trained to be a chef in "a much better place."

And the great city swelled to accept its visitors. The partially built walkway along the Bund overlooking the Huangpo River slept over six thousand souls the night before the race. Some were even forced across the Huangpo to the ever-dangerous Pudong to find a place to sleep—from which many never awakened. Brigands still controlled the Pudong, and travellers were not welcomed in their midst.

The night before the race the skies cleared. The gentle breeze from the west blew the incinerator smoke away from the city, lifting it, like so much silk, and flinging it down the river to the sea.

In the garages of the eight entrants final preparations were well underway, and the sound of hammers gave a strange note of preparation to the day. Roosters cried the dawn into morning and the thousands of peasants sleeping on the streets roused themselves and stood in the spots where they had slept, claiming their place in the day. Across the cracked pavements shadows moved with a silent grace as thousands performed their morning Tai Chi exercises. The hawkers were out in full force selling breakfast gruel—at almost seven times the normal price. The five-spice egg sellers were doing a brisk business, as were the water shops selling sheets of toilet paper and access to their "facilities." Police began to line the route, pushing people back from the course itself. Every rooftop along the way was filled with people—and the betting shops had sent their people into the dense crowds to facilitate yet more wagering. Before nine o'clock there had already been three million dollars bet on the race. A book Charles Soong published, detailing the assets of each car and driver, had gone into its sixteenth printing the day before and was now being sold by young boys on the street—at a healthy markup.

Food, wagering, crowds—hysteria swept through the city at the Bend in the River, as a two-man junk made its way slowly up the Huangpo to a wharf near the Bund. There, despite regulations, the grizzled Captain wrapped the boat's bowline around a heavy iron cleat. Then he sat back on a coil of heavy, braided rope and took out a Snake Charmer cigarette. Lit it. And waited patiently. He had been paid a huge sum of money directly from a *Fan Kuei* who, he had learned, was named Silas Hordoon. He was to take this man and a single object that the man would carry far up the Yangtze, where evidently he was to be met by other men who would take the *Fan Kuei* overland—to somewhere, somewhere better—a better place.

———

Edward had served a sumptuous breakfast of butter-filled pecan waffles with clotted cream and fresh field berries to his patron and the man's retinue earlier that morning. The man and his followers had both eaten and complimented him with great gusto. Then they'd hurried out into the street to assume positions on the race course that had been reserved for them by forty peasants, all of whom received handsome rewards for their efforts.

Edward oversaw the clearing of the dining room and then, once satisfied that the cleaners knew what they were doing, donned a sweater and
stepped out into the morning air. He was a black-skinned man—a true rarity in the city at the Bend in the River, where Africans were seldom seen—
tall and broad across the shoulder, with a smile so bright that it lit up the
morning. The waves of humanity parted as he approached, then filled in
behind him, in his wake, with a loud, gibbering commentary. Fortunately
for Edward he could not translate the streams of sarcastic comments, excla-
mations of horror, and the odd statement of wonder at his size—and his
potential jade spear size. Edward just moved on through the crowd with a
smile on his face, wondering at the number of people all around him. He
eventually slid and cajoled his way through the throngs to a very sharp
turn in the race course, where a tall, curved wall—like a wave about to
break—had been built. He noticed dozens of children sitting on the very
top of the wall. He stepped out into the street, ignored the stares of the
crowd and the shouts of a Sikh police officer, then, to the delight of the
children, ran up the concave of the wall. He pulled himself to the top and
sat between the children there, not one of whom was more delighted with
the view than he was.

chapter fifty-one
Getting the Tusk

Silas was surprised that he was not alone. Since Mai Bao had been secretive in every detail of her instructions, he'd simply assumed that Jiang's, which he knew she now owned, would be empty when he arrived to collect the mysterious "large, curved object." The seven-foot-tall Laughing Buddha stood by the door, its upraised left arm hollow and ready to receive the upper end of the object through the hinged flap cleverly hidden in the folds of its robe. Although the streets were almost deserted, as every ambulatory Shanghainese had many hours ago claimed a viewing place on the route of the race, there were three Han Chinese males waiting for him in the reception room of Jiang's.

One of whom he recognized.

Without speaking a word, the Master Carver shambled over to Silas and put out a hand. Silas tentatively extended his, and the two men shook. The Carver's strong grip impressed Silas. Then the Confucian stepped forward and shook hands also. Silas turned to the third man, who, to Silas's surprise, spoke.

"You'll need help getting the Tusk into the statue?"

"Tusk?" Silas blurted out.

Tension suddenly surged in the room. The man who had spoken rebalanced his weight and his hand slipped toward his swalto blade. Then Mai Bao entered the room and said simply, "Show my husband the relic."

With a solemnity that surprised Silas, the three men moved aside a table with a Go board on it, opened a velvet-covered box bench, and produced the remarkable object. The instructions he had received from Mai Bao concerning the length and curvature of the object now made sense, as did the answers to his questions about the strength of the object and how to keep it safe. What he did not understand, and knew better than to ask, was why this object needed to be spirited out of Shanghai and hidden. But he didn't need an answer to this question. Mai Bao and these men were clearly not frivolous individuals. They were fine representatives of their race—practical people who were asking a favour of a practical nature. An important favour that evidently only Silas Hordoon could accomplish for them.

A favour that Silas was willing to grant, first because he loved his wife, but on a deeper and more important level because he felt he owed it to Shanghai, his home. As well, in a hidden recess in his heart, he wondered if doing this favour might somehow expiate the sins that he had accrued while doing the Devil's work.

"These are the members of the Ivory Compact, husband. You are the only person not a member of the Compact who has ever—in the over two-thousand-year history of the Compact—met the Chosen Three, and the Carver."

"I am honoured, Mai Bao."

"As well you should be," said the Carver, who then added, "Let's secrete away the Tusk while the entire city is looking the other way."

The Tusk was removed from the box bench and wrapped in a gossamer silk.

"Is that strong enough?" Silas asked.

"The tears of many women make it extremely strong, husband."

Loa Wei Fen guided the Tusk into its hiding place in the Laughing Buddha. They carried the statue carefully to the curb.

There the men hoisted the large statue into the front seat of the automobile, where they secured it with guide wires while Silas cranked the engine into life. The wonderful thing burbled, then spat, then caught. The engine's spinning settled into a dull roar, and Silas slid behind the wheel. He looked back at the steps of Jiang's. He remembered as a young man walking up those steps, first to see the plays of the History Teller and later to experience women—always Asian women, as his father's Scottish assistant had so charmingly noted. He remembered his brother Milo taking those steps two at a time and the welcoming squeals from the women when he flung open the door. He remembered the drunken American who had told him of an impending civil war in America that would raise the price of cotton. Bringing this information to his father had been one of the few things that had made his father smile. All from this house! And now Mai Bao, the Carver, the Confucian, and the Assassin were standing on the steps, stock-still, staring at him, as if he were about to take their photograph.

He checked to make sure that the large rug was in the back seat of his car, then released the clutch. But before the gears could engage, Mai Bao ran up to him and kissed him, hard, full on the mouth—then handed him a large package.

"What's this?"

"Your book," she said, "your father's journals."

He kept his foot on the clutch and took a long, final look at his wife, then released the clutch, and the gears engaged. The car picked up speed slowly.

As it did, it passed the solitary figure of a young man standing in the shadows. This young man was born in 1893 in the small town of Shaoshan, in Hunan Province. Li Tian, the master fireworks maker, had taken the young man under his wing and made sure that he had read the classics, while on the side teaching him the basics of fireworks making. He had then insisted that the young man work for three years in a library. But those three years were up, and the young man was now in Shanghai. It was the first time he had come to the city, and he was amazed by what he saw. He pencilled a note in a small book with a red cover. The young man's name was something of a joke. You see, Mao means—cat.

chapter fifty-two
The Race

Silas was having fun—the last thing he'd thought would happen. As he drove the lead car slowly around the circuit he basked in the applause from the huge crowd. Cheers, howls of delight, screams of pleasure erupted from the people when they saw the Laughing Buddha, arms outstretched, coming toward them. And it was more than just pleasure he sensed. He felt them grateful. Thankful that the race would be blessed by their deity, by one of their own.

Silas turned north, past the great curve in the road, and was surprised to see a large Black man sitting amongst the children on the top of the safety wall. He wanted to stop and tell them to get down from there but there was no way—and no time. The large Buddha strained against the guide wires that held it in place as he took the sharp curve without gearing down, and for one terrifying moment he thought it might actually fall, or pull the car over. But neither happened, and the Laughing Buddha, with the Sacred Relic secreted inside, continued its strange, stately voyage around the circuit that would eventually shed the name of the Fabulous Shanghai Road Race and become known to history as the slightly more modest Great Shanghai Road Race.

—

MacMillan cursed the roll bar as he smacked his head against it for the twentieth time getting out of the car. The lottery had given the Hordoon car the sixth place in the line of parked cars on the river side of the Bund. But that didn't worry him because he had arranged a new ignition system for the car that allowed him to start the car while it was in reverse. Since the rest of the field had to start in neutral then go into reverse, MacMillan was confident that he would be the first car on the actual course. He'd promised the little heathen that he'd wear his seat harness—God only knew why it was so important. He was confident in the speed of his car, if not the roll bar, which he silently cursed again as he took his position with the other drivers across the road, waiting for the lead car to finish its lap and the race to begin.

———

Silas passed by several raised pavilions. One he knew belonged to Gangster Tu, another to the Americans, Oliphant and Company, and a third to the French entry. The Vrassoons, the Dents, the Jardine Mathesons would no doubt watch the proceedings from the safety and comfort of the roofs of their headquarters on the Bund itself or from the roofs of their stores on Bubbling Spring Road. Charles Soong had erected a covered scaffolding from which he and his wife, Yin Bao, and their children could view the race from a safe distance. His three daughters had grown up very fast and were far too interested in young men for his taste—and young men were interested in them as well—so Charles usually kept his brood aloof from or, in this case, above, the fray.

Silas made the final turn in the course and headed toward the start/finish line at the far east end of the Bund. He knew that if he wanted he could make a second circuit of the course, but as he turned onto the Bund at its eastern end he decided against it. It was time to put his plan into action, to send the arrow into the air—hoping he knew where it would land.

So as the cheers swelled he pulled the lead car with its Laughing Buddha over to the north side of the road and parked just behind the eight parked race cars. He stood and waved. The crowd cheered. And although Silas smiled broadly, he was not really waving to the crowd. He was straining to see if the two-man junk was tied at the wharf, awaiting him and his "baggage."

A man with a large red paper megaphone stepped into the centre of the road and hollered. The crowd went silent. Completely silent. *Such an odd thing,* Silas thought. *Silence at the Bend in the River.* He was not sure he had ever heard that before. The man shouted, "Take your marks! Set!" Then he fired his pistol into the air, and the eight drivers sprinted across the road and leaped into their cars.

———

MacMillan got to the Bugatti quickly, avoided the roll bar, ignored the seat harness, hit the ignition and backed out quickly. As he had predicted, he was the first one on the course itself, and he used the Bund straightaway to gain speed, although he wasn't moving fast enough to need to gear down at the sharp left turn onto Bubbling Spring Road. He took the turn with a wave to the crowd that drew cheers and hollers that could be heard well into the incantatory interior of the Pudong. He was quickly followed by Jardine Matheson's Simplex Racing Car and the Vrassoons' Rolls Royce Silver Ghost.

Silas watched carefully as every eye followed the progress of the cars. When he was sure that no one was watching, he drove his car, with the Laughing Buddha, forward, then down the narrow alley leading to the wharf.

On the second lap the cars slowed and carefully took the sharp turn with the large safety wall. As Silas had predicted, the first few times past the Bubbling Spring Road turn the drivers would be careful and not take the curve at speed. As long as they did so, the steering wheel of MacMillan's car would not spin quickly enough to engage the knife that would cut his front tire and cause the car to roll.

The Stanley Steam Car belonging to Dent's was the first casualty of the race. Something happened and the thing suddenly just stopped. Then it rumbled, and steam shot from its hood as a large, hot puddle formed beneath the car's rear wheels. The driver cursed as the other cars swerved to get past the stationary vehicle.

Silas drove as far along the narrowing alley toward the wharf as he dared. Then he dismounted and stared at the alley behind him. Empty. Almost silent. Only the cheers and shouts from the course itself filled the void. He unrolled the carpet from the back seat and set it on the ground in front of the car, then released the relic from its hiding place, put it on the carpet, and rolled it up carefully.

When he went to hoist it to his shoulder he had a shock. It was much heavier than he had thought. And he had thirty yards more of the alley and then almost two hundred yards to cover on the open wharf with the thing on his shoulder. He took a deep breath, bent his knees deeply, and managed to settle the relic on his shoulder. Then he stagger-walked to the very end of the alley. Sweat poured from his forehead and momentarily blinded him. He swiped it away with his free forearm. He stopped and waited. For almost two hundred yards he would be in plain view of anyone who cared to look away from the race as he moved along the wharf to the two-man junk. It was the most dangerous part of his exit from Shanghai—and the reason he had gone to all the trouble to get his own car to roll over, with MacMillan hopefully safe inside, strapped into his seat harness.

—

MacMillan was having as much fun as he had ever managed. Silas's car was swift and handled beautifully. He could see the Rolls Royce Silver Ghost belonging to the Vrassoons and the Simplex Racing Car belonging to Jardine Matheson in his rear-view mirror, and they were coming on fast but having trouble finding a place to pass him. He took the turn onto the Bund to complete his second lap, and a large placard with a huge number two was placed over the start/finish line. With the width of the Bund, the other cars slid to the outside trying to pass, but MacMillan slammed his foot down on the gas and managed to keep their challenge at bay as he sped past the great trading houses on the Bund and headed toward the one sharp turn in the course—a logical place to try to pass another car, something that MacMillan was not going to let happen.

As he approached the turn onto Bubbling Spring Road he hit the accelerator at the same time as he slammed the gearshift from third to second, to gain some traction. Then right in the curve itself, at the base of the large safety wall, he shoved the gearshift into first and furiously spun the steering wheel to the left.

Beneath MacMillan, the silk cords attached to the gearbox and the steering column came as close to each other as they could, thereby hooking the lever that engaged the blade that Silas had secured there. The blade pivoted as he had intended and dug deep into the racing car's right front tire.

MacMillan felt something give and suddenly he was spinning up the safety wall, somersaulting left to right, completely out of control. The only thing he remembered seeing was something that he assumed was a delusion: a Black man throwing himself at the car with dozens of Chinese children cowering behind him.

—

Edward saw the car's front tire blow out and the car begin to spin up the safety wall. It turned over and over like a chicken on a rotisserie, he thought. Then he heard the screams of the children all around him and saw the car barrelling toward them. He threw himself at the car with all his might and managed to change the direction of the car just a little, just enough that it did not hit the children—although Edward, the African from Boston, was so badly hurt that his voyage to the better place was swift, and sure.

———

Then Silas heard it—the screams. He sensed the movement of thousands of people as they ran toward the accident. He hoped that MacMillan was okay. Hoped that none of the children on the safety wall were hurt. He gave no thought to the large Black man he had seen there as he carried the Tusk inside the blanket as swiftly as he could along the wharf and into the two-man junk—all, he believed, without a single eye seeing his going.

chapter fifty-three
Silas Onboard

Late that night, Silas came on deck for the first time and wondered if somehow, in the moonlight, he was dreaming. But he stopped wondering when the Captain approached, wiped his raw, veined nose on his filthy sleeve, and said, "I was told to put those on deck in open display."

"Those" were thirteen other ivory tusks, strapped beneath the gunwales on both sides of the junk. Before Silas could ask, "By whom?" the ship swayed in a deep swell and Silas's stomach rose. He teetered and grabbed at the mast for support. The junk's Captain was completely unaffected by the pitch and roll of his vessel.

"I was told not to answer questions but just to get the Tusk you carry and put it in with the others."

Not knowing what else to do, Silas nodded.

The Captain returned to his tiller, readjusted his course, and lashed it off. Then he said, "You are not as clever as all that."

"Meaning what?"

"Did you really believe that no one would figure out your plan? That no one would follow this very ship and try to steal the relic?"

Silas suddenly broke out in a cold sweat. All his planning, and yet ... "How did you know...?"

"Shanghai is not a good place to keep secrets secret. But let that stand. The real danger to the relic is you, Mr. Hordoon. So be quick now because our time is short. Bring the Tusk up on deck."

Silas found himself somehow unable to control the motion of his legs and arms as he went below deck, knelt down, and pulled the Tusk in its Takrit carpet from beneath the berth. As if still in a trance, Silas carried the Tusk up on deck and then followed the Captain to the port side, where several other tusks were hanging. One set of straps in the midst of the other tusks dangled free. The Captain pointed to them, and Silas unwrapped the Tusk from the carpet, guided the relic into the waiting space, and belted it into place.

"Now, lad, be smart, turn the relic so that the back, not the opened portals, faces the deck."

Silas shook his head at his own idiocy and did as the Captain requested. Then he stepped back. In the shadows cast by the overhanging railings no one would be able to see the filigree etchings on the Tusk's surface, so it would appear to be just one of the many ivories destined for the carving factories upriver.

Silas turned to go, but the Captain's massive hand pulled at his belt buckle. "If you return to your berth you will not see the morning. On this, trust me. There is a bumboat lashed to our port side. It is already manned. Take it and get safely off this ship. I will meet you with the Tusk at Chinkiang—the City of Suicides—in two days."

Silas stared at the Captain. "And just leave the relic ...?"

"With God. Yes. Now hurry." Then the Captain pointed astern. Two large war junks were closing on them quickly. "The men in the bumboat think you are going ashore to find a concubine." The Captain smiled. "The best lie I could come up with on short notice. Hurry now. You are the greatest danger to the Narwhal Tusk. Get into that bumboat—time to stop doing the Devil's work."

Silas glanced at the Captain. It must have just been the light behind him, but he seemed to glow slightly. He turned and headed toward the bumboat but stopped when the Captain called after him. "Don't forget this," he said, holding out the packet containing Richard's journals. Silas was in a hurry or he would have realized that the packet had grown since Mai Bao had given it to him—grown by the weight of a Bible.

"But who are you?" Silas finally demanded.

The man just smiled. Finally he said, "I am who I am. That will have to be enough for you. Now go."

As Silas scrambled over the side of the junk, the Captain returned to his tiller and awaited the assault.

———

Gangster Tu's ships closed fast on the two-man junk, and in moments the smaller ship was grappled, bow and stern, and pulled tight to the larger ships. Tu Yueh-sen stepped onboard the small junk. The grizzled Captain demanded an explanation.

Tu answered simply, "Do you want to keep the eyes you have in your foolish head, or not?"

The Captain backed away, allowing Gangster Tu and his Red Poles, one of whom was Loa Wei Fen, to come aboard.

The Assassin saw the etched filigree of the Sacred Tusk catch the moonlight and he gave a quick prayer of thanks that earlier in the week he had carved the cobra on his younger son's back. The boy had accepted the pain without a whimper. Loa Wei Fen had then instructed the boy in his duties in the Ivory Compact should something happen to him. And he knew that something was going to happen on this tiny, rocking junk. Something that might propel his son into the Compact very shortly.

Gangster Tu ordered two Red Poles to light torches and the others to unleash the ivory tusks. One after another the valuable tusks were presented to Tu, who tossed them aside like so much rubbish. Then his men brought forward the Narwhal Tusk.

Loa Wei Fen's hand slid to his swalto blade and he stilled his breathing. The torches in the hands of the Red Poles cast roving shadows as the small boat bobbed on the swell of the great river. For a moment Loa Wei Fen felt his father's touch on his shoulders, his gentle voice in his ear. He remembered touching his own son's shoulders and the look of pride in the boy's eyes. The swalto blade turned in his hand and found purchase. The great snake on his back filled with blood and its hood flared.

"Bring the torches closer!" Big-Eared Tu shouted.

The Narwhal Tusk was suddenly in the full glare of the torchlight. Tu Yueh-sen let out a cry of joy and pointed to the exposed relic.

Loa Wei Fen didn't hesitate, he leaped high in the air and grabbed a torch with one hand while he stuck his blade deep into Gangster Tu's throat with the other. Blood sprayed across the men on the boat and lathered the Tusk. Before a Red Pole could bring out a weapon, a second, then a third lieutenant lay dying on the floor of the boat.

Loa Wei Fen heard his name called and he whirled around just in time to see the Captain throw himself at the remaining Red Pole, whose torch fell into the water as his pistol rattled to the deck. Loa Wei Fen cut the junk's bonds to the other boats, then hurled the torches onto their decks. "Turn the boat, open your sails, and head before the wind," Loa Wei Fen yelled at the Captain as he swung up to the larger ship, using the rope he had unhooked from the junk's bow.

One ship caught fire. The other had to deal with the Assassin, who killed seven more of Tu's men before a volley of rifle fire tore his sturdy frame into a dozen pieces.

But before the men on the ship could reorganize themselves without Gangster Tu to lead them, the two-man junk—with the Narwhal Tusk—had escaped.

* * *

TWO DAYS LATER the gruff Captain met up with Silas at Chinkiang. From there they and their precious rug-enwrapped cargo continued together for another three days, until Silas met his caravan for the long trek across the great desert and along the Silk Road—another Journey to the West, worthy of only a History Teller's telling.

Silas's journey lasted many months. And of the glories he saw and the wonders revealed to him only one moment stood out in his mind: the night he discovered both the Bible the junk's Captain had secreted amongst his father's journals and an entry in his father's journals he had never read before.

chapter fifty-four
Richard's Journal: The Bible

Silas was shocked when he read the entry. Beneath the blue dome of the desert night, leaning against the rug-shrouded Narwhal Tusk, with his caravan companions gathered in the distance around a small manure-fuelled fire, he once again opened his father's journals. The night was so clear that he could, with only a little effort, read by the light of the moon and stars. He shuddered. He thought he had read every entry in his father's journals, but somehow he had missed this one. And he read it in the blue glow of the stars—then read it again.

When he had first learned that his father was Bible-read he was surprised. But this journal entry staggered him. For a moment he felt a deep ache in his heart. Why had his father kept all this to himself? Why had he never taken Silas into his confidence? Why had they never talked about the important things in their lives?

The diary entry was entitled simply "The Covenant," and Silas saw quickly that his father's handwriting was not the tiny spider twitchings that he made while writing under the influence of opium. Here the letters were round and full, and written in Farsi. It began:

.. .. ..

So either God made a promise, then broke that promise, or there was no promise made. In either case, the Covenant—the oh-so-ballyhooed Covenant between Him and us—is clearly null and void. More likely it was just a fantasy of a heated mind anxious to unite a disunited and argumentative tribe.

—

Then there was a space on the page. When the writing picked up again, the colour of the ink was slightly altered. The completion of the entry evidently happened at a later time.

.. .. ..

The bargain agreed to was, as related in the Book, quite simple. Jews obey all the rules God sets out and God protects His people. So either Jews disobeyed a whole lot of rules or God didn't hold up his end, because the Assyrians and the Babylonians and the Romans certainly were not defeated by God. They trounced the Israelites. They destroyed the land. They vanquished the "chosen" people. Probably because the people were not chosen at all. Probably because there was no covenant. Probably because the fabulists from the desert were invoking a hoax to unite the people under the rule of priests who claimed divine direction. All one need do is meet these "holy men" to know one of two things: Either these men are just charlatans, or God is a fool to entrust His word to such individuals. Either way leads to disaster.

I have never denied that I am a Jew. But I am not a Jew like you. I am not a covenant Jew. I do not believe I or we have a special place at the side, at the feet, or in the heart of the Almighty. How could we, to the exclusion of others? If we are the chosen, then they are not. How could the obvious and overwhelming goodness of Lily, for example, go unrewarded because she says the wrong prayers in the wrong order and bows in the wrong direction, or doesn't bow at all? Lily's very life is an act of holy contrition. How could she not have a heavenly reward? Because she is not one of the chosen? Idiocy! Although, I do believe there is a God. But I believe our holiness is here. Our sacredness is ourselves. I do not believe He is worthy of our worship. I believe that we are actually here to fight against that overweening power of His and all His agents on this earth. That His whimsical, profane potency is the enemy of man and all that man does. "We are the gods' tennis balls." Well hit me, and I hit back. We live, we thrive, we work—and when we cannot work any more, we return to the earth, to the mighty spirit that lives there. In opposition to the whimsical, capricious power of the God of the desert, the spirit in the ground is our very wellspring. Once you see that, it's all actually quite simple. Farcically simple. It's all one. One of which we are all a part.

———

Silas closed the journal. His caravan companions had long ago smothered their fire with sand and gone to sleep. The blue darkness and a profound silence enwrapped him. Silas stretched out on his side, his back against the length of the rug-covered Narwhal Tusk. The deep blue dome of the desert sky was pierced by a new moon low on the western horizon. And as Silas drifted off to sleep, he sensed a presence softly pad toward him. But he did not stir as the great desert lion approached and gently sniffed his ear.

———

Two months later, Silas, with the Narwhal Tusk still hidden in its carpet but now easily carried on his shoulder, walked into the great city of his father's birth—Baghdad.

chapter fifty-five
An Ancestral Home for a Sacred Relic

Silas sat quietly on a bench across the street from Baghdad's largest syna-gogue. The cold winter sunshine cleanly etched the outline of the build-ings, as acid does on copper. Silas waited patiently, something his long trek had taught him. He checked his pocket for the letter of introduction he had from the rabbi he had employed for the little synagogue in the Garden.

The large doors of the old building creaked open and black-hatted men appeared, putting prayer books and taphilen along with prayer shawls into blue silk pouches. The men talked as they left morning prayers, and passed by the strangely dressed man on the bench without giving him a look.

That was fine with Silas. He wanted to see the head rabbi, not these men, and he had crossed river and mountain, desert and dusty plain to get here with what he now thought of as his two sacred objects: the Narwhal Tusk and his father's journals. He had left Shanghai in spring, and now it was the dead of winter. He had protected the Tusk from thieves and brig-ands, from the curious and the dangerous. He had slept on it, beside it, with it clutched in his arms. It had never been out of his sight these ten months. He was thinner than he'd ever been—and stronger—and more aware of the world beyond the Bend in the River than he had ever thought he would be.

The door of the synagogue opened slowly and an elderly man, bent by years, turned to close the door behind him. Silas climbed the steps quickly with the large rug under his arm and said in Farsi, "Is the Rabbi still in the synagogue?"

The man stared at him, then said, "Say that again?"

Silas repeated his question, and the man laughed, a deep belly laugh.

"What is it?" Silas asked.

"Do you really speak like that? I haven't heard Farsi spoken that way since my great-grandfather died."

"I'm sorry, but it's the only Farsi I know."

The man shrugged his shoulders and pointed within. "He's in there. You can't miss him." He turned to go, then turned back and said, "Say something else to me, will ya? No one will believe me when I tell them how you speak."

Five minutes later Silas was standing in the Rabbi's private office watching the old man read the letter of introduction. The old man handed the letter back and looked at Silas.

"You were waiting for me? Waiting until services were over?"

Silas nodded.

"Why not come into services?"

Silas bowed his head and let out a long line of breath. "I am a Jew by birth, not by inclination. If I am still a Jew, it is not the kind of Jew that you are. I don't believe God made a covenant with us as a people, or if He did He surely broke it."

The Rabbi chuckled.

"Is my Farsi so funny?"

"It's wonderfully archaic. They should keep you in a museum. And your thoughts are not new to me, or to any Jew who thinks." He got up from his desk. "Now, what is it you want from me?"

Silas showed him the deed to the house that the Vrassoons used to own and that his father had given to him. He told the Rabbi of the need to hide a valuable object in that place.

"Are there people living there now?" the Rabbi asked.

"Yes, to the best of my understanding, a large family called the Abdullahs."

"Are they squatters?"

"I don't care. I don't want to take their home from them. I only want them out of the house for a month. It is after all my property, not theirs."

"And when they are gone for the month?"

"I want a trustworthy architect to hide what is in this rug in that compound."

The Rabbi made a few notes on a pad of paper, then called for an assistant. Tea was brought, strong black tea, not the delicate oolong that Silas so favoured. They chatted while Silas waited to be informed of what was going on.

A full half hour later three well-dressed men arrived and were introduced to Silas. The first was a lawyer, who examined the deed to the compound and said curtly, "How long do you want them out?"

"For a month at most, and I am willing to pay for their hotel expenses while they are gone, and whatever you think fair as recompense for their trouble."

The lawyer shrugged and said, "It's a good deal you offer. The Abdullahs are merchants, so I assume they'll know a good deal when they hear one. I see no problem. I'll go see them now." He left.

The second man, an architect, listened to Silas's request: that the object in the rug was not to be taken from the rug but was to be hidden in the compound in such a way that the residents there would never suspect that it was there. The architect nodded and said, "Once they are gone, this is not a problem. I will do the hiding myself. I'll find an appropriate place, have my men do the heavy lifting, and I will go in myself in the night."

"With me," Silas said.

The architect was clearly surprised but quickly agreed, then left with a promise to start work as soon as the Abdullahs were safely in a fine hotel.

That left the Rabbi, Silas, and the final man. The man never introduced himself but started right in. "This is a significant favour you ask of us. And what do you have in mind for payment in return?"

Silas was prepared for the question. What he offered was sanctuary for fifty of the finest Jewish scholars in all of the Diaspora, their fare to the Garden, and their room and board in the Garden for as long as they wished to stay.

The attorney was obviously pleased with the offer. The Rabbi nodded, then added, "And we will bury ten of our sacred scrolls in the compound with your sacred object."

Silas stared at the man.

"God's wrath is growing and will crash upon us, perhaps even in my lifetime. We have sinned against the covenant that you don't believe in."

———

The work on the compound went faster than Silas had expected, so he found himself on a cold night only a few days later carrying the Narwhal Tusk in the rug through the streets of Baghdad, right past the house in which Teacher had raped Maxi, to the Abdullahs' compound. A peacock's shrill cry greeted his knock on the front door. The architect met him, and shortly after the Narwhal Tusk was safe in its new hiding place.

And Silas was free to go home to Mai Bao, who at that very moment stood at the door of his study watching three pages fall from the topmost shelf of her husband's bookcase and land face up on his desk. She crossed to the desk and shook the dust from the pages. She recognized the writing as that of Silas's father, but she could only guess at the language. These were certainly not Mandarin characters or the elegant scrawlings of Farsi. She knew many English words but recognized none on the pages. For a moment she considered asking others—then rejected the idea. Instead she smoothed out the three pages on Silas's desk and secured their edges with small pieces of jade. They would just have to await the return of her husband.

chapter fifty-six
Return of the Pilgrim

Silas Hordoon's return to Shanghai was as modest as a monk's arrival in a tribal village. Silas had had an uneventful two-month return trip, initially overland to Abadan, then aboard ship in the Persian Gulf, through the Gulf of Oman and into the Arabian Sea, passing the southern tip of India north of the Maldives and entering the Indian Ocean, through the dangerous Straits of Malacca, then turning north, past the wild territories of Malaysia and Borneo and Viet Nam before entering the Celestial Kingdom at a point guarded by the Triad-dominated island of Hainan. Eventually his ship passed the entrance to the Bogue access to Canton, then farther up passed Taiwan on the starboard side, continuing until finally Woosung appeared one morning on the port side and the mouth of the mighty Yangtze River beckoned him, as it had the British Expeditionary Forces in 1842.

A day later Silas stood on deck and watched the far reach of the Yangtze as it passed by the mouth of the Huangpo River. He allowed his eyes to scale the cliff on the south side of the mighty river, knowing that three graves and one mound looked down upon him as he returned. As the European towers on the Bund slid into view, Silas felt the exquisite rush of a traveller finally returning home. With only a small canvas bag containing his father's journals and the Bible the junk's Captain left him, he walked down the gangplank, no more impressive than any man who had travelled to the Middle Kingdom in steerage.

He had not cabled ahead.

He arrived as the sun set and sidestepped the proffered rickshaw rides. He didn't head toward his office on the Bund or his offices on Bubbling Spring Road. Instead, he walked slowly through the drizzling rain in the general direction of the Garden. The heat of the day had finally backed off a pace, although it would most assuredly return with the dawn. The evening was just beginning to soften. As he walked, he marvelled at the human reality that was Shanghai. His home. He passed by sidewalk barbers cutting the hair of customers seated on small, three-legged bamboo stools; sidewalk bicycle repairmen, often referred to as "maestros," who busied themselves stuffing fat red rubber tubes back into tires; sidewalk cobblers repairing shoes while surrounded by neat rows of upturned high heels from women's pumps; sidewalk seamstresses working on their foot-powered sewing machines; sidewalk physicians practising their ancient art. His heart swelled. Shanghai lived on its sidewalks. Silas passed by sellers of sugar-covered fried dough and soup and full meals prepared by cooks who carried their kitchens on their backs. Old couples sat on ratty chairs with their pant legs rolled up to their thighs. A five-spice egg seller blocked one nostril with a filthy thumb and discharged the contents of the other nostril onto the cracked pavement just millimeters to one side of her cook pot, then looked up at Silas. "You missed," he said, as laughter filled his voice. An attractive young woman paraded as if she were the only person with shapely legs in the Celestial Kingdom.

Passing into the French Concession, the ratio of automobiles to rickshaws increased, as did the number of pimps selling their wares. His eye was drawn to a shop window almost entirely covered with snakes coiling upwards, their blunt snouts pushing against the uppermost pane. He'd always liked snake—in brown sauce, naturally. The large glass jars of dried country roots and herbs in the next store bespoke magic and history in bottles. A country woman carrying a filthy baby barely covered in rags approached him with a hand out and a plea for help. He gave her all the money he had in his pockets. She was astonished and probably would have kissed him if he hadn't been a *Fan Kuei*. The over-pruned sweet olive trees in front of a walled French estate released their scent to the night air, adding a sweetness not there only moments before. Silas stood still and felt the world turn. For the first time he realized a lightness about him. The great burden had been plucked off his shoulders and was no doubt, even now, being carried by the wind, down the Yangtze, to the sea.

Two elderly Go players attracted a crowd filled with Shanghai's most abundant commodity—unsolicited advice. A young street-sweeper with a mask across her mouth moved her bound-twig broom slowly as she breathed in the street fumes that would first make her prematurely old, then collapse her lungs before she turned thirty. The heat backed off another pace, allowing in the gentle breeze from the mighty Yangtze. A child in new clothes played with a large wooden toy to the glee of his parents and all four grandparents.

In darkened doorways couples stole kisses—hands caressed curves and clutched hardness—only to be laughed at by the local crone. Silas wanted to cheer. A young man held onto a lamp post and vomited in the gutter as others watched, but no one helped. The fear of disease was now alive on the streets of the great city.

A dark alley's mouth emitted sounds of anger and a whimpered apology. Floral wreathes outside a storefront announced the opening of a new business and pleaded for good luck from whichever gods had not yet forsaken the city at the Bend in the River.

He passed by the Temple of the City God and the Old Shanghai Restaurant, then turned down an alley and emerged at the Garden. He removed his key from his pocket and opened the back gate—and stepped inside.

The entire compound was silent. He looked up; the moon was setting. He entered his house and saw a light coming from beneath his study door. He opened the heavy oaken door and there, on his desk, his green baize lamp threw a pleasing square of light onto the three pages Mai Bao had put there.

He rubbed his eyes, took off his coat, and sat. Immediately he recognized his father's handwriting—his sober handwriting, large and round. But for a moment the language stumped him. Not Farsi, not English— Yiddish!

He pulled the first page toward him and slowly translated his father's words.

•• •• ••

I told you of your mother. But I never told you of my sister. My sister Miriam—whom I begged Eliazar Vrassoon to take instead of me. I even offered him Maxi. Even then I was doing the Devil's work.

Vrassoon took Miriam and raised her as his own. But as she grew she became beautiful, and he moved her to his bed.

They had a daughter that he took from her and sent to be raised in the English countryside around Hereford.

My dear sister, Miriam, descended into madness and lived the rest of her wretched life where Vrassoon had put her, in Bedlam.

I don't know exactly when she died. And all I know of her daughter, your first cousin, is that she was named Miranda.

I have done the Devil's work. Do not do the Devil's work.

———

Silas found himself on his feet, not knowing how or when he stood. His head began to move involuntarily back and forth. Tears struck the floor at his feet and the word *Miranda* came from his mouth, over and over and over again.

Out the window the slash of red flowers that marked Milo's fall on the racetrack seemed suddenly alive with light. Silas backed away from the window.

Then he felt it.

He was closing down. Returning to the place he had been as a boy. Milo murdered. Impregnating his own cousin. He was falling, falling, falling to a dark, sealed place within himself.

He raced to the attic and threw open the window. He saw Shanghai, but suddenly and completely he was not *of* Shanghai. He ran out into the Garden. He smelled its dense, exotic aromas, but they did not touch his heart. He heard the sounds of the city as one hears a familiar but unimpressive singer. It was only when he realized that as he walked he was breathing the air that Milo had breathed and that his body was breasting aside the same air that Milo's body had breasted that he had a momentary surge of feeling—but it did not last.

He went to the door of the Garden—and locked it.

He never left the Garden again.

Silas Hordoon was adrift in the currents of the world. Even Mai Bao's delicate touch could not bring him back to life. He awoke the next morning well before the sun and installed an extra lock on each gate to the Garden.

That first morning he summoned MacMillan. "I am glad to see you are well," he said.

"Aye, Captain. Quite well."

"Good," Silas said, and then he arranged to have his entire business operation moved to a small house on the north side of his estate. And there he began the process of cashing in all his assets.

"And doing what with them, Captain?" MacMillan asked.

"Use them for my bank," Silas replied.

"The Shanghai Macao Bank?"

Silas laughed.

"What?" MacMillan demanded.

"It's an awful name," Silas said, "rename it. The Shanghai part stays, but use some other Chinese city with it."

"You want me to pick the other city, Captain?"

Silas thought about that for a moment, then said, "Sure. Pick another Asian city to go along with Shanghai for the bank's name."

He spent most mornings with his children and grandchildren and tried as best he could to love them. But he was fading and he knew it. The old curse of not feeling was returning with a startling urgency.

He awoke every morning drenched in sweat. He often missed meals simply because he forgot to eat, no longer taking any pleasure from the delicacies his master chef created.

It wasn't until three years after his return, while he was tending the hydrangeas blooming over the spot where his brother had fallen to his death, that he looked up and saw Mai Bao standing, watching him. He asked, "Who won?"

"Won what, husband?"

"The car race."

"You mean the Great Shanghai Road Race?"

"Is that what they called it?"

"It is."

"So who won the Great Shanghai Road Race?"

"The Vrassoons' Rolls Royce Silver Ghost came in first, and the Jardine Matheson Simplex Racing Car second."

Silas nodded and returned to the hydrangeas.

Mai Bao watched him for a long while. Finally she said, "Does it bother you that the Vrassoons won the race and the prize money you supplied?"

Silas didn't lift his eyes from his labours but shook his head slowly and said, "No. Why should it? It's all one, Mai Bao. I see that now. It's all one."

chapter fifty-seven

Interlude—And Time Passes

Late 1911 to February 22, 1934

And time passed quickly, as it did sometimes in the vast history of the Middle Kingdom.

The Manchu Dynasty fell, or, to be more precise, simply crumpled. Dr. Sun Yat-sen momentarily became president of the Republic of China, but that was short-lived as he found himself beholden to local warlords wherever he went—one of whom eventually assumed the presidency and promptly attempted to start a new dynasty. Eventually the foolish Doctor accepted a post as Minister of Railways in the new government.

An American journalist who travelled with the good Doctor shortly after his Cabinet appointment was appalled to see the foolish man take a map of China and simply draw straight lines on it from east to west and north to south.

"And what would those be?" the journalist asked.

"Railways. This is my plan for a new railway system for China."

The journalist stared at the lines on the map. They crossed mountains and rivers and deserts without a hint of understanding the difficulty presented by the topographical realities. When the journalist pointed these out, the good doctor replied, "Yes, but they are the most direct routes."

The good doctor managed to alienate his financial backer, Charles Soong, by first taking on Charles's youngest daughter as a secretary and then, without asking Charles's permission, marrying the girl, who was young enough to be his daughter. Not to be outdone by his nominal commander, Generalissimo

Chiang Kai Shek married Charles's eldest daughter, once again without asking permission. As these events were causing havoc in the Soong household, the middle Soong daughter was secretly spending time in the company of student revolutionaries in the growing Chinese Communist Party.

These three western-dressed Chinese women, as predicted by the Narwhal Tusk, had much to do with the unfolding history of their country. Eventually they became known as the Three Sisters—"She Who Loves Money," "She Who Loves Power," and "She Who Loves China."

Charles himself, by the mid-1920s, had handed over much of his personal power to his sons and, not unlike Silas, retreated from the fray.

Three Men with a Book—Gangster Tu, Silas Hordoon, and Charles Soon(g)—had played their part in the expanding tapestry of Shanghai. But a fourth Man with a Book was ascending, and he would eventually enter Shanghai at the head of a great army—and change everything at the Bend in the River. Although first he would have to march far to the north to avoid slaughter at the hands of Chiang Kai Shek's Kuomintang army, avoid the duplicity of the Russian Communist Party officials, and build an army to rival the Taipingers' before taking on the Japanese invaders.

book three

The End of the Garden

Wherein the invasion and expulsion of the
Japanese forms the background against which
the end of the story of the Hordoons is
played out. It also presents the final challenge
for the Chosen Three and the Carver. As well,
the New History Teller and the boy, Zhong
Fong, are introduced before the Age of Dry
Water descends upon the city at the Bend
in the River.

chapter one

The Final Dream of Silas Hordon

Silas saw them only as shadows in the far corners of his bedroom. At first he assumed they were his victims, Milo and Miranda—but he was wrong. As the sands of his life escaped in swifter and swifter flushes, the light in his darkened room seemed to intensify, and the shadow he'd thought was Milo awaiting his chance for revenge turned out to be, in fact, the stooped and aged figure of Charles Soong. Silas had been even more wrong in thinking that the other figure was his first wife, Miranda. Not only was the figure revealed by the growing light not Caucasian, it was also male. The man turned and approached the foot of his bed—it was the bloodied, sneering Gangster Tu.

The old thief broke the silence in the room. "'Bout time y'er joinin' us," he mumbled in a language that should have been Mandarin or perhaps Cantonese but oddly sounded more like Yiddish than any other language that Silas knew.

Then the palsied figure of Charles Soong turned toward Gangster Tu and said, "What d'ya mean, join *us*? I'm not dead, yet."

Silas nodded his agreement, although he was astonished that Charles Soong had replied to Gangster Tu in what was now most certainly Yiddish.

"I'm dying, then?" Silas asked, also in Yiddish.

"Did ya' think you'd be the first person to live forever?" Gangster Tu asked.

"I admit I'd considered that possibility," Silas acquiesced, astonished that he knew the Yiddish words for "admit," "considered," and "possibil-

606

ity." Not exactly words that come up in everyday speech, he consoled himself, then wondered why he was consoling himself, and what the Yiddish word for "console" was.

"Well, be that as it may," Charles said, "the truth remains that we were irrelevant—all three of us—a tease, a distraction from the real show. Nothing more."

"How do you mean?" Gangster Tu asked.

Silas sighed deeply. "We were just the catalyst," he said, amazed that his Yiddish vocabulary contained that arcane word.

"Explain it to him, old Jew," Charles said, without the least hint of rancour.

Silas opened his mouth but no words came, so Charles supplied the vital explanation. "A catalyst is an element that must be present to allow a process of change to occur. If the catalyst is not there, then no change can take place. But the catalyst itself never changes, it is always the same. With the exception of allowing the change to take place, the catalyst has no other purpose in nature, and is always left behind in the process. The catalyst is the necessary uselessness needed for change and growth to happen, but is itself of no value and is ultimately discarded by both man and nature once the process of change is complete."

"So," Tu snarled, "we, the three of us, were just ..."

"... catalysts to allow change and growth at the Bend in the River."

Tu harrumphed. "Now we are as useless as nipples on men."

Silas thought about that. Then about the grizzled junk Captain who must have put the Bible in with his father's journals, then about the ancient lion that had whispered in his ear in the blue desert night. He thought about the rumours of a search for a Man with a Book. He looked at the other two men. He hadn't noticed before that Gangster Tu was carrying his much-thumbed copy of the *I Ching* in his right hand and Charles was holding a copy of his newest publication in his left. To Silas's surprise he felt something in his own hands. He looked down and saw that he was holding his father's journals.

"Do you want me to read to you again, husband?" Mai Bao asked gently as she took the weight of the journals from his hands.

Silas stared at her. When had she come into the room, and where were Charles and Gangster Tu?

She repeated her question.

He shook his head.

"Then what, Silas? Tell me."

When he opened his mouth no words came at first, then they tumbled out. "Am I speaking Yiddish?" he asked.

"If you were I wouldn't be able to answer you, Silas."

"Then I am speaking Shanghainese?"

"And very beautifully, as you always have done, husband."

"I am dying, Mai Bao."

"Yes, Silas, as we all must."

Then he asked her, "Was it all for nothing? Was I just a catalyst?"

But this question she couldn't answer, as it was asked in ancient Farsi.

Silas grabbed her arm and, with surprising strength, pulled her close to his lips. "Find the Man with the Book, Mai Bao, find him! The Man with the Book is what we have led to all along."

But as much as Mai Bao tried to understand Silas's growingly agitated pleas she was at a loss as to what to say, since she didn't even recognize the language he was now speaking, let alone what it was he wanted from her. In fact, she knew only one word from the language Silas was speaking—a very good word—a word that at times provided a relief denied even to prayer: *Oy.*

And she said the word—and Silas smiled, then was no more.

chapter two
The Funeral of a White Chinaman

1936

The city at the Bend in the River had never seen anything quite like the solemn procession fronted by the horse-drawn trundle cart upon which sat the black-draped coffin of one Mr. Silas Hordoon—multi-millionaire, builder of the Garden, cotton baron, opium baron, real estate baron, banker, Jew, lover of Shanghai—murderer of his brother, Milo. The cortège made its stately way down Bubbling Spring Road toward the right turn onto the Bund, where Silas had once ordered a large, concave wall built to protect the citizenry before the Great Shanghai Road Race. The wall had succeeded in its assigned task. Not a single Shanghainese was hurt when the Hordoon racing car flipped over at that precise point of the race course. Even the driver, MacMillan, had escaped harm, despite the fact that he had not worn his seat harness. Only an African cook had died. An African cook who was later buried with honour and tears by another man of power and wealth in the city at the Bend in the River, one Mr. Charles Soong. And in a city that had no secrets—whose vast spy networks quickly converted the hidden into the exposed—no one had yet been able to bring to light the reason for Charles Soong's extraordinary reaction to the death of a simple African kitchen worker.

The horse-drawn cart carrying Silas's unadorned coffin slowed for a moment to allow the long line of mourners to catch up. First in the procession behind the cart were Silas's twenty adopted children, their spouses, and their children. Three had grandchildren in arms. All were dressed in the traditional white worn by Chinese mourners but none cried out or wept—all maintained vigilant control of their emotions.

Next in the procession, unaccompanied and several paces behind the children, Mai Bao, now known to most Shanghainese as Jiang, walked slowly, head bowed.

She had not slept for days and time was collapsing on her. The past and the present were intermingling, and she was periodically lost in the shifting images of what was and what is. But she didn't mind. It helped her remember. And as she looked at the pavement moving beneath her feet she was remembering. Remembering how shy this man had been. How he had begged her to show him how to please her. How he had reddened when she'd turned on the light in his bedroom and insisted that he watch her disrobe. Then how she had undressed him and taken him in hand. How gently he'd tried to love her. How disappointed he had been that she did not become pregnant, how it hurt her to have to fool him. There had never been a member of the Ivory Compact who was not a full-blooded Han Chinese. Although it was true that the Compact could not have continued without Silas's extraordinary journey to Baghdad, that still did not qualify him as a member of the Ivory Compact—and that hurt him too. He had so many successes—and failures. She remembered how his beard had tickled her thighs. *But why all these pillow thoughts now?* she wondered. *Because the pillow is the opposite of the place where your gentle husband now lies—and will continue to lie until he is fully returned to the earth*, she answered herself, in a voice that she knew belonged to her and to her mother and to her grandmother and to all the Jiangs before her.

As Mai Bao listened, other voices intruded—curious voices, hurtful voices—from the large crowd. Why was she walking alone? Why was her number-one son not by her side to hold her arm? Were the rumours true about the adopted twin girls? Were they really her natural daughters? How could she bear to sleep with the *Fan Kuei*? Didn't they stink? And on and on, as she marched her own Via Dolorosa toward the big turn in the road where she would briefly slip away from the procession.

She passed a delegation of high-ranking Japanese diplomats and felt their searing eyes penetrate her white robe and yank at her old breasts, pulling hard, trying to hurt her. She took a quick look and found herself falling into one of their young, handsome faces. Abruptly, something icy stopped her fall. The man's cruel, dark eyes gave the lie to his soft cheeks and bowed mouth. Then he spat at her.

The man's spittle hit the pavement just to her left.

She stopped for a moment and composed a curse, then stomped on the spit, to send the curse deep into the earth. She looked at the man a second time, and his almost lipless mouth creased into a smile—his dark eyes twinkled, and she saw his lips form the word *whore*.

The funeral procession passed the imposing facade of Dent and Company; then, farther down the Bund, passed the portico, guarded by stone lions, of the Scottish trading giant Jardine Matheson; then, after a hitch in the famous avenue, passed the marble steps leading to the kingdom of the Vrassoons. The steps of every Bund building were crowded with men in their Sunday best. All raised their top hats as the cortège approached. And Shanghai quieted, not to silence, but to a kind of reverent murmur seldom heard before at that hour on its teeming streets.

In that murmur, memories of the deceased filtered through the crush of humanity as incoming tidewater does through a pebbled beach—leaving no trace but filling the air with echoes. One high-pitched, many-voiced echo cheered at seeing Silas driving the lead car with the Laughing Buddha around the racecourse before the Great Shanghai Road Race. Another echo, this one old and feminine, whispered of the sheer gall (in Mandarin always a comparison to the size of a man's testicles) it took for Silas to marry his Chinese mistress and then take in twenty street children. "Cantaloupes, he must have had cantaloupes down there." "No, he had watermelons—three of them—I saw them." Another echo, this one male and stern, asked the question, "Where did he go?" Yes, Silas Hordoon's extended absence from Shanghai had not gone unnoticed. Although rumours had raced through the city, no one except the Chosen Three and the Carver had any idea where the Jewish *Fan Kuei* had gone for all that time. Other dark, sibilant echoes whispered of perversion and human sacrifice behind the high walls of the Garden—especially after the arrival of the fifty odd-looking men in dark suits with side curls. A chorus of women's echoes asked the question, "What man would allow his wife to run a brothel?" This echo was immediately answered by a chorus of young men saying, "I'd marry a courtesan if she would have me—and Mai Bao is not any old courtesan. She is Jiang!" But beneath the tenor and soprano echoes there was a deep bass undercurrent insisting that Silas was a murderer—that somehow he had murdered his brother, Milo.

But these were the murmurings of the people on the street—the Han Chinese.

The trading community standing on their elevated perches murmured as well, but their murmurs were not echoes—they were open sighs of relief. A pro-Chinese voice—no, *the* pro-Chinese voice in their midst—had been silenced. Some even spoke of it being God's will that "the heathen leave this earth." No one bothered to mention that if that were God's will, He had certainly taken His sweet time, since Silas had expired as one of the oldest men in Shanghai. "Aye, but God's will is God's will nonetheless," countered the voice from Oliphant and Company out of Philadelphia. Neither time nor experience in the Celestial Kingdom had altered the opinions of the House of Zion one jot—their beliefs were their beliefs. They brooked no questioning. Neither their failures nor their successes with the people of the Middle Kingdom had altered an article of their faith—or enticed them into any form of rational thought.

But these Christian musings were cut short by the howls of Taoist monks, accompanied by the banging of drums and the clash of cymbals. The ear-shattering noise was designed to pull thoughts from the specific deceased person to the general, all-encompassing truth that death awaits us all. The clatter said in no uncertain terms: *It is time to think of your own death before you are where this man is.* The horns, drums, and howls were as subtle as a slap in the face. As they were intended to be.

As Mai Bao's section of the procession neared the great turn from Nanking Lu (Bubbling Spring Road, still, to the *Fan Kuei*) she stumbled. Immediately, people stepped forward from the crowd and surrounded her. Under their cover, she slipped out of her white mourning garment, revealing a simple water-seller's tunic. She pulled her long, long hair into a bun and pinned it on the top of her head and slid out of the crowd around her, her place taken by a faithful maid, about her height, now dressed in white, with her long hair obscuring her face.

Mai Bao, in her disguise, pushed through the crowd. She passed a street doctor and two beggar men, who stepped aside and then assisted her into the basement of a tailor's shop. She had not used this entrance to the Warrens before and for a moment had trouble orienting herself. Then she heard the river to her right and knew which way she needed to travel.

Quickly she found the statue of Chesu Hoi in its niche and entered the once-secret chamber. The middle-aged Confucian and Loa Wei Fen's young, powerful son awaited her coming, with anxious looks on their faces. All knew that it was dangerous for Jiang to leave the funeral procession, but over and over again in their past it had proved valuable to meet at times of change. Delaying meetings could cause them to miss crucial opportunities to complete their task and bring on the Age of the Seventy Pagodas. So the Confucian had devised the plan, and Jiang had executed it to perfection.

"What does this do to our position, now that the second Man with a Book has died?" asked the Assassin as soon as Jiang had caught her breath.

"I don't know," she replied, thinking that the third Man with a Book, Charles Soong, was not long for this earth. "The next moves may not be ours to make," she said.

"The Japanese," the Confucian stated. The others agreed. The strange creep of racial distrust entered the chamber, and a profound silence followed. The Confucian allowed his eyes to move about the subterranean hall that had at one time housed the Narwhal Tusk. But the dank chamber held no answers. The silence elongated. The Carver, who often led meetings of the Chosen Three, was not in attendance as he was gravely ill and had yet to pick which of his sons was to carry on the obligation of the Ivory Compact.

"The Japanese must be seen as an opportunity. An opportunity to find the Man with a Book," the Confucian said, then quickly added, with an odd smile, "as the Taipingers were an opportunity to build up the population here. Don't you agree?" His smile stayed on his face for an instant, then disappeared into his traditional solemnity.

Jiang nodded, although she was not sure what kind of opportunity the Japanese offered the Ivory Compact. She was more troubled by the partially hidden look on the Confucian's face. As a business person, she had often had to deal with people who were not completely sincere. She had found that insincerity revealed itself most often in a person's not knowing whether he had spoken too little or too much—a confusion that was now evident on the Confucian's face.

Jiang turned to Loa Wei Fen's son, the Assassin. "Is the Guild preparing?"

The young man nodded but didn't bother to add that the preparations of the Guild of Assassins were, as he and his father had planned, not only underway in the Middle Kingdom but also moving quickly on the "island nation" of Manhattan, as people from that part of the world considered it.

Again silence descended upon them. Finally Jiang said, "This was dangerous and foolhardy."

"Perhaps," the Confucian said, his true expression once again hidden beneath his scholarly demeanor.

Jiang stared at the man for a long moment. The Confucian stared back at her, a wry smile coming to his face.

"I must return to the procession," she said, and then she moved quickly out of the Warrens, exiting the underground world into the south end of the Bird and Fish Market.

She could hear the sharp clashes of the Taoists' horns and cymbals over the screech of parrots, the songs of nightingales, and the trills of thousands upon thousands of other birds awaiting sale in their delicate cages.

Mai Bao stood very still in the midst of the calls of the birds and allowed a simple prayer to fall from her lips. "May these birds sing you to Heaven, dear husband."

A wren landed on her shoulder and shrilled in her ear.

Alone in the Bird and Fish Market she said his name aloud—"Silas!" It seemed to her that the birds all around her picked up the sound of the word and cawed and cooed and shrilled it until the cacophony seemed about to lift her off the ground. Then they abruptly stopped.

Silence.

Unheard of in the Bird and Fish Market—silence.

She felt time collapse again and turned slowly and there he was.

"It was my proudest hour, Mai Bao, my very proudest, and I am so glad you were there to play a part."

She nodded, and a smile came to her lips. She remembered, and treasured the memory as one does the details of an early love affair.

—

It was August, just over two years earlier.

"You don't like me," Vrassoon had begun that day.

"That's not true," Silas had responded

Mai Bao, sitting quietly to one side, knew that it was not true simply because Silas had as yet had no dealings with this whelp. She knew Silas did feel a natural antipathy to the young man's dark, well-deep eyes, which were startlingly like those of his grandfather, the old Patriarch, Eliazar Vrassoon. The young Vrassoon began laying out ghastly photographs on the study's rather large desktop: a horror gallery of starved and whipped and shot and mutilated and enslaved European Jewry.

Mai Bao watched as Silas scanned the images slowly. Finally he said, "It's true, then?" He let out a long sigh—an ancient sound from slaves long ago—a moment of breath asking, *Will it never end?*

Vrassoon said, "It's true, Mr. Hordoon." He indicated a large envelope in his pocket. "I have more, and far worse than those."

Silas nodded and turned away.

Mai Bao understood that these were European Jews, and her husband did not consider himself a European anything.

"Are they trapped, these Jews?" he finally asked.

"Not completely, not yet."

"They must be streaming toward the ports."

"They were."

"'Were'? Why past tense? Why 'were'?"

"Because boatloads of them have been turned back by the English, the Americans, the Canadians, the Australians, and the New Zealanders."

"Don't want their 'whiteness' tainted, do they?" Silas said in a whisper.

"Not the way I'd put it, Mr. Hordoon, but the idea is basically correct."

A long silence followed.

"We have power here, Mr. Hordoon. We could take in many of our kind."

Part of this Silas agreed with. He looked at the hawk-nosed young man across from him, then turned to Mai Bao. He smiled. She returned his smile. In rapid Shanghainese he said, "Serve tea, Mai Bao, and look this young man right in the face."

Mai Bao was now in her late middle age but had lost none of her elegance. Her walk across the room was an exercise in grace itself.

She pushed a beautiful teacart with delicate oolong tea brewing in a fine porcelain teapot that was so translucent that the dancing strands of tea leaves left slender, intertwining shadows on the surface as they slowly yielded their flavour to the heated water.

She held out a cup to Vrassoon, who promptly turned his head from her.

"I am not a serving girl, Mr. Vrassoon," Mai Bao said in a voice that, although soft, was full of fury.

"You are not my wife or sister or daughter," he began, but Silas interrupted him.

"Absolutely right—she's my wife, and she offers you the finest tea in the Middle Kingdom served with grace in the most delicate onyx cups available anywhere in the world—and you avert your eyes, Mr. Vrassoon, as if she were a leper. Is this the behaviour we are to expect if I help you extend hospitality to 'our fellows' and bring them to the Bend in the River?" Silas turned his eyes to the horrid images on his desktop. "If I helped you bring these people to our home here—to Shanghai—would they treat my wife as foully as you do? And would they deny that if Mai Bao and I had children they would be Jews? Would they do that, Mr. Vrassoon?"

Vrassoon sighed deeply, then spat out, "Don't do this! Your children would not be Jews because your wife is not a Jew. Is that not simple?"

"Extremely simple and extremely stupid. Everything in nature says intermix. Look at the health and beauty that the mixing of the races brings. Are you blind?"

"I am not blind, Mr. Hordoon, I am a believing Jew. I do not look at women who are not of my family, and I do not question the rules and wisdom of the Bible."

"Even if it leads you to exclude people of value? People who could renew your world? Perhaps even bring it into the twentieth century?"

Vrassoon reached forward and collected his photographs. As he did, Silas's face darkened. Mai Bao knew that another set of photographs—doctored images showing this man's uncle brutalizing a young Chinese girl—had once crossed this very desk. Those photographs had cost the Vrassoon family their monopoly on direct trade with China, and this man's uncle his life. Silas had spoken to her of this, of his doubts about the morality of that action of his father's—and now here was, perhaps, a chance for him to repent for that sin, to lessen the load of souls on his back.

Silas nodded.

"Is that a yes, Mr. Hordoon?" the young Vrassoon asked, joy and shock vying for pride of place on his swarthy features.

"It is. Between the two of us and our co-religionist thieves in Burma we should have enough money to help many."

"And we will help them."

"Yes. We won't let happen to them what happened to the Russians," he said.

Waves of displaced Russian aristocrats had arrived in Shanghai after the Communist takeover in 1917. At first they'd strutted around Shanghai's crowded streets as if they were rulers of a great country. They'd stayed at the finest hotels and eaten at the finest restaurants—until their money ran out. The Chinese were never fooled by these foul-smelling White people. They clearly did little with their time, knew less, and after selling off their furs and jewellery—almost always at ludicrously low prices, since they believed that buying and selling was beneath their lofty station in life—they reverted to the only form of gainful employment for which they seemed to have any real aptitude: whoring. Elegant, long-legged beauties of the pampered courts of Moscow and St. Petersburg quickly found that their ability to play the pianoforte, speak French, and indulge men in clever repartee had no monetary value in the city at the Bend in the River.

The paleness of their thighs, the narrow length of their backs, and the conquest they presented to both White merchants and Chinese men of every social stratum did, however, have a value that finally put some money in their pockets.

It's a rare moment in history when a shop boy can sluice a member of a royal family, or a merchant can push a duchess to her knees with impunity and a smile on his face.

While their women whored for them, the aristocratic Russian men did the only thing that aristocratic Russian men have done well for centuries—philosophized and drank and plotted dark revenges that even they knew would never come to pass. And when their women fell prey to the inevitable diseases inherent in their new profession, the men promptly called them sluts and left them to rot on filthy mattresses in rooms so cold in winter that water froze in the basins and so hot and humid in summer that mushrooms grew on the floorboards—and from the bodies of the dead who were thought to be just sleeping off a night of excess.

"We'll pool our resources," Silas said, "and try to figure out how many we can house and feed."

"But how will they get here?"

"By your ships and my ships and overland. Put out the word, Mr. Vrassoon, that Jews are welcome in Shanghai and they will find their way here."

Vrassoon put out his hand to Silas.

Silas did not take it. "But, Mr. Vrassoon, these newcomers will respect the Chinese of this city if they are to live here. Do you hear me? They will respect the owners of this place. They will! And they will not insult my wife. Now raise your head and stare into the eyes of beauty. Do it!"

And Vrassoon looked at the pictures in his hands, then up into the deep wells of Mai Bao's eyes. Mai Bao allowed the centre of her being to sift down from her eyes to the fullness of her lips—and then smiled.

"Welcome, Mr. Vrassoon." Then she added, sadly, "I've heard so much about you."

———

The wren pecked at her cheek and drew a pinprick of blood.

Mai Bao touched her cheek and the wren took flight. She watched it disappear in the distance and said, "I'll miss you, Silas."

And just as suddenly as the noise of the Bird and Fish Market had stopped—it returned.

Mai Bao listened for a moment to the raucous cries of the birds, then let down her long hair. She shook it free as she put back on her white mourner's robe and then, to the surprise of the huge crowd, re-entered the mourners' procession after thanking her stand-in. A Taoist cymbal crashed right behind her. For the first time it occurred to her that Silas might not understand why she had him buried in her tradition, not his. She hoped he would. She also wondered if those watching noticed—or cared.

As she fell in beside her eldest adopted son she noted the cold eyes of the surprisingly young General Akira, who headed the formal delegation from Japan.

The Japanese had taken Manchuria several years before and installed a puppet emperor. That had been this young General Akira's doing.

———

The young man nodded at Jiang, then, under his breath, said to the even younger counterpart at his side, General Yukiko, "It is time."

General Yukiko smiled at Jiang as well. "These Chinese are in disarray. The nationalists in Nanking are more worried about the Communists in the north than they are about us. Warlords control almost half the country. The Chinese are weak and foolish—it is definitely time to strike with all our forces. It is time that the superior culture of Nippon showed the way to this old, dying harlot. It should take us less than three months to occupy the whole country."

General Akira did not respond. Old images of Japanese disunity arose in his mind. All the wasted time in the 1920s as Japanese prestige declined precipitously while they waffled dangerously between new Western ways and the restoration of the Meiji Emperor.

"Thanks to young officers like us, the Emperor is back on his throne and in control of the destiny of the Floating Island. And the Emperor wants war as much as either of us," General Akira said.

"More," General Yukiko said.

"China is ours for the taking—all we need is an excuse to extend outward from Manchukuo into the rest of the Middle Kingdom."

"Yes," General Yukiko said, "and excuses for war are always easy to come by. Like that soldier over there," he said with a smile, pointing at one of the Japanese corporals who had accompanied the two generals to Shanghai for the funeral—an old aristocrat's son, a lazy, over-privileged slug of a soldier. "If he should, say, disappear—not a hard thing for either you or me to arrange—we could claim that the Chinese took him. We demand an apology, but after our taking of Manchukuo, they will no doubt refuse to offer us one. Then we attack in an effort to get back our soldier. We have every right to keep our military personnel safe. In fact, it is our duty to do so."

General Akira smiled. "What if one of our soldiers were to disappear from, say, the Marco Polo Bridge?" His smile creased more deeply into his face.

"The bridge leading into Beijing?"

"The same."

"That would then leave us no choice but to cross the bridge with the silly name and subdue their ancient capital in an effort to rescue our soldier ..."

"... and prevent similar reoccurrences in the future."

The two young Japanese generals contained their smiles. It was a funeral procession, after all, to which they had been invited. But they were unable to control the expressions of shock on their faces when the final marchers in the procession came into their line of view. The two young officers openly gawked at the fifty or so black-hatted, long-black-coated men walking slowly, bobbling awkwardly, muttering some guttural sounds that they assumed could not possibly be a real language.

———

Charles Soong's family pavilion was closer to the end point of the procession—what Charles thought of as the finish line. It was, in fact, just past the start/finish line of the Great Shanghai Road Race. So, as the Japanese watched the Jewish scholars doven at the very end of the procession, the cart with Silas's remains was just passing the family of Charles Soong.

Yin Bao stood proudly in her raised viewing stand, two of her three grown daughters on her left and her three sons to her right. Charles languished in his wheelchair, his head now in constant motion from the cruel end game that Parkinson's plays upon its victims. But he was content. His three daughters were the three most famous women in all of China. His eldest son had smoothly taken over the running of his business empire and was the Finance Minister in the Republican government in Nanking.

Charles's financial backing had, years ago, helped to push aside the creaking machinery of the Manchu empire, and that pleased him—although he was furious when, shortly after that success, Dr. Sun Yat-sen gave away his power to Yuan Shikai, a former Manchu general. The man had eventually declared himself China's new Emperor, but died shortly thereafter. He was the one and only Emperor in his own dynasty—the shortest in Chinese history. The memory of that pleased Charles, and he grunted a laugh.

There had been other betrayals that still rankled. His youngest daughter had married the old, foolish Dr. Sun Yat-sen—and that he just could not forgive. But that was long ago, he reminded himself. The old fool had departed this world more than ten years ago, leaving his wife to carry on his utopian vision of China. Then there was his eldest daughter, who had married the Generalissimo, Chiang Kai Shek—again, against his wishes. But this was a wild girl—a girl who just might live forever, he thought. A girl who could give as good as she got. Charles Soong did not envy Chiang Kai Shek's lot in life with such a wife. Those two had made their choices and would now have to live with the consequences. But his middle daughter concerned him most. Since the May Fourth movement in 1919 she had spent much of her time with radical students, and he believed that she knew much about the movements of the Chinese Communist Party—even, perhaps, the thoughts of the upstart librarian, Mao Tze-tung, who now controlled a Marxist state in northern Kiangsi province. He had not seen this middle daughter in over ten years. Her absence left a hole in his heart.

Yin Bao leaned down and touched his shoulder. He willed his shaky left hand to cover his wife's, but his arm refused to obey him. She pointed toward the cortège. In a long line behind the horse-drawn cart carrying the coffin marched the twenty street children that Silas and Mai Bao had taken into the Garden. They were children no more. Most had children of their own. One man loped with the poise of a fine athlete, but it was two of the young women who had drawn Yin Bao's eye. Two elegant young women—clearly twins. They were tall for Han Chinese women and moved with an unmistakable elegance—an elegance that infuriated Yin Bao, who instantly recognized their grace as that of her older sister, Mai Bao.

"So the virgin managed it," she whispered.

"Managed what, dear?" Charles asked.

"Nothing, dear. Sleep. Nothing of importance is happening here."

———

One of Mai Bao's daughters felt someone staring at her. She looked up to a high viewing platform and found Yin Bao's eyes boring holes in her. She tapped her sister's arm. With a shock, Mai Bao's daughters recognized that their aunt, Yin Bao, had spotted them. The girls communicated silently with each other and slowed their steps until they were on either side of their mother—then they linked arms with her, and the city knew their secret.

Shortly thereafter, the Buddhist monks finished their parting prayers, and the body of Silas Hordoon was committed to the fire.

* * *

AS THE SUN BEGAN TO SET that day, Mai Bao climbed the last of the hills leading to the far reach of the Huangpo River where it joined with the mighty Yangtze. She stared at the four graves, belonging to Silas's *amah*, his first wife, his adored brother Milo—and of course the mound that was his child.

She knelt and allowed the wind to blow her hair. She pulled it back and tucked it down the back of her gown. Then she began to clear the weeds from the graves. They were especially thick and hardy on Milo's grave. She reached for a tall weed with a purple flower and pulled hard. The thistle, rare for this part of China, cut deeply into her hand and she let out a quick gasp that the wind plucked off her lips, lifted high in the air, and then flung toward the Yangtze and the great sea waiting to the east.

The amount of blood coming from her hand surprised her, but Mai Bao didn't try to staunch it. Rather, she stood and moved her hand across Milo's grave, allowing her blood to fall on the mound. Then she moved to the *amah*'s, then Miranda's, and finally to the unborn child's. She salted each with the crimson from her hand. It was only when she went to pick up the urn with Silas's ashes that the bleeding finally stopped.

She walked close to the edge of the cliff, and the breeze suddenly whooshed up from below, billowing her white mourner's garments away from her still-slender frame. She put down the urn and, in response to an impulse older even than the Jiang family, she slowly removed her mourning clothes, one garment at a time—with absolutely no erotic intent, just a desire to be naked when she received her husband's remains.

Alone and naked, the great river far beneath her, she removed the top from the urn, raised it over her head, and inverted it.

She hadn't imagined what it might feel like, but she was surprised by the shower of dry ash, and the warmth she felt deep within.

———

That night Mai Bao sat alone in her husband's study, sensing him in every corner of the room. Then her eyes were drawn to an open drawer in his great desk. There she saw his father's large stack of handwritten journals, topped by a pile of old letters.

Carefully she slid the letters from their resting place, and that night Mai Bao—Jiang of the Ivory Compact—used the English that her husband had taught her and read first the letters of the famous English opium eater, Mr. Thomas De Quincy, and then the entirety of the dream journals of Silas's father, the great opium trader, Richard Hordoon—and, in death, she knew her husband better than she had in life.

As the dawn swept up the river, Mai Bao opened the shutters of her husband's study and stared at the riot of red flowers marking the spot of Milo's death.

She sighed. The Tusk was safe, and she had the deed for the Baghdad property in a fine hiding place. MacMillan and her two eldest adopted sons could run the family banking business, and her own brothel business had never been better. But she was anxious. She caught an image of herself in the full-length mirror in Silas's water closet and examined herself. Time had thus far been gracious to her, but she knew that time was ultimately cruel and disrespectful. With the Tusk gone from Shanghai, the Chosen Three would not need to meet as often as before, but even so Mai Bao knew she would have to choose between her two daughters, and that choice would have to be made sooner than later. Now that Silas was gone she felt no compunction about introducing her daughters to the Colombe family and Jiang's—a business that one of them would have to run if she was to assume the obligations of the Ivory Compact.

chapter three
Japanese Plans

Even as the two young Japanese generals waited for their vehicle, visions of a brilliant future danced before their eyes. "The greatest of the White thieves is in the ground." General Yukiko said under his breath as he stepped into the large touring car. "His family is in chaos, and our spies tell us that the Vrassoons' power in London is on the wane."

"And the Chinese are in their usual state of confusion," General Akira said as he stared at the young corporal who was supposed to race around to his side of the car and hold the door for him.

"Your name, soldier?" he demanded.

"Corporal Minoto, sir."

General Akira smiled—the same loafing man he had seen earlier. Yes, Corporal Minoto's death would be far more useful than his ludicrously privileged life had been, he thought.

The young corporal felt a wave of cold enter his bowels—and stay there.

General Akira stepped up into the car and sat beside General Yukiko. The men looked at each other. They knew what they would report. And they knew their words would carry weight with the Emperor. Both of these young men knew that it was their time to rise. It was time for Japan's glory—and for the world to change. And they would do the changing, starting with China.

A lead car, carrying Corporal Minoto, led the way. As the generals' car pulled away to follow, General Yukiko suggested, "Three months to take the whole country?"

"If that. What little in the north that we don't already control is in the hands of warlords who fight amongst themselves. Chiang Kai Shek and his ridiculous Republic rule from Nanking and are concerned with only one thing: annihilating the Chinese Communists up in Kiangsi."

"Our spies tell us that the Russians actually kidnapped Chiang Kai Shek in Xi'an and wouldn't let him go until he swore that he would fight us, not the Chinese Communists."

"Was that before or after the Communists retreated all the way up to the north-west?"

"It's hard to tell. Chinese history is an art, not a science."

The men shared a laugh at that.

"Is that place they went to called Yen'an?"

"It's something like that, but who cares? They say the Communists lost sixty thousand of their men running away from Chiang Kai Shek's army. They started with eighty-five thousand soldiers and fifteen thousand party officials."

"What's a party official?"

"A parasite who lives off the backs of real soldiers."

"Do the Chinese have real soldiers?"

"Not that I've ever met." The two men laughed like drunken teenagers.

"Weren't there some women who made the march?"

"Thirty, I think. Some tough women to service all those men."

"If those men who died had stayed and fought they could have at least taken some of their enemy with them, rather than just starving to death in the cold."

"True, but the Chinese are better at running than fighting."

"Agreed. That's why I think that three months is more than enough to take the whole country."

Their car braked to a sudden halt and car horns began to sound. The young corporal leaped out of the car in front of them and approached their vehicle, no doubt to apologize for the traffic. The driver beeped his horn loudly. The young corporal jumped out of the way. The generals looked at each other. Then Akira said to the driver, "Don't run over him here—he'll be more useful to us up in Beijing."

Yukiko smiled and nodded slowly as the car swerved up on the sidewalk and passed by the young corporal—and the generals helped themselves to the liquor supplied by the Imperial Court of the Japanese Emperor, and selected for them by the Emperor himself.

chapter four

*On and Beneath the
Marco Polo Bridge*

1937

The Marco Polo Bridge spans the Yongding River fifteen kilometres south-west of the centre of Beijing, and at the time was the only route out of the city that led to the Kuomintang strongholds of the south.

On either end of the bridge stand two imperial stelae—large stone slabs etched with historic calligraphy. The one on the west—where Chinese troops were massed—bears the inscription "Moon over the Lugou Bridge at Dawn" in the handwriting of Emperor Qianlong, while the one on the east end of the bridge—against which Japanese troops lounged—celebrates the restoration of the bridge in the reign of Emperor Kangzi in the late seventeenth century. Stone elephants guard the ramps to the bridge, while the eleven arches of the bridge itself hold their burdens under the silent, unmoving vigilance of four hundred and eighty-five stone lions, all in different poses, atop one hundred and forty balusters. In the tradition of hyperbole common to the Beijing area, it was often said that "There are too many lions on the bridge to count."

By 1937 the Japanese had already cut deep into Chinese territory. In 1931 they took Manchuria, called it Manchukuo, and set up the last Q'ing Emperor, Henry Puyi, as its puppet leader. Although the Republican Kuomintang and the international community had adamantly refused to recognize the occupation, both had signed truce agreements with the Japanese later that same year. A year after that, Japanese forces routed a poorly equipped and trained Chinese army and took Chahar province, giving them the western accesses to Beijing. In 1933 they annexed Rehe and gained all the area north of the Great Wall, including the northern routes to Beijing. They then added Hebei province in 1935, thus gaining control of the east, south, and north-west routes to Beijing … and the west end of the Marco Polo Bridge. All that remained was to take the east end of the bridge and the town there, Wanping, which billeted the Kuomintang's gathered forces, and Beijing would be undefended.

The Japanese army was well trained and mechanized. Tanks led every attack while many Chinese soldiers went into battle little better equipped than their ancestors who had first attempted to keep Maxi Hordoon's irregulars from the cities of the Celestial Kingdom.

In early July the Japanese began a series of military exercises near the west end of the bridge. The Chinese Kuomintang garrison watched closely.

"Good," General Akira said, "I'm pleased they are watching."

"They have much to learn," General Yukiko responded, then added, "about everything … even their own history."

"How do you mean?" asked General Akira.

"I mean naming a bridge in China the Marco Polo Bridge."

"Yes, that is odd, I agree."

"What self-respecting country would name a major bridge after a foreigner?" General Akira asked, as he brushed a fly from his beautifully constructed sushi.

"A foreigner who never even came to the country," General Yukiko replied casually as he moved the pickled ginger atop a rolled piece of rice and fish.

"What do you mean, never even came to the country?" General Akira demanded.

"Just what I said. I don't believe this Italian Polo person ever came to China," General Yukiko said, keeping his tone conversational.

General Akira laughed so hard he almost fell from his three-legged bamboo stool.

"No, listen to me," General Yukiko said, dipping another exquisite piece of sushi into the delicate sauce. "This Italian claimed to have been in the court of the great Khan for almost fifteen years, right?"

General Akira only managed to nod his head—his laughter continued.

"Fine. You laugh—go ahead and laugh. But if this Marco Polo had actually been in the court of Kublai Khan for all that time, how could he have failed to mention in his endless writings that Chinese noblewomen had bound feet, or that the Chinese don't use letters but characters in their writing. And then there is the minor fact of the Great Wall. How exactly could these little items have escaped his observation?" General Yukiko demanded.

General Akira stopped laughing and looked at his younger counterpart. "None of these things are mentioned in the Italian's writings about his years in China?"

"Not a single mention in all those pages of any of those things. A bit suspicious, don't you think?" General Yukiko asked, and extended his chopsticks for another artistically assembled piece of sushi.

"Really?"

"Really ... sir."

The two men ate in silence as their adjutant silently removed used plates and filled their sake cups before they were emptied.

Finally General Yukiko asked, "So how did this Marco Polo get the information that he included in his books on China?"

"From Silk Road traders would be my guess. The Italian lived in Venice. Chinese silk had been arriving in Venice for decades before he wrote. Persian traders met Chinese traders on the western stretches of the Silk Road and carried the goods to Europe—and no doubt stories too."

"So you think that this Marco Polo, who had been commissioned by his government—he *had* been commissioned by his government, hadn't he?"

"Yes, certainly."

"You believe his writings were fraudulent. So what do you think he did with that money?"

"I assume he pocketed a pretty penny from his government and in return he produced a book. An exotic tale of the Orient. Without ever venturing east of Venice."

"So where was he during those fifteen years he was supposed to have spent in China?"

"Probably safely ensconced in some Venetian whorehouse, where he bought stories from horny traders with the money his government had given him to go to China."

General Akira shook his head, then said, "And for that he gets a bridge named after him?"

General Yukiko raised his sake cup and said, "The Chinese are fools. This place is a disgrace to all of Asia. But we can change that."

"No," General Akira said. "We *will* change that—and shortly."

There was a polite knock on their door. General Akira checked for the rusted needle-nose pliers and the surgical scalpel in his pocket, fingered both, then looked at General Yukiko. The two men stood, lifted their sake cups, and saluted each other.

"To the glorious future," General Akira said.

"To the end of the salacious past, to the end of the former Middle Kingdom," General Yukiko replied. The two men drained their cups.

General Akira turned to the door and barked out, "Come."

The door opened, revealing the young corporal from Shanghai. The terrified youth took a step into the room, clicked his heels, bowed his head, then kept his eyes firmly on the floor just in front of his shoes.

"Speak," General Akira ordered.

"Honoured General, Corporal Minoto reports, as requested."

"Ah," General Yukiko said, clasping his hands behind his back and beginning to pace. "Do you really?"

The soldier ventured an upward glance, then quickly snapped his head back toward his polished boots. "Yes, sir." Corporal Minoto sensed the two generals slowly circling him. As they did, he felt his entire body go cold. He had never wanted to be a soldier. It had only been to please his powerful father that he had accepted a minor commission in the army. But he detested the army, and he feared these two generals who inexplicably kept cropping up in his life—like an ugly sister. Then he felt a sharp pain in his leg. One of the generals had kicked him with his heavy boot.

General Akira kicked the man a second time, and this time the Corporal's knee buckled under the heavy blow. But before the man hit the floor, General Yukiko caught him by the hair and yanked his mouth open. General Akira then trapped the man's tongue between the jaws of his needle-nose pliers and pulled it far out of his mouth—then he grabbed his scalpel and slit the young corporal's tongue down the centre.

Pain shot up behind the young man's eyeballs as blood filled his mouth. He opened his lips to speak, but somehow two snakes were loose behind his teeth—and neither made the sound of horror that screamed in his head.

"Close your mouth, soldier!" General Akira ordered. "Your tongue's been slit, not your throat. Swallow the blood and you'll live. You won't ever speak properly or cry out loudly again, but then, we all do our part for the greater glory of Japan."

General Akira looked at General Yukiko and the two men smiled.

"I think we have our missing man, don't you?"

"I do believe he was taken by the Chinese on the east end of the bridge."

"That mustn't be allowed to go unpunished. Kidnapping a soldier of the Japanese Imperial Army is an insult to the entire Japanese nation!"

General Akira summoned his adjutant. "Take this traitor to the small room beneath the third arch of the bridge, where we were yesterday. Stay by him. He is not to leave, and no one is to see you. Is that clear?"

The adjutant grabbed hapless Corporal Minoto under the arms and hauled him to his feet. "Yes, General," he said as he pulled the man from the room.

"Well, the first step is taken," General Akira said as he removed a formal document from his desk. "Now, to step number two."

*   *   *

LATER THAT DAY, to the dismay of the Kuomintang forces guarding the east side of the Marco Polo Bridge, General Akira and General Yukiko led a battalion of men, complete with four tanks, across the bridge and demanded to see the Chinese commanding officer.

The Chinese troops pulled back, allowing their commanding officer, General Zhang, to step forward. The sun was setting and he was able to see the Japanese only in silhouette. They seemed like fiends coming from the sun itself. Then they were speaking—no, yelling. Demanding the return of some soldier. One of the officers spat at his boots.

"Enough," General Zhang said, in a surprisingly strong voice. "If an officer of the Imperial Japanese Army has been taken by my troops he will be returned, unharmed."

"Not enough. This outrage has gone on too long. We have further demands that must be met, or our forces will invade Beijing," General Akira said.

He handed over an elaborate document. It demanded that the Kuomintang wipe out all anti-Japanese organizations and stop all anti-Japanese activities inside the cities they controlled. That the Kuomintang take full responsibility for the safety and the return of the Japanese soldier, and that Supreme General Song of the Chinese 29th Army apologize publicly to the Japanese.

The date was July 31, 1937.

Six days later, Corporal Minoto had still not died, although he had undergone the most rigorous torture that the two generals could devise. The sound of the man's pain filled the room for hour after hour, and with every sibilant scream the man's shattered mouth emitted, the two generals were sent into further paroxysms of fury that moved them to increasingly cruel acts upon the man's body—which seemed to accept pain as a beach palm does the ocean wind. It both thrilled and infuriated the two generals. In the dark of that small room beneath the third arch of the Marco Polo Bridge they had crossed a very serious moral line, and both of them knew it. The soldier's disappearance had given them everything they needed to force concessions from the Chinese, and no doubt to invade the ancient capital shortly after. And yet the two generals were not satisfied. They found themselves coming back to their tortured captive's room over and over again. Something bestial was happening there. Something that stank but sang to them of ancient glory and power. Something that said they were beyond man and man's laws. Something beyond the gods was happening in the room beneath the third arch of the Marco Polo Bridge.

General Yukiko and General Akira were not country bumpkins or uneducated labourers. They had both been schooled in the West. They both had experience in the world. They both could quote from Milton as well as from the great poet Basho—but nothing in their lives would ever match their time in that dark room, where a fellow human being begged them to end his life as they inflicted more and more pain upon his person. And each time a session finished and they returned to the bridge, they were amazed that the sun still shone and that the night would come at its appointed hour and food would arrive and taste good—that they had "crossed over," but only they knew.

By the end of the week General Zhang had accepted the first two demands but said that he could not speak on behalf of Supreme General Song so he could not offer up either an apology or a statement to that effect.

The Japanese generals assembled their troops, and on August 10 they crossed the Marco Polo Bridge and took the town of Wanping. Just over a week later the Japanese Imperial Army, with Generals Akira and Yukiko in the lead, marched unopposed into Beijing. On the twenty-first of August Tianjin fell, leaving the entire northern plain of China open to the mechanized divisions of the Japanese Imperial Army—and nothing stood between the Japanese and total control of China except the possible defences they would meet in the large cities, such as Shanghai and Nanking.

On the morning of August 22, General Akira and General Yukiko returned to the small room beneath the third arch of the Marco Polo Bridge. The ferocity of their attack upon the young corporal was an almost sexual experience. In fact, just before Corporal Minoto finally drew his last breath through his split tongue, he saw a red rage, molten as liquid iron, flowing from the blast furnaces of their eyes ... as their tails slapped against the walls of the small room and their talons clacked against the stone floor.

chapter five
Beijing

Chesu Hoi stepped back into the massive crowd that was standing with uncharacteristic stillness along either side of the wide avenue as the Japanese tanks passed by in slow formation. The great city—the ancient city—had fallen in less than a week, and now, for the first time since the Manchu invasion, a foreign power had control of both the city and the city within the city—the Forbidden City.

Years ago the Japanese had put the final Manchu ruler, Puyi, on the throne in Manchukuo. That was one thing. But marching into Beijing unopposed, a foreign power in full regalia, was something completely different—and every silent Chinese citizen standing on either side of the wide avenue knew it.

Chesu Hoi pushed his way through and away from the crowd. He'd seen something that really frightened him. More than the invading army. More than the death that was now so close. Two Japanese generals sitting atop one of the advancing tanks, as if they were gods. Something about these two young generals struck deep at Chesu Hoi's consciousness. Like a large icicle dropped from the eaves of a house as the spring finally pushes the cold from Beijing, the coldness plunged deep into his heart—and froze him to the bone. He turned back quickly to get a second look at the two Japanese generals. Could his eyes have been mistaken? No. He'd seen it. They were not human, somehow. He knew what he had to do. The Chosen Three and the Carver must be warned.

But warned of what? The Middle Kingdom had seen invaders before and all eventually had been salted by the great sea of China. But this was different, and Chesu Hoi knew it was different. He stared at the proud young officers as they climbed down from the tank and strutted in front of their troops. No, this was not a simple invasion. There was something evil here—something evil loosed upon the land.

* * *

THE NEWS OF THE FALL OF BEIJING and the movement of Japanese armoured divisions southward set off the predictable panic in Shanghai—but there was nowhere to run. The countryside was no safer than the city.

In the Foreign Settlement the great families met and decided to watch developments carefully but continue to trade. The American embassy had been in constant contact with the Japanese and had been given an assurance that "should Shanghai become a target, all care will be taken to leave the Foreign Settlement alone—after all, the Settlement is foreign sovereign territory, and neutral." This last the Japanese envoy had said with a smirk that the American ambassador decided he would not communicate to his superiors.

So Shanghai continued its dance, and the traders traded and the vendors vended and the street sweepers swept, but everyone was waiting. The air reeked of imminent change, and this time even the *Fan Kuei* smelled it.

* * *

THE SMELL WAS THE FIRST THING that struck the young missionary watching the bustle in the harbour as his ship, after almost three months at sea, finally made its way toward the access of the Huangpo River. A breeze blew the young man's brilliant red hair back from his astonishingly pale skin, and he clutched his Bible close to his heart. Ever since his ship had approached the mouth of the Yangtze, something ancient had been singing in his ears—a song of return. *I am coming home,* he thought, as he tied a thick rope into a complicated knot with one hand, without looking at the rope or thinking about what he was doing. Then Maximilian, for no reason he could accurately articulate, smiled, showing his large, white teeth.

* * *

THE KUOMINTANG BEGAN TO ORGANIZE defences around the city, and the Chosen Three met in the now empty secret chamber in the Warrens.

The Confucian was almost forty but still hardy. The young Carver, new to the Ivory Compact, had met the Chosen Three only once before. The Assassin was in his early twenties and a man of many secrets. But Jiang— Mai Bao—was now a very old lady, and she needed help from all three of the men to climb the final steps into the chamber.

The men waited while Jiang caught her breath. Then she said, "This is the last time you will see me in the Compact. I will name my successor tonight."

The silence in the room expanded and seemed to push the walls back against the surge of the river.

Jiang coughed gently, but when the men moved to help her she held up a hand for them to keep their distance. She nodded and said, "So, how are we going to deal with the Japanese?"

"They haven't taken Shanghai yet," the Carver said.

"A detail," she responded.

The Assassin quickly agreed.

Jiang raised her head and inhaled deeply. The others watched her. She let out a long line of breath, then said, "The smell is denser now than this morning." They all smelled the intense reek of ozone in the air and knew it presaged significant change. Exactly what change was the issue before them.

The Carver told them of Chesu Hoi's strange message of "evil loosed upon the land."

Everyone in the room weighed Chesu Hoi's warning against the possibility that the Japanese presented some sort of new opportunity. The two did not sit together well in the same thought.

"There's change everywhere," Jiang said. "Last week I was brought to the theatre. I haven't been in a very long time."

The others allowed that to hang in the air. Everyone knew that Jiang, while she was still called Mai Bao, had been one of the most famous arhu players ever to grace a Shanghai stage.

"A very long time," Jiang repeated. "But what I saw shocked me."

"Was it a Long Nose play?"

"No. Who would wish to punish themselves with such trivialities as the British parade on the stage? No, it was a new opera. A new Peking Opera devised and directed by a man they are now calling a History Teller."

The intensity of the silence in the chamber deepened. The last History Teller had been the eldest daughter of Jiang's grandmother—and that had certainly been a time of significant change at the Bend in the River.

"Just idle talk?" the young Carver ventured.

Jiang thought about that, then slowly shook her head. "No. This man's work touched me deeply. In a way that I have never been touched by such things before."

The Assassin said, "His presence is a sign. A marker. Change is upon us."

Again silence invaded the confines of the chamber deep in the Warrens. The sound of the Huangpo River seemed somehow louder, angrier.

Finally the Confucian spoke. "I've been thinking about the three girls in the second portal. The image was of these three girls *and* the Man with a Book." All eyes turned to him. He was different from many of the men who had held his position in the past. He was, naturally enough, educated in the Chinese classics, but he was also well read in modern political theory. Like his predecessors he was a deeply private man, but unlike them he didn't necessarily look only to the past for answers to the day's problems—or so it seemed to the others in the Compact.

"They are Charles Soong's daughters, aren't they?" he said.

My nieces, Jiang thought.

"She Who Loves Money, She Who Loves Power, and She Who Loves China," the Assassin said, reciting the oft-repeated maxim about the three Soong sisters.

"Well, She Who Loves China married the fool Sun Yat-sen, and now that he is dead, has no value to us. But She Who Loves Power is with Mao and his Communists in the north, and She Who Loves Money married Chiang Kai Shek and is a real force in the Kuomintang government."

Jiang nodded slowly; ideas were coming together in her mind as raindrops form patterns on a windowpane. When she finally spoke, her voice was whisper-silent. She chose her words carefully.

"Charles Soong, a Man with a Book, dies and leaves three daughters, the three girls in the second portal of the Narwhal Tusk. Each of the girls has influence over a powerful man. Sun Yat-sen has been dead for a decade, and he was hardly a Man with a Book. Chiang Kai Shek is powerful, but I doubt he can even read. Then there's Mao Tze-tung. Copies of his writings have been available for years in Shanghai—he was a librarian, after all." She looked slowly at the Chosen Three. "Mao is a powerful man—a Man with a Book—and it is rumoured that he has a Soong daughter, a girl from the second portal, at his side."

She waited for the others to speak. No one did, so she spoke again. "Perhaps Mao is the Man with a Book, and we must support him."

"If he will allow it," the Carver said.

Jiang chortled a quiet laugh and coughed into her palm. "The Ivory Compact uses people, will they or not. The only issue is getting to him."

"I believe I can look after that," said the Confucian. That surprised everyone in the room, but before anyone could ask how, he explained, "We Confucians have been around for a very long time. Just because the powers that be say they do not need us, or our philosophy, does not mean that we go away. We simply go underground. We find other work, we marry, have children—and pass on our birthright. We also stay in communication. There are highly placed Confucians in both the Kuomintang and the Chinese Communist Party. I will contact them, and they will contact the Soong sisters."

Jiang heard something in this, something hidden, but her old mind couldn't figure out exactly what. She looked at the Assassin. "And what will you do?"

"War is approaching. The Guild is ready."

"To fight?"

"To fulfill the First Emperor's prophecy."

"Will you help defend Shanghai?"

"Perhaps. Our allegiance is to the Ivory Compact."

"As is ours," the Confucian retorted, although with less enthusiasm than the others had expected.

The Carver thought of Chesu Hoi's warning.

"Once the Guild is identified it loses much of its power," said the Assassin, "so I want to unleash my men at the most crucial time."

"And how will you know when that is?" the Confucian challenged.

Jiang spoke before the Assassin could answer. "Because he and his kind have always known such things."

chapter six
Jiang Passes the Mantle

That night, Mai Bao summoned her two daughters to what had been her mother's, her grandmother's, and her great-grandmother's bedchamber.

It had been years since she had slept in the old bed in what she thought of as her mother's private chambers in the brothel. But here she was, propped up on half a dozen pillows, staring at her two handsome daughters. Both tall, both strong, both seemingly ready to bear children. But she had made up her mind a long time back. The younger of the two would succeed her.

She turned first to her elder daughter and took her hand. "Say goodbye to me, but do not mourn me. I have had a very long and happy life—and you are part of my great happiness. So please, no tears."

Her daughter kissed her sweetly and said, "I honour you and your wishes, Mother," then she retreated from the room.

Mai Bao, whom the world now called Jiang, turned to her younger daughter and, after a deep breath, began the story of the Ivory Compact. The girl's eyes momentarily widened, then returned to their normal size as she took in the details, one at a time, with a startling equanimity—as Mai Bao had hoped she would. During times of war the members of the Chosen Three had to be pragmatic, and this one was nothing if not that.

"You may have to make choices that are painful. Chesu Hoi has warned us that there is an evil loosed upon the land. People, perhaps many people, will be hurt. But you must not lose sight of the goal: the raising of Shanghai as a great city. Seventy Pagodas to lead the Black-Haired people back to power. If we fail—if the Ivory Compact fails—China will be picked apart by carrion birds. Remember that. Always think carefully. Consider the facts, but weigh them against the possible result. A good gambler bets against the potential winnings, not against his opponents. And every morning, look east toward the Holy Mountain and remember your obligation to the Compact." Mai Bao lay back on her pillows, a sheen of sweat across her brow.

"What, Mother?" the girl asked.

Jiang shook her head, then spat out, "Be careful of the Confucian."

"Why, Mother?"

Again Jiang shook her head, but this time she didn't speak. The girl sat on the bed, then put her head on her mother's chest and breathed deeply. Finally she asked, "What can I do for you, Mother?"

Mai Bao pointed toward a small vial on her dresser. The black liquid in the vial bespoke the death it would cause. "That," she said.

Her daughter brought the potion to her mother, who put it by her side, then said to her daughter, "Time for you to go. Time for me to be alone. Even a whore ... *especially* a whore ... deserves a little privacy at the end."

chapter seven
The Confucian

He had been the Confucian representative in the Ivory Compact for almost twenty years. And every day of those twenty years he had added to the Confucian Book of Knowledge that he would pass down to his son, who would in turn pass it down to his son, until Confucians rose to power and their wisdom was published for all to see.

He enjoyed the secrecy of it all, and the sense of being at the end of a very long line. That he was never alone, never. They—the Confucians in the Compact before him—were always there, their writings a constant comfort. Their presence never forgotten, nor his duty to return China to a place of Confucian power.

From his position as head of the Shanghai civil service he was able to observe two powers on the move—the corporeal and the spiritual—and he had no doubt which was more profoundly powerful.

From his study he looked at the great river as it turned toward the sea. Was it time? Was now the time?

The Confucian allowed his elegant fingers to slide down the smooth surface of the ancient writing stone—the one upon which his ancestor had first seen the reflection of the White Birds on Water, now almost a hundred years ago. He knew that with the stone and his pen he would set in motion change—but like the archer who does not know exactly where an arrow shot into the air may land, he did not know exactly where the change would lead. What he did know was that a missive answering his message should arrive before too long, and it would all begin—a return to Confucian power.

Still legion in the Middle Kingdom, Confucians guarded a tradition older than Q'in She Huang, the First Emperor, himself, a tradition that had survived Q'in She Huang's purges of scholars and the burning of their books, survived attacks by later dynasties. The tradition had gone underground and thrived. Old traditions did not disappear—they never disappeared—they only waited for the coming of the light.

The Confucian smiled and allowed the ink to flow slowly down the surface of the writing stone and pool in the well at the base. He watched eddies form and then melt into the calm surface. *Like us,* he thought. *Now the warlords, the Kuomintang, the Communists, and the Japanese are trying to silence us—a lot of enemies.* Confucians simply retreated, regrouped, and did what Confucians and most Chinese did so well—they waited patiently. And while they waited, they reinforced their lines of communications. He cooed softly, and the carrier pigeons in the cages that lined the balcony of his study overlooking the far reach of the Huangpo River cooed back.

He thought of Chesu Hoi's warning—then dismissed it. There was no doubt evil loosed upon the land. But he was the one to stop that evil Confucians rectified evil. Only Confucian principles of order could set the Middle Kingdom back on the road to power.

He took the rice paper from his desk and dried the ink with a simple wave of his hand. Then he folded the paper in upon itself, over and over again, until it fit neatly into the tin capsule that he affixed to the carrier pigeon's leg. Finally, with a pat and a coo he released the bird to the first leg of its mammoth journey—and hoped the Confucian with Mao Tze-tung was still on this earth.

He repeated the process with a slightly altered message and sent the next bird on his way upriver to the Kuomintang capital, Nanking.

Then he sat back and allowed the late-fall sun to touch his skin, warm his face, and bring dreams of power—and he pondered one simple question: How could he convince the Communist Mao Tze-tung that he needed a Confucian like himself at his side as he rid the Middle Kingdom of the *Fan Kuei?*

His wife came in with tea. *At least, after all these years, she has learned to be silent,* he thought. Then another idea entered his head. *A man of power, such as I am about to be, ought to have a younger wife—a younger and prettier wife. Much prettier.*

chapter eight
Missives

Madame Chiang Kai Shek's personal secretary was careful to keep his eyes away from the windowsill as the great lady—first daughter of Charles Soong—completed her instructions. He nodded and took notes, as any efficient personal secretary would. Then he smiled—and she smiled back at him, turned, and left the elegantly appointed room.

The personal secretary made himself sit very still and recited the first twenty verses of a Tang Dynasty love poem silently, to pass the time. Upon completion of his recitation he glanced once more at the door. It remained shut. He rose and opened the window, then scooped up the pigeon that waited patiently there. Quickly he unsnapped the small metal canister attached to the bird's left leg and removed the note. He read it twice, then returned to his desk. On the back of the same piece of paper he wrote: "Message received, awaiting further instructions." Then he refolded the paper and inserted it back into the tin tube. Two minutes later the pigeon was winging its way back to Shanghai and its owner, the Confucian of the Ivory Compact.

* * *

LATER THAT SAME DAY, an exhausted carrier pigeon alighted on the railing of a farmhouse far to the north-west of Shanghai. The bird had flown for over ten hours without stop and was now close to death. The scholar who lived at the farm retrieved the canister and read the message.

Five minutes later he had affixed the canister with its message to one of his own pigeons and launched it farther northward.

It would take six pigeons sent by six Confucians to finally get the Shanghai Confucian's message to the far north-west of China, where Mao's forces were amassing.

The final pigeon flew right by the open window of a party meeting in which Charles Soong's second daughter was speaking while a very young Confucian kept accurate minutes. The bird finally ended its voyage on the lip of the coop kept by this young Confucian outside his mud hut.

When the meeting ended, the Confucian saw the pigeon walking slowly around the outside of his coop. He slid a practised hand between the pigeon's legs and unhooked the canister, which he slipped carefully into an inner fold of his quilted coat. There would be time later to read the message—time was easier to find than privacy—and he instinctively knew this note required privacy.

That night he walked back through the hills into the empty countryside. He sat beneath the stars and struck a match. By the flickering light he read his orders to get close to Charles Soong's second daughter, gain her confidence, and await further orders. Then there was an imprecation, threatening what would happen should he fail in his mission, and an urging of all haste in this matter. The young Confucian tried to calm the pounding of his heart. It was rumoured that Charles Soong's second daughter was Mao Tze-tung's mistress!

He swallowed the missive and turned his head toward the stars. Winter was already in the air. The desperate cold of winter was held in abeyance for only a few months of summer in this part of north-west China. Those months were ending, and a new cold was approaching. He recited a few verses from Lao Tzu to calm himself, but they did little good. Charles Soong's second daughter was perhaps the most unapproachable of all the people to have survived the retreat to the north-west. And even if she were not Mao's mistress, the crazy sexual restrictions of the Communists virtually forbade any contact between the sexes—except, naturally, in the upper echelons of the party. Her sexual relationship with Mao made it even more dangerous to approach her. Even more dangerous than to approach any powerful woman in the Chinese Communist Party would usually be.

The young Confucian put his head in his hands and tried to clear his mind. He felt like weeping. How could he accomplish this task? When he went to stand he looked to the hills of the south, and there, silhouetted against the huge moon, was Charles Soong's daughter—her hands raised, as if in some atavistic prayer—her naked body splashed by moonlight.

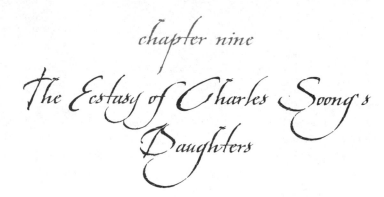

chapter nine
The Ecstasy of Charles Soong's Daughters

Charles Soong's second daughter—She Who Loves Power—allowed the chill Gobi Desert air to encircle her naked body. Slowly she spun, eyes shut, moonlight turning her skin a leonine gold, and thought of her time in America. Of her four years of isolation at Wesleyan College; her three months on a stinking freighter in the San Francisco harbour when she was denied access to the Golden Mountain because she was Chinese; her struggles with American idiomatic English; the thrill she'd felt when she heard of the fall of the Manchus and the rise of the Chinese Communist Party; and the glory of returning home after all those years of silent smiling amongst the *Fan Kuei*. She thought of her lover—and his jealous and dangerous wife. Then she thought of the fight she'd had with her aging father.

"But I did all this for you and your sisters," he had protested.

"Not for your sons, Father?" she'd snapped back, shocked by her own rudeness. She saw the flare of real anger in her father's already rheumy eyes.

"Is this the disrespect they taught you in America?"

"You sent me there, Father. I never asked to go!" she shrieked. Again she was shocked by her willingness to be vulgar in front of her father. But she was also pleased. As she had been urged to do at the meeting the previous night, she was resisting authority. She was starting her fight against the powers that were keeping China in chains: filial piety, ancestor worship, religion, and the authority of elders. The "Four Authorities"—political, theocratic, clan, and husband—had to be banished forever from the Middle Kingdom.

"Is this the loyalty that I deserve from a daughter?" he demanded.

"There is a difference between loyalty and obedience," she spat back. "Slaves obey orders, Father. You have to earn the loyalty of free women and men."

Charles Soong nodded slowly. Already the Parkinson's was elaborating every movement of his head, and it embarrassed him. This girl, of all his children, he feared. His eldest daughter, She Who Loves Money, he understood. Even as a child she'd had a taste for expensive things. His third daughter, She Who Loves China, was his heart's delight. But his second daughter, this daughter who stood before him, a scowl on her face, her hands in tight fists pressed hard into her hips, her legs spread wide like a man—this daughter he had never been able to reach. No amount of attention or praise or encouragement or bestowing of gifts had earned her approval, let alone her trust. But then why should she trust him? It was she who, as a young teenager, had barged into his study to find the partially clothed courtesan on his desk.

"What is this whore doing in Mama's house?" she had demanded.

Naturally enough, he'd had no answer. For an instant he'd thought of telling the girl of her mother's courtesan pedigree, but then he'd thought better of it. It was bad enough to incur his daughter's anger, no need to invite his wife's considerable wrath.

And now this girl was marching back and forth in front of his desk, barking out a political manifesto of some sort. Exhorting him to raise up the proletariat. To join the great movement of the people. "To do your part, Father, in unshackling China."

He wondered if she understood that it had been his money that had financed the fall of the Manchu Dynasty. Did she grant him no credit for his years of sacrifice, and the danger he'd faced?

"Father, turn your newspapers over to the workers who produce them."

He almost laughed when he thought of what would have happened to his newspaper empire if he had turned it over to the drunken student whom he'd first hired to write for him. Then he shivered as he thought of his last meeting with that poor man.

"Devote the power you have amassed to the good of the people, Father. And do it now, before we force you to do it."

Ah, he thought, *there it is. "Before we force you to do it." And that word: power. It's the only word that fits cleanly in this one's mouth.* He smiled. He'd known what it was to be powerless. To clean vomit from the floor of a Boston bar. His children had never known such powerlessness. Nor, for that matter, the exultation he had felt when the Irishmen dressed in orange had come singing into the bar, and the glory of the fight that had followed.

"Why do you smile, Father?" she demanded.

Then he said something she didn't understand. "I was thinking of a fight in Boston."

Boston. She had no idea what he was talking about—nor did she care. He was the enemy, the enemy of the people.

That very night she struck out against the enemy. She stole her mother's jewellery, pawned it, and delivered the money to the man she thought of as the Librarian. Shortly thereafter she became his lover.

She stretched her arms high above her head.

The wind picked up and flung the airborne grains of Gobi Desert sand against her nakedness.

Then she glanced over her shoulder and saw him—saw him watching her.

The young Confucian.

She spread her arms and turned slowly in his direction.

* * *

AT THE SAME TIME, in a massive warehouse stocked to overflowing with goods the Kuomintang army had taken in the Republic's name from private homes, her elder sister, Madame Chiang Kai Shek—She Who Loves Money—turned from her inventory of "the take" to her wasp-waisted Generalissimo and said, "Where to when Shanghai falls?"

"Are you so sure it's going to fall?"

She looked at him as if he'd asked if water were wet ... and finally said, "Yes. Aren't you sure?"

He ignored her rhetorical question and barked, "West." Once again he was surprised by the control this somewhat homely girl held over him. He had been a famous womanizer for years, with his pick of the beauties of southern China, yet this cow-faced woman had him in her thrall.

She picked up a vase that her expert had tagged as "Ming Dynasty," tilted it so it caught the light, and smiled. She liked it. She liked real things. "Move all our forces to Nanking?" she suggested.

"No. It's indefensible. We'll go farther west."

She looked directly at him for the first time. "To attack the Communists again?" she said, clearly disappointed, since west of Nanking there was very little wealth.

"No. They are farther north."

She thought about that. Her Generalissimo had ordered five major expeditions against the Communists—the last three led by German generals. Finally the Communists had given up and fled to the north-west. A rout, she thought, but she was smart enough not to dismiss the Communists and their Librarian leader. Although, giving perfectly good land and merchandise to imbecilic peasants struck her as madness. She wondered how much her idiot sister had to do with the choices the Communists made. Then she dismissed the thought. Number-two sister was just a stupid girl. She looked at Chiang, who was still speaking about something or other. Finally he concluded whatever it was that he was saying with, "Time to get ready to leave."

"No need. It's done." For the past ten days she'd had twenty servants steal everything of any value within a ten-mile radius, and now she was simply deciding which items would be carefully moved from this warehouse and stowed on her private railway car.

* * *

THE THIRD SOONG DAUGHTER—She Who Loves China—stood outside the house in the French Concession that she had shared with her now deceased husband, Dr. Sun Yat-sen. She sighed as she remembered her husband's tenderness—and his foolhardiness. She had almost left him once, when, in a vain effort to keep peace amongst his loose revolutionary coalition, he had given over the presidency of the new Republic to the Manchu General, agreeing in return to accept the cabinet post of Minister of Railways. Over and over, in their front parlour, she had been forced to look at maps upon which he had drawn perfectly straight lines while he'd explained to her, as if she were a simpleton, "The shortest distance between any two points is a straight line."

"The shortest distance?" she'd echoed.

"Yes, my child, the shortest distance to the New China."

She'd tried to protect him, but it was hard. The man was a fool, and everyone knew he was a fool. In fact, now that he was gone it was easier to stand up for his ideals than it had been while he was alive. She thought of the final days with him in the awful room upstairs. His insistence that he was freezing—despite the intensity of Shanghai's August heat. Then the cries. Cries for his mother.

She thought of her father's hurt silence when she had returned from her elopement with the good doctor. Then she thought of her two sisters—one backing Chiang Kai Shek's Kuomintang governing party, and the other who, she assumed, was a power broker in the Chinese Communist Party. Two sisters in opposition to each other. China in the balance. She closed the door of her now empty house and thought, *Yes, but I hold the deciding vote—I hold the balance of power in the Soong Dynasty.*

chapter ten

Attack on Shanghai

It was a child who first approached the half-buried bomb behind the apartment building on what the *Fan Kuei* insisted on calling Hamilton Road, despite the fact that the street was in the midst of the Old City. The boy touched the exposed rear fin and announced, "It's hot." Then he heard a whistling and looked up. A large grey thing was racing across the sky. He shielded his small eyes from the sun—then he heard the massive explosion a few blocks away.

Seventeen hundred lives ended in an instant as the powerful bomb ripped through the upper storeys of a huge department store on Bubbling Spring Road.

Moments later, a terrified woman came running out of her apartment on Hamilton Road and grabbed the little boy away from the unexploded bomb, both relieved that he was alive and furious that he had terrified her so.

That was August 13, 1937—only four days after a Japanese officer, First Lieutenant Isaw Oyama of the Japanese marines, had improperly attempted to enter Hungchiao Airport. He was stopped by the Chinese Peace Preservation Corps, a unit formed after the 1932 ceasefire agreement in which the Japanese had insisted that Shanghai be demilitarized. The young Japanese officer was furious that his path had been impeded and struck one of the Chinese Peace Preservation Corps officers. Then, as his superiors had hoped, he was shot through the heart with a single bullet. The next day, August 10, the Japanese Consul General demanded an apology and went on to insist that the Peace Preservation Corps be removed from the city, and that all of Shanghai's defence works be dismantled.

The Chinese listened patiently, but said nothing.

Before the end of the day Japan had sent reinforcements to Shanghai. Twenty-four hours later Chiang Kai Shek moved Chinese troops into greater Shanghai in direct violation of the Shanghai ceasefire agreement. Although there were negotiations, no one was surprised when, the next day, a day the Chinese eventually called Bloody Saturday, Japanese bombs fell on the great city while Japanese planes flew low overhead, strafing the population.

At 9:00 a.m. on August 13, Chinese forces fired on Japanese emplacements in Zhabei, Woosung, and Jiangwan districts. The Japanese responded and brought their ships in the harbour to readiness, and that night the Japanese Imperial Navy began a bombardment of the city at the Bend in the River.

Immediately the Foreign Settlement and the French Concession were deluged with refugees. The Japanese, on the whole, were attacking only the Chinese sections of the city, and the Shanghainese knew it. By the thousands—the hundreds of thousands—they sought shelter with the *Fan Kuei*, just as they had during the maraudings of the Taiping Revolt.

Early the next morning Chiang Kai Shek ordered General Zhang Zhizhong to mount a counterattack. The Chinese had numerical superiority but were badly outgunned. They had virtually no navy, and the Japanese completely controlled the China Sea. Although they had some air force they had no infrastructure to replace downed aircraft, while the Japanese had the foremost aeronautics industry in the world. More importantly, the Chinese had inadequate artillery and few mechanized vehicles—very few tanks.

———

From the roof of their offices on the Bund the great *Fan Kuei* traders sipped their after-dinner drinks and watched the flashes of light bloom beneath them, just outside their district.

"The Chinese will root the Japs out of their nests, then drive them back into the sea," the head of Russell and Company out of New York said as he helped himself to a generous amount of cocktail sauce for his skewered shrimp.

There were choruses of agreement from most of the other traders—but not all.

An ominous silence came from William Dent and his associates, who had been paid substantial bonuses to build the Japanese machine-gun bunkers within the city limits. Dent knew that the cement of the bunkers was too thick for the small-calibre artillery shells of the Chinese army—a fact that was playing out on the ground just a mile away, even as the *Fan Kuei* traders drank and deluded themselves with visions of a swift Chinese victory.

———

General Zhang Zhizhong's counterattack began with an assault on the very bunkers that Dent's company had built for the Japanese. The General had assumed that the removal of the hundred or so bunkers would take less than a day. He was badly mistaken, and his men paid the price of his miscalculation with their blood. For three days they assaulted the bunkers and the other fortified Japanese positions in Shanghai, concentrating much effort on the Japanese army headquarters near Zhabei. The fighting often came within earshot of the borders of the Foreign Settlement.

Finally, after three days of fruitless attacks, the General ordered his men to take and clear the streets around the bunkers, then set up sandbags to encircle the Japanese positions. This initially worked well—but then the Japanese brought in their tanks, and quickly the Chinese called off their advance.

For three days there was an unnatural calm—then the Chinese attacked the Japanese positions on the docks on the north side of the Huangpo. But the Chinese troops were inadequately trained in combining infantry with artillery movement. They ended up blockaded behind their own tanks on street after street—infantrymen exposed—and the Japanese used flame-throwers in combination with well-placed machine gun fire to drive the Chinese back. The Chinese suffered terrifying losses. The streets were littered with the corpses of scorched, bullet-ridden Chinese soldiers.

The next day the Japanese outflanked the Chinese troops with a large amphibious landing. After putting up brave defences, Japanese air power finally forced the Chinese to abandon the crucial towns of Baoshan, Luodian, and the lynchpin village of Dachang. The Chinese bravery astonished the Japanese. What the Japanese had thought would take only a week or two, at most, had ended up taking in excess of three months—time enough for Chiang Kai Shek to move major industry and his troops farther inland to the west.

By the end of November what remained of the Chinese army had evacuated the city at the Bend in the River, and the Japanese Imperial Army marched, uncontested, into the largest city in Asia.

———

Charles Soong's youngest daughter, Dr. Sun Yat-sen's widow, heard them two streets over, on Yen'an Lu. She pictured the Japanese troops parading down the wide avenue, Asian conquerors of the mother Asian nation.

Rifle shots cracked through the air.

She cringed. Hopefully it was just the Japanese firing their guns in the air—although she knew that bullets fired in the air in glee often fell to earth to cause much sorrow. She also knew that the Japanese were a parsimonious people, and she doubted the soldiers would be permitted to waste bullets. So, she knew, it was more likely they had fired on a pocket of resistance that they had failed to clean up.

The firing stopped as quickly as it had begun, and the silence that followed carried the quiet of death.

She closed her door and thought about bravery—and her duty to her country.

chapter eleven

The Naked Man

Rumours of the emergence of a new History Teller had surfaced in the city at the Bend in the River in the early 1930s. Many dismissed the very idea that there was a History Teller in their midst. Most who first met him thought him to be freakish. On subsequent viewings of his work, though, most found him to be unusually gifted. And they watched closely as he grew in stature from a distinctively styled young actor who specialized in playing females, especially courtesans, to a Peking Opera creator. His was a talent that sought the light and demanded to be shared. It was a unique but recognizable talent.

At the relatively young age of forty-eight, he took over the company itself.

But that was nine years and seven new operas ago—a span of time that brought him from obscurity to his present fame. From poverty to respect and modest fortune. A time from before the Japanese occupation to now.

It was a time span that began when missionaries were given a wide berth but respected, despite their folly, and brought us to now, when, to the History Teller's amazement, a young, red-haired, ghastly white-skinned missionary pulled a Japanese soldier off a fallen Chinese peasant woman and shoved him hard against the wall of an alley off Julu Lu.

For a moment the History Teller wondered if his eyes were deceiving him. He looked around. A crowd was quickly forming—and they were seeing what he was seeing. A white man attacking a Japanese soldier in order to save a Chinese woman.

—

Maximilian had seen enough. He remembered the day his father, Malachi, had stopped whaling. He'd come home and announced, "I'm finished with the violence of whaling. Finished with it." Well, Maximilian had seen enough violence since his own arrival in Shanghai eight months earlier. He had watched Japanese brutality increase daily. And now this. This soldier holding a bayonet to the breast of a prone, pregnant peasant woman who had done nothing more than disobey his traffic directions. Directions that, in all likelihood, the woman couldn't understand. It didn't matter how loudly Japanese soldiers shouted their orders, their words remained incomprehensible to most Mandarin speakers.

Maximilian had been surprised when he felt his pulse snap hard against his forehead. He knew the serpent vein there was throbbing, like some thing anxious to break the skin and escape. He looked down and was amazed to see his fists clenched and ready. But what most astonished him was the sweet taste in his mouth and the surge of joy that raced around his heart. A smile creased his handsome face. He was going to fight, and he couldn't wait. He didn't remember crossing the seven or eight yards that separated him from the Japanese soldier, but Maximilian would never forget the fear that flashed in the soldier's eyes as he yanked him from the peasant woman. Then Maximilian was on him, fists pummelling like pistons, his eyes alive with fury, the soldier's nose breaking, then an orbital bone crushing beneath the red-haired missionary's fists. Maximilian arched his back and a cry of elation escaped his lips—just as he felt the desire to bite deeply into the man's face.

The Chinese crowd couldn't believe it. A missionary fighting on the filthy pavement of a Julu Lu alley. From the dozens of windows facing the alley, most obscured by laundry satayed on long bamboo poles, came shouts of "*Hoa!*" and other more raucous encouragements to violence. With his limited Mandarin, Maximilian was not able to guess the exact nature of these shouts, but he was sure they were all urging him to kill the Japanese soldier.

And he really wanted to kill the man, but he stopped himself. He knew in his heart that he was no killer. He stood, the skin of his fists split and bleeding, his knuckles swollen, his black clerical shirt sticky from the soldier's blood, but his eyes still afire. Cheers rained down on him from the windows above, shaking the strung sheets and shirts as if they, too, applauded his work. Maximilian smiled. His large, white teeth momentarily reflected the brilliant noonday sun. And he found himself somehow more alive than he had ever been—and somehow finally completely home.

The first bullet went straight through his shoulder, and then a rifle butt crashed into the side of his head just below his ear. He whirled and threw the soldier with the rifle against the alley wall. The man bounced off and landed on his beaten comrade. Sirens sounded and whistles blew—and then there were six Japanese soldiers, their drawn bayonets only inches from his heart.

Maximilian didn't move. His shoulder throbbed and his head leaked, but he didn't move. He was aware of the faces in the alley windows above retreating to the safety of their squalid rooms. He heard shutters snapping to and noticed that even the satayed laundry retreated to inertness.

Then a sharp pain. Something or someone had hit him square in the face and blackness encircled him, slowly blotting out the harsh sun. The last thought he remembered was a reminder to himself—one his mother had repeated endlessly—*Your skin is very fair, stay out of the sun.*

———

He awoke two days later.

The first thing that occurred to him was that he was somehow both cold and hot at the same time. He went to pull his long, red hair out of his face but found that his hands were chained to a post stuck into the ground. When he moved, shards of pain shot through him. Hot pain. It was night, and he was chained to a pole—that he understood. He thought, *So the night air is the cold. And my skin—my sunburned skin—is the hot.*

He took a moment and realized that he was sunburned because he was naked. He could hear the sound of water lapping against a dock to his left. The night was moonless. He was desperately thirsty. Naked and thirsty—and, to his mind, doing God's work.

———

The History Teller had been watching the naked missionary on and off for the past two days. He had cancelled rehearsals, something he had never done before. Rumours that he was terminally ill spread quickly. They made him smile, but he refused to deny the stories. He spent more and more time in the presence of the naked, starving man: he sensed that something important was happening. Something worthy—something that could inspire art. And as he watched the naked man from across the wide street, over and over again phrases and pieces of phrases fell into his mind—words as colours and music. Combinations of words that he had never used before—combinations that no one had ever used before. Then new words themselves—words formalized from slang—words crystallized and split and reformed in new patterns, not only in his head but in his heart. He felt full of fire, and he noticed out of the side of his eyes that people had moved away from him. In Shanghai, where a person never had much space to himself, the History Teller stood—in the midst of a large crowd—completely alone. But he knew he was not alone. He was communing. Communing with the naked white man chained to the pole, who, clearly, the Japanese were going to allow to starve to death in public as an example to the population at the Bend in the River of what would happen to anyone who interfered with the actions of a Japanese soldier.

And each day the Chinese gathered to watch—and were confused by what they saw. The Japanese were the enemy. Well, so were the *Fan Kuei*. But hadn't the naked *Fan Kuei* tried to save a Chinese woman? What most confused them was the naked *Fan Kuei*'s refusal to beg.

Then, near the end of the third day, the naked *Fan Kuei* did the unthinkable.

He managed to get to his feet—and began to peel long strips of his brutally sunburned skin from his body, to entertain the Chinese children who cheered and ducked past the Japanese guards to grab the missionary's strange offerings.

———

Maximilian smiled as the young boy's hand touched his just before he grabbed the piece of sunburned skin. The boy, for an instant, stopped and stared into his eyes. Maximilian tried to speak. He wanted to say, "Don't be afraid. Don't fear to do what is right. Don't be afraid." But his tongue had swollen in his mouth, and he realized that if he didn't get water into his system soon his tongue might well bloat to such a size that it would cover his windpipe. Would Saint Peter laugh if he arrived naked, striped, and his mouth full of his tongue? He didn't know.

———

Another man observed the scene—and this one had a very different reaction to that of either the children or the History Teller. This man recognized the power inherent in such a public display of resistance. The Assassin knew a rallying cry when he saw one. And Maximilian's public pain and his refusal to cringe or whimper or plead was just such a clarion call. He watched the brave man, willing to die bravely, and thought, *There are better uses for a man's courage than a public death.* He watched a second boy dodge by the bored guard and grab a strip of skin from the man's outstretched hand. It was the missionary's third day without food or water—he would perhaps last another day—perhaps not.

One of the guards yawned openly.

Watching a man starve to death is a slow and boring process—especially if the prisoner refuses to beg.

The Assassin tilted his head slightly in the direction of three young men across the way. One of the three placed his hand over his heart and splayed his fingers, keeping his ring and baby finger together. The Assassin returned the hand signal with his middle and index finger touching—yes, there would be death today. He felt his swalto blade, like something alive, shift in his inner pocket, as if it ached to find its way to his hand.

And it did, late that very night, as the Assassin led a simple but daring raid on the Japanese guards who kept watch on the starving, naked man. The Japanese were overconfident in their power and so were unprepared as he silently slipped back the sewer cover behind them and castrated the nearest guard with a single slice of his blade. Then he and the three young assassins were everywhere—everywhere the Japanese weren't looking—and before a rifle trigger could be pulled or breath forced through an alarm whistle, the naked man was lifted and carried away.

———

He'd heard the voice first when he was a child. At his mother's grave, the old men mumbling prayers, he'd heard a gentle laugh. Then a strange, somehow foreign voice spoke: "Step forward and say goodbye to your mother."

He'd been frightened to say a word. Frightened because his mother had taken ill and died so quickly. Frightened because his father was not there, summer storms delaying his ship's return. Frightened by all the old men with beards and black coats. And him just standing there—and people looking at him.

"But I'm just a boy," he'd whispered to the voice.

"Yes, but she was your mother, and you'll never see her again."

"I will in Heaven."

The voice laughed again. It was a gentle laugh, but a laugh nonetheless. Maximilian liked the sound of the laugh. And wished he could laugh too. That the laughter would stay with him. Hoping to please the laughing voice he surprised everyone by pushing his way past the old men in front of him and approaching his mother's grave. The pastor stopped his mumbled reading and looked up.

"Step back, boy."

But Maximilian didn't step back. He stepped forward, then knelt beside his mother's grave. He stared at the simple pine box deep in the hole. Then he said, "Goodbye, Mother. Goodbye, goodbye, goodbye ..."

He waited for the laughter to warm him, but none came.

Maximilian took a handful of wet earth and threw it at the pine box.

The muck hit the coffin lid with a loud thud that echoed in his ears. He wanted to hear the laughter again. For it to tell him what to do. But the only voice he heard belonged to the old pastor, who said, "Stand up, boy." And somehow he did, and returned to the assembled mourners—where the laughter greeted him with the simple words "Be brave, boy."

He thought he had heard that gentle laughter other times in his life, but he wasn't sure. Even at the seminary he'd never admitted to anyone that he had what he thought of as a laughing guardian.

Then, on the evening of his third night, naked and scorched and tied to the post on the Bund, he heard the voice again. "Wake up, Max. We're not going to die roped to some post like a dog. Time to do a bit of magic." Then that laugh.

He opened his eyes and was amazed to see one Japanese guard fall, then another, and then the third. Hands were on him, a knife blade glinted in the moonlight, and the rope that bound him slithered to the ground, then strong arms were holding him and guiding him gently, head first, down a manhole into Shanghai's sewer system.

chapter twelve
The History Teller

The very night the Assassin and his Guild members freed Maximilian, the History Teller walked home from his theatre on Beijing Lu through what the Chinese called Shanghai's No-man's Land. The evening's performance had been a lesson in failure. Somehow the pain of the sunburned man had thrown everything he had done in his new opera into a paltry light, virtually a shadow. He had always been aware that this piece was not his best work, but that evening he found himself wincing at what he saw around him on the stage—whining instead of pathos; cleverness replacing thought; and, worst of all, his actors pretending, everywhere faking feeling and intent. He couldn't wait for the evening to be over, and he felt oddly joyful as he posted a notice that there would be no performance for the next three weeks. "How can we perform nonsense while a naked man bravely starves to death on a street of our city?" he demanded of the shocked company.

As he left the theatre he felt a gnawing deep in his gut. He smelled the deep, acrid air of change, and he knew that things were in motion—and that the naked man had something to do with that.

He turned a corner and was ordered to stop by a Japanese patrol. He produced his identification documents and his permission to be out after curfew. The leader of the patrol took his time reading the documents, then ordered him to get home quickly. The History Teller nodded, careful not to bow to the occupier, and headed down the street. He crossed through a small park with a bronze statue of a *Fan Kuei* boy at play. Long ago the etched plate on the statue's base had been filed down. So now the *Fan Kuei* child played in total anonymity.

He exited the park, turned another corner, then another, and was surprised to hear Japanese voices calling from the darkness of an alley for him to stop.

"Coolie! Stop right there, coolie."

He stood very still and allowed the men to approach him, in much the way one does crossing a bicycle-filled Shanghai street. Three dishevelled Japanese soldiers came out of the alleyway. He wondered if they had been to the famous brothel down there.

"Coolie!" one of them shouted again as they emerged from the shadows into the brightness of the street. In the harsh sodium light, any thought that they were simply soldiers on patrol evaporated. These were three drunken Japanese soldiers, no doubt from the Japanese countryside. Just spear-carriers and cannon-fodder in the Japanese Imperial Army. But to put peasants like these in charge of a sophisticated city like Shanghai sent a shiver of fear down the History Teller's spine.

One of them opened his mouth to speak. The History Teller could smell the disagreeable entwining of meat fragments and vomit on the man's breath. A lingering whiff of cheap alcohol hung on the still night air.

"Coolie, papers!"

For an instant he thought of complaining that he had just been stopped a few blocks before, but he decided against using logic with drunken peasants. Before he could pull his papers from an inner pocket, though, one of them threw him to the cracked pavement and began shouting at him. Then the soldiers encircled him and began to kick dirt at him as they laughed for no discernible reason. One spat on him—their laughter grew—while another fumbled with the buttons of his flies. The History Teller rolled just in time to distract the man's aim and the drunken man urinated on the feet of his compatriot. The wetted man let out a scream while the other two laughed as if this were the most extraordinarily clever thing that anyone, anywhere, had ever managed. The one with his penis still in his hand turned back to the History Teller but was surprised to find the man was no longer on the ground. He let out a grunt. The History Teller shouted in furious Mandarin mixed with just enough Japanese, "That's the ugliest one I've ever seen. Does it do anything but piss? I wouldn't imagine something that ugly has ever entered a jade gate." The Japanese were startled by the History Teller's words and were about to respond when a dark, female voice interrupted them in furious Japanese.

"Is this how you would act if you were in the presence of a great *shirabyashi*? Don't you dare look around. You will not look directly at me or my kind. If we were in Kyoto I would have you whipped. Now go."

The soldiers bowed low and grovelled their way back into the alley.

The History Teller waited until the soldiers were gone, then turned to his rescuer—and was astonished to see the young and already famous Jiang. He bowed quickly and said, "I am in your debt."

"True, and I in yours, for your art," she responded.

"What did you say to them?"

"The little Japanese I know—something about geishas and Kyoto—and their behaviour. I've had to learn such nonsense since their arrival in our city at the Bend in the River."

"Thank you again," he said, then turned to leave.

"Allow me," she said, and signalled for her palanquin. Her runners came up fast with the elaborate conveyance, and she opened the curtain for the History Teller, who entered quickly. She followed, closing the curtain behind her.

"I've never been in a palanquin before," he said, then added, "except on stage."

"I only went back to using them after the Japanese arrived. They seem frightened to stop a curtained palanquin for fear one of their generals' ladies is inside."

The History Teller nodded and said, "Clever."

"It is a time when, if we wish to survive, we must all be clever. Where were you going?"

"Home." He gave her an address, and she related it to one of the men. The palanquin was lifted and advanced at a sturdy trot.

In the moment the curtain was open the History Teller noticed the muscles on the man. He turned to Jiang. "These are not coolies."

"No. It is too dangerous for coolies. Surely you see that. They are members of the Tong of the Righteous Hand—and well paid to protect me."

He turned from her.

"You don't approve?"

"I have no opinion on the matter."

She looked at the shadowed face of the beautiful man beside her. "You portray women."

"You have seen my plays?"

"Of course. Actors and courtesans are first cousins. You move audiences of many, I move audiences of one."

He nodded.

"But you portray women. Why?"

"It is my gift. We must all be led by that which is given to us."

With that Jiang agreed completely. Completely. She parted the curtain, allowing the street lights to illume the History Teller's face in bands that appeared and disappeared as the palanquin moved. "You still wear your makeup."

"Curfew prevents me from taking the time to remove it."

"Does the makeup allow you to access us?"

"Us?"

"Women."

He smiled just as a band of light crossed his face. "You are asking me to reveal the secrets of my art."

She noticed he called it an art, not a craft. She'd always been surprised that actors called their work a craft while musicians never did. Finally she said, "Yes, I am asking you to reveal the secrets of your art."

His eyes hooded as his body shifted ever so slightly, his hip tilted, his feet turned in—and his lips became heavy. His hand reached toward her face, and when his fingers touched her lips, she was sure an ancient courtesan was touching her. The tip of her tongue touched his fingers, then she smiled and sat back.

"Very impressive, very."

Twenty minutes later the palanquin came to a halt. The History Teller pulled the curtain aside and stepped out. "I thank you for your kindness and, as I said, I am in your debt."

To his surprise Jiang's face was stern as she said, "Remember that, History Teller—you are in my debt."

He bobbed his head in acknowledgment and disappeared down an alley.

Jiang nodded knowingly; of course he had not told her his actual home address. *Good*, she thought, *you are careful. We must all be careful, now.*

The History Teller passed by the Temple of the City God and momentarily wondered what this City God had been up to these past months of Japanese occupation.

A Japanese armoured vehicle rumbled slowly up Tientsin Lu. He waited for it to pass. Shanghai's streets were unnaturally deserted. People waited behind closed doors and latched shutters—waited for what might happen next.

He stepped out into the street and crossed over into the French Concession. There would be no Japanese troops or armoured cars there. The smell of the sweet olive trees gave a lie to the tension of the night.

He passed by several expensive estates guarded by high walls. Some of these wealthy people had sponsored his operas. He had, in fact, performed solos in some of their homes to entertain merchants and *Fan Kuei*. The *Fan Kuei* would stare at his makeup, and didn't know what to make of the "women" he portrayed. But the Han Chinese, mostly Hong merchants, didn't stare. They would shout "*Hoa!*" and cheer and clap him on the back, then put up the money to sponsor his newest venture. He thought of some of them as friends, but did not trust them now. The Japanese had already identified potential collaborators, and there were many. It was not hard to find people in Shanghai who had scores to settle and would be only too happy to have the Japanese do their "settling" for them.

He stepped out of the French Concession and into the Old City. He passed by the Yu Yuan Gardens, now off limits to Chinese people. He saw a Japanese soldier pawing a Chinese courtesan and wished he had the courage to intervene, but he didn't.

Ten minutes later the History Teller stepped into the courtyard of his *shikumen* and was greeted by his old *amah*. She *tut-tutted* over him as she removed the last of the makeup from that evening's performance. He allowed her to fuss, then gently put her off. "Yes, tea would be nice."

"Shall I wake …?"

"No, no need to wake my wife. Bring tea to my study."

The tea was tepid and weak, but he didn't complain. The naked man had made him think of his daughter. Thoughts of her had haunted him all day. He sat there and thought of their last meeting.

His daughter, Chiao Ming, had joined the resistance movement exactly eight months earlier, when the Japanese army had begun its encirclement of Beijing. It was a natural evolution for her from Communist activities at the Shanghai Technical School. In her final year there, before the Japanese were even headed toward Shanghai, she'd spent more time in clandestine cadre meetings than she'd spent in classes. That was where she'd met her lover, Chen. Their affair had been secretive and intense—love at the dawn of war. There they had dedicated their young lives to the cause. In fact, Chen, she'd told him, looked upon the arrival of the Japanese invaders as an opportunity, maybe even a gift. A rallying point for the masses to finally get angry enough to fight back and claim what was rightfully theirs. And it was in Nanking that he planned to make his stand—their stand.

———

"Are you mad, Chiao Ming? Nanking? Now? There will eventually be much fighting there. The Japanese can't control the interior without Nanking."

"There will shortly be fighting everywhere, Father. Our lives are no longer our own." She stopped, suddenly unsteady on her feet. She lurched to his desk and leaned against it.

He stepped forward quickly, "Are you sick?"

"No. Just hungry, I guess."

"Then sit and eat."

She stepped back. "You have extra food while others starve, Father. How can that be right?"

More Communist foolishness, he thought, but said, "Take some with you, then, and give it to your friends."

"No. I have no time. I need to go."

Suddenly he opened his arms and said, "Stay, please, stay."

She looked at him with more pity than anger and said, "And do what? Become a silly actor like you, or write idiotic tales for the stage? What earthly good are you doing, Father?"

He suppressed a grin and said, "Must be some good, must be."

"Why is that?"

"Because, Chiao Ming, nature is extremely cruel. Anything that is not of value is discarded. But actors have been with us for a very long time. Only music, of all the arts, has been with us longer. But actors remain. Nature has not removed us—so we must serve some purpose."

"The only purpose now is to serve the state and free the peasants."

"Not fight the Japanese, Chiao Ming?"

"They are one and the same, Father. One and the same. And someone of your respected position should know better! Much better."

And that was that. He could think of nothing to stop her going.

"Perhaps you're right," he said—then tears came to his eyes. "I can't think of anything else to say."

She surprised him by putting her hands to his face.

"I'm an old man," he said.

"And I am not a child any more, Father. I know that in your plays you fought for China in your way, now I need to fight for it in mine. Why are you looking at me, Father?"

"Where did you get that necklace?"

"You gave it to me on my fifteenth birthday."

"Yes, I did, didn't I?" He smiled despite himself and thought, when Chiao Ming had first admired the necklace he had said to her, "But it is incomplete. It broke and is now missing some pieces."

"Yes, but those missing make those present more valuable," she'd said.

He had been pleased, very pleased—a true History Teller's point of view—the simple piece that makes the rest comprehensible.

Just so did she stand before him, wearing the necklace—it was the simple necklace that made her understandable to him. He knew that it was impossible to understand another being completely, even one you loved. But a necklace—that could be completely understood, and from that specific you could at least discern the outline of the whole. He nodded.

"What, Father?"

"I was just thinking of the necklace. Do you know the story it tells?"

Each of the glass globes contained a separate image.

"I assume, Father, that it is another of your fairy tales."

"The Black-Haired people's fairy tales," he corrected her.

"As you will, Father. As you will."

He nodded again but this time very slowly. "I'm going to turn my back now, Chiao Ming. When I turn back it would help me if you were gone."

"Won't you give me your blessing, Father?"

The History Teller felt himself spinning in time. For an instant he was back on a mountain—an old emperor raging against the cold—beginning to disrobe.

"In return for a kiss—anything."

As her lips pressed against his forehead, the necklace he had given her on her fifteenth birthday brushed against his shoulder.

Then he turned his back—and she was gone

chapter thirteen
The Chosen Three Decide

The young Carver convened the meeting with an abrupt clearing of his throat. Mai Bao's daughter, now Jiang, had found it difficult to avoid the curfew patrols, and in spite of having given herself hours to get to the meeting she had arrived just minutes before the appointed hour. The Assassin had come directly from his hiding place with Maximilian and his Guild members. Curfews and patrols were not an impediment to his movements. The Confucian had arrived early as well—and was oddly silent.

"We have serious decisions to make," the Carver began. "Have you set up communications with your Confucians?"

"Yes. I dealt with Madame Sun myself, and I have Confucians highly placed near both of the other two Soong sisters. They await my orders."

"*Our* orders," the Assassin said, with a deadly earnest.

"Yes, of course, our orders," the Confucian snapped back.

Jiang remembered her mother's warning about the Confucian.

"How do we proceed?" asked the Carver.

"Mao is the Man with a Book," the Confucian stated. "Are we agreed on that?"

Neither Jiang nor the Assassin wanted to believe that Mao was the Man with a Book, but he certainly fit the criteria.

"Good," the Confucian said, taking their silence for agreement. "Then how do we use my influence with the Soong daughters to support Mao?"

"First we get him to stop fighting with the Kuomintang," said the Carver.

"Chiang Kai Shek's forces are attacking the Communists, not vice versa," said the Confucian.

"Agreed," said the Carver, "So how do we get Chiang Kai Shek to stop attacking the Communists?"

There was a long pause as a possible answer rose in each of their minds: Find a common enemy that both need to fight. But it was the Confucian who stated the obvious.

"The Japanese have been occupying China for years, and that reality has never forced the Communists and the Kuomintang to stop fighting each other." He felt Jiang staring at him. He turned on her. "Time for you to speak, young lady. You haven't said a word. Your mother was never hesitant to speak her mind. Now it's your turn."

Jiang felt like crying because one potential answer leaped into her head. Create a catastrophe so awful that the two sides would have no choice but to join together. But the horror would have to be so great … but it was all too early. Not enough was known to make choices. She had no idea what role the Compact had to play—and neither did any of the men standing in the Warrens. Mao might well be the Man with a Book, but he seemed to be assuming power on his own, without their help. The Kuomintang forces had pulled out of Shanghai and were now farther west, the Communists were in the north—Nanking lay between the two and needed to be taken by any power that really wanted to control China. Nanking was obviously the next city the Japanese had in their sights, but what could the Compact do to determine the outcome of that inevitable battle?

Jiang stepped forward, her elegance graced by the flickering light. She took a deep breath and let it out slowly. This would be her first statement in the Ivory Compact, and she knew it ran counter to much of the historic thinking of the group. Her long fingers seemed to pluck ideas from the air much as her mother had plucked music from her arhu.

"The Japanese are not like the Taipingers. Or the Manchus. Chesu Hoi has warned us that there is an evil loosed upon the land." She paused and put her hand up to stop the Confucian from interrupting her. "And I believe him. It is time for us to ride the dragon's tail."

The old phrase came from deep in the collective memory of the Black-Haired people. When overwhelming forces were at work, you could do little more than ride the dragon's tail.

"So you propose we do nothing?" the Confucian demanded.

"Absolutely not," Jiang shot back at him. "I propose we track the dragon and see where he leads. Even the strongest of dragons eventually sleeps—and when he does, we will use our influence to have him killed."

The Carver nodded, as did the Assassin. But on the Confucian's face Jiang saw, just for an instant, something that could have been rage.

chapter fourteen

Getting to Nanking

The new Captain came onboard the junk at the south end of the Grand Canal, just past Chinkiang. Chiao Ming was startled by the man's appearance. One eye socket was empty, and the skin there was translucent, revealing a pulsing vein and splaying capillaries. An odd thought crossed her mind. *If I put my finger into that socket I could feel his brain.* She dismissed it as just more nonsense imposed on her by the raging hormones that were feeding the life within her.

Chen came up quickly behind her and grabbed her elbow, supporting her. She hadn't realized that she was tottering, but she quickly recovered and said, "I'm fine," then smoothed the cloth of the apron that covered her growing belly.

"Good," Chen said, "because this new Captain is one of us, and intends you no harm."

"If you're trying to avoid harm you're heading in the wrong direction," the one-eyed Captain said, and spat far out into the fast-moving waters of the Yangtze. "There'll be much harm in Nanking, before too long."

"Have you been there?"

"This junk's a trader, boy. Nanking is a major manufacturing centre, so of course I've been there."

"That's not what I meant, and you know it," Chen fired back.

"Ah, you meant have I been there lately?" the Captain asked and turned away.

"That," Chen said, not trying to hide the annoyance in his voice.

The Captain turned his single eye toward the young couple. The fact that her belly was slightly distended beneath the cover of her apron didn't escape his inspection. Finally he said, "No one will be going to Nanking soon—the Japanese will, no doubt, block all river traffic east of the city." He spat a second time. "If the Japanese want to rule the Middle Kingdom they have to take Nanking. They have no choice." He looked closely at these two young people, then said, "But that's where you're heading, isn't it?"

Chen nodded.

Chiao Ming thought she felt a stirring in her belly—then a strong kick. She almost winced.

"The Japanese are demons," the Captain said.

"No they are not, Captain," Chen said. "They are just indoctrinated peasants who don't know who their friends are."

The Captain's single eye opened wide, and he laughed.

"What?" Chen demanded.

"Are you going to Nanking to educate these demons?"

"Yes."

"They'll cut off your head and put it on a pike."

"Reason is …"

"Reason is nonsense in a war. If you are going to Nanking, it better be to kill Japs—period."

chapter fifteen
The Fall of Nanking and the Rise of the Dragon

Nanking—capital of the Tang and Ming dynasties, for ten years Chiang Kai Shek's Republican seat of government, and for Hung Hsiu-ch'uan and his Taiping followers the Heavenly Capital—fell to the Japanese after less than four days of resistance.

Neither Mao's forces nor the Kuomintang came to the defence of the city, so, on the evening of December 13, 1937, although small pockets of resistance remained, Generals Akira and Yukiko walked on foot into the city at the head of a column of tanks—without bothering to unholster their weapons.

——

That night, as Chiao Ming helped her comrades reinforce their barricade, she caught a glimpse of her lover's face. The deep lines of betrayal were still there, somehow more prominent than ever. She would never forget the moment when the Japanese soldiers had pulled out pistols from their uniforms and aimed them at him.

"I came here in peace," he'd said, "as a comrade—a fellow worker."

They hadn't laughed—but they might as well have. Two of the younger students whom Chen had convinced to come with them had quickly found themselves on their knees, one with his head lolling at an unnatural angle from his neck. A second had had a small hatchet buried deep in his chest.

It was almost comic—but blood and screams are seldom very funny for very long.

Chiao Ming had pulled Chen aside just in time for them to escape down an alleyway.

All he had ever said about the incident was a single sentence: "I came to Nanking to help workers, to help them." Then he had returned to his silence.

The baby kicked inside her.

Rage swelled in him.

Although the Japanese easily overpowered most of the under-armed Chinese resistance, the small Communist unit that Chen and Chiao Ming had joined held its ground. All around them Chinese fighters fell back, often throwing their antique firearms aside as they scurried, like rats from a flooded boat.

The Japanese tried to assail the Communist position three times, then decided to simply encircle it. The Communists bolstered their defences, preparing for an onslaught. Their backs were to the Yangtze, so the young Communists could have escaped if they had wanted, but they had come to Nanking to fight—not run.

On the second day of the occupation a stray bullet ricocheted off an alley wall and pierced the neck of their leader. Despite their best efforts the man bled out in less than an hour. Suddenly there was panic in their ranks. To everyone's surprise, Chen stepped forward and took command. And he led by example. That very evening he headed a raiding party against the Japanese and came back with both food and ammunition. The next morning he did the same, with even better results. What little opposition there had been to his leadership vanished.

Chen deployed his men carefully. Every morning as the sun rose he attacked the Japanese west of their position, and as the sun sank low in the sky he attacked the Japanese to his east—each time coming out of the sun. For three days the tactic worked. Then the Japanese had had enough and they called in aircraft to strafe the Communist enclave while the Japanese Imperial Navy bombarded the site. Under Chen's leadership the unit held its position, although their numbers were depleting quickly.

On the final day the naval shelling was so thick—and accurate—that almost every building in the area of Nanking that they held was flattened. Then the Japanese army's shock troops mounted a final assault.

"You have to go," Chen screamed at Chiao Ming.

"I came to fight, like you," she screamed back at him.

"And our baby? Did it come to fight too?" He turned quickly. There were three Japanese soldiers cresting the pile of rubble to his left. They all shot at once. Two shots tore into his chest. The third hit Chiao Ming in the shoulder and bored out a large hole as it left her body. She staggered back. He grabbed for her. She saw his eyes go wild and he mouthed the words "hiding place" and "boat."

They had fought about the damned hiding place and the damned boat. She hadn't wanted it. He had insisted. "If things get crazy, you head to that boat and get out of here."

"Why, because I'm a woman?"

"No," he'd said, "not that."

He'd never said, *Because I love you*. The only man who had ever said he loved her was her father, whom the world now called the History Teller. And thinking of her father, and the baby in her womb, she staggered toward the entrance to the basement of what they had prepared as "the hiding place." And there she waited while the Japanese tanks rattled overhead, flattening what little was left of their unit's defences. Night fell, and she waited, and listened for the telltales of Japanese soldiers' footfalls, but none came. Slowly she allowed herself to relax, and then the pain took her. She lay back on the blankets that they had prepared and gingerly felt her wound. The baby kicked. She smiled—then fell into darkness, unconsciousness saving her, momentarily, from present agony.

* * *

SHORTLY AFTER THE REMOVAL of the Communist resistance, the madness of Akira and Yukiko spread from them and entered their men and Hell opened its maw and belched forth horror.

The graceful streets of the Old City quickly began to reek like a charnel house in the still of August. Flies buzzed constantly in the chill air and grew fatter and fatter until many couldn't fly. Great black vultures gathered from the mountains and circled endlessly, at times blotting out the winter sun, impatiently awaiting their turn. Dogs ran mad in the city and could be seen scurrying away into the shadows with slimy mouthfuls of what could well have been slabs of human liver or kidneys.

The Japanese shat in the holy wells and forced mothers to throw their children from the city walls. The upper Yangtze turned pink, then red, then glowed crimson in the sunsets—oddly beautiful—as it made its majestic way eastward, toward the sea.

And no one slept, not victim or torturer. For days, weeks, the terror continued until neither Chinese or Japanese could tell if they were awake or asleep, dreaming or staring into the abyss.

For six weeks the Japanese army raped and murdered with a frenzy never before unleashed in the Middle Kingdom.

Somehow the Japanese were enacting upon the people of Nanking a revenge for their entire history as "China's second son." All the years of perceived slights and insults, the boasts that Japan was nothing more than a bastard colony of the Celestial Kingdom. All the taunting: that Japan had not even invented its own writing system or civil service or ... But those were reasons, and reason had nothing to do with what happened between December 13, 1937, and early February of 1938 in Nanking. Reason has no place where a father is forced to rape his daughter in front of his son. Reason has fled a city whose walls are festooned with the bodies of old men allowed to die slowly, twisting in pain around and around large spikes that nailed them to walls, their feet off the ground. Reason is laughable in a place where over three hundred thousand civilians are murdered in less than six weeks. Reason is an obscenity in a place where bayonet practice was held every morning using live Chinese men as targets. Reason is an insult in the world that was Nanking for six weeks at the end of 1937 and the beginning of 1938.

And the great birds drifted lower and lower over the city, hiding the sun's face. And the screams of the victims only infuriated the conquerors. And—like Akira and Yukiko beneath the third arch of the Marco Polo Bridge with young Corporal Minoto—the Japanese had crossed a moral line, and had left humanity behind them. And in its place they could not be differentiated from either the marauding packs of wild dogs or the swooping vultures or the fat flies that could no longer fly and crunched underfoot. They were horrors themselves. And each horror they inflicted pushed them a step further into the darkness, until the Komodo dragon that sleeps deep within every man was finally loosed, and they paraded openly on their four powerful legs, their talons clicking on the stone streets of the ancient city.

And men all behaved like dogs.

And the shit came down so heavy you needed a hat.

And the violence hid in the hallways.

And it clung to the curtains.

And death reared its blackened jaws on its scrawny neck and laughed to the heavens, but the stars averted their eyes and the sun wept such fat tears that it could not see—and the god in the Temple of the City God wept blood. But nothing stopped the carnage.

Babies were ripped live from their mothers' wombs with knives and impaled on boards leaned up against the houses of their families. On the main streets there was not a lamppost without at least three men hung from the armature. Women were gang-raped, then gang-raped again—then shot as they were clearly now unclean. Men had their arms cut off at the elbow and then were harnessed to oxcarts and made to pull soldiers in a bizarre parody of chariot racing.

And beneath it all—pushing it, thrusting it forward and upward, challenging the heavens—was the madness of Akira and Yukiko, now permanently white with rage, insane from lack of sleep. And both—now with hunks of human offal hanging from their rubbery Komodo lips and unsheathed claws, now permanently crimson—strutted before their men and demanded further horror.

King cobras were let loose in nurseries as the Japanese soldiers bet on which child would be bitten first. Men were buried to their necks and run over by the treads of tanks. Wild dog packs were guided into the homes of the aged and infirm while Japanese soldiers cheered on the slaughter. And no one slept—and the night and fog went on and on and on.

* * *

CHIAO MING KNEW that she had to get help. She was weak, but her baby was still alive. She could feel him grow within her, although he kicked less now. Her food was running low and she doubted the drinking water they had secreted in the hiding place was still good. She grabbed hold of a pole and pulled herself to her feet. Something sharp arched into her belly—the baby kicked, angry with the pain as Chiao Ming made her way back up onto the horrifying streets of Nanking.

* * *

"EVEN IF HALF of what we hear from Nanking is true, it's enough," the Assassin said.

"And what will the Guild do?" asked the Confucian.

"That for which they have trained so long," said Jiang, stopping the Assassin from answering the Confucian's question. Then touching the Assassin's shoulder she whispered, "Safe journey and return."

* * *

IN NANKING the horrors continued, unabated and unopposed, until a junk downriver disgorged its twenty-six men, who under cover of night clung to makeshift rafts and swam their way into the city.

A safe house awaited the Assassin, the men of his Guild, and the red-haired *Fan Kuei,* Maximilian. Once they had secured the place they immediately started their work.

And that night, a new force entered the terrifying world of Nanking under Japanese occupation: the Guild of Assassins. Seventy Japanese soldiers were severely wounded or killed before the sun rose—and the people of Nanking held their breath. They knew the Japanese would retaliate, and they did. Seventy Chinese men were forced into a Taoist temple and the building was set ablaze while their families were forced to watch and hear the screams of their loved ones.

But the next night the assassins were on the darkened city streets again.

Night after night the assassins struck. Day after day the Japanese retaliated—ten, then twenty Chinese died for every Japanese hurt or killed.

Every night the Guild's presence was felt by the Japanese. The Guild members were not particularly subtle, and they preferred to use the double-edged piercing knives they called swalto blades. Maximilian had heard their leader, the Assassin, reminding them that they did not need to kill Japanese—maiming was often more valuable. "Make them fear the coming of the night and the night will belong to us." They had been doing just that for almost a week and had lost only two of their members. The Japanese toll was closer to four hundred killed or maimed. But each morning the Japanese would bury their dead and savagely attack the populace in ever more horrifying ways. For every Japanese soldier killed or maimed, thirty Chinese males were crucified or staked out in public squares, their bellies split open so the rats could do their nasty work. The Japanese built a firepit and boiled water in a large cauldron into which they tossed Chinese boys, whose screams pierced the unearthly silence of the city for hour after hour.

It takes a long time to boil to death.

* * *

MAXIMILIAN PUT ON THE PARACHUTE HARNESS that the Assassin had given him as a souvenir of the previous night's raid. He threaded the long silk rope he had found through the front ring, tied a knot that somehow his hands knew, although his mind did not, and tossed the end over the rafter beam. Caught it, threaded it through a pulley, then twisted it through the front ring and pulled.

He was not surprised that he rose smoothly from the ground. Nothing about Nanking surprised him. Every night he wandered the streets and listened to the city moan in the throes of pain. Maximilian knew this place—everything about it. He had never been here before but he knew exactly where everything was and how everything worked, even knots.

He pulled on the silk rope again and rose to the level of the upper windows.

He looked down on the sleeping men in the room, the twenty men of the Guild of Assassins and their leader. Most slept, some talked quietly, all waited for the darkness, and the call to do their deadly work.

During the day the Komodo dragons strutted down the ancient streets, but as night fell the dragons retreated to their lairs and prayed for the dawn.

* * *

TWO WEEKS OF NIGHTLY KILLING hadn't changed the Assassin's demeanour even a little, despite the loss of two fingers on his right hand. Maximilian had seen him cauterize the wound with the white-hot end of a log he had put in the fire. The smell of roasting flesh had nauseated him, but, like the pain, had had little effect on the Assassin.

Maximilian knew that eventually the citizens of Nanking would yield to Japanese pressure and betray them. He told the Assassin as much. The man responded, "Why is this important?"

"Because we can't go on like this forever, that's why," Maximilian said, trying to control his now ever more present temper.

"Perhaps you'd like to hit me," suggested the Assassin, with what Maximilian was beginning to understand was the man's version of a smile dawning on his face.

"I hardly think that'd be fair, considering you are missing two fingers from your right hand," Maximilian replied, with a smile as well.

"I'd cut off two of yours if it would make you happier, to satisfy your *Fan Kuei* sense of fair play."

"Very clever, but our position here is precarious and you know it. You lost another man last night. It's actually amazing you haven't lost more. We need help from outside."

"Outside doesn't care about silly Chinks." The final word slid through his almost completely closed lips like something slimy and foul—which it was.

"Maybe. But if they knew what the Japanese were doing here. If they knew …"

"Then they would laugh. One set of heathens killing another set of heathens—what business is that of theirs? They still get silk and tea shipments from the Middle Kingdom, that's all they care about. We've already built their railroads for them—it's all that Slants are good for, as far as they're concerned."

Maximilian didn't deny that. How could he? He'd heard those sentiments often enough from the lips of the men who had sent him to the Celestial Kingdom. But he rallied himself to the task and put his hand on the Assassin's face. "We have to try. We have to tell the rest of the world of the horror of Nanking."

The Assassin looked at the red-haired *Fan Kuei* and nodded slowly.

Two nights later the entire Guild gathered round a small fire down by the river and the Assassin repeated Maximilian's argument. The men considered it—as only thoughtful men could consider things—in silence. Finally the youngest of the assassins spoke.

"My family lives just above a newspaper kiosk. Every morning hundreds of people come to that one kiosk. Those who can't read wait for someone to read the news to them. They all look at the pictures. And that's only one kiosk in Shanghai. There must be thousands there."

"Yes, but the Japanese control all publishing in Shanghai."

"Not in the Foreign Settlement or the French Concession," said Maximilian.

"True," the Assassin said.

More silence.

In his broken, although quickly improving Mandarin, Maximilian asked the youngest man to repeat what he had said. Maximilian listened carefully and, after asking for a few clarifications of words and meanings, said, "Pictures. More people look at the pictures than read the paper. Pictures are more powerful."

"More ghastly," the Assassin said.

"So we need photographs," Maximilian said, "it's that simple."

"Do you have a camera and film, Mr. Missionary?" the Assassin asked.

"No, but ..."

The Assassin ignored Maximilian and turned to the men. In rapid Shanghainese he ordered them to search out cameras, film, and other photographic equipment in that evening's "roamings." Then he dismissed them, kicked dirt on the fire, and was asleep within minutes.

By the end of the following night there were three cameras and some accessories sitting on a table in the safe house.

"That's all?" Maximilian asked.

"Apparently the Japanese confiscated every camera they could find," the Assassin said, keeping his voice matter-of-fact only with some effort.

Maximilian carefully inserted rolls of film into each of the cameras, then handed one to the Assassin and one to the young Guild member who had spoken first.

"Who gets the third one?" another Guild member asked.

"Me," Maximilian said.

He quickly instructed them how to aim and shoot, how to get the focus right and keep the iris open to allow in as much light as possible. They would be shooting at night and they'd need time for the exposure to work. He handed each of them a simple tripod and showed them how to mount the camera. Then he said, "One man to watch the camera, two to guard him. It could take upwards of five minutes to get the shot to work."

"No," the Assassin said. "That's too dangerous. The Japanese are looking for us already. Our weapon is stealth, not standing still taking pictures. I won't allow it. These are brave men and I will not senselessly risk their lives."

"But—"

"No. And that's final. We're not going to stand around waiting for light to mark paper while the Japanese gun us down like dogs. No."

There was a protracted silence. Finally Maximilian said, "What if we could take pictures in an instant, in a flash?"

"Then fine, but you just said that we needed to wait for up to five minutes—"

"But not if we have a flash of light, like the phosphorus they use in photographic studios."

"And do you know where we could get some of this phosphorus?" the Assassin asked, clearly ready to end this conversation.

"I think I do. Do you remember the parachute harness you brought back for me?" The Assassin nodded. "Those men parachuted in at night, didn't they?"

"You know they did, or we wouldn't have caught and killed them."

"How did they see where they were going at night?"

The Assassin stood and took three long steps away from the young missionary. "With flares—flares made of phosphorus."

Two nights later they were ready. Their cameras were equipped with phosphorus taken from flares stolen the night before from parachute troops, and their swalto blades were sharpened.

The rain began early that night and fell in sheets.

"Can we take photographs in the rain?" the Assassin asked.

Maximilian had no idea. He understood only the principle of light on photo-sensitive paper.

The rain proved more problematic than he had thought. They couldn't keep the water off the lenses, and they knew that what few photographs came out would be next to useless.

"It's not just the rain that's the problem," the Assassin said.

He didn't really have to elaborate. Both Maximilian and the young Guild member had faced the same dilemma: shoot the picture or save the victim?

"It's easier if they're dead," the young Guild member said.

"But not as effective," Maximilian said, and instantly regretted his comment. Two of the Guild members spat in the fire. The hiss was unusually loud.

"Enough," the Assassin said. He turned on the *Fan Kuei*. "Would you feel the same way if white-skinned, red-haired people were lying there in pain while you did nothing to help them—just took their photograph?"

Maximilian nodded.

"No, now it's important for you to speak."

"Yes," Maximilian said loudly. "Yes, their skin or hair colour doesn't matter to me. They are human beings being treated like animals—worse than animals. So yes and yes again."

Maximilian was sure the Assassin was going to throw the cameras in the fire and be done with the whole damned thing. But he didn't. Instead, he picked up his camera and said, "Maybe tomorrow it won't rain."

For seven nights they photographed the horrors of Nanking. Then, on the eighth, they met with a man who was identified only as a riverboat captain. No one had to be told the man was a pirate.

"Can we trust him to get the photographs to Charles Soong?" Maximilian asked.

The Assassin smiled and invited the man to the far corner of the safe house. "Turn around," he ordered his men. They did, and he removed his shirt. The pirate looked at the cobra on the Assassin's back and grunted. The Assassin took out two sets of pictures. Loudly he said, "If these photographs don't get into the hands of Charles Soong ..." Then in a whisper, referring to the second set of photographs, he said, "... and these into the hands of Jiang, I will personally see that you and your sons all feel the wrath of the serpent on my back. Is that clear?"

The pirate nodded, and the deal was sealed. Hopefully the world would see the obscenity of what was happening in Nanking, and Jiang could get the photos to the Soong sisters, whose men could join forces and put an end to it.

But the horror continued in what passed for the light of day. Only as the sun began to set did the Japanese retreat, hunker down, and await death from the darkness.

And each night the Guild of Assassins attacked. And days passed, too many days ... and the Assassin was not the only one who knew it.

"The photographs mustn't have gotten through," Maximilian said.

"Perhaps," the Assassin said, suspecting rather that the rift between the Communist forces and their Kuomintang enemies was too great for even the catastrophe of Nanking to bridge the gap.

"We have to create a safe zone—a sanctuary. A place where we can protect the remaining populace from the Japanese," Maximilian said.

"And how exactly would we do that?" the Assassin demanded. He waited for a response. When one was not forthcoming, he sharpened his swalto blade and curled up in the corner, seeking sleep before the night's work.

Maximilian had no answer, but he sensed that he would find one soon. He had been on the rooftops every night since they'd got their cameras and had travelled great distances above ground—distances that, somehow, he knew. On his first night on the rooftops he'd spied a tall post atop a hill in a city park. The next night he'd found two more poles that, along with the first, formed an almost perfect equilateral triangle. The next morning he'd asked the Assassin what the poles were for and the Assassin had replied, "They were watch towers of some sort. There are wild stories about a *Fan Kuei* general of the Taiping who flew on ropes from one post to the other, but it sounds a bit fanciful, don't you think?"

Maximilian didn't think it was fanciful, and the laughing voice in his head kept encouraging him to *Search, search for it, bring it to light.*

The next night Maximilian ventured out on the streets of the city. He moved quickly into the shadows of alleys and made his way to the westernmost tall pole. When he reached out and touched it a thrill raced down his arm and circled his heart. He looked down and was surprised to see his hands set into fists, then he tasted the blood in his mouth. He was ready to fight. No. He was *anxious* to fight. But fight with what? With light? He stepped back from the pole and his heel hit the curb. He turned and stared at the curb. He kicked it a second time, and this time he heard it clearly—a hollowness. Then he smelled it. Oil.

It took him two more nights to find the opening to the half-foot-wide channel on the under-edge of the street gutter, and a third to open it up. He followed it. The channel led directly to the second tall post, then to the third.

But the oil smell was gone.

He made his way slowly back toward the first post, then laughed out loud. Unless there was a pumping system of some sort, whatever flowed in those channels would have to move by the force of gravity. So all he had to do was find the highest point on the triangle outlined by the three posts—and dig.

It took him another night of searching to find the spot, and three more to do the digging—but there it was, the source of the oil smell: a substantial reservoir of oil, with a simple wooden block holding the liquid in place. The block could easily be smashed by a rock, releasing the oil into the channel. There was even a convenient rock, waiting, awaiting the right hand.

* * *

CHIAO MING HAD FOUND a hole in which to hide, inside what used to be a Buddhist temple. The elderly couple who had remained to look after the place took pity on her and did their best to help her. But her wound was festering, and fever crept upon her and seemed to still her baby.

* * *

JUST PAST NOON the next day, Maximilian squatted opposite the Assassin, a cold bowl of rice between them. Maximilian told him about the oil reservoir.

"How do you propose to use what you have found?"

Maximilian thought, *Komodo dragons control the streets of the Heavenly Capital. What could scare a Komodo dragon?*

And in a whoosh, he knew—fire.

The voice inside his head laughed.

But more important than fire, godliness.

The voice paused, then laughed a second time, but this time with great gentleness.

Maximilian said, "You can't keep on going the way you've been going, and clearly no one is coming to save us. Eventually the Chinese who know where we are will betray us. They'll give up this hiding place to keep their children from being raped or boiled to death. They'll stand in line to give us up. And you know it."

The Assassin nodded slowly and reached for a small hand scoop of rice.

"So you'll help me use the oil to set up a sanctuary?" Maximilian pressed.

The Assassin did not move for a full five minutes, ten minutes, then he nodded and put out his right hand, the one missing the two fingers.

Maximilian took the extended hand and the two men stared into each other's eyes. "Good," Maximilian said, "then maybe it's finally time to tell me your name."

The Assassin seemed to think about that for a long moment. He said, "Loa Wei Fen," then added, to Maximilian's surprise, "now, it is Loa Wei Fen."

* * *

CHIAO MING MANAGED to get to the bank of the great river, managed to push aside the brush that hid the boat, and pushed off into the fast-moving current of the Yangtze. Standing in the bow of the boat she suddenly felt a rush of liquid and reached down. Her pants were soaked through, as was her smock. "My waters ..." She took a step, slipped, and almost cracked her head against the gunwale before coming to rest on the damp boards of the round-bottomed boat. And there she lay as the life within her began its voyage to the light.

And she dreamed a strange dream, a waking dream. She was in a great city square, the largest she'd ever seen. And there were young people. Young people her age and Chen's—so many of them. And they were singing and calling out. And somehow she knew that this was later—much later—and that the baby in her womb—no, not the baby in her womb, but the baby that he would sire—was standing, alone, in front of a huge Japanese tank—no, not a Japanese tank—a Chinese tank. He was just standing there. A whole line of huge Chinese tanks had just stopped—and he stood there—carrying only a flower.

And the boat was taken by the current—turned and spun and paused in eddies, rocked by the hand of the river god—and headed downstream, toward the water access of the safe house that housed the Guild of Assassins in the ancient capital of Nanking.

* * *

AS THE ASSASSINS CAME BACK from their night of killing they retreated to the river to bathe away the gore. And there—like a baby in a basket of reeds—the boat slowly appeared through the morning mist. Immediately the assassins were on their guard. Two plunged into the cold water and swam to either side of the boat. Mounting at exactly the same time, they found Chiao Ming on the wet floorboards.

Ten minutes later the girl's body was laid out on the one mattress in the safe house, and Loa Wei Fen signalled Maximilian to approach.

He immediately saw that the girl was not dead, but her breathing was terribly shallow and her colour ghastly white. "She's in shock," he said, "and half starved."

"And pregnant," Loa Wei Fen added.

"What?" Maximilian threw back Chiao Ming's smock. "Jesus, help me," he muttered. Then he ripped open her sleeve and saw the extent of her shoulder wound. The wound smelled like cheese left out in the sun. The discoloration on the arm and shoulder were pronounced, and the infection had clearly spread down to her torso.

"So?" Loa Wei Fen asked.

He shook his head. He was no doctor. He knew rudimentary first aid—and even that he hadn't paid much attention to. Besides, he didn't have any bandages or sutures or even a scalpel. Then he saw the womb expand and re-form. "The baby's alive."

Loa Wei Fen pressed his fingers deep into Chiao Ming's protruding abdomen. His fingers seemed to crawl across her womb, then they paused at the top of the expansive belly. He looked up at Maximilian. "It's the head. It hasn't turned."

Maximilian reached over and tried to feel what the Assassin had, but couldn't. "Are you sure?"

Loa Wei Fen nodded—for the first time since Maximilian had met him, something that could have been fear crossed the older man's face as he removed his swalto blade and held it out to Maximilian. "Cut out the baby or it will die with its mother."

Maximilian was shocked. "You do it!"

"No. I kill things, I don't bring them to life. That is for the likes of you."

The sharpness of the blade amazed Maximilian, as did the founts of blood that rose with each cut. Then Chiao Ming's womb was open and a perfect child turned its head and stared up at him. He reached into the womb and put a hand beneath the infant. For an instant it slipped, but Maximilian shoved his other hand beneath and lifted the baby from his now terrifyingly still mother. He didn't remember cutting the cord or cleaning the child. He just remembered that he was tired, so tired, and saying, "He needs some milk."

Later that night, with the baby swaddled and quiet, Maximilian stared at the lifeless form of the baby's mother on the floor of the safe house. What had no doubt at one time glittered in this soul had now gone—a flame extinguished. The only sparkle of life about her was the unusual necklace she wore around her neck. He gently lifted her head and unsnapped the clasp.

The thing came loose in his hand and he held it up to the dawning light. The glass beads cut the light into rainbows that formed, then re-formed—a concerto of colours—across his palm. He noticed the intricate carvings in the heart of each bead, then realized that the necklace was missing some beads. He assumed they had broken off over time, although no remnants of them clung to the silver thread.

The baby let out a howl.

He went to it and put it in his lap. As he gently rocked him, the baby opened its eyes and for the first time they stopped their roaming and seemed to focus—on the necklace that Maximilian still held in his hand.

He moved the necklace slowly toward the baby's face. The boy's eyes traced the movement of the baubles. Maximilian looked from the necklace to the infant, then back again. Finally he said aloud, "It's your inheritance, little one, something of your mother's that you can keep." He snapped the necklace in two and then retied both strands. The small one he put around the baby's neck, the larger he put around the mother's wrist.

When later that day Maximilian and two of the Guild assassins committed the woman's body to the river, it was taken by the current quickly, and soon all Maximilian and the baby could see of the body was the glint of the brilliant sun off the delicately cut glass.

Maximilian rocked the baby in his arms and felt the surge of the boy's life within—his godliness—and knew how to create the safe zone he needed to save the remaining Chinese citizens of Nanking.

He put on the parachute harness, looped his silk rope around the overhead beam, and pulled. The cord slid smoothly through the pulley he had positioned there and he rose—baby in his arms—a godly thing.

* * *

CHARLES STARED at the photographs in front of him. "How did you ...?"

He never completed his sentence, as the Hong merchant who presented the photographs put a finger to his lips and said simply, "They are from Nanking—you can see the famous tower in one of the pictures, the temple of their city god in another, and many other recognizable features of the old capital. Turn to the last picture."

Charles did.

A man whose hands had been cut off and who was chained to a wall had a Nanking newspaper in his lap, with the date prominently displayed: seven days earlier.

"Thank you," Charles said. "Do you want ...?"

"Money?" Suddenly the man was laughing.

"What could possibly be funny here?"

"Money—money is funny—is ridiculous, when things like that in those pictures are happening to our people."

———

Jiang pushed the photographs aside and felt a cold rage growing in her. She instantly wanted to call her twin sister, but her mother's words of warning filled her head: "Your allies now, your only allies, are the Chosen Three and the Carver."

She summoned the Carver and the Confucian. Both gasped at the pictures. The Confucian stood up and did that walking-lecturing thing that she found so annoying, just as her mother had before her. Then he said, "I will contact the Confucians with the Soong girls."

"You said you already did that when we heard rumours of what was going on in Nanking," Jiang said. Then she stared at the Confucian. "You didn't do anything, did you?"

The Confucian thought, *I do not take orders from a whore. The time was not right for Confucians to reassume their position of power.* But all he said, with a smile, was, "They were just rumours, then. Now I have proof."

———

Charles had no way of running the photographs in his Shanghai papers, since each had to pass a Japanese censor, but he had many contacts in France, England, and America—and each received copies of the photographs with a personal note verifying their authenticity and a plea for them to be published and widely disseminated.

———

The Confucian waited patiently for the youngest Soong daughter—She Who Loves China—to return home. The photographs were tucked away in his front pocket. It was getting late. Curfew had already passed, and he had no desire to be caught out after ... Then a modest automobile turned the corner and the young woman stepped out. She turned back to the car and gave the driver a *yuan* note.

The Confucian stepped out into the road just as the car turned the corner. "Mrs. Sun," he said.

She was instantly on her guard. "You again?"

"I intend no harm. I am only a Confucian scholar who has something important for you to see."

It took a little more persuading, but shortly the Confucian was sitting at a delicately inlaid lacquered table, his photographs laid out for the youngest Soong daughter.

The woman gasped, then picked up one of the photographs. Tears sprang from her eyes and she turned away. "So it's true?"

"Absolutely, I'm afraid."

"Why do you show me these things?"

"You are a Soong daughter. Your sisters are powerful women. I want you to talk sense to them."

———

The few papers in the West that ran the photographs carefully blacked out the most offensive parts and all carried warnings that the photographs might not be legitimate—that "those people" were "prone to exaggeration"—a sentiment the western press would repeat a few years later when the agony of another group of "those people prone to exaggeration" was presented to them.

* * *

MAXIMILIAN WAITED for a moonless night. The assassins all assumed their positions, Loa Wei Fen, rock in hand, by the oil reservoir.

Days earlier the assassins had strung the strongest silk ropes they could find to the pulleys on each of the three poles, as Maximilian had instructed them

Now Maximilian waited for the laughing voice to come—and it did. He fastened the last of the buckles of the parachute harness and grabbed hold of the loose end of the rope that was attached to the pulley with one hand while he held Chiao Ming's baby with the other.

He signalled his readiness, and the assassins began to smash garbage can lids, pots, pans, sheets of metal, woks—anything that made a racket—and sure enough, the Japanese patrols from all over Nanking came running. Maximilian had walked the routes and timed them night after night: ten minutes was not enough time for the Japanese to get there, but twenty minutes would give the soldiers time to interfere with his plans.

He began to count.

When he reached five hundred he heard shots and shouts, but he continued to count. He needed many, many Japanese to see what he had in store for them. Too few and their word might be doubted.

By six hundred and fifty he saw the flash of rifle muzzles piercing the darkness, and by seven hundred he heard the rumble of tanks.

He continued to count. At seven hundred and eighty he saw the youngest assassin take a bullet in the face and fall directly backward against a stone wall. At nine hundred he shouted his command to Loa Wei Fen—the first time he had ever ordered the Assassin to do anything.

Loa Wei Fen released the oil from its reservoir with one swift swing of the rock.

At eleven hundred he shouted, "Now!" and the remaining members of the Guild of Assassins lit their supplies of phosphorus and plunged them into the huge equilateral triangle of oil beneath the streets.

For a moment nothing happened.

Then flames shot thirty feet into the air, turning night to day. The Japanese dropped their weapons in confusion and stared at the wall of flames. Then they looked up—and in the midst of the flames, seemingly suspended in space, they saw a red-haired White man holding a baby aloft, shouting in perfect Japanese, "This is God's territory. The fire demarks God's sanctuary. Be gone from that which is God's."

And the Japanese, knowing a godly event when they saw one, stood like statues in the fire's light as their reptile skins and Komodo lips became once again the lips and skin of ordinary men. And a sanctuary that would keep almost four hundred thousand Chinese alive and safe within its two and a half square miles was born.

chapter sixteen
Shanghai Under Occupation

And the sanctuary held, although very little news came out of Nanking, as the Japanese controlled the railroads and the great river. But whispers filtered out. A cousin was still alive, a grandfather had found refuge—a red-haired *Fan Kuei* had flown with a baby in a ring of fire.

In Shanghai the uneasy peace between the Japanese occupiers and the Foreign Settlement proceeded one day at a time. Incursions from both sides were not uncommon, but the invisible boundary basically held.

The Japanese secured their hold on Shanghai and ignored the Concessions, and a kind of normality returned to the city at the Bend in the River. But the Foreign Settlement was truly "a lonely island."

The Palace Hotel replaced its shattered windows, and businessmen could be seen playing tennis—and even golf. Ironically, a production of Pearl S. Buck's *The Good Earth* was drawing large crowds to the Grand Theatre to see Luise Rainer's star turn.

There were, naturally enough, some new complications to life in Shanghai. Japanese soldiers were stationed at several crucial intersections in the city, and every Chinese person who passed them had to bow. If the bow was considered not deep enough or disrespectful, the Chinese man, woman, or child was immediately beaten. Trams were stopped as they passed Japanese guard posts, and all the Chinese onboard had to bow. *Fan Kuei* were exempt from this treatment, although if their chauffeurs were Chinese and they drove past a checkpoint, the Chinese chauffeur had to stop the car, get out, and bow properly to the Japanese soldiers.

Strangely, the business of entertaining the populace of Shanghai had never been better. Cabarets and bars were filled to overflowing, and places like the popular nightclub Great World were in such demand that people lined up in the street for hours to get in. It seemed that as Shanghainese worries increased, their desire for diversion grew.

In 1938, the first of the expected rush of European Jews began to arrive. Initially most were German or Austrian, but they were followed shortly afterward by Polish Jews. The Jews' exit point from Europe was often Genoa, and their month-long trip on the Italian Lloyd Triestino liners brought them past such ports as Port Said, Aden, Bombay, Ceylon, Singapore, Manila, and Hong Kong—but they were not permitted to set foot ashore in any of these places. The Italian shipping line charged them twice the normal fare, and since the Nazis permitted them to leave with only one bag and twenty Reichsmarks, they all arrived in Shanghai disoriented and impoverished—and about to experience yet another shock. They were not permitted to disembark at the Bund wharfs, which belonged to the British and French, since refugee Jews were not permitted to set foot in those countries either. So the last part of their arduous journey was in a Chinese junk that charged them a minor fortune to take them the two miles from the Bund, up the river to the Japanese-controlled docks on the Suzu Creek.

Shanghai's Iraqi Jews came to their aid. The Vrassoons, the Ellises, the Kadooris, and Silas Hordoon (through his adopted daughter, Jiang) supplied the lion's share of the money. Many of the new immigrants were settled in bombed-out tenements in Hangkow—although the Vrassoons were eventually shamed into offering up what few unrented units they had in their fashionable Embankment House. The wealthy Sephardic Jews supplied milk for the children and soup kitchens to get the newly arrived families going.

Because many of the Jews who escaped the Nazis were people of wealth and education, they hung out shingles and began to work. Doctors found employment quickly, as did engineers. Some academics were taken into the Chinese universities. The Vrassoons and the Hong Kong Canton Bank (the name Silas had momentarily landed on for his banking enterprise) gave loans to others, who reproduced some of the life they had left behind. Some opened factories (one, a very large margarine-making concern); others opened watch-repair shops and clothing stalls; and European-style restaurants appeared, like Café Louis on Bubbling Spring Road and the expensive Fialker Restaurant on Avenue Joffre, which offered fine Viennese food. The Black Cat Cabaret on Roi Albert Avenue presented the same cynical, biting satires that could be found in clubs on

Berlin's Unter den Linden. Sachertorte and strudel were suddenly available in the city, and the newest Hollywood films appeared, as if from nowhere. Within a year the Jewish community had a newspaper, a radio station, an orchestra, and regular theatrical performances, many of which were extremely critical of capitalists like the Vrassoons, Hordoons, Ellises, and Kadooris. Debating societies—which served no real purpose, since every Jewish dinner table was actually a debating society where socialists clashed with capitalists, the religious with the non-religious, the old with the young, Zionists with cosmopolitans—sprung up like weeds in an untended garden.

Not every Jew adapted to Shanghai. Between the demands of the climate, the loss of status, and the terrible crowding of Hongkew, the dock district by the Suzu Creek where they all initially stayed, suicide was an all too common occurrence amongst the formerly powerful. But on the whole, Shanghai Jews realized that they had literally found a port in the storm, and they made the best of their new surroundings. Only Japanese-controlled Shanghai opened its doors to these dispossessed souls. The Allied nations—Great Britain, America, Australia, New Zealand, and Canada—turned ship after ship of Jews away.

But the twenty-eight thousand Jews in Shanghai were an insignificant number compared to the vast numbers of Chinese in Shanghai—and Chinese lives under the Japanese were getting more and more difficult. The Japanese set up the Kempie Tei—their version of the Gestapo—and ruthlessly set out, under the political cover of the quisling governor, Wang Ching-wei, to eradicate all Chinese patriots. Their reign of terror began in February of 1938 with the public decapitation of the prominent Chinese editor Tsai Diao-tu—right across the street from a major entrance to the French Concession. Daily, Chinese businessmen and journalists believed to be patriot sympathizers received packages with severed fingers and decayed hands as a warning that they were on Kempie Tei's lists.

Only the remains of Tu Yuch-sen's Tong of the Righteous Hand, reverting to their initial anti-foreigner purpose, fought back. They shot at Chinese businessmen they thought were too close to the Japanese. One was wounded right outside the Cathay Hotel before his White Russian bodyguard returned fire. Tu's men also sent packages—these usually contained axes. If the warning was not heeded another axe, not unlike the one in the package, would find its way into the chest of the collaborator.

The Kempie Tei, from their headquarters at 76 Jesse Road, known to everyone simply as Number 76, intensified their wave of terror. Seven newspapers were firebombed. Newspaper staff, to protect themselves, barricaded themselves in their buildings. Printers and editors slept on their desks. News items came to them by phone or telegraph or as typed pages wrapped around stones thrown through open windows on upper floors. No one came in or went out—in one case, for years.

And the world continued its descent into madness.

Hitler invaded Czechoslovakia and "took back" the Sudetenland. Glass tinkled in the night and a new horror began. The Nazis took Poland. Britain, France, Australia, and Canada declared war. The Nazis took Denmark and Norway, France, Belgium, Luxembourg, and the Netherlands. The Japanese signed a peace pact with Germany. The little man with the nailbrush mustache strutted openly in the streets of Paris. German bombs landed in London, Southampton, Bristol, Cardiff, Liverpool, and Manchester. The Japanese entered Indo-China over the objections of Britain and the United States. A polio-afflicted president was re-elected in America. The Americans began to supply arms under a lend-lease program to the British and Soviets. The Grand Mufti of Jerusalem went on Berlin radio to support Nazi efforts to eradicate Jews. A massive air raid on London lasted two days and two nights, but St. Paul's Cathedral, miraculously, was untouched. Inexplicably, Hitler attacked the Soviet Union. Yellow stars appeared on the chests of European Jews. A canister of gas was released in a sealed room in a small Polish town. The Germans took Kiev and murdered 33,771 people wearing yellow stars. Odessa fell. Kharkov fell. Sebastopol fell. Rostov fell. But Moscow and Leningrad did not. All the while, America stayed out of the "European" war.

In July of 1940, the quisling Wang Ching-wei published a black list and set loose a new wave of assassinations.

At the same time, the Japanese closed Chinese gambling houses and opium dens—and opened their own. Jiang lost three major properties that were outside the French Concession in a week, but considered herself lucky to still have her main business, Jiang's, just down the street from the Colombes' House of Paris. But she was not beyond expressing her distaste for the actions of the conquerors. Often she thought of calling her sister, but always resisted. Her mother, Mai Bao, had chosen her to control the family fortunes and enter the Ivory Compact. But these were hard times, unlike any that her mother had experienced. And she had more of a temper than her mother—much more.

"This is Jiang's, not some Tokyo noodle shop," she said to the drunken Japanese officer.

The man made a face and signalled to his translator, who told his superior officer what the beautiful madam had said to him.

"You are no geisha," he slurred, then laughed to himself.

Before the translator could speak, Jiang, recognizing the word *geisha*, said, "I cannot imagine that a pig like yourself ever had anything to do with a real geisha." She looked at the translator and said, "You're a translator, so, translate!"

The translator did.

The Japanese officer suddenly reddened, then screamed something unintelligible.

The translator responded with a quick, deep bow. Clearly he had apologized.

"Tell your commanding officer," Jiang said, "that this is the French Concession, not Fang Bang Lu—he has no power here. Here he pays for services that I will or will not supply as I deem fit. This is Jiang's, as I said before, not some limp noodle house in Tokyo."

The man left in a stony silence, and Jiang retreated to her private room. She was angry with herself. She had lost her temper—a bad thing to do in times of war when your side was losing—and she had an obligation to the Ivory Compact.

A few months later the Foreign Settlement was shocked by the departure of its entire complement of English and Australian military, all of whom had been ordered to more pressing theatres of war. In July 1940, the day after France fell, the French Concession came under the control of the Vichy government. The next day the Americans evacuated all of their female nationals, and most American firms sent everyone but vital personnel home. Most head offices were moved to Hong Kong.

Many British families ignored the pleas of their government to come home and stayed, unwilling to give up the "good life" in the Orient. Back in Britain, few of them could have come near to affording the lavish, servant-filled lifestyle they enjoyed at the Bend in the River.

It is a choice they will all come to regret, the Confucian said to himself as he allowed his fingers to riffle the edges of the ancient text on the table. He knew the history of the Ivory Compact better than any other living being. When the second window was opened, he'd known with a certainty that he himself was the Man with a Book—books, actually. He had the rarest collection of the twenty famous Confucian texts, known collectively as the Analects. They had been carefully maintained and handed down from one generation of Confucians to the next when the obligation of the Ivory Compact was passed on. But it was another, even rarer manuscript—of which there was only one copy—that assured him that he was the Man with a Book. This book had been added to by every Ivory Compact Confucian through the years. It contained a detailed description of each Carver, Jiang, and Body Guard who ever swore fealty to the First Emperor's vision. As well as these details there were impressions, flights of fancy, and often profound doubts about the whole enterprise. The Confucian on the Holy Mountain, for instance, had believed the First Emperor to be completely out of his wits, mad as a Canton cook. As he wrote, "Only a lunatic would have ordered the executions of thousands of Confucian scholars and the burning of all their books."

The Confucian read the first entry in the book again, which was dominated by doubts about the relic and the task ahead of the Chosen Three. The first entry ended with a question: "Why did the First Emperor never harm me or burn my books?"

Because he did not dare! The Confucian thought as he closed the book. *We are a deep stream running beneath the entire structure of the state—to be respected, or the whole edifice will fall.*

He carefully turned the ancient text to its final page and dipped his brush in the ink of his writing stone. He would continue to support the Compact, as all the other Confucians before him had, only if the Compact was going to produce a China in need of Confucians—no, *ruled* by Confucians.

He allowed the excess ink from his brush, then wrote his notes on the figures in the second portal, identifying himself as the Man with a Book and pointing out the potential importance of the Soong sisters.

He set out to find everything there was to know about Charles Soong's daughters. He received reports from dozens of different sources. Every report about the eldest daughter, Madame Chiang Kai Shek, confirmed the fact that she was completely obsessed with her desire to possess every article of value she saw. The evidence entirely supported her popular name: She Who Loves Money.

The reports on the third daughter, the widow of Dr. Sun Yat-sen, bore out her selfless goodness. She was evidently, in both word and deed, She Who Loves China.

But it was while investigating the second daughter, Mao's mistress— She Who Loves Power—that he came across valuable tidbits, tantalizing clues to a dark soul. A Confucian scribe reported that one of his young, handsome classmates had become a "favourite" of She Who Loves Power. And the Soong girl had pursued him to the point of appearing, uninvited, in his bed. He had resisted her advances, but she had insisted and had her way with the young man—and, the next morning, with the young man's even more handsome brother. Three different Confucians detailed incidents confirming that Soong's second daughter had inherited her mother's, Yin Bao's, sexual appetites. And finally there was an odd report from a

Confucian who had seen her slip into a bumboat in the depths of night and head toward the Pudong, with its mountebanks, pirates—and abortionists.

The Confucian sat very still and allowed the various pieces to align. A sexually aggressive Soong daughter who was presently the mistress of Mao Tze-tung, and his need to find a powerful soldier as an ally. Could he use the Soong girl to harness this soldier—to ride him to glory?

He had his Confucians in place, and even the support of the Chosen Three and the Carver—naturally without their knowledge of his deeper ambition. Now he needed to settle on and activate a plan.

He took his brush from his writing stone and composed a note to the young Communist Confucian. Then he dressed carefully, as he had an appointment with Madame Sun Yat-sen, She Who Loves China.

He looked in on his sleeping sons. Almost from the time of his younger son's birth he'd known that this boy would succeed him, and so he had insisted that he be schooled early. At nine he already knew much of the Confucian canon and was fluent in Cantonese and English. He would shortly be ready to assume his place, at his side, as Confucians ruled China.

As he bathed he reviewed his situation. The Assassin was still in Nanking, where rumours of a sanctuary were finally being confirmed. Jiang was busily running her brothels that now had to cater to Japanese tastes—not always easy—and several times she had come afoul of the authorities. "Good," he said aloud, with a viciousness that would have surprised him had he heard it from others.

Thinking of Jiang, he rubbed the smooth quartz stone over his body and stretched. It was going to be a good day. A good day for China—and a good day for Confucians.

As he made his way past a Japanese guard post he bowed deeply—he had no desire to arrive at his appointment bloodied and beaten. The Japanese guard waved him through, and as he walked he sensed every other Confucian walking behind him—toward their destiny.

* * *

From the Notebook of the History Teller:

Only in darkness are myths forged.
From dreams of power—monsters.
From dreams of justice—monsters.
Control banishes nightmares but ends dreaming.
I am the seed of dreams.

You will chase me away; hunt me down; but I live inside your nightmares and I light the fire that shows you the monster's face in the mirror of your bed-chamber.

Rebirth comes—I feel its icy approach—whether from the melting snow of spring or from ashes of burned flesh—but what baby is born from such a birth?

Fire cleanses and makes way for the purity to come—or the horror.

The History Teller looked up from his writing and said "horror" aloud. The wind picked the word from his lips and carried it east—toward the sea. The intense midsummer sun beat down on his shoulders, but it didn't warm him. He felt it approaching—from far away it was coming—and he knew it. His hand shook as he reached for his brush.

* * *

AS THE CONFUCIAN WALKED THE BUSY STREETS he relived all the insults that the city at the Bend in the River had heaped upon him. How Confucians' positions had been taken from them. How their knowledge of traditional literature meant nothing here—their years of study meant nothing to these merchants. How newspapermen and pornographers were the only writers valued in this place. How merchants now paid for courte-sans while scholars were left alone in the gardens under trees, mocked, as they pined for what was rightfully, and had historically always been, theirs. That the Flower World whose very underpinnings and mythic reach came from scholars was now a place for petty whores, *Fan Kuei* sailors, and merchants—always merchants. And the romantic centre of the Flower World that scholars had fostered with centuries of their writing was ridiculed with harsh laughter and brutish sex, no more elevated than a bull mounting a cow.

A vision of Jiang floated through his head, and he allowed himself to revel in her presence, but could not maintain it. He cursed. Only money mattered here. Only that. In this place at the Bend in the River, in this Shanghai, a scholar was a useless appendage—like a sixth finger.

He sidestepped a beggar and ducked into the cool dampness beneath the wharf. It was not quiet—nowhere in this awful place was there any real quiet—but it was at least not roaring. He sat and pressed his forehead against the cool, damp timbers and thought of the task ahead.

It was time to visit the martyr's grave in the Pudong to offer his thanks and there to think carefully about his next move. All Confucians eventu-ally visited the grave, when faced with crucial decisions. Its secret existence and location were in the private notes that each Confucian in the Compact passed down to the next.

He heard a loud buzzing beside his head. He reached out and cupped the large dragonfly in his hands. He smiled as he felt its life flutter against the skin of his palms before he slipped it into his shirt pocket and buttoned the flap.

A good omen, he thought, *a very good omen.*

He rose and walked quickly through the dense crowds on the Bund toward Beijing Lu. At the corner he spotted a scribe taking dictation from an illiterate workman—very likely a letter back to his village. The Confucian cleared his throat. The scribe looked up at the Confucian and then dismissed him with a wave of his hand and a large, dark puddle of spittle.

The Confucian controlled his temper. Scribes, of all people, should acknowledge Confucians. *And they will,* he promised himself. *Who would have taught these imbeciles to read and write but Confucians? Were we not their teachers?* He took careful note of the man's face and stepped on the spittle, sending a curse into the ground. Then he said, "Soon enough you will all be put in your places—for good."

He turned from the scribe and proceeded up Beijing Lu. Finally finding a street tailor, he told the crippled man what he wanted. The man nodded and produced a long needle that he threaded with a length of black yarn. The Confucian held out a coin, which the tailor took before handing over the threaded needle.

The Confucian returned quickly to the wharf and waited for an appropriate boat to take him across the Huangpo to the Pudong, where the martyr's grave awaited his offering.

He reached into his pocket with his thumb and index finger and withdrew the live dragonfly. For a moment he watched the insect's rainbow wings thrum the thick Shanghai summer air, called tiger heat by the locals. Then with his other hand he took the threaded needle and jabbed it through the insect's thorax. The eye of the needle, in Chinese the nose of the needle, needed a quick, sharp tug to get it through the living flesh. The dragonfly arched against the pain, but the Confucian ignored it. He pulled the yarn all the way through and tied a large knot tight against the insect's body. He held the needle end and released the dragonfly. Instantly the creature sought its freedom, only to come to the end of its tether and be jerked to a halt, making it fall before it righted itself and tried to fly away again. Over and over it snapped the yarn to, then fell. Until finally it flew to the end of the thread, then circled around and around, above the head of the Confucian—who smiled. The dragonfly had learned its place. This was good, this was very good.

He selected a boat and barked a command at the boatman, then ignored him for the rest of the crossing, keeping his eye on the endlessly circling insect on the end of the thread.

Once in the Pudong he headed east and north. Two hours later he found the five banyan trees that had been carefully planted in a circle within sight of the river. The tree's ancient aerial prop roots formed a kind of boundary within which the grave lay.

Since the Boxer Rebellion, every Confucian in the Compact had made this journey. Every one had sought advice and solace here.

The dragonfly buzzed angrily over his head as the Confucian used his hand to dig into the loose earth of the grave. In a few moments his fingers found what he sought. He pushed the ground aside and extracted an old photograph in a glass-fronted frame. He gently brushed the debris aside.

The young man in the yellowed photograph stared right into the camera's lens. He had a large blotch on the left side of his face—a discoloration that, if the photograph had been in colour, would have stood out as a lurid raspberry stain.

"We are coming—we are ready to assume our rightful place," the Confucian said. "We all appreciate the effort you made all those years ago. But this time," he paused as he looked up at the angry dragonfly over his head, "we will not fail." He took the needle and threaded it through the hook at the top of the photograph's frame, then covered it with earth once again, so that only the circling dragonfly marked the grave of the martyr.

The Confucian had never even heard of the diaries of Richard Hordoon, but he would have agreed with the famous opium addict's warning: "When the peasants get together with the scholars, the end is near."

"We are rising as one great thing," he said. "All that is needed is a leader, and a Confucian to guide his hand."

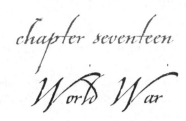

chapter seventeen

World War

It was early in the morning of December 7, 1941.

A Japanese submarine was spotted trying to enter Pearl Harbor. Then a second submarine was seen.

7:02 a.m.: Opana Radar Station. Privates Joseph Lockhard and George Elliott sight Japanese planes 132 miles north-east.

7:20 a.m.: Lt. Kermit Tyler dismisses radar sightings as B-17s due from California.

7:49 a.m.: Admiral Fuchida radios his planes to attack using the command. *Tora Tora Tora*.

7:55 a.m.: The first wave of 183 Japanese planes led by Fuchida attack Pearl Harbor from the north-west.

9:00 a.m.: The second wave of 167 Japanese planes led by Shimazaki attack Pearl Harbor from the north-east.

9:45 a.m.: Of the 96 ships in harbour, 18 are sunk or seriously damaged. Of the 394 aircraft at Hickam, Wheeler, and Bellows airfields, 188 are destroyed and 159 are damaged. Of the United States military personnel, 2,403 are killed (1,102 onboard the USS *Arizona*) and 1,178 wounded.

.. .. ..

More importantly for the people at the Bend in the River, the United States and Britain declared war on Japan the next day, and Japan promptly declared war on the United States and Britain and ... Japanese soldiers crossed the invisible boundary between Chinese Shanghai and the Foreign Settlements, and so took complete control of the city at the Bend in the River.

One hundred and one years after the signing of the shameful Treaty of Nanking that created Shanghai, the city was finally unified under an Asian flag—the Japanese flag.

The *Fan Kuei* awoke to the sound of sirens. The British gunboat *Petrel* was ablaze in the harbour, and the American ship *Wake* was swarming with blue-shirted Japanese soldiers.

Within hours of the bombing of Pearl Harbor, diplomats from every foreign power were put under house arrest in the Cathay Mansions in the French Concession.

And that very evening, the Japanese officer whom Jiang had shamed appeared in her foyer with his interpreter.

Jiang approached with a nod and a small smile.

The officer turned to his interpreter and said, "Tell the whore she is to take me to her most private and most soundproof room."

Jiang did, passing by the bouncers she had drawn from Gangster Tu's men, and that night she experienced what so many Chinese women had experienced at the hands of their conquerors—rape and a beating that left her near death for almost a week. All that she thought about during that awful week was that she had not yet produced a girl child for the Compact. It kept her alive.

Life changed quickly for foreigners in Shanghai. They were all forced to register as "enemy aliens" and wear armbands that identified their nationalities. The Japanese froze all foreign bank accounts. The Shanghai Club, a British favourite that boasted the longest bar in the world, was taken over by Japanese officers, while the American Club became the headquarters of the Japanese Imperial Navy. The Union Jack that flew proudly over Silas's Hong Kong Canton Bank was replaced by the Empire of the Sun's red-and-white flag. *Fan Kuei* cars were confiscated.

The Japanese closed all foreign newspapers, although the British *Shanghai Times* and the American *Shanghai Evening Post* were allowed to reopen because they agreed to publish only Japanese editorials. Radio stations were closed, and a new station, XGRS, filled the airwaves with German propaganda. XGRS featured two programs of skits that mocked Allied achievements—one performed by two Americans identified only as Bill and Mack, and the other by two British subjects, a Mr. Gracy and a Mr. Johnston.

All short-wave radios were confiscated, although, oddly, American films were still allowed to be shown, as long as the theatres played a twenty-minute Japanese propaganda short before the movie.

The Japanese systematically took over all foreign businesses, and liquidated them or seized their assets. Everything that could be shipped back to Japan was. All metal, machinery, boilers, and radiator pipes were ripped from buildings and sent off to support the war effort.

And the name "Bridge House"—designating an eight-storey building on the Hongkew side of the Garden Bridge—entered the now quickly growing Shanghainese lexicon of fear.

The Kempie Tei used Bridge House to torture journalists, businessmen, and common Chinese citizens. Few survived the beatings, the water torture, the disease, and the starvation that were common in that place.

And things got darker. On Christmas Day, 1941, Hong Kong fell, despite the valiant efforts of the Royal Scots Regiment to defend Kowloon. Nationalist radio claimed that a Chinese army of fifty thousand men was on its way to liberate Hong Kong, but like so many of Chiang Kai Shek's military claims, this proved to be a lie.

The Japanese took Singapore, Malaya, and Burma and threatened Australia by crossing the Owen-Stanley Mountains in New Guinea.

Photo exhibits showing Japanese successes and Allied failures appeared on hoardings at major intersections, always under the titles "The New Order of East Asia" or "Asia for Asiatics."

In June 1942, Jimmy Doolittle's daring raid on Tokyo shocked the Japanese. But their revenge was quick. Many of Doolittle's pilots didn't have enough fuel to get back to base and ditched in the ocean. They were all picked up by the Japanese and brought to Shanghai, paraded half naked down Nanking Lu to the Bridge House, and forced to dig their own graves. All were shot in the back of the head.

Finally, in August 1942, two ships arrived to repatriate civilians. American and Canadian nationals left on the *Gripholm* while the British were taken away on the *Kumukuru Muru*.

But neither ship was nearly big enough to carry all of the foreigners anxious to leave the Middle Kingdom. Shortly after the ships left harbour, the Japanese began "relocating" enemy nationals to concentration camps.

In February 1943, Heinrich Himmler, the Nazi Gestapo head, sent Josef Meisinger—who had so successfully overseen the butchering of one hundred thousand Jews in Warsaw—to Shanghai to enact the "Final Solution."

Over a formal dinner, Meisinger suggested to his Japanese hosts, "It is really very simple. We wait until their Rosh Hashanah, when they all go to pray. Give them ten minutes, then barricade the doors and burn down their synagogues, complete with the rabble inside." He looked at the stunned faces of the Japanese. He turned to his translator. "What's the problem?"

The Japanese were amazed. As far as they could see, this Meisinger looked as Jewish as any other White person. In fact, the Japanese couldn't see any difference between White people whatsoever. More importantly, the Japanese believed the Nazi propaganda claiming that Jews ran the United States, and, knowing that they would eventually have to make peace with America, the Japanese wanted to be able to point to their good treatment of Shanghai's Jews to prove they were a reliable peace partner. So over the following months the Japanese did a lot of smiling, the Germans a lot of fuming and fulminating. Finally the Japanese agreed to force the Jews who came to Shanghai after 1937 into a mile-square ghetto in Hongkew.

Meisinger considered it at least a partial victory. He then suggested, "Give them twenty-four hours to move their asses into the ghetto."

The Japanese didn't understand the rush, but it seemed to be important to their ridiculous ally, so they ordered the move. Jews were given ninety days to leave every residence outside Hongkew and "get their asses" into the ghetto.

.. .. ..

FROM THE HISTORY TELLER'S NOTEBOOK:

A Japanese armoured vehicle crawls up Tienstin Lu. In front of it trudge three European families carrying suitcases, some leather and expensive, others cheap cardboard. All bulge as if their contents are anxious to spill out onto the street.

The forlorn Europeans are suddenly lost in this foreign land.

A woman stumbles. A Japanese soldier screams at her. A tall man, I assume her husband, steps forward and is forced back at bayonet point. I look at the man's face and record the shock and shame in my mind's secret memory chamber, which, like these forlorn people's suitcases, is crammed full. But I find a place—an honoured place, because the Europeans' countenance carries a profoundly Asian look. A look of helplessness in the face of overwhelming force—the stuff of another Peking Opera. But I am observing, apart, alone with it. It exists. It is—and I just watch——and sense the approach of the cold once again. I hope I am strong enough.

The History Teller closed his small notebook and reached into his pocket. Its emptiness bothered him. There was clearly something missing—and he knew it.

.. .. ..

Jews obeyed the order and moved into the increasingly overcrowded ghetto in Hongkew. Many ended up back in the public shelters, called *heimes,* that they had first occupied upon arriving. Most had sold almost everything they owned and worked furiously to get out of those filthy places, but they were literally back to where they had begun.

Food quickly became a problem, and the tension between the general Jewish population and the Orthodox yeshiva community became intense. Many of the Orthodox yeshiva Jews were receiving a stipend of thirty American dollars a month from wealthy American Jews. Thirty American dollars was enough to buy eggs and milk and fresh vegetables and meat, while their fellow Jews made do with cabbage and fell prey to dysentery and typhoid and other opportunistic infections that always await the malnourished.

Soft hands, pasty complexions, and rounded bottoms demarcated the yeshiva families.

Germans were now a noticeable European presence in Shanghai. The History Teller had actually been approached by a fish-faced German officer who wanted him to perform an opera by a man named Strauss. He had listened to the music on a gramophone for as long as he could stand it, then asked, "Is this Electra singing or just in terrible pain?"

The German had spat out some slander and then barked in execrable Mandarin, "They said you were the opera expert here."

The History Teller had bowed slightly at the compliment but declined to introduce Strauss to Shanghai. That night every window in his family's compound was smashed and the front entrance boarded and nailed shut. *Small retribution for an insult in wartime,* he thought as he stood in the middle of the street, but he knew it was just part of the approaching cold.

———

A small boy, not yet five, named Zhong Fong, saw the attack on the History Teller's home while he and his cousins were picking up night-soil honeypots. When the attack was over, he saw the History Teller staring at the shattered windows of his house.

He wanted to say something, to help the older man, but he found his mouth dry and his pulse racing. The previous day his gentle father had taken him to see this man, the History Teller, play the Princess from the East in *Journey to the West,* and he had been enthralled by the singing, dancing, tumbling miracle that is Peking Opera.

He took a step toward the History Teller's home, but the strong hand of his grandmother landed on his shoulder and she barked in his ear, "Is that your home?"

"No, Grandma, but that's the History Teller's ..."

"Then why get involved? You have a family of your own that needs every strong back we can get."

"But ..."

"Your business is your family. Not these people. Now pick up the rest of your honeypots and be quick about it or I'll send you to Hongkew and make you pick up *da pitse*'s—Big Nose's—shit again. The dawn's coming."

Fong hurried down the darkened city streets. He passed several bodies lying on the pavement. He hoped they weren't dead, but he knew they were. He'd already seen a lot of dead bodies.

"Do they hurt, Papa?" he'd asked.

"No. They are beyond hurt, Fong."

Fong wondered if being beyond hurt was a good place—he doubted it was, despite the rictus smiles on some of the dead faces.

Fong picked up his pace, frightened that his grandmother would catch him loafing and beat him.

* * *

THE NEXT NIGHT, the part of Chiao Ming's necklace that Maximilian had put around her wrist—wrapped in cheap paper and weighted by a rock—sailed through the History Teller's shattered balcony window.

When he pulled aside the paper, it brought tears to his eyes and his writing brush to his hand. Instantly his confused thoughts began to take form.

That necklace had originally appeared on his makeup table one night. He'd been writing all day and had arrived at the theatre late, so he was rushing to put on his makeup for the Princess role. In his haste he slathered some of the white, pasty base into his left eye. He let out a yelp and grabbed for a towel. And when he'd cleared the makeup from his eye he found himself staring at the necklace hanging from a corner of his mirror—where, he was pretty sure, it had not been before. He leaned in close and marvelled at the seventy carefully carved structures trapped inside the balls of glass.

Even as his hand reached for the necklace he felt himself near to something special, something holy.

As his fingers touched the necklace he tasted burnt orange on the sides of his tongue and knew the fit would be upon him shortly. He stumbled to the door and locked it. No one had ever seen him in the throes of a grand mal fit—and no one was ever going to see him like that. He steadied him-self against the door and made sure the area in front of him was clear. He didn't fear the fit, but he dreaded smashing his head against the edge of a table or knocking over a gas lantern as he fell. But the area was clear—the floor awaited him.

He took a deep breath and closed his eyes.

Then it took him, like a bull lifting a man on its horns. It picked him straight up in the air and whipped him to one side. As it did, his eyes flut-tered open and he was amazed to see in his makeup mirror a beautiful, tall woman holding him in her outstretched arms. She took the glass-bead necklace and put it around his neck as she whispered, "You do my play great honour."

And that's all he remembered, until the midst of the performance, when he saw his hand—the one that carried the bamboo stick to indicate that he was riding a horse—inadvertently cut the silver strand that held the beads, and all seventy of the glass baubles fell to the floor, where they bounced and rolled into the audience.

The audience leaped to their feet and shouted their approval of this new invention in the role of the Princess from the East as they hustled for-ward to grab a bead or two.

The rest of the performance passed without incident, although it was generally received as one of the History Teller's very best.

Only afterward, outside the theatre, when the night-soil collector offered him back the necklace beads, did he recall a striking detail about the beautiful, tall woman who had held him and put the necklace around his neck and told him, "You do my play great honour." The beautiful woman in his vision had a crimson line of blood around the base of her ele-gant throat.

He remembered giving Chiao Ming the necklace on her fifteenth birth-day. She'd seen him wear it on stage and had loved it. Her wanting it had made it of inestimable value to him, and as special as a song from heaven. Her face had lit up when he placed it by her plate at her birthday dinner. "I'll never take it off, Father. Never," she'd said, and she had been true to her words, even as, just a few years later, she had lectured him about being a "capitalist roader"—the exact meaning of which he never under-stood.

And now, part of it was here in his hand, not around her neck where it belonged. Now it was here in Shanghai, while she ... she was in Nanking. He looked down at his hand holding the brush, then past the bristles to the paper on his writing desk. He had drawn a long, angry slash across the page with two characters: *cold* and *alone*. Chiao Ming was cold because she was dead, and alone because we all make the first and last voyages of our lives in absolute solitude, without guide or signpost.

He lost his balance and fought off the coming of another fit.

Chiao Ming dead—this could not be. It must not be. He looked at the beads in his hand ... but it surely was.

He reached for the paper that had packaged the necklace and was about to throw it away when he noticed a broad ink line on its underside. He turned it over and spread it flat—and there, in crude bold characters was written, "*What Was Ours.*"

He stared at the characters.

He dipped his brush in the ink, then turned the bristles against the stone's slant so that the excess ink fell from the brush and pooled in the well. *Like tears in oolong tea,* he thought. Then he lifted the brush and wrote "*What Was Ours*" on the title page of what he knew was going to be his last and most important work.

* * *

THE JEWS STAYED PRETTY MUCH UNBOTHERED by the Japanese in their very congested, disease-riddled ghetto in Hongkew.

Not only were the Japanese in no hurry to enact the Nazi "Final Solution," they set up a system run by an officer, Kanoh Ghoya, who awarded Jews passes, allowing them to leave the ghetto during the daylight hours. Blue passes were good for a month and pink for a week—and they were given out totally on the whim of the diminutive Ghoya-san. On one occasion, after making hundreds of Jews wait for an entire day in the freezing cold, he drew himself up to his full four-foot, eleven-inch height and announced to the frozen Jews seeking passes that they were "lucky as hell" that he was "the King of the Jews." No one laughed. No one dared. These people had seen short Nazis be as cruel as tall ones.

With their passes, most Jews sought out work that was hard to come by. Many scoured the garbage for scraps of food. Many others begged. Some prostituted themselves. And in one notable case, a young girl was given over to a wealthy family in exchange for medication that was desperately needed for the girl's mother.

Living conditions throughout the vast city were deteriorating quickly. Corpses were piling up on the streets, garbage was no longer picked up, and beggars were everywhere. Only the resourceful Zhong clan kept up their business—night-soil collecting.

And yet there was still luxury in the city at the Bend in the River. The nightclubs were now filled with Japanese and German and Italian soldiers—and every conceivable luxury good could still be bought on the black market.

* * *

THE CONFUCIAN PACED SLOWLY back and forth across his balcony. He had been searching his Analects for days for an indication of an appropriate time to move. Today seemed as propitious as any. He took two pigeons from their cages and released them, one to the south to Canton and the Republican Confucian there, and one to the north-west to the Communist Confucian.

He watched the birds as they dwindled to white dots, then disappeared. Then he looked down at the murky waters of the Huangpo River that led to the Yangtze, which in turn led to the sea. It had defined direction, he reminded itself, unlike the arrow that he had just launched into the sky. Then he turned from the river and allowed a smile to his thin lips. It was a beginning—a beginning to the rightful return of Confucian power.

* * *

FROM THE HISTORY TELLER'S NOTEBOOK:

I walk slowly along the Bund Promenade. The great trading ships are dwarfed by the ships of the Japanese Imperial Navy. But in my mind, both sets of ships are dwarfed by the story that is slowly uncoiling in my mind and working its way first to paper then to stage. I stop exactly where the naked Fan Kuei was tethered to a post. There are conflicting stories—of course there are, this is Shanghai!—as to what fate befell the naked man. Some say that he took off so much skin that he slipped his handcuffs and swam to freedom in the Pudong, across the Huangpo River; others believe that the Chinese Communists freed him, others that the Japanese killed him in the night and dumped his naked body into the river.

I doubt that any of these is correct. There has always been something at work in Shanghai that is beneath the surface, unseen but undeniably here—like an underground river, not seen but constantly felt. Exactly what that something is, I cannot guess—but it's old—very old. It is not the cold I sense approaching, because this is vibrant and alive. At times as I write I tap into the subterranean current and find myself pulled along, sometimes pulled under, by its vast, ancient strength.

I reach into my pocket and remove the remains of the necklace I gave Chiao Ming on her fifteenth birthday. It has been in my pocket since it arrived with the simple three-word note: "What Was Ours." She loved that necklace. Why, except in death, would she part with it? I hold the baubles up to the brilliant sun. The light parses then parses again as it traverses the glass. "Into its essence and its shadow," I say in a loud voice.

Your essence remains with me, Chiao Ming, although I know you have followed your shadow into the darkness. I look down at your necklace. The light no longer penetrates the glass. My tears prevent that.

I unsnap the latch and lower the necklace, bead by bead, into the hole into which the pole was buried, to which the naked man was tethered.

Somehow I know that the two of you must be together, intermingling—joining—to make something new, never seen before beneath the heavens.

A coup de théâtre.

A miracle birth.

* * *

THE ORDER HE RECEIVED from the Shanghai Confucian was so dangerous that it almost made the young Communist Confucian sick. But he obeyed, and every night when the second Soong daughter, Mao's mistress, came to him, he whispered suggestions in her ear—even as they brought on the clouds and rain in what was, except for his words, complete and utter silence.

Their first meeting had been the very night he saw her naked in the moonlight. The howling of the wind and the blowing sand had covered her movements and swallowed the creaking of his hut door as she pulled it open. "Who's there?" he'd whispered as he felt beneath his bedroll for his weapon. When he'd cocked it she spoke from the darkness for one of the few times in their encounters: "If you shoot Mao's mistress, his wife will no doubt kiss you, but the Chairman of the Communist Party of the People's Republic of China will rip your heart from your chest. Now put that gun away and lie back." The wind had swirled into the hut and made it hard for the young Confucian to be sure what else she had said that night, but he thought her final words had been, "... and enjoy it."

And, despite the risk, he had enjoyed it.

During the days their paths often crossed as he went about his official record keeping for the Party, but he did his best never to look in her direction. Although he found it hard and often caught himself staring at her.

"Read me back that last question," demanded Deng Xiao Ping.

Suddenly Mao snatched the pen from the Confucian's hand. "Wake up! Wake up or I'll have you woken up."

The Librarian's large face, not yet familiar to the people of China, let alone the entire world, was inches from his. He'd never noticed the slightly reptilian blotchiness of the Chairman's little-girl-smooth, clearly very sensitive skin. *Like a toad's belly,* he wanted to say, but managed to look down at his notes and read, "But we were routed, despicably defeated. What else would you call our retreat all the way to here, the middle of nowhere?"

He spoke slowly, entirely without inflection, and was greatly relieved when Mao turned away from him and addressed the men and women around the table. There was an odd grin on his face as he said, "A victory. I would call it a great victory for the human spirit."

It was then that the young Confucian sensed her smiling. He'd never seen her smile before. Or was she laughing at him? It suddenly occurred to him that, through her, he was connected—albeit in an odd way, as any lover is related to a cuckolded husband—to the strongest man in China. He tore his eyes away from the Soong girl and looked to Mao.

"All our defeat needs is a name," Mao said. "A romantic name."

The faces around the table remained impassive. No one was willing to commit until it became clear where all this was going.

"A way for the people to be proud of it."

"So they won't remember the huge losses we suffered?" asked Deng Xiao Ping.

The air in the room snapped with electricity as the two men, who had been comrades in arms for almost twenty years, stared at each other. No one dared look at either man. Then Deng Xiao Ping smiled, lifted his hands, and said, "Why not? What name do you suggest?"

Now that it was clear which way the wind was blowing, suggestions were offered by many around the table.

That grin crept across Mao's broad features again. "The Long March," he said. "From now on, we will refer to our retreat by one name and one name only—the Long March." He took out the small red book he always carried with him and made a note. Then he added, "Even the longest voyage begins with a single step."

The young Confucian could have told him that this was a bastardization of a well-known Taoist saying, but even if he could have corrected Mao, he would not have done so—sleeping with his mistress was dangerous enough.

Mao quickly eyed the men and women around the table, always on the alert for telltale signs of opposition. There were none. They all remembered the fate of General Zhong, the last man to seriously challenge Mao's power. He and Mao had argued publicly over the wisdom of continuing north—on the Long March. Zhong had eventually taken his army west toward Russia, only to be massacred by Moslem tribesmen well before he and his troops got anywhere near the Russian border. There were persistent rumours that Mao had sent word to the tribesmen on General Zhong's route that allowed them to ambush and kill almost half of the General's men. Most of the rest of his soldiers starved to death in the western wastelands. General Zhong himself, in an unexpected appearance at a colloquium held at the University of Toronto in 1971, confirmed Mao's treachery. Until then, it was believed that he had died with his men. But he had in fact been running a dry-cleaning store, without fanfare, for years in a small place called Don Mills, Ontario—a place that had one very good Chinese restaurant.

Like Hung Hsiu-ch'uan, the Taiping leader, before him, Mao continued to distribute land to peasants wherever he went. The "new landowners" formed the wide base of the pyramid upon which his power rested—that and his knack for public relations.

Mao made another annotation in the small red book, then asked, "Are there any other items of business?"

"What of Nanking?" the oldest of the soldiers around the table asked.

"The Japanese control it, and we are not yet powerful enough to dislodge them," Mao said dismissively.

"And the horrors there?" the old soldier bravely persisted, although it was clear Mao did not wish to pursue the topic.

"They will eventually stop of their own accord. Even horror needs creativity to feed its fire."

That stunned the people around the table. What did creativity and horror have to do with each other?

The old soldier stood. "I have fought at your side since 1921."

Mao nodded but did not speak.

"I have obeyed orders, never questioned the wisdom of my political betters."

Mao nodded again.

"We should join Chiang Kai Shek's Republican forces and free Nanking—then Shanghai."

Everyone felt the tension in the room rise again.

Mao controlled his rage and walked around the table to face the older man. "Would that we had a thousand more like you, old friend," he said.

The room visibly relaxed, but both his wife and mistress heard the edge of anger—no, fury—in Mao's voice. "Plans are already in the works for just such a meeting."

The young Confucian put down his pen in confusion. Then he noticed his lover, Mao's mistress, Charles Soong's middle daughter, smile and nod in his direction. So she had taken his whispered advice after they'd brought on the clouds and rain and passed it on to Mao! It took his breath away, and he had to fight the impulse to vomit. He had followed instructions from Shanghai—and now, to his amazement, he had influenced history. The meeting between Mao and Chiang Kai Shek that the Shanghai Confucian had urged him to push through his sexual contact with Soong's middle daughter was going to happen—because of him!

* * *

"NONSENSE," Madame Chiang Kai Shek said to her Generalissimo, as she scowled at the stoneware on her elegantly appointed dinner table in their Canton mansion.

"Then why?" Chiang Kai Shek demanded.

"Because, sweetness, it makes sense, and if you think about it, dear, you'll know that I am correct about this, as I have been about so many other things." She tapped a long fingernail to a wine glass—no *tink*—an expression of deep hurt crossed her face.

Chiang Kai Shek was tempted to ask his wife what was the matter, but knew better than to enter such open-ended conversations with Soong's eldest daughter. Instead, he stayed on what he thought was the topic by demanding, "What do you know of such things?" But even before the words were out of his mouth he knew that he could not win this conversation with his forceful, horse-faced wife.

"I know everything of such things, as you well know, dear. Let my sisters and me work this all out. And ... while I do," she looked up brightly, "shoot whoever bought this tableware. It's atrocious."

Just for a moment Generalissimo Chiang Kai Shek wondered if his wife was kidding—but then he dismissed the idea. His wife never joked when it came to expensive things.

* * *

MADAME SUN YAT-SEN, She Who Loves China, bowed slightly as the Confucian entered her home. He had been there often. Unlike her deceased husband, the good doctor, this man was almost a contemporary of hers. And they had become strangely close. He shared confidences with her, and she had begun to reciprocate.

Finally she asked, "But you are married, are you not?"

The Confucian canted his head slightly as if to say, "A technicality," although he carefully said nothing.

She served tea. He listened to her concerns about the fate of China and finally said, "But perhaps China's fate is in your hands. Your sisters are both aligned with powerful men. One married the Republican leader. The other …" He allowed his voice to trail off in a conspiratorial manner.

Madame Sun Yat-sen blushed.

"I have been in touch with both of your sisters. They are close to agreeing to meet with you."

She was startled by both of these revelations. How had the Confucian gotten close to both of her sisters, and why had her sisters agreed to meet with her? But before she could give voice to either question, the Confucian took her hand and asked, "How is your mother?"

"Not well, I'm afraid."

"Ah. I am sorry to hear such." In truth, the old whore got sick, then got better. Got sick and got better, over and over again. She had the constitution of a—well, of an old whore. Now the Confucian needed her death as a final excuse for the Soong sisters to come together—and usher in a Confucian-friendly future for the Middle Kingdom.

"I fear that she will not live out this year."

He touched her hand again and muttered a standard Confucian platitude about the necessity for the old to step aside to make way for the young. Not something he personally believed.

She nodded. And before she knew it, she found herself buried against his chest and anxious for the Confucian's arms around her. The Confucian smiled inwardly and guided Soong's youngest daughter to a brocade sofa, the coffee table in front of which had the most detailed topographic maps of the Middle Kingdom he'd ever seen.

"These are lovely," he said.

"My husband's," she said softly.

"Ah."

"They are one of a kind—the only truly accurate mapping of the topography of the Middle Kingdom."

The Confucian knew a thing of value when he saw it. He said, "They are exquisite."

"As the Minister of Railways, my husband commissioned them. I am ashamed to say that commissioning the maps was the only wise thing he did while heading that Ministry." She pointed at a series of straight lines drawn roughly on the top map and said, "Then he seemed to ignore the precision of the topographic information that they presented."

The Confucian had heard tell of unrealistic railway plans, and perhaps that was what she was indicating. "But they are beautifully done," he ventured.

She seemed to brighten. "You like them?"

"Indeed," he said, doing his best to keep any hint of excitement out of his voice.

"Then have them, please. Keep them for the people of China—keep them for the people for when they are finally free."

* * *

YIN BAO'S EXTRAORDINARY SPIRIT—her voracious consuming of life and living—came to a sudden halt amidst a banquet she was throwing for her three sons. Her eldest son, T.V. Soong, Chiang Kai Shek's Finance Minister, looked at his mother and actually giggled as he said, "Such a funny face, Mama."

But his mother, the famous Yin Bao, wasn't making a funny face, she was sensing a paralysis enter the muscles of her cheeks. She stared at T.V. and then reached for him. Her hand missed and knocked over a porcelain bowl that fell to the floor and shattered. She stared at the jagged pieces—then keeled over and struck the floor, her beautiful head making a loud clunk, her bound feet, obscenely loose from their tiny slippers, exposed to the air.

* * *

LIKE CHARLES SOONG'S FUNERAL, Yin Bao's was lavish and private—and Christian. And from the point of view of the Confucian, the long-awaited reason for all three Soong sisters to finally find themselves in Shanghai—at the youngest sister's house.

The Confucian had offered his services as minute-taker of the sisters' conversation. He was pretty sure that he knew which camp he was going to back, but, with the whole future of Confucianism in his hands, he wanted to be sure. As he paced his balcony, awaiting notification of the first meeting of the sisters, he reminded himself that the Communists controlled only a small section of the north, and Chiang Kai Shek an insignificant part of the south. All of central, essential, China was in Japanese hands.

But perhaps not for long. From hidden short-wave radios he'd accumulated news of the outside world. It was becoming clear that Japan was losing the greater war beyond the borders of the Middle Kingdom. This seemed to be confirmed when, a few months back, in early 1943, many of the younger Japanese soldiers in Shanghai had been replaced by older men, sometimes disabled men, who could not control the city at the Bend in the River.

Chinese patriots began to slip back into Shanghai. One such patriot had a snake carved on his back and was accompanied by a red-haired *Fan Kuei* who had a young Chinese boy in his care.

Many a morning now brought to light the body of a Chinese collaborator hung from a lamppost, or a Japanese soldier slumped against a wall, his head sitting on his shoulders, not his neck.

* * *

THE MEETING OF THE CHOSEN THREE and the Carver, the first since the Assassin had left for Nanking over six years ago, was an exercise in steely silence. The Assassin had clearly aged, and the deep lines of war had etched their way across his face. Jiang had grown into a truly beautiful woman who carried her own scars of the war with a surprising grace.

The Confucian had trouble taking his eyes from her.

The Carver said, "Curfew is soon, we should start."

But no one knew where to begin. Only the Confucian knew of the upcoming meeting with the Soong sisters—and it was not a bit of information he was willing to share. And of course the Tusk was in far-off Baghdad, so there was no way to re-examine it.

"The war will end soon," Jiang said finally.

The Assassin nodded. Both he and Jiang looked to the Confucian.

The man kept his eyes carefully lowered as he said, "Perhaps."

For twenty more minutes the Chosen Three spoke, but said nothing of importance. They were strangers to each other. Finally the Confucian said, "Well, if we have nothing else, I have pressing business."

The Carver left shortly after the Confucian.

Jiang put a gentle hand to the Assassin's face. "You have seen horrors."

"Be careful with the Confucian. He looks at you with hunger."

Jiang nodded.

"He's secretive," the Assassin added, although he didn't mention that he and his father had set a secret plan in motion too. The Guild was, even now, growing in Lower Manhattan—growing and waiting—to retrieve the Tusk. The Assassin turned to Jiang. "He's been in Shanghai all this time, while I wasted away in Nanking."

"You didn't waste away, you saved many lives."

The Assassin stared at Jiang. Something was wrong. "What is it?" he asked.

"Excuse me?"

"Tell me!"

She looked away from him and said, "We have all paid for our country's failure. Each in his own way." She took a deep breath. "I bore a rapist's baby—and bear the scars of his beating."

"Where is the child?"

"It is not necessary for you to know that."

"Was it a girl?"

She nodded.

"She must not be named Jiang upon your passing."

She withdrew her eyes from him. She understood the standing orders of succession to the Ivory Compact as well as he did, but she was not sure that they were immutable—and her sweet, mixed-race baby, the outcome of a vicious rape, might indeed, she felt, play an important part in bringing on the Age of the Seventy Pagodas.

She turned from the Assassin, then turned back to him. "Is it true you have the red-haired *Fan Kuei*?"

The Assassin nodded. "He is being kept safe."

"And is it true he has a baby?"

"Yes, but that baby is almost six and is being trained in the Assassin's art."

"Was this the child of the fire?"

"It was."

"And what race is this boy?"

"Han Chinese, but English is his first language—and when the light strikes him in a certain way I could swear he has red hair."

* * *

IT WAS TIME for the Confucian to act, to pick a side and back it. So as he laid out his brushes and paper on Madame Sun's surprisingly simple dinner table between the two beautifully carved jade figures, he listened closely to the words of the Soong sisters. He had never witnessed so much open hatred between siblings. Madame Chiang Kai Shek tried to dominate the proceedings using her seniority and her marriage to the Generalissimo as reason enough for her pride of place. But the other two were not having it. The middle sister, fresh from the beds of both Mao and the young Confucian, had the wind of power in her sails, and she clearly felt its urgings.

"You and your Republicans are loathed by the people of the south," she said bluntly. Before her elder sister could respond, she added, "While we are growing daily. We can now field an army of over two million men— men willing to fight to keep a quarter acre of land, access to a communal field and newly dug well, a piece of the Middle Kingdom to call their own."

"Stolen land."

"No. Land they deserve. Your Kuomintang army is led by senior military men but populated by conscripts, many of whom are just waiting for a chance to desert to our side."

The first day ended in an out-and-out screaming match reminiscent of the best mud-slinging episodes of their courtesan mother—which had, in fact, been the genesis of their father's great fortune.

As the two great armies of her sisters massed, Madame Sun Yat-sen's concern for the "greater good of all the people" seemed simplistic, if not just foolish.

———

On the second day, as the Confucian was laying out his brushes and paper again, he noticed that one of the jade figures was missing from the table, and then, just before lunch, he saw Madame Chiang Kai Shek slip the second one into her Parisian handbag.

The conversations—or, more accurately, the acrimony—went on for three days.

It was clear to the Confucian that the Kuomintang and the Communists would eventually unite to force the Japanese out of the Middle Kingdom, but once the external enemy was gone the two Chinese armies would be at each other's throats. So he still had to choose whom to back.

It was a simple choice.

Now it was a matter of how to get Mao to see how badly he needed a head Confucian, and getting the voracious Republicans to more quickly follow the road to ruin upon which they had been marching for years.

The latter was relatively simple. Put food in front of a glutton and he will gorge himself. Put wine within reach of a drunk and he will drink until he pees his pants and vomits down his shirtfront. Put gold in front of a covetous woman and she will follow it to her folly.

But how to ingratiate himself, first, then make himself important to Mao was far more complicated. He had been watching the second Soong daughter closely. He saw shocks of sexuality in her that were missing from the other two. Something close to her mother's thrusting, lunging approach to life. Yes, there was much of Yin Bao in this middle child.

How could he use that?

The plan slowly formulated as he completed his notes for the Soong sisters. When they were done, he gave them to his younger son to make two copies, so that each sister could have a record of what was said—or at least what the Confucian had written down that each had said.

All three were surprised when they read that they had agreed that the Confucian should deliver a copy of this text personally to both Chiang Kai Shek and Mao Tze-tung.

"But you all agreed to this," he said, when one of the daughters questioned the statement.

The animosity between the sisters was so great that they could not agree that they had not agreed on anything, so they acquiesced, and three days later the Confucian got off the train and onto a mule that two days after that deposited him outside the headquarters of the Chairman of the Communist Party, Mao Tze-tung.

Mao was deep in conversation with a half-drunken *Fan Kuei* who was introduced as a Doctor Bai T'une—or something like that—and the ever-present Deng Xiao Ping. The men were discussing something over an old set of maps.

The Confucian congratulated himself on his foresight in taking the maps upon which Dr. Sun Yat-sen had made his silly railroad markings. The markings were ludicrous, but the topographic maps were the finest to be had in the Middle Kingdom. The Confucian had studied them carefully and understood the strategic bind in which the Communists found themselves—between mountains and rivers, they seemed to be trapped. But Sun Yat-sen's topographic maps clearly showed that if Mao were to lead his men farther north there was an open plain that would lead him out of the trap.

After being quickly introduced by the middle Soong daughter, the Confucian offered his set of maps as "perhaps a way of clarifying the discussion before us."

The Doctor, who came from some place called Gravenhurst, Ontario, protested, but the Soong sister silenced him with a withering stare.

Within weeks the Confucian's gift of the maps and his clear organizational skills had allowed him access to Mao.

Access that, at the next full moon, he used to awaken the great man and show him his mistress and her young scholar, locked in the coils of lovemaking.

It secured the Confucian a place at the side of the most powerful man in China. Now all he had to do was wait—and he would stride into Shanghai at the head of the largest army the world had ever seen.

He was content. He had fulfilled the expectation of his ancestors and brought the Compact back to its logical goal: the restoration of full Confucian power.

* * *

FOR THREE DAYS the Assassin had been trying the usual means of contacting the Confucian, but he had not received a reply of any sort. On the second evening he and two of his Guild members soundlessly broke into the Confucian's fine house overlooking the far reach of the Huangpo River—and found only the Confucian's wife and two sons asleep in their respective beds. No Confucian.

The next morning he contacted the Carver, who had not seen the Confucian for ten days.

On the third night he re-entered the Confucian's house and silently closed the door to the boys' room, then stepped into the Confucian's bedroom. The man's wife snored gently, her head tilted toward the balcony window. A soft cooing came from the window. The Assassin stepped out onto the balcony and was surprised to see an extensive pigeon coop. He turned toward the window and stared at the Confucian's wife. Then he saw it, as if buried deep in the thick glass of the window—a carrier pigeon heading directly toward him. He turned just in time to see the exhausted bird alight on the balcony railing. The small tin cylinder attached to its hind leg glinted in the moonlight. He reached over and gently scooped up the bird—much as his ancestor the Fisherman had lifted his birds from the water—then plucked out the message. As he read it, his hand trembled. "Dearest, it is just a matter of time until the Communists take Shanghai— then we Confucians will resume our rightful place. Prepare yourself and our house—for history's sake."

He looked at the bird and nodded. *Only a Confucian would see the benefit of using the old systems,* he thought. *Who would think of pigeons when there are telephones and telegraphs?* He answered his own question. *Someone attached to the old ways, locked in thinking from the past.*

He allowed the paper to flutter from his hands. The wind picked it up and threw it up the river, toward the sea.

Then, in July 1945, a new sound filled the skies over the Bend in the River—the drone of American B-29s, from their airbase on Okinawa.

chapter eighteen

A Flash of Light

The two crowned willow warblers perched on wires on opposite sides of the dojo's roof—their *kikinashi* calls the first step in their creation of a new life. The male hopped three times to his left and then lowered the register of his song. The female's tail feathers flared and she whistled shrilly. The male puffed out his chest, opening his wings to display his full glory. The female stuttered two steps, then took flight. She flew high into the air, then, with a remarkably sweet song, headed earthward—and the male met her halfway.

In mid-air they circled each other.

Below them, life in the large city was just beginning. Shinto priests were completing their morning ablutions; wives wrapped kimonos around themselves and lit the morning fires.

The two crowned willow warblers touched beaks—then …

With a flash of light,
everything in Hiroshima—
and the world—
changed.

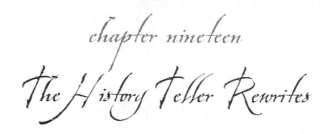

chapter nineteen

The History Teller Rewrites

The History Teller's writing pad suddenly took light. He stepped back, then looked at the brush in his hand as he wrote:

Momentary high noon brilliance
where there had been only murky dawn ...
then a profound darkness, to shame the night.

The History Teller turned to the east, then rose and walked out onto the balcony of the second floor of his *shikumen*. He scented the air—and discovered something new there.

Something new in the world has been born
a brilliant light ...
that brings on an infinite darkness.

He shivered. The reek of ozone had been replaced by something for which he had no name. He returned to his writing table and took a fresh piece of rice paper. He felt the world spin beneath his feet—and he began—at the beginning—something new—something new for a new world. He watched the characters form on the beautiful paper:

Something born; slouching—no,
relearned,
unchained,
and now at large and hungry—in the new world.

He looked carefully at the characters. He thought of the naked *Fan Kuei* on the Bund all those years ago, then of his daughter's necklace that now rested in what he thought of as "the missionary's hole in the ground." Then he wrote the phrase that he had written more than any other:

What Was Ours.

And he thought of a brilliant light that brings darkness.

He felt it approaching—faster, now. So much faster.

He permitted his mind to still—then beckoned it. *So it is this new darkness that I have sensed coming toward me for so long,* he thought.

Then it wormed a cold tendril into him.

Good, he thought. His kidneys suddenly ached and his bladder contracted, but he resisted the urgent impulse to urinate. He lost all feeling in his feet but he refused to put on shoes. The evil was testing him. Thinking him weak and frail. Frail perhaps, but not weak. "Come on, all the way in," he coaxed. "Grow in me, then enter the halls of my temple—there we will do battle—and I'll gain access to your secret self, to your hidden self, to your interior darkness where your poetry lies, awaiting my light."

Then it bloomed icy fingers in him—racing along his veins, reaching, clawing—singing to him, luring him, seducing him to the sanctuary of sleep—but he fought off the temptation and took his brush in hand.

The icy tears streak the maiden's face
As darkness falls upon the world.

He held up the rice paper and the wind fluttered it dry. He placed it on his writing desk and put a small jade stone on its centre. As he did, he looked at his right hand—his writing hand. The top joint of his thumb had turned in and large, hard nodules were quickly forming on the knuckles of his index, middle, and ring fingers. Only his baby finger remained untouched. He smiled and said, "To remind me what beauty was—what I have lost—*What Was Ours*—very clever."

He reached for a second sheet of rice paper and stationed it on his writing table.

This time he wrote no words, just allowed the brush to lead him. The ink formed a mountain, with a high alpine lake, a woman in front of her frozen laundry staring at her hands—and soldiers, soldiers everywhere.

He'd dreamed this before—so had many Han Chinese over the past twenty-one hundred years.

He lifted the paper and committed it to the wind, which plucked it from his fingers and flung it toward the river. "That takes it to the sea," he said aloud. Then he repeated the phrase.

He grabbed another sheet of paper, ignored the pain in his hand and wrote:

To the sea on the day of darkness
All creatures run.

Then he secured this sheet beside the other with another small jade stone.

He thought of the earlier History Teller's classic play, *Journey to the West,* of the devotion of the Serving Man and the futility of his love for the Princess. His performance of the Princess had been his first major success. He'd played it several times since, always to more and more acclaim.

He allowed his back to arch and his feet to point as he lifted his head high on his neck—and felt the woman he became as the Princess turn to fight the darkness he had allowed into his body.

"The flash of light is hope itself—the profound darkness, the challenge to hope," he said aloud, not even noticing that he had written the same thing he'd spoken. He looked down and smiled. Then he wrote the Mandarin word for hope—*xi wang*—three times.

He stared at the words, then wrote:

From the tears of Nanking
A hope to view the sea
And regain What Was Ours.

The darkness inside him shifted, bolts of angry cold shot through him, he felt a light tingling in his forearms—a tingling he knew presaged a serious attack on his hands. He allowed the brush to fall from his fingers to the floor. He had no desire to soil a fine piece of rice parchment.

He waited—watched his fingers twist and turn as if they were trying to free themselves from his hand—but he ignored the pain.

He managed a smile as the grand mal fit took him. He had found the way through the darkness—hope would lead him to the dawning of the sea—to that which was his—not his, *What Was Ours.*

chapter twenty

Surrender and After

The loudspeaker that had been set up at the intersection of Nanking Lu and the Bund was cranked up to such a volume that it distorted wildly—yet its message was clear to the thousands of Chinese who had gathered to hear what the world had in store for them. The words "new and most cruel bomb" pierced the static, then the high-pitched voice of the "Sacred Crane," Emperor Hirohito, paused. Static followed, and then clearly the words urging his subjects to "bear the unbearable." This somewhat contradicted the famous edict of his war minister, Koreichiki Anami, who had vowed that "The great soldiers of the Japanese Imperial Army will fight to their last breaths, even if it means chewing grass, eating dirt, and sleeping in the fields."

How easy it is to commit soldiers to their deaths from the safety of a government office.

Shanghai immediately began to celebrate. Blackout curtains were ripped from windows and dress clothing that had not been worn for years was donned as every citizen at the Bend in the River who could danced in the streets. Bamboo victory banners appeared, and firecrackers filled the sky well into the night.

A Communist army was within two days' march of Shanghai and would have accepted the formal surrender of the Japanese, but Chiang Kai Shek and his troops beat them to the city with the help of a massive American airlift.

Chiang Kai Shek's first order upon accepting the Japanese commander's surrender was to give control of the city back to the Japanese, whom he entrusted with keeping the peace. So the soldiers of the defeated Japanese Imperial Army patrolled the streets of Shanghai and accepted the jeers of the locals. While they did, their superior officers loaded ship upon ship to the gunwales with goods they had confiscated from the *Fan Kuei* and wealthy Chinese. Bonfires burned all day and night disposing of evidence from Bridge House. Once all proof of their perfidy was nothing more than piles of charred paper, the Kempie Tei torturers removed their uniforms and disappeared into the human sea that is Shanghai.

By the end of the week, American ships of the Seventh Fleet entered Shanghai Harbour to wild cheers. When the American flagship *Rocky Mount* anchored at the number-one buoy, the cheering grew so loud that it could be heard miles away.

Quickly American GIs were everywhere, smiling, giving out chocolates, dancing in the cabarets, pulling rickshaws—seeking out Shanghai's famous prostitutes.

American aid flowed freely into the city and was distributed by a United Nations agency, which, as is usually the case, was completely unprepared for the complications they faced on the ground. It didn't take long for the lion's share of the aid to go directly into the pockets of such powerful families as the Soongs, Kungs, and Chiangs—and from there directly to the black markets that had sprung up faster than mushrooms in the fall.

Over three billion dollars of authorized aid effectively disappeared. T.V. Soong caused most of this, as he, in his capacity as Finance Minister of the Kuomintang, insisted that all aid be distributed by his Chinese Relief and Rehabilitation Administration. As several American newsmen noted, "Within a day of receipt, UN goods were being sold at ludicrous prices from newly erected stalls whose merchants didn't even bother to remove the UN or Red Cross labels before sale."

As T.V. Soong had this scam working in high gear, the rest of Chiang Kai Shek's Republican comrades went on a theft spree without precedent in the history of the world. Anyone of any wealth was named a traitor, and all their goods were confiscated by the Nationalists. Others lost their businesses to the Kuomintang with the accusation that they were Communist supporters. Within weeks the Nationalist government had seized virtually every business in Shanghai. Anyone who had stayed in Shanghai during the occupation was considered a collaborator. Every lawyer who had come to the bar between 1942 and 1945 was immediately disbarred. In fact, few actual collaborators were brought to trial. Those that did were sometimes given light sentences and then invited to join the Nationalist government. The quisling Wang Ching-wei died of natural causes a few days before the bomb fell on Hiroshima—the last jest of the gods of justice who had utterly abandoned the city at the Bend in the River.

Quickly the Shanghainese realized that their Kuomintang liberators were just different persecutors ... and Mao's forces were on the move.

* * *

"WE HAVE BEEN BETRAYED," the Assassin said, in a flat voice that matched the flat distance in his eyes.

Jiang sat quietly with her Japanese daughter on her lap and nodded slowly.

"Never before in the Ivory Compact—"

"To the best of our knowledge," Jiang interrupted. "To the best of our knowledge, no one of the Chosen Three in the past has betrayed the Compact." Her words sounded like an echo of some ancient voice.

"Our Confucian fancies himself to be the Man with a Book," the Assassin said.

"Men with photographs and scholars with books ..." she muttered, then cooed to her daughter.

"What?"

"Nothing."

"I repeat, our Confucian believes—"

"Ridiculous. Mao Tze-tung is the Man with a Book."

"Of course."

"But think, Loa Wei Fen, although the Confucian may be trying to betray us, he is still, despite himself, fulfilling his obligation to the Ivory Compact. Mao and his men will take the city at the Bend in the River and give it back to the Black-Haired people, who are the ones who must build the Seventy Pagodas—so we are still in concert with the First Emperor's wishes."

"But he tried to betray the Compact. And he must die for that."

"Why? He is still doing the Compact's bidding, even if he doesn't realize it."

"For now."

"What does that mean?"

"He does the Compact's bidding for now, but as soon as he has power he will create a future for China that is good for him and his kind, and you know that."

Jiang nodded slowly.

"And you and I would stand in the way of that, wouldn't we?"

That sat in the air between them like something hot and angry. Finally Jiang said, "Perhaps the Compact has never been betrayed before by one of the Chosen Three, but certainly, no member of the Compact has ever killed another. You are not to be the first, Loa Wei Fen."

"Agreed. But it will not be me who moves against the other members of the Compact. It will be the Confucian."

"Why?"

"Because we endanger the one thing he values."

"Which is?"

"Power."

Jiang nodded slowly, then picked up her little girl and nuzzled her chest. Her Japanese daughter giggled.

The Assassin looked away.

"Don't," she snapped.

He turned back to her. "I meant no—"

"I am not ashamed to love a child, a Japanese child—and you should not be offended to watch me love her. We are living after the light—things must change—or the darkness will return and never leave."

The Assassin took a breath and then said, "Have your people accepted your child?"

"No, but they will. They must. My stepfather married my mother, outraging both his Jewish community and my mother's Han Chinese family. It was not a perfect marriage. What marriage is perfect? But it was an important marriage, it turned the entire city around—just as a great Indiaman sailing ship turns slowly into the wind."

"Another kind of White Bird on Water," the Assassin said with a nod.

Jiang stared at him for a moment. Finally she said, "Rumours are spreading that the red-haired *Fan Kuei* is with you and the Guild and that he has a magic child."

"A Han Chinese boy, not a magic child."

"He loves this Chinese boy, doesn't he?"

"Yes."

"Ah, a red-haired *Fan Kuei* raising a Han Chinese boy, and a Chinese courtesan raising a Japanese girl—surely we are after the light."

It was the kind of talk that made the Assassin uneasy. "So we support Mao's entrance into Shanghai, even with the Confucian at his side?"

"Mao is the Man with a Book, so we support him. It won't be hard. The people of Shanghai are already furious with the corruption and incompetence of the Kuomintang government, and if Chiang Kai Shek were to show his face he would be pelted with garbage."

"Agreed. But should we hurry things along?"

"Naturally. That is what the Ivory Compact does. But the Confucian is not to be killed—he may well be more valuable to us as Mao's advisor."

"He will turn on you and me and the Carver. He cannot permit us to continue to exist and still hold his position."

Jiang thought about that and nodded, but then she added, "For now, we do nothing about him."

"But he is committed to the return of Confucian rule, not to the building of the Seventy Pagodas."

"I agree. But Mao is more anti-Confucian than Chiang Kai Shek, so we shall wait and see how this plays out. Prepare the way for the arrival of the Man with a Book and perhaps the Seventy Pagodas are closer than we think."

* * *

ZHONG FONG rubbed his eyes with his little hands.

"Don't, Fong, your hands are dirty."

"Papa?"

"Yes, who else did you think it would be?"

"I don't know, but my eyes hurt."

"Because you're tired."

"Aren't you tired, Papa? We worked all night long." Suddenly Fong propped himself up on his small elbows and stared at his father. "Why aren't you sleeping, Papa?"

"Don't be frightened, Fong."

"Why are you dressed? Is it time to work already?"

"No, Fong, it's not time to work." Fong saw his father take a deep breath, then he heard him say, "It's time for me to go."

"Go where?"

"Shh—you'll wake your cousins."

"But where are you going?"

"Be brave, Fong."

"Why, Papa? Why do I need to be brave? Why are you dressed? It's not time for work. Where are you going?"

"To fight, Fong. It is time for me to go and fight." Before Fong could speak, his father put his index finger to the boy's lips. "Remember the Peking Opera I took you to?" Fong nodded. "Remember how sad you were when the Serving Man didn't get to stay with the Princess from the East?" Fong nodded again. "Remember how unfair it was that the Serving Man couldn't marry the Princess? Remember you asked me why the Princess couldn't stay with the Serving Man?"

"She loved the Serving Man and he loved her, but she had to stay with the Prince of the West who didn't even like her."

"Exactly. So you remember?" Fong nodded and began to cry. His father wiped away his tears. "Do you know where I'm going?"

Fong nodded.

"Where, Fong, where am I going?"

"To a place to make things fair."

"Right, Fong. I'm going to fight so that the Serving Man can marry the Princess of the East if they love each other. That's a good idea, isn't it?"

"Yes, Papa," Fong said, but his tiny body began to shake.

"Hold out your hand, Fong."

Fong did, and he looked up into his father's kind eyes. Then he saw the two delicately cut glass beads his father held out to him. "For me, Papa?"

"Yes. The very first time I saw the History Teller play the Princess from the East his necklace broke in the river-crossing scene. The glass beads scattered, and many went into the audience. Some people wanted to keep them, but I insisted that they belonged to the History Teller. People gave me their beads, and I gave them to the History Teller at the end of the performance. He thanked me and gave me two of the glass beads to keep— which now I give to you, my special son, my gift above all gifts."

His father held him and said, "I have to go because it's the right thing to do. It's time that the Black-Haired people knew a little bit of fairness. You agree, don't you?"

Fong's head nodded. His father leaned over and kissed him on the forehead. Fong's tiny fingers went into his father's hair and held his face close to him. He smelled the deep odour of his father, then he let him go. But as his father got to the door, Fong called out, "But who will protect me from Grandma?"

* * *

SHORTLY AFTER FONG'S FATHER, and thousands more like him, slipped out of Shanghai to join Mao's forces, the Nationalist government hit on the idea of printing enough money to keep the people "happy." By the end of 1946, four and a half trillion new Chinese dollars had been printed. Inflation soared to the point that the money was literally worth less than the paper upon which it had been printed. One American dollar traded for over a million Chinese dollars. By 1949, the figure would reach six million Chinese dollars.

Prices were raised four times a day. Stalls were set up outside banks so that people could withdraw money and immediately spend it while it had some value. Many workers insisted on being paid in rice.

Ironically outsiders thought that Shanghai was prospering. People dressed well and ate out—they had no choice. The money they made on Monday would be worthless by Friday, so everyone spent on anything they could find. Overnight, straw sandals, the traditional footwear in Shanghai, disappeared, to be replaced by the far more expensive leather shoes.

White-collar workers and salaried employees left their offices for labourers' jobs, or they starved. To further complicate matters, over six thousand refugees arrived in the city every day, quickly swelling its population to over five million—two million more than when the Japanese marched into Shanghai less than a decade before.

Some of the truly wealthy were quick enough to avoid the Kuomintang net—big money has always been peripatetic.

The *Fan Kuei* traders initially tried to revive their businesses but quickly saw the futility of such actions. Vrassoon sold off all his Shanghai holdings and moved them, and himself, to the Caribbean. Once there, he reinvested his wealth in South America. Most of the traders followed Vrassoon's example and got out of the city at the Bend in the River.

Shanghai's inflation was a direct result of Chiang Kai Shek's refusal to share power with the Communists. It forced him to spend over eighty percent of his budget on his army. Despite American efforts to broker a peace between Chiang Kai Shek and Mao Tze-tung, by July 1946, any talk of reconciliation between Chiang and Mao had stopped and the civil war began in earnest.

America withdrew all its troops, although it continued to supply materiel and money to the Republican cause.

Mao's troops swelled to almost three million men, and by 1948, he was poised to take Manchuria and the Nationalists' cities north of the Yangtze. But it wasn't his troops that were giving Mao victory—it was the support of the people.

In a final idiotic financial manoeuvre Chiang Kai Shek declared a gold currency pegged at one new gold *yuan* to four American dollars. Three million old Chinese dollars could buy one gold *yuan,* and everyone—everyone—was required to convert all their savings to the new currency. Chiang put his son Chiang Chiing-kuo in charge of the program—and like his father, the son resorted to terror and the ransacking of private homes to enforce the new law.

Wages and prices were frozen.

The ruse worked for less than a month. Value is value and will not be denied by government fiat—a lesson that even Communists eventually learn.

Chiang's last supporters in Shanghai, the middle class, rose up against him. They had surrendered their life's savings for yet more worthless currency. It was widely believed that the whole point of the gold *yuan* conversion was to further line the pockets of the powerful.

When Chiang's son, evidently in a fit of conscience, went to investigate these accusations, the trail quickly led to such powerful families as the Kungs. Hearing this, his mother, Madame Chiang Kai Shek, flew to Shanghai and publicly slapped her son—putting an end to what little effort he had expended to make the system fair.

Meanwhile, the Chiangs, the Soongs, and the Kungs were transferring all their wealth, stolen and personal, to the United States for safekeeping. In one notable incident, a plane from Chunking heading for America had to ditch due to mechanical difficulties. When American General George Marshall came to the rescue, he and his men were stunned to find the plane stuffed with American currency that the Soong family was sending to its bank accounts in the United States.

And the Soongs were modest in their theft compared to Madame Chiang Kai Shek and her husband.

And the people knew—so the end was inevitable.

Important Republican generals began to defect to the Communists, complete with whole battalions. The rest was just a matter of time.

Hsuchow fell, leaving Nanking open to attack.

Then Tientsin—then Beijing surrendered peacefully to General Lin Paio's Red Army.

Ten days earlier Chiang Kai Shek had resigned, "for the good of the nation." Of course, it made no difference. His plan to rape and rob China of its vast wealth and transfer it to Taiwan was almost complete. The final movement of this extraordinary thievery happened in the dead of a February night when, without explanation, the length of the Bund was blocked off and, within clear view of people in the Bund's buildings, the entire horde of gold bullion from the Bank of China was carried in buckets at the ends of coolies' poles down the great street, out onto the public wharf, and put on a freighter that left before dawn for Taiwan.

The last few weeks of Nationalist control of Shanghai were the worst. Martial law was enforced viciously. The remaining soldiers stole anything they could get their hands on before removing their uniforms and disappearing. Daily executions of "Communist sympathizers" took place. Many young men lost their lives to Kuomintang firing squads.

Mao's troops crossed the Yangtze River in mid-April, took Nanking without a fight, then turned toward Shanghai.

The Nationalist troops left the city for Woosung, at the mouth of the Yangtze, in an action that many described as their most successful manoeuvre in the entire war.

By noon on the twenty-fourth of April, 1949, gunfire could be heard in the suburbs of Shanghai. By evening it had stopped.

The great city held its breath.

Just after midnight, the vanguard of Mao's peasant army marched into the city at the Bend in the River. They stared at the movie palaces and the towering hotels and stores bursting with goods—and the thousands upon thousands of starving citizens.

Then they passed the high wall of the Garden, and stopped, and awaited orders from Mao's Shanghai commander, the Confucian.

Slowly, the people of Shanghai came out to greet their new liberators. One, a young boy, ran for miles along rooftops looking intently at the soldiers' faces, searching.

The next morning, the Red Army marched, rank after rank, down Bubbling Spring Road. Seemingly from nowhere huge red banners proclaiming Shanghai's new freedom appeared across every intersection, and street wardens, carefully chosen, specially trained, and given their positions by the Confucian, took control of every large building. These new officials were of "good peasant stock," and they loathed the sophisticated city of Shanghai and all its residents.

And the people saw new rulers slide into place. Many cheered. Others remembered the old saying about the devil you know.

All the while, one young boy strained to get a better look at the faces of the soldiers—to find the gentle face of his father, who had left to "make things fair."

* * *

THE CONFUCIAN set himself up in the Vrassoons' headquarters on the Bund and summoned the forty Confucians who would be his lieutenants.

"We will subdue the tendencies of this sinful city. Every trace of the *Fan Kuei* influence will be removed. Every non-Chinese element will be removed. Remember that everyone, everyone at the Bend in the River has been infected with the *Fan Kuei* disease. Be merciless. These stiff-necked people will obey the rules coming from this office or they will feel the righteous wrath of the Revolution."

After another half hour of this ranting he sent them away. Then he called in another man, a rat of a man, and asked simply, "Is it secure?"

The man nodded. He had, as instructed by the Confucian, taken a large piece of land on the western reach of the Yangtze and had his men begin to build a prison. It would eventually be the largest political prison in the world, and its very name—Ti Lan Chiou—would make even the bravest of the citizens at the Bend in the River think twice before breaking a rule, no matter how ridiculous or petty.

* * *

FONG'S GRANDMOTHER found him weeping in the corner of the room he shared with his six cousins. He held the two small glass beads in his hands. She snapped, "Work time. New rulers shit just like old rulers."

"Where's Papa?" Fong asked through his sobs.

"Dead probably, that one ..." Her voice trailed off into nothing.

"He was your son, Grandma."

"He was a fool getting involved in other people's problems. Now get up and get your brushes. Communist night-soil smells as bad as Republican night-soil, but both pay for us to cart it away—so let's go."

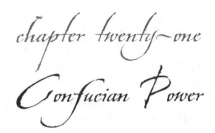

chapter twenty-one
Confucian Power

Once the Red Army had secured the streets, the real job of controlling Shanghai began with a swiftness that surprised everyone. The Confucian brought organizational skills to the Communists that they had never had before—and his burning hatred of the city fuelled the ferocity with which he attacked his task.

He found that women from the country bore an even greater grudge against the city dwellers than their men folk, so he put them in charge of housing and encouraged them to make all former building owners live in the most cramped, dampest, and smallest of basement spaces. Merchants were to be put out on the street and street people put in their homes.

Every alley had peasant guards who checked the identification documents of everyone who came or went, although many could barely read. Most intersections were made into checkpoints, and a pedestrian could be stopped as many as three times in a single block by the shouted order, "Papers!"

The wardens all reported to the Confucian's horde of street scribes, who then reported to his forty Confucian lieutenants, who in turn reported back to him directly—and quickly. Even for a city used to vast webs of snitches and complex spy rings, the Confucian's city-wide system of informants was something new.

And each of the spies had been told to search for a man with a cobra carved on his back.

The Confucian was aware that the Compact members would know of his duplicity soon enough and would move against him. He would not have that. Now that he was near his goal, he would not have it taken from him. It was one thing to assume power, he knew, and quite another to keep it.

The first thing the Confucian had done after setting up his office was deal with the Carver. He ordered the man's entire collection of ivory and jade sculptures confiscated "for the state." Then he had the man's workshop taken from him. Finally, the Carver was brought in shackles to the wide steps leading to what had been the heart of the Vrassoons' empire.

The Confucian made the Carver wait in the cold rain for three hours before ordering the soldiers to bring him up.

The Confucian, dressed in his traditional blue robe, stood with his hands clasped behind his back, looking out the floor-to-ceiling window that provided a glorious view of the Bund, its promenade, and the still wild Pudong across the Huangpo River.

The Confucian dismissed the soldiers, then allowed a long moment to pass before he turned to the Carver.

The artisan stood calmly, his naturally aristocratic bearing still intact.

It threw the Confucian, who had expected the man to be at least partially humbled. The opening that he had prepared seemed petty now, specious. He discarded it and strode to his desk, sat, and threw open a folder.

The Carver didn't bother moving, although his eyes followed the Confucian. Finally he said, "Do you know what you are doing?"

The Confucian looked up and said, "Absolutely." But he heard the waver in his own voice, and it infuriated him.

"Perhaps you are inadvertently still in the service of the Compact," the Carver suggested.

"How would that be?" the Confucian demanded.

"The Red Army has no love for the *Fan Kuei*. Perhaps they will rid the city of the Europeans and return it to the Black-Haired people."

The Confucian nodded slowly and rose. "Perhaps."

"But that is not your intent, is it? You seek the restoration of Confucian power. It's a foolish thing to want. History may circle itself, but it never returns to a discarded option. History tests various solutions, and those that fall short are thrown in the river. Your dream is a fool's dream."

"Where is the Assassin?"

The Carver allowed a slow smile to come to his face, then he nodded. "Yes, you're right to be concerned about the Assassin's whereabouts. Without a doubt he plans your demise."

"So where is he?"

"He is smart enough never to have divulged such information to me, or, I assume, to anyone else."

A withering look from the Confucian stopped him. "Would you like to have your carvings back ... your workshop?"

"I would."

"Then tell me where the Tusk is hidden."

"In Baghdad."

"Where in Baghdad?"

The Carver lifted his shoulders and shrugged. "I have no idea where in Baghdad the relic is hidden, and you knew that before you asked."

The Confucian stared at the Carver for a long moment, then said, "Do you know what Ti Lan Chiou is?"

The Carver nodded, and for the first time his confidence seemed to falter. "The new prison."

"Yes, the new prison. If I commit you, you will never see the light of day again. So I want you to think about where the Assassin is and how I can discover where exactly in Baghdad the Tusk is hidden."

The Carver looked down at his hands. Rough, scarred, workman's hands. The same hands as his father's, and his father's father's—and all the Carvers before them. Then he glanced at the Confucian's soft palms and pudgy fingers. Hands that had never known calluses, never carved in stone, let alone in ivory. He lifted his head slowly. "I have already told you that I don't know. And no threat or bribe or torture you could devise will—"

The Carver heard the sound of his skin ripping before he registered the pain in his cheek or the trickle of blood—or the small knife in the Confucian's hand.

The Carver's smile broadened. "You cannot make me know what I do not know."

"Take that smile from your face!" the Confucian screamed. But he knew he sounded foolish—like a disappointed child. "Guard!" he called. "Get this man out of my sight!"

* * *

IN EVERY SPARE MOMENT Fong searched for his father—but the city was full of soldiers, most assigned to specific tasks, many confined to their barracks, all of whom had been instructed not to interact with the Shanghainese. It was getting harder and harder to move around the city. Fong was surprised to find that all the new wardens spoke hideous Shanghainese or none at all, and openly despised the people of the city at the Bend of the River.

Fong would finish his night-soil work as quickly as he could so he would have as much time as possible to search for his father. Soon his grandmother figured out what he was doing and added more streets to his daily route.

"Why, Grandma?" he demanded.

"Because it needs to be done, and with your father gone, who else is going to do it? Your cousins' fathers are doing their work. Only your foolish father saw fit to leave his family and his responsibilities for someone else's concern. So his work is now your work, permanently."

"Why permanently?"

"Because he's not coming back. Grow up. Your foolish father is dead."

So Fong's route now included sections of the Old City that he had never cleaned before. And it was on the first day in the ancient city that he found something peculiar about the honeypot of one of his new "clients." It smelled unusual—but he recognized its odour. As punishment, a year ago, his grandmother had made him work in the *jutaning* ghetto in Hongkew. Quickly he'd learned that Chinese night-soil smelled different from *Fan Kuei* night-soil—just as their skins smelled different. It had something to do with the strange *Fan Kuei* willingness to eat cheese and cow's milk. *And they think what we eat is peculiar!* Fong thought. But now, here in the heart of the Old City, in the most densely and exclusively Chinese section of Shanghai, was a night-soil honeypot that smelled like the ones in Hongkew.

He noted the address and made up to his mind to come back and explore this curiosity. Then, not knowing exactly why, he reached into his pants pocket and felt the two glass beads that his father had given him before he'd left to fight for "what is fair," and said aloud, "I know you're not dead, Papa, I know you're not dead, Papa, I know you're not dead, Papa."

As he did, a Han Chinese boy a few years his senior watched him closely as his hand went to the glass beads around his neck.

* * *

THE SOLDIERS SEEMED TO TAKE particular joy in smashing to bits every piece of furniture in Jiang's. Only the box seat that had housed the Tusk was spared. Jiang read the order presented to her and retreated to what she still thought of as her mother's room. Well before the Communists walked into Shanghai, she had moved most of her valuable pieces and had informed her best clients where they could find her in the future. Despite some misgivings she had settled on a small building in the Pudong, then hired ten men from the Tong of the Righteous Hand to protect it. As well, two of the Tong members manned a boat that was reserved for her clients to make the journey from the Bund to the Pudong.

A loud knock on her bedchamber door drew her to her feet. When she opened it she was surprised to see the Confucian. She had assumed he was a coward who would have others do his foul work.

"Come in," she said.

He stepped into her bedchamber and closed the door behind him.

Thank god my daughter is safe with my sister, she thought.

"Have you spoken to the Carver?" he demanded.

"He contacted me after the delightful conversation the two of you had in your office. What does it feel like to sit in the chair of the great Vrassoons?"

He ignored her and said, "So I ask you the same questions I asked him."

"And I offer you the same answers he gave you. I have no idea where the Assassin is, nor do I know the address in Baghdad where the relic is hidden."

The Confucian took another step into the room, then slapped her hard across the face. "You are not properly dressed to entertain a scholar."

Jiang blanched, then canted her head slightly to one side. "There is tea on the table. I will return in a moment—more appropriately dressed."

The Confucian sat and watched her elegant figure leave the room. The tea was excellent. He felt himself returning to something important—his rightful place.

Then she re-entered, dressed in the formal attire of a courtesan.

He stood, for a moment, his breath locked in his chest.

"Have you read *The Dream of the Red Chamber*?" she asked, and flared her fan.

———

A week before the Communists actually walked into Shanghai, Jiang had met with the Assassin.

"The Confucian will close my business down. The Communists have a bizarre puritanical streak to them—although the Confucian's actions against me will be entirely personal."

The Assassin raised a single eyebrow. "Does he have feelings for you?"

"He thinks of me as a courtesan and himself a scholar."

"As in the old books?"

"Just so. But I don't care what he does. I have already moved my business."

"Good," the Assassin said as he reached for his tea. "You are no real danger to him, so you are safe. It is I whom he fears." A darkness crossed his features. "I have moved my family out of the city."

"Would the Confucian ...?"

"Think, Jiang. He will need what every ruler of the Middle Kingdom has needed since the First Emperor himself—legitimacy. The Tusk can give him that. And he could use my family to ..." He didn't bother to complete his sentence. "Did you bring the deed for the Baghdad property as I asked?"

Jiang hesitated.

"If you keep the deed you are in great danger. You are a brave woman, but you have a child, and physical pain is not something everyone can bear."

Jiang looked silently at this hard man across the table from her, then reached into her sleeve and withdrew the deed for the property in Baghdad that hid the Tusk.

"Have you read it?" the Assassin asked.

"No. Even if I had wanted to, it's in Farsi script, and I can neither read nor speak that language."

"Good," he said, pocketing the deed. "Now prepare yourself. The Confucian will come to your door before long."

"And you prepare too, old friend," she said.

"My whole life," he replied, "has been one long preparation."

* * *

SHANGHAI HAD ALWAYS BEEN a cauldron that spewed out rumours. All sorts of rumours kept the people at the Bend in the River entertained—and safe. The Chinese are a practical people, and if a rumour continues, they reason, there is probably some truth in it. And the rumours that swirled around the great city kept returning to a moment in Nanking—and a red-haired *Fan Kuei* who flew above a fire with a Chinese baby in his arms.

The Confucian had ordered his people to investigate the story and they had come back with, naturally enough, contradictory information—but most of the details supported the unlikely story.

Alone in his great office, the Confucian contemplated the possibility that the hysterical tale of a flying *Fan Kuei* with a baby in his arms could be true. He considered what he knew of the Japanese and tapped the windowpane with his long fingernails. He asked himself a simple question: "What could have stopped the Japanese marauding in Nanking? What would have made them give up a section of the old capital as a safe zone for Chinese?" He came back to the image of a *Fan Kuei* with a baby. He had no idea what to make of the stories of a great fire that surrounded the eventual sanctuary; it sounded oddly like a story from the Long Noses' Bible.

Still, he was not dismissive. No, with the Assassin still on the loose his position was too precarious for that.

Then he remembered the red-haired *Fan Kuei* who had been stripped naked and tethered to a post on the Bund. He recalled that the man had disappeared just before the Assassin and his Guild headed toward Nanking. Could it have been the same man? And if it was, was he with the Assassin?

He summoned his aide and issued a single order. "Find the red-haired *Fan Kuei* and bring him here." The aide nodded and turned to go, but the Confucian stopped him with a clearing of his throat. "And the boy. If there is a boy, bring them both to me." The man nodded again, and the Confucian gave him a limp-wristed wave of his hand. "And be quick about it."

The city's thousands and thousands of prying eyes turned and began searching for the red-haired *Fan Kuei*. But it was a small boy who found him first—found him because a honeypot in the Chinese Old City smelled like a White man's.

* * *

FONG WAS WORRIED that he wouldn't be able to continue to watch. He was very tired. He had finished his rounds as the sun rose, then done his chores around the Zhong house before disappearing to look for the White man in the depths of the Old City. It was not hard to watch the door from which the honeypot had come. There were many street people, and he simply sat on the curb across the way and waited. But it was already late in the afternoon, and he had nodded off several times. If he didn't get some sleep he wouldn't be able to complete his route that night, and his grandmother would beat him. He was about to give up when he saw a young boy—a Chinese boy with beautiful, delicate features, maybe two or three years older than him—emerge from the house across the street. But it wasn't the boy that drew his eyes. It was the set of glass beads he wore around his neck.

Then the boy turned to him, and Fong knew he had been spotted. He leaped to his feet, but a strong hand grabbed him by the scruff of the neck and ran him across the street.

The man had a cobra tattooed on his wrist.

Fong tried to struggle, but the man was very strong, and quickly he was hauled into a sub-basement and shoved against a wall.

The door was slammed shut and a lamp lit. The man with the cobra on his wrist demanded, "What are you looking for?"

Fong didn't really know what to say so he said the first thing that came into his head. "My father."

Loa Wei Fen absorbed that, then said, "Your father is not here, boy."

"Your son has a necklace," Fong blurted out.

The man with the cobra tattoo called out a name and the boy stepped into the room. "This boy was trying to steal your necklace."

"No," Fong protested, but before he could say more a very White man with red hair stepped into the room.

Maximilian said in English, "What's going on here?"

"Loa Wei Fen thinks he was trying to steal my necklace."

The *Fan Kuei* stepped closer to Fong and wrinkled his nose. In very good Shanghainese he said, "You don't smell so good, son."

Fong answered in Shanghainese, "Neither do you."

The White man laughed at that. "So I've been told. So I've been told many times."

Fong reached into his pocket and pulled out the two glass beads his father had given him and he said to the boy, "I have beads too."

The Assassin had them from Fong's hand in a second. "Where did you steal these?"

"I am not a thief. My father gave them to me."

"The father you're looking for?" asked Maximilian.

The boy nodded, then tears sprang to his eyes. "Please help me find him. He's my father, and I haven't seen him for so long."

Quickly Maximilian drew the story of his father's leaving from Fong, then returned to the glass beads. "You say your father gave these to you?"

"Yes."

"And where did he get them?"

"At the theatre."

"He bought them at the theatre?"

"No. They fell."

"Fell?"

"From the History Teller's neck. He was wearing the necklace when he played the Princess in *Journey to the West,* and it broke and the beads fell—and my father picked them up."

"And stole them."

"No. No. No. My father would never. He returned them to the History Teller after the play was over and the History Teller gave him two to keep, and he gave them to me just before he left to make things fair."

"I believe him," the boy said in English to Maximilian.

Maximilian was nodding. "As do I, son." Then he turned to Fong and said, "Tell me how you got the beads again."

Fong told of the Peking Opera, *Journey to the West,* that his father had seen the History Teller perform. And of the stick indicating that he was riding—and the stick coming up and cutting the necklace from the History Teller's neck.

When Fong had finished his story, Maximilian turned to the boy at his side and said in English, "Those beads that you wear came from your mother's neck. This boy's beads came from the History Teller. The beads are unique. I've never seen their like. Your mother may have something to do with the History Teller."

The boy's hands touched the glass beads around his neck and said, "My mother and the History Teller?"

"Perhaps."

Loa Wei Fen broke in. "We still have a problem. This boy here has seen you. There's a reward for your capture."

"I'd never tell," Fong shouted, "never!"

Maximilian was tempted to laugh but thought better of it. He sat beside the boy and said, "I believe you, but others might force it from you."

Fong shook his head so violently that Maximilian was frightened the boy would hurt himself.

Fong looked at the boy and said, "Is the *Fan Kuei* your father?"

The boy shook his head and said, "He's my father now. My other father's dead."

Suddenly Fong drew a quick breath and a huge sob came from him. "So is mine. So is mine."

Maximilian pulled Fong close and ran his fingers through his hair. "Don't be frightened. You're among friends here."

Fong turned his head into the White man's chest and sobbed until he couldn't cry any more.

* * *

IT WAS VERY LATE, and Jiang heard a sound at her bedroom window. Then she felt the breeze as the Assassin swung into her room. Jiang lit a lamp and said, "There are doors to this place, Loa Wei Fen."

"And guards on the doors who would be only too happy to collect the reward for my capture."

"True. Why are you here?"

He told her of Fong, and of the reward on the street for the capture of Maximilian and his boy.

"How old is this boy of his?"

"Eight. He was born in Nanking."

"Huh," she said, "twice the age of my daughter." She watched carefully to see if there was a reaction forthcoming from the Assassin to her Japanese daughter—there wasn't one. "Hiding the Chinese boy won't be too hard."

"He won't leave the *Fan Kuei*. He thinks of him as his father."

"That makes it difficult." She rose from her bed and poured herself some hot water from a thermos and took a sip. Finally she turned back to him and said, "There is someone who is in my debt who may be able to help us hide a very White man in an Asian city."

———

The History Teller was shocked when he turned to see Jiang in the back of his theatre during rehearsal.

He put the actors on break and walked up the gentle rake of the audience to where Jiang stood.

Without preamble, Jiang said, "You owe me a debt."

"True," the History Teller said.

"I want my debt repaid."

Warily the History Teller said, "If I can, I will."

"You can. Trust me. You can." She turned and called gently. A shy, bespectacled, Japanese-featured girl came forward and took her hand. "You have to go back to my sister now," she said in passable Japanese. The girl nodded. "This is the famous History Teller, Akiko. Say hello."

"Hello," the shy girl said in Shanghainese.

"And this is your ..."

"This is my daughter, History Teller, and the repayment of your debt will arrive after moonset this evening. Prepare yourself."

———

Jiang delivered her message to Loa Wei Fen in person.

"Tonight?" he asked.

"After moonset."

He nodded.

"What?" she asked.

"And our young intruder?"

"After the red-haired *Fan Kuei* and his son are gone, you can disappear?"

"Easily."

"Then there is no reason to hold the night-soil collector."

The Assassin thought about that. There was something to this boy that touched him. But he nodded.

An hour before moonset, Loa Wei Fen brought Fong back up to the street. "If you come looking for us, we will not be here. So just go home, boy."

Fong hesitated.

"What?" the Assassin asked.

"Can I have back the beads my father gave me?"

The Assassin reached in his pocket and put the beads in Fong's small hand.

"Thank you," the boy said, then turned to go—took two steps and stopped. Then he was in Loa Wei Fen's arms, holding him close.

Loa Wei Fen patted the boy's head gently and said, "Be brave, boy. It is time for us all to be brave."

Fong nodded, although he was already tired of being told to be brave. He looked down at the beads in his hand, and when he looked back up, Loa Wei Fen was gone.

As the moon set, the dust from the old seats filled the shafts of light coming from the stage, making the air sparkle. On stage the History Teller, in full Princess attire, executed a complex series of steps, then reached up and pulled down a long peacock feather from his headdress and put it in his teeth. He arched his back, turned toward the seats, and struck a one-legged pose that took the Assassin's breath from him.

Knowing it was a man in woman's costume somehow made it that much more fascinating.

The Assassin let out a hearty "*Hoa!*" and the History Teller, still in his pose, swivelled his head in Loa Wei Fen's direction. Then he turned away, completed another series of intricate steps, somersaulted—seemingly without touching the stage floor—drew his bamboo stick with the horse-hair trailing from it, and travelled across the stage with such grace that his head never bobbed—as if his feet were not actually moving.

Jiang offered her "*Hoa!*" this time, from the darkness behind Loa Wei Fen, and the History Teller stopped. The scarlet lines of his makeup had begun to run into his white underpaint, looking for all the world like blood-tears.

Then the Princess from the East magically became the middle-aged History Teller as he walked forward and sat on the edge of the stage, a towel around his neck.

"Are you ready to repay your debt?"

The History Teller nodded slowly. "An honest man repays his debts."

Loa Wei Fen gave a low whistle. A side door opened. Maximilian and his Chinese son came through the door quickly and shut it behind them. They stood in deep shadows.

The History Teller stood and walked quickly into the wings of the theatre. The stage lights snapped out and a single light bulb on a stand in the middle of the stage came on.

The Assassin tensed, then turned. The History Teller was behind him. "I have seen you before," he said.

"Where?"

"Years ago, somewhere else, long, long ago, in a play."

Loa Wei Fen was aware of his famous ancestor who had indeed performed for an earlier History Teller, but he dismissed the idea that it was this to which this History Teller referred.

The History Teller turned to Jiang and said, "I owe you much thanks."

"For what?"

"I have learned much about playing a princess from watching you."

Jiang, for the first time in a very long time, blushed. "You honour me."

The History Teller touched her face with fingers so light that she wasn't sure he had really touched her, but a shock of desire shot through her. Then sadness—such deep sadness that she turned from him, not wanting him to see her face.

The History Teller stepped back and said, "Bring my guests to the stage."

Moments later Maximilian and his son stepped onto a stage for the first time. The single light bulb behind them put them into silhouette and threw long shadows into the audience.

From the darkness of the auditorium the History Teller said, "Can you lift the boy?"

Maximilian did and held him in his arms.

Loa Wei Fen tried to figure out what the History Teller was doing.

"Now turn slowly to stage right. No, that's stage left, turn to your right. Good. Now lift him above your head."

Maximilian did as he was instructed.

"*Hoa!*" the History Teller shouted, then bounded up to the stage.

Maximilian put his son down and looked at the slender, middle-aged man in the Princess costume and full makeup and didn't know what to say. But he managed, "Thank you for helping ..."

"You were the naked man who tore the skin from his body, weren't you?"

Maximilian looked to the Assassin, then answered, "Yes."

"And this is ...?" he said, looking at the handsome, delicately featured Han Chinese boy at his side.

"My son," Maximilian said.

The History Teller looked at the boy, who met his gaze without blinking. Then the History Teller turned to the darkness of the audience and said, "Did you bring your Japanese daughter, Jiang?"

Loa Wei Fen responded, "It was too dangerous."

"Ah," the History Teller said, then looked back at the red-haired *Fan Kuei* and his Chinese son and said, "It is a new world when a White man can have a Chinese son and a Chinese woman can love a Japanese rapist's child."

Something caught his eye—a glitter from the boy on stage. "What was that?" he demanded, his voice suddenly harsh.

Maximilian reached for his son, for the first time sensing a threat.

"I said, what was that! What are you wearing around your neck, boy?"

The boy stepped forward and said, "The beads from my mother's necklace."

The History Teller ripped the necklace from the boy's neck and some of the beads tinkled as they hit the wooden stage floor. The History Teller brought them to the single light bulb and looked at them closely. Then he arched his back, magically becoming the Princess from the East, pulled both peacock feathers from his headdress into his mouth, struck a pose so exquisite that the air itself seemed to still—and he let out a cry from the depths of his heart, which, through the transcendental miracle of Peking Opera makeup, stayed alive and vibrant in the minds of the Assassin, Jiang, Maximilian, and his son until the very end of their days.

———

In the History Teller's dressing room, over steaming cups of tea, Maximilian told the story of the birth of his son, the finding of the necklace, and the death of Chiao Ming.

The History Teller bowed his head and there was a long silence. Finally he looked at the boy and said, "I have a grandson."

"And I a son," Maximilian said.

The History Teller nodded slowly. "It truly is a new world when a Chinese boy can have a red-haired father and a black-haired grandfather."

"A better world," Maximilian said.

There was a pause. The History Teller reached for a towel and began to remove his makeup. The exquisite Princess of the East disappeared, revealing the deep, hurt eyes of the History Teller. "I have one more task I need to ask before I put you in stage paint to keep you safe and begin your training."

"Training for what?"

"To perform."

"Perform what?"

"In my new opera. You cannot stay in the theatre if you cannot act."

"And what am I to act?"

"A lost peasant with a son—naturally—who confronts the Monkey King. But to my task first." He told them of putting his part of Chiao Ming's necklace into the hole that held Maximilian's post.

Loa Wei Fen said, "I'll get that …"

"No," the History Teller said. "Chiao Ming's son and his father and his grandfather will get *What Was Ours*."

* * *

AT HIGH NOON the next day the Bund Promenade was alive with peasants and soldiers. Street wardens were everywhere, checking papers, making sure that there were no vendors or peddlers. And eyes were watching—many eyes, looking for the red-haired *Fan Kuei*.

Mao stood in his window overlooking the Bund, anxious to be done with Shanghai and return to the north. The Confucian stood at his side.

Then a boat coming from the Pudong headed directly toward the Bund docks. Immediately the river patrol boats swung to intercept it, but the boat was swift and dodged them. As the boat approached the wharf one of the strangest sights that would ever greet the eyes of the newly Communist people at the Bend in the River came into view. Jiang, dressed in full ancient courtesan costume, stood on the prow of the boat—holding the hand of her Japanese daughter—and singing.

A sudden silence allowed her beautiful voice to carry the words and melody of the ancient song, "Tears of Time," all the way to the Bund Promenade. Then the silence broke and was followed by an enormous commotion as bodies pushed against each other to get a better look at this most unCommunist of sights. Angry shouts and loud cheers intermingled, and three beggars, their heads swathed in rags—one a grandfather, one a father, and one both son and grandson—quickly dug into the dirt and extracted a necklace that had been *What Was Ours*.

chapter twenty-two
Mao

It was a bitterly cold day when the History Teller knocked on Mao's door, as he had been instructed, and entered the huge room. It was almost vacant except for a raised dais upon which sat a large desk and an ornately carved chair. Behind the chair stood the Chairman of the Communist Party of the People's Republic of China. The cold breeze from the Yangtze blew the curtains into the room like the sails of a great ship taking the wind. The History Teller stood calmly, his hands crossed in front of his waist. He rolled gently on his feet—and waited.

Mao finally turned to him and said, "You're older than I thought you'd be."

"I would apologize, but my age is not my fault."

Mao stared at the History Teller for a moment, then said, "I am unimpressed by glib cleverness, of this you can be sure." The History Teller canted his head to one side. "I have seen your plays."

That surprised the History Teller. "Did you like them?"

"No. I found them hollow and self-serving. Egotistical and sentimental."

The History Teller heard the implied "but" in Mao's words, although he couldn't tell what the "but" would lead to. "I'm sorry you did not enjoy them."

"Ah, but I did enjoy them. You asked if I liked them, and I didn't."

The History Teller nodded again, but said nothing. He had been summoned to Mao's presence, and he assumed he was not there to talk about the difference between "liking" and "enjoying" his plays.

Mao sat and said, "I want you to create a play to celebrate the great victory of the people over first the Japanese and then the Nationalist traitors."

It didn't escape the History Teller's eye that Mao, who might think of himself as a man of the people and dress like an ordinary soldier, had chosen to sit in an elaborately carved chair on a raised dais—like any emperor of old.

"Do you have anything you would consider appropriate?" Mao demanded.

"As it happens, I have been working on a new piece—very new, and quite different from anything that has been seen on the stages of the Middle Kingdom."

"Good," Mao said. "And what do you call this new opera?"

What Was Ours, the History Teller thought, but he chose to say, "*Journey to the East—To the Sea.*"

Mao smiled. The History Teller smiled back. Mao said, "You may go. I will see you and your opera on the final night of the New Year's celebration."

"At the end of the Lantern Festival?"

"No. The Dragon Dance."

The History Teller nodded. That gave him just over a month to uncoil the story that had wrapped around his heart and bring it to the life that only Peking Opera could offer.

The History Teller turned and left the grand room that had at one time been the private domain of one Hercules MacCallum, the gout-afflicted head of the Scottish trading company Jardine Matheson.

After the History Teller left, the Confucian entered through a hidden side panel.

"You heard?"

"Yes, Chairman."

"And your thoughts on this matter?"

The Confucian chose his words even more carefully than he usually did. "The History Teller has a unique talent—but he is not a man of the people. He has dangerous bourgeois tendencies, and unless his work is harnessed to your purposes, I would suggest you abandon this project."

Mao looked at the man before him. *Surely this Confucian has read my anti-authoritarian writings,* he thought. *So he must realize that once his usefulness to me is over I will discard him—and all his creed.* But what he said was, "Although discipline is essential, the human spirit needs at times to break free of all restraint and revel in its own excesses. The Red Army has exacted a great victory—now we will let the people celebrate that victory." Mao knew that taking away hope from the people was the act of a fool. He was still the people's favourite, and he would need their support to sweep aside Old China, and all of its Confucians, and replace it with a new order—an order for which he had been tinkering with new names, romantic names. Although he kept coming back to one: Maoist—Maoist order.

Moments after the Confucian left, Mao heard a female voice say, "You have a sly smile on your lips."

Mao looked down into the stern eyes of his wife. Then he looked away. A great ruler like himself deserved better than this woman—far better. But she was useful, for now.

"Have you completed your task?" he demanded.

"Yes," she said, and clapped her hands. Three men in army fatigues brought in large cardboard boxes, put them on the edge of the dais, then exited. Each of the boxes was filled with numbered and lettered files.

"They are all there?"

"Surely many *Fan Kuei* left after the Japanese were defeated. Many, but not all. The numbered files are those who are still here, the lettered those who left."

"How many of them are still in the Middle Kingdom?"

"Before the Japanese were defeated, five thousand British, three thousand Americans, two thousand French, more than fifteen thousand Russians, and over twenty thousand Jews. That is as of 1941." She was having fun, and he knew it.

"Fine. And now?"

"Some British, a few Americans, a few French, almost no Russians, and only a handful of Jews."

"Numbers, damn it!"

"Maybe eight hundred, all told."

"Good. And these files tell us where they all live?"

"Where most of them live."

"Fine. Where most of them live. Prepare the ship we talked about."

"For when?"

"At the end of the New Year's festival—after the new opera."

"Fine. From the Suzu docks?"

Mao thought about that, then shook his head. "No. From the Bund. I want them to see what they are losing."

His wife laughed—one of the first times he'd heard her laugh since that unpleasantness with the Soong girl.

"Something else?" she asked.

Mao turned from her, stepped off the dais, and pulled a curtain aside. Holding the swath of expensive fabric, he stared at the Huangpo River. He allowed the long curtain to slide through his fingers, then said, "Do we have any old ships—with white sails?"

chapter twenty-three
Journey to What Was Ours

A sudden drop in temperature in Baghdad in late December made the ivory contract, rapidly widening an existing crack—revealing a line of new figures in the second window, headed by an elegantly dressed, tall Han Chinese woman with a serious but beautiful face. As did all those lined up behind her, she carried an actor's mask in her left hand, and from her outstretched right hand dangled a necklace—of seventy glass beads.

* * *

THE FIRST DAY of the fifteen-day New Year's celebration dawned bright and cold in Shanghai. For centuries, the opening day of the New Year's festival was a time to welcome the gods of heaven and earth, but now, with banners everywhere proclaiming that religion was a plot to enslave workers and peasants, the Shanghainese didn't know exactly what to do—anger the gods or anger the Communists? Some people retreated to private places and continued the ancient rituals, but many did not—although almost everyone abstained from eating meat that first day, as doing so ensured a prosperous and happy life. A vegetarian dish called *jai* was front and centre on most tables, and although it was never mentioned, people were careful not to cut the noodles, as they represented long life.

The History Teller spent the first day of the festival hunched over the tatters of his new script, in prayer. But it was not the city god or the kitchen god or even the Jade Emperor to whom he prayed. Rather it was to his artistic ancestor the History Teller who wrote the original *Journey to the West*.

———

The second day of the festival presented similar problems to the Shanghainese, as it was supposed to be devoted to prayer to ancestors. Many abstained, although almost everyone was kind to dogs, since it was believed that the second day of the new year was the birthday for every dog.

New complications arose on the following day, which was traditionally a time for sons-in-law to pay respect to their wives' parents. But the great red banners draped across almost every major intersection exhorted the young to challenge parental authority. Many homes were the scene of quiet and tense dinners that night.

———

It was on the fourth night of the festival that the History Teller threw out the entirety of his draft, returned to his initial notes—and started again.

———

On the seventh day of the festival, farmers from miles around came into the great city to display their produce. The Communists greeted them with open arms and lauded them as the real heroes of the Revolution. The farmers, often confused by the attention, did what they had for centuries. They made a drink from seven different types of vegetables. Many found the drink that year terribly bitter. Without much ceremony, everyone in the city at the Bend in the River ate noodles with raw fish that night. The noodles for long life and raw fish for success.

The eighth day brought another serious problem, as it was a day meant to be devoted to prayers to Tian Gong, the god of Heaven. Few such prayers were offered in public, although, behind closed doors, the Shanghainese felt it wise to continue the old tradition despite the new rulers.

———

Late that night the History Teller completed three full days without sleep—and the last act of his newest creation.

———

The ninth day was traditionally devoted to adulation of the Jade Emperor who ruled Heaven. It proved to be a markedly quiet day in Shanghai and for years after was thought of as the most unnaturally quiet day of the entire decade.

———

The History Teller slept the entire day, but as night fell he carefully left the safety of his home.

———

"You frightened me!" Jiang said as she tied the sash of her robe.

"I'm sorry," the History Teller said, moving the suitcase he carried from his left hand to his right, "but your people ..."

"Didn't know what to do with you, so they sent you in to me?"

"Yes," the History Teller said.

"Well, you are here now."

"Yes. I haven't been to the Pudong for a long time. Do you like it here?"

"It's different."

"A prudent move from Shanghai?"

"Considering our new rulers, yes. Prudent."

"But do you like it on this side of the river?"

"I miss the place my mother and her mother and her mother before her called home."

"The magic of the Pudong doesn't impress you?"

"Magic—here in the Pudong?"

The History Teller laughed. "I guess you aren't impressed."

"Tell me of this magic."

"The ground here is fecund. It's ready to give birth, to shake off its evil and thrust upward—seventy times—I can feel it."

She stared at him. *Seventy times?* she thought. *A coincidence of numbers?* Finally she spoke. "Why are you here, History Teller?"

"Tomorrow we start preparing to perform for Mao."

"I know. How do you think your two newest actors will manage?"

"They will be clumsy, but that may have its own charm."

"You know that's not what I meant. Will they pass?"

"What choice do they have? They should be safe for a while. Hopefully until the performance."

"And after that?"

"Ah," sighed the History Teller, "only fools think beyond the opening night of a new play."

Jiang nodded. "I look forward to seeing your newest creation."

The History Teller nodded and moved the suitcase back to his left hand.

"Why are you here?" Jiang asked a second time.

The History Teller smiled, then said, "To watch you dress."

"Excuse me?"

"To watch you dress. I will play the Princess just one more time—and this time it must be perfect—everything must be perfect." He unlatched the suitcase and pulled out his elaborate Princess costume, complete with the two long peacock feathers for the headdress.

"And you want me to ..."

"To put it on, so I can watch you dress. You are, after all, the only Princess I know." He walked to the far corner, sat in a straight-backed chair, crossed his legs, and waited.

Slowly she reached for the sash of her robe and loosed it. Her robe whispered to the floor, like petals from cherry blossoms. Then she crossed to the costume, unconcerned about her nakedness, picked up the first undergarment, and fastened it around her waist.

* * *

Rehearsal, Day One

The History Teller wasn't pleased with his company's response to the unexpected arrival of the two new cast members. Some actors were too curious, others were annoyed at the realignment of roles. The actor playing the Serving Man, the lead in *Journey to the West*, already unhappy that he appeared only briefly in the new opera, was openly hostile. "I'm just there to be killed. I come on, say, 'Hey, look at me,' then the fuckin' Monkey King eats me or something."

"Actually, we don't know how you die," the History Teller said, although he wanted to say, *We don't care how you die just as long as it's very quiet and extremely painful.*

"Look," the actor said, riffling through the pages of the script, "my part is so small you could replace me with a lamppost and no one would notice."

Replacing this actor with a lamppost struck the History Teller as a suggestion worthy of consideration. He'd seen a marked change in the man over the years. As his own fame had grown, this man had become more and more bitter—and since the arrival of the Communists there was something new in the man's look, something vaguely feral.

"It's time to start rehearsing," he said, "we play for the King in six days."

The History Teller's implicit criticism of Mao did not go unnoticed by the company. Maximilian, standing as unobtrusively as he could in the back and struggling not to touch the makeup on his face or the dark wig that covered his red hair, thought it unwise for the History Teller to literally—*mao* meaning cat—"bell the cat." But he said nothing. In fact, he seldom spoke to the actors unless he had to. His Mandarin was excellent, but his accent could still betray him.

His son, also in makeup, stepped closer to him and took his hand.

"Let's look at the final scene from *Journey to the West*," the History Teller said. "That's where the new play begins." Then he looked at the actor playing the Serving Man and said, "You'll like this, you're the lead in this section."

"Yeah, for two fuckin' minutes," he muttered.

"What was that?" the History Teller's voice snapped in the thick air between the two men.

"Nothing," the Serving Man said, and donned his headdress.

Maximilian and his son retreated to the back of the auditorium as the History Teller got down to serious rehearsal—arduous, exacting, and, at times, magnificent.

* * *

Night One

The actor playing the Serving Man stood patiently outside the Confucian's office door—waiting for the great man. He was not used to waiting. He was a star—or he used to be. In an unusual moment of insight he thought, *Is there a more dangerous person in the world than a man who was at one time thought to possess genius?* Then the door opened. The Confucian was standing, in his traditional blue robe, by the window. *Not a bad look,* the actor thought.

—

The History Teller stood in the door of the small prop room and watched his grandson sleep on the mat he had placed there. Maximilian approached with two steaming mugs of tea. "He's beautiful," Maximilian said.

"Like his mother," the History Teller replied.

Maximilian didn't say anything. The Chiao Ming he had seen was in the advanced stages of starvation—and gangrenous.

"You do know that they'll find you?" the History Teller said. "You can't wear the makeup and wig forever—and eventually the actors' curiosity will overcome them and they'll find you out. Even I can't keep actors' curiosity in check. It's their nature."

Maximilian nodded and took a long drink of his tea. "It's very good."

"It is. It's oolong. Enjoy it. I fear it will be a long time before we will see its like in the market places of Shanghai again."

"That's a bit pessimistic."

"This from a *Fan Kuei* hiding in makeup and wig?"

"You use a peculiar rhythm in your speech sometimes."

"Do I really?"

"You do." The History Teller turned from Maximilian. "Why do you say that about there being no oolong tea?"

"Our new rulers hate us. We offend them. Everything we do offends them, as a library offends one who cannot read. They are frightened of our joys—our pleasure offends them. They will take our pleasures from us first—our city later. The tyranny of the many needs be no more just than the tyranny of the few."

The History Teller looked from Maximilian to his grandson. "Do you have your rigging set?"

Maximilian was aware that the History Teller had changed the subject abruptly but answered, "Yes. The silk is easily strong enough to hold us both."

A darkness crossed the History Teller's face as he whispered, "Silk, that which is made from women's tears."

"Excuse me?" Maximilian asked.

"Nothing. Just an old thought." He sipped his tea, then asked, "And you did as I suggested?"

"Yes, I rigged it all the way up to the rafters beneath the trap door in the roof. Why not just rig it to the overhanging grid?"

The History Teller ignored his question and asked one of his own. "How did you make the circle of fire in Nanking?"

* * *

753

Rehearsal, Day Two

The soldiers arrived first thing on the second day of rehearsal.

"It's to be expected," the History Teller said to Maximilian, "Mao is going to attend the performance, and they are going to be sure that things are safe. Just keep your fingers out of your makeup and stay back in the wings and you'll be fine."

But the presence of six wardens with the soldiers was ominous. *How far behind could the authorities be?* Maximilian thought as he retreated farther into the darkness of the wings and adjusted his headdress.

Then, one of the wardens, a sugar-fat peasant, sat down in the front row and made it clear that she was not leaving.

The History Teller caught Maximilian's eye and nodded in the woman's direction.

Maximilian turned to his son and said quietly, in English, "Remember. If they catch me, you are going to claim you don't know me—right?"

His son looked away and then slowly nodded his head. Rehearsal continued. The History Teller's temper was shorter than usual. He was particularly concerned with the Monkey King scene but seemed to relax when loud snores came from the cavernous mouth of the peasant warden, who had draped her large upper body over two seats and her fat legs over a third in the front row.

The actor playing the Monkey King said, "Our first critic."

Or our last, the History Teller wanted to say, but chose to say, "She may be right. This scene needs work."

———

Later that same day the first government notices were delivered to *Fan Kuei* citizens of Shanghai. Their presence was no longer wanted at the Bend in the River, and transport would be supplied in five days, at the end of the New Year's festival, for their departure. They were to be ready and were permitted one bag per family of no more than twenty kilos in weight.

Any door that was not opened was promptly broken down, and all the contents of the home or office were confiscated "for the state."

The notices were not really a surprise. But most of the *Fan Kuei* who remained in Shanghai had known no other home. They were not Shanghailanders who'd come to rape the Middle Kingdom. Almost all of them spoke Mandarin, lived in harmony with their Han Chinese neighbours, and loved the vast city. But they had been smelling the reek of change in the air for some time.

* * *

Night Two

"Because I need them," the History Teller said. He wasn't used to explaining himself to anyone.

The Assassin was surprised that the History Teller had come to him. "How did you find me?"

"Jiang," he said simply.

The Assassin nodded and said, "Of course."

"The night-soil boy has the only two remaining beads. My grandson willingly gave me his. Now, to make Chiao Ming's necklace complete, I need those two beads from the boy."

"Why?"

He sighed. "It's going to be my final performance as the Princess, and I want to wear the complete necklace. I know it sounds ..."

"Petty? Yes, it does. But I'll retrieve your beads for you." He thought of Fong and asked, "Can the boy be allowed to see your play?"

The History Teller nodded and said, "I'll arrange for him to watch from the wings."

"Good. I'll try to find him."

The Assassin got to his feet, then turned to the History Teller. "When you add those two final beads, how many beads are on the necklace?"

"Seventy. Why?"

———

Fong found himself lifted from the ground, and before he could call out, a strong hand covered his mouth. The honeypot he'd been cleaning fell from his hands and emptied its contents on the doorstep. He heard his grandmother shout his name, then he heard a soft voice in his ear, "It's me, Fong."

Fong jerked his head around. He saw the Assassin and his eyes lit up.

Loa Wei Fen removed his hand from the boy's mouth and said, "Come with me, quickly."

Ten minutes later Fong understood what the History Teller wanted and gave his two glass beads to Loa Wei Fen. "Can I get them back?" he asked.

"I don't know. That's up to the History Teller."

Fong thought for a moment, then said, "That's fair. They were his to begin with."

"Five nights from now, come to the west door of the History Teller's theatre, the one down the long alley, and you can watch his play."

"His new one?"

"Yes."

"Will you be there?"

Loa Wei Fen heard the need in the boy's voice.

An old woman's scream pierced the night, "Zhong Fong, you lazy creature, where are you?"

"My grandmother," Fong said.

"Sounds pretty angry."

"The pot spilled when you picked me up. I hope it didn't crack."

"I'm sorry."

"I'm not," Fong said.

Loa Wei Fen saw the boy's smile in the moonlight. He smiled back. *This one is going to find his way,* he thought.

"I should go," Fong said.

"Yes, you should."

But Fong didn't move. He suddenly understood that, like his father, he might never see this man again.

———

Late that night, the Assassin pushed open the History Teller's dressing room door. The man never went home when he was working, and he seemed never to sleep.

"You wanted these," Loa Wei Fen said, holding out the two glass beads.

The History Teller took them and said, "Thank you," then turned back to his mirror. "It's you they are looking for, not the red-haired *Fan Kuei,* isn't it?"

Loa Wei Fen nodded.

"So if you leave, my grandson would be safe?"

"He's safer with me here."

"Why's that?"

"I come from a long line of bodyguards. I'm very adept at bodyguarding."

"I see."

"Do you?"

"Yes, I think I do." The History Teller looked at his feet for a moment, then directly into Loa Wei Fen's eyes. "What have you done to make the authorities hunt you down?"

"Nothing. But they know I like people to keep their promises."

"Be careful. When a new regime takes power it dictates which promises need to be kept and which ought to be broken."

Loa Wei Fen smiled. "I'll consider that."

"Do. For now, hide yourself well, and thank you for retrieving these."

Loa Wei Fen left and ten minutes later was on the theatre's roof. Had he looked toward the river the Assassin would have seen a sight that would have taken his breath from him—an Indiaman sailing ship in full sail was turning the far reach of the Huangpo and heading toward the Bund docks. But he didn't look toward the river. He pried open the roof's trap door and slid back into the theatre, touching down on a high rafter as lightly as a sparrow alighting on a wire. And there the Assassin—like a predator in the high reaches of a bamboo stand—awaited the dawn, awake and watching.

At first light the Assassin finally spread his weight evenly along the ceiling beam and shut his eyes. As sleep took him, he thought of the hidden channels the History Teller—after he'd received Fong's two beads, and well after he thought the theatre was empty—had directed his two technicians to build into the perimeter of the stage.

Images of fire filled Loa Wei Fen's dreams—and the snake on his back uncoiled, ready to strike, while his swallo blade turned and sought his hand.

* * *

Rehearsal, Day Three

The third rehearsal day began just after sunrise. The actors were out on the sidewalks and in small parks stretching, performing Tai Chi exercises, and warming up their voices for the long day of work ahead. Some juggled balls or fighting clubs as they went through their morning preparations. Everyone knew they had better be ready when they took the stage—the History Teller was already wearing that possessed look he got when things were not going well.

Back in the theatre, the History Teller sat cross-legged on the stage looking at drawings on the floor. A middle-aged man stood over his shoulder. The Assassin crept forward on his rafter beam and looked down.

"It needs to be bigger," the History Teller said.

"How big?"

Loa Wei Fen was shocked that he recognized the man's voice. Then his posture and his strong, heavy hands.

"I'd like it from floor to ceiling," the History Teller said.

The man glanced up into the fly space above the proscenium arch.

Loa Wei Fen saw the Carver's serene face. He felt the earth spin. Then it settled. *Is it all coming to this?* he thought. *Everything distilled down to one place, one moment in time?*

"What if it's all head, no body?" asked the Carver.

The History Teller smiled, "Identification would be no problem that way, to be sure. Would that make it easier?"

"It would make it possible," the Carver said. "And you want another?"

"There's a Prince of the East who gives away his daughter and a Prince of the West who ignores her—so two powerful men, yes."

The Carver nodded. "It can be done ..."

"Good," the History Teller said. "The first one rises and shatters, the second one should fly in."

"I'll make the first out of thin shells and the second from starched paper."

"Can the second be made of silk?"

"A face made of women's tears?"

"Yes, of women's tears." There was a moment of silence between the men, and then the History Teller asked, "Does silk readily burn?"

"Yes, it can even be treated to burn in patterns."

"Can it burn in a circle, or two circles?"

"Like Li Tian's famous fireworks?"

"Yes!"

The Carver turned away and mumbled, "Tears again."

"Yes, my friend, tears again. Treat the silk that way."

The Carver nodded.

"Can we have them soon?"

"No," the Carver said as he gathered up his drawings. "You can get them when they're ready, and not before. You're not the only one who takes pride in his work."

The History Teller smiled and canted his head. "Fine. When do you think that might be?"

"Four days hence at the earliest."

———

That day's rehearsal was gruelling. The History Teller put up a scene, and before two minutes had passed he called out, "Enough. God, stop!" He marched up the centre aisle shoving soldiers and wardens aside, muttering to himself. He grabbed his script, ripped out pages, flipped them over, and began to write. The actors gathered round him with their scripts and tried to get the changes as he shouted them out. As the day progressed it got worse. One seven-line sequence he changed thirty-one times before he had it the way he wanted it.

Chiao Ming's son stood in the wings for the whole day—amazed, awestruck by the art of his grandfather—and was filled with pride.

* * *

Night Three

The Chin family had always taken on the responsibility of building the dragon and then manning it for the climactic end of the Lantern Festival and the New Year's celebration: the Dragon Dance that scares away evil and brings in good luck. But when they arrived at the old warehouse down by the Suzu Creek they were surprised to see that hundreds of bamboo stalks had already been cut to size, the paper had been painted, and bolts of silk were hanging to stretch along the north wall.

Then they saw the small man in the filthy cassock.

Behind the small man, a craggy-faced fellow, probably a mariner, stepped forward and in coarse Shanghainese told the representatives of the Chin family that they were relieved of their duties, at least for that year.

"Why?"

"New rulers," the craggy-faced man said, "want things done in a new way."

"Who are you?"

"I am who I am."

For just an instant the Chin family members bridled, but then they smelled the reek of ozone in the warehouse and knew that change was upon them—and they retreated, leaving the chore of building and then dancing the New Year's dragon to this new team.

When the Chins finally left the warehouse, shadows appeared from the walls—and as they took bamboo shafts in their hands they assumed corporeal form. A handsome *Fan Kuei* with an opium pipe, a tall Han Chinese with a strange version of the Bible, a woman without ears or nose, a man with a wine stain on his left cheek, a large African with a smile that lit up the room, an elegant man with jasmine-scented breath, and a dozen more. But of the strange visitors in the warehouse the strangest was a tall man with long braids, a deep scowl, and the bearing of a man of great power. He raised his hand and a wind swept into the warehouse. "Desert wind. Madness wind," he said in a harsh whisper. Then his braids were picked up by the wind and thrown against his cheeks, making a distinctive *thwap, thwap thwap.*

That night, backstage, the boy opened the older man's dressing room door a crack and watched his grandfather, the History Teller, lean over a hooded lamp. He held one bead after another of the glass necklace in front of the intense, bright light. As he moved the beads closer to the lamp, sharply etched shadows filled the far wall.

* * *

Rehearsal, Day Four

The panes of the Vrassoons' windows shook with the fury of the Confucian's screams. "How hard can it be to find one red-haired *Fan Kuei*? He must stand out like a beggar in the snow!"

The forty Confucian lieutenants said nothing. They had already seen six of their ranks replaced when they hadn't succeeded at tasks the Confucian had assigned them.

"So go! Find me the red-haired *Fan Kuei!*" Then the Confucian thought of the actor who had come to see him three nights before with the bizarre claim that the red-haired *Fan Kuei* was now a member of the History Teller's acting troupe.

———

"No!" the History Teller yelled.

Maximilian turned and, lifting his shoulders, said, "I'm sorry but—"

"Don't apologize—get it right."

They'd been working on Maximilian's scene with his son and the Monkey King since sunrise.

Maximilian, as the Peasant, enters with his son from downstage left. The Monkey King corners them and is about to attack when the Princess appears upstage right. The Monkey King leaps in her direction. Maximilian's character wants to take the opportunity to steal away, but his son convinces him to help the Princess. When they find her, she is holding the remains of the Serving Man's bloody clothing and delivers the evening's most haunting aria. As she finishes, the Monkey King leaps at her, but the Peasant and his son distract the Monkey King—in a most unusual way—allowing the Princess to escape.

But no matter how simple the History Teller made the sequence, Maximilian couldn't seem to master it.

"I'm sorry," Maximilian said a second time.

"More with the sorry," the History Teller said. "Forget that. Think of what you want from the Monkey King—how entranced you are by the Princess—not the footsteps or the words. Think the thoughts, swallow the thoughts, say my stupid words."

———

The Confucian was surprised when Mao summoned him to his office, but he waited as patiently as he could manage for the great man to speak.

The Chairman of the Chinese Communist Party was staring out the window at the confusion that was Shanghai. He let out a long sigh and said, "I cannot wait to leave this awful place."

"Yes, Comrade, this is an awful place," the Confucian agreed, still wondering why he had been summoned.

"I leave the night of the play, right after the ship."

"I will prepare myself."

"No," Mao said, with a finality that chilled the Confucian. "You—and your kind—are to stay here. You will teach these Shanghainese a lesson. We will squeeze them so hard that even water will lose its moisture. We will make this abomination a desert—by ignoring it. We will allow it to fall apart. Piece by piece it will crumble into the muck, while the rest of China rises."

* * *

Night Four

"It was my mother's favourite fan. It belonged to her mother before her," Jiang said. The History Teller looked awful. "You need sleep, not more instruction," she said.

"I need a moment of perfection, just one, before it is all gone."

"Before what is all gone?"

"All of it. Before it's all, all gone."

She looked at him more closely. His eyes were rheumy and yellowed at the corners. His skin was almost translucent. Then, to her surprise, she saw that he had fallen asleep, with his eyes wide open. She tilted him over onto the bed and began to remove his Princess costume. It confused her. She knew he was a man, a handsome man, but she was undressing a woman in the privacy of her room. Then she lay down beside him—her— and they slept till the dawn.

———

In the warehouse by the Suzu Creek they worked slowly, methodically. Bamboo to paper insert to silk stretched tight. Bamboo shafts to form the dragon's spine and support the massive head. Long poles to support the great beast's hundred-foot length. No one spoke. Everyone obeyed the ancient rules. The dragon took form.

* * *

Rehearsal, Day Five

Despite large sections that he wasn't happy with, the History Teller knew that he had to give his company a chance to run the play—to get some sense of its rhythm and breadth. The Carver's creations hadn't arrived yet, but the History Teller had lots of other concerns.

The run started well, since it began with a scene that they had played for many years, but as soon as they got past that, things began to unravel.

Then the dress rehearsal was stopped by the entrance of the Confucian at the head of a large contingent of soldiers.

"Perform!" he ordered. "You work at the behest of the people, and we are the people, so perform!"

The Assassin rolled over on his rafter. An ancient voice whispering in his ear, "*From above, always attack from above.*"

"Fine, we'll go back a bit," the History Teller said.

"No. Go on. Don't let us disturb you. Continue!"

Next was the Monkey King scene, with Maximilian and his son.

"We'll go back," the History Teller repeated.

The actor playing the Serving Man shouted, "Let's complete the thing at least once before we put it in front of an audience."

It struck the History Teller as an odd thing for the Serving Man to say, since his character, as he had so accurately noted, had already completed his work in the piece. Then he saw that feral look again and thought, *You called the Confucian, didn't you?* but what he said was, "I'm adding a new scene here."

A hearty grumble came from the company. The History Teller ignored them and turned to the Serving Man. "You'll be pleased, since you are the centre of the new scene."

"Really?" he asked, clearly not as pleased as he ought to have been.

"Absolutely. No point allowing your role to be such that you could be replaced with a lamppost—is there?" Before the Serving Man could answer, the History Teller announced, "We're going to re-enact your death at the hands of the Monkey King—after all, you are the hero."

The company had seen the History Teller drive an actor hard, but never like this. In rapid succession the History Teller set up the killing scene, then staged the fight with a stark realism that shocked the company. Twice the Serving Man hit the floor with so much force that the thud echoed through the old building. Both times the History Teller stood in the audience and shouted at the Monkey King, "It looks fake. Awful. Really throw him. Hard. Throw him hard. Kill him. Kill him for us. In front of us. That's what they really want to see, so let's give it to them. Kill him for us."

Maximilian watched closely as the fight between the Serving Man and the Monkey King increased in intensity, until finally the Serving Man backed off. He turned toward the auditorium and shouted, "I know what you're doing!" and ran from the stage.

———

Later, in his office, the Confucian looked at the Serving Man and asked, "Are you sure?"

"No. But as I said before, it makes sense. There are posters up every-where, everyone's looking for the red-haired *Fan Kuei*—but you haven't been able to find him. Where can you hide a White man in an Asian city?"

The Confucian nodded and smiled. Even as this little man was "tat-tling" on his fellow actor, the Warrens were filling with water—a plan that the Dowager had advocated long ago. As the river water rushed into the tunnels, the Confucian's men were working their way methodically from the south toward the Bund. *No red-haired* Fan Kuei *yet—but soon,* he thought, *very soon. And the* Fan Kuei *will lead me to the Assassin. And once Loa Wei Fen is dispatched, my position will be secure—Confucians will be secure. And I will have fulfilled the oft-repeated request of the ancient Confucians' writings: "Make China safe for us to govern."*

———

The Carver watched the water rising in the tunnels and knew that there was nothing he could do to save the statue of Chesu Hoi. *It's stone,* he reminded himself. *If the tunnels hold, it will survive.* But he knew it was a big *if.* The pressure of the onrushing water would break through walls, and the water itself could undermine the stability of the earth holding the ceiling panels in place. The entire Old City sat atop the Warrens. It could sink if the tunnels gave way. Then it occurred to him that the Confucian didn't care if the whole city sank—perhaps that was exactly what he wanted.

He discarded that thought and returned to his work on the History Teller's two large faces. He completed them just moments before the light dawned on the day before the performance.

* * *

Rehearsal, Day Six

Maximilian's eyes snapped open. The History Teller was in his room, the Monkey King's costume in his hand.

"What are you …?"

"Time for you to change character."

"But I'm still—"

"Miles away from mastering the Peasant. That's an understatement."

"Then why?"

"Because I think they know about you."

"How did they …?"

"Have you been watching the actor playing the Serving Man?"

"Not much."

"Well he's been watching you—far too much. Now get up and sit here while I put on your Monkey King makeup."

"What about the actor playing the Monkey King?"

"I gave him the morning off. He seems jittery, something's wrong there too. He keeps saying someone is watching him, but I don't have time for that now. Sit over here and let's get going."

———

Rehearsal that day was run by the stage manager. The rehearsal began strangely and got stranger and stranger as time passed. The Serving Man's absence was never mentioned but was on every actor's mind. And where was the History Teller?

Then the Confucian struck.

With surprising efficiency, every door and egress from the old theatre was shut, bolted, and guarded as the actors were herded out onto the stage by soldiers who were none too gentle.

The soldiers lined the actors up across the front of the stage and told them to stand still.

In the darkness at the back of the auditorium the Confucian turned to the Serving Man beside him. "So?"

The actor paused only for a moment, then ran to the stage, pointing directly at the Peasant.

Soldiers immediately threw the Peasant to the stage floor and pulled off his wig.

The Serving Man stepped back. Something was wrong. The man's hair was traditional Han Chinese black. "Scrape off his makeup!" he shouted. A filthy rag was brought out and the Peasant's makeup was swiped from his face—and there was the History Teller, smiling at the actor playing the Serving Man.

"What is this?" the Confucian demanded of the Serving Man.

"I swear ..."

"No, I swear that you had better be careful not to forget that you are no more than an actor—just an actor. Now put on your paint. It is no doubt time for you to learn your role—since the new role you tried to assume is clearly beyond your ability."

The Confucian turned on his heel and left the theatre.

Maximilian, in his Monkey King costume, released his son's hand and let out a long breath.

"Are we all right, Father?"

"For now, thanks to your grandfather."

Above them on his rafter beam Loa Wei Fen put his swalto blade away and felt the snake on his back uncoil, its hood fold, and the great serpent return to its resting place.

"Enough," the History Teller said. "Let's run the last half, and with a bit of pace this time. We haven't earned even half of the pauses we're taking, not half." Then he said softly, quoting the oldest of old theatre wisdom, "They can't all be great, but they can all be faster."

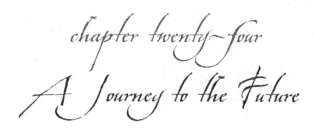

chapter twenty-four
A Journey to the Future

Mao marched at the head of the Lantern Festival as it made its illuminated way through the maze of streets in the Old City. It was bitterly cold and had begun to rain. A flick of lightning momentarily brought Mao's face to light. He did his best to smile. At the theatre he waved a brief goodbye to the crowd and walked up the old steps to the front door.

The entrance made by the Chairman of China's Communist Party was choreographed with as much care and executed with as much pomp as the arrival of any emperor to a public performance. A special dais had been built in the centre of the auditorium for him—so that his view was not obstructed, and to keep others at a distance.

Upon Mao's entrance the entire theatre rose to its feet and applauded. A large red banner praising the great new leader hung over the proscenium arch—a last-minute order from the Confucian that the History Teller had simply had no energy to fight.

Mao took his seat and then, after an appropriate pause, signalled the audience that they might sit also. As they did, Red Army soldiers with weapons drawn filled both side aisles. Several more leaped up onto the stage, pushed aside the edges of the large curtain, and took up places in the wings.

This part of the Confucian's plan was carried out exactly as he had diagramed it four hours earlier in his office, after the actor playing the Serving Man had returned and insisted that the red-haired *Fan Kuei* was still in the acting company. The Confucian doubted this, but when the actor mentioned that the History Teller had a necklace with seventy baubles on it, he mobilized his forces.

The musicians entered from prompt-side, sat downstage in front of the stage curtain, and, as is their ancient tradition, tuned their instruments with absolutely no regard for who was sitting in the audience waiting for the evening's festivities to begin.

This was fine with the History Teller, who was still busy backstage with his technicians figuring out how to use the second of the Carver's set pieces. He finally thought he understood exactly how it worked, and he signalled the other actors to take their positions. He ignored the soldiers who were standing at attention in the wings and sought out his grandson. The boy waved at him. His smile blossomed beneath the magic of his Peking Opera makeup. The History Teller waved back, then turned from the boy and took a deep breath. He looked at the empty stage. It had been his home for a very long time—and now it might well be his grave. He loved the moment before the curtain rose. Before it all began. Standing there in no man's land—not actor's territory or audience territory—open, unmarked space, the place between.

He took another breath and smelled the slightly oil rich air. His eyes traced the perimeter of the stage, sighting the opening to the channel.

He touched each of the seventy baubles of glass around his neck, one at a time.

He nodded to the stage manager, who gave the musicians a signal, and they stopped their tinkering.

Jiang, near the back of the auditorium, lifted her Japanese daughter onto her lap. Above, Loa Wei Fen shifted on his rafter beam. Fong, in the wings, stepped past the soldier who was blocking his view, his eyes big as rice bowls.

A moment of utter silence. Then a cymbal clashed and the house lights snapped out. As the echo of the cymbal faded, the lights slowly rose on a tableau that the History Teller's celebrated ancestor had made famous.

———

The Serving Man is downstage, the Princess upstage—parted by their mutual fate. The Prince of the West's servants and sycophants enter to the sound of horns and begin the dance that whisks the Princess away to the royal harem. It ends with the Serving Man alone, all the way upstage centre, and a single sustained note from the high string of the arhu. The Serving Man's head drops to his chest, his shoulders slump, and he looks to the heavens. A truly moving image of a man profoundly alone, the woman he protected and loved now gone, forever. The music abruptly stops—then he takes his first step—the first of many thousands in his journey to the east—back to his master—and the sea.

Howls of praise come from the audience. Jiang's daughter bounces up and down on her lap and claps loudly. The piece is executed with a confidence that comes only with years of performance. The elegance of the Princess, the fortitude of the Serving Man—the repetition—like prayer, familiar and comforting.

Fong, in the wings, wants to cheer but doesn't know if it is permitted.

* * *

THE CONFUCIAN pulled his coat tightly around him to keep out the rain that was now closer to sleet. He surveyed his troops and smiled. The bulldozers and other heavy earth-moving equipment were in place, all around the high walls of Silas's Garden.

A sheet of lightning lit the western horizon.

He picked up his field phone and dialled a number. His lieutenant, down by the Bund docks, picked up on the first ring.

"Are they all there?"

"Yes, sir, 688 *Fan Kuei* are now registered."

"Is that the lot?"

"We are missing only a few, and I'm sure they will be found."

"How long have you made them wait?"

"Some as long as six hours, sir."

"In the rain?"

"Yes, sir, as you instructed. None were permitted to stay in cars or wait in buildings."

"And their umbrellas?"

"Taken from them, as you ordered."

"Good. Now throw their hats and coats into the Huangpo."

"Yes, sir."

"Another thing."

"Yes, sir."

"Throw their suitcases in the river too. They are to leave the Middle Kingdom with nothing but the sodden shirts on their backs."

* * *

IN THE SUZU CREEK workshop they heard the cheering as the last of the lanterns passed them by and knew the time was upon them. One by one they entered the belly of the dragon—the old Emperor at the head—Brother Matthew, almost a hundred feet behind him, supporting the very tip of the tail.

———

The music picks up—the arhu strikes a haunted pitch and the lights change. The History Teller, now in full courtesan costume, enters the harem. A red banner descends from the flies: "A Princess Humbled."

Cheers rise from the audience. It startles the History Teller, until he realizes that they are from the Communists, who would have no problem with the humbling of a princess.

The History Teller lifts a foot high in the air, then brings it down as the first step in a long dance run. Without scenery or props, the audience follows the Princess as she runs to the extremities of the room, then bounds back toward the opposite wall. Each time she turns, more and more women, dressed very much like her, step forward, until the stage is littered with courtesans. She who is special is made mundane by repetition.

The entire stage is aswirl in colour and motion. The sequence moves from dance to song to a complex tableau of women asleep.

The arhu sounds a long, mournful note, and as it extends, the sleeping women roll away from the centre of the stage, leaving only the Princess, asleep. There is a pause—no music, no motion. Then a shadow elongates from stage left and crosses her body.

Jiang holds her daughter, who, terrified, buries her head in her mother's chest.

Fong takes a step back, while the Assassin stands on his rafter beam to get a better look.

Mao shifts uncomfortably in his elevated chair.

Lights slash across the Princess's sleeping figure. Horns scream. The shadow grows—the danger approaches.

Then the lights snap out. Darkness.

A low-angled shaft of light hits the Princess from upstage, bounding past her into the audience, momentarily blinding them. The audience, as one, gasps. A huge figure rises from the upstage floor with a gentle clacking.

A cymbal crash.

The light turns from the audience to the Carver's huge figure.

The audience gasps again—it is the face of Chiang Kai Shek! The audience immediately makes the connection between Chiang Kai Shek and the indifferent power of the Prince of the West. The Princess leaps to her feet, grabs a feather from her headdress, bends it into her mouth, and strikes an astounding pose. She holds it for a long breath, then screams a single word, "Devil!" She backs away, lets out a second, even more ear-piercing scream and races toward the huge face. At the last moment she leaps high in the air toward its centre. Her body goes through the thin shell visage right between the monstrous eyes. Chiang Kai Shek's image shudders, then shatters into a thousand pieces, and the audience—led by Mao—rises to its feet as one great thing and howls its approval.

This time Fong doesn't care if it is allowed—he cheers his voice hoarse.

Jiang's daughter claps her little hands until they hurt.

Loa Wei Fen on his rafter beam reaches for his swalto.

* * *

ON THE HOUR, the Confucian's street wardens, backed by Red Army troops, went door to door arresting every Chinese person who had ever had anything to do with the *Fan Kuei* and shipped them off to Ti Lan Chiou Prison. Then they set about pulling down every non-Chinese street sign, every non-Chinese poster, shop advertisement—every vestige of English, French, German, Dutch, or Russian from the city. Many foreign words were painted on storefronts, so the windows were smashed—thousands of store windows were shattered.

Quickly the ominous sound of tinkling glass filled the night as bonfires of foreign books and clothes and newspapers and banners sent plumes of rank smoke into the darkness to mingle with the growing reek of change.

* * *

THE NEXT SCENE is serene—and solo. The Princess dances her way out of the confines of the Prince of the West—the whole thing is accompanied only by the unearthly cries of peacocks.

The History Teller's mastery is not lost, even on those who have never seen Peking Opera. His Princess is a gift of the gods—an elegance in human form—a whisper of hope.

The evening proceeds. Some scenes are better than others. All are completely original.

Finally, at the beginning of the fourth hour, the Princess finds herself approaching the mountains where the Serving Man saved her from the Monkey King. She begins a lament.

The audience quiets in a way that Chinese audiences seldom do. The History Teller's pure tenor voice floats effortlessly through the air. When he finishes, there is a silence even more profound than before. So simple, so intimate, that the audience know they are in the presence of something most unCommunist, something overpoweringly personal.

* * *

DESPITE THE STORM the dragon was greeted with howls of delight as it ended the Lantern Festival parade. As it danced down Bubbling Spring Road, red packets containing tiny amounts of money were at first thrown at it, but when the dragon turned on those throwing money and a deep growl came from its mouth, the old custom ended.

Taoist horns sounded in the distance, and the dragon turned toward the Old City—and the History Teller's theatre.

* * *

SILAS'S WALLS RESISTED the bulldozers, so the Confucian called in artillery. Shells roared through the night, ripping great holes in the walls, which the bulldozers quickly enlarged. Then more fire, as the twenty homes and buildings were put to the torch. The walls tumbled, and the bulldozers pushed the rubble evenly across the vast gardens. Shortly, all that remained alive in the Garden was a single, startlingly red hydrangea bloom that stood out against the destroyed landscape to mark the place of Milo's final fall. The Confucian stared at the thing and thought it an insult to nature. He was going to yank it from the ground but was momentarily distracted by a fork of lightning striking a tall building two blocks away. When he turned back to the flower—it was gone. He kicked at the dirt and swore to himself. Then he announced, "The people have reclaimed their city. This obscenity of *Fan Kuei* power is now declared Renmin Park — People's Park—and it will belong to the people at the Bend in the River forever."

The workers and the soldiers did their best to cheer, but in their hearts they knew that they had destroyed something special and replaced it with something banal.

The Confucian yelled to his driver, "Get me to the theatre."

* * *

THE MUSIC CHANGES to bells and percussion. Maximilian does one final check of his harness, then enters with his son. Instantly the audience laughs. There is something so ludicrous about Maximilian's awkward attempt to be a Chinese peasant that laughter rolls from the audience to the stage. Maximilian catches the History Teller's eye in the wings. He mouths, "You knew this was funny!"

The History Teller nods and mouths back, "*Fan Kuei* are always funny trying to be Chinese."

A snapping snarl comes from the musicians—the Monkey King leaps to the high platform.

In the wings, Fong gasps and grabs the hand of the actor beside him.

The audience leans toward the stage.

Loa Wei Fen moves forward on his rafter beam and stares down at the stage—at the Monkey King. Somehow he knows every move, gesture, and sound the man is going to make.

The Monkey King rounds the stage in more and more aggressive and tight circles and finally traps the Peasant and his son.

Then the Princess enters.

The Monkey King leaps back up on the platform, entranced by the Princess.

The Peasant turns to run, but his son convinces him to save the Princess.

The Princess comes out from beneath the upstage platform with bloody clothing in her hand—her Serving Man's clothing.

Again, only the arhu accompanies her song—more a memory than a song. A voice of things lost—irredeemably lost—tears in an ocean.

The Confucian enters the theatre just as the song ends and the audience rises to applaud. As the applause crests, the Monkey King leaps down to attack the Princess. The Peasant and his son bound forward. Maximilian grabs the guide wire and attaches it to his harness. He picks up his son in one arm while he pulls on the rope end with the other—and they rise as one extraordinary thing. The Monkey King stares at them, his mouth open. He howls, then begins his slow retreat to the place of nightmares. The audience erupts in applause. Maximilian can feel his son's pleasure, but when he looks down to the stage he is shocked that by mid-applause the History Teller has not acknowledged the audience. He just stands, his shoulders heaving, looking at Maximilian and his grandson eight feet above him.

Something is very wrong.

The Assassin sees it right away. Jiang shrugs her daughter from her lap and stands.

The History Teller's makeup is running—tears are flooding from him.

The stage goes to dark—and holds.

Fong steps forward.

The musicians don't play. The audience begins to stir, and then a light comes from the stage, all the way downstage, only three feet from the first row of seats. A single, tall flame. A real fire from the floor of the stage.

The audience stirs uncomfortably. Shanghai has known its share of fires.

"Stop this outrage," Mao hisses. The Confucian signals his lieutenant.

The History Teller takes a deep breath and steps up to the fire. He nods to the technician and the man lowers the second of the Carver's set pieces. It descends slowly, finally filling almost the entirety of the upstage area.

The audience struggles to make out its features with only the downstage firelight.

The History Teller glances into the wings. The soldiers are gathering there. He looks up at Maximilian and Chiao Ming's son.

Maximilian sees the soldiers in the wings unholstering their weapons.

Under his breath the History Teller says, "It's time to fly."

"That's why ...?"

"It is time to fly," the History Teller says a second time.

Maximilian reaches for the loose end of the silk cord and pulls hard. He and his son rise another four feet, then another four.

"Say goodbye to me," the History Teller calls.

"Goodbye," Maximilian says.

"Goodbye, Grandpa."

The History Teller reaches up and puts a hand on his headdress. He signals to the stage manager.

Lights slam on, bringing the Carver's creation to life— a floor-to-ceiling face of Mao Tze tung in translucent silk.

The History Teller steps behind the flame, and now the audience can see him and his huge silhouette on the image of Mao.

"Yes, but the tyranny of the many is no more just than the tyranny of the few!" he screams, then he reaches up and pulls off his headdress. With a single swipe of his sleeve he removes most of the stage paint from around his eyes. Then he takes the beads from around his neck. "But from death, rebirth—and change will come, no matter how long or hard you resist it!" he shouts.

"Stop him!" Mao roars.

"Too late!" the History Teller screams back. He turns to Maximilian and shouts, "Go. Now!"

And to the amazement of the audience, Maximilian and his son rise above the proscenium as the first shots from the soldiers ping off the bricks of the old theatre. Forty feet off the ground they hold, momentarily—then gunfire erupts all around them.

"Hold tight," Maximilian says to his son as he yanks hard on the silk rope. As he does, he looks down.

The History Teller lights a taper and runs to the side of the stage. He flips open a panel and shoves the taper into the gap. For a breath, nothing happens ... then a ring of fire ten feet high springs up on either side of the stage. The soldiers retreat, and their gunfire momentarily ceases.

"Go!" he yells at Maximilian.

Maximilian pulls hard again and he and his son ascend toward the trap door in the ceiling.

The History Teller grabs the beads of the necklace and shouts, "Behold the past that will inevitably lead us to a future that no man or government can control! A future that belongs to all the Black-Haired people."

He puts the beads, one at a time, in front of the flame.

They cast hard-edged shadows of History Tellers of the past in full costume. Seventy peacock-feather–topped images parade on the flat surface of Mao's image in the wavering light of the ring of fire.

They hold for a moment.

Maximilian pushes open the trap door and hauls himself and his son onto the roof just as the western sky explodes with a massive curtain of sheet lightning.

On stage a shaft of brilliant lightning from the trap door pierces the darkness upstage, bounces, and thrusts intense beams of light through the glass baubles from the other side—the upstage side ... and the images all change.

No longer are there images of seventy History Tellers projected on the face of Mao—now there are the silhouettes of seventy buildings etched on the very walls of the auditorium.

The audience rises as one great thing and slowly turns to take in the miracle all around them.

Jiang holds her daughter up as high as she can and asks, "What do you see?"

"Pagodas, Momma."

"Yes. Seventy Pagodas, and the end of a great task."

Building after building—seventy of them. Seventy buildings as if on the far side of a river. A skyline unlike any that has ever been seen in the history of the world. Tall, elegant buildings, each unique, each fighting for attention as they assault the sky.

On his rafter beam, the Assassin kneels and drinks in the vision of the Seventy Pagodas. And something within him releases. Years of tension drain from him and he slumps against a crossbeam. A smile comes from deep within him.

Fong feels a strong hand on his shoulder. He does not know it, but this is the Carver, whose smile matches that of Loa Wei Fen. Then tears come.

"Why are you crying?" Fong asks. The Carver's tears continue, but he manages to say, "Because the Compact is successful. See the Seventy Pagodas?"

When the Confucian sees the Seventy Pagodas on the walls all around him his mouth opens wide but no sound comes. An ancient wind seems to turn his face first to his left, where Jiang, seemingly generating light of her own, stands transfixed, and then up to the rafters, where Loa Wei Fen meets his gaze, the smile luminous on his handsome face.

The silence in the building is complete.

Then Jiang sees something bloom in the fury of the Confucian's face—the Confucian in power, and great suffering. Executions of thousands—famine—great famine, to rival the death toll of the Taiping Revolt—a slaughter in a huge public space.

The doors of the old theatre swing open and, to the amazement of the audience and the History Teller, the huge silk, bamboo, and paper dragon dances down the centre aisle. About twenty feet from the stage it stops. Silence.

The First Emperor stares at the vision of Seventy Pagodas through the eyeholes of the dragon and turns the dragon's head upward. He sees Loa Wei Fen on his rafter beam, then the Confucian standing beside Mao, and then Jiang with a beautiful Japanese girl in her arms. He nods, and the head of the great dragon does the same. Then he says softly, "Not yet. Soon, but not yet."

And the dragon charges the stage.

The History Teller steps back.

The dragon passes over the single downstage flame and in one loud *whoosh* is afire. It makes one large circle of the stage, then runs right at, and through, the image of Mao.

The History Teller feels intense heat. He looks down. The flames from the dragon have ignited the hem of his costume.

His stage is a world of dancing flames. He looks up. Maximilian and his grandson are at the open trap door in the roof. He sees Loa Wei Fen standing on his rafter beam. He senses Jiang in the back of the auditorium with her Japanese daughter. He sees the night-soil boy with the Carver in the wings—and the dragon, fully aflame, leaping wildly upstage.

Then he feels something hot on his face and realizes that his stage paint has caught fire. The smell of his burning flesh surrounds him, but he doesn't care. He continues to hold the beads to the light. The images of the Seventy Pagodas are now imprinted across the massive silk visage of Mao

Tze-tung. Then, through the flames, he sees figures approaching—the first History Teller, a gentle fisherman, a red-haired *Fan Kuei*—and more, many more. They hold out their arms to him—and he steps toward them.

Then Mao's image catches fire. One outer band burns clockwise while an inner band burns counter-clockwise, and the Seventy Pagodas disappear, like Li Tian's blood-tears in a darkening sky. Like dreams in the dawn.

* * *

MAXIMILIAN AND HIS SON got to the Bund docks just in time to be rowed out to the great Indiaman sailing ship. He held his son in his arms as the topgallants took the wind and heeled slowly to port—and the buildings of the Bund slid slowly by.

"Is Grandfather ...?"

"Yes," Maximilian said, "he is with the Ancients now."

"And us?"

"We're going home," Maximilian said.

"But Shanghai is my home, Father."

"Yes, it is," Maximilian said. "Your home, son."

"I will be coming back here, Father," the boy said.

Maximilian looked at his son. A new hardness had entered the boy's face. His eyes were obsidian. Then he repeated, "I will be coming back."

Maximilian could not meet his son's eyes. He felt the truth of the boy's words and sensed a wave of pain approaching. "You will do great things here, of that I'm sure." Looking to the buildings on the Bund he continued, "But I and my kind will not. My family's time in the Middle Kingdom has come to an end. I am the last Hordoon who will live in this great city."

Then he noticed it—the flower in his son's hand. A vivid red hydrangea.

"Where did you get that?" he asked.

"The night-soil boy gave it to me for good luck."

Maximilian nodded. A beautiful flower from a night-soil boy. It was perfect—perfectly Chinese.

———

"It might be time for the Tusk to return to the Bend in the River," the Carver said as they continued to climb.

"Not yet, but in good time," Loa Wei Fen said.

"What do we do now?" asked the Carver.

"We wait," Jiang said.

"For what?" asked the Carver.

"For the Confucian to complete his task. In his arrogance, he is not able to see that he is still in service of the Compact."

"You're not going to …?"

"Kill him for betraying the Compact?" Jiang asked. "No. The city at the Bend in the River has survived the Age of White Birds on Water and is now in the hands of the Black-Haired people—the only ones who can build the Seventy Pagodas."

"But the Communists …"

"Are just another foreign fish in the great sea of China."

Loa Wei Fen turned to the Carver. "You must leave Shanghai. The Confucian will surely punish you."

"He's already taken my workshop and every piece I've made. What more can he do?"

"Bring me your son," Loa Wei Fen said.

"What will you …?"

"He will come with me and my sons."

"And where …?"

"Away. Far away, to get ready for the return of the Sacred Relic. Do not ask me where we will go. I will not tell you."

The Carver nodded and agreed to bring his son before the dawn.

Finally, at the top of the hill, Loa Wei Fen turned to Jiang. "Will the Confucian harm you?"

"I think not."

"Why?"

"Because he thinks he loves me."

The Assassin nodded. "May I ask one last favour?"

"Surely."

"Let me hold your daughter."

Jiang nodded.

Loa Wei Fen took the Japanese girl's hand, then lifted the child gently in his arms and kissed her forehead.

Jiang went to speak, but Loa Wei Fen put a finger to her lips. "It's something I should have done the first time I saw her."

Jiang wiped away a tear. "Will we …?"

"No," he said, "we will never meet again. But our children or our grandchildren will—and with the Tusk they will oversee the building of the Seventy Pagodas and complete the First Emperor's vision at the Bend in the River. Now look."

From their position on the top of the rise at the far reach of the Huangpo, the Carver, the Assassin, Jiang, and her Japanese daughter watched as the mighty ship accepted the wind and, like a great White Bird on Water, took the *Fan Kuei*, after over a hundred years, out of Shanghai—down the great river, toward the sea.

Epilogue
The Age of Dry Water

Nestled safely in its Baghdad hiding place, beneath the floorboards on the second storey of the Abdullahs' family compound, the sacred Narwhal Tusk continues its voyage of revelation. Although there is no one to see it, the First Emperor's prophetic plan continues to reveal itself as the Tusk rots slowly in the dry desert air of Mesopotamia.

Then the great Tusk cracks.

And the alignment of the filigree on its surface re-forms and brings a new idea to the world. The classic characters spelling out "Age of Dry Water" magically form above the Man with a Book portal. And although the Tusk remains in Baghdad, as if the phrase was carried on the desert winds, madness winds, from the west, the citizens of Shanghai begin to refer to the new time after Mao's arrival—the time when Beijing actively ignores the city at the Bend in the River for forty years— as the Age of Dry Water.

Historical Note

Shanghai: The Ivory Compact is a work of fiction. It uses some of its historical facts and characters with accuracy, others with much liberty.

To start with, there are no Warrens in Shanghai. They would be a physical impossibility with the Huangpo River so close. However, the streets are as described and most of the buildings are correctly placed. The Old Shanghai Restaurant is real, as are the intricate foods eaten in the scene with Charles and Silas. The Temple of the City God, the Yu-Yuan Gardens, the various tea shops, and the Long Hua Temple are quite real and, I believe, accurately portrayed. The Pudong was for a long time a place of substantial wildness and danger. Shanghai was not known, however, as the city at the Bend in the River.

The depiction of the opium trade is basically accurate, and the great Shanghai trading companies named in the novel did exist. A monopoly on direct trade between China and England was granted to one such company (represented here by the Vrassoons) and was subsequently lost, but this happened at a much earlier date, and there is no indication that there was extortion involved.

The First Emperor, builder of the Grand Canal linking the Yangtze to the Beijing basin, did unite China for the first time, and his accomplishments are much as described in the novel. He also hunted down and murdered Confucians and burned their books, and sent people to the ends of his wide realm in search of a stone that would grant him eternal life. It is reported that the First Emperor was found frozen to death on the top of a holy mountain—naked, with a round stone pressed to his crotch.

It would have been hard to concoct behaviour more outrageous than that of the real Dowager Empress, who did, in all likelihood, murder emperors and her own child. She did outlive her last emperor—and apparently celebrated her victory much as described in the novel.

Silas Hordoon did exist, and he did marry his Chinese mistress (outraging both ethnic communities). The story of how they took in twenty street children and raised them as their own inside a large walled garden is a true one. Richard and Maxi Hordoon, however, are fictitious characters. And there was no Great Shanghai Road Race.

A real Charles Soong worked in a Boston bar as a boy, attended seminary school in the southern United States, and arrived in Shanghai as a Southern Methodist missionary, where he eventually ran a printing house of some sort. He became the wealthiest man in China and provided financial support to Dr. Sun Yat-sen's revolution—but no one knows exactly where all that money came from.

Soong did indeed have three daughters, who were referred to as She Who Loves Money, She Who Loves Power, and She Who Loves China. One became Madame Chiang Kai Shek, and another married Dr. Sun Yat-sen. Soong's middle daughter was, in all likelihood, a Communist supporter, but it's unlikely that she was Mao's mistress. T.V. Soong, Charles's eldest son, was Finance Minister in the Republican government and by many accounts the architect of one of the greatest thefts of all time.

Gangster Tu was a real person, and the Tong of the Righteous Hand was—and is—quite real. Big-Eared Tu was certainly as ugly as described in the novel.

The depictions of many of the historical events in the novel—the Boxer Rebellion, the Taiping Revolt, the Hong Kong Typhoon, and the battles between the Shanghailanders and the European Shanghainese—are rooted in fact, though liberties are taken in their telling.

The events in the book relating to the Rape of Nanking are fictional — but quite true. There is a difference between a History Chronicler and a History Teller, but neither has a monopoly on truth itself, especially when it comes to horrors like those that took place in Nanking.

There is a Peking Opera called *Journey to the West,* but it is completely unlike the one described in this book.

And of course (unless it is indeed very carefully hidden) there is no Narwhal Tusk dictating events in the Middle Kingdom—although when you look at the history of China, it is not hard to imagine that there is some extraordinary guiding hand at work. China was the wealthiest nation on earth until 1842; nations throughout Asia paid it tribute. Opium brought this nation to its knees—but it is rising—and the Seventy Pagodas are proudly on display in the Pudong even as you read these words.

Acknowledgments

You can't write a large book like this without a tremendous amount of support. First and foremost from my wife, Susan Santiago, without whose patience and encouragement this book would never have come into being. Then from Michael Levine, my agent and friend, who has been in my corner for many years now. Then from the fine folks at Penguin Canada — David and Helen and Lisa and Catherine and Tracy—their expertise can be readily seen on the pages of the book. Then there are my prelim-readers and researchers, Charles, Suzanne, and Wayne, whose input was greatly valued. Thanks as well to my translator, Zhang Fang, my business partner at the Professional Actor's Lab, Bruce Clayton, and all those who so freely opened their hearts to my, all too often, foolish inquiries. And finally, a note of gratitude to two teachers: a grade school teacher named Mr. Patterson who read to us every Friday morning before class and a high school teacher who showed me the glory contained within the word, Mr. Gallanders—back then we didn't know our teachers' given names.

David Rotenberg
Toronto, 2008

Pied Beauty

Glory be to God for dappled things—
    For skies of couple-colour as a brinded cow;
        For rose-moles all in stipple upon trout that swim;
Fresh-firecoal chestnut-falls; finches' wings;
    Landscape plotted and pieced—fold, fallow, and plough;
        And all trades, their gear and tackle and trim.

All things counter, original, spare, strange;
    Whatever is fickle, freckled (who knows how?)
        With swift, slow; sweet, sour; adazzle, dim;
He fathers forth whose beauty is past change:
        Praise Him.
           —GERARD MANLEY HOPKINS, 1877

For my Canadian, Puerto Rican/American,
Jewish/Agnostic, Christian son, Joey, and daughter, Beth—with
much thanks to them for bravely being who and what they are.